THE COLLECTOR'S EDITION OF

VICTORIAN LESBIAN EROTICA

First Magic Carpet Books, Inc. edition March 2006

Published in 2006

Manufactured in the United States of America
Published by Magic Carpet Books, Inc.

Magic Carpet Books, Inc.
PO Box 473
New Milford, CT 06776

Library of Congress Cataloging in Publication Date

The Collector's Edition of Victorian Lesbian Erotica
Edited By Major LaCaritilie
$17.95 /Canada $24.95

ISBN# 0-9755331-9-3

Book Design: P. Ruggieri

INTRODUCTION

Contrary to what our stereotypes might lead us to expect, the Victorian era offers an untapped wellspring of lesbian erotica. Indeed, given the wide range of vivid and creative nineteenth century writings on all forms of lesbian pleasure, one might say that lesbian erotica has advanced very little in the past century. Plots and pastimes that one might have believed to be the invention of subsequent generations were in fact alive and well in the age of the Queen Victoria. There even existed how-to books on lesbian sex, *The Horn Book*, and travel guides, *The Pretty Women of Paris*, that instructed where one might enjoy such pleasures.

Moreover, the quality of these writings was quite high. While works by Anais Nin, Henry Miller and D.H. Lawrence were still decades away, the fiction in this collection can compare favourably to these authors in its psychological insight, stylistic fireworks and arousing prose. Indeed, hints of the formal experimentation that would come to define the modernist era can be seen in works like *Beatrice* and *Parisian Follies*, both of which adum-

Introduction

brate the innovations of future lesbian writers like Gertrude Stein and Virginia Woolf. While the identities of the writers of these works will forever remain a mystery, it is the privilege of this collection to bring such masterpieces as these back into print.

One might worry, as I did, that the sexual encounters represented in these works would seem tame or quaint by modern standards. I can assure you, however, that this is not the case. The array of sex toys available in the Victorian era included all manner of dildo (inflatable rubber, leather, and strap-on), props such as handcuffs, riding crops and costumes, and toys that we do without, such as a phallus that ejaculates warm milk when squeezed. There are stories that involve the use of nascent photographic and recording technologies to capture the pleasures of sexual encounters, as well as stories of cross-dressing, gender bending, and voyeurism. A wide range of tastes and proclivities are represented. Authors, though anonymous by name, can be easily distinguished by their various enthusiasms. While one author may describe oral sex in loving detail, another might delve equally deeply into dildos, spankings or role-playing. Indeed, with stories involving everyone from streetwalkers to aristocrats, nuns to fugitives, it can be said with confidence that this collection contains something for everybody.

In his influential study *The History of Sexuality*, Michel Foucault argues that the Victorian era, far from being more repressed than our own, actually offered more sexual freedom because it lacked the rigid categories of identity that define us today. For the Victorians, Foucault suggests, it was what you did that mattered, not what you were. The Victorian woman was therefore free to do one thing on Monday and quite a different thing Tuesday. Instead of being pigeonholed by labels like homosexual or heterosexual, she was free to explore all facets of her desires. This collection focuses on their desires for one another, and records the stories of women who freely express affection for all manner of sexual activity.

Victorian erotica is relatively free of what we would today call true lesbians. The novels of heterosexual love and marriage that make up so much of mainstream Victorian literature have no lesbian equivalent. The works that make up this collection aren't so much about women who have chosen to be lesbians as they are about women who enjoy sexual activity with other women. While there are all-female secret societies and country houses where women may retreat for the exclusive company of their own sex, their activities are not linked to a political agenda or a larger set of lifestyle choices. First and foremost, these are stories of the pleasures and relationships that women have amongst themselves.

Of all the various paraphilias represented in this collection, the most prevalent is sadomasochism. Indeed, the reader might be forgiven if, reading works like *Beatrice* and *Parisian Follies*, they forget that these were written a full half century before groundbreaking works like *The Story of O*. While it can hardly be surprising to find a preponderance of spanking in a collection of English Victorian writing, the psychological insight and the lesbian nature of these works will likely exceed the reader's expectations. Furthermore, some of these works, set at the ancestral homes of prominent English families, contain a quantity of incest that will likely surprise the reader. Yet this may be seen as simply another example of the way that these courageous writers took on taboo topics and put them front and centre in their novels. Indeed, many of the narratives about cousins and other relations include a tender affection quite unlike that found in comparable works that lack a familial dimension.

Those expecting purple prose and hackneyed clichés will also be pleasantly surprised by the quality of the writing contained in this collection. While some of these works have no literary pretence above that of a steamy

Introduction

page-turner, others work in the tradition of established Victorian genres like the epistolary novel, *The Adventures of Grace and Anna*, *School Life in Paris*, *Catherine*, and *Maudie*. There are even works that could qualify as modernist masterpieces *avant la lettre*. Works like *Lady Chatterley's Lover* and *The Story of O* will seem less audacious once you have read their literary antecedents. It is to the credit of the underground writers, editors and publishers of the Victorian era that they could keep quality work plentiful while working under the veil of secrecy and the risk of arrest.

Dr. Major LaCaritilie

TABLE OF CONTENTS

CAROLINE

Having overcome my reticence about my tribadism, I can now plunge boldly into the tale.

My mother died giving me birth, and by reason of this my father, Thomas Powerscourt, lord of the manor of Woodbury and deputy-lieutenant of the county of Warwickshire, imbibed a certain dislike for me, which showed itself, not indeed in harshness, but in a studied indifference to my existence. He had married my mother rather late in life, and the loss of her so soon after their union was so much of a blow to him that he seemed determined to vent his displeasure on me, whom he unjustly regarded as in a way the author of his misfortune; and, wrapping himself up in the literary and scientific studies to which he was addicted, seemed to forget altogether that he was a parent.

I was brought up under the care of a middle-aged and kindly but somewhat taciturn Scotch nurse. None of the other servants were permitted to converse familiarly with me, and I had scarcely any young friends my own age—none, indeed, to speak correctly, so that by the time I was past eighteen years of age I was about as innocent of the mysteries of human life as one much younger than me, and any curiosity that I had evinced upon such matters had always been severely checked, both by my nurse and by the governess who was afterwards engaged to instil the first principles of learning into my mind.

At the period I am speaking of, I was sent to college at Devonshire, and in more ways than one the change was a very eventful one for me. The school had been selected on the advice of my father's greatest friend, Colonial Rutherford, whose own daughter was a pupil there.

It was arranged that a day or two before going to school I should proceed to Rutherford's home, so as to travel down with him and his daughter; and, accordingly, I was dispatched with my luggage to Everton Grange in Wiltshire, where the Rutherfords lived.

I was greeted most kindly on my arrival, and found it a very different household from that which I had left behind, the only point of resemblance being that Caroline was an only child. Colonial Rutherford and his wife, Lady Florence, were both of them amiable and society-loving, and the dinner table, at which Caroline and I were given seats, presented a great contrast, with the lively conversation that took place there, to the silent and gloomy meals I had been condemned to at home.

I found that it had been arranged for me to sleep with Caroline for the sake of company, and I was not altogether displeased at the prospect. She was a tall and elegant girl, and I took a liking to her from the first.

At about ten o'clock we bade 'Good-night' to the Colonel and Lady Florence, and retired to our bedroom, which was a large and very comfortable apartment at the rear of the house.

Caroline talked to me very kindly as we undressed, and at length we got into bed. The feeling of strangeness which is natural amid new surroundings kept me from feeling very sleepy, while Caroline continued her animated chatting. At last there came a pause in the conversation, and I was beginning to wonder whether Caroline would put out the light, or let it stay on all night, when I felt her hand wander down, pull up my night dress and rest on my thighs. She did not make any further movement for a time, apparently waiting to see whether I should say or do anything in response. However, finding I remained quite still and silent, Caroline threw off the bedclothes, and next instant was kneeling over me.

'Don't get in a funk,' she said, smiling, 'I only wanted to have a look at you.' Getting a hold of my nightdress, she began to pull it off. I made a faint resistance with my hands, scarcely knowing what I was doing, so much was I taken by surprise, but she gently though firmly overcame my efforts, and, unbuttoning the garment at the neck and wrists, deftly drew it over my head, leaving my lying on the bed quite naked.

'I say, you are a fine girl, Maude,' she said, and, sitting down beside me, she let her eyes rove all over my body with very evident admiration, and passing her hands over my breasts and legs and arms.

I said or did nothing, overcome by the strangeness of the situation, but let her do as she liked, and her examination of me seemed to give her great pleasure, for she persisted in it for quite a long time, making remarks about the smoothness of my skin, the soft fleshiness of my limbs, and so on, till I thought she would never stop.

Caroline

At length she made me turn over, and ran her fingers over my back, my neck and my calves. Presently, turning me on my back again, she lay down by my side, with her right arm around my neck, and we stayed so for a minute; then her left hand stole down, crept slowly over my belly, and came to halt between my legs.

I was silent. I had never experienced anything of this sort before, for even my own hand had been trained not to touch there anymore than was necessary. Though I did not feel sure whether it was wrong or not, a keen sensation of pleasure came over me, suggestive of some extraordinary enjoyment connected with the parts she was touching.

Finding I did not protest, she raised herself up, saying, 'I must have a better look at it,' and, kneeling down at the foot of the bed, she bent forward and gloated over me with eyes and fingers in an ecstasy of delight, while I lay with my head back on the pillow, full of this new joy that had taken possession of me.

How long we were so I do now know, but presently there was a downward motion on her part, and next moment I was conscious of a warm feeling between my thighs. Looking down, I saw to my intense astonishment that she had begun licking me between my legs and was sucking with the greatest avidity. Then I found my voice.

'What are you doing?' I whispered.

She lifted her head.

'Don't make a row,' she replied; 'this is fine. I learned all about it from my cousin, who got to know how to do all this sort of thing when she was staying in Paris.'

Without waiting for my reply, she bent down again and went on licking. All this set up in my voluptuous sensations of a kind entirely new, and beneath the warm, moist influence of her tongue, my pussy began to wet itself quite thoroughly.

Finally, I could contain myself no longer, but raised my head up to speak to him.

'Is yours wet like mine? Let me see, will you?' I said; and without a word, she pulled up her nightdress and exhibited herself to me.

After my amazement passed, I began to collect myself somewhat and I altogether forgot my humiliation as I saw a young woman like myself undress for the first time. Caroline laughed and stooped down to kiss me until I thought she would suck the breath right out of my body; and I had to laugh out loud as I tried to thrust her off. Then she got back on the bed, which was a very big and soft one, and my curiosity soon got the better of all my other feelings. She took me in her arms, but I insisted upon kneeling up and having a look at her. She was an awfully pretty girl, with beautiful dark hair, and deep-blue eyes, almost black, and a very white, smooth skin. She had big round breasts like little mountains, and firm as anything, while her titties stood up stiffly. But of course what I was most anxious to see was lower down. I had always wondered about certain feelings I had felt, but now I had no doubt. The urges inside me made it clear I would always love women in a way I would never love me. This was my first cunt, and Caroline was giving me a grand opportunity, and you can stake your life I took advantage of it. She let me do just as I liked, and didn't mind how I pulled her about.

She had a lot of long, soft dark hair on the lower part of her belly, and in the middle of this I could see the slit which I knew was the opening of her cunt. So different it was from mine! I parted the hairs with my hands, so as to get a better view of it. I pressed the red lips apart and gently inserted a finger. Then I let my finger play with her clitoris, moving it about and rubbing it in different ways. While I was doing this, I had two fingers in Caroline's cunt, and was groping about in the interior regions, exploring all the secret corners of this new country, and rubbing the inner surface as I did so. I had only been engaged in this for a very little while when all of a sudden Caroline began to twist her legs and heave her belly, and before I could guess what was going to happen, she gave a little scream, her cunt seemed to close up, drawing my fingers right in, and next moment a regular stream of fluid poured out over my hand. I pulled my fingers out hastily, fearful at what I had done, but she sprang up and caught my arms, clasping me tightly, and saying, 'Oh, you darling! What a little love you are!'

Then, to my further amazement, she made a request. 'Kiss it,' she said, pointing to her cunt. The idea pleased me at once, and I put my lips to it. Caroline's immediately responded by pressing her thighs tighter against my face, and some hidden instinct led me to push apart the lips of her slit and thrust in my tongue. Her bottom seemed to shiver as I did this, and in the excitement of the play I pushed in my tongue as far as possible, and curled it about in all directions inside. Her legs twitched nervously, and she wriggled her bottom and belly from side to side as I continued to tickle her cunt with my tongue, and squeezed her legs her legs with my hands. This did not last long before she began to give a little tremble; I felt my tongue pinched, and then a further quantity of her love juice gushed out and ran down my throat. Her legs closed tightly around my head, so that I was obliged to swallow the stuff, and I didn't think it appeared to me to be nasty; and, as she kept me as I was before, I went on tonguing her again, until after another interval there was a further outpouring of warm cream, drenching my face, and it was not until I had had time to lick her cunt dry that Caroline removed herself from me.

I had not any idea of the feeling of her crises until she did to me what I had done to her and I felt my own crisis of the first time, holding her tongue to me as she had done mine so that I could feel this delicious feeling again and again.

* * *

After an hour I was able to recover my composure, and by bedtime was restored to my curious self.

'What have you arranged for tomorrow night, Caroline? I asked, but she didn't answer.

We had repaired to bed. You can imagine that after what had just happened, I no longer felt shy, and as she sat beside me I put my hand underneath her nightdress and felt her cunt. But she didn't seem the same as she was the previous hour, and I had hardly had my fingers between her warm thighs more than a minute, before she got up, kissing me tenderly with a peculiar look.

I was wondering what was the matter, and why she had changed, but I said nothing, guessing that she would explain herself presently. And I was not far out, for after an interval she took her place beside me again and, putting an arm around my neck, exclaimed, 'I am very much troubled to know what to do tomorrow night, Maude. You see, I belong to a kind of women's club, which meets tomorrow evening, and as I am one of the principal members I ought to be present.'

'Well, couldn't you take me?'

'Oh, would you. I should be most comforted.'

'I would love to,' I replied.

'Oh, you jewel!' she cried, kissing me again.

As I was not a member, Caroline instructed me to impersonate one, choosing a name from the roll book that she was quite confident no one had any knowledge of. The next evening, I was disguised before we sat down for dinner. While we partook of the meal, Caroline instructed me in my part, making me repeat everything after her, to show that I thoroughly understood. She said that she would introduce me as a friend, and that it was also understood that no member's friend (or, indeed, long lost member) need take an active part in the proceedings, if not so inclined. Caroline suggested I invoke this privilege, as it was my first time and she didn't want me overwhelmed so soon. She took particular care to impress this upon me, warning me that I should resist all overtures that might be made, however pressing, while she on her part would plead my youth and inexperience as an excuse; and she assured me that if I kept proper watch over myself there would not be much risk of detection. 'I shall say that you have lived all your life in the country, and have never been to such a club before; so that will be a sufficient reason for your appearing bashful.'

At last I convinced her that I was thoroughly up in my part, and eventually we left the house and drove off in a carriage, which took us some distance, stopping in front of a large house in a quiet by-street. The man in uniform at the entrance evidently knew my companion, for he gave her a deep salute, and we were at once admitted, passing through two doors, each presided over my several men, and finally reaching an elaborately decorated hall. Several lackeys came towards us, but Caroline lightly declined their offers of assistance, and tripped gaily up the broad and richly carpeted staircase while I followed. On the second floor we arrived at a green-baize door, on which Caroline knocked, and presently a little panel was opened and a voice of enquiry came through. Caroline gave her name, which once again had a magic effect, and in a few seconds the door was unbolted, and we entered a small lobby or anteroom. Two women, dressed in something like those who sell programmes and show you to your seats in the theatre, were in charge here, and we left our wraps with them. There was yet a further door to pass, but this was not locked, and on going through we found ourselves in a very large apartment, fitted up in the most lavish style, with great mirrors and painted panels on the walls, and rich heavy curtains drawn across the windows. The floor was covered with a carpet of velvet pile, so thick that the feel sank into it, and the furniture seemed to consist mainly of large, low divans and couches, plentiful supplied with cushions.

There were present here a score or more of ladies, all young and good-looking and all beautifully dressed, and these came crowding up to greet Caroline, at the same time regarding me curiously, but as soon as my friend had introduced me as the long-lost Elise, the whole of them in turn insisted upon embracing me and kissing my cheeks, which I quite enjoyed. Then we all flocked together to the end of the room, where a table was spread with wines and cakes and other dainties. I sat between Caroline and a girl whom the others addressed as Isabelle, and the latter seemed a very lively sort, and kept talking at the top of her voice, and at a tremendous rate.

Presently, Caroline asked, 'Hasn't Helen come yet?' but the words had scarcely left her mouth when the door opened and a tall, fine-looking woman with a lot of reddish hair came in, accompanied by another woman, slighter and younger. My neighbours immediately rose and advanced to the newcomer, Caroline whispering to me on the way that the tall woman was the president of the society. I felt a bit abashed as Caroline introduced me, and Helen's rather bold eyes fixed themselves on my face.

When the late arrivals had partaken of some refreshments, Helen got up from her seat and said, 'Come! Let us prepare for the business of the evening.' I threw a quick glance at Caroline, who turned to the president, saying, 'My little friend Elise does not feel equal to taking part in the ceremonies of this evening. She would prefer to remain only a spectator, and I am sure that you will not mind her doing so on this occasion. You see, she has led a life of such utter seclusion up to the present that it is hardly fair to impose too much upon her all at once. Dear Helen. You will great this small favour, won't you?' 'Certainly,' Helen replied, 'she shall do exactly as she likes. We must not expect too much of one so young; and I am sure that next time she pays us a visit she will not refuse to join in our pleasures.'

I felt very much relieved on hearing that this difficulty was over come, and the remainder of the party retired through a door at the opposite end of the room to that by which we had entered, Caroline telling me that they would return shortly. I passed the time while they were away in munching bonbons, and in about a quarter of an hour they all came back. When I tell you that everyone was perfectly naked, you can fancy the state of my feelings. My heart suddenly started to beat like a hammer, and my legs were all of a tremble with excitement as I watched the procession of nude forms, and mentally compared the merits of the various big round bottoms, firm swelling breasts, and well-fringed cunts that were presented to my astonished but delighted gaze.

Caroline came over and took her seat by my side, whispering, 'Whatever you do, don't betray yourself.' I gave her a meaning nod, to imply that I was sure she could depend upon me, but we had not opportunity for any further private conversation, as we were joined by Isabelle, who immediately started with her frivolous chatter. Here was I, wedged in between these two naked females, with an uninterrupted view of all their most secret charms, and the situation was a highly exciting one. Isabelle held me round the waist, and taking my hand, placed it between her thighs, squeezing her legs together. 'You are silly not to join us,' she said, wriggling her cunt against my fingers. 'There is nothing to be frightened of, and there is no harm in one enjoying oneself.' 'You must not worry Elise,' interposed Caroline, though I was thinking much of what Isabelle said. 'You heard what Helen said,' 'Oh! I don't want to interfere with the arrangement,' replied Isabelle, with a saucy pout. 'I was only saying what I thought.'

Just then Helen called out, 'Isabelle, you and Angela are the first on the list. Are you ready?' Isabelle sprang forward eagerly, walking to the centre of the room where she joined the other girl, Angela, who was a pretty brunette. They each placed themselves at full length on a low couch, while one of the company sat down and began to play a slow dreamy air on a grand pianoforte which stood at one side. Helen turned to Caroline, saying, 'Bring your little friend here, so that she may be able to see properly all that takes place, and she will then know what there is in story fore her should she make up her mind to join or society at another time.' I was placed midway between the two couches, so that I had a good view of what took place on each, but as the proceedings were similar in either case I need only describe them as regards Isabelle. Caroline and another knelt down on either side of her, and took her teats in their mouths, sucking them, and tickling her neck and shoulders with their hands. Helen placed herself at the foot of the divan, and began to titillate Isabelle's clitoris, parting the hairs with her hands, and at the same time thrusting her long, pointed tongue dart-like in between the lips of Isabelle's cunt. A most lascivious scene followed, Isabelle turning and twisting about something like a serpent, in the greatness of her excitement, while her breasts rose and fell with great spasms; and she kept up a running fire of little comments expressive of her feelings. This gradually ceased, however, and she relapsed into silence, only twining her body and drumming on the cushions in time to the languorous music. Her energy even in this began to fall off after a time, and she lay quite still for a few moments, then suddenly shook violently and started screaming and laughing, subsiding into long-drawn sighs as a thick volume of fluid poured out of her cunt. Angela followed suit soon after, only with less palpable emotions, but the tow who were tonguing them did not relax their labours and kept their patients on needle-points of unbearable voluptuousness, crying and tossing up and down in a perfect madness of lust, until their overwrought natures found relief in a further crisis.

Then Helen directed the four girls who had been sucking Angela's and Isabelle's teats to take their places on the couches, a couple on each, in the position of sixty-nine. Angela and Isabelle took no further part yet, neither did the others, but Helen, in company with the girl who had already been playing, performed a duet on the piano, and while they were doing this, Caroline sat on the floor between the two stools and, putting her hands between their thighs, tickled the clitoris of each at the same time. I walked across to watch them, and it was awfully funny to see the expression on their faces as they strove to fix their attention on the music in spite of the distracting effects of Caroline's fingers; although they did their best, they were unable to avoid a flat note now and again, while, when at last the pangs of delight began to rack their bodies, they lost control of themselves altogether, and the tuneful bars of the duet ran off into a second discord of loud jangling noise, as they rocked to and fro on their seats and their brimming cunts gave down a copious shower of warm liquid. After witnessing this finale, I returned to the couples on the couches, who had meanwhile been tonguing each other with great zest. They were in the deep throes of the keenest pleasure, wrestling with each other in a heated embrace, their faces buried between one another's thighs, and I could see that the engagement had already had its affects, for a white froth besprinkled their hairs, and the overflowing fluids that escaped their mouths was running in tiny rivulets down their legs.

By this time, as you might think, I was so hot myself that I imagined my own thighs as wet as theirs. I could barely contain myself, and was only just distracted from the urge to join the proceedings by Helen's next pronouncement. Helen cried, 'It is now the turn of Yvonne. You all know that she has come here tonight for the purpose of sacrificing her virginity. To you, Caroline, I assign the task. You can prepare at once.'

While I was wondering what the new item was to be, the girl addressed as Yvonne, a delicate-looking, golden-haired creature who appeared to be rather younger than the others, came forward and placed herself on one of the divans, while the others gathered round her. The next thing I noticed was the Caroline had fetched a leather case, which she opened and from which she took an instrument covered in cream-coloured velvet and shaped like a man's member, with tow balls hanging underneath, and the whole attached to a stout belt. I went up to her in order to examine this better, and she told me, with a smile, 'This is what we call the godmiché or dildo with which we can manufacture an artificial man, almost like the real thing, and not nearly so troublesome, eh, Helen? Poor Elise looks surprised, doesn't she? I am sure she has never seen anything of the kind before,' and she looked archly at me as she spoke. Some warm milk was brought and poured into the balls, which were of India-rubber, and when this was done, Caroline arrayed herself in the belt, which, when it was on, gave her the appearance of what is called a hermaphrodite—that is, you know, a creature half-man and half-woman. As soon as she was ready, she advanced on Yvonne and places herself on top of her, Helen guiding the end of the dildo towards the glowing entrance of Yvonne's cunt. As it glided in, Yvonne laughed nervously, and appeared to be in great suspense.

Caroline waited for an instant, and then sank down with all her weight on the girl below. The latter rolled her eyes in her head and gave a shriek of pain as the instrument penetrated right into her, but after this first shock she made no further sign of distress, and Caroline commenced to thrust quickly backwards and forwards just as a man might do. I got as close as possible, in order to watch the novel operation, and I could see by Yvonne's face that

Caroline

all her thoughts had now given way to pleasure, and she twined her legs round Caroline as the last-named continued her pushes. The end soon came, and as Yvonne cried out that she was spending, Caroline quickly seized the balls and squeezed them, sending the hot milk they contained into the younger woman's belly. Yvonne seemed as if she were almost dying with delight, but she held to Caroline so tightly that the latter could not disengage herself. When she did eventually, she drew out the dildo, dripping with mingled fluids, and as Helen saw me looking on open-eyed, she said, 'This is quite new to you, Elise, isn't it? You see how we can dispense with men. No man can give such a big and strong discharge as this little instrument. I hope you will give us a chance of proving that to you someday.' I smiled and blushed.

Helen did not stay to embarrass me with further conversation, but turned to Caroline, saying, 'Come, my dear! I cannot wait any longer. You must let me ride you a la St George.' Caroline offered no protest, and as soon as the dildo had been cleansed and charged again with milk, she lay on her back, looking rather funny with the big white thing sticking up from her thighs, and Helen quickly mounted on the divan, facing the other and squatting down over her so as to bring her quivering, bushy cunt immediately above the dildo. When she had got into the requisite posture, she sank lower, letting the dildo enter the lips of her grotto, and gradually pressed down until it was engulfed to the root. Then she began to rise and fall, to obtain the necessary amount of friction, and while she was doing this, Isabelle inserted a finger into Caroline's cunt and proceeded to rub the inner surface with a quick motion. Helen looked a full-blooded woman, abounding with lustfulness, and I was not surprised when in a very few minutes she gave a quick signal to Isabelle, who at once squeezed one of the balls with all her and Helen quivered as the stuff shot up into her with the force of a jet from a hand-pump, while her own hot liquor poured down in a torrent over the dildo and spread in streams on Caroline's belly. She did not cease her movements, however, but on the contrary, they became more rapid, and it was not until she had discharged twice more, and all the milk had been squirted into her, that she at length made up her mind to get off. Caroline, too, had come plentifully, and, as soon as Helene gave her the opportunity, Isabelle bent down and licked up with much enjoyment the thick abundance of her fluid that coated her thighs and still welled out of her palpitating cunt.

Several of the others had now accoutred themselves with dildos. These found ready partners, so that when I turned to observe what they were doing, I found them dispersed in couples in various parts of the room, abandoning themselves to a regular debauch of sensuality, writhing and panting as they wrestled with one another, and subsiding into a chorus of hysterical screams and sighs as one after another the well-springs of their sperm gave way and they deluged each other with their spendings, until the hot exhalations from their bodies and the smell of spilt milk seemed to combat and overpower the scents and the perfume of the flowers with which the room abounded. It was a scene of abandon such as I had never imagined, and it did not cease until all had become utterly worn-out and exhausted.

Helen at last notified the closings of the proceedings, and the members went into the adjoining room to dress, leaving me once more alone. Glad of the momentary escape from being observed, I quickly slid my hand under my petticoats and felt my own cunt, but I was too fearful of being surprised to do it properly, and the only result was that it felt more inflamed when the ladies returned than it had before they left. It would be the next day before I could fully get my relief.

Caroline

* * *

On emerging from the bathroom the next morning, we found our meal ready, and on finishing, we went into the boudoir, where my friend, at my request, gave me some music. When we had been there about half an hour, a member of Caroline's house staff named Marie came in to say that a young person giving the name of Julie Melnotte was waiting to see Caroline. 'Show her in,' said the latter; 'it is the girl that the club promised to send me. I told them that I wanted someone to assist you, Marie, when we are at college. I said that I should like one as young as possible, so that she would be easier to teach her duties to, and they replied that they felt certain they could entirely suit me. I hope that is so, but I have no doubt that under your tuition, Marie, she will quickly accustom herself to our ways. Let us see her now!'

Marie left the room and presently returned, bringing with her a girl of our age, quietly but respectably dressed. She was rather pretty, with a clear-skinned, child-like face and brown hair, and she wore a very shy and innocent expression. She appeared to be greatly impressed by the situation in which she found herself, and kept her eyes fixed on the ground. 'Make your respects to the young gentlewoman!' said Marie, placing her hand on the girl's shoulder. She reddened at her forgetfulness, and dropped a somewhat trembling curtsey. 'You wish to enter my service?' interrogated Caroline. 'Yes, if madam will be good enough to take me,' the girl replied nervously and in a low voice, as if repeating a lesson. 'Very well,' Caroline answered; 'I have had a very good recommendation of you, and I hope you will prove worthy of it. Marie will assure you, I know, that I am not a bad mistress, and I have the interests of all my servants at heart so long as they try to give me satisfaction.' 'I shall do my very best to please you, madam,' responded the girl in the same low voice. 'That is right!' said Caroline; 'let that be your motto, and you will never regret having entered my household. I shall engage you, and you may stay with me as long as you like. You will have very light work to do, as I shall only need you to assist Marie. She will let you know all that is required of you, and I hope that you will endeavour to prove a diligent pupil. I shall expect you always to look clean and neat, and Marie will supply you with all the clothes you will want.'

Caroline paused, leaving the girl standing there motionless, not knowing whether to remain where she was or go. Marie advanced, looking at her mistress questioningly, to see what her orders might be. As she approached, Julie took it as a sign of dismissal, and, with another curtsey, was preparing to turn away, when Caroline exclaimed, 'Wait one moment! I like to know that my maids are well made as well as good featured. You will therefore oblige me by undressing, and giving me an opportunity to satisfy myself on this point.' The girl blushed up to the roots of her hair and said almost in a whisper. 'Oh, please, madam! I cannot.' 'Good gracious, child. Why not?' cried Caroline, with much affected amazement; 'you make me apprehensive. Surely, you have nothing the matter with you, have you? I could not have anyone about me who was not perfect.' 'Oh, madam! It is not that at all! But the shame, to uncover myself before people,' and she threw a nervous glance around the room. 'Shame!' echoed Caroline; 'I do not like you to use such a term before me. There is no one here that you need be afraid of. You cannot object to myself or to Marie seeing you; and as for Maude, though she is not part of the household, she is my very dear friend and there is no occasion for you to be ashamed. If I do not deny her the privacy of my chamber, you need not be alarmed at her being here. Besides, it is not as if she were a man. But, dear me! Why should I stop to argue with you thus? Come now, and obey me! Marie, help her if she wants any assistance.'

Caroline

Marie began to loosen Julie's dress, and the girl was too frightened to resist, but burst into tears, covering her face with her hands. Caroline said nothing, watching her calmly, and Marie quickly carried out her task, until Julie stood before us in only a cotton shift reaching midway to the knees. Marie's next work was to remove the girl's boots and stockings, lifting up one foot at a time in order to do so. There now remained only the shift, and Marie caught hold of this next to remove it, but as Julie felt that the last vestige of her attire was about to be dragged off her, she broke down altogether and fell on her knees, weeping bitterly. This had not effect, however, on Marie, and she rapidly stripped off the shift. No sooner had she done this than Julie fell forward on the floor, her boding rocking with violent sobs. 'How very ridiculous she is!' exclaimed Caroline in a hard voice; 'Marie, pick her up and bring her here.' Julie seemed to have no strength left whatever and remained in a state of collapse, limp and still crying, while Marie lifted her in her arms and laid her on the couch between Caroline and me. She stayed motionless, with hands pressed to her eyes, and damp cheeks, while we overlooked her. She had a well-made body, soft and clear-skinned. Her breasts were small and resembled those of a much younger girl's. Her despair was so great that she remained quite passive as Caroline subjected her to a critical examination, pulling her about and turning her over unceremoniously, and as she lay on her face I noticed that she had a very respectable-sized bottom. 'Why should you have made such a fuss?' said Caroline, when she had done overhauling her; 'there is nothing at all wrong with you. I am very glad, I am sure, and you ought to be, also, as it only confirms me in my intention to engage you. Come, calm yourself! Or I shall be vexed.'

Caroline placed Julie on her back again, but she did not appear to be able to recover from her distress, and continued to give vent to deep sobs. I took advantage of her supine condition to make a more close inspection of her form. She had a fat, hairless cunt, and the clitoris was small and had not yet arrived at its proper condition. I touched her with my hands, pleased at this opportunity of investigating a female member other than my own that was free from any concealment through natural growth around it. As she felt my fingers between her thighs, she broke into still more profuse crying, and I looked at Caroline, but she signalled to me that I might proceed. Julie's slit was so small and tight that I had some trouble forcing my fingers inside, but I at length managed to do so, and began to work quickly in and out, at the same time scratching lightly at her little button. The latter began to stiffen after a time, and her cunt relaxed and closed up now ad then as I went on rubbing between the portals. Apparently, in spite of her terror, she could not help experiencing the natural instincts of her sex. She had not ceased weeping, nor removed her hand from her face, but as the final moment arrived, she gave a shrill scream, and raised herself up with a sudden bound, almost falling off the couch. Simultaneously with this, her cunt tightened, and I felt my fingers running over with moisture. She had spent.

As I looked down I saw a thin trickle running down and dripping on to my hand. Caroline motioned me to make way for her, and, bending over Julie, she pressed her legs apart and opened her cunt as widely as possible, sucking the wet lips and burying her tongue in the hot aperture. Julie uncovered her tear-stained face and glanced down to ascertain the cause of the new sensation. When she was what was taking place, she cried with a gasp, 'Oh, madam! What are you doing?' 'Keep still child!' replied Caroline, pausing for a moment to speak, and then resuming her occupation, while the girl, forgetting even to cry, tossed and sighed with painful emphasis as she was brought to cognizance of sensual emotion for the first time. 'Oh, madam! Please do not. I shall faint! I shall die!' she cried at last, as her virgin orifice gave down its dew for the second time. 'There, my dear child!'

said Caroline, as she acceded to the girl's wishes and rose. 'Why do you permit yourself to become so agitated. You ought to thank us for showing you the hidden secrets of your nature. Come, tell me! Was it not pleasant?' 'Do not ask me, madam,' Julie answered, having now recovered a little from her discomposure; 'it was delightful, yet it was dreadful. I feel as if I had done something terrible; the kind sisters never taught me anything about this.' 'You have now entered the world, Julie, and it is right that you should know what things are in it, and the capabilities which you have in yourself,' replied Caroline. 'The sisters willingly renounce the pleasures of human life as an act of sacrifice, but, as you are not going to take the veil, you are not called on to do so, and I do not choose that you should remain in ignorance of the most wonderful works of the *Bon Dieu*. I would wager that you could not tell me what the in reality a man might do to a woman. Well, I intend that you should have a practical demonstration at this moment.'

'Madame, you frighten me again!' exclaimed the girl. 'The sisters always warned us to be careful not to have anything to do with the male sex. Oh! I feel so troubled and perplexed; I do not know what to do. And, madam, you would not surely have me do anything wrong?' 'I am glad to see you are so prudent, Julie, and have taken to heart so much of what the good sisters have told you,' responded Caroline; 'but as I explained, their rules are rules which are primarily made for those who intend to pass their lives in the cloister. You are not going to do so; therefore, there is no sin in your being made acquaint-ed with the governing principles existing in the outside world. In fact, it is only right that you should know, otherwise how can you expect to combat the evils which you will have to face sometime or other? Besides, you must allow me to know what is best. Indeed, while I shall educate you fully, I no man will be involved. Please remember that I have your good at heart.'

Julie gave in to Caroline's reasoning, and Caroline turned toward Marie and said, 'Julie is a virgin, as I have had occasion to ascertain. I do not think it advisable to let her remain so, as the thought would continually prey on me. Besides, it is a deprivation from pleasure which she would be well to be rid of. There would be no fitter time than the present for her to undergo the ideal. Kindly conduct her into my sleeping-chamber and place her one the bed. I will get ready at once, and shall be there in a few minutes.' I followed her to her dressing room, where she begged me to assist her in unclothing herself. When she had undressed completely, she opened a drawer and took out from amongst its contents a dildo similar to those I had already seen, but of much smaller dimensions. This she fixed on, and when she had adjusted it, directed me to follow her into the bedroom. Julie turned her face towards us as we entered, and stared with big-eyed amazement at my companion's appearance, as the latter approached.

I doubt whether Julie had any idea of what she was intended to undergo, but possibly some dim perception entered her mind as her eyes rested on the protruding instrument attached to Caroline's front. 'What are you going to do, madam?' she asked, tremblingly. 'I am about to admit you into the freedom of a new life and a larger existence,' replied Caroline. 'Do not be frightened. You may perhaps feel a little pain at first, but that will very shortly be altogether forgotten and swallowed up in such joy as you have never known before. Now! You need do nothing but remain as you are; I shall do all else that is required.' Caroline mounted the bed as she spoke, and placed herself across Julie's body. The girl appeared very ill at ease, and gave a start of terror as Caroline lowered herself until she had brought the dildo against the shivering lips of Julie's cunt. 'Oh, madam!' she cried, 'you must not. Indeed, I could not bear your putting that thing into me. Oh, please let me alone!' and she began to whimper again, and attempted to push her mistress away from her. 'Be silent, child!' cried Caroline; 'Marie, hold her hands!' The maid did as directed, keeping the upper part of Julie's body still, while Caroline, as she lay over her, effectually prevented her from moving her legs. Feeling herself thus helpless, her presence of mind again deserted Julie, and she cried and moaned as she was conscious of the dildo touching and pressing against her outer orifice. But this did not deter Caroline in the slightest, and she made a slow but irresistible forward push. Julie gave a loud cry as the instrument entered into her, followed by a yet more piercing shriek as Caroline bore downwards, tearing open with the dildo, as she did so, the last defences of the girl's maiden citadel. The shriek dropped directly afterwards into a babble of sighs, and Julie's body was convulsed for a minute or two as she seemed to be endeavouring to break away from the cruel thing that pinned her down. She became a little quieter then, although her head moved slowly from side to side, with a sort of bewildered look in her eyes. This gradually deepened, but presently there came a sudden change, and they lighted up with a fixed and wonderful glance, as she felt the strings of her being touched.

Caroline noticed the expression, and increased the force and quickness of her movements. Julie raised her face slightly, no longer rocking it, but staring straight in front of her with a rapt and expectant look. Her brow and eyelids contracted, and she seemed full of an intense impatience of anticipation; she placed her hands flat on the bed and heaved upwards in an effort to cooperate with Caroline's actions. This rapidly brought the affair to a climax, and presently she almost leaped aloft, then fell inert and listless on her back with a long-protracted groan. Seeing that matters had come to a head, Caroline quickly got hold of the balls of the dildo, and syringed the whole contents in one powerful jet into Julie. This acted as the last straw on the girl's already over strung frame. She gave a muffled scream, and vainly attempted to raise herself, threw up her arms in spontaneous wildness, and the subsided into immovability. Caroline at once took herself away from the prostrate form beneath her, and as she drew out the weapon with which she had accomplished Julie's ravishment, I noticed that the moisture which covered it was streaked with crimson, while a further glance showed me that thin streams of blood mingled with the other liquor that oozed out of the part where she had been invaded.

At that moment, I became keenly conscious of the fact that this was the fate that awaited me. Indeed, once my real identity was revealed, my next visit to the club was sure to mean the end of my virginity. Next time it would be my blood flowing gently after being pierced by Caroline's dildo, but that story will have to wait for a later volume.

SUSY

It all began when Zilla, a member of my household and my Sapphic conspirator, received into her charge a pretty young girl to train as lady's maid. She was the orphan daughter of a soldier, Susy by name. The governess was greatly pleased when she heard of it and said it would be such a treat to see her in the bath with me and hear us talk together, and "my Queenie knows the kind of talk that will please her old Charlotte best.'

I planned the matter with Zilla, who was to be her initiator in the first instance and who promised carefully to report progress to me. She therefore brought her to her own room, and they slept together the first night. Next morning when

Susy

Zilla attended me as usual she told me she had no difficulty in obtaining Susy's fullest confidence; that she had a charming little cunt with smooth lips and just a suspicion of light silky hair at that part of the projection where the slit begins; that the little rosy clitoris was very sensitive and easily excited, and that altogether, from her disposition and previous learning, she was fitted and prepared in no ordinary degree for all kinds of amorous sports and enjoyments.

Zilla also found out that although Susy had not as yet been regularly fucked, she was perfectly familiar with the act and knew the names of all the parts employed with men as well as with other women — and liked to talk about them too; that she had seen her mother fucked by other men besides her own husband as well as numerous women; and that one of her mother's maids had frequently petted and looked at her cunny and taught her to bring herself to crisis at will. I said I would like her to attend me when taking my midday bath, and went on, "You may tell her, Zilla, as if from yourself, you know, that the more free and unconstrained she is with me, the better I will like her, and that nothing would please me more than to hear from herself a full and minute account of all she has ever seen and heard of these interesting matters, for I am exceedingly curious about such subjects.'

The old governess was delighted when I told her all this, especially when she heard that Susy had a smooth little fat cunt with scarcely any hair on it. 'How I shall enjoy,' she said, 'seeing her naked with you in the bath!'

So on the following day, I had the governess snugly ensconced in the towel press, seated on a chair and able through a slit in the door to see and hear all that passed in the bathroom.

I was soon *puris naturatibus*, but I observed that she hesitated about pulling off her shirt.

'Why, Susy!' I said, laughing, 'You don't mind my seeing you naked, I hope; it is natural enough to be ashamed before men, but it is excess of modesty for women to mind one another, for I expect we are all furnished pretty much after the same fashion. That's right,' I continued, as she drew her shirt over her head, 'and certainly,' I said, drawing her toward me and putting one hand on her bottom and the other on her smooth plump little cunny, 'you have no reason to hesitate, for you seem very nicely furnished for so young a lady; come: let us compare together.' of course my object was to make the girl display her young charms in the fullest manner, and to lead her on to lascivious talk so as to give more gratification to my dear old Charlotte, who was, I knew, at the moment, rubbing up her own old cunny as she feasted her eyes on this budding cunt.

I drew her forward to race the press, and passing my hand over her pretty rising mount, asked, 'Is it long, dear, since these silky hairs began to sprout?'

'No, missy, it is only within the last month that I have begun to need to shave it to keep my youthful appearance.'

'I'm quite glad that you keep it thus. These fat round lips are very soft, and this funny little lump between, how it slips about, do you often pet it with your finger?'

'Sometimes, miss,' she said, as she laughed and blushed.

I laughed too, and as I frigged her, said, 'Susy, you and I will be good friends, I think. And now, let me assure you that the more confidence you have in me, the better I will like you; and besides, I know very well what girls are, and that no matter how demure they are before men, when they are among themselves, they delight in unrestrained liberty, both of speech and action. And moreover, I don't think the worse of a girl, provided it be done wisely and discreetly. Now tell me, dear, was this pretty little chink every touched by another woman?' I asked, still continuing the frigging, so that she twisted and started as often as I pressed the sensitive top of her tiny clitoris.

'Yes, miss, Oh!'

'By more than one?'

'Yes, miss.'

'Often?'

'Yes, miss.'

'Ah! I thought so and I like you all the better. Now let us take our bath, and we can finish our talk afterward.' We then stepped in and enjoyed the refreshing effects of the cool water while we dipped and splashed about.

Susy grew more familiar as we played and toyed together, and became quite affectionate as she dried me afterward.

Before we put on our things again, I said, 'Sit down here with me awhile, Susy; lean back and open your thighs, you have a charming little loose chink and I want to get a good view of it; now tell me, who touched it first, and how did he do it; but first tell me, do you know my name for it?

'I do, miss, but I am ashamed to say it?'

'Why need you be ashamed? Is it cunt?'

'It is, miss.'

'Well, say it.'

'Cunt.'

'And before you proceed, what is a cunt for?'

'Oh, it is for—for—'

'Out with it.'

'Well, it is for fucking.'

'With what?'

'La, miss, you want me to say everything.'

'Of course I do.'

'Well then, fucked by a prick of a man.'

'Good girl, but is it for anything else as well?' I asked, saddened by her limited view of its utility.

'Well, miss, the first woman who touched my cunt was Miss Joyce. My mother was her washerwoman and she used to send me to carry home her clothes. Miss Joyce always got me to put them away for her in her drawers. She knew the time of my coming and generally had cakes and something nice for me to eat. One day she kissed me and called me her pretty little maid. She quickly saw that I felt flattered, for at that time I thought it a great thing to be kissed by a lady. Then she got me to sit on her knee and tickled me, first under my arms then between my things; at last she got her hand upon my cunt, and after awhile she prevailed on me to lie back, open my legs and let her look at it; and what do you think, nothing would satisfy her but to kiss and lick the inside with her tongue! Was that not horrible?'

'Not at all, dear Susy, it is quite a natural thing for a grown woman to kiss and suck the cunt of a nice girl like you; but go on, what did she do? Did she show you her cunt at all?'

'Indeed she did, she coaxed me even to unbutton her dress, and put my own fingers inside, and then she got me to kiss her and suck her cunt; one day she stopped me stark naked, and placed me across her lap with my cunt across her knee.'

'Did she ever try to get her fingers into your cunt?'

'Yes, often, but I was quite small and she could only get one inside.'

'Did you ever see anyone fucked, Susy?'

'Oh, dear yes, I saw my mother fucked, and indeed most of the women in the barracks. Sometimes when there were no men present, I saw them do such things to one another.'

'I am so glad; tell me everything and all about it; but, I declare, Susy, I do believe you are spending—stay let me taste it'; and putting my hands under her plump little bottom, and my face between her widely spread thighs, I rubbed my nose in the sweet savoury chink, and lapped up the hot rich juice that exuded from its excited depths.

'Dear miss, how pleasant that is,' she said, wriggling about, 'how kind and good you are! I never felt anything so nice; let me kiss and suck your sweet cunt in return.'

'Here then, Susy, I will hold it open for you while you suck it, and slip the tip of your finger into my bottom, I love to be tickled there at the same time, yes, that is very pleasant.'

I lay back, so that Charlotte might have a good side view of my cunt while Susy sucked it, and as she leaned forward, her own pretty little bum with its round hole just over the rosy chink of her cunt was turned to her too.

'Oh! Susy dear! I am spending now, suck it, love, suck my cunt,' and putting down my hands, I pressed her head between the wide-spread thighs as I felt the sweet suction of her lips on the clitoris and the point of her tongue darting into the sensitive orifice beneath.

'That is a good girl. You gave me great pleasure, Susy.'

MARY

Rebecca declared that of all the randy girls she ever saw, she never met the equal of quiet, demure, modest-looking Mary Bond.

She had also a particular fancy for looking at and playing with the cunts of other girls. She assured her that there was scarcely a young lady of her acquaintance whose cunt she had not seen and handled and that she liked even to kiss and suck them.

Rebecca asked her if she generally found it easy to prevail on them to allow her to take these freedoms?

She replied, that of course most girls more readily yielded their hidden charms to the enterprises of the other sex, and were more inclined to trust them, too; yet, as they all liked the thing itself, she usually found that, by gaining their confidence and by skilful allusion and suggestion exciting their imagination and providing their desires, she could mostly get them to meet her halfway; especially as they knew that with her they ran no risk of a big belly; and as she was always ready to gratify them with a similar inspection of her own belongings, she seldom experienced much difficulty. Rebecca told her how delighted she would be if she could witness one of these inspections without being seen herself.

She promised to gratify her if she could. So one day she told her that a young lady, Miss Madge Stevens, whose cunt she had often seen and petted, was to visit her next morning; and as she always brought her special visitors to her own room, she would hide her there first if she could spare the time.

She said she would arrange that, and promised to be there at the time she fixed. So accordingly, remaining home the next day under plea of a headache, she quietly stole upstairs to Mary's room, and by her direction, concealing herself under the dressing table; in the cover of which a slit was made to enable her to look out and see as well as hear all that passed.

Soon afterward, Mary and Madge entered the room together, with their arms round one another.

'Come sit with me on the bed, Madge, I have not seen nor petted your little fanny for nearly a fortnight; how is it getting on?'

'First rate,' replied Madge, 'how is your own?'

"Just as troublesome as ever; it is for all the world like a bird in a nest opening its mouth every moment expecting some tidbit to be popped into it!'

Madge laughed, 'I suppose that most girls, who know what the tidbit is like are in the same sort of expectation and desire; and true for you, Mary, your cunt is in a most excited condition; oh my! How hot it feels! And how red it looks. I am certain you have had a fuck lately; now tell me all about it like a darling. Ah! You are laughing! You can't deny it. You may trust me, dear.'

'Well, lie back first and perhaps I will tell you; draw up your thighs, and poke your bottom out that I may see it all, as I like a good sucking and kissing.'

The bed was opposite the table and window, so Rebecca had a magnificent view of Madge's splendid arse, with its great fat cheeks bulging out on either side, and a most delicious hairy randy-looking cunt gaping in the hollow below.

Mary pulled open the lips with her fingers as widely as she could, showing the rich carmine of its interior folds all glistening with the dews of love. Then drawing up her own dress behind, so as to indulge Rebecca with a view of her own naked posterior, which she knew she greatly admired, she kneeled on the floor and plunged her face between Madge's wide-spread thighs, and kissed her cunt with such vehemence that she caused that voluptuous young lady to exclaim in a loud voice, 'Oh! Mary you drive me wild! You make me long for a prick! Have you not got one! I would tell you to stick it in and poke it up to the last inch.'

'Hush, Madge if anyone heard you, what would they think?'

'What would they think? They could only think that we were a pair of love-stricken maids that were ripe and longing to be fucked, just as their mothers before them. But Mary, in sober earnest, I never did feel in such humour as now! Where is that dildo you were talking of! Fetch it, my dear, anything at all in the shape of a prick to give one some relief.'

Rebecca had already given Mary one of those precious instruments, and when she had to save her own over-taxed energies, she enjoyed watching her endeavours to satisfy her cunt with that inanimate substitute for the living tool. Not that I mean to repudiate or make light of the dildo. It has its own peculiar excellences and good qualities. It is more under command, and does not need the coaxing and the humouring which the living article sometimes requires. We can make it move fast or slow, just as we like, and it will retain its stiffness as long as we desire. It will discharge too at the precise moment when we can meet it with our own. But, at the best, it is still only a poor substitute for the living, throbbing organ of bliss wielded by a man we like, thrust into our quivering cunts by successive heaves and driven home by the mighty push of a vigorous backside.

But to return. Mary said, 'Well, remain as you are while I unlock my drawer and take it out of its hiding place.'

As she turned around she glanced toward the dressing table, and catching Rebecca's eye peeping out through the slit, she smiled and put her finger on her lip to warn her to keep quiet.

Then quickly returning she reoccupied her former place between Madge's wide-spread thighs and holding up the dildo, cried: 'Is not this a pretty plaything for two innocent maids like you and me, Madge, to amuse ourselves with! Now I will give you a taste of its performance, but I must stiffen it first,' she said, blowing into the tube and then screwing up the nozzle.

'Let me feel it in my hand,' said Madge, taking it up and rubbing its smooth red head to her lips; 'and, Mary is this an exact resemblance of a man prick? I did not think it was quite so large, but you can tell me about it, I am sure.'

'Don't be too inquisitive, Madge; one thing at least you may depend on, it is intended to be an exact resemblance, and as to its size, you can best judge of that when you have it in your cunt; now open it as much as you can; once we get the head in, the rest will be all plain sailing.'

She spread open the lops of the randy-looking cunt, and standing so as not to interrupt Rebecca's view, took the dildo again, and having moistened its top pushed it against the tender opening.

'Oh! Mary! Oh! It does feel very big, ah! You have got it in… that is a relief… how well you work it… yes, I like that… oh! It is beginning to feel very nice, go on push it in further… faster, harder.' Mary worked the dildo with one hand, while she frigged her own cunt with the other, panting at the same time, 'I am fucking you, Madge, and frigging myself. Oh! Prick… cunt… bottom… piss… fuck… fuck!' Throwing herself forward on Madge she hammered her own cunt on the butt of the dildo, while they both squirmed about in all the voluptuous wriggles of full enjoyment.

Rebecca described this scene as having a most overpowering effect upon her. It made her cunt flow like a river, while her heart beat audibly, and her breath came fast and hard. Yet the fear of frightening Madge and offending Mary caused her to use every effort to restrain herself; but at last she could endure it no longer; the view of Mary's splendid arse bounding between Madge's voluptuous thighs fairly conquered her. So slipping out from under the table she crept upon hands and knees behind Mary, and seizing her round the thighs began to kiss the soft cheeks of her bottom. Mary seemed almost to have expected her approach, for she did not start, nor utter any cry, but quietly spread her legs further apart and bent her bottom more to her face.

Under any circumstances Rebecca could not fail to have been moved by this extraordinary sight, but in her present excited state, it appeared absolutely celestial. She could just distinguish the fat lips of her cunt spread out on the end of the dildo, close to the little round hole of her arse, with its delicate pink edge wrinkled up, and fringed by fine silky hair and flanked on either side by the resplendent semi-orbs of her glorious bottom, lasciviously quivering with amorous excitement.

She applied her mouth without hesitation to the sweet little orifice, sucked it with vigour, and thrust in her tongue.

This was a treat Rebecca had not given her before, and she enjoyed it immensely. She pressed her bottom on her lover's face, and relaxed the constricting muscles, to allow her tongue to penetrate more deeply into that highly sensitive entrance.

Just then, a loud knocking at the door made them all jump. Rebecca, without saying a word, rushed back to her shelter, Madge smoothed down the bed and threw herself into a chair, while Mary fumbled at the door to give them time. When she did open the door her mother, who was standing outside, asked: 'What on earth are you two girls about? Making such a noise! And your door locked and your faces like scarlet and your dresses all tumbled!' and she glanced from one to the other. 'What I wanted was to ask whether you know anything of Miss Rebecca? A messenger has come from the hospital for her, and she is not in either of her rooms, thought I thought she had not left the house.'

'How are we to know? You don't expect to find her here, I hope, mamma.'

'I don't know as to that, my dear,' she replied laughing, 'for when two such skittish girls as you and Madge Stevens get together, if you have not a young man with you, I am quite sure you might have conscripted a woman instead. I say, what sort of a thing is that?' she said, with a twinkling eye, and a knowing look, as she pointed to the dildo lying on the floor at the bedside where it had fallen.

'Oh! Mamma,' groaned out Mary, covering her face with her hands, 'how horrible! What ill luck brought you in?'

'Ah well, dear,' said Mrs. Bond mildly, not wishing to make her presence disagreeable, 'you need not mind me so much; don't I know very well that it is not at all unnatural to like this sort of thing, and most girls have an itching for it, more or less, whatever they may say; and indeed, if they only amused themselves with such innocent playthings as this' — taking up the dildo — 'it might be much better for them. But which of you was trying it, may I ask?' As she spoke, she passed it through her fingers with a loving kind of touch, while her eyes glistened with amorous excitement.

Mary made no answer, but she and Madge looked at one another, and seeing the turn that matters were taking, they broke out into an uncontrollable fit of laughter; the events which followed, however, shall require a chapter unto themselves.

MRS. BOND

Mrs. Bond was fat, fair and forty; but she was something more, for not only had she a very imposing presence, and a remarkably find physique, but she was possessed of one of the hottest, randiest and most insatiable cunts that every poor widow was plagued with; but, at the same time, she was clever enough to maintain a character of the greatest decorum and respectability.

On this one occasion, she felt that having caught the girls in flagrante delicto, she might safely indulge her favourite passion; besides, she had been listening for some time at the door, and had heard sufficient to agitate very keenly her prurient inclinations.

So, sitting down on the bed, she joined in the laugher, and invited the girls to sit by her side. Then, placing her hand with lascivious pressure on Madge's soft thigh, she said: 'You really must give me a lesson in the use of this clever invention. I need to make up for the pleasures that have been taken from me, while you employ it in anticipation of pleasures you hope to enjoy in the future; and which, if report is to be relied on, you at least, Madge, will soon have to the utmost your desire. Let me feel how you are furnished up here. You know I have had great experience in these matters,' and stooping forward she ran her hand up under Madge's petticoats.

'Oh! Mrs. Bond, how can you!'

'What a luxuriant crop you have! This is a larger bush than mine though I am twice your age; and such a pair of luscious lips! How they will suck in the dildo, and cling around it with loving delight! Oh, Madge, I envy you your first fuck; but very likely you have tasted that pleasure already, eh Madge? You are quite as roomy here as I am.'

'Oh, Mrs. Bond! How you talk!'

'Why not, dear, I was myself fucked many times before I was married, by as many dildos as men, and my good husband was never the worse for it; of course, I was not fool enough to tell him, though he got the benefit of it, all the same, for I knew beforehand what would gratify him much better than if I had been a poor innocent unsophisticated girl. And now, as I want you both to be quite at your ease, I will, if you wish, give you a full account of how and when I was first fucked.'

'Do, dear Mrs. Bond, it will be delightful.'

'Very well, but let us place ourselves in position; I can talk more freely when I am looking at a cunt, and when somebody is petting mine. Tuck up, Madge, and let me see it, and place your hand here.'

'Oh, Mrs. Bond, what nice soft silky hair you have; and the mouth feels as hot as fire! May I see it?'

'Yes, dear, if you wish,' and pulling up her petticoats she displayed a pair of fleshy thighs, and between them a cunt of extraordinary luxuriance and extent, its great lips pouting out in the most wanton manner as if ready for anything.

'Oh, Mrs. bond, what a grand affair you have! Mary, did you ever see such a glorious love-chink?' and drawing the lips apart with her fingers, she exhibited its glowing interior.

Mary looked at her mother's cunt at first with a sly kind of interest mingles with feelings of shame at its exposure to the prying eyes of Rebecca, who, she knew well, was then regarding it with most lustful desires. But when Madge went on manipulating it, rubbing the large distended clitoris, pressing together, then opening wide, the fat pouting lips, her libidinous propensities overpowered her natural disinclination to make free with her mother's cunt, and with a sudden dash, she placed herself between her mother's widespread thighs, and having regarded for a moment the mysterious portals through which she had passed into life, she pressed her lips on the secret spot, drew the soft clitoris into her mouth, and probed with her penetration tongue the hot folds of the passage inside.

Mrs. Bond laughed with pleasure, as she pushed her tingling cunt against her daughter's mouth, and said: 'Why, Mary, Mary. Are you sucking your mother's cunt? I must see that your own sweet little pussy is soon gratified in the way it likes best. I have no doubt that if Miss Rebecca was here, she would be quite ready to repay it for the pleasure you are giving me; and I would place her cunt in my mouth and tickle her bottom while she tongued your cunt. And now that I think of it, when I finish my story, we need search for her, for I am sure she is in the house, and if she is, she may enjoy you at once, and we will all be happy to assist at the demolition of your maidenhead by a thing such as this,' she said, holding up the dildo.

Mary kept her head down, and said nothing, so turning to Madge, Mrs. Bond asked: 'What's your opinion, Madge, don't you think that Rebecca, who often passes whole evenings alone with her, has already explored her maiden secrets, and made her acquainted with the power of her Sapphic ways?'

'Indeed, it is highly probable; and as I was saying to her before you came in, in spite of her innocent looks, I am sure she has been often fucked, and could tell us all particulars of Rebecca's cunt, if she pleased. But in the meantime, don't forget the story you have promised us.'

'Well, my dears, let me say, by way of preface, that I am a great admirer of what the Americans call going the whole hog, that is, if I go in for a thing at all, I go in for it altogether; I mean what I say, and say what I mean. I am not ashamed to call a cunt, a cunt; and a prick, a prick. I enjoy fucking, and I like to talk of it. I delight in frigging and being frigged; and I find great pleasure in looking at and petting a nice cunt, like yours, Madge, and to have my own cunt at the same time caressed and sucked by my darling child is heaven itself.' Here she laid her hand most lovingly on the back of Mary's head as she licked between the fat unctuous lips and darted her tongue into the recesses.

'I sometimes think,' she continued, 'I must have been born with an itching cunt, at least, I don't remember any time when it did not. I have always loved to fiddle with cunts, my own and those of others, and suck them in my mouth, and was always gratified when their owners repaid the compliment by inspecting and kissing my little nest, as they called it. I had a governess, and used to tease her with all sorts of queer questions: what was a virgin? What was a eunuch? Why was it wicked for a woman to lie with another woman? And what harm could it do her? Her attempts to evade my questions only made me all the more curious. As I grew older, nature made me feel that my little slit was evidently so formed that something might enter it, and whatever that something was, I felt sure it would be a source of great pleasure and enjoyment. And I determined that if any opportunity ever presented itself, I would not fail to make the most of it. Well, my dears, the opportunity came in the shape of a slave girl, named Dinda. My uncle had a plantation in the hills about six miles from Kingston, where we lived, and I sometimes rode on my donkey to visit her. On such occasions I was always attended by Dinda, as the donkey was her special charge.

We usually took a short cut across the wild part of the country through which a small stream flowed rapidly down. One very hot day, we were passing near a deep pool in a retired part of the river. Dinda asked permission to take a dip to cool herself. I didn't understand her request for privacy, but I obliged and dismounted a little way off and told her I would mind the donkey while she was bathing. I soon heard Dinda splashing about in the water and the temptation arose in my mind to creep among some bushes that lined the bank and watch her as she sported naked in the water. The shrubs were pretty thick and enabled me to come quite close to the edge which overhung the water some four or five feet. I was delighted with the view of her black shining body and queer-looking breasts swaying from side to side as she rolled about enjoying the refreshing coolness of the stream. She had unusually large breasts for so young a lass. She touched her chest and cunt with her hand. Oh, I said to myself, that is the very thing I want to kiss. How nice it would feel on my mouth, and putting down my hand, I squeezed my lips and rubbed the clitoris. Her further proceedings were still more attractive, for leaning against the bank right opposite hiding place she commenced frigging herself with her own fingers in the most deliberate manner, just as if she was being herself fucked.

Mrs. Bond

In my eagerness to see all I could, I incautiously stretched too far over the brink, and to my terror and dismay, the bough on which I was leaning gave way, and I tumbled head-foremost into the water. I gave a cry as I sank below the furnace, but in a moment I felt myself borne up by the arms of Dinda, taken to the other side and drawn up the sloping bank.

Beyond a good fright, and a thorough wetting, I was uninjured, so, looking at Dinda's rueful countenance, I burst out laughing, as I said, "Dinda, what shall we do? I am wet to the skin.'

'Missy must take off her wet things or she will catch cold; leave them here and I will dry them on the rocks.' And she turned as if to go away.

'Stay, Dinda, I want you to help me; I am so drenched, that I never could get them off by myself.'

I turned my back to her, and after a deal of tugging and twisting, we got them all off except my stockings and shirt. I then sat down while she spread them on the rocks to dry. Shivering with cold, I called Dinda again, 'Dinda, you must help me off with these also, they make me quite chilly. Thanks. Now come and give me a good rubbing, as if you were shampooing me.'

I stood with my back toward her, while she rubbed my arms and legs. I knew by her quick breathing that she was growing very excited. I pushed my bottom up to her, and felt her fingers poking against me. She put her hand on my buttocks, and rubbed the cheeks; then passing between my thighs, rubbed softly up and down. The side of her hand touched the lips of my cunt; I opened my thighs a little and she touched my cunt again, and yet again, each time pressing more firmly against the lips. She passed her other hand round in front and placed it on my mons, just beginning to be overspread with silky down. One finger slipped in between the lips. 'Oh! Dinda, that tickles me.'

The other hand passed swiftly round, and with both together, she pressed my bottom into her. Then she shifted and I felt her mouth where her hand had been, and her tongue poking stiffly between my thighs, and rubbing up against the lips of my cunt. She opened the lips with her fingers, and her tongue went deeper than I would have believed any tongue could.

'Oh! Dinda! How it smarts! Oh, how strong you are! Hold me—I cannot stand against you.' She leaned forward, and let me down on my hands and knees, and grasping me firmly by the hips she resumed her licking me from behind. My cunt opened, and, oh girls! How delicious it felt.

The joy I felt in giving down my own share of love's essence was so great that I fell prone on my belly, with Dinda over me, pressing on my bottom, and her fingers taking the place of her tongue on my soaking in my cunt.'

'Oh, Mrs. Bond, I'm coming, too!' cried Madge. 'Rub your finger in the entrance. Oh! I'm coming. I'm coming.'

'Straddle over my face then, Madge, put your cunt on my mouth and let me taste your spending.'

Mary too resolved to share in the common ecstasy as she gazed with pleasure at the voluptuous prospect Madge presented with her mother's mouth buried in her cunt. So pulling up her skirts behind, she turned her naked arse in all its attractive beauty toward the table, while she frigged herself with her finger and lapped up the rich streams which now began to flow from her mother's fountain of delight.

Rebecca described this scene as being the most exciting spectacle she had ever witnessed, and though she had spent twice but a short time before, her cunt was overflowing with love juices and she felt consumed with vehement desire. She had a shrewd suspicion, which she afterward found was correct, that Mrs. Bond was perfectly aware of her presence, and was in fact only endeavouring to draw her out from her hiding place.

She was naturally of a prying disposition, especially in such matters, and by listening at doors and spying through peep-holes, she had made herself acquainted with all that was going on between Rebecca and her daughter; and had been for some time planning how she could turn her knowledge to account in gratifying herself by a participation in their joy.

On this occasion she felt certain she was in the room, and her sagacious eyes at once fixed on the dressing-table as the only shelter that could afford her a sufficient hiding place.

She accordingly arranged the little scene on the bed and told her exciting story, both with the intention of drawing Rebecca out and then profiting by her excitement to obtain for herself the gratification she desired.

She did not succeed however as she expected, for Rebecca, wishing to hear more of her extraordinary confession, by a great effort restrained herself.

Among her other distinguishing qualities, Mrs. Bond never allowed that she was beaten. Apparent failure only nerved her for renewed and stronger effort.

So after resting a few moments on the bed, she sat up and said, 'My dears, we all want something to give us fresh spirit; run Mary to the pantry and fetch a little of my French liqueur.'

Mary soon returned with a decanter and glasses. The effect of the strong and highly spiced stimulant was soon apparent; Mrs. Bond tumbled the two girls on the bed, tossed up their clothes, smacked their bottoms and kissed their cunts. They retaliated in like manner upon her, to her evident satisfaction.

'Now Mary,' she cried, 'I must have a good look at your own pussy; lie across the bed with your head resting on the edge, and I will straddle over you and suck your cunt while you watch Madge giving me a taste of the dildo.'

Mary placed herself in the desired position, and her mother, after fastening up her skirts, stooped over her and buried her face between her upraised thighs. Her object evidently was to favour Rebecca with a full view of her splendid posteriors bulging out like two creamy globes on either side of the furrow where nestled her moist cunt and inviting arsehole.

Madge also tucked up her dress at Mrs. Bond's request, and then with Mary's help worked the dildo in her salacious cunt.

Mrs. Bond was one of those whose pleasure is intensified by the consciousness that all the secrets of their cunt and bottom are open for inspection. So she exclaimed, 'Dear girls, that is most delicious, are you both watching?'

'Oh yes, dear Mrs. Bond, we see all your fine bottom, and your cunt sucking in the dildo! Could you go on with your story now, or shall we wait until you spend?'

'Oh! I can tell it now, if you wish; keep the dildo where it is, and only stir it a little now and then.'

Here, as luck would have it, some stray hair or fly tickled Rebecca's nose that, in spite of all her repressive efforts, she delivered a tremendous sneeze. Mrs. Bond jumped from the bed, ran to the table, thrust her hand under the cover and caught hold of the first thing that met her touch, which was nothing other than Rebecca's left nipple.

'Hallo! What have we here? Murder! Thieves!' and tightening her grasp on the exposed limb she tugged with such force that Rebecca was compelled to crawl forth, trying to look droll, with her finger in her mouth.

'Oh! Rebecca! What a shocking lass you are! Prying into the secrets of us poor women. What shall we do with her, girls?'

'Tie her to the bedpost,' said Madge, laughing, 'and let Mary be the executioner, for I guess she is more to blame than she is.'

'Capital, the very thing Madge, you are worthy of your salt. Come here, my young lady, and don't stand there in that barefaced manner before these innocent girls. Face about, we will make you bare-bottomed as well as barefaced,' she said, tucking up her shirt behind, while the girls tied her hands firmly with towels to the bedpost.

'Now, Madge, off to the garden, and fetch a bundle of good stout twigs, and do you Mary go to the house closet for some strong cord to tie them up.'

Having thus got rid of the girls, she turned to Rebecca.

'Now, Madame, I want your serious answer, by a strange stroke of luck you have go behind the scenes; now I want you to assure me that you intend to act honourably by my daughter Mary. If you give me your faithful word then you shall be welcome, not only to enjoy her anew, but to share in all our private amusements.'

(This was a trying question, and very craftily put. According to my notions, Rebecca answered wisely and well. She had found an agreeable, clever, well-educated girl, devotedly attached to her and of a temperament warm and lascivious as her own; and that knowledge, which might have repelled others, she wisely judged, only secured for her that freedom that such a relationship would have been to her insufferable; hence her reply.)

'Well, dear Mrs. Bond, my answer is ready. I love Mary. She is just the girl to my taste. As soon as I have a home to take her to, I will take her to live with me as honourably as any man ever could.'

'All right, I always knew you there was a true lady behind your decadent lesbian exterior; now we will try to gratify you as much as we can,' and she placed her hand lovingly on her next, and pressing up to her, gently delved within it.

Rebecca looked up at her hands, and said, 'My hands are tied, or I would return your kind caresses.'

She at once reached up and untied the knot; in doing so, her fine swelling bosom was brought close to Rebecca's face, she kissed the voluptuous globes, and at once placed her hands on the older woman's bottom and cunt. She leaned back on the bed, her thighs expanded, she slipped her hand in between; her fingers against her open cunt; she pushed it, it entered; her fingers all inside and her palm pressed against her bottom. They heard steps approaching; Rebecca stopped heaving. 'It is only the girls,' she muttered, 'don't mind them; finger me, give me all you can, quick.'

Mary entered and could hardly believe her eyes when she saw Rebecca on top of her mother, and the sight did not please her. Rebecca looked around and smiled, while Mrs. Bond said, 'Mary approach. Rebecca has given me her promise to make an honourable lesbian of you, and this is her reward.' Mary still looked doubtful. When Madge returned with the twigs and heard the last words, she rushed into the room with a merry shout; 'Hold her, Mrs. Bond, Hold her... now's your chance, Mary — punish her — punish the wretch; after promising herself to you, the very first thing she does is fuck your mother! — did anyone ever see the like?'

She hastily tied up the twigs, put them into Mary's hand and pushed her toward Rebecca's naked bum, which presented itself in the most suggestive manner as she leaned over to get her hand inside Mrs. Bond.

She looked smilingly at her, and said, 'Do it, Mary, I deserve a whipping.' But Mary had evidently no heart for the office, and she applied the twigs in the softest way to the buttocks of her lover.

Observing which, Madge pulled the bundle of twigs impatiently out of her hand saying: 'You are no good; give it to me, I'll punish her,' and she laid on Rebecca's arse with such a will that she made her jump again, to Mrs. Bond's manifest delight.

Rebecca fucked with her whole hand as she had never fucked before. 'Oh! Madge, have you no mercy? Stop you vixen!' and Mrs. Bonds fully spent.

After a few minutes of rest, during which they all arranged their tumbled

Mrs. Bond

dress, Mrs. Bond said, 'Now, my children, we must separate for the present; but as Madge has promised to remain for the day, we hope that you, Rebecca, will join our party this evening.'

'Thanks, Mrs. Bond, I will be most happy,' replied Rebecca; while Madge added: 'And then, Mrs. Bond, you will favour us with the continuation of your interesting story.'

As luck would have it, the rest of the evening was spent with social obligations which forbade the telling of the end of the story, and soon after Rebecca was off to make the life in which I was to join her. That life, I am happy to say, continues and will be the subject of my future literary endeavours.

FRANCIS

I invited Jimmy to come to us again, both for her gratification, and as a diversion for Lady Ferrars and my husband. Jimmy had decidedly Sapphic tastes, and declared that while she enjoyed amazingly the prods of a sturdy prick in her cunt, yet her pleasure seemed increased tenfold when she could at the same time pet and suck the cunt of another woman in as randy a state as herself. So to gratify her, I used to lie on my back across the bed with my head resting on the edge; then she would bend over me with her belly resting on my breasts and her open cunt right over my face. Then she would encircle my thighs with her arms, holding open the lips of my cunt with her hands, would suck the clitoris while she frigged the passage with her fingers.

Once while at Jimmy's country house, she had allowed me to watch her with her cunt pressed on the mouth of one of her lovers, who seemed to sup up with peculiar zest the unctuous drops which exuded from that lustful gap. When she had finished licking round the sides, and had probed the hot juicy passage with the full length of her penetration tongue, she told her to lie back with her legs drawn up and her bottom turned toward a servant named Sally.

Then addressing her charwoman—who might be correctly termed her cuntwoman, she said, 'Now, Sally, my dear lady, give me a good bellyful of dildo while you feast your eyes on Susan's randy slit.'

Sally did as she was told until Jimmy had been plugged and spent many times over, and finally She turned her bottom toward me in my hiding place, still holing her thighs at their widest stretch. I had been frigging her own cunt with the middle finger of my left hand, now emerged from my hiding place and dipped the four fingers of my right in the slit of her Jimmy's cunt and rubbed them up and down the open chink.

'Oh, that's grand! I'm going to spend.'

'Will you ladyship get over me and spend in my mouth, while I frig my own cunt and tickle your ladyship's arse.'

She did as I had requested over Susan with a knee on either side and her cunt pressed down on her face. I could hear the sucking of lips in my cunt while she frigged away at her own and thrust the forefinger of her other hand into the hole of Sally's arse. Then my whole body seemed to writhe in voluptuous contortions as she poured into Jimmy's mouth the rich liquor of her cunt.

Then they lay side by side to rest, with all the interesting parts of their palpitating forms still uncovered and in full view of everyone present.

You can me sure I was looking forward to Jimmy's arrival, but I have gotten ahead of myself. Before my letter had even reached her, a strange denouement occurred which I will now proceed to relate.

Lady Ferrars was visited almost every day by a very handsome boy, dressed in naval uniform, who she called her middy. He had beautiful violet eyes, and a profusion of flaxen curls. He generally came in the morning and remained some hours in Lady Ferrars' room, writing her letters and making up her accounts — as he told me. I took a fancy to the boy and often tried to get him to talk with me, but he seemed very shy, and evidently avoided meeting me as much as he could.

Lady Ferrars always spoke most kindly to him, and in every way treated him with marked consideration.

When I questioned the Lady concerning this youth, she told me she had picked you up at an English seaport, and as he could keep accounts, understood the management of a yacht and had a decided taste for the sea, she retained him in her service as an attendant companion.

This explanation did not quite satisfy me, and my curiosity becoming more aroused, I set myself to probe the matter, and find out the true nature of the connection.

Besides, I was piqued at the youth's indifference to myself; it was a new sensation to me to meet one of the other sex who appeared totally unaffected by my charms; and what increased the mystery was that in spite of my admiration of his good looks, there seemed some subtle influence pervading him that repelled us mutually, just as if we were two similar poles of a magnet; and the cause, I determined to find out.

So one day, getting my husband to take Lady Ferrars out of the way about the time when the middy usually called, I opened the door for him myself, brought him into my boudoir and closed and fastened the door.

Frances

He seemed surprised, and sat down with great reluctance on the seat I offered him, looking around as if prepared to bolt at the first opportunity.

In order to set him more at his ease, I sat down beside him, and looking kindly at him, said, 'My young friend, I am so pleased with your constant attention to Lady Ferrars that I wish to know something more about yourself. First tell me how old you are, then your name and how you came to meet his Ladyship.

'I am eighteen years old, my name is Francis Gripton. My mother kept a lodging house in Southampton, and Lady Ferrars used to stop with her when she remained on shore. She often took me out in her yacht, and finding me useful, she asked me to enter her service.'

'You seem greatly attached to Lady Ferrars.'

His eyes flashed as he quickly replied, 'Why should I not be? She is very good to me and to my mother also. She is constantly sending her presents.'

'I like you all the better for it; we are all fond of her here.'

A look of scorn passed over his beautiful features as he said, 'Yes, but you are a married lady, and have not any right to be thinking thus of Lady Ferrars; you ought to be fond only of your own husband.'

I was both surprised and amused at the earnestness of the boy, and I thought, more than ever, that there was something underlying this and I must discover what it was. So I said in my kindest manner, 'Why, Francis, you need not be angry; at all events, if you are so much attached to Lady Ferrars, you ought to be pleased at our being fond of her, even as we love our husbands as well; and we would like to be fond of you too' — and I put my hand on his shoulder.

He drew back with a frightened air, 'Oh, please, don't trouble your head about me; I am not worth thinking about.'

'But you are, Francis, and I like you very much,' and I tried to draw him towards me.

'Please let me go, Mrs. Harpur; you remind me of Potiphar's wife,' and he smiled in a curious way. 'I am not, however, going to fly from you like Joseph, but I really have duties which I must attend to.'

He arose as if to go, but I held his arm with my right hand, and passing my left down his front before he suspected my object, I pressed it between his thighs; as I expected, there was no appearance of what Shakespeare calls his codpiece there; all was smooth, with the exception of a rounded fullness, which told me how luxuriously the want was supplied by a pair of pouting lips.

'Why, Francis, you have been deceiving us all; you are a girl,' and I put my hand on her breast to make sure.

'Oh, Mrs. Harpur, what shall I do? If Lady Ferrars knows that you have found me out, she will be terribly vexed. She will hate me, and perhaps leave me behind when she sails away,' and she burst into tears.

'Ah, well, don't cry, dear, I will see that she is not vexed with her little mistress—you are a brave girl—I admire you for your devotion to Lady Ferrars, and if you let me, I will love you as a sister, but you must conceal nothing from me—there must be candour on both sides, and then we shall be the best of friends; and let us begin by being mutually free with each other. Pet my fanny with your pretty little hand,' I said, lifting my dress and spreading my thighs as she pushed her hand up to my region of delight, 'and I will investigate the sweets and capacities of your own little love chink,' proceeding to unbutton her trousers and open them down the front. Inserting my fingers between the moist lips of her fat little slit, I said, 'Of course, you know this is your cunt, and you are familiar, I have no doubt, with all the terms and expressions of love.'

'Yes, I think I know them all pretty well. Lady Ferrars likes me to use them; do you like to hear them too?'

'I do, dear Francis, it not only saves trouble and beating about the bush, but I find, as most everybody does, that the free use of bawdy terms has an extraordinary effect in stirring up amorous emotions and creating sexual desire. So, let us talk freely of pricks, and cunts, and fucking, and bottoms, and arses too. What does Lady Ferrars prefer? What would she have you do to her? And how often does she request it?'

'Almost every day, and sometimes oftener. In the daytime, she is fond of having me on my knees before her, lapping up her fluids without her even disrobing; but at night, she loves to have me quite naked, and she fucks me with her collection of dildos in every imaginable way and position, though I think what she likes best—at least, when she is fresh—is to have me lying while she mounts my face and I kiss her cunt.'

'I know the position well, it is a general favourite. Did you ever suck a woman's cunt before Lady Ferrar's, Francis?'

'No, I had never had the opportunity, but I find that I cannot get enough of it and I am quite willing to suck yours, if you like.'

'Well, we shall have a mutual suck by and by; the salty taste of a nice cunt like yours, Francis, is very pleasant. But tell me, would you be very jealous if you saw Lady Ferrars with me?'

'No, not now that I know you. She can't be with either of us exclusively. I once thought she might have devoted herself to me alone.' Here, her beautiful eyes became suffused with tears. 'But that,' she added, checking herself, 'was, I suppose, great presumption in me; yet it was a pleasing dream.'

'Would you mind, dear Francis, telling me how her Ladyship first obtained the enjoyment of your favours?'

'Not in the least, Mrs. Harpur, but remember it is in strict confidence. As I told you, her Ladyship used to lodge in my mother's house when staying at Southampton and I often waited on her. She was very kind and gentle in her manner to them, and gave me nice presents. I liked her. I loved her. I was then only a silly girl. I allowed her to hold my hand and kiss me. One evening, we two were alone in the house; when I brought in her tea, she took me in her arms, told me that she loved me, and called me her own Fanny. She kissed me, drew me on to her knee, and put her hand under my neckerchief and felt my breast.

This did not alarm me, for I thought it was quite *en regle* for a Lady to befriend a pretty innocent girl such as I in whatever way she pleased—most of the novels I was in the habit of reading had some such circumstance for their plot; and then, her manner was so seductive, and her touch so delightful, that I felt intoxicated by her love, and unable to oppose her as she went on from liberty to liberty until she had explored my cunt with her fingers and, having pulled up my dress and separated my thighs, was at last gazing on its virgin bottom.

It was the first time anyone, man or woman, had meddled with me there, and I felt as if my whole being was concentrated in that one spot. My cunt thrilled as she rubbed about the clitoris, but when she pushed her fingers up the as-yet-unbroken passage, I started, and exclaimed, 'Oh, my Lady, what are you doing to me? I never felt like this before.' I wriggled my bottom, while the lower part of my belly and all between my thighs tingled with voluptuous heat mingled with pain.

'Does my finger hurt you, darling?'

'It does, my Lady, but I like it,' spreading my thighs and turning up my bottom to her, "only it makes me feel so queer.' And that was as much as she did with me that day, but since we have done much more.'

'Why, Francis, you have told that in the most charming way. You know what love is—you were born for it. Cupid must have had something to say to the getting of you. You are worth a score of the mawkish, half-dead-and-alive women one meets nowadays. But, let us now have a little taste of tribadism together and first let me have a good view of your little fanny, I am sure her lips must be watering after all this talk,' and I made her lie back. Then lifting her shirt, I uncovered all her smooth white belly. 'Open, love, spread wide open the book of your secret charms. What voluptuous development is here! Lady Ferrars made a wise choice in you, Francis, for here is cunt to perfection, and plenty of it. People say that little women have the largest cunts, but I never saw yours excelled by big or little. Your light hair too enables one to see more of its luxurious shape, and the extreme whiteness of your skin sets off its most lascivious lips which look as if they were just going to speak of dildos, pricks and fucking; and this clitoris shines like a piece of sensitive coral, and this crimson furrow seems the very avenue of bliss. And how moist it is! And how extremely hot inside! It makes me wish I had a dildo to satisfy its cravings. However, I will do what I can with my mouth and tongue,' and stooping down, I kissed and sucked the fragrant lips.

'Dear Mrs. Harpur, it is your goodness makes you praise my little fanny. I am sure your own is much nicer—won't you get over me and let me have a suck, too.'

'I will, my pet, but not just now; I have a plan in my head: let us take a bath together, and when we are quite naked we can enjoy one another with more satisfaction. Go in there; I want to give directions to the servants, so that we may not be disturbed. You can meanwhile undress, and I will be with you in a minute.'

I then ran to the surgery, where, with my usual good fortune, I met Rebecca and Lady Ferrars, who had just come in.

'Hah! My Lady, I have found you out; your pretty little page turns out to be a blooming mistress, and I commend your taste, for she is a choice little piece.'

'Well, Queenie, I knew it would happen sooner or later. But how does the little pet bear the discovery herself?'

Oh, she shed tears enough when I forced her secret, but she brightened up when I promised to lover her myself and make all square with you; so you will have to be kind and indulgent; and if you don't object, she will form a very pleasant addition to our social party.'

'That is just what I was planning, my dear Queenie. I meant to offer her as a tidbit to my friend Rebecca as a small return for her kindness in another matter.'

'Right, my Lady; and Rebecca, I promise you a treat, for she has the most charming love-trap I ever saw. She is now in my bathroom undressing. I am going back to her in a few moments, and if you and Freddy care to witness a little love-play between two women, you may betake yourselves to the spying place which you and Rebecca so cleverly contrived.'

They were both delighted with my plan, and went off to my husband's dressing-room, which opened into my bathroom by a concealed door by means of which anyone in either room could hear and see all that passed in the other.

Meanwhile I gave instructions to the servants not to admit visitors, nor allow us to be disturbed, and then hastened to rejoin Francis—or Frances—as we must now spell it. I found her undressed with the exception of her shirt; she blushed when I helped to draw it over her head, and the lovely girl stood revealed in all her naked charms.

Her shapely limbs, so smooth and glossy, shone like alabaster. Her delicious belly spread itself like a voluptuous plain between her firm strawberry-tipped bubbies and the rising mount sacred to Venus. And the mount itself, covered but not obscured by light silky hair, divided into two remarkably full and sensuous lips which curved down between her swelling thighs, while the inner furrow gleamed as a crimson streak, the rosy clitoris protruding its tiny head at the upper end.

I noticed these particulars as she stood before me helping me remove my clothes.

When all was ready we entered the bath together; and then commenced a scene of sportive play which must have displayed in fullest perfection whatever beauties or feminine charms we possessed. The invigorating effect of the bath joined with the lascivious ideas produced by the touch and view of our naked bodies threw us both into a state of extreme amorous excitement.

So when we came out and had dried one another, with particular attention to our cunts and bottoms, I took her in my arms and turned her up on the couch. As I stooped over her with my head between her up raised thighs, she pressed me down until my cunt rested on her mouth. Then the mutual suction of our lips and the active penetration of our tongues caused us to turn and twist our bodies in all the circlings of voluptuous enjoyment. We rolled over and over, alternately taking the upper side, all the while tightly enfolded in each other's arms; until at last a copious spend subdued our excitement and cooled us down.

Then we rested, I placed Frances so that her moist and rosy quim was turned towards the concealed door, and asked her to favour me with a full account of how she came to assume man's attire, and of some adventures which she said she had encountered while endeavouring to conceal her true sex; and I added, 'Call me Queenie, like everybody else.'

Then Frances embarked on her long story. This is what she said:

After Lady Ferrars had taught me to know and enjoy the delights of love, I clung to her with all my heart. Her image filled my soul, and devotion to her became the guiding principle of my life. How I used to long for the friendly covering of the night, when I could steal unobserved into her room! How fast the happy hours speeded by as I lay encircled in hers arms! How my fond and curious hand wondered over her manly frame, and with what delight I handled her noble cunt, and kissed it as an expression of my adoration. She often lighted a number of candles that she might view me naked. Then with what pleasure I spread my thighs to allow her to see and examine all my hidden charms. How willingly I turned and bent my body to let her view my cunt and bottom in different aspects. I frigged my cunt. I piddled before her, and to please her, called it pissing; I contrived different ways of fucking, and invited her to put her fingers and dildos into my cunt in the most outlandish positions I could imagine.'

Thus a few weeks passed rapidly away; and then I fancied she was growing tired of me, for she spoke of going to sea. I burst into tears and said she did not love me, otherwise she would not think of going away and leaving me.

She assured me, she had not intention of leaving me; that her great desire was to have me with her, and that she had been planning how she could get me away without a commotion, and then provide for my security and comfort.'

She told me that she had a lady friend at Brighton, who would take charge of me at first, and in whose house she could see and enjoy me as much as ever; that she was purchasing a new yacht and intended to engage a different crew, who would not recognise me. Then she suggested my assuming man's attire and sailing with her as a middy.

I hesitated about the male costume, but as, on talking it over, that it seemed the only feasible plan, I consented. So Lady Ferrars got her friend Mrs. Simpson to write to my mother inviting me to pass some time with her and offering to complete my education and bring me out in good society. She was highly pleased, and thus all was satisfactorily arranged.

Lady Ferrars started for London, and in due course I arrived in Brighton and was met at the coach office by a smart young lady who introduced herself as Miss Anna Simpson, the youngest daughter of Lady Ferrars' friend. We took a cab and shortly arrived at a quiet house in a retired street where I was cordially received by Mrs. Simpson and another young lady.

I did not fancy them much for they seemed a good deal over dressed and not very refined in manner; however, they were Lady Ferrars' friends and that was enough for me.

Mrs. Simpson told me she had instructions from her Ladyship to provide me with a middy's uniform, something like that of the Royal Navy, and everything necessary for a sailor's outfit; and she handed me a letter from her in which she stated that she was detained in London, but would rejoin me at Brighton as soon as possible and meantime to make myself at home, call for all I wanted and enjoy myself in every way I could.

Anna attended me to my room, and as she was a very merry girl, we had great fun together. She soon made me understand that she knew all about my connection with Lady Ferrars, but, she said, that was nothing uncommon, for nearly all the girls of her acquaintance had some lady friend whom they especially liked, and whom they often favoured by yielding to their wishes.

While saying this, she was trying to get her hand up under my petticoats.

'Why do you push away my hand?' she asked. 'Come dear, don't be over modest—don't I know very well that your little fan is well used to being petted, and looked at, too—there—let see it; now must have a kiss—open your thighs—open more. Oh, how nice you are! No wonder, Lady Ferrars is so fond of you! Do you know,' she rattled on, 'we often have ladies to supper, and plenty of drink, and then we have no end of fun. They love to tumble us about and see our bubbies, and our cunts and bottoms too; and then, of course, we retaliate by pulling out their cunnies and titties; and then we are sure to fall under them and our cunts get crammed with dildos in no time. We expect such a party tonight; will you join us and share in the fun?'

'Oh, no, Anna, I would be sorry to let any woman touch me there except Lady Ferrars. How could you let any woman make free with you in that way except you loved her.'

'My dear Fanny, what a child you are! Nobody could get on with such a notion as that. In the words of the poet:

'The mouse that always trusts to one poor hole can never be a mouse of any soul.'

The way to enjoy life is to be free with everyone who treats you well and pays you well.

There are two more of us in this house; we find it convenient to live with Mrs. Simpson, for she is respectable, takes good care of us, manages all our business and on the whole treats us fairly and well. We all like her, and call her mother, though none of us are really related to her.

'You will only be with us for a day or two, but my desire is, don't make yourself singular; enjoy life while you can, and depend upon it. Lady Ferrars won't think the worse of you. She knows this house and the company one may expect to meet in it, for she has been often here herself; and more than once, I have had her for a whole night in my arms, and I can tell you, she was not idle there—now, what do you say to that? So make your mind easy on her account. Most of the ladies about town keep mistresses, and more than that, many of them like, now and then, to exchange with one another for the sake of variety.'

This extraordinary revelation took me aback. An uneasy sensation crept over me as I, for the first time, realized my position. I threw myself on the bed and sobbed aloud.

Anna seemed to pity me; she put her arms round me and whispered in my ear, 'Don't fret, Fanny, you are a sweet girl. These things are perhaps strange to you, but nobody will harm you; you can do just as you please while you are here.

Lady Ferrars warned us to treat you with every consideration, and to make you as happy as we could. She is very fond of you. So dry your tears, and come with me, I will show you some funny scenes that will amuse you and drive away those melancholy thoughts.

We have a habit here of bringing our lady visitors to our own rooms where we can have them all to ourselves. But Mrs. Simpson has made spying places for viewing all that passes in each apartment. We all know this very well, and none of us minds having prying eyes watching us as we sport with our lovers, exposing our cunts and turning up our bottoms. In fact, I enjoy a good fuck ten times as well when I know that there are wistful eyes watching how I heave my rump, and hold my woman as she works up and down, driving my tongue into her cunt.' But perhaps, dear Queenie, I am only boring you with this long recital, and you don't care to hear a description of what Anna brought me to see.'

'On the contrary, I am deeply interested, in fact, you are giving me such pleasure, darling Frances, that my cunt is just on the flow, and if you care for a suck, now's your time.'

'Here I am, then, dearest Queenie, draw up your legs and let me get my hands under your bottom, so that I can push my mouth well in between the moist lips of your quim.'

As she buried her face between my drawn-up thighs, I so managed that her beautiful arse should be in full view of the aperture in the concealed door. This opening though large was covered by a tall mirror, which could be moved on a sliding frame. As I looked toward it I saw that the glass was being noiselessly pushed to one side, until there was space enough for a large dildo with a glowing head to be projected in. it was Lady Ferrars' dildo, one that must be quite familiar to Frances, yet that she could hardly recognise under these circumstances.

Lady Ferrars and Rebecca told me afterward, that having taken off their dresses on account of the heat, they both stood close together intently watching us through the aperture; that the full exposure of our cunts and bottoms, and above all our wanton talk, had excited them in the highest degree and, as they pressed together, their cunts became so moistened that their legs were quite coated; that Lady Ferrars' hands found their way round her in front of Rebecca where they naturally encountered and found their way into her cunt; that as she pressed against her naked bottom, while gazing over her shoulder at the exciting scene in the bathroom, her Ladyship's fingers struggled hard to find a lodgement in Rebecca's arse. What happened after that, I cannot say but I fancy she succeeded.

Meanwhile, Frances, in the most randy manner, wriggled her arse as she drew from me the soft effusion and I heard Lady Ferrars gave a suppressed grunt of satisfaction and delight.

The looking glass was then moved back nearly to its place, and Frances and

I settled ourselves on the sofa. I made her lean back with her cunt and bottom well in view; and she put her hand on my cunt as she continued her story.

Anna first brought me to a closet adjoining a room which she told me was occupied by a girl named Ellen, who was considered the beauty of their party; that a short time before my arrival, her favourite lover, the rich old Marquis of L—, had come to pay her a visit, and had been taken as usual to her room, so we might expect to see them together.

The peep-hole was over a couch, so that parties could recline as they watched what was going on in the room. Anna and I lay along the couch and she told me to look through; meanwhile, she raised my dress behind that she might rub her belly and cunt against my bottom.'

Here, I could not help smiling as I thought how funny it was that the very same dodge which Frances described was now being practised with regard to herself. She observed the smile, but thought it was caused by what she was doing in my cunt; so giving my clitoris an extra squeeze, she went on.

Looking in, I perceived that Ellen, with the exception of her silk stockings and laced sandals, was perfectly naked. Her black hair was down and streamed over her polished shoulders; and her beautiful bottom, under which I could just perceive the pouting lips of her cunt, was turned toward me as she stooped forward in the act of sponging with water the languid tool of the most noble marquis who was seated astride a bidet.

'Then she carefully wiped it, and when she stood up, she remained on her knees that she might hold it to her mouth. She first rubbed its read about her face and over her eyes, then she took as much as she could into her mouth while she worked his balls with one hand and tickled his bottom with the other.

Meantime, Anna got her hand on my cunt, and pressed me into her as she kept rubbing her mouth against my bottom.'

'What are they doing? Tell me everything you see,' she whispered, still frigging my clitoris and pounding my bottom.'

Anna's movements now become very energetic. She banged herself against my bottom. She worked her finger in and out of my cunt, and muttered, "Oh! If it were a pri-i-c-k!' spinning out the word prick, 'to fuck your cu-n-t; or perhaps you would like it here,' inserting another finger in my bottom-hole, 'to fuck—fuck—fuck your arse, or, best of all, to have both together—two pricks fucking arse and cunt at one ant the same time.'

'Oh! Anna! You are sending me mad! There, that will do, you have made me spend twice already.'

'So I perceive. You have given down a lot. You are the very devil at spending and your little cunt is all in a glow. We may leave this, however; there will be nothing more to see here, at least for the present. Come, I will show you another scent.'

She then took me to the room of a girl named Sarah, whom she described as the fat girl of the house, and said that younger men fancied her, for she was strong and lusty, and was never satisfied unless her men were as lusty as herself.

We found the same arrangement as before; but this time, she applied her eye to the peeping-place, and I rubbed against her bottom from behind.

'Keep your finger in my cunt and rub your belly against my bottom, and I will describe for you all that I see. Now they are having a wash, and are busy sponging one another. Pinch my clitoris, Fanny, frig—frig my cunt—right.'

I really felt I had had enough for one bout, and longed for a little rest, but this girl, Anna, seemed insatiable, and hurried me off to another place of observation. This next was the grandest bedroom in the establishment, that of Mrs. Simpson herself.

Frances

This lady, who in spite of her vulgarity was much patronised by the aristocracy, laid herself out to humour and gratify all their peculiar whims and fancies. Amongst other modes of pandering to the tastes of the numerous customers, she always had a supply of young girls just entered on their twenties, when their cunts were sufficiently developed to take in a good-sized prick but were not yet shaded or obscured by hair.

In this matter, she had especially in view one of the most refined of her visitors, a distinguished nobleman who had been for many years ambassador to the Sublime Port at Constantinople.

I had there made the acquaintance with the Circassian ladies, well trained and accomplished in the art of love, though ignorant of everything else. Following the example of the opulent Turks, she secured by purchase a choice harem of these celebrated beauties who are taught to consider themselves brought into the world for no other purpose than to please man and minister to her delight. These ladies, knowing the gratification it was to their Lady to kiss the lips of their quims, made it a regular practice to extract every hair as it grew, so as to render the whole surface as smooth as they could contrive to make it.

And indeed, I too have sometimes thought what a pity it is that our cunts are so covered up. Admittedly, the hair so grows that it never prevents a good prick finding its way in, but for all that, I cannot but think that it would be a more gratifying object to look at, and to handle too, if it were free from the rough and often tangled hair which hides it from view and obscures whatever beauty of form it may possess.

Well, my dear, what you say is very just; but you see, nature evidently intended us to go naked; it was in that condition that the first woman was presented to the first man; now if our cunts had no natural covering, the effect of their free exposure would be so exciting to men that they could think of nothing else; so in mercy to them, and to save us from continual worrying, nature has so covered our cunts that although the exact shape is concealed from view in ordinary position, yet when required for use the way is plain enough, while the slight concealment imparts the additional charm of requiring some effort to gain the soft retreat; at least, that's my notion.

MADAME RINALDO

Monsieur Rinaldo, the Spaniard, had a small family, consisting only of one maidservant and his wife, who was some twenty years younger than him. She spoke my language well, having had been born in England, whither her father had gone as agent for an Italian company. This led to my passing of my time with her, and we soon became very intimate. From the first, she inclined to take me into her confidence, telling how much older her husband was than herself, and that although a very kind old fellow, she was not able to give her full satisfaction, and hinting that if she could meet a good-looking chap, such as I was, who would be inclined for sport, she might be easily won.

I knew what she was driving at plainly enough, but thinking I might safely amuse myself with her, I pretended not to understand her. On which, she became still more eager and outspoken, and, one day, when we were sitting together on a lounge, she asked me if I had ever had a sweetheart: I replied that I never had, and indeed did not care to bother myself in that way.

Then she asked, 'Did you ever make free with a girl? Of course, you would not require a sweetheart for that, although a sweetheart would be much nicer.'

'No,' I answered, 'I don't want to have anything to do with girls at all for I have observed that they are always causing quarrels and leading young fellows into mischief.'

You are quite right, Frances, as regards common women, and I am very glad to hear you say so, but don't you know what a pleasant thing it is to meet with a nice sensible woman, who could be kind as well as trustworthy. Oh, Frances, you surely know the pleasure such a woman can give to a young man like you?' and she put her hand on my arm.

'I have never yet found such a woman as you describe,' I said smiling but drawing away from her a little.

'Perhaps, you have never looked for one,' she answered, moving after me; "tell me, what sort of woman would you like?'

'Oh, I don't know. I have never thought about it at all.'

'Ah, I think I know; shall I describe her for you?' she said, glancing at me with an arch expression; 'she should be a brunette and moderately stout; she should have a sprightly manner and be sensible in her talk; and above all, she should have a special fancy for yourself; now, is not that the kind of woman that would please you?

'Why, I declare, you are describing yourself, Madam Rinaldo, in everything except the last particular.'

'Now, there you are wrong, Frances, for let me tell you, and you know an honest confession is always a good thing, I am very fond of you—perhaps I should say, foolishly fond of you—and I would like above all things to enlighten you as to the pleasure a loving woman can give to a young fellow who has the courage to avail herself of the opportunity.' Here, she put her arm around me, and gently drew me toward her, as she whispered; "Now tell my truly, is it not a fact that you have never touched a woman?"

'Of course I have touched them when handing them into a boat, or putting my arm round them when dancing.'

'Ah, you know very well I don't mean that kind of touching, you are only pretending to misunderstand me; or do you want me to speak more plainly?' she asked, as she kept pushing up against me and squeezing my arm with her fingers.

'No, I assure you, my dear madam,' yielding a little to her pressure, for I felt amused at her eagerness, and expected that it might furnish me with something funny to tell my Lady on her return, 'I do not really understand what you mean, as I have never felt inclined to touch a woman in any other way than as I have said.'

'How charming to meet with such innocence! How happy I shall be if you, like a dear boy, will allow me to teach you what is the truest joy and the greatest happiness of life.' Here she took my hand and placed it on her thigh; "don't you know that every woman has a little treasure which she keeps carefully covered up, and the touch of which causes most men great delight; would you not like to feel it for yourself?' and she pressed my hand down between her thighs.

'I don't much care,' I replied, resigning my hand, however, to her wanton guidance. 'I really am unacquainted with the pleasure you speak of.'

She seemed almost irritated by my slowness. 'What,' she asked, with amorous fire blazing in her eyes, "sort of stuff are you made of? Perhaps you have no article at all! No masculine organs to infuse some heat into your cold blood! Let me try.' She suddenly dived her hand between my thighs.

'Oh, don't,' I responded, firmly closing my legs together, 'I cannot let any other woman touch me there. I promised my dear mother when leaving home that no woman should make free with me until I came back to her again; and I mean to keep my promise.'

Her face flushed. She had gone too far to recede, and fearing she might be balked at last, she seized my hand and thrust it under her clothes. 'Well, at all events, put your hand on my cunt,' she cried in her mad excitement. 'You made no promise not to do that! What more can I do except let you see it? Here, Francis, I can refuse you nothing. I know how young fellows like to look at a woman's cunt—see, here it is—this is my treasure, hidden from all the world except my husband, and I show it to you; put your hand on it,' she said, drawing up her petticoats, and spreading her thighs.

To humour her and carry on the joke, I placed my face on her very pretty and nicely formed quim. Its lips, which pouted out in ripe luxuriance, were thickly covered on the edges by a skirting of black hair, very crisp and curly. They were not as fair as mine outside, but were brighter red within, while the clitoris, the fullest I ever saw, projected like the prick of a little boy, and was of a deep ruby tinge. Rubbing my finger down the slit, I said, 'And so, this pretty looking mouth is your cunt! And is it through this you piddle?' I asked, looking very innocent, and touching her clitoris.

'No, I don't know what that is for, only that I like to have it rubbed; the little hole for piddling is lower down, in the middle of the slit, just here.'

'How funny! Then you must wet your cunt every time you piddle; I like the way a boy is made much better, for he can piss without himself; but I wonder why such a big mouth is necessary for such a small stream to come out of.'

'You little goose, or you little humbug, I am not sure which! Don't you know that the cunt is made for a prick such as you have, or ought to have, if you are a boy at all.' I started, fearing she had made some discovery, but it was only a random hit, for she went on. 'And perhaps, in your simplicity, you think your prick is only made for piddling too. I wish you would let me put my hand on it, and I would soon teach you the difference.'

'I would gladly let you, my dear Madame Rinaldo, but for my promise, for I would like to please you. Meantime, tell me, as you are so king, how the prick goes into the cunt, and what sort of feeling you have when it gets in; and if you wish I will go on rubbing this part while you are telling me.'

'Well, Francis, I never met anyone like you before, but I will enlighten you so far as you will let me. I suppose you know what it is for your prick to grow large and stiff, and stand up; that is called an erection; and a prick is no good, in a woman's estimation, unless it can stand up, firm and strong. Now if you were fond of me, and your prick in good order, you would take it out for me to see and handle, then you would get over me and I would lean back and let you in between my thighs. Then you would open the lips of my cunt and place the head of your prick at the lower end of the slit and push it up the passage. Then you would work it in and out, which is called fucking, driving it up again, while I would hold you in my arms and keep kissing you and saying how much I enjoyed the motion of your prick in my cunt; and heaving up my bottom, I would cry, fuck me, fuck me, my love, oh, what pleasure! Oh, what delight! And you would grunt and cry out as the pleasure went on increasing. And when at last you felt the hot spunk leaving your cods and darting through your prick, you would give a shout as the great thrill of pleasure agitated your whole body; then plunging your prick as far as possible into my cunt, you would like panting on my belly.'

'Oh, Francis! You are giving me such pleasure! Rub the clitoris harder, now press up your two fingers together, or three if you like.' Here we were both startled by a shuffling noise outside the door. Madame hastily put herself to rights, muttering between her teeth, what a nuisance when she felt she was just coming. I jumped up, and quickly opening the door saw something like the skirts of the maid, Juanita, disappearing at the end of the passage. I did not tell Madame Rinaldo what I saw, for I thought it better not to arouse her suspicions against her maid, but only said I could see nothing to account for the noise; yet it would be wiser for me to leave her for the present I said, with a significant smile, as I went out and closed the door.

Curiosity, however, induced me to follow the maid, treading as softly with my slippered feet as I could. She had gone to her own room, hurriedly shut the door and thrown herself on the bed.

The door was imperfectly fastened and by a gentle push I opened it sufficiently to get a view of Juanita, with her clothes tossed up, her thighs spread open, her head thrown back and her eyes turned up, frigging her cunt with the middle finger of her right hand. In the midst of her muttered exclamations of pleasure, as she endeavoured by energetic friction to satisfy the importunate cravings of her love chink, I fancied I heard the sound of my own name. This of course naturally increased the interest I felt in watching her performance; and besides, she seemed so terribly in earnest, and so carried along by pleasurable emotion, and her cunt looked in such a bursting state of excitement, that I, familiar as I am with the cunt and its longings, could not help admiring her and sympathising with her wanton exercise. So pushing my hand through the opening of my full wide trousers, I placed it on my own chink of delight, and by the friction of my finger speedily allayed for the moment the intense excitement into which I had been thrown by these two exhibitions of wanton female nature.

That very evening, Juanita made up to me in the most unmistakable manner. She even charged me with deceiving her, and told me, in her own beautiful language, which seems specially adapted for giving utterance to the emotions of love, that I had spoken to her too kindly and looked at her in such a loving way that I had gained her heart and made her expect and long for some more palpable evidence of love.

I smiled, and offered her a present, she smiled in return, but refused the present and, coming close up to me, said, 'That is not the proof of love I wish for. It is you I want,' she added, looking down, while a roseate flush suffused her face.

'My dear Juanita, you have indeed gained my goodwill by your attention, and I enjoy conversing with you in your own language, for you are so kind in correcting me, and take such pains to get me right; but as to love, you know, I am only a boy, and won't be thinking of marriage for many years to come.'

''I don't expect you to marry me, and I don't want you to marry me; I don't think marriage makes people fonder of one another; I know it foes oftentimes the reverse. I do want you to love me, and to love me without force or compulsion.'

'My dear Juanita,' I said kindly, for I really felt for the poor girl, while I pitied her infatuation, 'What proof of love do you want?'

'What a question to ask me! You tell me, I am pretty; I know I am young. I am healthy. I am a woman, and I tell you I love you and crave your love in return; what can I say more?'

She put her arm round me, and drawing me to her, pressed me to her bosom, and burst out sobbing as she laid her head on my shoulder.

Madame Rinaldo

Well, thought I to myself, this is a pretty fix! What am I to do? What excuse can I make? I must carry on for the present, however, as well as I can, and contrive to get away before she drives me to extremities. So knowing well the soothing effect of such attentions as she was evidently desiring, I first pushed my knee in between her thighs (oh, how readily they opened!) I pressed it up on her seat of love (with what joy she responded by pushing hard against me!) I stooped and raised her petticoats (she made no objection), I ran my hand up between her soft warm thighs, and I reached her bush. The lips seemed to open as I pressed my finger in. The chink was very moist and glowing with heat, and the clitoris felt stiff and springy as if endued with life. Wishing to give her all the pleasure I could, I passed my other hand beneath her clothes, and grasped the firm round cheeks of her bottom, while I frigged her cunt as skilfully as I could.

'Oh, my love! Now you understand me. Won't you put it in? Where is your prick? Let me find it. I will pet it for you and then you can fuck me, if you will.'

'No, dearest Juanita, not just now. I never care for a fuck while hampered with my clothes, wait till I have you naked in bed, then we shall take our fill of love. Meantime, let me frig your nice juicy cunt… there, do you like that?'

'Oh, my love! You know how to frig faster—harder—oh! I'm coming—push your finger up. Oh! Oh!'

She kissed me rapturously, while she hugged me in her arms, then as I gently disengaged myself, I said, 'Now, darling, leave me and if I can I will come to you at twelve tonight; but if I do not come at that time, don't expect me, for I might be prevented.'

She left me with reluctance, and I prepared to go out. I had promised to meet on that evening two young men — one whom I will call Henri, a lieutenant in the Italian navy, and the other, Julien, an officer in the marines.

I made their acquaintance the day after the robbery, when I had to appear in the police court to give my evidence. They were present and took a fancy to me. I passed many evenings in their company, for I thought it a good way of perfecting my education as a boy, though I found, as you may imagine, extreme difficulty in the concealment of my true sex. We generally went to the theatre, or some other place of amusement after which they usually finished up in the arms of some of their favourite mistresses.

I was perpetually solicited by those ladies to join in their amusements, but always excused myself on some plea or other.

On this evening, I had reason to expect that a more determined attempt would be made to overcome my opposition, and compel me to prove my manhood.

I should mention that as I often returned late at night, I obtained from Monsieur Rinaldo a latchkey with which to let myself in without disturbing the house.

I was just sallying forth with this key in my pocket, revolving in my mind various plans of escape from the importunities of my friends, when Madame Rinaldo met me in the passage, and putting her arm round me, without ceremony drew me into her room, and having shut the door, whispered, 'My dear Francis, don't fasten your door tonight, for I intend making monsieur's evening glass stronger than usual, and I will come to you when all is quiet; you won't turn me out—will you, dear?'

'Oh, how mad you are! What would you do if Monsieur Rinaldo were to wake up and find you absent from his bed?'

'Oh, he'll not wake up. I'll take care of that; and if he does, I can easily make an excuse, so don't be afraid. I will come, and be sure that you keep yourself fresh and wholesome for me, and don't stay out too late. Now kiss me, and goodbye for the present,' she added, quoting my own expression.

As I passed out, I thought, how the plot thickens! How strange, to be so beset at once by two most lascivious women, both dying to be fucked! Now, I bet if I were a hot young blade with a glorious prick of my own, instead of being only a poor girl with nothing but an innocent little cunt to boast of, such good fortune would never have happened to me; but somehow, things always go in this world by the rule of contrariness. I decided that given the direction that events were bound to head, I should extricate myself with haste, and wrote to my dear Lady Ferrars explaining my situation with great candour. After delaying matters further for a several more days, I finally got a letter from my dear Lady, informing me that I might expect her in the course of the day, and directing me to lose no time in getting the yacht ready for an early start.'

***

It so happened that I called for Frances the next morning, being anxious to ascertain what evil consequences had followed my discovery of her true identity the day before. I confess to an additional desire: to play the doctor with the girl's budding cunt. I instructed the servant to address her thus: 'The mistress wants to see you, Frances, but don't fear, she means well, and my advice is give her your full confidence; and if you can, let me know the result, by and by.'

Frances was directed to my room and I found her sitting on the sofa. She looked kindly at her and said, 'Why, Frances, how you manage to steal the hearts of all Lady Ferrars! She raves about you. I have been wishing for some time to have an opportunity of telling you that you need not fear jealousy, in fact, I am quite happy for the both of you. I consider it the wise plan to allow a certain amount of liberty, yet under some control and prudent direction. Now I have heard from your stories that you are very particular as to whom you admit to your embraces, and I am sure that if anything was wrong with you, you would not suffer our young women to incur any risk of infection. Is not that your own feeling, Frances?'

'It is indeed, my Lady; and as you have spoken with so much kindness and consideration, I am ready to trust you in all these matters. I do try to be very select, and I seldom have a connection without a thorough ablution as soon as possible afterward. But if you have any wish to examine me yourself, I have not the slightest objection.'

I replied, 'I am glad to find that I have not been disappointed in you, Frances. You seem to be a good sensible girl, and as I wish to have your full confidence, I accept your offer. I confess, too, that it will gratify me to see and inspect the little cunt which Lady Ferrars tells me gives her more satisfaction than any she ever fucked. So lean back and open your legs.'

Frances obeyed, and I proceeded to raise her clothes and expose all her belly and thighs.

'What a quantity of hair you have, Frances! It covers all the lower part of your belly! Your whole cunt, too, is large and well developed, and the lips are unusually plump and full, while the inside lining is exceedingly hot and moist. You must be a very lascivious girl, Frances, and I am certain you are very fond of being fucked! Are you not'

'Yes, I am fond of fucking,' replied Frances, laughing. 'I know of nothing that can be compared with having one's cunt crammed with a sturdy dildo or a long tongue.'

'Frances, you are right,' I responded. 'The mercenary spirit of some women is detestable. Now I understand why the women are all so fond of you. And I am sure your cunt gets a good share of admiration too. Do you enjoy having it petted and played with?'

'Yes, I love to feel a woman's fingers fiddling about my cunt. It always causes me a pleasant thrill and makes me wish for a fuck. But somehow your frigging, my Lady, has a stranger effect. I suppose that is because you know that exact spot—which others seldom do. Oh, that is so nice!'

'Do you like having your cunt sucked, Dolly? A tongue frig is generally very agreeable.'

'Oh, yes. I think a tongue frig delicious! I always try to get every woman to suck my cunt; and sometimes the sucking is the best part of it.'

'Do you think I might suck your cunt, Frances?'

'Only if you care to, Madame.'

'I most certainly would. I like it very much—especially when the cunt has plenty of feeling like yours, Frances, and above all, when it is kept nice and sweet. Would you like me to suck yours?'

'I would, my Lady, if you don't dislike it yourself.'

I spread her cunt open with her fingers, pushed in her mouth and ravenously sucked her clitoris with her lips and tongue, while Dolly twisted about her bottom and muttered, "Oh! How nice! Oh, dear. How you suck! Oh, your tongue is setting me wild! And now I feel your finger up my bottom! This is beyond a fuck! Oh, my cunt! Oh, my bottom! Oh, my arse! I'm spending! Oh, I'm spending,' and Frances with a might groan lay back, while I grasped the quivering cheeks of her bottom and licked up the sweet juices that poured from Dolly's fountain of delight.

After a while, Frances came to herself and said, 'Dear Lady, I never enjoyed anything like that. And now you must favour me with a full view of your own cunt and bottom, and I will suck everything you have.'

I lay back in her turn and spread her thighs wide open while Frances pushed a pillow under her, and said, 'Why, my Lady, you have a beautiful cunt of your own, with red-brown hair, the colour of gold, and a luscious chink, as hot as an oven and steeped in voluptuous dew!'

'Oh Frances, your are sucking my cunt and tickling my bottom very skilfully and pleasantly,' I told her before I spent myself and vowed to keep Frances and Lady Ferrars in my hospitality as long as I possibly could, for delicacies such as Frances were hard to find, and I was certain Lady Ferrars would not begrudge me the usufruct of her pleasure.

A GIRL'S GUIDE

Female Solitary Masturbation

Oft times this habit begins when a girl moves excitedly about on her couch, until her bolster or any other object gets between her thighs. She may rub it against her swollen clitoris and move up and down until she loses consciousness in pouring forth her sweet essence. In such cases, they begin again and again their pretty little games, which give a taste of the pleasures of paradise and finish up by finding the spot which, thus rubbed, is capable of renewing for them the heavenly joys of emission. The hand wanders to the palpitating cunny and nature teaches them to do the rest. The budding lass makes her finger do the office of a man's tool, or seizes a candle, an empty needle-case—heaven only knows what!

She has no need to wet her fingers, either when rubbing her clitoris (which resembles, as I already mentioned, the top of the male organ, but is considerably more sensitive), or when pushing it into her cunt, for these parts are naturally always slightly damp. Indeed, the masturbating maid is soon ready. She whips up her petticoats or simply slips her hand through her pock-et-hole, or any other mysterious slit in her gown, for I must not forget that the feminine dress-pocket changes its spots, like the leopard, once in every decade, according to fashion decrees. Her slender third finger goes to work, lightly pressed on the magic button, and sometimes insinuating itself more or less in the cunny, where it is worked in and out, quickly or slowly, follow-ing the gradation of the pleasure she feels until she attains the venereal spasm and the delightful discharge, of which the proofs are rarely abundant.

Some doctors have even doubted whether the female really ever emitted, pretending that what we take to be a gush of sperm is only a flow of liquid which does not emanate from the seminal canals, but is only secreted by the prostatic glands, resembling that which appears at the top of the man's prick when he gets an erection, serving to render the manipulation of the foreskin more easy, or if he has some weakness or inflammation. This colourless liq-uid is not the real seed and has no prolific virtue. Nevertheless, whether women have real spunk or only prostatic liquor, it is certain that, when they spend under the influence of any venereal act whatsoever, they have as much and more pleasure than their lords and masters, and as they lose less at a time, they can begin again more often and with much less fatigue. Thus it is that women are noted to be generally more able to resist reiterated assaults extending over a short space of time.

Let me add that a man can only copulate when he has an erection. Without a cockstand how can his prick find shelter in a cunt; but woman is always ready to receive the peacemaker. She requires no preparatory erection, and as soon as she feels her stiff darling coming up the passage, his friction and her imagination does the rest.

A woman can procure for herself the pleasure of the discharge, just as we can, by other means than manual ones. She has also the resource of the bolster and other similar objects which she can squeeze between her thighs, and rub her greedy furrow and her saucy clitoris against anything that comes in her way, from a brass knob or a bedstead down to an odd finger of an old kid glove stuffed with wool. Some girls like to see themselves frigging and enjoy the solitary act seated in front of a looking glass. A feather or a camel's hair brush produces enervating results and prolongs the salacious sensations. All is fish that conies to the female frigging net, as long as it resembles in some slight degree the manly organ; any round wooden case, a carrot, a turnip, a saveloy, and Creole girls in tropical climes make a very tidy false cock out of a banana.

But enough on this head, or rather tail; I will lose no longer any time in discoursing upon what you understand, I am sure, perhaps better than I do myself?

Maud.—I think that you have drawn a satisfactory picture of the pleasure that each sex can enjoy alone without the help either of the opposite species, or of his own, and that selfishly, as you truly stated. Now paint for me as well you can the image of the delights experienced by two persons of the same sex: two males alone and then two women together.

Tribadism, or Women with Women

D o not think that women are less extraordinary in their pleasures among themselves without the help of the male. Those who fear the approach of a man, or prefer their own sex, are still more madly depraved than unsexed men. They put into play every resource of their frame and use foreign bodies too, to procure for themselves the happy dispatch, the sole desired end of male and female libertines. No stone is left unturned to obtain the spermatic result. They frig mutually, rubbing the clitoris with their fingers, which they introduce into each other's cunts, exchanging kisses, pressing bubbles, bottoms, and every part of the body, not forgetting to stick their digits up each other's little bum holes. They force into each other's crack anything shaped like a prick. They get on top of each other, entwine their thighs and rub their cunts one on the other, pressing their hairy bushes till they are entangled together, clasped in each other's arms as if they are both of different sexes, and move and shake as hard as they can in convulsions of lubricity until they obtain the supreme happiness of the discharging crisis. Be it their liquid prolific quintessence, or simply prostatic, as some doctors say, the result is the same in the supreme moment of joy and they start off again until tired nature gives out. Oft times they wear a dildo or godmiche, which is an ingenious little machine fashioned in the image of a man's cock, with hair and balls all complete, more or less artistically got-up and of different kinds of material, but sufficiently elastic, soft and smooth, and fastened by ribands or a strap to the lower part of the belly, exactly where the manly organ sticks out. The lady carrying the artificial weapon becomes the husband of a lecherous little bride, introducing into her cunt this peculiar machine which is a hollow tube of wood, tin or ivory, of a goodly size in thickness and length, and covered in leather or velvet. At the rounded top there is a little hole, the same as in the genuine article. The tube is filled with warm milk or any other syrupy liquid, and a piston, as in a syringe, serves to throw a jet into the vagina, at the psychological moment, when the woman whose parts are plugged up is about to discharge herself.

Nowadays these dildoes are made of India-rubber, with a ball-bag of the same. As this material is cold and hard, it is generally left to soak before using in some hot soapy water. And then the balls are pressed and the instrument is filled with liquid. It now suffices to squeeze the balls at the proper moment to make the liquid spurt out by the hole in the acorn-top, absolutely like the true essence of virility. What gives great enjoyment to the woman in the use of this secret toy is that she can obtain a tremendous quickness of the movement to and fro, impossible with a man, however young or active he may be. But, of course, nothing equals the real thing, if it will only remain stiff and not collapse in the middle at the slightest pretext. A woman can strap the dildo on her heel and turning over on her back, dig away in her privates to her heart's content, and there is no act of parliament to prevent either sex being buggered with it. I have seen some very small ones for little girls, or for teasing men's bum-holes and some of remarkable size for especially large Messalinas. Some are even arranged with a covering over the glands, imitating the foreskin. These are made for rich Jewesses, who out of curiosity want to try an uncircumcised pego without committing adultery. There exist also double ones, representing two pricks joined at the root and separated by a double set of balls, so that two women can each have an imitation prick in their cunt, or arse-hole, as they choose, and so spend at the same moment as if they were hermaphrodites, male and female in one. If each girl presses the false testicles belonging to the India-rubber prick, each receives at once, or separately, the desired emission of the liquid they have put into the hollow canal.

Imitation cunts have likewise been manufactured. They are made of India-rubber and are painted and bedecked with false hair exactly resembling a cunt. They can be pushed upon the prick with the hand, or the man can lie over them and simulate a genuine fuck.

Sodomites also use single and double dildoes in their orgies, either to take the place of exhausted pricks, or simply out of sheer lubricity, such as having them shoved up their backside while they are being sucked and frigged.

Women often suck each other simultaneously, by lying over each other. One will be on her back, and, kneeling over her, the other will lick her cunt and press her own orifice down on the lips of the woman she is sucking. The clitoris is tickled with the tongue, which is held out stiffly and made to quiver quickly on the sensitive button and all round the cunt and inside it, where they take as much of it as they can in the mouth and draw it up with an inward movement of aspiration. The nose, the chin goes in too. They also tickle the arse-hole, and put in there their noses, tongues and fingers. They pinch each other, lick each other all over, and playfully nibble the cheeks of the arse and every other part that tempts them. Then again one will straddle over the other; either on her titties and ask to have her clitoris tickled with a rosy nipple, or else will sit or ride upon her mouth where the lips and tongue do their office as in the case of the "Sixty-nine" diversion I have just described, and during all this their hands are not idle; they travel everywhere, giving rise to voluptuous feelings by the sweetest titillations, varied and reiterated. There are no possible positions, or lascivious touches that they do not practice, every secret nook of their bodies is looked at, caressed, admired, kissed, pressed, pinched, sucked and nibbled. They try to become as one being and force their way into every opening of the body, exhausting their imagination to invent new methods of exhaustion of the body, by repeated discharges evoked by the most voluptuous and salacious games.

These creatures treat each other as lover and mistress, or as husband and wife. Some prefer to play the masculine part and are always the "men' in this comedy of passion: others are ready for either sort of work, etc. They are called "tribades' or "anandrynes,' from Greek words signifying a woman who is not for a man or who prefers her own sex. They are also known as Lesbians, gamahuching girls, and suckers, because they generally lick the genitals, a taste formerly supposed to be peculiar to the women of the island of Lesbos.

Some of these licking ladies do it out of sheer vice and devilry, others with mercenary motives. A poor Lesbian may sometimes get a rich woman into her power and force the latter to keep her in clover, either because the wealthy one is pleased to reward her for the pleasure found in sucking or being sucked, or else it is a case of blackmail. This passion is more flourishing than one might think, but it is very difficult to detect for obvious reasons. In all schools, workshops, convents, etc., there is more or less cunt-sucking going on, and governesses and servants often enjoy licking the virgin clefts of the girls left in their charge.

CATHERINE

I am not—as I trust shall become clear—a woman given to bawdy talk or mere faithless, wanton ways. I have never indulged in the loose and immoral speech which nowadays cloaks so many novels. I find such productions crude and tasteless, lacking entirely in finesse and given to unlikely descriptions of equally unlikely behaviour by characters who are no more than cardboard people.

Even so, I am not a prude. Prudery is for those who fear the consequences of their own desires, however errant such desires may be. Neither will I countenance hypocrisy. There are always to be found a number of mealy-mouthed and self-inflated persons who would suppress all references to the most satisfying of physical pleasures. It is not my intention to do so here, but neither will I proclaim that they should be widely copied unless such art and sophistication is brought to them as I have been fortunate enough to be able to engender.

For I must make no bones about the fact that the comforts of wealth have provided often enough the wherewithal for many of my amorous luxuries. I call them that since they appertain to such voluptuous aspects of good living as the less well-to-do must mainly do without.

I am told by some that this view is false. All views to some are false. One can do no more or less than hold to one's own. I have known some quite pretty and adorable girls of the working classes. I have known, too, some doughty young males from the same milieu who could be counted upon to dispense with the normal crudities of their behaviour when in the presence of ladies. Removed temporarily from their drab surroundings and mean streets and brought into an atmosphere of luxury, their amorous abilities improved vastly, though ever requiring tuition.

But I must not delay my narrative too long by philosophising and shall commence—with the many secret diary entries I have made throughout my life—beginning when I was eighteen. It was the year 1882—that selfsame year when our dear Queen gave Epping Forest to the nation and the British Fleet bombarded Alexandria. I was proud to note such events in my early years, but as wisdom grew and the world progressed even more, so I devoted my immediate recollections to more personal events.

In the midsummer of that year, I was staying for a long weekend at the country house of one of my uncles. I needed not therefore to be accompanied by a chaperone, for my aunt played that role, or would have done had she been more alert to what was afoot all about her. The dear lady lived in dreamland, however, and this perhaps was all to the good insofar as it concerned my immediate education. The world is made up for the most part of fools and knaves, as the second Duke of Buckingham remarked. He was a writer indeed upon whose pleasantries I would have much cause to ponder in those next few days for it was he who first coined another phrase which was to become commonplace among those who neither knew nor cared about its source: 'Ay, now the plot thickens very much upon us.' This—for those whose learning would extend as does my own—occurs in the third act of his play, *The Rehearsal*.

Among my cousins was one Elaine. Six years my senior, she possessed my own medium height. Her ankles and calves were slender, her thighs well-fleshed as befits a woman. Her development otherwise tended to the 'bold,' as we called it, for she more than amply fulfilled her dresses in respect of her breasts and bottom. Her eyes were large and her lips of medium size but fully plump—a delicious peach of a mouth to kiss, as I was to discover. Infinitely more knowing then than I, she was to teach me much.

I should say that in the grander houses of the time, two distinct types of weekend parties were held. The most general was that at which up to sixty or even seventy people might be invited—invariably during the shooting season. On the whole I found these boring. There were too many people to encounter about the house at odd hours—and sometimes to embarrass one.

The other type of party was arranged only in more knowing circles. The guests were fewer and more selectively chosen. Discretion was total, for all knew that the merest buzz of scandal beyond the porticos of the mansion would eventually ruin other such occasions. Within this understanding, certain delicious license was permitted and orgies were not unknown. I am speaking of gatherings, of course, of no more than a score of guests, including the host and hostess.

Catherine

Perhaps I should say also that these were country gentry whose morals had altered not a wit from those of their immediate forebears. They preserved their traditions. If a young woman was to be 'trodden,' it was accepted that she should be. She was expected to return the virile salute of the lusty penis with the same passion that it was accorded her. Many a fair bottom have I seen wriggling for the first time on a manly piston while murmurs of encouragement spurred its flushed possessor on.

Often if a girl were shy, she would be coaxed and fondled by several of the ladies into receiving her injection. This attention from the fairer sex interested me especially. Flushed cheeks and snowy breasts were exposed— an apparently burning anguish showing in the eyes as her skirts were raised—all such were salt to the occasion. Girls too bold in their ways provided little sport for an expectant assembly, and such as might have been were given sufficient hints in private to bring them to struggle and sob with great realism while they were laid open-legged upon a dining room table or a waiting divan, there to receive their first dosage of ardent sperm.

But I digress—a habit I must in these early stages of my memoirs avoid. It is of a late hour that I speak and I would not have wandered from my room on that Saturday night, so far past midnight, had the servant not forgotten to fill my bedside carafe of water.

Wine had made me thirsty. Believing all to be asleep, I opened my door quietly, padded in my nightdress along the corridors and began to descend the wide, curving staircase. At mid-point, however, I stopped. There was a light below. It shone from the dining room where the door stood half open. I heard voices—a faint laugh.

'No, Harold—not here!' I heard, and recognised the voice immediately. It was that of my Aunt Helen, whose husband was nowhere to be seen. Of less than fully-matured years, she was about thirty-seven, as I fancied—a brunette of some distinct charm.

Crouching down behind the railings of the banisters then, I saw her. There was it seemed a playful chase going on. A hand seized her arm as she made apparently to flee. Her long dark hair appeared already tousled. There then came into my view the owner of that hand. It was Mr. Witherington-Carey, whose acquaintance I had made only yesterday at tea. His evening jacket, tie and collar had been cast off and his braces dangled from his waist. In a moment, with no more pretence of flight, his victim was seized and thrust back over the table.

I could scarcely believe my eyes. In every fleeting second I feared discovery by another guest wandering from their room, or worse the appearance of my uncle or one of my cousins. Fate was kind to me, however, for there came no interruption to the proceedings. Despite her fiercely protesting whispers, Helen's skirts were raised up high.

Ah, what a voluptuous spectacle presented itself! In the fashion of the times her stockings were richly patterned and of a dark blue shade. Sheathing the curving columns of her well-turned legs they rose to mid-thigh and there were ringed by broad garters. Above, the vista was even more enticing, for in affecting split drawers, as she had done that evening, the victim's posture showed in all their appealing nudity the two plump cheeks of her bottom which the broadly-separated halves of her garment exposed. I noted my own special affection for the lady's body. I spent little effort thinking of the men involved and focused my rapt attention on the members of my own sex.

A last febrile attempt by her was made to rise. I know now of course that it was but a token movement. My uncle's hand had in any event fixed itself strongly upon the back of her neck while, with his other, he groped at his breeches.

Catherine

A muffled cry—quickly choked back as if by practise of discretion—sounded from her throat as the crest of Mr. Witherington-Carey's staff inserted itself within the inviting valley. My aunt's hands clawed for a brief moment at the polished top and then her face sank sideways—fortunately in such a manner that she could in no wise raise her vision to mine, even had she been able to discern me up on the dark stairway.

I had seen enough, however, too much indeed for my inexperienced eyes. I dared stay no longer. At any moment they might, I feared, turn to the door. Discovery would present such a horror as I could not face. Gathering up the hem of my nightgown so that I would not trip over it, I tiptoed to the top of the stairs, all thoughts of my earlier thirst having vanished. Fully dizzy with what I had seen, I felt a curious, warming moisture between my thighs as I neared my door and was aware that my nipples had risen, teased by the cotton of my garment.

I had left my bedroom door on the latch, but saw now even in the gloom that it was ajar. Some errant draught had disturbed it, I thought, though my mind was really too distracted for such matters and my pulses were racing still. Pushing open the door I gave a little cry which I endeavoured as best as possible to suppress.

Lying upon my ruffled bed was a white-robed figure that stirred and rose up at my entrance.

It was my cousin, Elaine.

* * *

Oh, what a fright you gave me!' I gasped.

Quick as a flash, Elaine had bounded up from the bed and closed the door even as I faltered in the entrance.

'Shush! Do not make a sound! How you are trembling! Did I frighten you so? I could not sleep, Catherine. Forgive me, do, but I am so restless.'

All this being said in a rush, and I scarcely having recovered from my double shock, she led me to the bed and drew me down upon it, passing her arms about me so to comfort me for my aroused fears, as she thought. Indeed, I trembled violently, though not so much from the scare she had given me as from the aftermath of what I had witnessed. Alas for feminine intuitions, I was not long to remain guardian of my secret.

'What have you been doing? Where were you?'

All such questions being thrown at me, I knew not how to reply for a moment. Her body being warm to mine and pressed thighs to thighs against me, I do not doubt that she could feel the risen perkiness of my nipples against the firm gourds of her own breasts.

'I, too, could not sleep—I went to get some water,' I muttered.

At that, Elaine laughed and kissed me on the tip of my nose. 'Oh, you have seen something—I know you have. What is going on down there?' she asked.

Fretfully I tried to stir from her embrace, but curiosity had awoken devilment in her and she clasped me the tighter, I becoming aware of the silky feel of our bellies together through the cotton of our nightdresses and the fact that my nipples were stubbing against her titties.

'Nothing, I have seen nothing—what is to see,' I blustered.

'I know you have. That is why you are trembling, and beside I can feel your excitement,' Elaine laughed. With that she insinuated one hand between us and so manipulated my breasts and felt my hard nipples that I gasped and twisted for the caress was more enervating than she knew and my burning globes swelled to her touch.

'I have not—oh, I have not.'

I blustered fiercely and would have gone on doing so had she not then closed my trembling lips with hers. How sweet her mouth was! Never before had I kissed mouth to mouth with anyone, nor had I ever thought I would be so fortunate to do so with another girl.

'I will make you tell, Catherine!'

Moist and full, her lips engaged mine more deeply. The sensation, coupled to the blatant wandering of her palm all about my thinly-covered breasts, caused me to surrender utterly. I responded. The tips of our tongues met. In that first moment of the true uncovering of my desires, Elaine knew beyond doubt—as she afterwards conveyed to me—that my heated mind held secrets that she was intent upon devouring. Knowing full well even then her capacity for seduction, she commenced easing up the hem of my nightgown while I all too feebly attempted to obstruct the effort.

'Come, darling, come, for you must be longing for it. Did you see them at it?'

'I am not—no! Oh, Elaine, what a naughty thing to do! St... stop f... feeling me... AH!'

Of a sudden I was bared to my hips. The tip of her forefinger engaged the oily lips of my nest and found my button. I twisted, writhed. I absorbed her tongue. My protestations fled. At the first ardent rubbing of her finger I was lost. Or rather, I should say, found. Oft since have we talked about that moment and how the net of fate ensnares us by the most casual of events. I refer of course to the fact that Elaine had caught me in that moment. My hips wriggled even as her own mother's had done. My legs parted, enabling Elaine to slip full-length upon me. Withdrawing her urging finger as she did so, her furry nest sidled moistly against my own. I felt the rubbing of our love lips, the tingling merging of our pubic hairs. Coiling her arms under my knees and raising and thrusting my legs back, she caused our honey pots to meet and rub fully. I gasped within her mouth, I clasped her shoulders. Our bottoms squirmed in mutual delight.

In a moment a violent shuddering seized me and my belly felt as if invaded by bursting stars. Lashing her tongue wickedly all around my own, Elaine sprinkled my bush in turn with her own spattering love joy and then kissed me tenderly all about my hot face.

Alas, that one can never come within distance of such moments with mere words. Long have I practised such in my diaries, yet ever despairing of describing even the touch of lips to one's own in a manner that will communicate to the reader—even to myself. I who hold the dear memories of a thousand such moments of ineluctable bliss can frame them more closely in my mind than mere words can draw. The words provide but a sketch, the frailest outlines of reality. I trouble myself too much about it, perhaps. To Elaine I appear to possess a mastery of prose such as she can never attain to. Time and again in the years that have since passed after that first night of voluptuous discoveries, she has asked me again and again, 'What did you write about it?'—referring of course to whatever event had last occurred. She has been party to almost all I have written, her eyes positively glowing as she has perused my diaries, while for myself I have fretted openly to her that I have failed to capture the fleshly bliss.

'Oh, if I could but write like you, I would write very naughty books,' she has oft times declared.

I have never been flattered by her praise, however. I know my faults, my shortcomings, the midnight wrestlings with words upon which I afterwards gaze with disappointed mien. However, I digress again and must return to the first ruffled bed in which we found ourselves alone and palpitating.

My nest throbbed. Our bodies were sticky together. With a sigh Elaine rolled off of me, though still continuing to cuddle and caress me. That I made no bones about letting her do so—and even returned her lascivious touchings—was the full sign that I had been drawn at last into my future realm. Hot-nippled as our breasts were, they rubbed together where our nightgowns had been drawn up to our armpits.

'Tell me now. What did you see? Who was it?'

I giggled foolishly, still somewhat naive as I was. That long night was, however, to temper me much in my attitudes and ways of thought. I recall not what I replied for I durst not tell her—as I then thought—that her own Mama was one of the participants. Indeed, in my own ridiculous fashion in those first moments of aftermath, I thought she would not believe me or would be shocked. Such veils of unknowing were soon to be rent from me. Persistent in her questioning and never ceasing to keep me thoroughly aroused between my thighs, Elaine at last after many hesitations and denials on my part drew from me by simple methods of elimination of names the identity of Mr. Witherington-Carey. Indeed, I bit my tongue and hid my face upon uttering the name. However, to my uttermost surprise, my cousin remarked with a charming laugh, 'He is quite handsome, is she not? I hear that he has such a big one, too. How did he have at her? Were her drawers full down?'

'Oh, she had none on,' I replied, realising for the first time that Auntie had worn no such garment. Even as I spoke my breath was bubbling out again for upon Elaine's wicked forefinger as my dell was, I was yet about to come again.

It was over the table, I said. Who was the man, she demanded to know. Do not make me tell, I begged. At that she laughed and rolled me under her anew.

'I know—it was Mama. Oh, she is a naughty one!' she declared, to my perfect astonishment.

'Oh, it was Mama, then. I know it from the look on your face.'

'Ah, Elaine!'

She had me exactly as she wanted. I was lost to her entirely. Raising my legs of my own accord, I wound them round her slim waist. Her words sang in my brain even as we kissed and rubbed and rose anew to a peak of bliss.

'How... how do you know?' I gasped, for all manner of thoughts were now raging in me.

'You sillykins, you do not know much, do you? Oh, you naughty thing, you are making me come again—is it not lovely?'

I could not but agree. The word painted but a ghost of the sensations I was prey to. The thorns of our nipples seemed to spin about one another's. Our lips indulged in the most lascivious kisses. The curls of our quims became matted with our merging spendings.

'We will do everything together, shall we not, Catherine?'

'Yes,' I choked, though I knew not then the full import of her words, nor to what scenes of libertine delights they were to lead us. Quieting ourselves at last, we lay quiet. In the milky gloom, Elaine bent over me and regarded me solemnly. Then, rising, she discarded her nightdress and bid me do the same. There being a flask of liqueur such as was kept for all guests in a side cabinet, we indulged ourselves by drinking from the neck of it. I knew not the time, nor cared.

'Shall we be naughty together?' Elaine asked. We sat up, our legs curled under us, hips touching.

'What can we do?' I asked naively.

'Everything, Catherine. I have long thought of it. Have you not wondered that I am not yet wed? It is of my own choosing. I may do so in a few years time, but for the nonce I do not mean to fetter myself to a man. I have learned too much for that, how utterly boring it would be! I need my fill of a woman's sex before I could ever dream of contentment with a man. Even Mama has confided in me that a woman makes a superior lover to a man. She takes the occasional man for diversion, I think. I am certain now that you share my feelings, or will soon do so, therefore I mean to confide in you. Do you know how many ways there are in which pleasure can be taken?'

I shook my head. I was all agog with wonder and so tremulous from the experiences of the night that I was ready to follow her in all.

'Let us consider, for I have read many naughty books that I filched from Papa's study, though he knows it not. Were all the things therein to be brought together, what exquisite pleasures one could have! Even in those books, there are myriad joys between ladies, such as we have just had and which are ever renewable. You were very easy to seduce, my love, for you were already in a fine fever for it. Supposing, though, that one seduced a girl who was not. What fun!'

'Oh, but she might hate it and make a fuss, Elaine!'

'Of course she would not—not for long. Girls are very understanding among themselves you know, and if she were a novice her delights would be threefold and we could teach her much.'

My mouth parted, I could not believe what I was hearing, yet Elaine spoke not in a coy fashion but a very plain and practical one that stilled the amazed response I might otherwise have given. Indeed, I was dumbstruck, which she—perceiving my silence to be halfway towards assent on my part—took quick advantage of.

'It is perfectly possible, you know, for I have heard about it being done at hunt balls and such. It is called being put to the cock, but it is really being put to a cock-shaped phallus of rubber or leather and many a fair young lady has been initiated thus during the revelry. Alas, Mama feels she must appear very prim and proper, you know, and so has never let me attend one, nor my sisters. I have endeavoured to wheedle her into letting me, but she has resisted. For my part, of course, I have pretended ignorance to her of the goings on, merely saying that I wished to attend a grand affair, but she will not have it, saying they are by invitation only. All the world knows that, of course, but it would trouble her nothing to arrange our presence.'

'But in that case you would see nothing, for surely it is not done before the whole company and your Mama could scarce be present when you did.'

'You see how I have to educate you, my pet! Mama need not mind any more than it bothered you that she was not putting herself to Mr. Witherington-Carey. Did it bother them? Not for a second, Catherine. The pleasure is all. I mean to bring you to my way of thinking on this.'

'You said he had…'

I could not finish the sentence no more than I could stop myself from uttering it.

'A big one? Well—has he not? How I know this I do not intend to tell you as yet, which I know will tease you much and therefore to listen to me ever more carefully. But truthfully my interest is in the dildos, which are even bigger still, and manned, so to speak, by a fair lady who knows what delights it can bring. So you see, as to bringing a girl to cock is more easily done than you would think, although the moment and the atmosphere must be right. I have witnessed it once, as you have, and found a perfect pleasure in doing so. What more could be gained than by gazing upon the intimate conjunction of the parts, by listening to the sighs, the moans, and seeing the rolling of the eyes and the passionate merging of lips.'

'Yes, that is true,' I exclaimed, for the more I then thought upon it, the more I wanted to see what she was describing. For as exciting as I found Mr. Witherington-Carey's pursuit of Auntie, it would have been so much more so if it had been another member of her own sex trying to pierce her with a larger-than-life phallus.

'Well, then, and so is much other than one can think and read of. What a waste were we to let it all pass by us, Catherine! What utter boredom to find oneself too early wed and the doors of adventure closed. Listen now, for there is much more than I have already said. To birch a girl is quite delicious, for instance.'

'Oh, but that would hurt her!'

'My tender one, it would sting and burn her, yes, but if wielded properly—as from all I read—the ensuing pleasures are a perfect delight and not by any means to be scorned. The twigs burnish the bottom, cause it to become fervently heated and the cunny to moisten, and so all is well prepared for the amorous assault that needs follow.'

'Is that true? Oh, I suppose I can imagine it a little! Papa has never birched me, though. Has yours?'

'No, my pet—he has been too busy on other ventures with other females to think of baring my bottom. But wait, for we have not by any means reached the end of our lists. There is riding, for instance— mounted on the same horse as another agreeable lady—may rub each other as they raises her bottom to the jogging of the horse. The reading of such an event much excited me, as I'm sure it would you. There is then also the binding of a girl by ropes or straps when she may be made to take the dildo. I have heard it said that some girls are well held by other ladies to the same end at such occasions as I have mentioned, so I see little difference in the matter save that by more elaborate means of bringing a girl to her fate one may take more time and have more enduring pleasure in it. But I see you are looking doubtful about it,' declared Elaine, taking another swig from the flask and passing it to me.

Whether it was the headiness of the liqueur or that of her words, I knew not, but found myself shaking my head in denial. I averred only, and rather weakly, that it seemed a trifle cruel.

'That is because you have not thought about it, my pet, as I have. The girl would be well prepared beforehand by being tickled and kissed and teased, just as you have been this very night. Did you not surrender and willingly? I have no doubts at all that any sporty girl put to such mischief would soon enough take as much pleasure from it as you did. Think you now of other things, however, that one might do, as for instance entertaining two dildos at once.'

My exclamation at this was such that she burst into laughter.

'I forget, Catherine, that you have not even been threaded yet and know only of the real pleasures by proxy. I must warn you though that they are not always brought forth with such voluptuous skills as you have witnessed, and indeed that bout itself was of brief duration from what you tell me. This is not to say that one might not sport briefly oneself of occasion—out of a sense of mischief, perhaps, if nothing else. We must ourselves enjoy all that we speak of, and more, or we shall remain as novices. What say you, cousin?'

What could I say? To venture her a negative reply would have been ludicrous, yet I teetered on the edge of all such wickedness's as she had spoken of,—though a continued tingling in my cunny surreptitiously announced my pleasure at the thought of them. Nor was that all, for as Elaine had told me she had garnered many very naughty ideas from her father's secret store of books and had memorised them all.

Making not too much of my wondering silence, she stroked and fondled me, well seeing that I was all a-quiver still to receive her tongue and her fingers. Ere dawn broke, Elaine had tasted my honey pot with her mouth and

I hers. We trickled and spurted our pleasure between each other's lips. After doing so, we coiled our tongues together so that we might take a further taste of all that was mixed.

'Is it not more delicious than the finest of liqueurs? Come, leap with me into a divine course of wickedness. Say that you will!'

'Yes!' I assented. The die was cast. Never would I turn back.

* * *

First you must be threaded, darling, and have your cunny filled to the brim with the thick leather shaft,' Elaine murmured to me before departing for her own room. The sheet was long twisted under me from our rompings, yet I felt no discomfort from it. My passions stirred upon all the things of which we had talked. Amidst my musings I saw ever again and again the sturdy shaft that had reamed dear Aunt Helen. The vision of her in the throes of ecstasy enflamed me still. I toyed with myself and fell into the most vivid dreams wherein all earthly cares are cast aside. Upon waking at the entrance of a housemaid bringing tea the next morning, all churned up again within me, yet I could scarce believe it had all come to pass, The fevers of the night seemed to my drowsy mind but tattered emblems of a wild imagination. Indeed, a certain morbidity would, I believe, have seized me, had not Elaine once more entered upon the scene.

Attired in a pale pink peignoir adorned with lace, she looked perfectly lovely. Her legs, elegant as they were and full womanly at their juncture, twinkled palely through the gap in the fine, silky material. Her eyes were warm. Seeing my expression, she gave a loving smile and sat beside me, taking my hand.

'I meant all that I said—be not in doubt of it. Long have I waited to have an accomplice such as you,' she declared. 'You have such an air of angelic innocence and prettiness as will disguise many of our escapades. Your passion will know no more bounds than mine. Say that you are still of the same mind, Catherine, oh do!'

Such was the pleading in her tone that I laughed almost in relief at being lifted from my cloud of doubt. Taking this for all the assent that my expression was intended to reveal, she kissed me warmly.

'Repeat now the final lesson I taught you,' she demanded. While I hesitated, she tapped my lips playfully with her fingers, saying that if the words did not come out she would tickle me to distraction. 'Cock must come to... Come on, Catherine!'

I must have looked puzzled because she clarified, 'Not a man, silly girl, but a cock of the sort that a woman might utilize.' I hid my face but could not suppress a grin. Her hand moved to tickle me beneath my armpits and I jumped.

'C... c... cock must come to cunny,' I whispered.

'Yes—go on!' The excited impatience in her voice was evident.

'C... c... cock must come to bottom—lips must come to cock—pussy must come to pussy—lips must come to pussy... oh, Elaine, I forget!'

'Oh, you story, you do not—but that will do for the moment. But you have forgotten one thing: it does not matter the words, the meaning is clear enough! There, you see, it sounds like a little song! But listen, for I have a most wonderful idea. You remember that I told you that I wished to attend one of the private gatherings and that Mama would not take me? Of course you do. Well, we shall exercise our devious powers, my pet, and to the advantage of us all. Mama is much smitten with you, as I happen to know, for 'tis always she who ensures your invitation here. Yes, you may well blush, but that is the truth of it. Now, as to my plan it is really very simple. I shall make it known to Mama—indeed, we shall do so—that you are much taken with the idea also. Of course, she will believe us innocent in the real affair of things, but no matter. The idea will come far more fetchingly from you and I feel certain she will not then resist.'

I became almost pettish at first at the idea which I thought merely hotheaded, I confess.

'Elaine, we dare not, for whatever passes there will be seen by your Mama as much as we, and I would have no face to put upon it, let alone you.'

'Have I not thought of that, my darling muddle head? It will be known, of course, that Mama and I are kin and so discreet arrangements will be made to ensure our separation. I shall be whisked away—I have no doubt of that—but hence will still enjoy myself and, who knows, with the help of one or other may yet still peep in upon the proceedings. As for you, 'twill be quite other, for Mama will be discreet enough to withdraw from you, I know.'

'Oh, Elaine, what boldness! I could not!'

'Ha! See how you scurry to your rabbit hole as soon as we begin!' Elaine jeered and made to rise, which reaction from her caused me to seize her wrist, for then—as now— I would never be taken for a coward, however bizarre all seemed to me then.

'I do not! I will do it, you will see,' I blurted, much to her satisfaction, for she embraced me and declared that she had really known it all along.

'Really, you have no need to bother about Mama any more than I, Catherine. She knows perfectly well what is afoot at such gatherings and will be well apprised when something naughty is about to begin. At that she will no more be able to face you than you her and so will take to one of the bedrooms with some lady of his choosing. To put not too fine a point upon it, the occasion will give her fair opportunity to do so.'

'Yes,' I countered, 'but she will know that we know.'

'Make not too much of that, my sweet. Mama may then see in you and I accomplices of a sort—already compromised by his own lights—and may see us well out of the affair. It would not come amiss were she to buy me the pearl necklace he has long promised!'

'Oh, you wicked one!' I declared, but could not help laughing at her boldness and her quaint determination. I have long thought that innocence was upon her in some part even then, and knew not the trepidations—which she afterwards confessed to me—which she experienced in embarking upon her course. My own uprising sense of mischief and daring gave strength to her. We were as wall and ivy, the one complementing the other in our upward Teachings.

Reflecting upon the affair now, as I often still do—for it is as well to know our own motives in all things—I perceive that one or other of two qualities would have carried me through. I refer to naivety on the one hand and the full knowledge of experience on the other. Either would have done to decide me upon the path I trod then. Had I veered between both states, as many foolish women do, I would in all probability been too utterly shocked to entertain such ideas, or on the other hand would have wavered feebly and come to nothing but inertia. Thus naivety is put to good purpose while experience finds its own. Elaine had divined this instinctively during all her readings and daydreaming. Males who invariably consider themselves the lords of the universe could never have done as we. Nor could even the most determined of young women contrived on her own what we accomplished.

That I was destined to pleasure myself as I have done has long been clear to me. It will be seen however that none suffered in the process and many gained enduring delight from my precepts. That I occasionally surpassed her in my daring fretted her not. Untold measures of hedonism can be found within us all. In the beginning we shared everything, whether by our mutual presences or by our confidences afterwards. Each of us in a sense was the other's fervent disciple.

Our first plot—which I confess made my heart palpitate madly—proceeded with an ease born of the selfsame fate which directed our footsteps.

'We shall stroll a little in the garden, Mama, will you not join us?' Elaine asked her after breakfast. I had not until then thought of Auntie in any sense of being an admirer of myself, but now that the thought had been put into my mind I perceived with what interest her eyes passed all over me. She had been minded, I believe, to do something other, but as it chanced this proved her first opportunity to converse with me beyond the hearing of my uncle.

Upon her approval, therefore, the three of us took to the sward whose green and springy surface floated comfortably beneath my feet. Elaine seemed unduly quiet to a point at which I thought she was regretting her idea. Once out of sight of the house, however, she quickly broached the point, saying that I was much minded to enjoy my first festive evening with dancing and company.

At this a shadow passed across my aunt's brow. She hesitated much before replying.

'I fear, my dear, that your Papa would think it very strange were I to take you both. No, I do not think it can be thought of. Moreover, there are Catherine's parents to be consulted.'

One quick glance from Elaine and I knew that I must speak. Somewhat to my surprise I then heard my own voice declaring that Mama and Papa would make no ado about the matter and indeed were minded that I should enjoy myself.

'Ah yes,' my aunt replied. She was clearly in a dilemma. Walking on the other side of him, Elaine took her hand playfully.

'Will you not, Mama? It is a trifle deceitful, I know, but we could always tell Papa that we were attending some other function. After all, no harm will come to us for you will be there to chaperone us. Dear Mama, say yes!'

Her apparent innocence was perfectly judged in tone and manner, while my own could equally be in no doubt. My aunt, glancing at me as we made our way through a shrubbery, appeared flushed of visage. I would have given much then to read her thoughts. She was most obviously at a loss, since she must either forewarn us of the consequences or simply refuse. The smile that I afforded her appeared to swing the balance.

'I do hear,' she declared, 'that there is to be a small reception at the Eastwoods on Saturday evening. I must mention, however… well, that is to say… they are very lively.' Her voice appeared hoarse, her visage strained.

'I have so heard also, Mama, but that is to the good is it not; for we mean to enjoy ourselves,' replied Elaine who could scarce conceal a smile of victory.

'Yes, my pet, but… '

'Then it is settled, Mama. Besides, I have a topping idea. We will apprise Papa that we are attending a séance. You know how such things fret him and that he will have nothing to do with such events. Oh dear, I have no kerchief about me and must fetch one. Pray excuse me!'

With that she was gone, leaving me in full knowledge of the fact that it was but an excuse whereby I might wheedle the more into her Mama's favours. Alone with her, however, I knew not what to say and felt my tongue quite twisted. She for her part appeared ruminative and frequently on the verge of saying something which she could not bring himself to speak. I surmised, of course, what was on her mind and finally found voice as we came upon a rustic seat outside a summerhouse where she seemed as pleased to rest as I.

'As to the—er—reception, my dear, I fear that neither Elaine nor your sweet self know of the nature of such— er—functions,' she observed hesitantly.

Catherine

'Oh yes, we are fully apprised, Auntie. There is dancing and music and general merriment such as perhaps may not take place at more formal gatherings. Be certain that we are fully prepared to enter into the spirit of things.'

Had I spoken too boldly? Her eyes searched mine—her hand encompassed mine where it lay on my lap. So far from imagining it, I felt her knuckles graze not unpleasant against my belly where I had inadvertently parted my thighs a little. Wearing as I was a light summer gown with naught but a chemise and stockings beneath, the warmth of my body in such an intimate region communicated itself to his hand immediately.

'Yes, my dear, but there is a certain—er—freedom… '

She appeared to have difficulty in finding words. I interrupted her sweetly.

'Society puts upon us, does it not? No one can truly understand what it is like to be a lady in these times, can they?' I replied. Keeping my lips parted I gazed at her with such lustrous innocence that she knew not how to answer and indeed made no attempt to do so in words for with the swiftness of a swallow her mouth came upon mine, causing me at first to hold my breath.

'How young you are—you know not what you are at. At least I didn't. I was such a naïve girl at your age,' she murmured, though appearing to do so himself by passing her hand up until it all but encompassed my left titty. Responsive as my nipples have always proved, she was in but seconds in no doubt of their springiness which made itself apparent through my gown. I gulped, I swallowed. Even so I made no attempt to avert either my mouth or her hand which wandered first from one mound to the other and weighed the gelatinous hillocks amorously.

'Oh, you must tell me what you mean, please,' I begged as our lips parted.

Appearing then to realise where her hand was, she placed it instead upon my upper thigh where her fingers savoured the ridging of my stocking top through the fine cotton of my dress.

'I meant not to kiss you—yet how delicious you are,' she muttered. 'You must be shocked to find out that women do these sorts of things to one another.' Her desire to be encouraged was obvious.

'Dear Auntie, if you mean to kiss me, you shall, for I see no harm in it. It is not a very wicked thing to do, is it?'

'Nor this?'

With something of an eager grin she replaced his cupping hand, this time upon my other breast, allowing it to swell in her grasp as had its neighbour. I confess that I had no prior clue to her Sapphic tendencies, but I was quite happy to have discovered them.

'I cannot call it wicked, Auntie, for it feels pleasant. Do wicked things feel unpleasant? There will not be unpleasantness at the reception, will there?'

'One may gauge it so or one may gauge it not, Catherine. The most wicked things are invariably the most pleasant. Even so, I hesitate still to take you there for your innocence will be confounded and undone, I fear.'

'Oh!' I ejaculated and pursed my lips so prettily thereby that she could not help but lavish more kisses upon me, all of which I received with a certain coy pleasure while wondering whether Elaine intended me to draw her out upon the subject or not. I could find no words, however, to frame a question in such a way that would not betray my foreknowledge. Making great play of being petulant and sulky, I pushed her hand away. 'Then I shall not let you kiss me, for if we do not go we shall not have any fun,' I exclaimed, leaving her much in the dark as to what I knew or did not know. Seemingly, however, she was satisfied since, having made several attempts to dissuade us both from our course there would be no one to blame but ourselves. Thus guile did win the day, and thereupon also did Elaine reappear.

'How flushed you look, Catherine! Has Mama been at you?' she asked merrily in a manner that could be construed by two meanings. At her remark Auntie flushed heavily and told her not to speak nonsense for she had—she said carefully—no need whatever to upbraid me.

Coming then, as I felt it tactful to do to his support, I averred that we had been talking together very nicely and that she had finally given her full assent to our attendance on the Eastwoods.

'Why then, we shall all have fun,' Elaine said as she smiled artlessly. 'I have told Papa, so there is no hindrance to the matter. We may even be late in returning if we wish for I have had him believe that the spirits do not rise well before midnight.'

This remark causing us all to laugh, though not in an unkindly manner, eased the atmosphere much, though a certain agitation evidenced itself in my aunt who upon some excuse soon made his departure, walking with a rather curious gait. I had no doubt that she would have been pleased to accompany me alone to the Eastwoods' private party, but was anxious at the intended presence of his daughter. Indeed, the matter appeared to have played upon her mind for that selfsame day he succeeded in cornering me in a passageway upstairs close to my room, saying that she would have converse with me. A nearby linen closet being unattended I allowed myself to be escorted within, my aunt closing the door with solemn mien.

On either side of us were shelves upon which sheets and towels and other necessities were stored. The space between was such that we were brought to stand close together, I making no demur when she passed her arms about my waist and drew me against her.

'My dear Catherine, my sweet child, there is a matter of some import I must convey to you. It concerns the reception which you and Elaine would have us attend.'

'Yes, of course, Auntie, what frets you? Oh, what a pretty kiss! Have you brought me in here only for this?'

'No, my pet, but you are truly irresistible and therein lies the crux of the affair, as much also as it appertains to Elaine, who is as thoroughly excitable and as carefree as yourself but knows not the consequences thereof.'

'Pray do tell me, then, for naught shall pass my lips of what is said here,' I replied with great solemnity while she, passing her hand down from my waist, made bold to caress the rondeur of my bottom.

'There are country pleasures of which you know not, Catherine. The guests on such occasions are given to great frivolity. I hesitate to say to what extent. Suffice perhaps to tell you in all confidence—and such of course must never reach the ears of my dear husband—that the ladies are given to doffing much of their attire, and playing amongst each other with great fervour. There follows much amorous play, of course, for in select and well-chosen company such is accepted as a pleasurable pastime and no ill is thought of it. You see my dilemma?'

I feared at first to speak, not so much out of modesty but because in speaking she had slowly gathered up my skirt at the back and—first fondling my bared thighs and the sleek silk of my stockings—succeeded in cupping my bottom cheeks which protruded boldly upon her hand. Appearing much confused I pressed myself as if protectively against her and hid my face. My drawers being of fine batiste permitted the warmth of my derriere to exude over her hand which searched the hillocks somewhat feverishly. It was an amusing situation, for I swear that the poor woman was struggling twixt desire and the need to advise me of my future fate, as also that of Elaine whom clearly she knew little despite her occasionally bold manner.

'Shall we then need to take our drawers off?' I asked while not permitting her a view of my expression.

The question caused her to sigh, making her arousal quite clear to me.

'Those and much else,' she replied thickly, whereat her febrile fingers loosed the ties of my drawers and caused them to slither slowly down my legs. 'It will be so, you see,' she went on, raising my chin with her free hand and passing her lips across mine. I quivered and strained, for the seeking of her hand beneath my bottom cheeks caused me to rise up on tiptoe. A sweet, sickly sensation invaded me. By passing her forefinger under my derriere she was able to touch the soft warm lips of my quim which moistened instantly. The impress of her mouth upon my own grew stronger. My lips parted. I received her tongue. Roaming her hand all about, she then brought it to the front between our bodies and fondly cupped my pulsing nest. 'It will be so, my love, while you in turn will be required to take dildos in your quim and kiss the nests of other girls.'

My belly swirled. I could not help but widen my thighs as much as my fallen drawers would permit to allow her finger to seek up between the lips of my love nest. I know not what words passed between us in those brief moments save that on her part they were lewd and on mine excited. I moved my hand gently and tentatively across her body. My senses reeled. Second by second, I could feel my cunny moistening the more. Our tongues flashed together in such utter yearning that the moment clearly could no longer be delayed.

'You must know how it will be, Catherine, must you not?'

'Yes!' I assented, though I scarce recognised my voice as my own. I felt myself being borne back. We fell together upon the floor, she taking care that I would not harm myself in doing so. Without more ado my drawers were ripped from my ankles. With a certain roughness that thrilled me exceedingly, she thrust my legs apart, and began ramming me hard with a whole fistful of her fingers.

'You will be put so upon the floor, or upon a couch, and fucked, Catherine.'

'OH!' I moaned. Our lips meshed. I was in such an ague that I wriggled my bottom to obtain more of her fingers, though to my aunt the movement must have appeared evasive in intent for she seized me strongly about the waist and embedded her fingers the more so that in some magical wise my cunny expanded to receive them.

'You will be thoroughly fucked by dildos larger than my fingers, Catherine—do you wish to be?'

'HAAAAAR!'

I could not speak. I was filled with her. Her lips savaged my own. With a passionate jolt her fingers were fully inserted and then all but withdrawn so that I near cried out for their return. Her face appeared haggard and flushed. I saw the lust and desire a woman can have for a woman.

'You wish to be—you wish to be!' she exulted.

'Oh, Auntie—oh!'

Some inner wisdom in me told me not to respond directly, though I would have fain have cried out that I wanted her fingers to work me strongly. Some measure of modesty must be present at all times in the first moments of erotic bliss. Such draws the hunter on to excite the hunted the more.

'You do, you do—confess it! What a luscious little cunt you have—how tightly it clasps it and sucks upon my fingers. Ah my god, yes, work your bottom!'

In my fever, I was doing so without knowing it. It mattered not. We were lost in that world wherein fulfilment is all. I gloried in each powerful stroke of her hand. My spendings sprinkled her all the way up to her wrist. I implored her tongue the more by twirling my own in her mouth. I was as one who drowns in passion and seeks to do so. Cupped now upon her broad palms, the tight cheeks of my bottom rotated savagely, though it was then to my gain that she thought me endeavouring to fight free from under her by so doing and hence her fingers rammed in and out the more lustily.

Her questions poured upon me. It was my first lesson in discovering how an older woman will try to draw the lewdest words and phrases from a younger one, seeking to find beneath her apparent innocence the hottest pits of desire. I answered not except by chokes and sobs. Advised by instinct that she would think me otherwise a schemer, I held back the lascivious responses that would fain have come to my lips. It is no folly to use them when one knows one's lover, though all should be spoken haltingly and not in too great an efflorescence of words, for such would render the female common. The lure must always be that all is not said which it is wished to be said by one's partner. Thus is she kept in thrall, ever convinced that she will finally succeed in drawing one out to confess all one's innermost desires and—indeed—prior adventures. One is not so foolish, however, as to disrobe one's mind fully in front of, or indeed underneath, others.

My legs lay limp, my knees slightly bent. Her praise for the tight sleekness of my cunny was ever expressed. I continued to moan. I evaded her mouth from moment to moment as though in inner conflict at what I was permitting. Her kisses rained upon my cheeks and neck. I felt the tempo of her thrusting fingers increase, as if she herself were coming to a frenzy with the fucking.

'It will be so, if you come,' she croaked.

I AM coming, I thought—but told her not. I bucked, I clung, my soft cries grew ever wilder. All that had been promised to me by Elaine was true. With a last rattling cry I received my joy. Our mouths fastened together again, for I could refuse her not in that moment. The strokes of his fingers grew shorter. Panting, she thrust it in to the full and lay all too heavily upon me for a long moment until she stirred. I felt the slow withdrawal of her fingers with infinite regret. Had another hand taken the place of Auntie's inside me then, I would have welcomed it. Drawing me up, her eyes searched mine. I hid my face and affected great confusion.

'You will not tell her?' she demanded hoarsely while caressing my long brown hair with a certain tenderness. I quivered and pressed in, my skirt being caught up still, the warmth of my belly wet by her fingers which rested on it.

'No,' I comforted her softly, 'yet what of the reception? Oh, pray say that only you will do it to me if I have to take my drawers off.'

The apparent naivety of my words—tinged as they were with eroticism—struck exactly the right note, as I had intended they should. She laughed and mussed my hair, awarding my yielding lips a long kiss.

'Only I, my pet, but you must pray warn Elaine. Would that I could take you alone.'

'She may not believe me, Auntie, but I will try. How am I to say that I have come upon this knowledge, though?'

Her brow furrowed. 'That is true. I had not thought of it, for there is scarce a guest here who would venture such confidences even if they were to know of them. I know not what to say.'

I had expected her to proffer the name of Mr. Witherington-Carey, whom I suspected knew much of such things, but discretion in her obtained. It was a small but pleasing sign that she had become not so flustered as to completely forget herself. One must beware ever of the possible indiscretions of lust.

'Say naught, Auntie, for whatever will be, will be, and it is too late now to dissuade her or she will think it my fault. We may hide ourselves away there, may we not, so that whatever else passes happens not before our eyes.'

'By Jove, yes, that is the only solution to the matter. What a delightful and resourceful girl you are! Did you like what we just did?' she asked as if in apparent anxiety.

I giggled. I pressed my cheek to hers. 'I believe so. If you do it to me again at the reception, I shall know better and tell you. But haste, we must not stay here or a servant may discover us. Pray go first and then I will follow.'

'You minx, I truly believe there is more to you than anyone could imagine,' she chuckled and thereupon made his way out. I had not long followed when Elaine appeared as I was about to enter my room.

'I have been looking for you. What have you been at?' she asked curiously.

'Oh, nothing. I am about to find a book to read,' I replied. Perversely no doubt I did not mean to tell her of my amorous engagement on the floor of the linen room. Later on we would exchange all such secrets. With a strange expression on her face she shrugged and passed on. It occurred to me only afterwards that she had probably similarly encountered her Mama on the stairs in his descent.

* * *

As might be imagined, I dreamed much that night of what had passed and became restless for more. My cream puff had been well filled with Auntie's fingers, but sought extra dosages. I was not to be lacking in them, as will be seen—nor was Elaine. That which we immediately ventured upon was wicked in the extreme and I doubt not that had I demurred in the linen room and been of lesser daring, my Aunt would have sought some excuse not to take us, for it was apparent to me that she saw in her daughter a mischievous but innocent girl who knew as little as I had seemed to her to do about the ways of the world.

Time floats and passes, however, and soon enough the hour was upon us, I affecting a dark red dress and Elaine a blue one. Our stockings matched our gowns, for we had decided upon that in terms of appearance, were we to be disrobed. I had no doubt now that we were to be and told my cousin so.

'What will you do, then, if your Mama sees you without any drawers on?' I asked. I had not forgotten what she had said about her dildos and was still very curious about it.

'Well, she must not, for you must divert her,' she answered and I am sure quite believed herself. 'Besides, Catherine, I am sure that there will be quite a crowd there and in all the bustle and gaiety no one will notice what others are at. If Mama does see my bottom I shall be careful to keep my face hid and she will know not who it belongs to, for I swear I will not dance about without any clothes on — and neither must you,' she added with remarkable solemnity.

'Oh, as to that, I am sure excitement will overtake us if it is all that you say, but what a lark it will be if all is rumour and nothing happens!'

'You silly, of course it will, as soon as everyone is in their cups. Be sure that you see to Mama if anyone lifts my skirts.'

'Of course,' I replied demurely, though it seemed to me even then that Elaine was containing herself too much and I already thinking ahead of her. It was scarcely to be imagined that the three of us could attend such an event without several untoward events occurring. As I had learned even briefly in the linen room, the fevered imagination quickly rises to a pitch at which all things are possible. In the immediate aftermath they drain away and become dissolved, for there is a momentary peace and a delicious sense of floating. Soon enough however the imagination soars again and no bars are to be put then upon such enticements as enter the mind. Thus I thought and most curiously in so doing was a step ahead of my cousin who but hours before had been my mentor. A desire arose in me to see her being exercised, as we were prone to call it. Had her Mama not weakly conceded to her wishes then all would have been different and mayhap fewer opportunities would have arisen to put her philosophy to the test.

We affected no gaiety upon our departure at eight of the evening in question, for it was to be seen by my uncle that we were upon solemn business. By good fortune he was a rather vague man and would no doubt have forgotten by the morrow what the purpose of our outing had been.

The house of the Rt. Hon. Edward Eastwood and his family was one of the grandest in the neighbourhood. It was said often enough in joke that all looked up to them, for their mansion stood upon a slow rise among many rolling acres. The jogging of the carriage as we made our way there did nothing but encourage my now passionate temperament, for my bottom bounced up and down all the while as did Elaine's. It being dusk already we could see little enough of her mother who accommodated himself on the seat opposite, but I did not doubt that her thoughts of the advancing night were as much as mine.

The house was well lit as our carriage at last approached the entrance. But a single aged servant appeared to be about the place, though the reason for this soon struck me. All others had been dismissed for the night, perhaps locked in their rooms with their supper or packed off to an inn. Thus there were to be no witnesses as to what followed other than the assembled gentry.

As Elaine and I had already surmised, they were not many. I counted many ladies as well as a few gentlemen and found the score not greater than fourteen. Among the former were several beauties of local distinction. By good fortune I knew none of them. All were perfectly polite and utterly discreet, as I discovered. Mrs. Eastwood was a lady of remarkable charm, approaching then her fortieth year, who herself met us in the hall and took our cloaks without the faintest hint of embarrassment.

'You have come well provided for,' she said with a laugh to my aunt while gazing both Elaine and I up and down most approvingly. 'You have advised them well, I trust, for there are to be no understandings.'

Such boldness took me as equally by surprise as it did my cousin. We exchanged the most furtive glances. A purplish hue spread meanwhile over my aunt's features. The doors to the drawing room being closed, we all stood alone.

'Ah, as to that, perhaps we might converse privately,' she said. Her voice sounded exceedingly strained. I stared at my feet, as did Elaine.

Mrs. Eastwood shrugged in a languid manner. 'If you wish ' she declared and led Auntie into a small side room, though leaving the door ajar of a purpose, as I surmised. A muttering came to our ears and then a faint laugh from our hostess.

'My dear, discretion is all here. You above all should know that. I make no demur myself about the presence of Elaine and nor will anyone else. What? I cannot hear what you say, and really I cannot keep the others waiting. She must be put up as needs be, as we all are. That is the sport of it. You had no need to bring her, my pet. Let me speak with her for I do not wish her to enter upon the proceedings in total innocence, though should she wish to make play upon struggling a little that will be all the more fun. As to the other very pretty young lady who accompanies you, I will have her no more in the dark than Elaine.'

'Oh, I say! But Mavis…'

All was lost, or all was gained, depending upon one's philosophy, for my aunt's interruption was itself interrupted by the emergence of our hostess who clearly was determined to have no break in her evidently smooth affairs.

'Elaine, my dear, there will be much pleasantry tonight for which you must forgive us, as I am sure that— Catherine, is it not?—will also. Within half an hour or so when all have been well warmed with wine we shall call upon the ladies to present themselves, by which I mean you will doff as gracefully as possible such outer attire as you have, including of course your drawers.'

A gurgling sound came from behind her as these words were spoken. My aunt stood in the doorway of the side room as might have Lady Macbeth. No sooner had this sound struck softly upon us than Mrs. Eastwood, persuading herself between us, took us both by the elbows and steered us towards the drawing room, talking as merrily meanwhile as if we had been attending a fete.

Within was such a bubbling of voices and laughter as immediately warms the senses. Though the hall had been well lit, the drawing room was otherwise. A single chandelier had been lit in the centre of the ceiling, the gas mantles being dimmed so that while the middle of the room was sufficiently illumined, pools of shadow lay all about around the sides which gave a cozy atmosphere. The room was naturally commodious, there being some five large sofas and divans placed about the walls for such comfort as would be required. A huge sideboard accommodated piles of tiny sandwiches and canapés together with an impressive number of bottles and glasses.

'You, my dear, are one out, for we have an even number of ladies, but as such you make a piquant addition to our party. You will not be put out if you are attended to simultaneously by more than one lady? Of course, you will not, for there are many couples here who like to dally with a young woman together before disporting themselves,' our hostess said calmly enough to Elaine.

Before Elaine could gather herself to reply—though I know not what she would have said—we were surrounded by admirers and drinks placed in our hands.

'All are known by names other than their own, of course, so you may use any pseudonym that you wish,' remarked Mrs. Eastwood helpfully and then disappeared to the other side of the room the while that my aunt made his hesitant entrance and stood regarding me. I moved towards her upon instinct and stood by her side. Elaine, throwing me a somewhat frantic glance, found herself sandwiched between a lady of some forty years and a young woman scarce older than herself. Even as we watched I heard the girl declare, 'Let me kiss you, for you have such lovely lips.'

At that, and while others watched the trio as fondly as might parents observing their children at play, Elaine was embraced by the looping of the girl's arms about her neck. I believe she might have started back, but all happened so quickly that there was naught for her to do but surrender to the moment. As if to encourage them a beautifully attired couple standing by merged to one another as if they had waited long for this moment and exchanged the most lascivious kisses which all then fell to partaking of save for my aunt and I who stood apart as two who enter a room and see no one but strangers before them.

As may be thought, this state of immobility lasted not long. Moving swiftly behind Elaine, the lady whose female partner was impressing ever more passionate kisses upon her lips, raised her skirt so quickly that she had not time to retreat—nor any space to do it in—before her shapely legs were fully bared and her proudly-filled drawers were displayed to all. Giving her no time to wriggle from between them, the lady then fumbled through a bag she carried for a dildo she deemed proper for the occasion.

'Down with their drawers!' a voice cried, whereat several of the ladies made great play of shrieking and endeavouring to run all about, though not with such energy that they were not quickly made as captive as my cousin who could be seen moving her face agitatedly from side to side while the lady into whose stomach her bottom was pressed, held her waist tightly and so allowed her companion to further her endeavours by unfastening Elaine's corsage. Isolated in a corner as I seemed to be with my aunt, I could but watch dry-mouthed as my cousin's lustrous firm titties were brought into view while the ladies dildo moved to and fro between the backs of her bared thighs.

All was now as a scene painted in one's own erotic dreams. All about were to be seen suspender stockings, corsets, arid emerging breasts and bottoms as the females everywhere were being disrobed. Some fumbled for their partner's dildos at the same time while others pretended a ridiculous coyness which however did not abate the strip-pings. A cry from Elaine announced that her own drawers were being descended. Quite without thinking I sank down upon a sofa in company with my aunt whose arm stole about my shoulders. I turned my flushed face to hers. Our mouths met in the wildest of kisses.

Moans, cries, laughter, squeals, came to our ears while blindly our tongues met and whirled. Feverishly Auntie fondled my breasts and then, dipping one hand into my corsage, sleeked her palm over the silky swollen surfaces to taunt my stiffening nipples. I fell back, encouraged by the seeking of our hands, unbuttoning her dress as I did so. Auntie was quite suddenly wielding a leather shaft of momentous dimensions such that I believed would never fit inside me. Yet I was as one possessed. Forgetful that she thought of me as naught but a novice, I rubbed the great leather shaft fervently, while hands sought my gown and threw it up, tearing at the waistband of my drawers.

'Let me kiss her. How pretty she is!' a voice sounded dimly from above. My aunt moved from me, allowing me to see who had spoken. Above us, legs astride and with a well-puffed mount displayed, stood a beautiful woman of about thirty whose attire consisted solely of a fetching black waist corset, stockings and shoes. Lying half beneath my aunt as I was, I had not time to stir nor rise before she lay down alongside me and captured my lips in a breathless kiss. Therewith my aunt stirred and must have slid to his knees so that she knelt beside the sofa and, pressing back my legs, applied her mouth to the succulent haven of my cunny.

'What is your name?' she asked amid fervent tonguings.

'Rose,' I gasped for want of anything else to reply, while her hand dipped as freely in my gown as my aunt's had. My bottom being cupped and slightly lifted now on her tender hands, I wriggled madly at the invasion of her tongue between my love lips.

'Let us have her things off,' the unknown murmured, causing me to feel somewhat like a piece of property, though all was such and I so feverish by now in my responses that I made no demur as I was drawn up between them and quickly bereft of all save my shoes and stockings. My titties, bottom, thighs and cunny all being caressed the while, I was in a perfect fever to be fucked as was evident in the way I rejoined our triple embrace once more upon the sofa. Even so, I had not failed to glimpse Elaine and neither, from the rubicund hue on his face had my aunt. Having surrendered to the opportunities of the moment as quickly as I, she was upon her hands and knees on the floor receiving a sturdy dildo from the rear. All about us indeed were such scenes of libertine delights, the ladies all being by then universally in a great state of nudity.

'I adore kissing young girls while they are being fucked,' my female companion declared, and so it seemed, for while we pecked amorously at each other's lips and caressed each other's breasts, my aunt made ready with the dildo while her naked form pressed against my quite tingling nipples. Davina—as she appeared to be called—breathed teasing words into my mouth even as the lusty shaft drove up into my cunny.

'Is this your first, or have you been a truly naughty girl?'

'My f… f… first,' I stammered. All my senses reeled. The dildo plugged me where Auntie's hands had previously. Our three tongues joined. My legs being drawn up, I wrapped them about his waist. We jogged, we writhed. The dildo sluiced in and out, causing me the most exquisite raptures which were all the more enlivened by the caresses that Davina and I lavished upon one another. The triple kisses in the very midst of being so fully pleasured added to our bliss.

'She is coming,' breathed Davina who with seeking fingers could feel the rippling in my belly. Her tongue plunged into my mouth anew. My aunt's fingers sought her bottom, causing her to churn her hips, bending as she was then with one knee on the edge of the seat. I came, I sprinkled, I melted, I urged his thrusts with sensuous movements of my bottom. Our moans resounded, mingling with those all about us, though in my lowly posture I could see naught.

Davina announced her own delirious pleasure by tonguing our mouths in turn. Febrile quivers shook us. My tight cunny seemed to suck upon the embedded dildo until, in withdrawing at last, the well-soaked too smeared my thighs with my own juices. I floated. Warmth and satisfaction spread in easy waves throughout my uttered charms. With a soft gurgle, Davina eased herself off of my aunt's probing finger and sat up languidly to look all about.

'Ah, Elaine is having her dosage of the shaft,' she declared to my full surprise at having so casually uttered my cousin's name. With something of a satisfied grunt my aunt removed her weight from my body. I drew up my knees and swivelled on to one hip, leaning into a corner of the sofa. Auntie's eyes were transfixed as were my own for a moment on Elaine who now lay with her head and shoulders beneath a large oak table, couched beneath a formidable lesbian manning an equally formidable shaft of rubber.

'How well she takes it,' Davina murmured, having seated herself on the other side of my aunt so that she was between us. Her hand stroked Auntie's thigh. Her eyes appeared glazed. Kneeling beside Elaine was the young woman who had first kissed her and who was now entertaining a rigid dildo in her bottom. But a few feet away—and all at the centre of other heaving couples— our hostess was having her cunny kissed.

The scene blurred, came clear, and then blurred again before my eyes. Stealing my right hand sideways I mischievously stroked my aunt's quim the while that Davina dandled her titties.

'See how she wriggles her bottom,' Davina said of Elaine who, while she could not possibly have heard and indeed must have been utterly lost in her sensations, appeared at that moment to twist her lovely face all about and gaze directly at us across the carpet. At that my aunt's jaw literally gaped for she sensed that their eyes were locked even though I felt certain Elaine would have seen nothing but a swirling of bodies and faces. Elaine opened her legs wider by letting her feet slip to the floor. A species of snorting moan escaped my aunt. She was quite driven beyond ecstasy, a state that we all thoroughly shared for the rest of the night.

* * *

A touch of fate occurred but two afternoons later which was to prod our destinies, for I at least was surprised by the arrival of the self-same lady who had assisted my aunt in ramming me with her dildo. Her true name was Pearl and the nature of her visit showed me much of how things were veiled, for even my uncle was well acquainted with her, as was Elaine.

Naturally I showed all modesty in greeting her and, while my uncle was otherwise occupied—for Pearl, it seemed, was too old a friend to require formalities—the three of us repaired in feminine fashion to Elaine's room. Quite astonishingly Elaine had been unconscious of Pearl's presence at the orgy, but this was to be accounted for by the dizzy eagerness with which she had succumbed to several amorous assaults.

Whether Pearl—or Lady Mathers, as she was properly called—was aware of this really mattered not, for she was plainly intent on broaching the subject, first complimenting me upon my 'performances,' though being discreet enough not to mention the names of my partners on that particular battlefield of love.

'Oh! Were you there, then?' Elaine asked her.

'You did not notice me? Ah, but, my dear, you were rather too occupied. I know not who was the more agile and passionate of you two. You are both much to be congratulated on your entry into the lists, for all spoke of you with high praise and your return is looked forward to. Praise be it that your Mama was not backward in bringing you.'

'Oh, but say nothing to her, I pray, or she will discover all,' begged Elaine, causing me thereby some hidden mirth which Pearl shared more openly.

'Really, what a silly you are for I swear he thought you looked quite adorable,' declared our companion who was obviously able to speak of such matters as if they were everyday events. Seated about the bedroom as all three of us were, Elaine duly became the focus of attention for such dismay was spread upon her face as could not be disguised. I need not however repeat her expostulations, for they were as quickly swept aside as is a cobweb, Pearl declaring that if Elaine were to play the hypocrite then her true nature had not been as her actions had revealed.

Seeing my cousin's confusion and feeling not a little sorry for the way she had vainly endeavoured to cloak herself in illusions, I made what best of it I could by falling upon her and tickling her, this having been done many times to me in the past by my Mama when I was in poor salts. In vain did Elaine endeavour to fend me off, for I think she would sooner have affected misery than pleasure. Pearl watched at first with amusement, thinking us—as she said—quite like two kittens at play, but no sooner had I got my cousin to giggle at last than Pearl declared the best place for such amusements to be upon the bed.

Elaine then became—not too unwillingly, I should say—our victim. Being duly raised up and hustled upon the counterpane, she was trapped between us, I attending to the waving of her arms and her increasingly weak protestations while our companion raised up Elaine's skirt and set about to tickling her between her thighs.

Being as susceptible as I to such a caress, Elaine succumbed, though saying that she knew not what devils had got into us as I unbuttoned her corsage and set to teasing her nipples with lips and tongue while Pearl, thrusting up Elaine's legs, began to gamahuche her deliciously.

'Oh, oh, Papa will come!' protested Elaine who could not help working her cunny against Pearl's mouth.

'That he will not, for your Mama is diverting him. She knows how our womanly fun must be disguised from his dour eyes,' replied Pearl in a muffled voice. Giving Elaine's quivering clitoris a final lick and having made her spend already, Pearl then clambered up upon her and lay belly to belly with her, having raised her own skirt for the pleasure. Then in a triple embrace while I lay beside the pair did we fall to exchanging tongues and lips. Pearl's hand roamed about my naked bottom which I presented to her. A fervour of pleasure seized us. Pearl's lips passed from one to the other of us. The lewdness of the moment was all. We exchanged as many hot words of pleasure as we did kisses.

'Ah, that we might be naked,' I murmured.

'Soon, my pet, we shall, for all will be arranged,' said Pearl, dipping her long tongue between my lips as she spoke while at the same time rubbing her quim fervently all around that of Elaine who was as lost as I.

Catherine

And so it was that we did all end naked and spent, the taste of each other's quims on our tongues and the pleasure of our ecstatic gasps resonating between these walls. Scarce thirty minutes had passed in all since we had entered the bedroom, and yet as so often the pleasures seemed as of an eternity. Elaine followed more slowly which caused Pearl to nudge me in a manner I well understood. It was time to go and she left it to me to persuade my cousin to make a timely return to her Mama and Papa.

* * *

It wasn't long before Auntie herself joined the proceedings, unable to resist the pleasures we were having. Auntie, Pearl and I took advantage of the moments when Elaine was occupied with her Papa and snuck off. On one such occasion, Auntie had just reached her crisis and rolled off of me, lying on her back, spent. She thus permitted Pearl to come upon me in turn. Between my open thighs she lay, rubbing her cunny madly to mine and exchanging such a torrent of erotic phrases as I returned in full.

She squirmed upon me, full knowing that I was ready as ever before to spill my excitement anew. In this she was right. The rubbing of our love lips and our pubic curls made me soar again to heaven. Blind in our hungers we mouthed and tongued. I felt her wetness. Yet again she trilled out her sparkling juices as did I until the hairs of our cunts meshed oiled and wet together. Uncaring of the condition of the eiderdown which would betray our pleasures we then lay still as might two babes. Murmuring gently we exchanged kisses as soft as doves.

'Ah, you are well fitted for it,' Pearl sighed. A laugh escaped her as then my aunt stirred and came upon her, bringing our heat up yet again. Finally, well delayed on the purported errand that had taken us away, we forced ourselves to return to Elaine and my uncle. My uncle greeted us with a jovial absentmindedness, but Elaine was no where to be found. Finally, I came upon her huddled up on the bed.

'Oh, what have you been at?' she asked crossly. Evidently she had slept, for her hair was all disarrayed and her skirt up. I suspected something of that and, before she could rise, threw myself merrily upon her and reached my hand so far up her thighs until I could feel her quim. There was such a stickiness there that I knew well what she had been about.

'You have enjoyed yourself,' said I.

'But not as much as you, I am sure,' she replied pettishly. Blushing deeply, she pushed my hand away, got off the bed and went to her dressing table. Determined to break her mood, I bent over her from behind and, sliding my arms beneath hers, cupped her breasts.

'What naughty thoughts did you have?' I asked, whereat she had the grace to giggle.

'None—and you have not told me what you were doing. I suppose you were conversing again,' she said sarcastically. I turned her face—moving my free hand all about over and beneath her proud titties—and kissed her. She felt my fervour, my affection. Her lips returned the compliment.

'Yes, it may be called that,' I murmured. I had no cause to blush, nor she. 'It was nice to have it in your bottom, was it not?' I asked, referring to the dildo I saw sticking from her at the party last week, my lips continuing to brush her own while her neck was turned about to me.

'No,' she said softly, but I knew the word not to be taken at its face value nor indeed any value. I told her then what I had heard the Madame say to Pearl before we were put over the bars. At that, Elaine's hand clutched mine and held it over her left breast.

'Is that really true?' she asked.

'Of course. Why else do you think it was done? That dildo was divinely formed to open up our furrows so that the larger ones might follow. It tingled me at first, but it was nice. I am sure you felt the same.'

'Oh, then have you…?' she asked, referring of course to my absence and well imagining, I am sure, that her Mama's dildo had breached the same route.

'You have not told me whether you liked it or not,' I countered. At that I raised my head and pressed her face to my breasts while feeling for the little velvet buttons of the front of her dress.

'Yes, all right, I did, though not at first. I wished she had kept it in longer. You had the best of it,' Elaine confessed.

Little by little I had freed her breasts as she spoke. My fingers roamed now over their glossy swollen surfaces. Her nipples, quickly risen, stubbed against my fingertips.

A little awkwardly I drew her up, but she following easily, we moved sideways together back cross the room and fell pell-mell upon the bed. Her mouth was moist and hungry. Licking at her nipples while she sighed and let her arms loll above her head, I raised her skirt and dwelt my eyes with pleasure upon her mount. The dark hairs were crisp and well-fluffed up. The lips were oily with the excited thoughts she had apparently sustained. Working my tongue into the whorl of her navel, I caused her to giggle and double up her legs. Upon her doing this, and having her bottom half hanging over the edge of the bed, I dropped to my knees and— holding her without resistance, plunged my pointed tongue back and forth in her pussy.

Elaine squirmed and moaned, but pressed into me, quite mushing me with her pubic hairs.

'Did she fuck you? Tell me, oh tell me,' she quivered.

'Of course—as she will you tonight.'

She hid her face, enjoying my tongue as the sly movements of her bottom showed. Rolling her upon her back and forcing her thighs askew, I plunged my mouth in deeper. She was on the point of coming as I could tell by all the little febrile movements of her body. Her stockinged legs stirred passionately, waving this way and that. The slurping of my tongue sounded.

'Oh, no, I cannot!' she moaned.

Gliding my luring tongue without, I rubbed my chin all around her clitoris, this coming as an inspiration to me and proving most effective, for she bucked the more and let me feel her tricklings.

'You silly, you must, for else you will be birched and your hot bottom put up to them one by one. Many a girl is so treated at the Comte's, I hear.'

'Oh-woh!' Elaine's knees spread themselves over my shoulders, the heels of her shoes digging between my shoulder blades. Her back arched. She came again, this time in a fiercer spurting whose fine rain spattered against my chin. Her legs slumped down either side of me and remained open. Her eyes stared at the ceiling. I was upon her like a tigress. Our stocking tops rubbed together.

'Say yes, for I would not have you birched,' I begged.

'Yes!'

Whether she even heard herself speak, I know not. She kissed divinely. Our quims rubbed together as sensitively as the strings of violins. So wriggling and squirming together we released our juices which mingled in the oiling of our thighs. Quiescent then in the pale mists of fulfilment, we lay panting. Moving half off of her I toyed with her slit. My left leg lay across hers.

The night would soon enough come upon us. I whispered to her of what must come to pass. She hugged me, answering me not; her eyelashes fluttering against my cheek.

Catherine

* * *

One day Pearl was making inquiries on the progress of Elaine's development when I came upon the interview and accelerated the process of getting at the truth.

'Elaine has already had the forbidden fruit,' I said mischievously, causing my cousin to squeal and shush me.

'It is as well she did. Such barriers put up by a hypocritical society are not for us. There are only two rules whereby we guide ourselves. The first is complete refusal to participate in the body's pleasures, for ultimately the proclaimed will of the individual must be respected. The second—as I need hardly say—is that the giving of pain must be avoided at all costs.'

'Oh, but Mama stung me with the birch!' interjected Elaine.

'Stuff and nonsense, girl—she but burnished your bottom. You had not a mark to show upon it afterwards and naught but pleasure in the outcome. For the most part, young women of your age receive such admonitions of the birch through their drawers and conceal thereby their ultimate modesty. Many a girl at boarding school receives the birch, the cane or the strap before her Mama lays hand in turn to her bottom. Such as are brought to so-called illicit delights in that way may count the birching a part of the bargain, for it persuades the girl to a submissive posture and a readiness to succumb. Finding that the dildo rides pleasurably in her and that she is frequently afterwards fondled and rewarded for her compliance, all is then well. Such is far better than that she may be taken to the marriage bed in ignorance and without having first tasted the pleasures of other women. Come, Elaine, sit upon my lap and tell the truth. Did you not like it?'

My cousin, obeying, found her thighs and pussy immediately prey to Pearl's caresses and thus answered in heat more quickly than she might otherwise have done that she had found it indeed to her liking.

'And the birching? It did not really pain you? You were not in torture?'

'Oh, no. It stung me and bit me, for some of those twigs had awful tips to them, but once I was made to... to... to do it, the stinging became a lovely glow and I felt the better for it.'

'You were held and plugged, my pet—that is how it should be after your bottom has been well-warmed. A girl must be taken quickly if she is to succumb, else she may entertain all sorts of doubts and wriggle her way out of it. Once the dildo has found its niche in her cunny or bottom and she is so held, then the outcome is certain. A gentlewoman is one who will then fuck her lovingly that she might partake of the delicious sensations and so be brought to the full sport of it. Shyness has a certain charm, however, and I wish you not to lose it. Come, Catherine, the minx is coming on heat. Attend to her bottom while I make her spill!'

Thus saying, Pearl drew up the back of Elaine's dress and raised it to her waist so that my cousin's bottom bulged out over Pearl's thighs. This allowing me perfect access to her nether charms, I threw myself down beside them and worked my forefinger delicately up into her bottom hole while Pearl tickled her clitty.

'Oh, oh, what are you at?' gasped Elaine who jiggled this way and that but—being firmly held—could not escape.

'A little introduction, my pet, to what two dildos may feel like though I fear that our fingers are rather small for it.'

'HAAAAAR! I c... c... could not!' my cousin moaned, though seeming to like the intrusion of my finger she weighed down upon it and so forced my finger in past the first knuckle while Pearl equally inserted her own into her slit. Then instructing me briefly, Pearl told me to feel for the sheathing of her own finger, at which I was to withdraw mine to the tip. At the emerging of hers, I was then to allow mine in turn to act as the 'poker.' Thus did I gain the art of it, and Elaine too, emitting an 'OOOH-AH!' each time we deftly worked our digits alternately. Indeed, there were moments in my haste when I could feel the pressure of Pearl's finger through the membrane that divided the two orifices and from this I also learned the purpose of so pleasuring in this way.

Clutching at Pearl's shoulders, Elaine seemed unable to speak, though she several times attempted to. Her hips pumped and her breath literally whistled out.

'Ah! She is coming!' cried Pearl whose fingers were already well lubricated while I sensed upon my own a filmy moisture such as in my own case had much improved. This, Pearl said afterwards, was a secretion provided by Nature when sufficient titillation was provided, though in the case of male penises some warm sweet oil was always to be recommended, for then it afforded immediate pleasure to both parties.

After such enervating trials as she endured in the next few minutes, Elaine slipped from our grasp and lay quietly curled up upon the floor, Pearl nudging her playfully with her toes and winking at me.

Such were our adventures that whole season. More parties and more ladies, each taking Elaine and I far beyond our imaginations, but never beyond our appetites. We were never again so satisfied as we were by those parties, the newness of which would eventually where off, though we would never tire of attending them.

AMANDA

Good news, Amanda,' my mother exclaimed upon reading the message she'd just received from a friend in Dieppe. 'Your father has escaped France in safety.' We hugged each other, overjoyed to know that he would avoided the inevitable fate, which, as an aristocrat, would have befallen him at the hands of the purging Republicans. Then a look of distress crossed her face. 'But until we get news from England to enable us to join him there, I hardly know where we can look for refuge. I suppose we're guaranteed a temporary home, for my younger sister, Agatha is Abbess of the convent of St. Bridget, but now there is talk of suppressing convents and priests altogether. My other fear pertains to you, my dear girl,' she said, wringing her hands. 'Taking refuge and protecting you from danger is one thing; but how to smuggle you, a famed nonconformist, a reputed lesbian even, into a convent full of young nuns is a perfect puzzle to me.'

'Nonsense, Mother!' I exclaimed. 'Before the convents are suppressed, we'll be in safety in England, and as for getting me snugly into the convent, we're about the same height and resemble one another, so you must dress me up the best way you can and introduce me as your sister, or niece, or friend, or something or other.'

'You are impudent for imagining any such idea,' replied my mother, laughing, 'but you forget one thing. It will be impossible to deceive my sister, Agatha. She knows you too well, my dear girl.'

'Try, anyway,' I said, 'and if the worst comes to the worst, we must let her into our secret and trust to her kindness.'

'Your plan is bold, if not rash, but as I can't think of anything else, we'll try it,' she agreed with some misgivings. 'Let me see,' she continued in a musing tone, 'I'll present you as the niece of your father's wife, a girl named Augustine who Agatha has never met. But even then Agatha may have her suspicions, but we'll risk it.' She wagged a finger at me. 'Mind you don't look so bold, and stride so wide in your walk as you usually do, and keep away from the nuns, especially the novices. I'll dress you suitably tomorrow morning.'

I shook my head. 'We don't know what may happen this afternoon or tomorrow morning. If we are discovered here, we shall never see the Convent of St. Claire, or any other place of refuge.' I gathered up my jacket and walked to the door. 'There is plenty of time left today, so while I go and hire a coach, why don't you lay out suitable apparel for me."

'You are right, Amanda, or rather Augustine, as I must now call you,' Mother said. 'Go quickly.'

I lost no time in getting a conveyance, the driver of which I knew I could depend upon. And upon my return in twenty minutes with my mother's assistance, I was completely metamorphosed. We packed up my mother's jewellery and some of our most valuable attire and prepared for the street. We had previously given my mother's chambermaid a holiday. When she returned and found us gone, the clothes and jewellery missing, she would take it for granted that we had either attempted to make our escape to join my father, or that we had been arrested and thrown into prison.

Our plan proceeded without difficulty, and before sundown, we arrived at the back gate of the convent of St. Claire. We were most cordially welcomed by my aunt, the Lady Abbess of St. Claire, who, however, could not help lamenting the necessity which there was for us to take refuge with her. I noticed that she stared at me with great curiosity and whispered apart to my mother. The answer that she received seemed to be only partly satisfactory. She shrugged her shoulders and smiled slightly as she glanced at me. 'I do not doubt your step-daughter's discretion, but I hope that she will recollect that she is Mademoiselle d'Ermonville, and will behave as becomes her rank and sex.' This was addressed to me with very pointed emphasis. I remained silent; my only reply was a low, sweeping curtsey, at which feminine performance my mother could not repress her smiles.

'But my dear Henriette,' commented the Abbess, 'I fear that I must now treat you inhospitably, and turn you out of the room. I am momentarily in expectation of the arrival of the Mother Superior.'

'Oh, I know her very well indeed,' replied my mother, appearing to me rather confused, 'and there is no necessity for my leaving the room unless you want a very private interview with him, Agatha!'

'None of your banter,' replied the Abbess tapping her sister's cheek. 'The Mother Superior is coming here on duty.'

'She is always 'on duty,'' muttered my mother. Just then we were interrupted by a tap at the door. After the Abbess gave the necessary permission, a tall, attractive young nun entered. First she made a lowly obeisance to the Agatha, and then a slighter recognition of my mother and me.

'I have come, Holy Mother, to receive my punishment,' she said quietly.

'You have done well to keep your time punctually, daughter Emilie,' replied the Abbess not unkindly. 'It shows some degree of penitence, although the degree of the penance must rest to a great extent with the Mother Superior. Yet I think I can promise that you will not be treated very severely.' She arched one eyebrow. 'But stripped you will have to be, and I think slightly whipped. So you had better begin to undress yourself at once in order to save time.'

'Will these ladies remain to be spectators of the proceedings?' asked Emilie, alluding to my mother and me.

'It is rather unusual to allow strangers to be present,' replied the Abbess, 'but as these ladies are my sister and niece, I think I may venture to grant them the privilege.'

'Certainly, I should like it,' replied my mother. 'I have a great curiosity to see what penance the Mother Superior, whom I know very well, will impose on a fine girl such as sister Emilie. What fault has she been committing?'

'Oh, dear Lady Agatha, please don't tell your sister,' exclaimed Emilie, 'or I will die of shame.'

'Nonsense, my child,' replied the Abbess. 'Proceed with your disrobing, find a rod, and then go and kneel upon the divan in the corner. While you are waiting, you may repeat one of the penitential psalms to get yourself in the right frame of mind before the arrival of the Mother Superior.'

I might mention here parenthetically, that I had, on my first entrance into the room, observed this so-called divan, and wondered what its use was! It was provided with pillows and cushions, and covered with black velvet. At each corner, moreover, it was furnished with leather straps and buckles.

Before this device the beautiful young Emilie stripped, my eyes devouring her nudity. She was most curvaceous, her hips wide. Her breasts were full and pendulous and capped with rosy buds that swelled under my intense stare. Her milky thighs swept up to the mossy juncture that was of the greatest interest to me. The hair on her mount was thick and bushy; below this mass, there peeped a most delicious pink slit that invited penetration. I felt a stirring beneath my dress and longed to kiss and tongue that moist love nest.

On this black altar then, which set off the dazzling whiteness of her skin most charmingly, Emilie knelt down, a victim for sacrifice, and after depositing the switch between her spread legs, proceeded to her devotions.

Never in all my youthful experience had I seen such a sight as the young novice, Emilie — the swell of her breasts, partially concealed by her posture, her long graceful legs, and above all, her delicious cunt, looking like a garden of black moss pierced with vermilion and placed between two puffy cushions of satin texture and snowy whiteness.

Surely, the Mother Superior can never be such a brute as to flog that lovely rump, I thought to myself. As these reflections were passing through my mind, my aunt told my mother about the fault for which Emilie was to suffer. It appears that, because of her complaints of poor eyesight, she was allowed an extra quantity of candles in her sleeping apartments. When the Lady Abbess was kind enough to visit her in the middle of the night, and to her intense consternation, instead of finding the young novice wrapped in slumber, she was lying partly uncovered with her legs spread lasciviously open as far as they could get. A large candle rammed about nine inches up her cunt, which Emilie was driving in and out most furiously, and heaving and wriggling her rump about as if she was possessed by the devil.

Of course, any attempt at concealment or excuse was utterly useless, as Lady Agatha was an eyewitness of the transaction. Indeed, at the very minute of her entering the apartment, shuddering spasms overtook Mademoiselle Emilie and she released the flood of her self-induced passion. Emilie sank back upon the pillows in a half-fainting state, leaving her candle to drop out of its come-moistened sheath at its leisure.

Now, the Abbess was not a severe woman — on the contrary, she was especially indulgent to the young ladies under her charge. But, upon the discovery of Emilie, she was aggravated into being rather severe, as Emilie on being scolded, retorted with some impertinent remarks about handsome young confessors, and the superior privileges of the convent superiors.

All this my aunt related to my mother in a half whisper, not altogether unheard by the beautiful culprit on the cushion whom, as I perceived as I closely watched her, could hardly restrain her laughter. She didn't act very afraid of the Mother Superior, I thought, and I was right — she wasn't.

At last she arrived, but before paying any attention to the naked girl huddling in the corner, she saluted the Lady Abbess with what I suppose she considered a 'holy kiss' on her lips. Then she turned to my Mother with delight and surprise. 'My dear Madame d'Ermonville, what brings you here? And who is this — this — young lady?'

This she said with some emphasis and I saw in a moment that she had found me out.

But my mother prevented any outbreak at the moment; she drew her to one side and spoke to her in a whisper. This conversation was not long. At its end she said, 'Then, Henriette, will you promise? If so, I will not only keep the secret, but do my best for you in the bargain!'

This agreement was ratified by half a dozen kisses given and taken, which somehow seemed to me to be less chaste than they should have been. But I supposed my mother knew best.

'Now I think, Mother Superior, that poor girl has been on her knees waiting her penance long enough,' she remarked, 'and in common charity you ought to inflict her punishment, whatever it is. Only don't be too severe upon her!'

'If only for your sake I will not, lovely Lady d'Ermonville,' replied the nun, whom I perceived was a woman with some hidden Sapphic proclivities. 'You shall be witness for yourself.'

I must say that she was a very handsome woman, but for her nun's habit. It was not a becoming costume. What seemed strange to me was that she wore no breeches, or undergarments of any description. But I soon found out that this was intentional.

Turning around, and regarding with lustful complacency the lovely posteriors and perfect charms displayed by the kneeling girl, Mother Superior briefly asked the Abbess if she had confessed her sin and promised repentance. Being answered in the affirmative, she remarked he would not use the whip but would merely administer a few gentle slaps, then whisper forgiveness, pour in a little holy oil, and the younger sister might consider herself absolved and purified.

Nothing could be milder in the way of penance than this, and to my astonishment, Emilie absolutely appeared to like the gentle slapping. Instead of shrinking from it, she stuck her naked rump upwards and outwards as if to meet the infliction. She did not long dally over this part of the ceremony, and I could easily perceive the reason why, for as the Mother knelt down to approach his face to the novice's white buttocks, her frock fell a little open in front, and the most lush thatch of hair covering her nest was revealed, right at Emilie's eye level. As it was quite clear to me how all this penance would terminate, I could not help thinking that Mademoiselle Emilie would find it a rather different affair to masturbating with the tallow candle.

Her 'whispering forgiveness' as the Mother Superior called it, consisted of her putting his tongue up her tight little slit from behind, and gently sucking it. The tip of his tongue worked all the way from the topmost portion of her trembling thighs to the curving line of her buttocks, then underneath again to that mossy nest that glistened with his moisture and her own. She flicked at the young sister's cunt lips, laving them thoroughly and plastering down the hair, then darted inside the slit, once, twice, and again until Emilie shuddered from fear and luscious anticipation. When she fancied she had sufficiently opened and lubricated Emilie's pussy for his purpose, she proceeded to administer what he called his 'holy oil.' He meant simply that she pulled an enormous dildo from her habit and introduced it in the entrance of her dripping tunnel and proceeded to ram the full length of the shaft into her. Then she began to fuck the girl with the dildo in the fashion of dogs. To better ease the passage, she ground the dildo in a tight circular motion, which served to open the poor girl's cunt even wider, if that were possible.

Emilie, on her part, bore it very well, much better than I could have considered possible. After two or three natural expressions, such as 'Ah! Oh!'

brought about by the huge dildo first forcing an entrance, she ably reciprocated the Mother' lunging shoves. I particularly noticed that she bent down, so that by looking under her belly she could see Mother Superior's entire performance. I, too, watch, enraptured by the performance and more hopeful than ever that for a lesbian, St. Bridget's would prove a most rewarding place indeed.

I dared not look at my mother, but as I stood in one corner with my arms around my aunt's waist in an attitude of fear and intimidation, I could not for the life of me help putting my hands into her robe. I groped around until with one hand I felt the lowermost swell of her generous tits. I fairly crushed the soft globe as I searched for the pebble-stiff nipple that soon rose beneath my insistent encouragement. My other hand was equally busy, raking her belly and exploring downward until it found the warm cavern entrance covered with a forest of growth. I ran my fingers through the silky hair, then allowed one digit to probe the slit that seemed to bloom eagerly — and greedily — beneath my fumbling explorations. She never so much as whispered an objection, even though she must have been feeling something rather queer.

To my disappointment, just as I was beginning to think that I could proceed to extremities with my handsome young aunt, the Mother Superior, brought his delightful punishment to a close.

Emilie meekly submitted, which she showed by sinking down from her sturdy kneeling posture, until she was all but prostrate on her belly. Mother Superior, of course, kept the dildo buried in her while she sank to the floor. Her hands were clamped firmly on her hips as she continued to ram her for several more minutes. Then she gently withdrew the dildo while warmly kissing her plump buttocks. She assured her of entire absolution and complete forgiveness.

Amanda

Tucking her dripping phallus back into her frock, the Mother Superior turned to my mother, and looking towards me in a very expressive way, said that she wished to talk with her on a certain subject privately. My aunt said her room was at her sister's services, and she would stay and help Emilie to dress.

'It is too much honour for me, dear Lady,' said Emilie. 'Perhaps this young lady would lend me a little assistance; she looks very good natured, and I should so like a glass of wine, for I feel very much exhausted!'

'Naturally, my child,' responded my aunt, 'I will give you wine.'

So saying, she left the room, turning around as she did so with rather a quaint expression on her face, as if she was rather uncertain what my assisting her novice to dress might lead to. I, as may be easily imagined, had no objection to act as lady's maid to the beautiful young lady, and I was so affectionate in my trembling attentions that she quite overlooked my clumsiness. I was sure, though, that she was very much aware of how my hands lingered over her quivering breasts and their jutting nipples ... how they brushed her curvaceous bottom-cheeks and intruded on the fringe of her drooping pussy lips.

'Dear mademoiselle,' she remarked, 'you are so kind, as if you enjoyed my ordeal more than most.'

'Perhaps,' I replied, in a bantering tone, 'you would have no objection if I enjoyed it?'

'Well,' she coyly replied, 'I confess that I should like it if you did.'

'And what if I should enjoy an encore?' I hinted.

She coloured slightly and averted her eyes. 'After the scene you have just witnessed, my friend, it would be useless for me to affect any prudery. Of course, it was the duty of the Abbess to be present, but I think it was rather in bad taste for her to inform you and your mother of my fault and allow you to witness my punishment.'

'Don't be angry,' I replied kissing her. 'It was a very pretty sight indeed, a most luxurious spectacle. Did the holy mother hurt you at all?'

'Why, no,' she replied, 'as long as the penance lasted I rather enjoyed it. But now I do feel rather inflamed and sore.'

'Permit me,' I replied, 'to wipe your secret charms dry with my handkerchief. I will do it gently and you will find yourself much more comfortable.'

Without waiting for her permission, I knelt down before her, lifted her robe and proceeded to dry the delicate lips of her pussy and the lightly-mossed adjacent parts. I wiped gently over the swollen lips, pausing to admire the pouting pinkness of the orifice. The musky fragrance was arousing; I felt my too-long-deprived piston start to stir under my clothes. Not eager to quickly finish the job, I tended her slowly, brushing the down on her mount with each movement, and seeming, as if by accident, to have my fingers open the bruised lips of that abused cunt. Indeed, I very nearly had one digit buried up to the knuckle before I remembered my situation and casually withdrew. As I predicted, she found great comfort from this operation and was profuse in her gratitude. I protested that it was a pleasure to be of service to such a splendid girl as herself.

This remark of mine led to unforeseen results. Emilie immediately replied that such a compliment from me was very valuable inasmuch as I was one of the finest and tallest girls she had ever seen. While saying this, she endeavoured to feel my body.

I regarded her with much amusement, and put my hand on her cunt as she lay at my side. She was pleased at this mark of attention, and opened her thighs to give me more room. She said that, as a rule, she was not particularly aroused by a woman's private parts. But on this occasion, she confessed that there was something in my touch. Indeed, putting my fingers in her love chink felt as if I had put them on an electric box. It seemed actually throbbing with amorous fire. The lips were exceedingly full, prominent and open; the clitoris protruded boldly out from between them and felt very large, strong and wonderfully hot; it slipped about under my fingers as if endowed with life. I felt irresistibly drawn toward it, and bent down my face. She turned on her back and spread her thighs as I passed between them and stooped to kiss her hot recess. Drawing open the lips, I buried my mouth in the moist charm. As soon as she felt my tongue playing the clitoris and penetrating the passage, she muttered: 'Oh, Augustine! You are very good... I cannot tell you how much I am enjoying that. It is better even that a fuck. Oh... Oh! Augustine, I'm spending... oh! Oh!' and a hot gush of the sweetest and most lascivious feminine spunk I ever tasted filled my mouth. I really at first thought she was pissing but the thick unctuous flavour testified as to its true character.

She was ready to favour me with the deeds I had just done to her, but a light footstep was heard in the corridor. She dropped my petticoats just in time, as my aunt entered the room carrying some wine.

'I have brought you some refreshment, as I promised, my child, but upon my word you don't seem to require it. You have got quite a colour in your cheeks, thanks I presume to the kind attentions of my niece Augustine. But mind, my dear niece,' she wagged a finger at me, 'I don't approve of even young ladies being too affectionate, it sometimes leads to nonsense, even to mischief.'

This, of course, was meant a broad hint for me to be careful, but alas the 'mischief' was half done already.

'But pray, Lady Mother,' said Emily, 'may I not take Mademoiselle Augustine to some of our sisters to introduce her around St. Bridget's? They will be glad to see a fresh face and hear some news about society.'

My aunt frowned, apparently not much liking the proposition. 'Well! I grant permission on strict condition that you do not neglect chapel or any of your other duties, and that you bring my niece to my room for vespers, as she must sup with her mother and me.'

'Your commands shall be punctually obeyed, Madam,' replied Emilie making a low reverence. Then she took me by the hand and we left the room together.

As we went down the corridor, she broke into a short laugh and said, 'The Abbess is quite jealous; she guesses something about you, and if it had not been for my happy idea of introducing you to the other novices, I should not have been able to enjoy the pleasure of your society, certainly not alone. But I will bring you into the company of Louise and Adele, who are pretty playful girls, and almost as lascivious as I am.' She stopped for a moment and faced me, a knowing smile on her beautiful face. 'By the way, I hope you do not consider it immoral to sleep with your aunt; for she most certainly will make you do so tonight. If all accounts are true, she'll give you such a sampling of voluptuous and even obscene lust that it's likely you'll never forget it. The scene you just witnessed in the penance room is nothing to what you will experience.' We continued walking and arrived at one of the young lady's rooms.

'Adele and Louise, my dears, here is Mademoiselle Augustine d'Ermonville, whom the Superior has allowed me to bring here as an addition to our society this afternoon.'

Both of the pretty girls who had been sitting at embroidery frames rose from their seats and kissed me warmly on the cheeks.

'We had better make the most of her company, for her aunt, the Abbess, fancies there is something manly in her appearance,' said Emilie.

'So there is,' exclaimed the two girls together.

'And she intends her to sleep with her tonight, and you know what the consequences of that will be. Augustine will be much too exhausted for us to have any fun with her tomorrow.'

'Adele already knows,' said Louise. 'It is a pleasure which I have yet to learn.'

'Tell us all about it, dear Adele,' I said. 'It will amuse me greatly and help me look forward to the coming evening.'

'Since you ask, I will tell you,' said the sweet girl, 'though I am rather ashamed. The Lady Superior reported herself ill and nervous, and wished someone to stay in her room all night. She chose me. I gladly consented, taking it as a compliment, and went to her room where I found her already in bed. She desired me to undress and come to bed, leaving the lamp burning. No sooner had I done so, than she thrust her hand between my thighs. She roved over the soft hairs that sprouted upon my pussy, but did not linger very long. Instead, she proceeded to shove a couple of fingers into my tight slit and spread the clasping lips as she worked in and out. I knew very little about such lustful games and submitted meekly as she continued to plumb my most secret depths. She did not continue this long before she altered her position, kneeling with her belly upon my breasts, her shapely rump resting upon my face, and the lips of her cunt applied to my mouth. Then she asked me to shove my tongue into her pussy, and work it well in. And, though I was more than half smothered, I was able to comply and did my best to give her pleasure. I licked her again and again as a dog laps at a bowl of water, only this nectar was far more sweet than any I had tasted. I flicked at the bedewed lips, catching up all the pearly drops, then dove inside the slit scouring the tender membranes hidden within.

'I must acknowledge that the Abbess did her best to return the pleasure, as, according to our relative positions, her head naturally fell between my thighs. She put her tongue into me as well as she could. It wriggled about like a snake in my cunt passage, stroking and sliding and seeking every hidden corner. While I didn't feel full of it there in my cavern, still I was aware of the most pleasant sensations that began in my toes and slid upward with sensuous warmth to the very top of my head. Of course, she could not do me the justice that I did her, but she did enough as I very soon found out.

'As for her, whether I did my duty by her or not may be judged from the fact that in a few minutes, after some convulsive lifting and wriggling of her bottom, my mouth was filled, and my face and throat drenched, with a warm oily liquor of her passion. When she was finished, she lazily rolled off of me, and lay for a few moments with her naked legs on the pillow, and all of her person exposed. I thought it advisable to get a towel and wipe my face and her rump … and when I had done so, she thanked me feebly and asked me to pull down her chemise and make her comfortable in bed. This done, she wanted her medicine, which I found on tasting to be neither more nor less than orange liqueur. After this libation, she went to sleep.

'I hoped for a quiet night's rest but I was never more mistaken in my life. At about two o'clock in the morning I was awakened by the Mother Superior kissing me, which I was obliged to take as an honour, though I was very sorry to be disturbed.

'She then asked me if I was a virgin. Upon my assuring her of the fact, she proceeded to raise my shift and satisfy herself by inserting her finger into my pussy as far as it would go. Finding an obstacle, she announced her intention of taking my maidenhead. How she intended to do this I hardly knew, but I was speedily enlightened. Stripping off her chemise, the Abbess took from one of the pockets a curious thing that looked like a thick ivory ruler, about nine inches long, and partly covered with red velvet. This apparatus had an elastic

Amanda

appendage shaped like a ball, which she filled from a vial. The whole thing was promptly strapped around her front by using a strong bandage. She told me to lay down on my back, with my thighs as wide as they would go, and a bolster under me to elevate my rump, she proceeded to shove this instrument up my cunt, forcing my virgin barrier without mercy or remorse. Indeed, I'm certain that my exclamations of pain and half suppressed cries gave her the utmost delight. Unnatural delight it must be surely, though I can understand a man in his lust violating a girl even against her will. But, when she began to find from my movements an unmistakable sign that my woman's nature was beginning to get the better of my feelings of pain and shame, and that I was enjoying the proceedings, she placed one hand under her buttocks and squeezed the ball I mentioned before. It spouted a jet of warm milky matter right into me as far as my kidneys. This ended the performance for that time.

'But she was not satisfied even with this, for before I left her in the morning, she told me to fasten the device upon myself, and fuck her with it as strongly as she had done me. I was very clumsy in strapping on the curious instrument, but she assisted me. I may safely say that she assisted me also in the actual performance. When I had got this thing she called a 'dildo' fairly rammed into her eager slit, I began to push as best I could, but I might almost have saved myself the trouble. For clasping me around the waist, she heaved herself up so vigorously that she more than met me half way as she impaled herself on the smooth shaft. She became almost bestial in her wrigglings, shrieking and grunting and moaning as the long smooth object drove into her grasping cunt. With each stroke, its passage was eased, so that soon I was ramming it into her with the same ferocity a man would drive his cock into a pussy. Seeing the cold hardness covered with her cream was exciting, and she urged me to continue the assault with unabated energy. At length, giving one powerful wriggle of her buttocks, she screamed out, 'Milk, Adele, milk!'

'At first I hardly knew what she meant. But then I remembered what she had done. Imitating her action as well as I was able, I squeezed the ball at the base of the cock and injected the precious fluid into her as far as it would go. I certainly must have given her great satisfaction, for when she recovered herself, she kissed and dismissed me with thanks and benedictions. And that is my story. What do you think of it, dear Louise? You may depend upon it, since it is just what you will have to endure. As for you, Mademoiselle d'Ermonville, you will enjoy the same from the Abbess this very night.'

I promised her I would take her warning into consideration, and Emilie then reminded me that it was time for me to keep my appointment with my aunt. If I did not do so punctually, I should get her into trouble, and would not be allowed to visit any of the fair young sisters any more. So, guided by my lovely conductress, I reached the Abbess' apartment, where I found a table laid, and my mother and Mother Superior in company with my aunt.

* * *

The night had passed as they had foretold, with me in the service of my ravenous aunt, the abbess, and her dildo. Instead of inviting me to her chamber, she came into my room after midnight with a triumphant expression. She had something in a small box which she mysteriously produced. It was labelled: 'One Superfine Dildo'.

She locked the door and, opening the box, revealed an India-rubber article about the size of a man's shaft ready for action. She explained to me what it was and said she had got it from her milliner as a great favour and had paid her five hundred francs for it. She was all eagerness to try it on me.

But I vowed to play coy and not reveal my Sapphic experiences with such tools. 'But, Auntie,' said I, most disingenuously, 'I'm not going to be a nun forever, and if I do this, and if I should ever get married, my husband would know it.'

'Oh!' she said, 'Not to worry. You could easily fool him.'

Having filled the dildo with warm milk and fastened it upon my loins with the straps attached to it, she prevailed upon me to act the man's part. She pulled me into bed and seemed perfectly familiar with the proper manner for me to mount her. So far from being hurt by the thing, the abbess seemed to enjoy every movement of it, from the time I thrust it into her till she gave a dying sigh and subsided.

After a while she was ready to perform the same office for me. When she had got it adjusted I felt the warm thing enter in a little way with a sensation rather divine. Then she gave a thrust with all her might and I could not suppress my shriek. Though she worried I had been hurt, it was rather an expression of my ecstasy. The rest of the night was spent thus, and I found myself quite worn the next morning.

After breakfast, my aunt summoned Emilie, and gave me into her charge. She told her to introduce me to the pleasantest and best looking of the young ladies, and that we might amuse ourselves with embroidery or other similar work. And so she dismissed us, to the great delight of Emilie. Actually I'd been afraid that my aunt's rest and refreshment might have restored her lust to such an extent that I would have to service her once again. I was hoping to gather my strength for the benefit of the young ladies in whose company I planned to find amusement and gratification.

When we were in the corridor Emilie threw her arms around me and kissed me rapturously, saying how glad she was to see me.

'I hardly expected to see you looking so healthy after passing the night with our Lady Superior. How did you like your bedfellow? Was she very lusty?'

And so she rattled on until she had extracted from me an account of part of the night's amusements. She was thrilled to hear of them.

'Oh,' Emilie exclaimed, 'that sounds really delightful. Indeed, while you were busy with your aunt, we were busy making plans a sister Louise, for she is so prudish and sanctified and such an old maid that we will all be glad to hear that the pride and formality will be taken out of her a little. Perhaps you will help us in our conspiring against her. I'll take very good care that if there is no impropriety going on when she visits our apartment, there very soon shall be. I think I can guess what your aunt will do when she sees her thus. She will get Agnes safely into her chamber with you under pretence of hearing her complaints, and then with your assistance strap her down on the edge of the bed with a leg fastened to each of the foot posts. If she is placed in that convenient position, I hope you'll split her cunt up handsomely with that dildo of your Auntie's. If you don't, I'll never forgive you. And, speaking of bedrooms, I suppose there can be no impropriety in one young lady showing another her sleeping apartment,' she laughed. 'Perhaps you'll come and see what a nice little room I have got. It's close at hand.'

I followed her into her snug little chamber, where her first action was to bolt the door. The second was to put her hand up my petticoats and penetrate my slit, while she kissed me and murmured some broken sentences in my ear to the effect that she had been dreaming of me all night. She had hoped that day before that I might have managed to serve her, but circumstances prevented it. She was afraid that similar circumstances might prove an obstacle today if I didn't seize the moment. She longed for me, she moaned. In fact, she begged and prayed me to do as I would to her as if it was the greatest boon Heaven or earth could grant her.

I was by no means indifferent to her entreaties. She evidently was passionately fond of me, and I was more than eager to fill her wishes. I thrust my hand up her petticoats as she had hers up mine and what I felt certainly urged me on. For the lips of her cunt were open; the moist tunnel was burning hot. Upon pushing my finger well into the interior, I felt her clitoris asserting itself like a little cock. My fingering procured the expected results; her canal became a slick and drippingly eager receptacle and my prick stood stiff as an iron bar. Without further delay, I dragged her clothes up to her armpits, pushing her at the same time upon the edge of the bed. That done, I leaned down and began kissing the lightly-mossed lips of her cunt. Meanwhile I shoved my fingers into her, right up to my wrist with my very first thrust. This produced a single exclamation of 'Oh!' from the young lady. I slowly withdrew my fingers until they resided just within the juicy folds, and then I leaned forward so as to clasp her heaving breasts while plunging in once again. I could feel my fingers scraping the tender inner membranes as I penetrated to the core of her belly while I tongued her. I began slowly lapping her clit with steady tempo, gradually increasing the length of the strokes and pressing as hard as my tongue could. Eventually she shrieked and squirmed and wriggled until she spent most spectacularly.

After we'd rested a bit, hastened to arrange our dresses, after which we exited Emilie's room. 'You know,' she said. 'I think you might manage to fuck Louise under the pretence of its being some innocent little game you were playing with her. She not only has no experience, but she doesn't seem to have any ideas on the subject. She is totally ignorant, but I think you may open her eyes!'

'By opening her thighs I suppose,' was my reply, at which she laughed.

Together we entered the morning room that was occupied by some of the novices.

There were seated Adele, Louise, and a third party I didn't know, who seemed to be a lay sister instructing the young ladies in the mysteries of some sort of needlework. As we entered, she rose and retired and I was affectionately received by Adele and Louise.

After some talk of no consequence between a few girls in company, Adele began half in jest, half in earnest, to ask more pointed questions. Adele, of course, was the novice who had the honour, experience and pleasure of passing the night as the bedfellow of the Mother Superior. She specifically wanted to know if Lady Agatha had fingered me, if she had made me finger her, if she had used a dildo on me, and if she had taken my maidenhead. To all of these questions I gave the best answers I could. I informed the girl that although my aunt did some fingering, all the dildo work was of a new method that my aunt admired very much. Indeed, Emilie agreed that there was much to be admired. In fact, she revealed herself to have obtained her own dildo, which she had in this very chamber. She asked if I would be kind enough to instruct her on its usage. This caused quite a stir in the room. I don't think Adele would exactly have broken her heart with vexation if I had at once announced myself to be ready to put it on and to fuck her on the spot! But with Louise, it was necessary to use a little caution. Of course, both girls expressed a curiosity to see the novelty. Adele impudently proposed to take up my petticoats and strap it on me at once. Louise more slyly hinted that if I would be so kind, she would like to see what sort of a thing it was.

Emilie checked Adele's ardour by telling her that she already had experienced such pleasure and that she herself had been well fucked by Mother Superior in the course of her penance the previous day. The sly monkey did not say anything of the loving performance in which she had shared just half an hour before. Therefore, it was only fair that both she and Adele should give the first chance to Louise, who had never had either a real cock or an imitation, and who could not begin her experience under better circumstances. For this, Louise thanked her and timidly asked what she was expected to do?

'First of all, my love,' replied Emilie in a dictatorial tone, 'you must raise up your frock and your underclothing, so that Mademoiselle d'Ermonville can make complete investigation of your secret treasures. When she has done so, it will be easier for her to operate upon you. She will then attach the apparatus to her loins and you will experience more pleasure than pain. We don't want this to be one of those cases where a dildo has been rudely or carelessly inserted, and the girl operated upon has suffered needless pain and felt sore for two or three days afterwards.'

'Certainly,' chimed in Adele, 'when Lady Agatha poked me with that dildo of hers, I was obliged to use milk and water for two days afterwards. My poor tender little pussy was quite raw.'

'Don't frighten Louise with your nonsense,' interrupted Emilie severely. 'I'll guarantee she'll not have to endure any such disagreeable consequences from my instrument. It's not like a coarsely made ordinary dildo. I assure you I would only accept the best of them. Come, child, lift up your petticoats and let Mademoiselle Augustine take your measure.'

The blushing girl obeyed her, pulling up her shift and undergarments, disclosing an alabaster belly and thighs between which nestled her fuzz-bedewed little cunt in all its maiden purity. Upon my gently unfolding the orifice with my fingers, it resembled nothing so much as a rosebud first opening through dark brown moss. Of course, this had the effect that Emilie had designed, for she knew right well that I should require some stimulant after my recent attack upon her. So under the influences of seeing, feeling and kissing the innocent Louise's sweet cunt, I became so excited myself that I wished to plunge the dildo inside my own quim. But duty called in the form of Louise's upturned bottom.

Our relative positions were thus: Louise stood with her legs apart, while Emilie held up her clothes and soothed and caressed her. I, on my knees, was with my mouth and fingers preparing the pretty, velvet-lined sheath for the reception of the protrusion strapped to my front, when Adele crouched down between Louise's legs and dragged up my petticoats. She amused herself with inspecting my dildo. The lascivious girl proceeded to fondle and suck and then wrap her lips and tongue around the noble tool. She cared for the toy as if it were flesh and blood. But this lascivious show was a mere distraction and watching it was a poor apology for not taking her young friend's maidenhead. I accordingly thought it high time to proceed to business. I intimated as much to Emilie, who asked me in what position I would like the innocent victim of lust to be placed.

Looking around the room, I could see nothing better than a low divan without back or sides. I suggested that if the sweet girl was laid down on that with a pillow under her rump, and that if Emilie on one side and Adele on the other would each hold up one of her legs, her position would be most satisfactory. This would enable me to get well into her with as little trouble as possible to herself. Also, that would afford the spectators a fair and full view of the entire proceedings from beginning to end. Louise lay down on her back, and drew her clothes up as high as they would go. That way there would be nothing intervening between my belly and hers. They held her legs up tolerably high, and as wide apart as a virgin's could well be pulled without hurting her.

'And now,' said she, 'if you think you have wetted her orifice with your tongue sufficiently, charge into her and good luck to you!'

Amanda

I didn't need further urging than the sight of that enticing slit awaiting me. I reared back and buried the dildo between her taut lips. The very first push I made elicited a scream from Louise. This elicited a laughing remark from Adele, who said, 'I think we ought to wish 'good luck' to poor Louise instead of this Sapphist, for she'll be dreadfully sore after all this perform-ance. Upon my word Emilie, I think we had better put a handkerchief or two between her rump and the divan or it will be all stained with blood.' This they effected, though with some difficulty, for Louise really had not strength enough to raise her rump because of my vigorous pushes. I didn't mean to give her any unnecessary pain, but any one who has had the pleas-ure of snatching the maiden treasure of a fine, well-shaped, vigorous girl just budding into womanhood, must be quite aware that it is not accomplished without occasioning some trouble and perhaps a little soreness to the vic-tim. In our case this was especially true — for not only was Louise natural-ly small and tight, but she had never been a participant in any of the amuse-ments so much favoured by the young ladies of the convent. I don't even think that she had ever been fingered. No matter her discomfort, though, she could be thankful that it was a woman doing it and not a man, for I could easily remember my own lost maidenhead and did everything in my power to minimize the distress without detracting from the experience.

I think that it was about the fifth or sixth heavy push that the dildo broke down her barrier and got fairly into her. Louise faintly screamed and begged me to have mercy upon her and draw myself out of her. But while she was uttering these broken exclamations, she clasped me tightly around the neck and pressed her lips to mine. I didn't think it necessary to comply with her wishes further, so I drew out about four inches, then plunged in again with renewed vigour up to the hilt of the phallus. Her sheath clasped it tightly, milking it with each piston-like stroke. Her protests faded into sighs of pleasure as I began the steady pumping motions designed to release her reservoir of pearly nectar. I forced myself deeper and deeper until our mounts fairly ground together, the hairs mingling and our bellies scraping. So constricted was her passage around the shaft that that three or four strokes were all that was required to have Louise release a flow of warm fluid that fairly erupted from her nearly filled slit and mixed with the blood of her broken maidenhead to ooze down her milky thighs.

As I lay prostrate on Louise's body, I thought with a sort of languid satisfaction of this being the first maidenhead that I had ever had the pleasure of enjoying.

* * *

One night found Emilie telling stories of her lustful adventures, much to our delight. Emilie's story, I noticed caused a good deal of agitation among the young ladies of her audience.

For instance, Adele was kneeling with her head between the Abbess' thighs; what she was doing I could not exactly see. Emilie herself was sitting with her legs open, perfectly unconcerned, while Louise was fumbling about her secret parts.

Meanwhile, Agnes cuddled up close to my side and suffered me to explore all her charms with my hand. During Emilie's description of a particularly naughty encounter, my fingers toyed with the curls between her thighs, and, as the story went on, parted the curls and felt of the lips beneath. She was turned partly on her belly against me so that this by-play was not observed.

My fingers were encouraged by the sister's hand until two of them made an entrance and were completely enclosed in the hot, moist tissue. The little protuberance which all women have within the orifice, and which is the principal seat of sensation, was in her remarkably developed. It was as large as the end of my little finger. I played with it and squeezed it and plunged my fingers past it again and again; she manifested her pleasure by kissing me on the neck, where she had hidden her face.

When Emilie described her first thrill in the bedroom my fingers were doing all in their power to complete the Agnes's gratification, and this, too, with success, for they were suddenly bathed with moisture, and, at the same time, the Abbess drew a deep sigh, which was not noticed, for all supposed it to be in sympathy with Emilie's story. Then she withdrew my hand and lay perfectly still.

My head was still pillowed on the plump breast of my old friend breast, who stooped and kissed me. She was about medium height, graceful and well rounded, and her skin visible under the habit where it had gaped was as white as alabaster. Her features were of the perfect antique mould and were lighted with fine grey eyes. Her glossy black hair was all brushed back to a knot just below the back of the neck, from which but a single curl escaped on either side and toyed with her firm but finely rounded bosom.

The deep vermilion of her lips compensated for the faint colour of her cheeks, whose tinge was scarcely deeper than that of her finely cut ears. She was about twenty-two, and ripe to yield a charming embrace, but before I could progress with her, my aunt very sensibly remarked, 'I think, Emilie, my love, you had better stop a little, for I perceive that narration of your delightful adventures with the handsome young page and the consequent loss of your maidenhead has produced the usual effect upon the minds and bodies of the young ladies present.'

I do not know what effect it was producing upon the minds of the young sisters, but I do know what effect it was producing upon me. I was hungry for a new quim to kiss and another tongue to bathe my slit. That, however, I could not find very easily, as I had fucked the Lady Abbess and every girl in the room excepting Adele; but as Agnes was sitting upon my knee, I had not far to search for the requisite accommodation. How easily my course is made clear for me! As I began to make known my lustful intentions, to shift the position of Agnes' naked rump upon my knees, she blushingly whispered in my ears, 'Dearest Augustine, I am so sore. I fear that I cannot bear your loving embraces any more today.' To which I replied that I would rather tongue her than anybody else, but that my animal passions had got to such a pitch that I must really quench the heat and fever with some girl's warm pussy. I told her also that I had had every girl there except Adele, and she, I had reason to think, was kept by my aunt for her own unnatural purpose. This Agnes declared to be nonsense.

In the meantime, my aunt, who had been whispering to Adele, called to us and demanded to know what we two young folks were talking about.

'Indeed,' she said, 'Augustine, we are all rather jealous of Agnes. You have been monopolizing her for the last half hour. She has been sitting, as I can see, with her bare bottom on your bare lap, and St. Bridget only knows what you may have been doing to her before all our faces.' She said all this very good humouredly, but with a little evident spice of jealously.

I replied that neither she or any of the charming girls around us need be in the least degree jealous, for however good my will might be, my sweet friend (upon which Agnes kissed me) felt very sore, and I had too much consideration for any charming girl to force the Abbess's dildo into her tender cunt hole when she was sore and bleeding.

I'm afraid, of course, that this was not exactly true and that if there had been no other girl or woman in the room but Agnes, she would have had to suffer either in front or behind, sore or not sore.

As it was, my considerate speech was very well received. Adele especially was very loud in her commendations and thought I was quite right; no young girl ought to be fucked more than once, at least not on the first day at any rate.

The sly girl knew that I had passed the night with the Lady Superior, that I had fucked Emilie in the morning and subsequently had taken the maidenheads of Louise and Agnes.

So not unnaturally, she thought and hoped that perhaps her turn was coming. And I have no doubt but that she expressed herself to this effect in the whispered exchange which I have alluded to as taking place between her and my aunt.

My aunt raised herself from the sofa, saying, 'My love, do not distress yourself, you shall have it! I want you to dildo me, for you have had some little experience, more than any of the other young ladies.

Agnes kindly assisted my awkwardness so that when Adele returned to the room stark naked with the dildo strapped around her waist, my aunt was ready to receive her and I to fuck her.

'Ah, you did right to strip yourself,' murmured my aunt. 'Your stockings contrast very well with her creamy skin, don't they Augustine? And I hope you have got the dildo strapped so as not to interfere with Augustine tonguing you from behind. I will get myself into the most suitable position — you'll take care of me, and my niece with the long legs and long tongue, will take good care of you, I'm sure.' Taking this hint, I knelt down, pulling open her buttocks to get a clear view of my dinner in her tight little crevice.

The dildo was strapped well on her belly, the road to her cunt was free, and I reached under and pulled the lips open. They were smooth and moist; the inner folds had the hue of conch, all pink and shiny. My aunt, in the meantime, had, with the assistance of Emilie, laid herself down on the table so that her rump touched the edge. When Adele approached her, she threw her legs over the young girl's shoulders, and Adele immediately thrust her hips forward and shoved the ivory velvet-headed tube into its destined receptacle. I, on my part, lubricated with my tongue the sanctuary I was going to violate with my fingers, licking all around and within the smiling lips and then, much to her shock, introduced my entire fist. I found that the position Adele was occupying relative to my aunt was an admirable one for my penetrating the very innermost parts of the fine fat-rumped novice.

Moreover, if I had desired additional pleasure, I had further gratification in admiring my aunt's finely curved legs and ripe bosom, to say nothing of the sensual gratification expressed on her face as Adele began to warm into her work, assisted no doubt by the vigorous shoves and plunges with which my fist was penetrating her person. I should mention here that when I made my third drive into her widely stretched pussy, which was a vigorous one, she gave a slight scream; the only sympathy which that elicited from the others was, 'Open your thighs wide, my sweet friend!' from my aunt, 'Don't mind her screaming, Augustine! She has got no maidenhead. I took that. Fuck her hard with that dainty fist; the road's clear enough!' So I began to ram her brutally while reaching around and crushing her swaying tits with my grasping hands.

Just as Lady Agatha had got worked up to her utmost ecstasy and required the two or three last heavy thrusts and the injection of the warm cream from the dildo, Mademoiselle Adele found herself in exactly the same predicament! This I perceived by her beginning to catch her breath, to wriggle her bottom about violently, to call upon my name with every term of endearment, and to seem to be entirely forgetful of her Superior's open cunt before her. All this was because she felt the rapturous effects of my glorious fist behind her, pounding into her love cave with dogged regularity. All this time my aunt was exclaiming, 'Push harder, Adele, harder, you silly girl, and give me milk.' But it was too late. I felt Adele losing her rhythm almost helplessly.

Amanda

Already I felt her warm love stream spouting forth and deluging my fist up to the wrist. I saw there was no time to be lost. I caught her firmly and gave two or three tremendous shoves so as to force the dildo into my aunt's belly as far as it would go. Then, applying my hands to the elastic balls of the instrument, I effected the required ejection to my aunt's great delight. She murmured, 'That's very nice. I feared I was going to miss it!' and sank down upon her pillow in a dreamy state of enjoyment.

At the very start of the proceedings, I had heard Emilie say to Louise, 'Go, dear and fetch me a candle, a good large one. Never mind whether it is lighted at a shrine or not, bring it here.' And away ran Louise.

On her return, she found Emilie upon the sofa lately occupied by my aunt, her petticoats drawn up, and one long leg stuck over the back of the sofa while the foot of the other rested upon the floor. Of course the exposure of the person was as complete as anyone could desire. Her pink little pussy slit below the generously thatched mount was full open to my hungry gaze and so occupied any glances that I could spare from my immediate business.

On Louise's making her appearance with the candle, a huge one, Emilie told her to insert it in her gaping orifice, a hint which Louise, perhaps inspired by the scene she saw enacted on the table, or a grateful remembrance of my services to her, was not slow to take. She shoved the candle well into Emilie, at least as far as she considered safe. Then she commenced to work it with the judgment of an expert practitioner. And what was poor Agnes doing all this time?'

I rather think that very charming and virtuous young lady was regretting that she had ever pleaded soreness as an excuse for not being fucked. The devotion she was exhibiting toward my person led me to suppose that she would not have been very sorry to have been in Adele's place, sore cunt and all.

At any rate, she was the only person among us with any presence of mind or energy to do anything. I sank down in an easy chair, Lady Agatha remained on the table, Adele lay down on an ottoman and Emilie and Louise lay together on the sofa with their arms around each other and their lips pressed together. The candle still protruded from between Emilie's thighs while the melting wax mingled with her own juices. It was an interesting group certainly; a painter or sculptor might have searched the world over for an exhibition of more splendid limbs, or more graceful shapes. A libertine would have been driven frantic at the display of white rumps, mossy cunts, fat thighs, plump bosoms and blushing nipples, all displayed without pretence of concealment.

The effect of this display was heightened by the air of voluptuous languor and total abandonment exhibited by all of us. The only exception was Agnes. She evidently thought that something should be done to preserve a semblance of decency. She first of all turned her attention to me, and I gratefully acknowledged her kindness in slipping my frock over my head and fastened it loosely. So I was pretty comfortable, especially after I had gone to the buffet and helped myself to a tumbler of champagne.

Agnes pulled Louise off of Emilie and requested her to put a wrapper or loose frock of some kind upon Adele, at the same time removing the candle and drawing down Emilie's petticoats, so that she was pretty decent. Then she turned her attention towards her Lady Superior, who being pretty well accustomed to such attacks, was not in a very deplorable state of dress. But she gratefully acknowledged Agnes' kindness in drying her cunt and bringing her a glass of wine. My aunt proceeded with her help to robe herself and managed, to my surprise and admiration, to appear in a few minutes as if nothing had happened.

When order had been thus partially restored, the Abbess remarked, 'I hope, Emilie, you do not feel too fatigued to continue your story. Ah, you naughty girl,' she continued half laughing, 'the candle again. I suppose you'll frig yourself to death if you don't take care.'

'I beg your pardon Madame,' replied Emilie in a languid tone. 'On this occasion, Louise did my business for me, and very nicely she did it too. When she has a little recovered from her violation, I'll do as much for her.'

'All very fine,' responded Lady Agatha, 'but in the meantime, as Louise got the candle, which I see is one of the largest and best in the nunnery — and it is a mercy it was not broken by your wrigglings and heavings — she had better go and put it where she took it from, and light it again, and you can go on with your story.'

But just as Emilie was about to recommence, the door opened and there entered Mother Superior and Madame d'Ermonville

Thanks to Agnes' presence of mind, the room and its occupants were better fitted to receive visitors than they had been ten minutes before, but still there was a certain air of disarrangement about the room and furniture. Most decidedly there was something dishevelled in the appearance of the young ladies. Their dresses, though somewhat arranged, were hardly tidy. Agnes and Louise had flushed cheeks and sparkling eyes for their desire had not been gratified, while Adele and Emilie were pale and their eyes heavy. An air of unmistakable sensuality pervaded all four of them. As for me, I tried to look as unconcerned as possible, sitting with one arm around Agnes' waist, with her head resting on my shoulder. I suppose we presented a picture of two affectionate young ladies.

Mother Superior seemed determined to carry out the farce and approached me, laying her hand upon my head. 'I rejoice, my daughter, that you have made choice of one so holy and virtuous as Sister Agnes for your companion! May your friendship be a close and a lasting one.'

I assured her most conscientiously that I intended it should indeed be a close and intimate one, giving Agnes a squeeze around the waist that she understood very well.

Meantime, Madame d'Ermonville, after saluting her sister, remarked that she had been taking a walk around the garden with Mother Superior and was beginning to feel hungry and tired, so they had come into lunch. 'But I see,' said she, 'that we are too late as the lunch has been removed from the table to the sideboard.'

The Abbess was going to remark that the lunch had never been on the table when she fortunately checked herself on my mother's remarking, 'But you should take care, Agatha, not to let careless people spill melted butter on your handsome table cover. Look here!' And she pointed to the very spot on the edge of the table where her sister's rump had rested, and which had been plentifully bedewed, and which had been neglected in the general robbing and cleaning up. My aunt took the allusion very coolly; saying that it was careless, but that she thought it was milk. She requested Adele to wipe it up and invited her sister and Mother Superior to take some refreshment. This they gladly accepted, the Mother Superior in particular eating and drinking as if she meant to restore her wasted energies.

As they were eating, Madame asked her sister how they had been amusing themselves, and how I had behaved myself. To this, the Abbess replied that I had conducted myself admirably, (she laid great stress on this word) and had inspired her and all the young ladies with the highest opinion of me. As for their amusements, Emilie had been telling them a short story, relating some adventures of hers, which though doubtless of the world and worldly, and even rather licentious, had doubtless a good moral, as they had spurred her to seek the shadow of the cloister.

Indeed, I think that such an understatement had never before been uttered. Unfortunately for me, my mother had come to inform me that our passage to England had been assured and the time had come to leave St. Bridget's. It is with my sadness that I report that events have never permitted me to return to that lovely convent and I have had to make my way through the quims of English ladies, leaving the French at the mercy of the Republicans.

LAURA

t was about eight-thirty and as I wandered down the street, wondering how to most enjoyably the evening with the small capital in my possession, I saw a train with the sign 'Wonderland' approaching, and acting on impulse of the moment, I ran out and boarded it.

Wonderland was an amusement park situated on the outskirts of the city. Here were cheap shows, skating rinks, carousels, and an infinity of catchpenny devices. On holidays, Saturdays and Sundays, the place was well patronized, but there never was much activity on weeknights, although many of the concessions remained open. It was reputed to be a fine place to 'pick up' girls, even the sort whose affection was not for men but for others like themselves. Though at this moment I had no other thought in mind than to kill an hour or two of time agreeably.

When we reached the park I got off, paid the small entrance fee and went inside. Few of the entertainment features were operating but here and there were signs of activity with barkers, pitchmen and touts shouting their wares or extolling the qualities of the entertainments. I idled along, indifferent to their supplications, for I had on previous occasions seen about all there was to be seen.

From a distant section came the strident but not unmusical notes of a mechanical organ, operating in conjunction with a merry-go-round, and toward the source of this music I wended my way. Under a blaze of coloured lights, to the tune of 'Sweet Rosie O'Grady,' tigers, giraffes, lions, horses, elephants and other gaily painted members of the animal kingdom were flying around in a dizzy circle, rising and falling with mechanical precision in what was supposed to be the equivalent of wild flight.

As I watched them flashing by on their never ending journey something caught my eye which instantly awakened more than merely passing interest. This something was a girl of youth and beauty, sitting astride a ferocious tiger which, with uplifted, menacing claws, swayed backward and forward, as it whirled about the course. The object of my interest was out of sight almost before I had gotten a brief glimpse of her, but brief as it was it was sufficient to hold me there for further contemplation.

A mass of yellow curls bobbed up and down with the swaying of the feline steed and with each downward movement a short dress billowed up in the air displaying a generous expanse of flesh above the top of her hose.

I watched this seductive bit of femininity with increasing interest till the contrivance on which she was diverting herself came to a stop and she clambered down, displaying further expanses of flesh and panties as she swung her leg over the bark of the wooden effigy. Departing through the narrow exit, she ambled down a passage between two rows of ring throwing and other swindle schemes with me close at her heels and watching covertly over my shoulder, to see whether there were any chaperones or older companions in the background. I saw nothing to indicate that anyone besides myself was interested in her movements, and as she paused to inspect a display of knick-knacks in a window I sidled up to her and murmured in her ear:

'Having a good time, cutie?'

She looked me over appraisingly and with not but brief hesitation replied:

'Not very. Nearly everything's closed up.'

'Like to take a ride on the roller coaster?'

'Sure!' was the succinct and satisfactory reply.

Something about this girl's appearance and the matter of fact way in which she accepted my invitation, told me I had a live one. As we made our way to the coaster an adroit question or two extracted the information I was most interested in, namely that she was alone. She lived but a short distance from the park, and was in the habit of coming by herself, to spend an hour or two in the early evening.

Carefully I sized her up, and the inspection tended to confirm my first estimate. Despite her baby face, there was something in her eyes which denoted sophistication. The dress she wore was extremely short, and displayed too well a pair of round mature legs sheathed in glistening black silk stockings, a luxury common enough for now, but rather unusual for young girls at that time. She also had on high heeled French slippers, something still more unusual for young misses.

Laura

When we reached the entrance to the coaster, I invested in a sufficient number of tickets to carry us around the track four times. The device in question commonly denominated as the 'Russian Mountains' was an inclined track which ascended to an elevation of some height. Little three seated cars were drawn up this track, and permitted to descend a winding course under their own momentum. It was extremely popular with young couples, and it was quite permissible for a gentleman to put his arm around his companion, as in assurance of protection when the cars shot down the steep incline which gave initial impetus and velocity to the journey. Moreover there were several enclosed sections constructed in the form of dark tunnels, located at convenient intervals along the course. Under cover of the darkness so provided warm lips could be discretely kissed, and if the circumstances were favourable, caresses of a still more intimate nature might be indulged in. Naturally, I had all this in mind when I suggested a ride on the coaster.

A scarcity of customers that night resulted in our obtaining the exclusive occupancy of a car designed ordinarily to accommodate three couples. As we slowly ascended the steep incline, I put my arm around my companion's waist. When the car started down the straightaway, gathering velocity with every second, she squeezed up to me, with the customary simulation of fright.

The first time around I contented myself with warm kisses pressed on half-parted willing lips in the darkness of the tunnels and caverns as we speeded through.

As we started on the second trip, I raised my arm over her shoulder and let my had rest lightly over one of her small but firm little bubbies, and as no objection was made to the contact, I ventured a bit further, and squeezed it softly.

On the third trip around, this same hand was on the inside of her bodice over her bare breast instead of on the outside. Its mate was under the hem of her short skirt lying on the smooth skin just above the top of her silk stocking—and disposed to go higher.

On the fourth and final trip the hand last referred to had deftly found its way up the inside of a panty leg and was in pleasant contact with something softly hairy, warm, and very moist.

All this had been accomplished with the complete acquiescence and entire complacency of the little miss with the baby face and woman's legs. City girls are more sensible than country girls.

When we got off the car I had become so aroused myself as to feel my wetness lubricate my thighs as I walked.

How to bring this fortuitous encounter to a satisfactory conclusion was the next problem. And, in a flash, there came to my recollection another charming feature of this amusement park which also greatly contributed to its popularity with young couples.

This feature consisted of a tiny lake where row boats were available for a shilling an hour. In the centre of this lake was a small island with a bit of sandy beach and about its interior a few trees and shrubbery. It was toward this island the boats carrying amorous couples were invariably steered and doubtless the trees thereon could have told many interesting stories of romances which had budded and come to flower beneath their discrete shadows on summer nights.

Elated I turned to my companion and suggested a ride on the lake. She was agreeable, but cautioned me that she must be home before nine-thirty, or her father would come after her. A hasty glance at my watch told me that it was then almost nine-thirty, but unscrupulously, I told her there was plenty of time. We hurried across the park grounds to the lake, and under a string of lights hanging above a floating platform to which were anchored several dozen rowboats I made the necessary monetary arrangements for the use of one of them.

Laura

The boatman winked knowingly at me, as if I were a rakish man rather than the sort of woman doctors called an invert, as I helped my little friend to seat herself. Seizing the oars, I quickly had the small craft skimming over the water. The moon was in first quarter, softly illuminating the scene, and a circle of electric lights around the lake twinkled brightly and were reflected back from the velvet surface of the water. I saw with inward satisfaction that there were no other boats out and unless some couple was already at the island we would have it to ourselves. I circled it once and found that, as I had hoped, it was unoccupied.

'Shall we rest a little while on the sand?' I insinuated softly.

'If you want to!' she answered, with a sly smile.

A bit of manoeuvring and I quickly had the prow of the boat close against the sandy shore. I jumped out, pulled the small craft up on the beach, and assisted my companion out.

We sat down on the sand. I knew from what she had said about being home early, that we had not time to lose. Placing an arm around her I drew her down so that her head was resting on my lap. I bent over her and as I covered her mouth with mine I slipped a hand under the edge of her dress, and up between her legs. And a moment later one of my fingers was inside the temple.

The road had apparently been travelled already.

'You've had it before, haven't you, cutie?' I murmured.

'Yes!' she replied shortly, her legs twitching under the effect of my fingering, 'Lots of times!'

'Who…?'

'Oh, some boys I know!'

'Ever a girl?' I asked.

'Only a few, but I've always preferred them.'

When I put my hand between this girl's legs I had first inserted a finger in her vagina to see whether the way was 'open' and after assuring myself on this point, I withdrew it, and felt for her clitoris, with the intention of exciting it. I found, to my surprise that it was a great deal larger than that of any female I had previously manipulated. Also it was of a different shape. Instead of being a small elongated ridge it was conical in shape and stood up seemingly half an inch or so. Under my touch it became perceptibly firmer. It was like a diminutive little cock and it seemed to me the tip must project out between the upper lips of her cunt. Its likeness to a cock was further apparent as I continued to finger it, for it pulsed and throbbed to the touch, standing out harder and firmer. Absorbed in this unusual phenomenon, I prolonged my digital examination, touching, squeezing, and feeling until my companion, frantic at the extended manipulation, exclaimed:

'I can't stand any more of that! Hurry up and let's do something!'

I straightened up and glanced out over the water. There was still no sign of other boating parties on the lake but the possibility that some might arrive at an inopportune moment suggested prudence.

'Let's go back behind those bushes,' I suggested, 'so that if anyone comes, they won't see us.'

'All right!' she agreed, and jumped to her feet.

We retired to the relative seclusion of a clump of vegetation not far away, and which offered a slight shield from possible observation; there, raising her dress and holding it tucked under her chin, she began unfastening her panties.

As she fingered what seemed to me an interminable number of buttons, I dropped to my knees and endeavoured to assist in the operation.

Freed, finally, the garment fell to her feet and she kicked it to one side, at the same time twisting the lower part of her dress around her waist. It was a pretty picture which was revealed by the subdued light of a crescent moon as she stood there with her bottom, thighs and legs down to the tops of her silk stockings exposed to my eager eyes.

I was still on my knees before her, when yielding to a sudden impulse, I pressed my mouth to the exposed surface of her stomach, below her navel. The skin was so refreshingly cool and smooth that for some moments I continued to caress it. Then I became aware of the contact of the softest and finest of silken hair against my chin.

My heart leaped with excitement, and without wasting a moment in speculation or deliberation I slipped my arms around her naked bottom, drew her closer, and ... pressed my mouth right over her moist little cunt.

As I did so, I felt her hands on my head, trying to push me away.

'What are you trying to do?' she gasped.

But my tongue was already inside the valley.

Up and down between the wet lips it raced, pausing finally to centralize its caresses over and around the odd, tit shaped clitoris. And, as when I had petted it, it responded by stiffening out and increasing in size. I felt it throb violently each time my tongue passed over it, and my own cock began to jump in sympathy.

I stopped licking it, and getting the tip between my lips commenced to suck it.

'Don't do that!' she gasped again, but there was a strange disparity between her words and actions, for now, instead of trying to shove me away her fingers were entwined in my hair, and she was pulling me to her and at the same time had arched her body forward.

'Don't do... ah! Oh! Oh! Like that! Oh that feels nice! Oh! Oh! Oh! Don't stop! Don't stop!'

This clamour aroused me to a perfect frenzy, and I redoubled my efforts, intending to make her have orgasm once this way as quickly as I could, and afterward hope she might return the favour, though it did not seem a familiar activity to her.

Suddenly I felt the muscles of her thighs tense, her clutch on my head tightened, and I sensed something wet and sticky dripping from my lips and chin. My companion's legs gave way beneath her, and we were in a confused tangle of bodies on the ground, with her on top. We lay still for a few moments panting, and when we recovered she was kind enough to feel up my own dress and bring me to a rapid and satisfying climax.

As soon as she had finished with me, she pulled her dress down over her naked bottom and stood up.

'Hurry up!' she urged, 'it must be nine-thirty, and my father will come after me.'

* * *

My experience and observation lead me to believe that the lingual caress is gratefully received by most females, although many through a feeling of shame will protest hypocritically at first. Their opposition generally melts rapidly under a little persuasion, or perhaps the employment of just enough force to provide an excuse for submission.

Women, in my experience with lovers of both genders, are by nature more lascivious than men but the precepts and inhibitions which are inculcated in them from puberty to maturity exercise a powerful restraint, and they automatically assume a hypocritical prudery they may be far from inwardly feeling. Few are ever able to completely free themselves of the belief that this pretence must be maintained even with their fellow women who receive their most intimate favours.

Laura

I shall insert here a few episodes which though out of the chronological order of events I have attempted to follow in this biography, will nevertheless not be amiss as illustrations of the peculiarities I have made reference to.

Once, under a temporary domestic arrangement, I lived with a girl of very ardent disposition, who lent herself enthusiastically to every erotic fancy our youthful passions could suggest, and we were neither of us novices exactly. Indeed, she had confessed that her tastes ran towards members of her own gender. There was, therefore, no logical reason for the slightest degree of prudery between us.

It was my custom to arise at seven o'clock in the morning, and in order not to awaken her I always dressed quietly, and slipped out with the least possible noise. One morning I left our apartment at my accustomed hour, ate my breakfast in a nearby restaurant and was about to proceed to the school where I taught when I discovered that I had left papers in the apartment which I should have brought with me. So I retraced my steps and, supposing that Gabrielle, my companion, was still asleep, I turned the key quietly, intending to slip in and get my papers without disturbing her.

The door to the bedroom was slightly ajar and as I put my hand on it to open it wide enough to permit my entry, a sight was unexpectedly revealed which caused me t remain where I was.

Gabrielle was awake, but she was not aware of my presence.

She had thrown back the covers, and with her night robe drawn up over her breasts was lying on her back, knees drawn up and legs separated. One round white arm was resting at her side but the other, not so innocently occupied, was extended down over her abdomen, her wrist was moving vigorously—and the tips of two fingers were lost to sight amid the glossy tendrils of hair at the base of her stomach.

In plain, vulgar, everyday words, my little Gabrielle was jacking herself off.

The sight reacted instantly and violently upon my own emotions. My first impulse, after observing the spectacle for a few moments, was to take off my dress and delay my return to the school for half an hour or so, but it occurred to me that it might hurt her pride to know I had witnessed her act, thinking possibly I had intentionally spied upon her. But even as I hesitated undetermined, the episode came to a sudden conclusion. I heard a subdued gasp, the movement of her wrist was accelerated for a moment, then ceased and she relaxed languidly, closing her eyes. I slipped away from the door and quietly left the apartment.

The really curious termination of the incident referred to came a fortnight later. Family matters required that I make a trip from the city which signified three or four days absence from home. While I was discussing the matter with Gabrielle she remarked in a joking way that she didn't know how she was going to 'get along without it' during the period of separation, to which I replied:

'Well, honey, you can do what you did before you had me, can't you?'

She looked at me in a startled way, and said:

'What do you mean, Laura?'

'I mean, you've still got your fingers, haven't you?'

When the significance of my words dawned on her in a wave of crimson passed over her cheeks and to my astonishment she exclaimed with great indignation:

'Why, I never did that in my life!'

'What! Never?'

'No! Never!'

'Not even once, honey?'

Do you see how women dissimulate even to one another?

On another occasion I was discussing with a feminine acquaintance the subject of suppressed longings and inhibitions. She was twenty-five or twenty-six years old, had been married, but was separated from her husband.

I had expressed my belief that there was no person living, who did not carry in his or her heart a secret longing for some particular form of sexual gratification which had never been indulged, either because of lack of opportunity or inhibition through fear or shame. Something in the look she cast at me, or in the way she quickly averted her eyes, told me that in her case at least I had hit the nail on the head. Curious to confirm the supposition, I urged her to confess.

'Come now! Own up! Isn't there something naughty you've wanted to try for a long time, but never dared?'

She made no immediate reply but the colour of her cheeks was proof enough of the accuracy of my surmise. It took a lot of coaxing and encouraging, but I finally got the story.

When she was eighteen, she had known a young woman who courted her assiduously for a brief period, though in the surreptitious ways of lesbians in this era. The courtship had not resulted in anything serious, although she was a likable young girl and my friend had never quite forgot her. Later she moved from the neighbourhood and she had never seen her again, though she remembered her with some affection.

Some years later and while married, she had a dream in which this young woman figured prominently. In this dream she was standing naked before a tall mirror brushing her hair. While so engaged, the woman appeared in the room and kneeling on the floor before her, she separated the lips of her genitals with her fingers and sucked her clitoris until she had or dreamed she had orgasm. And ever since, had suffered an inordinate longing, a longing she had never before voiced, to have a woman do it to her exactly as in this dream—she standing named before a mirror, and the other kneeling at her feet while she brushed her hair.

Needless t say, I volunteered to help her convert the dream into immediate reality, but no quicker were the words off my lips than with flaming cheeks she fled from the room, and locked herself in the bathroom, and it was half an hour before I could coax her to come out.

Here was a girl who for years had ardently and passionately longed for a certain form of sexual gratification and yet, when the opportunity was at hand, shame prevented her from taking advantage of it.

Later, I employed more aggressive tactics of 'take it first and ask afterward,' and had satisfaction of 'bringing' her several times in rapid succession by the famous French method, although not supplemented by mirror or hairbrushes.

Another instance of feminine curiosity which for naïve simplicity and ingenuousness certainly took the prize, comes to my mind with the recollection of a little eighteen year old, whom I succeeded in coaxing into my room on several occasions while living in a boarding house her widowed mother presided over. Subsequently our meetings took place late at night after the mother had gone to sleep, the girl slipping into my room when all was quiet in the house. She was an innocent appearing little damsel and I hesitated to take full advantage of the situation until I heard from her own lips that she had already been initiated, and by no other person than her own uncle—a man of forty-five, and who lived under the same roof. Such an affront by a man so close to me brought out the competitor in me, and I vowed to show her how superior a young woman could be to an old man.

According to her story, he had been in the habit of fondling and caressing her, and fingering her genitals. One morning, some months before I had made her acquaintance, she had gone to his room to awaken him. He seized her, and pulled her down on the bed by him.

'He pulled my dress up,' she confided, 'and unfastened my panties and then he threw the covers off, so that he was all naked. His thing was sticking up, and he rubbed it between my legs. I tried to get away from him but he held me tight. And then he made it go clear inside me. It hurt awful at first, but pretty soon it began to feel kind of good, too. When he let me up there was blood all over my legs an on the bed sheet. He made me get a clean sheet and put it on the bed. And then he wrapped the bloody one up in a bundle, and hid it so mama wouldn't see it. And another time, one day when mama was gone, he did it to me again. He sat down in a chair and unfastened his pants and made me sit on his lap so his thing went up inside of me.'

After hearing this interesting history I lost no time in doing one better on my uncle, and thereafter on an average of once a week I enjoyed her company in the still hours of the night, while the rest of the household was wrapt in slumber.

On one of these occasions after she had slipped off her nightgown and was cuddled up in my arms, she whispered:

'If I asked you to let me do something to you, would you let me?'

'What do you want to do to me, sweetheart?'

'It's something ... oh, you'll think I'm awful if I tell you!' and she hid her face against my neck and began to giggle.

My curiosity was aroused as it always is when I see a woman giggling and blushing at the same time.

'I'm not easily shocked, sweetheart. What is it you want to do?'

'I won't tell you unless you promise to let me first!'

Rather suspecting that I was destined to be the object of an amateur experiment in gamahouching, I assured her that I was willing to take the chance, and promised my acquiescence.

'Well, I ... oh, I'm ashamed to tell you!'

Thoroughly intrigued, I encouraged with caresses and coaxing. When the secret was out my surprise at its ingenuous, almost infantile nature was boundless. She wanted nothing more or less than to masturbate me with her fingers so that, quoting her own words, she could 'feel it grab my fingers!' Speechless for a moment, all I could do was gasp.

'Is that all you wanted to do, sweetheart?'

Her eyes refused to meet mine, but she nodded her head.

'Well, there it is. Go to it!' and I turned over on my back.

With shining eyes, and flushed cheeks, she extended her hand, and began to work my clit in circles while her other fingers found their way all the way inside my nest, waiting for it to contract when I spent. All that was necessary for me to do to help her gratify her curiosity was to lie still and let nature take its course. And a few minutes later she was recompensed with the contracting of my cunt on her fingers and my groans of gratitude at a job well done.

These and other examples of female timidity led me to take the lead, especially when seducing women to inversion for the first time. For though I believe we all possess a degree of inversion, many are loathe to let it come out.

* * *

had been working for nearly a year at St. Margaret Girls' School when the headmaster who employed me summoned me to his office one afternoon.

'Laura, here is a little matter I want you to take care of. The wife's private secretary is away on vacation, and until the girl returns, I have instructed her to send for you once a week to assist her with household accounts.'

He could not, of course, have imagined the thoughts I had had about his wife. Indeed, I believe he was in total ignorance to the extent of inversion in his school. The electrical effect of this communication upon me may be easily imagined. At last an opportunity to be near, if but a few moments, to the hitherto unapproachable Goddess of my dreams. I could scarcely conceal my elation as I assured him it would be delightful to be of service to his wife, but how delightful he certainly did not suspect.

It must not be supposed that I was beguiling myself with any fantastic hopes. No; for once, and despite the success with which most of my previous amorous campaigns had been waged, I was infatuated with a woman I considered far beyond my reach. To me she was little less than a deity; the possibility that she might descend into my sphere of life and my sexual inversion was not entertained even in my wildest dreams. The lines of caste are well defined in England. She was the essence of aristocracy; I was a plebeian. She was a model wife; I was a deviant, completely outside her world. I expected nothing.

Six days later a message was laid on my desk requesting me to report at the house.

A taxi conveyed me through the city's most exclusive residential section, along flower-bordered streets under leafy bowers of foliage, and I shortly had my first glimpse of my employer's residence. It was a veritable castle of stone architecture, almost concealed under climbing ivy, beautiful vines and trees.

In answer to the clang of a heavy brass knocker, appeared a trim, luscious little maid gowned in a short black dress, over which a white lace edged apron was neatly draped. Her plump legs were admirably displayed in glistening silk and these, together with other obvious charms would have captured my heart in a minute, if it had not been otherwise occupied to fullest capacity.

Upon being informed of my identity, she ushered me into a reception hall, and while I gazed with admiration at the tasteful splendour, she went to notify her mistress of my presence.

On the interview which followed I shall dwell but briefly for intoxicatingly pleasurable as it was to me nothing transpired which fits well into this naughty biography in the intimacy of the small study to which my employer's wife conducted me, she seemed more delectable and desirable than ever, and it was with the greatest delight I found that my presence would be needed once a week during the absence of the secretary. The work was nothing more arduous than the figuring of domestic accounts, the writing and recording of checks issued in payment to merchants, and represented less than two hours of time. At its conclusion, she called the maid requesting that I be served with refreshments, and shortly thereafter I departed. During the interval we had been together her attitude toward me had been friendly, but entirely impersonal.

Four successive visits transpired, during which I feasted my eyes and tortured my soul with more or less surreptitious contemplations of her charms. On the fifth, last, and epochal occasion of our meetings, I was conducted into the little private study as previously and was soon engaged in putting the domestic accounts in order. It was to be my last visit, for the absent secretary was returning in a few days, and there would be no further occasion for my presence. The object of my idolatry entered the room and, seating herself in a huge leather cushioned chair near me, began to look over the tradesmen's bills, initialling them one by one, and handing them to me to be recorded for payment.

Glinting under the rays of sunlight which filtered into the room through the interstices of lace curtains, golden ringlets of hair, tied with a single ribbon at the base of her neck, rippled down over shoulders and back in riotous profusion. Draped loosely abut her body was a velvet dressing gown or lounging robe of black velvet, trimmed with a fringe of pure white ermine down the front and around the hem, sleeves, and neck. This strikingly beautiful garment was not buttoned, but was sustained with a silken girdle carelessly knotted about her waist. In a sitting posture the lower edge of this robe hung just below her knees, and her legs visible from the knees down, were clad in the sheerest of silken host through whose translucent weave, the snowy whiteness of flesh beneath was discernible.

The combination of circumstances that day seemed to have been arranged painstakingly by Destiny. Or did the lady herself have a hand in the arranging?

The intimate garment, her closer than usual proximity, the casual touch of a strand of hair light as thistledown against my cheek as she leaned over me to make an observation about an entry in the small ledger, all contributed to provoke in me a veritable torment. The room was scented by some perfumed essence emanating from her hair, body and garment, the air was vibrant with an undefined but palpable atmosphere of eroticism.

The chair in which she was sitting was one of those heavily padded, amply built affairs with an inclined back. A slight frown passed across her face as she glanced over a bill from an establishment which supplied most of her wearing apparel. I paused, waiting for her to conclude her examination of the account and as I waited, my eyes fixed on her, she changed her position slightly raising one of the silk clad legs across the knee of its companion.

In the position in which she was sitting, she was not fronting me directly but rather to one side. The movement she made in crossing her legs caused the folds of the lounging robe, loosely tied, to separate slightly and bulge outward above the cord around her waist. And through the aperture so fortuitously provided, immediately became visible an exquisitely rounded breast of alabaster whiteness, crowned with a tiny rosebud nipple.

Seemingly she wore no undergarment beneath the fur-trimmed robe! And as though this entrancing sight were not enough to suffocate me with emotion, the raising of her leg had also elevated the border of the garment, and above the purple silk band which supported her hose, a brief space of naked thigh was visible. Those bits of white flesh held my gaze like magnets, and with my eyes first on one then on the other, oblivious to everything else in the world, I continued to look, and as I looked a thought involuntarily formulated itself in my head.

'I'd give a year of my life just to put my mouth on her cunt!'

A prolonged silence suddenly impressed itself upon me and brought me back to earth. Guiltily I raised my eyes to hers. Those violet eyes instead of being fixed on the bill in her hands were contemplating me in a speculative, half sardonic manner.

Guessing that she was conscious to some extent of my emotion, the blood rushed to my face.

'What are you thinking about, Laura?' she asked dryly, while the ghost of a smile hovered about her lips.

'Beauty!' I stammered in reply.

She looked at me, apparently surprised at the ingeniousness of my answer and then suddenly broke into peals of silvery laughter. Relieved but still greatly embarrassed, I sat in silence, hardly daring to meet her gaze. When the laughter subsided she laid the bill down and murmured in a low, insinuating voice:

'Laura, what would you do for me?'

'Anything!' I answered fervently and without hesitation this time.

'Anything!'

'Anything?' and the word was repeated with a slow, deliberate insistence which I comprehended held some special significance.

I looked at her intently in an effort to divine her meaning, but though there was a smile on her lips the violet eyes were inscrutable.

'Anything!' I repeated, putting all the emphasis I could into the all-embracing word.

There was an interval of silence, unbroken except for the tapping of the pencil she still held between her fingers against the edge of the table. Her gaze now turned to from me, and through half close eyes she seemed to be looking off into space lost in introspection. She had not changed her position, and though she must now have been aware that intimate portions of her body were visible to me she made no effort to conceal them from my view.

There was no longer any doubt in my mind that this situation was replete with glorious possibilities and though I hardly dared venture a guess as to what might be in store my heart was pounding with anticipation.

Her eyes, which for some moments had been fixed unseeingly on the curtained window, were again turned toward me. From her lips fell the softly spoken request:

'Sit down by me here, Laura.'

And she motioned toward the rug at her feet.

I needed no second invitation, and rising from my chair I accommodated myself on the soft rug. The bit of snow flesh above the top of her stocking was now so close to my eyes that the faint, blue tint of tiny vein which traversed the rounded curve of that immaculate limb was perceptible.

She extended her hand, and I felt her finger-tips running through my hair, caressing my forehead, and temples. The intoxication of her nearness, the subtle perfume which emanated from her body, the exquisite intimacy, all contributed to embolden me. Reverently, but without hesitation, I doubled back a portion of the fur-trimmed gown, exposing her leg from the knee half way up her thigh, and laid my lips upon cool flesh. It was as smooth in texture as the finest silk.

The play of her hands over my hair and face continued, but otherwise she remained motionless under my caress. On the firm, smooth skin I pressed kiss after kiss. My hand itched to raise the brief fold of garment just a trifle higher but something counselled me to hold myself in check, and let her take the lead.

I heard a sigh fall from her lips. She withdrew her hand from my head and shifted her position. She had been half sitting, half reclining with one leg crossed over the other, and when I had taken my place at her feet I had seated myself close by the side of her legs. But now she lowered the leg which had been crossed above its companion, and at the same time moved her body in my direction so that I was directly in front of her knees, instead of at one side. The dressing robe, already well elevated, was pulled tighter by this movement, and further expanses of alabaster whiteness were revealed.

I looked into her eyes in an effort to read her wishes. She smiled faintly in response, and her fingers engaged themselves in the knot of the silken cord which girdled her waist. It was unfastened, and with one sublimely indifferent gesture, without hesitation, without the least semblance of hypocritical prudery she flipped the folds of the garment back, exposing her nude body to me in all its splendour.

Scarcely breathing, my whole being submerged in an ecstasy of delight before this extraordinary spectacle of celestial beauty, my gaze travelled up and down over her naked form from the tips of daintily and exquisitely moulded breasts, over the smooth, slim waist and stomach where a softly rounded promontory, covered with the silkiest of little curls and ringlets of curls of gold, heralded the proximity of the temple door.

Many a naked woman have I seen, both before and since, but never have I seen the physical perfection of this woman duplicated. Perhaps after all there is something in aristocratic blood different from that possessed by those of more lowly birth.

Silent, apparently indifferent to my rapture, she passively permitted me to feast my eyes freely upon the spectacle of her nudity.

Now, she moved her limbs again, so that one of her knees was on either side of me. Again she placed her hand on my head with a touch which gently but unequivocally bid me draw myself closer. What I had viewed before, while her knees were still close together, had been sufficient to hold me breathless, but what was now revealed was of a nature to inspire thoughts other than those of mere admiration for physical perfection.

Beneath the mons veneris, with its soft curls and ringlets, there now appeared, frankly and clearly, the coral folds of flesh which constituted womanhood's supreme treasure. So small and virginal in aspect were the petal-like lips, that it hardly seemed possible they had ever been distended by the intromission of a male organ.

Deliberately, she let her body slide lower in the chair until her thighs were extended well out beyond its edge, the flower of her sex close to my face, her legs widely separated on either side of my body.

I knew not what was expected of me.

The wish I had so fervently voiced to myself, the favour I had vowed to be worth any price, was about to be granted me.

I rested my cheek for a moment against the satiny flesh of one of her thighs. Then, I pressed my lips against her mons veneris. The hair felt as fine and soft to the touch as that of a new-born infant. Then, quickly and expertly, my tongue sought out and penetrated the perfumed valley below. And, an instant later it was playing over her clitoris with all the fervour and agility at its command. A slight sound issued from her lips— something between a gasp and an exclamation—and she shifted her body forward a bit to better accommodate me. Then silence, profound and absolute.

Under the spell of one of the most intense erotic intoxications I had ever experienced, I plied my tongue feverishly, first centralizing its activities upon her clitoris, then, up and down the length of the genital cleft, and even inside the vaginal aperture as far as I could project it.

But a few moments of such energetic stimulation as I was subjecting her to would have had most women squealing and kicking, yet I failed to observe in her any of the customary reactions. I glanced upward toward her face. She was lying with her head thrown back, her eyes were closed and her countenance as calmly composed as though she were sleeping. Not a gesture, not a facial expression, not a sound or movement to suggest that she was under the influence of any emotional stress. Her hands rested quietly on the heavily padded leather arms of the chair, her little, tapering fingers curved lightly around them.

This was something of a new experience for me, but I had received several surprises that day and I did not pause to analyze the apparent anomaly.

Applying my mouth more firmly against the coral folds I succeeded in getting her clitoris compressed between my lips and then imparted a vigorous suction to it. Almost instantly, the hitherto motionless form began to show signs of life. I felt vibrant tremors in the flesh of her thighs where they pressed against my cheeks and perceived the muscular contractions of body and limbs as her physical organism began to yield to my ministrations. Maintaining her clitoris a prisoner between tightly compressed lips, and without relaxing the suction I was applying to it, I again glanced up. Her eyes were wide open, distended, and fixed upon me with the intent, strained expression of approaching orgasm. The slender fingers, which before had rested idly upon the arms of the chair, were now clenched tightly around them.

My own passions augmented by the knowledge that she was near the edge of orgasm, I slipped my hands under the cheeks of her bottom and pressed her closer to me. This movement brought a quick response. There was a violent, spasmodic shivering in the thighs which were compressed about my cheeks, and a sudden flow of moisture bathed my lips. The pressure of her thighs increased for a moment, and then relaxed. I felt her fingers on my forehead, pushing me away. I arose to my feet, trembling from the effects of the intense stimulation. Again she was lying with head thrown back, eyes closed. Except for the rise and fall of heaving breasts she might have been one of those exquisite, little tinted porcelain statues one may sometimes see in private collections in Holland—jewels of erotic art in which no tiny detail of life and colour is omitted. The heaving of her breasts subsided. The violet eyes opened, and scrutinized me quizzically.

'Was that what you were thinking about, Gilbert?'

And then, little fingers closed over the edge of her gown and drew it around her naked body, veiling it forever from my view. A short-lived romance was over, and as I look back over the span of years, it seems more a dream than a reality.

* * *

While still dreaming of my headmaster's wife, I met Irma. One of Irma's charms lay in the uncertainty of her determinations. I never knew from one moment to another what was coming next.

Irma told me many surprising revelations as to how young maids comport themselves in boarding school!

The lightness with which she regarded this kind of play was looked upon may be judged from the following: An English girl named Mercy, daughter of a wealthy British importer of tobacco, received naughty pictures and novels by post from a girl in Paris. One day, between the pages of a novel received from this source, she found a 'French letter' or condom. This interesting but under the circumstances entirely useless gift was passed from hand to hand amid general laughter. A few nights later, another girl, a lively little French mademoiselle, upon turning back the sheets of her couch preparatory to retiring, found between them a banana of ample dimensions over which the rubber condom had been stretched.

Brandishing the rubber clad banana in her hand, she announced that she was going to 'get' the girl she suspected of perpetrating the joke. Accompanied by several of her friends Rosita slipped into the dormitory where the object of the intended assault was just getting into bed. Waving the banana in the girl's face she exclaimed:

'Just for this, I'm going to fuck you!'

'You're not going to fuck me!' was the defiant answer.

A tussle began, which, because of the determined resistance of the prospective victim, might indeed have been lost by the French girl, had not her friends, reluctant to be defrauded of the spectacle, come to her assistance. Between them they straddled the protesting one out upon the bed, and held her while the little mademoiselle made good her threat.

'And I was one of the girls that held her legs!' added Irma, laughing at the recollection.

She entertained me with various anecdotes of her experiences with girls and women and seemed amused at my surprise at the ease with which she apparently found females willing to participate in such adventures. I wished I possessed similar good fortune. When she stated that there was an unlimited supply of them, my amazement gave way to incredulity. I could scarcely give credit to the assertion and yet before many hours had passed I was afforded an opportunity to judge for myself. For the following afternoon while driving leisurely about she pointed toward a group of small girls carrying baskets of violets, and smilingly referred to our conversation of the previous evening. Often enough had I observed these pert little youngsters, and had been annoyed more than once by their persistent efforts to sell me flowers, but their extreme youth made it seem to me improbable that, aside from selling violets, they had other professions.

'Do you mean to tell me those little girls…?' I exclaimed incredulously.

'Every last one of them,' she replied. 'I'll get one to come to the house, if you want me to.'

'Get one!'

'All right! Wait till I see one I like!'

Ordering the coachman to circle the block we again approached the same group and as we came alongside of them Irma motioned the driver to stop and leaning from the window she called to one of the youngsters, a bright eyed, piquant faced child who couldn't have yet been twenty. The girl rushed up to her expectantly, and extended a tray containing a quantity of violets in little bunches. Irma selected one, eyeing her attentively the meanwhile, and gave her a small coin. Then, removing a card from her purse, she pressed it into the girl's hand and whispered:

'Come and see me tonight at seven o'clock, darling!'

The girl glanced quickly at Irma, then at the address on the card, then at me, back again at Irma, nodded her head, and backed away.

'Of course, she'll come,' replied Irma dryly.

And, as punctually on the hour though she had been waiting outside for the clock to strike seven before presenting herself, the girl was at the door. She wore a fresher dress, and with all the innate and natural coquetry of a born Parisienne, she had made infantile efforts to beautify herself.

Irma took her hand and led her inside.

If she was impressed by the luxurious and exotic surroundings she did not show it although she gazed with interest at the little statues, pictures and paintings with which the room was adorned.

'What is your name, darling?'

'Lucille, at your service, Mademoiselle.'

'Who do you live with?'

'With my mama, and my sister.'

'Does she sell flowers, too?'

'Yes, Mademoiselle.'

'Can you stay all night?'

'*Certainement!* If you desire, Mademoiselle.'

'Very well, Lucille. The first thing we are going to do is take a nice bath in the pool together. Then we'll have dinner and afterward we'll have a fine time. You can sleep here and go home tomorrow.'

'As you please, Mademoiselle,' was the courteous answer.

Placing an arm about the child, Irma took her to the big bedroom and while I lounged in the doorway, an interested spectator, the two undressed. When Lucille's garments were removed down to her little panties, she glanced uncertainly toward me, but Irma reassured her.

'Never mind her, darling. She's a nice lady.'

Off came the small garment, and Lucille was naked in the presence of her hosts. Only the hint of a round swell surmounted with tiny nipples marked the budding breasts. Here again after many years, I saw another fat lipped, naked little V with its vertical incision and cute little dimple.

Irma herself was now disrobed, and before my sight was a vision in contrasts of female nudity, one in the bold nakedness of girlhood, the other in the full bloom of enchanting feminine maturity. My own body, I confess, standing somewhere in the middle between these poles

With soap, perfumes, and towels, followed by me, they proceeded to the tiled pool, and soon were immersed in the limped waters. After fifteen or twenty minutes of splashing and laughter, during which Lucille was diplomatically rubbed, scrubbed and sponged, they emerged, and after drying themselves Irma perfumed and powered the child's body, dried her hair and dressed her in a pyjama suit which, though large, was pressed into emergency duty. Then she brushed and arranged Lucille's hair, tying it back with a pink ribbon and finally, with her own toilet accessories, she first powered, then touched up the juvenile cheeks with rouge. With a lipstick she traced a dainty Cupid's bow upon the mouth. The deft touches produced a complete transformation and I could hardly restrain an exclamation of amazement at what water, soap, powder, perfume, lipstick and rouge could do to a ragged girl.

During dinner I could scarcely take my eyes off of her, so incredible was the transition. She, except for brief replies to our questions, ate in silence. The mother, from what we were able to gather, was or had been a prostitute, Lucille and the younger sister referred to being the fruit of transient amours, fathers unknown. Now they lived entirely upon what revenue was derived from the sale of flowers, and on what 'rich ladies' gave Lucille and her little sister.

My curiosity as to what procedure such children followed to please the 'rich ladies' was unbounded. After dinner was concluded we went into the lounging room and here, after a few minutes, Irma left us, telling me that I might 'play' with Lucille, but not to 'hurt' her.

As soon as we were alone I took her upon my lap, where she sat passively while I loosened the belt of her pyjamas. Slipping a finger between the lips of her cleft, I made discreet exploration. Her maidenhead was intact and technically at least, she was a virgin.

Irma returned, draped in a kimono. She lay down on the big, plush covered sofa and called Lucille to her. The girl lay down by her, clasping her arms about the recumbent form and their lips united in an amorous kiss. From then on Lucille calmly took the initiative. She continued to caress her older companion and finally slipping one of her soft little hands inside the breast of the kimono, she exposed Irma's bubbies, and applied her lips to the nipples of each in turn. With close attention I watched this tender play, while Irma lay still surrendering herself to the child's ministrations. Young as she was, she had acquired, or possibly it had been born in her, a skill and artfulness beyond description. Her caresses were as light and soft as the touch of a feather. While I watched I began to get a better comprehension of certain things which had formerly mystified me.

Like a hummingbird flitting from flower to flower, the moist, red lips were being applied first to one, and then to the other of Irma's snowy breasts. I saw the nipples stiffen out, and erect themselves as the provocative caress reacted magically upon them. Lucille clasped her lips over one of them and raised her head. The nipple slipped back with an elastic jerk when released. She moistened the nipples with saliva, then twirled them between her fingertips, until under the tantalizing manipulation, Irma began to twitch and tremble.

Beneath the kimono which still draped her lower limbs, her thighs slowly separated themselves. As though waiting for some such indication the girl instantly threw the garment open, slipped one of her knees between Irma's thighs, bringing it up in close contact with her cleft. In this position, crouched over the naked body of her friend she hesitated, glancing toward me as though doubtful as to whether she should proceed.

'Hurry up, darling!' gasped Irma.

Without further hesitation, with a matter fact directness which indicated perfect familiarity with the task in hand, she twisted about on the sofa and the next instant her face was between Irma's legs. With my gaze now on Lucille's bobbing head, then Irma's face as she surrendered her body to the intimate caress, I watched the realization of the act, following every graduation of its effects upon Irma in her facial expressions. When I saw her hands suddenly dart to Lucille's head and perceived in her eyes that intent strained look which precedes orgasm I was almost on the verge of spontaneous orgasm myself. When the tensed thighs relaxed their pressure upon the girl's face and the hands withdrew from her head she sat up, reached for a towel and wiped off her lips. Irma lay with her head thrown back and eyes closed for a few moments and then with a languid movement drew the kimono about her naked legs. With a sly glance toward me she placed an arm about Lucille and drew her face down, whispering something in her ear.

Lucille slipped off the sofa and approached me. Before I had time to guess her intent, she stripped open the front of my skirt and began doing as she had done for Irma. As the tide rose in response to her soft manipulation I made no effort to restrain it and, sensing the impending crises, she sucked and fingered all the harder until I spent myself most enjoyably. She looked pleased, with a professional seriousness, like she had performed a like service for me.

'She's a perfect jewel, isn't she?' said Irma, her eyes on me, a quizzical smile on her lips.

'She's a treasure!' I agreed fervently. 'I'd like to adopt her permanently.'

'Well, we'll keep her here tonight anyway. I want another session or two with her yet tonight myself,' responded Irma.

We lounged there for an hour talking, joking sipping burgundy while Lucille, over her first feeling of restraint, entertained us with accounts of her adventures with 'rich ladies.' We induced her to remove her pyjamas and show us some of the positions and methods she was familiar with.

'Doesn't doing such things make you feel funny down here?' I asked, placing my hand over her little cunt.

'*Certainement!* Sometimes the ladies do it to me, too!'

'Ah! How do they do it, darling?'

'Voila! With their tongues! With their fingers!'

'Does it feel nice?'

'Yes! It feels good down there, and all down inside my legs! Sometimes I do it to myself, too!'

'Show us how, darling!'

'With my finger! Like this…' Suiting action to word, she pushed away the hand with which I was caressing her, spread her legs apart and placed the tip of a little forefinger on her clitoris, rubbing it with a circular motion.

She realized the exhibition with such an entire lack of self-consciousness, and in such a natural, matter of fact way, that Irma and I were both convulsed with laughter.

'Come on; let's all go to bed. You can show us some more there,' exclaimed Irma when we had recovered our composure.

Lucille and I followed Irma to the bedroom. They proceeded to make themselves comfortable on the big bed where I joined them as soon as I had undressed.

Despite the outlet to my passion which Lucille's slim little fingers had afforded but a short hour previously, the sight and contact of the two naked females soon restored my virility and wakened new temptation. I pressed up against Irma but then she jerked away.

Jumping from the bed, she ran out of the room, to return a moment later with some twisted silk ropes she had pulled from a set of portieres in the drawing room.

'What are you going to do with those?'

'I'm going to tie you up with them.'

'Tie me up?'

'Yes! Tie you up!'

'Go ahead!' I replied, much amused.

She pushed my down on the bed; obediently, I extended my arms and legs. First, she knotted the silk cord around one of my wrists and tied it to one of the corner posts of the heavy bedstead, repeating the process on the opposite side with my other wrist. Then she fastened my ankles in a similar fashion to the foot of the bed. When she had finished the job to her satisfaction, I found myself spread-eagled out in a position far from dignified but I consoled myself with the reflection that a good stout jerk would break the cords and release me at any desire moment. For the present I was content to let her go ahead with her play.

She surveyed her handiwork speculatively for a moment, and then began to laugh.

'Now I've got you just the way I want you, and this time, when you spend it will be when I want you to!'

'Make her wet inside, darling!' Irma told Lucille.

Sitting down on the edge of the bed near me, Lucille extended her hand and her fingers inside my nest. A few movements of her wrist sufficed to restore its lubrication. Irma, to my disgust, halted the pleasant manipulation. Accommodating herself on the opposite side of the bed, she began to discourse the advantages of self-control, and the art of prolonging erotic pleasures, punctuating her remarks at intervals by reaching over and fingering my clitoris. It was a tantalizing situation in which I found myself—straddled out on my back, arms and legs tightly secured, my clitoris throbbing impotently under the provocations of the two females, who took turns in toying and teasing it.

But this was nothing in comparison to with what was yet to come.

At Irma's suggestion Lucille got up on the bed and seated herself astride my chest, her knees doubled under her on either side of me and her cleft within a few inches of my face. The sight of this tempting morsel so close to my lips, the feel of her bottom on my chest and the pressure of her thighs combined to aggravate my condition.

'Now you can pay her back for what she did to me!' insinuated Irma.

More than willing, I raised my head, Lucille edged up closer, and in a few seconds my tongue was between the two little naked converging lips. I located a tiny clitoris without difficulty, and quickly demonstrated the fact that little clitorises are as responsive to an active tongue as big ones. And while Lucille was twitching and quivering with her genitals planted firmly over my mouth, Irma intermittently penetrated my slit with her fingers, pumping vigorously for a few seconds, then withdrawing cruelly. Lucille suddenly inclined herself forward, and I felt her thighs clenching themselves tightly about me. She clung to me rigidly for a moment and then jerked away. She had received her compensation.

The taste and humidity of her genitals remained on my lips, augmenting my own excitation. Irma's fingers were on my clitoris, but she was not moving it. I raised my hips in an endeavour to obtain sufficient friction to release the pent up tide, but she divined the purpose, laughed, and withdrew her hand. Hungrily, my eyes devoured the lascivious spectacle of her nudity, and as they rested inevitably upon the most intimate of her charms, she murmured teasingly:

'You've seen hers, now you want to see mine, too, eh? Voila! I'll let you look!'

And mounting on the bed, the exuberant Russian placed herself on her hands and knees directly over my face. With all the desperation of Tantalus, grasping for water just beyond his reach, I strained my neck in an effort to reach her cunt with my tongue.

'Ha!' she exclaimed. 'You're not satisfied with seeing it! Now you want to lick it! Well, lick it, then!'

And she sat down on my chest, as Lucille had done. And, as I had done with Lucille I did with her. I licked and sucked until she too had orgasm, and bathed my lips and cheeks with her offering to Venus.

This was the final straw and I decided that it was time for me to get a little satisfaction for myself. I pulled tentatively at the cords and when they failed to give I jerked at them with all my strength. To my surprise I was unable to break them and after a few more efforts while Irma and Lucille looked on laughing I discovered that I was trussed up far more efficiently than I had first imagined.

Irma assured me that she didn't propose to free me for 'hours and hours yet' and that I might as well make up my mind to stand it.

In part, she made good her threat, and during two solid hours, or more, I was subjected to such tantalizing manipulations and treated to such spectacles as nearly set me frantic. While I lay there alternately swearing and coaxing, she and Lucille diverted themselves in my sight by running the gamut from Lesbian and Sapphic embraces to mutual masturbation, pausing between whiles to sit on the edge of the couch, and tease me with naughty words and actions. About twelve o'clock, it became apparent that Lucille was exhausted, and Irma considerately carried her to an adjoining room, making her comfortable for the night. The girl had conscientiously lent her little body to every caprice of her hosts, and had well earned whatever recompense awaited her on the morrow.

Returning t where I was still stretched out on the bed Irma stood looking down at me a moment.

'Now see if what I told you isn't true!' she said. She got upon the couch, and placed her knees astride my body. First came the contact of her lips she nestled down upon me, then the warm, humid feeling of her breathe and tongue on my nest. Then without conscious volition on my part, I spent, making up for all the time I had waited with a climax that endured nearly a minute.

'Didn't I, ah… tell you it was, oh… better this way… oh… o-o-o-oh!'

* * *

Well, you tell me something now. Tell me some more about Paris!' said my latest target for conquest.

She listened with glowing cheeks while I described several of the spectacles I had witnessed in the French capital and when I had concluded, she whispered:

'Laura, do you suppose there are girls here in London who do that with other women, like those French girls?'

'Plenty of them, honey.'

'Laura …' she paused, and there was something in her tone which told me that another secret was going to be imparted to me, 'Laura, I … it sounds dreadful, but do you know… ' and she stopped again in confusion.

'Go on, honey.'

'Well … I'd like to have another woman do it to me … just once … I believe … ' and she began to giggle.

'What do you believe, sweetheart?'

'Oh, nothing!'

'Come on now, what is it?'

'Well, I bet a woman can do that better than a man!'

'I'm sure you're right and I'd like to show you myself.'

'But Laura, it can't be you, can it? Certainly you've never…'

I said nothing, but my guise of inexperience with which I had seduced her had been lifted.

'You fibbed to me the other night!' she added a moment later.

'Fibbed to you?'

'Yes; fibbed to me.'

'About what, honey?'

'When you said I was the first woman you were ever with.'

Not knowing whether it would be more discreet to deny, or confess my guilt, I hedged with another question.

'What makes you think I fibbed about it, darling?'

'Ha! You know too much for a novice. I realized that, after thinking about it a little. Don't think I'm so silly as to be jealous about what you did before you knew me. Not that I blame you. You should have been just as dishonest now. Asking me if you could do it to me that French way! Why didn't you just pull my legs apart and to it without asking me? I was crazy to try it, but I was ashamed to say so! You made me so darn mad! And asking me to let you see me naked— you're strong enough to lift my nightgown up and look at me all you want without my helping you, aren't you?'

This discourse was delivered so seriously, and yet with expression so comical on her face that it convulsed me with laughter.

'You may be right, in part, honey,' I said, when I had recovered my composure, 'but sometimes there are exceptions which might make that a doubtful rule to follow. A woman must be sure her attentions are welcome before she goes too far. And no woman wants to force anything on a woman against her wishes.'

'But I asked for it!'

'And I offered.'

'But I was too embarrassed. You should have just done it!'

'Maybe you're right, sweetheart. I'll follow your advice hereafter!'

'You old darling, you've been so good to me I don't believe I could really get mad at you if I tried.'

'Happy with me, sweetheart?'

'Happier than I ever was before in my life, even if you do tease me to do naughty things. Oh Laura … Do it to me, then, I can't be still a second longer!'

And then she received it French style for the first time, and I savoured the taste of her exquisite cunt.

'What did it feel like, sweetheart?' I asked her afterwards.

She sat up, looked at me for a moment, and then burst into laughter.

'It felt like somebody touching me with velvet on my most sensitive part! That's just what it felt like! Now is there anything else you want to know… or see… or try?'

The next day I took my time to pay a visit to a certain neighbourhood not entirely unfamiliar to me by reputation, which visit brought as its result an appointment with a petite little German Fraulein, who was presented to me under the name of Freda. She listened attentively to my words, smiled at some of my observations, and summed up her answer in the following concise terms:

'One pound, and one extra for going out.'

'We won't quarrel over price. There'll still be another pound if you manage well.'

'I'll manage it all right.'

'Very well. Be ready for me to pick you up here at eight o'clock.'

I telephoned to Edyth, and told her I would be a little late that evening, and would eat downtown, suggesting at the same time that she prepare herself for a real nice 'special' evening at home.

'I haven't forgotten the good advice you gave me!' I added in conclusion, and heard a silvery giggle in response as I hung up.

I reached the apartment about nine o'clock and the blond Fraulein was with me. Edyth looked from one to the other in surprise as I presented the girl, saying that she was a little friend of mine I wanted Edyth to know. She acknowledged the introduction in a friendly way though she continued to gaze questioningly at the visitor.

Acting on the suggestion conveyed by my telephonic references to a 'special' evening, she had dressed herself in coquettish dishabille, not dreaming, of course, that I intended to bring anyone with me. It was evident that she was burning with curiosity regarding the German damsel, and her eyes followed me reproachfully for my failure to enlighten her regarding the mysterious visitor.

After a bit of aimless conversation I suggested that she bring in some wine, and she arose and went into the kitchen. As soon as she was out of the room, I whispered to the fraulein I would speak to her alone a moment, and followed her.

As soon as I entered the room Edyth pressed up to me and said:

'Laura! Who is that girl?'

'Why, you expressed a wish last night, honey, to try something and I fixed it for you.'

'Laura … what on earth do you mean?'

'You said you'd like to have another woman French you once. You seemed to suggest that I wasn't adequate. That's what she's here for.'

'Laura!' she exclaimed, in horrified tones. 'I was just talking! I wouldn't let a stranger like her do that to me! I'd die of shame.'

'Oh, yes, you will let her, sweetheart. Remember, you gave me some good advice, too. Something about 'making' girls do things without asking permission first!'

'I won't let her, Laura! I won't even go back in the parlour while she's here!'

'Darling, you're going to let her even if I have to hold you down while she does it! You run into the bedroom now, and get ready! Here … drink your wine first!'

She was about to voice further protests, but I interrupted:

'I mean it, honey. There's no use arguing!'

She took the glass I was proffering her, drank its contents slowly and set it down.

'All right then, if you're going to start giving orders! I'll go in the bedroom and wait for her. But don't think you're going to watch! I couldn't, Laura! I just couldn't! I'd die of mortification! It will be bad enough, alone with her!'

It assuredly was no part of my plan to be absent while the experiment was in progress; however, I promised her that I would stay outside, promising myself at the same time that I would not be far from the keyhole.

'All right! I'll go in the bedroom but don't let her come in for a few minutes,' she added, blushing, 'until I fix myself up!'

She threw her arms around my neck, clung to me a moment, and murmured:

'I'd rather it was you, though! I was only half in earnest when I said that. I never dreamed you'd take it seriously. But I'll go through with it now!'

'Maybe there'll be some left over for me afterwards!' I said and I ran my hand up under her dress between her legs.

She slipped down the hall, and I heard the bedroom door close behind her. I picked up the remaining glasses, took them to the parlour, gave one to Miss Freda, and drank the other.

'What did she say?' inquired the girl, who was aware that Edyth had not at first known the purpose of her visit.

'She didn't make as much fuss as I thought she would. She's in the bedroom waiting for you now.'

'Are you coming in, too?'

'No,' I said regretfully. 'She drew the line on that.'

'Too bad!' said the Fraulein, with a half sympathetic, half cynical smile.

She arose and I conducted her to the bedroom. She opened the door softly, stepped inside, and closed it behind her. I remained in the hall, listening attentively. At first I heard nothing but the subdued tones of the lesbian's soft voice, answer in almost indistinguishable monosyllables by Edyth. 'You're awfully bashful, aren't you, darling? You don't have to be with me... I'm only another woman just like you... Oh, what perfectly beautiful bubbies... Why, your skin is simply marvellous! As smooth and white as a baby's! And no hair except where it ought to be... do you know, in my country when a woman's hair down here is soft and silky instead of crisp, they say it's a sign of aristocratic blood. Oh, you sweet thing! If you were mine, I'd just love you to death!'

I kneeled down to pear through the keyhole but rose again cursing under my breath. Something was draped over it from the opposite side of the door, and my vision was blocked. Again I pressed my ear to one of the door panels. Through it came the slight sound of rustling garments, the creaking of bedsprings as they ceded to the weight of moving bodies. 'Now you lie perfectly still, darling. Let me do everything. Just relax and enjoy yourself!' Then a silence, unbroken except for the barely audible movement of bedsprings.

At last a faint, but expressive and long drawn out 'Ooooh!' broke the silence, followed at short intervals by others subdued in tone yet pregnant with emotion.

The exclamations continued, and became more audible. The temptation was too much for me, and dropping my hand down on the doorknob I turned it softly exerting a slight pressure at the same time. The knob moved, but the door didn't. Again I had been outwitted, for Edyth had taken all the necessary precautions to see that I kept my promise, regardless of whether I changed my mind about it or not, and had latched the door.

The music on the other side of the door was now beginning to run the chromatic scale in a way which, by experience, indicated the proximity of orgasm. It culminated in a crescendo of vibrant moans and cries, and died away.

Another long silence and then I heard the sound of moving feet on the floor, the murmur of voices—words I couldn't distinguish. Quickly I straightened up, and returned to the parlour.

A few minutes later the door opened and the lesbian came out. She came alone. Edyth remained in the bedroom. The girl smiled, and nodded her head as though assuring me that all had gone well. She was evidently not disposed to linger, and when she had adjusted her hat over the blond curls I handed her three pound notes.

'Here is my address and phone number in case she wants me again,' she whispered, and she slipped a small card in my hand as I opened the door.

Edyth had not reappeared, so I went into the bedroom. A seductive vision met my eyes. She was lying stretched out on the bed with nothing to cover her charms except a short silk vest, which barely reached the upper border of the soft curls which the lesbian had called 'aristocratic.' The round, tapered legs were extended out languidly, parted just sufficiently to reveal the cleft which divided the two halves of the altar of Venus, faintly visible under the little curls and ringlets of chestnut hair which formed its natural curtain.

She said nothing, nor even attempted to cover her nakedness as I gazed down upon her. I was still tingling with excitement, and needed nothing more inspiring than this vision to stimulate me to quick action. I undressed as quickly as I could, and lay down by her. A second later my mouth was on her cunt, still moist from its recent spendings. She had not uttered a word and had hardly moved except to further separate her legs to better accommodate my caress, but within a few seconds after my tongue found her clitoris, the usual pandemonium was loose. I raised my head in dismay. My first thought was to make her hold a pillow over her face but, even as I reached for one, a better way to quiet her occurred to me.

'Here! Put this in your mouth and let's see whether it won't choke off some of that noise!' I exclaimed, and I turned around on the bed in a direction contrary to that in which I had been lying. My own clitoris now touched her tongue as hers touched my tongue, and without hesitation she licked it vigorously. And while her tongue licked up and down my slit, my own mouth again attached itself firmly to the humid aperture between her thighs. My tongue penetrated the most recondite depths; it played along the length of the valley and danced in circles around and over the little tit shaped protuberance which rose to meet it and then shrank back coquettishly. Almost unconsciously, my hips were moving forward and backward, and her tongue managed to penetrate far into my depths.

Did it stop the noise?

Not exactly, but it did transform it from highly audible shrieks to something of a more subdued nature, a sort of gurgling, gasping, glug-glug-glug, which might possibly be mistaken, if overheard, for the sound of water being drained from the wash basin!

I didn't try to delay things. As soon as I perceived that she was ready for orgasm, I let go, and as the warm essence from her ovaries baptized my face, her own lips received their recompense in my own feminine fluids.

A few minutes later I murmured in her ear:

'How was it that way, darling?'

'Oh, that was the best of all!' she exclaimed fervently.

'And the girl…?'

'Oh, it was wonderful!'

'Better than with me?'

'No… not better… but…' She began to laugh hysterically. 'The way she did it was wonderful, and the way you do it is wonderful, too!' was her ambiguous answer.

'Did she do it different from the way I do it?'

'Yes!'

'Different in what way?' I asked, somewhat perplexed.

'Well, she… oh, I can't tell you!' and she went into another fit of laughter.

While I was pondering over this mystery, her demeanour became serious, and she murmured in a rather preoccupied voice:

'Laura... tell me something... am I different in some way form other women?'

'Sure you are, darling! You're sweeter and nicer and you have prettier titties, and legs, and arms than any other... '

'Oh, Laura, you old exaggerator!' she interrupted. 'I don't mean in that way. I mean... down here... ' She motioned toward the juncture of her thighs.

'What makes you ask that, honey?'

'Well... that girl... there was something odd... she kept looking, and feeling... why, you would have thought she was a man, and I was the first woman she ever saw... she acted just like you did the first time you... kind of... oh, I don't know... as though there was something strange about me. Maybe it was just my imagination.'

I knew the answer to this of course, lay in her enormous clitoris, but fearing that, woman-like, she might regard the abnormality as a defect, I changed the conversation and, still curious, endeavoured to find out in what way the lesbian's caresses had differed from my own. But my questioning only evoked more hysterical laughter and the protest that she 'couldn't explain it.'

Possibly the Fraulein 'mounted' her, as I had frequently tempted to do, but on this point neither my curiosity nor yours will ever be satisfied, for just exactly what the girl did to her during those mysterious fifteen minutes they were locked together, I was never able to ascertain.

Very shortly, after this incident an unfortunate circumstance separated Edyth and me, temporarily as we supposed at the moment, but permanently as prescribed by fate. She received an urgent message calling her to her mother's side. A lasting illness kept her there, and before she was free to rejoin me, I received an offer to act as commercial representative for a British firm in New York, and offer made under such advantageous conditions as made it expedient to accept.

Of my several years in that incongruous land, where 'Liberty' and 'Prohibition' are bedfellows, I shall tell you at some future date.

BEATRICE

I do not like old rooms that are brown with the smell of time.

The ceilings in my husband's house were too high. They ran away from me. In the night I would reach up my hands but I could not touch them. When Edward asked me what I was doing I said I was reaching my hands up to touch the sky. He did not understand. Were we too young together?

Once a week he would remove my nightdress and make love to me. Sometimes I moved, sometimes I did not. Sometimes I spoke, sometimes I did not speak. I did not know the words to speak. We quarrelled. His stepmother would scold us. She could hear. In the large, high-ceilinged rooms voices carried as burnt paper flies, rising, tumbling, falling, drifting.

The doors were always half open. Sometimes—lying in bed as if upon a huge cloud—I would play with his prick, his cock, his pintle. Pintle… I do not like the set in it.

The night before I left we quarrelled. Our words floated about, bubble-floating. They escaped through the door. His stepmother netted them. She entered and spoke to us. The oil lamps were still lit.

'I will bring you wine—you must be happy,' she said. Her nightgown was pale and filmy. I could see her breasts. Balloons. I could see the dark blur of her pubis, her pubic hair, her wickedness.

'Wine, yes, 'twould be splendid,' Edward said. He was pale and thin. Like his pintle. I had nursed it in my palm even while we quarrelled. It was the warm neck of a bird. I did not want it in my nest.

I heard his stepmother speaking to the maid downstairs. The maid was always up. There was clinking—bottle sounds, glasses sounds. We lay still, side by side. His stepmother returned and closed the door, bearing a tray. She poured wine. We sat up like people taking medicine.

'Angela, dear, lie down,' Edward said. His father had married her when Edward was fourteen. During the past months then of his father's absence in India, she had encouraged him to use her Christian name. I judged her about forty. A woman in full bloom.

Wine trickled and spilled on the sheet as she got in. Edward was between us. The ceiling grew higher. The sounds of our drinking sounded. The wine was suitably chilled. My belly warmed it. We were people in a carriage, going nowhere. We indulged ourselves in chatter. The bottle emptied quickly. We must sleep, we must lie down, Angela said.

'I will stay with you until you sleep.'

I heard her voice say that. The ceiling came down. It had never done that before. I passed my hand up into it and it was mate of cloud. We lay down side by side on our backs. Our breathing came. There was warmth. Edward laid his hand on my thigh. He moved my nightgown up inch by inch. He touched. Into my fur, my nest, he touched. The lips were oily, soft. I did not move. His hand on the other side of him moved. I could feel the sheet fluttering there.

Our eyes were all open. I did not look but I knew. Soft, wet sounds. I tried not to move my bottom. Would the maid enter to remove the tray? Edward's fingertips found my button. I felt rich, forlorn, lost. My legs stretched down and widened. My toes moved. On the other side of him the sheet fluttered still.

Edward moved. His finger was oily with my oily. He moved on his hip and fumed towards me. I felt the pronging of his prong. His hand cupped my nest.

'Kiss goodnight, Beatrice.'

His voice was above me, yet far away—a husk blown on the wind. I moved my face sideways to his.

'Yes, kiss goodnight,' Angela said.

Her voice was far away—a leaf floating on the sea. His mouth met mine. His charger quivered against my bared thigh. Fingers that were not my fingers ringed the stem of his cock. His finger entered me. I moved not. Our mouths were pasted together, unmoving. I was running through meadows and my father was chasing me. My mother and my sister, Caroline, were laughing. I screeched. Their voices drifted away on to the far horizon and waved there like small flags.

Moving my hand I encountered Angela's hand—the rings upon her fingers that ringed around his cock. I moved my mouth away from Edward's and stared up at the ceiling. It had gone high, gone high again. Birds drifted through it. Edward's hand eased my thighs wider. I lay limp, moist in my moistness. The bed quivered as if an engine were running beneath it.

I found my voice.

'Kiss goodnight,' I said. My mind was not blank. There was coloured paper in it. A kaleidoscope. I watched the swirling, the patterns. Would love come?

Small wet sounds. Slithery sounds. I held my legs open. I was gone, lost. They did not know me. The bed heaved, shook. I turned my head. I looked as one looks along a beach at other people.

Did I know them?

In the night he slimed and mounted me. Drowsy in coils of sleep I did not resist. The oil lamps flickered low. Did she watch? From moment to moment I jerked my bottom in long memories of knowing. I wore drawers in my dreams. My bottom was being smacked. It was being smacked because there was a cock in me. In our soft threshing my legs spread. My ankle touched hers. She did not stir. Our feet rubbed gently together. Our toes were intimate.

Edward worked his work upon me and was done. The spurtings came in long, strong trills of warmth. Warm, wet. Sperm trickled down my thighs. I lay inert. I had not come. He had not pleasured me. My nipples were untouched.

In the morning I left. Was that the reason? No. It was not anything he had done or not done. It was men and women and I did not feel with men what I felt with women. I would go where I would be with women. He would be happier with Angela. She cared better for him. Angela smiled at me and said. 'It was the wine. We must make him happy.' Her bottom was large and round beneath her peignoir. Edward kissed us. We took breakfast with the windows open.

I kissed them both when I left.

I was kind to them.

* * *

Houses seem smaller when one returns to them after a long period. The rooms shrink. They carry dead echoes. One looks for things one had left, but the drawers have been emptied. Furniture is moved. Even the small pieces of paper one had wished to keep have vanished. I like small pieces of paper. My notes to myself. Addresses, birthdays, anniversaries.

My notes to myself had all gone. Did I take them? Two reels of silk cotton that no longer matched my dresses lay in the back of a drawer in my dressing table. One was mauve and the other a pale blue. They were pretty. Once I used to keep biscuits in a jar on the top shelf of my wardrobe. Someone had eaten them. I told my sister Caroline.

'Beatrice, that was three years ago. You ate them,' she said. No one looked surprised. It was always a quiet house. We hate those who shout. They knew I would come back.

'You should never have married,' Mother said. She looked at me sternly and added, 'Did I not tell you? How old are you?'

'I am twenty-five,' I replied, as if I were addressing a stranger. Dust swirled in the sunlight as I drew back the blue velvet curtains and raised the sash of my window.

'The maid does not clean,' Mother said. Did she see reproach in my eyes? She stood close to me and I could feel her authority. The gold of her jewellery gleamed in the pale sun. There was a silence because we like silences. A baker's cart trundled down the street. From the side entrance of the house opposite a maid appeared, her white cap askew on her head. She raised her hand and the baker's man reined in his horse. A cat prowled by the railings.

Mother stirred. She moved past me. Her thighs brushed my bottom.

'I must return soon to Madras, Beatrice. You will have comfort here.' Her finger traced dust on the top of the rosewood cabinet by my bed.

'I shall be comfortable, Mother. You will be gone long? Madras is so far.'

'A year, my pet, and no more. Your Aunt Maude will afford protection to you and your sister. Had you but returned before we might have walked with the early summer sun in the meadow.'

'Yes, Mother.'

My Aunt Maude lived close by. She had done so for years. We were close. Mother's hand was upon my shoulder. I felt smaller. She stood behind me like a guard, a sentry. Did I like Aunt Maude? I asked with my mind but not my mouth. They were sisters. There was kinship.

'Shall Jenny be there, too?' I asked. In my unmoving I asked. The baker's cart had rolled on with a tinkling of harness. The street lay quiet again as in a photograph. The maid had gone, loaf clutching her maidenhood. Into a darkness of scullery, a glowering of gloom behind windows. Fresh smell of fresh bread.

'Jenny has grown as you have. You will like her more. She is fuller of form and pretty. In her guardianship of her your aunt has moulded her well,' Mother replied.

My buttocks moulded. Beneath my long silk dress they moulded. Proud in their fullness they touched mother's form lightly, gracing her grace with their curves. I felt the pressure of her being. There was comfort between us as in the days before my marriage. We had lain in the meadow and seen the flashing of wings, birds' wings, the butterflies. I leaned back. Mother's hands touched my hair, the long gold flowing of my hair. The moulding of my bottom, ripe with summer.

'We shall drink wine. Come—let us celebrate your return,' Mother said.

I followed the first touch of her hand. We descended. The polished banister slid smooth beneath my palm. Caroline waited on us, neat on a chaise-lounge. At mother's bidding she drew the bell-pull. The maid Sophie appeared. Wine was ordered.

In the coolness of its bottle glass it came. Mother poured. The sofa received us. Like two acolytes we sat on either side of her. Sophie had gone. The door closed. In our aloneness we sat.

'We shall French-drink,' Mother said. It was a pleasantry we had indulged in before. I was but twenty-one then, Caroline eighteen. The wine glistened now again upon our lips. Our heads lay upon mother's shoulders. We sipped our sips while Mother filled her mouth more deeply and turned her face to mine. Her breathe tickled. My parted lips received wine from her mouth. There was warmth. Her hand lay on my thigh.

Mother turned to Caroline. Foolishly shy she hid her face until her chin was raised. I heard the sounds, small sounds—the wine, the lips. A wasp buzzed and tapped against the window as if seeking entry, then was gone. The gardener chased the long grass with his scythe. I waited. The wine came to my mouth again. A whispering of lips. The ridging of my stocking top through my dress, beneath her palm. The tips of our tongues touched and retreated. Did the French drink this way? Mother had been to Paris. In her knowing she had been.

Long did we linger. Caroline's dress rustled. I could not see. Across her form I could not see. The bottle emptied but slowly like an hour-glass. The wine entered my being. As through shimmering air Caroline rose at last, her face flushed. She adjusted her dress. Her eyes had a look of great foolishness.

'Go to your room, Caroline,' Mother said. There was yet wine in her glass. Silent as a wraith she was gone, her blushes faint upon the air like the smoke from a cigar.

'She is yet young,' Mother said. Her tone was sombre. There was wine on my breasts once when I was eighteen and she had kissed it away. The wine made pools of goodness and warmth in me. It journeyed through my veins and filled my head.

'We shall go to the attic,' Mother said. Her hand held mine—clasped and covered it. As we rose her foot nudged the bottle and it fell. A last seeping of liquid came from its mouth. We gazed at each other and smiled.

'You will come, Beatrice? It is for the last time.' There was a sadness.

We ascended, our footsteps quiet. The door to Caroline's room stood closed, thick in its thickness. The patterned carpet on the curving stair drank in our steps. Above the first floor were the guest rooms. In the old days those who wished had passed from bedroom to bedroom at nights during the long weekend parties my parents held. I knew this though my lips did not speak. At nights I had heard the whisperings of feet—a slither-slither of secrets. Arrangements were made discreetly with my mother as to the placings in rooms. The ladies of our circle always arranged such things. The gentlemen took it as manna. Bedsprings squeaked. I had told Caroline, but she did not believe me. There were moanings and hushed cries—the lapping sounds of lust. Small pale grey puddles on the sheets at morning.

No one had ever seen me go to the attic with Mother. It was our game, our secret. Our purity.

In the attic were old trunks, occasional tables my mother had discarded or replaced, vases she disliked, faded flowers of silk. Pieces of unfinished tapestry lay over the backs of two chairs. Sunlight filtered through a dust-hazed window.

We entered by the ladder and stood. In the far corner near the dormer window stood the rocking horse, grey and mottled. Benign and handsome—polished in its varnished paint—it brooded upon the long gone days. Dead bees lay on the sill. In my kindness I was unhappy for them. Mother's hand held mine still. She led me forward. My knees touched the brocaded cloth of an armchair whose seat had sagged. Upon it lay a mirror and a brush, both backed with tortoiseshell. They were as I had used of old up here.

Mother turned her back to me and gazed out through the glass upon the tops of the elms. A trembling arose in me which I stilled. With slow care I removed my dress, my underskirt, and laid them on the chair. Beneath I wore but a white batiste chemise with white drawers whose pink ribbons adorned the pale of my thighs. My silk brown stockings glistened. I waited.

Mother turned. She regarded me gravely and moved towards me. 'You have grown. Even in three years you have grown,' she said. 'Where shall you ride to?'

I laughed. 'To Jericho,' I replied. I had always said that though I did not know where it was. Nodding, her hand sought the brush. I held the mirror. With long firm strokes of the bristles Mother glossed and straightened my hair. Its weight lay across my shoulders, in its lightness. Its Boldness shone and she was pleased.

'It is good,' Mother said, 'the weather is fair for the journey. My lady will mount?'

We stepped forward. She held the horse's reins to keep it still. Once there had been a time when my legs could hold almost straight upon the horse. Now that I was grown more I had to bend my knees too much. My bottom slid back over the rear of the saddle and projected beyond the smooth grey haunches. Mother moved behind me and began to rock the horse with one hand. With the other she smacked my outstretched bottom gently.

'My beautiful pumpkin—it is larger now,' she murmured. My shoulders sagged. In the uprising of my bottom I pressed my face against the strong curved neck of the horse. It rocked faster. I clung as I had always clung. The old' planked floor swayed and dipped beneath me. Her palm smacked first one cheek and then the other.

'Oh! No more!' I gasped.

All was repetition.

'It is far to Jericho,' my mother laughed. I could feel her happiness in my head. The cheeks of my bottom burned and stung. My knees trembled. The bars of the stirrups held tight under the soles of my boots.

'No more, mother!' I begged. Her hand smacked on. I could feel the impress of her fingers on my moon.

'Two miles—you are soon there. What will you do when you arrive?'

'I shall have handmaidens. They will bathe and perfume me. Naked I shall lie on a silken couch. Sweatmeats will be brought. Slaves shall bring me wine. There shall be water ices.'

I remembered all the words. I had made them up in my dreams and brought them out into the daylight.

'I may visit you and share your wine?' Mother asked. Her hand fell in a last resounding smack. I gasped out yes. I fell sideways and she caught me. She lifted me until my heels unhooked from the stirrups. I sagged against her. My nether cheeks flared. In the pressure of our embrace my breasts rose in their milky fullness above the lace of my chemise. My nipples showed. I clenched my bottom cheeks and hid my face against her soft chest.

'It was good. I should bring the whip to you henceforth,' Mother murmured.

The words were new. They were not part of our play. Beneath my vision I could see my nipples, the brown buds risen. Had I forgotten the words? Perhaps we had rehearsed them once. In their smallness they lay scattered in the dust.

'It would hurt,' I said.

'No, it is small. Stand still.' I did not know what to do with my hands. She was gone to the far corner of the attic and returned. In her hands was a soft leather case. She opened it. There was a whip. The handle was carved in ebony, the end bulbous. There were carvings as of veins along the stem. From the other end exuded strands of leather. I judged them not more than twenty-five inches long. The tapered ends were loosely knotted.

'Soon, perhaps. Lay it for now beneath your pillow, Beatrice.'

So saying she cast aside the case and I took the whip. At the knob end was a silky smoothness. The thongs hung down by my thigh. A tendon stood out on my neck in my blushing. Mother traced it with her finger, making me wriggle with the tickling. Broad trails of heat stirred in my bottom still. The handle of the whip felt warm as if it had never ceased being touched.

I moved away from her. The thongs swung, caressing the sheen of my stockings. Mother assisted me in the replacing of my dress. Her hands nurtured its close fitting, smoothing it about my hips and bottom. Her eyes grew clouded. I stirred fretfully. My hair was brushed and burnished anew. Mother's mouth descended upon mine. Her fingers shaped the slim curve of my neck.

Beatrice

'It was good, Beatrice. You are grown for it—riper, fuller. The smacks did not hurt?'

I shook my head, but then smiled and said 'A little.' We both laughed. In the past there had been wine afterwards, drawn from a cooling box that she had placed beforehand in the attic. Now we had drunk before and it moved within us.

Her fingers charmed the outcurve of my bottom—its glossy roundness tight beneath my drawers. She recalled her own bottom when it was as mine. We kissed and spoke of small things. I would never come to the attic again, I thought. In the subtle seeking of our fingers there were memories. At last we descended. Mother took the ladder first. Halfway down she stopped and guided my feet in my backwards decent. Her hands slid up beneath my skirt to guide me.

Caroline was reading when we re-entered the drawing room. Her eyes were timid, seeking, brimmed with questions.

'There is a new summerhouse—come, I will show you, Beatrice,' Mother said. I shook my head. I must see to my unpacking with the servant. Mother would forgive me. Her eyes forgave me. They followed me like spaniels, loping at my heels.

'Your boots are re-polished—the spare ones,' Caroline called after me. It was as if she meant to interrupt my thoughts. Mother went to her and drew her up.

'Let us see if the workmen have finished in the summerhouse,' she said. Her eyes were butterflies on and on. I turned and stood of a purpose, watching her rising. Her form was as slender as my own. Her blue dress yielded to her springy curves. Through the window I watched them pass beneath the arbour. Three workmen in rough clothes came forward from where the new building stood and touched their caps. My mother consulted her watch and spoke to them. After a moment they went on, passing round by the side of the house towards the drive and the roadway.

Their day was finished, or their work was done. Mother seemed not displeased. Caroline hung back but mother drew her on. Her foolishness was evident to me even then. The sun shone through her skirt, offering the outlines of her legs in silhouette. She was unmarried, but perhaps not untried. I fingered the velvet of the curtains, soft and sensuous to my touch. The lawn received their footsteps. The door to the summerhouse was just visible from where I stood. Mother opened it and they passed within. It closed.

I waited, lingering. My breath clouded the pane of glass. The door did not re-open. The shrubs and larches looked, but the walls of the summer-house were blank.

Going upstairs to my room I fancied I heard a thin, wailing cry from Caroline.

* * *

When Caroline smiles I know something, but I do not know what I know.

The whip lay untouched beneath my pillow. Mother was due to depart. There was movement about the house. Trunks, valises. Two hansom cabs were needed—one for the luggage.

In the night before her departure I slipped my hand beneath my pillow and touched the whip, the smoothness of the handle, the coiling of the waiting thongs. My thumb traced the carved veins upon the penis shape. It moved to the knob, the swollen plum. After long moments of caressing it I got up and moved along the dark of the passageway. The door to mother's bedroom was ajar. I stilled myself and took an extra pillow from the linen cupboard, making no sound.

The door to Caroline's room lay half open. Normally it was closed, as was mine at night. In the night. I peered within, expecting her to sit up. In the milky gloom she lay sprawled on her bed. Her hair was fanned untidily over her pillow. The hem of her nightdress was drawn up, exposing her thighs and the shadowy thatch of ash-blonde hair between. Her eyes were closed, lips parted.

I moved forward quietly, expecting to surprise her. She stirred not. Her legs lay apart in an attitude of lewd abandon. Slender fingers curled lax upon the innerness of her thigh—the firm flesh of pleasure there. Between the curls the lips of pleasure pouted. In the pale moonlight it seemed to me that there was a glistening there, as even upon her fingertips. Her breathing was the breathing of a child.

I stirred her shoulder with my hand. Drowsily her eyes opened.

'You are uncovered. Don't be naughty,' I scolded. She prefers me in my scolding.

My hands slid beneath her calves, lifting them. As with the motions of a nurse I drew the sheet and blanket over her. Beneath her bottom cheeks a faintly sticky moisture. Throwing one arm over her eyes she mumbled something. Pieces of unfinished words.

'You were long in the summerhouse today,' I said. She answered not. The defensive movement of her forearm tightened over her face. 'We are bad,' I said. Her legs moved pettishly beneath the sheet and then lay still. An owl hooted, calling to witches.

'Bad,' Caroline husked. She was a child repeating a lesson. I bent and kissed her mouth. Her lips yielded and then I was gone.

The hours passed as white clouds pass. At three the next afternoon Mother departed. The gates lay open. The hansom cabs waited. The second carried her luggage piled high as if in retreat from days that were too long, too dry. In the hallway we were kissed, our bottoms fondled. There was affection. The cabmen waited. A smell of horses-manure and hay. A jingling of harness, clatter of wheels and she was gone. Gone to the oceans, the sea-cry and the vivid sun. The women would be bronzed, I thought. I would bronze my body—my nipples rouged, erect.

Caroline did not speak. Her pale fretting was evident. In the drawing room Sophie bobbed and called me M'am instead of Miss Beatrice. I was pleased. With Mother gone I now was mistress. We would take tea, I said, but no cakes.

'I want cakes,' Caroline said. Her look was sullen. I meant to punish her—perhaps for the summerhouse or for lying with her thighs apart on her bed. I knew not. We were like travellers whom the train has left behind. We drank unspeaking, our minds in clouds of yesterday. Sophie came and went, silent as on castors. Then the doorbell jangled. Its sound seemed to cross the halls, the rooms, and tinkle in the rockery beyond the windows.

Alice went, adjusting her cap but leaving her white apron askew. It was out aunt. Announced, she bowed benignly to us both. She was a woman of slightly ruddy countenance, neither tall nor short, strong in her ways. Her late husband had owned a small manufactory and numerous saddlers' shops that were scattered about the county. Sophie poured fresh tea. We spoke of Mother.

'Jenny has come?' I asked. My voice was an echo of my voice in the attic. My aunt nodded.

'She is settling,' she announced. 'Her training has been of use, I believe.'

'Was she not teaching?' I ventured the question. Her eyes passed over the fullness of my breasts and then upon Caroline's.

'You will come for dinner,' she declared.

It was not a question. I would have preferred it to be a question. Her hazel eyes were like Mother's. They sought, found and alighted. I felt their pressure upon my thighs.

'At eight,' I said. I knew exactly at what hour they dined. I rose. 'Aunt— if you will excuse me.'

Politely, as I thought, she rose in unison with me. Caroline's glances hunted and dropped. 'Let me accompany you,' she said. It was unexpected. I desired to say that I was going to my room, but I suspected that she guessed. The moment was uncanny. It was as if Mother had returned, wearing a different dress. I could scarce refuse. At the door to my room I hesitated, but there was a certain urging in her look. The door closed behind us.

'Beatrice, you will bring the whip,' my aunt said.

A bubble of no came to my lips, then sank again. That she knew of it seemed to me a treachery—bizarre, absurd. Her expression nevertheless was kind. Without seeking an invitation she advanced upon me and embraced me. I leaned against her awkwardly. She smelled familiar.

'I have to care for you, nurture you, Beatrice. There are reasons.'

I sought but could not find them. Delicately her fingertips moved down the small buttons at the back of my dress. My chin rested against her chest. With some absurdity I wondered what it looked like undressed.

'The whip—it has many thongs, has it not?'

She raised my chin. My eyes swam in her seeing. My lips parted. Pearls of white teeth.

'Lick your lips, Beatrice—you must learn to show them wet.'

Unknowing I obeyed: She smiled at the pink tip of my tongue. It peeped like a squirrel and was gone. I was in another's body, and yet it was my own. We moved. I felt our moving. Backwards, stiffly. My calves touched the rolled edge of my bed. Her right hand sought my bottom and slid beneath the bulge. She held me like Mother always had.

'Reach down and backwards for the whip. Beneath your pillow. Do not turn,' she said. Her fingers cupped my cheeks more fiercely. The blush rose within me. A tendon strained in my neck. Held about my waist by her other arm, I leaned back, I sought. My fingers floundered. She assisted me in my movements. The ebony handle came to my hand. It slipped. I gripped again. In a moment I held it by my side, still leaning back as I was told.

'It is good. You shall remain obedient, Beatrice, while in my care. I am doing this for your mother. Speak now, but do not move. I want you thus.'

'And Caroline?' I asked. Were the secrets about to be unlocked? There were cracks in the ceiling. Tributaries. I knew not what I spoke.

'It shall be. You must be trained. Upright now—come! Hard against me!'

I wilted, twisted, but to no avail. A hand forced into my back brought me up, slamming against her. She was so strong. My breasts ballooned. Her hand supported my bottom. Mother had not treated me this way. I had come to her arms and said nothing. In the attic we had whispered secrets, but they were small.

Then of a sudden she released me and I fell. Backwards upon my bed. Forlorn as a child. The whip dangled its thongs across my knees.

'At eight,' my aunt said. She was flush. I had seen my mother thus but had averted my eyes. I hung my head. There was a loneliness within me that cried for satisfaction. I said yes—hearing my voice say yes. My nipples stung their tips beneath my bodice.

My aunt departed, leaving gaps in the air. I rose and gazed down from the window as I had gazed with Mother. A woman in black carrying a parasol walked past holding the arm of a man. The cry of a rag-and-bone merchant came to my ears, long away, far away. In a distant cave. Below there were voices. Mumblings of sound. Why did Caroline always cry out? How foolish she was. I sat again, fondling the whip. In the attic I would have received it,

Beatrice

I knew. The horse would have rocked. My pumpkin raised, bursting through my drawers. I had shown Mother my nipples. We were bad.

In the moaning I would be alone, walking through the clear air.

My bottom had not tasted the whip. I turned before my dressing-table mirror and raised my skirts. Perhaps I would cease to wear drawers. Their frilled legs were pretty. Pink ribbons dangled their brevity against the milky skin of my thighs. Awkwardly I slashed the thongs across my cheeks. The sting was light.

I wanted to go to Jericho—to lower my drawers and let my pubis show. The curls were soft, springy and thick. The thongs would flick within my groove. I would clutch the horse's neck, the dappled grey, the shine of him, and cry. I would cry tears of wine. The dead bees upon the windowsill would stir. 'All shall be well with the best of all possible bottoms,' Mother had said to me once. We had laughed.

'Pangloss,' I declared. I knew my Voltaire. Pangloss and bottom gloss, Mother said. There was purity.

I repaired my disorders of dress and brushed my hair. I am never given to allowing servants to do it. In the drawing room Caroline sat as placidly as she would have me believe she always did. I deeded to challenge her. I went and sat beside her. She was surprised, I believe, at my composure.

'Did Auntie kiss you?' I asked. She shook her head. Her cheeks were bright red. 'Or feel your thighs?' I added. Her gasp sounded as I drew back her neck and kissed her. My hand sought her corsage. There was a loose butt.

Her nipples were stiff.

Loosing second and third buttons, my small hand squeezed within. The jellied mounds of her breasts were firm and full—only a trifle smaller than my own. Caroline struggled, but I am stronger than she. She endeavoured to raise her arms between us but the enclosure of my arm was too tight. Her lips made petal shapes of helplessness. Her breath was warm. My hand slipped down, cupping the luscious gourd. The ball of my thumb flicked the nipple.

'Between your thighs, Caroline,' I murmured. I did not say of what I spoke, nor of whom I spoke. Her head shook violently. Her eyes were lighthouses. Her expression became rigid with surprise. Her head fell back. I licked my tongue along her teeth and, laughed. I released her, leaping to my feet. 'How foolish we are!' I laughed. I funned and went before my disguise melted.

'Suck, Caroline.' Her voice would be deep and urgent, her head squeezed, ripplings of blonde hair through her forgers. Beneath her dress her breasts would lilt.

There was sin here, among the rubber plants, the rooms overcrowded with furniture, photographs of sepia in silver frames upon the piano. From the conservatory whence I fled I gazed upon the waving fronds of ferns. Mother's train would have reached the terminal. Her bags would be carried. The boat train at Liverpool Street would await her. Blinds would be drawn, expressions adjusted. The women would wear fine kid gloves, velvet-smooth to the touch on sensitive skin. Balls pendant. Veins.

'Suck, Caroline, suck.'

In my then I was alone in my aloneness. I returned to Caroline. She had not moved save to button her dress. The servant would enter soon with the oil lamps. Caroline stared down at the carpet and would not raise her eyes. I knew her moods. I sank to my knees and pressed my lips upon her thigh.

'Do not!' she said. Her voice was as distant as the far, the whistling of a train.

Kid gloves. The blinds drawn. Penis rampant. The knob of my whip. 'There is no sin. Is there sin?' I asked Caroline. Sin once had been giggling in Sunday School. Now there was desire between our thighs.

'I do not know,' Caroline said. Her voice fell like a small flake of metal. She was angry with me.

My desire became muted. I wanted to protect her. Soon, after we had bathed and changed for dinner, it would be almost eight o'clock. I looked up and she was staring at me. Perhaps she knew her fate as well as I.

* * *

Aunt Maude awaited us. She wore a black velvet choker. It suited her, I thought. Her dress swept back in a long train that was very modish. Her hair was piled high. Diamond earrings glittered.

My aunt was of a stature an inch taller than myself and full of form. Her breasts and bottom jutted aggressively. I took her for forty. Her eyes were kind but imperious. Though both were close to my mother, neither Caroline or I had spoken much with them through the years. Those of under age were always considered best unheard.

I spoke of Jenny. I was eager to see her. For a year we had shared a boarding school together.

'Later,' my aunt said. The dining room table was candlelit. My aunt preferred it to the smell of oil. Electricity had not then reached out from London and it was said that we were too far from the county town for gas pipes to be laid. Three years later magic would be wrought and they could come. My initiations—though I knew it not that evening—were to be by oil lamps in the old tradition. Frisky young ladies of Society were weaned on a bed with their drawers down, it was crudely said. Of cottage life and that in other dowdy dwellings, we knew nothing except, as we understood, that the males rutted freely.

Although married, and now separated, I still obtained innocence in many degrees, as shall be seen. At dinner my aunt spoke to us as if the past were still upon us. My aunt tutted severely when Caroline spilled a drop of wine. The servant was called of a purpose to mop it up.

'You will stay the night,' my aunt said after coffee had been taken. We sipped liqueurs and said nothing. Jenny had still not appeared. I wondered anxiously if she ate in her room. Had she been whipped? She had come to them in childhood. An orphan, it was said. One did not know. I sought for strength to object, to rise, to leave, but their eyes were heavy upon me.

At ten-thirty my aunt looked at the clock. 'Excuse me,' she said to Caroline, 'I must take her up,' she said. My palms moistened. I knew of whom she spoke, though she had not the delicacy to use my name. Caroline said nothing. Would she not save me?

The house was as ours except that the interior pattern was reversed. Perhaps that was symbolic. The stairs were on the left, as one entered the hall, instead of on the right. Entering as I had first done I had placed the whip somewhat furtively behind the large mahogany stand in the hall which carried occasional cloaks and walking sticks.

'Go to your room and I will follow,' my aunt said. I had been shown it briefly already. It lay as my own lay on the first floor. Left to right it was a mirror image. The curtains were brown, the drapes edged with ivory tassels. The air trembled. The furniture looked at me. I wanted the room to go away, the walls to dissolve, the air to take me high, free, floating in the blue dark of night. The carpet rolled beneath me like the sea. I moved, and moved towards the bed. Two pillows were piled high upon a bolster. Was my whip there?

I would not seek it. I refused. This was not my room. As by habit, I opened a small wall cabinet and found to my surprise that which I kept in my own—a bottle of liqueur and two small glasses. Pleasure traced itself across my lips anti then was gone. I turned, closing the cabinet. Auntie had entered. In her hand she held the whip. Moving she moved, towards me, she moved. She took my hand, the palm of mine shining with moisture.

'Beatrice, bend over—hands flat on the quilt.'

'Auntie—please!'

My mouth quivered. I did not want it to be my mouth. Her hand reached out caressing my neck and I gave a start. Her fingers moved, soothing.

'You will obey, Beatrice.'

The world was not mine. Whose was the world? Was Caroline in the dining room thinking of me?

'No one will come,' my aunt said. The door stood solid. We were on an island. In the attic Mother and I had stood on the top of the world. The whip moved. She passed the handle around and beneath the globe of my bottom, shaping, carving. I felt her breathe on my neck. I could not run.

'Auntie—please, no!'

I broke from her and stood trembling. The thongs swayed down to her knee like a fall of rain in slow motion. Her eyes were kind. Her arm reached out. She took my chin and raised it.

'There are things you need. There are locked rooms above. There are keys.'

I did not weal to blink in the meeting of our eyes. Go into the world clear-eyed and so return from it.

'Yes?' I asked. There was imperiousness in my voice. Dare I rebel? The whip slipped from her grasp and fell upon the patterned carpet. She would not whip me. She could not. I knew it. I felt happy. She waited further upon my speech, my quest, my questions.

'What is in the rooms?' I asked.

She took my hand. We walked. The stairs received us. Caroline had wandered perhaps into the dark garden—into the long grass which the garden-er chased by day. The grass would receive her. Her eyes would be loam, her nipples small blossoms. Her pubic hair would be moss. There was silence below in the house. Along the passageway of the second floor as we went my aunt rattled keys. A door opened.

The attic! They had made a replica of it! Except for the dormer win-dow—but it did not matter. The door closed—a heavy click—we were alone. My aunt's arm encircled my shoulder. I could not speak. Let me speak.

'The horse is the same. Only the horse, Beatrice.'

It was true. Trunks, boxes, broken pieces of furniture, old vases—all lay as they might have lain in our house.

Her hand stroked my back, warm through my gown.

'Go to the horse, Beatrice.'

I moved, walked, threading my way among the tumbled things—the love things, the loved things. The horse was large, bright, new. The stirrups gleamed, the saddle and the reins shone. The mottled, dappled grey was the same. I stroked the mane. On my own horse the mane was worn and thin where I had too often grasped it, but here it was new and thick. The leather smelled of new leather. Heady.

For a last moment I turned and looked towards the closed door. Caroline into the long grass gone. At breakfast she would return. Out of the caves of my dreams she would return, pure in her purity, the loam fallen from her eyes, her nipples budding, the moss of her pubis gold and curled.

I waited, humbled in my waiting. The sea moved beneath Mother. The timbers of the sailing ship would creak. The dark waters. Kid gloves soiled with sperm upon the waves. Salt to sperm. The licking lap of water.

Hands at my back. I did not stir. My aunt unbuttoned. The sides of my gown fell from my shoulders. The material dragged to my waist and heaped.

I stood still. Her hands savoured the outswell of my bottom, raising the skirt. My drawers were bared. A lusciousness of thighs. I fancy myself upon the silkiness of my skin.

'Mount,' my aunt said. I raised my leg. The skirt slip-slithered down again, enfolding my legs. As if tired my leg fell again. 'Remove your dress,' she breathed.

I wanted blindness but found none. The oil lamps, ranged around the room, flickered. Small messages of lambent light. My hair ruffled as I stripped off my gown. There was no one to brush it. My underskirt fell to my ankles. I stepped out of it as out of foam. The dark sea lapping. Silent in a cabin, my thighs apart.

Cupping my bottom as I toed the stirrup, my aunt assisted me in my rising. She knew not of Jericho. There were secrets still. The horse jolted, moving as if on springs rocking. The movement was smooth as velvet, soundless. I clung to the neck. My brazen bottom reared, my pumpkin warm.

'Ah!' I gasped at the first smack, and the next. There was a sweetness in the stinging I had known before. Because of my excitement perhaps. Was I excited? My hips squirmed to her palming smacks, my back dipped. I clung, I squeezed the cheeks, I squealed. Would Caroline hear? Under the deep lush grass would Caroline hear?

At the tenth smack—lifted down—foundered, falling, grasped in her strong grasp. Words tumbled, spun like pellets in a drum. Words polished in their spinnings. Hands clasped my bulging cheeks. I blushed, I hid my face. Her fingers drew the cheeks apart beneath my drawers. I strove to be still as Mother so oft had taught me. My heels teetered. Then I managed it.

'So,' my aunt said. She was satisfied. I closed my eyes, pretending myself in the attic. I was happy. The stinging in my bottom had made tears glint in my eyes. 'You are older now, Beatrice—it is better.'

I wanted wine. I wanted to go down to Caroline, to rescue her from the long grass. My aunt held me. My nipples peeped.

'Is it not better, Beatrice?'

Was I to answer? I knew not. I believe she expected it not. My silence pleased her. She sought confusion, girlishness there. My bottom cheeks weighed heavy on her palms.

'Raise your arms, Beatrice, and place them behind your head.'

It was a game—a new game. I obeyed. My left elbow nudged her soft cheek. Her breath was warm on my face. I was obedient. We had never done this in the attic. Once on Christmas Eve in the merriment of the night I had been carried up to my room, my drawers removed. Had I dreamed that? Tomorrow I would buy kid gloves, long and white to my elbows. The kid leather would be of the finest. Sensitive to flesh. A stem upstanding.

My aunt raised my chemise inch by inch. I was naked beneath. I quivered. My hips would not keep still. She raised it, raised it to the silky melons of my breasts. And then above. Dark nipples in their radiant circles.

'No!'

I jerked, twist-tumbled, gasped. I did not want to be obedient. The lacy hem of my chemise tickled my nipples in its rising.

'Auntie, no!'

I cried, I fell. There was carpet on the floor—purple with dull red patterns. In the attic there was no carpet. Dust rose to my nostrils. My chemise was crumpled over my polished gourds, my tits, my breasts.

My aunt fell beside me. Her hands pinned my shoulders. Gazing upon my gourds she gazed. She bent. Her delicate tongue licked my nipples. My back reared but she stilled it with a warning grip of hands.

'Shall you be whipped?' she asked.

Beatrice

My eyes were mirrors. They encompassed the world. I stared at her in my staring. My hair flowed upon the carpet. I must have looked a picture of extreme wantonness. There was wet on my nipples where she had licked. They strained in the rising. The floor moved gentle under me as waves beneath a tall ship sailing. In Madras the women would be bronzed, their hips supple.

'Lift your hips,' my aunt said.

My heels dug into the carpet. For a moment I lay mutinous. Then my knees bent, bottom lifted. I was arched. Her fingers sought the ties of my drawers, the pretty ribbons. Loosing they surrendered. Closing my eyes I felt my drawers being removed. The whorl of my navel showed. The impress of a baby's finger dipped in cream. Curls glinted at my pubis.

Then there was a sound.

The door had opened and a young woman stood there in a severe black costume. The toes of her black boots shone.

It was Jenny.

* * *

Jenny took me to my room. I carried my dress. The ribbons of my drawers had been tied again on my rising when she appeared. My aunt had risen and kissed her brow.

'We were playing games,' I said. I sat on the bed. I wondered how Jenny had arrived. Perhaps she had been here all the time hiding behind the wallpaper—a voice in the shrubbery. Owl calls. Night calls. She looked older, younger—both. The appearance of her costume was severe—high buttoned to her neck. Her face was Byzantine. By Giotto perhaps. Her long thick hair was swept back and tied with a piece of velvet.

'Games are nice,' Jenny said. She came and sat close to me, legs together, hands in her lap. I felt comforted. Had I betrayed myself upstairs? My aunt had followed us to the door, avuncular. Jenny was talking. There were words. I caught her words in the broad net of my mind.

'You must be kind to her, Beatrice. We must all be kind.'

'Have you just come?' I asked. My hands had not trembled. My voice was bright and clear. In the room with my aunt I had been speechless, mumbling. How foolish. The skin of my breasts beneath the low neck of my chemise was glossy, tight and full. Jenny looked at them. I saw her look. We used to undress together—when I stayed with her. When she stayed with me. But then I remembered something. Something I had never believed in.

One weekend when she had come to stay, six or seven years before, Mother had said to me, 'It is best if Jenny has the guest room tonight.' Jenny had looked strange, I thought—sitting, listening. She had nodded at me lightly as if she wanted me to say Yes.

I had heard sounds in the night, that night. It was midnight. I had looked at the clock—the small clock that says yes to me when I want it to be a certain time. There were sounds. Sounds like leather smacking. I thought I heard Jenny whimpering. The servants sometimes made noises in the night in their moving. But now the servants, too, would be abed.

A voice said, 'You are a good girl, Jenny.' It sounded like my mother's voice. My dreams were often strange. I sat up in bed. There were more leather sounds, little cries, a voice like Mother's voice. The sounds and the voices stirred and were mixed. I heard a woman-voice murmur: 'More— harder—a little harder. Ah, how sweet she looks.'

Oh, a little scream I heard, a screaming moan, then quiet. Sounds of breath like rushing waters. Bedsprings tinkled. Small bells of the night. Two men went past the house below—rough men, not from our neighbourhood. One shouted and I lost the sounds.

'I just came,' Jenny said now. 'There are clothes in your wardrobe. Have you looked?'

She drew me up. The mirrored doors, whose mirrors were tarnished, opened. From a shelf Jenny took black stockings of silk with a raised, ornate pattern that was run through with hints of silver. With it she produced a tiny waist corset of satin black. The small fringe of lace at the top that would fall beneath my breasts was silver, too. From the bottom of the wardrobe she drew out long high bests of the finest leather. The studs around which the laces wound were silver. The heels were slender, tall.

'Where is Caroline?' I asked.

Her eyes were glitter stones.

'You will look beautiful in these, Beatrice. Who?'

'Caroline.'

'Yes, I know. Remove your chemise, stockings and shoes. Put these on.'

She held them to me as a gift. I took them. The boots were light in weight. They would reach up to my thighs.

'It is late,' I said. I licked my lips. My aunt had wanted my lips wet. Jenny did not smile. She raised my chemise and drew it off my head. I shook my hair like a dog emerging from water. As carefully as if I were a nervous yearling she knelt and drew off my drawers, my shoes. Without my shoes my thighs looked plumper.

'Your pubis is full—a splendid mound,' she said. 'You are beautiful, Beatrice. Your hips have the violin curve that men adore.'

'I want to go home,' I said. I felt sullen. Caroline's face was my face. My lips brooded.

'You will be good,' Jenny said. She tickled me. She knew I hated being tickled. I squirmed, laughed, my breasts jiggled. I fell back on the bed, I rolled. She smacked my bottom. I yelped. The bright spreading of her fingers was upon it. It was a superb bottom, she said, the cleft as deep as a woman's heart. Her hands fell and pressed on it so that I could not rise. Her knee came into the small of my back.

'You will dress, Beatrice. You are not naughty, are you?'

'No,' I said. She had seen Auntie taking down my drawers. My pubis had been offered. On her entry into the room upstairs she had stopped and risen as if we had merely been conversing. 'What did you do in my mother's room?' I asked.

'What?' she asked sharply. She did not know my thoughts, my memories. Her palm tingled across my bottom again. 'Dress!' she commanded me, 'I like you in stockings best. You have the thighs for it—plumpish, sweet. Do not disobey. Get up!'

I obeyed her. The long boots were at first difficult to manage. They were tight. Their tops fell but three inches below the dark bands of the stocking tops. I would have difficulty in walking in them, I said. The corset nipped my waist. My hips blossomed. The corset framed my navel beneath an upward curve. My belly gleamed white.

'You will walk in them slowly and with stately tread—that is their purpose, Beatrice. Try.'

I moved from her. I walked. The high heels teetered. My legs were constrained. I felt the movements of my bottom, naked.

'Stand!' she commanded me. I stood, my back to her. She drew upon my wrists and brought them behind my back. A metal clink—a clink of steel. My wrists were bound. I wanted to cry and hide my face. Next she secured my ankles. Why?

'Lie down. Beatrice.'

Beatrice

I was bundled on to the bed, face down. 'I don't want to,' I said. I did not know what I meant. Jenny tut-tutted and arranged the tops of my stockings above the rimming leather. My toes were cramped in the boots. Jenny turned my face and bent and kissed my mouth. Full lips. Rose lips. She straightened and her eyes were solemn, full of night.

'You will stay so a little while,' she told me. She moved away. A chinking of metal as I tried to move.

'Please don't, Jenny.'

She was at the door. 'I always loved you, Beatrice,' she said.

'Please don't, Jenny.'

She did not hear. The door closed. I was alone with my aloneness. In the night. Where was Caroline? I listened as I listened when a child, on evenings when the curtains were drawn in my room against the evening light. I listened now, I heard. There were footsteps, soft voices. Voices heard, unheard. Was it the wind? I was half naked and bound, strange in my half-nudity and bonds. Jenny was naughty. She would come and release me and I would dress in my summer dress and we would picnic. Caroline would be tied to a tree. She would watch our small white teeth nibbling cakes. Lemonade would gurgle down our throats. The world would never come to an end.

Did Caroline remove her chemise in the attic?

I heard voices. Caroline's voice. She was laughing. Jenny was laughing. I knew I must not call out in my calling. They stopped outside my door and went on up. I imagined in my imaginings my aunt waiting for her in the attic room.

It was quiet again. The walls are thick. I dozed. Tight in my bonds I dozed. The door opened. Was it a dream? Through slits of eyelids I saw Jenny. She was dressed as I was dressed save that there was no silver in her stockings nor in her corset. She wore drawers of black satin, but they had no legs. Their lines swept up between her thighs.

Auntie entered behind her. The door was closed. From her ears dangled rubies in long gold pendants. Her mouth was carmine. In her hand the whip.

Aunt Maude sat now on the bed. I felt her weightiness. She rolled me onto my hip, my back to her. Her hand caressed my cheek and brushed my hair back where the strands were loose.

'Has she been good?' she asked.

Jenny stood as if she had been waiting to be asked. 'She has been good,' she said. I was pleased. They were going to release me. We would have our picnic. Jenny and I would hide in the shrubbery and Caroline would have to find us.

'It will take time,' my aunt said. Her complexion was as smooth as mine. Once when I was very young she was younger. She bent over me so that our mouths almost touched. Jenny stood still. I knew that Jenny was being good standing still.

'She was smacked,' Jenny said. I wanted to cry. I hated her. I glared at her and she smiled. My aunt continued to stroke my face and hair. Then she passed her long-tapered fingers down my neck and back. I shivered. I jerked towards her. Her eyes were kind.

'Twenty-five. She looks younger—she could be younger. Beatrice always had a fine bottom, did you not, Beatrice?'

My eyes said no-yes. Her fingertips floated my globe, my split peach, my pumpkin glory pale. The tip of her forefinger sought the groove. My lips quivered. Jenny did not look away. All hands should be hidden from people. My mother told me that. Hands can be wicked. My wrists were bound.

Beatrice

My aunt's finger tasted the inrolling of my bottom cheeks and wormed between them.

No—even my husband did not do that. Edward never did that. His stepmother was jealous of me. He bought her flowers. I remembered his cock. It was thin and long.

I made a noise—soft, small noise. The fingertip had touched my rose, my anus, my little bottom mouth that makes an O. My aunt smiled. She had turned my chin towards her. I bubbled little bubbling sounds. I jerked my bottom. My lips pursed in a long, soundless oooooh. The fingertip oozed in me and it moved. Back and forth, an inch of it, it moved.

My aunt took my nose pinched between her thumb and finger. I was like a fish. I had to part my lips to breathe. Rouge-scented, her mouth came to my mouth. Her tongue extended, licked within. I squirmed. Between my bottom cheeks her finger sank. In deeper sank. I was impaled. My breath hush-rushed. Her tongue worked. It worked its long wet work around my tongue. Her finger moved in-out, gently, like a train uncertain at a tunnel. Menace of dark and tightness.

Her finger felt itchy, strange. Then it came out. Her tongue came out. I tasted her rouge on my mouth with my rouge. I wanted to tell Jenny that but I hated her. My aunt gave my bottom a pat and stood up. She smoothed her skirt down.

'She should bathe,' my aunt said. 'Take her, Jenny.'

Jenny made me get up. Into the hallway I was led, along to the bathroom. As in those days it was huge—a fireplace within. The walls were draped with dark blue velvet all around. The bath was of white porcelain. Unshackled, my attire was removed. The water had already been brought in and emptied by the servants into the bath. It was lukewarm and pleasant.

'You know I love you,' Jenny said.

I sat down. The water lapped me with its tongues. I liked that. Jenny sponged me and poured scented water over me from a pitcher.

'Do you remember we learned wicked words at boarding school?' she asked. I wanted to ask things, but I did not. I nodded. Her eyes were bright and merry. Christmas tree decorations. 'What is cunt?' she asked.

'Con,' I said. I did not want her to think I did not know. I like the French word but not the English word. The English word is ugly. Its edges are sharp.

'And prick?' She held my head round so that I could look into her eyes. Her breasts were splashed with water. I wanted to nibble her nipples.

'Pine.' I knew I was right. I would never then say prick. Why are all wicked words sharp in English? Someone sharpened them. Anglo-Saxons with dirty beards and guttural voices sharpened them. My bottom squashed its cheeks into the water, plump. Is it too big?

'And sperm?' She would not stop. Jenny was often like that before, not ever stopping. She would tickle me in bed when we were younger and make me say things. In my imaginings I would say better things, naughtier things, but I never told her. Did she know? Was this punishment?

'*Foutre*,' I said. I knew she liked the word best. I liked the word best. It was like a ripe plum being chewed and then pieces coming out briefly on the lips before being swallowed. The word was thick bubbles around my tongue. Creamy bubbles.

'Have you not been whipped yet?'

It was Jenny asking me. At first I did not know that it was. I thought the voice came from the ceiling. I did not answer. I was mute. Her fingers moved over the outjutting of my breasts. My nipples had risen under the sponge. Jenny licked inside my ear. I giggled. It wasn't fair.

'I knew you hadn't been,' she said, 'get up.'

My feet slipped. She smacked me. 'Now stand still,' she said, just as Mother and Auntie said. She sponged my legs and made me open them. The sponge was squelchy and warm under my pussy. Did Jenny ever touch me there before? No, yes. In bed once, I think. That was summers ago. The ice cream has all been eaten since then, the plates put away.

'Move your hips. Rub them against the sponge, Beatrice. Did you often come over Edward's prick?'

'I hate you,' I said. There were tears in my eyes. She knew that I would not tell her. She became impatient with me.

'Oh, get out,' she said. She pulled me roughly from the bath and towelled me. She was brisk and quick as Mother used to be when I was young. Younger, young. Then she powdered me. Clouds of powdering me. The powder made me sneeze.

She led me back into my room. The house was silent. Had they all run away?

'I want champagne,' I said. I do not know why I said it. Bubbles. Jenny laughed.

'There should be rouge on your nipples,' she said. She had left the door open. From along the passageway came sounds, cries, whimpers.

'Please?' I asked. I felt as if I were speaking in a foreign language and that I only knew the beginnings of sentences. Then I recovered myself. 'I heard Caroline,' I said.

Jenny put a white linen nightdress over my head. It flowed to my feet. The hem was wide. 'You shall see,' she replied. She took my hand and led me along the corridor. The door to Caroline's room was half open.

Caroline was lying naked on her bed, face down. Her wrists and ankles were bound as mine had been. Aunt Maude was swishing a long slender cane lightly across her tight, pink cheeks. Caroline's face was flushed. At every contact of the cane she jerked her hips and whimpered.

'You will both sleep now,' Jenny said. She pushed me back into my room and closed the door. I heard the lock click. The tasselled curtains parted to my hands. I pressed my forehead to the cool glass and stared down into darkness. The baker's van had gone—the maid—the cat. Had the loaf been eaten?

My bed was soft and comfortable, the sheets scented with lavender. The oil lamps made shadows on the ceiling. I could not stir myself to extinguish them. A servant would come in the morning and attend to them.

Through the green-blue sea I floated. The dark shadow of a huge ship loomed above me. I reached and touched the planks and felt the barnacles. There was seaweed in my hair. Mother came floating towards me. My skirts billowed up to my hips in the deep, still waters.

No one could see.

* * *

The sun was warm when I awoke. The curtains had been drawn back—the lamps removed. Evidently I had slept heavily. Jenny roused me, smiling from the doorway where she stood. The gong below sounded for breakfast.

'You are late,' she said. She wore a long black skirt, the waist drawn in tight. Her blouse was white, the buttons of pearl. Beneath the silk of her blouse, her breasts loomed pinkly. A perking of nipples. They indented the material. Like a child late for school I was hustled into the bathroom and out again.

'I have no dress to wear,' I said. Jenny smacked my hand.

'You are late,' she repeated. The smell of sizzling bacon came to us. I was hungry. My mouth watered. The wardrobe doors were opened quickly. A thin wool dress of light brown colour, rust colour, was handed to me. 'Nothing beneath except your stockings,' Jenny said. She palmed my bottom and my breasts as I raised my nightdress. The sensation was pleasant. The dress cascaded over my shoulders and was worked tightly down over my curves. It was as if I were naked. I was preferred in boots today, Jenny said—black lace-up ones that came to my knees. The heels were high. I feared to fall down the stairs. I told her.

'Nonsense,' Jenny said. 'Brush your hair quickly. Show me your teeth. Are they clean now?'

I was taken down. Approaching the dining room we walked more slowly. My legs felt longer in the boots, the high heels. My aunt and Caroline were already seated. Silver tureens stood on the massive sideboard. Caroline looked up at me quickly and then attended to her bacon. We ate in silence as if some doom were pending. Neither my aunt nor Caroline spoke, even to one another. It was a penance perhaps. I ate voraciously but delicately. The bloom of health was upon me. The kidneys and mushrooms were delicious. The maids who served were young and pretty. I liked them. They avoided my eyes. They had learned their learning.

With every movement of Jenny's body her breasts moved their nipples beneath her blouse. Beneath the tablecloth my aunt's hand stole onto her thigh. It did not used to be like this, but I was beginning to understand what it had become. To be around such women. Jenny wore garters that ridged themselves slightly through her skirt. Auntie caressed them. Her palm soothed from one leg to the other. Jenny parted her legs beneath her skirt and smiled. I wanted to suck the tip of her tongue.

At a nod from my aunt we were dismissed. Caroline and I rose together and wandered into the drawing room. We were lost in our fondness. We held hands. Our fingers whispered together. In a moment, from a side entrance, my aunt appeared in the garden. A carriage had arrived, it seemed, but the visitors came not to the front of the house. They skirted the side and appeared where my aunt stood.

The woman whom she greeted was in her early thirties. I had a vagueness of seeing her before. Her flowered hat was large, of pale straw with a wide brim. She wore white kid gloves to her elbows. Were they my gloves? I had left mine in the sea at night. The fishes had nibbled at them. She was beautiful, elegant. Her dress was of white and blue, the collar frilled. Pearls glinted around the neck. Beside her came a servant neatly dressed in black with velour lapels to his jacket. She had an air of insolent subservience.

'She is beautiful,' I said to Caroline, 'do you know who she is?'

Jenny's voice sounded behind us. 'What are you doing?' she asked in a sharp tone. A tone that scratched.

'I was asking,' I answered.

Caroline moved. Her palm was moist in mine. 'I know her. She is Arabella Hayton—an actress. We have seen her at the Adelphi,' she said. Her eyes were saucers as she received Jenny's stare.

'You were not told to hold hands,' Jenny said. She jerked her head at me and said, 'Come. Beatrice, come.'

Forlorn, I relinquished Caroline's hand. Our own house was yet an ocean away. In the bedrooms women with bronzed skins and supple hips were lying. They would wear my clothes and steal my jewellery.

Jenny led me down the hall. To my astonishment we entered the linen room. It smelled of starch and nothing. 'You must learn—you must both learn, Beatrice. Do you not know?' Jenny asked me.

I blinked. I did not know who I was. Mother had lied perhaps. She had not gone to Madras. She was with the women in the rooms. They would French-drink. Their lips would taste of curry. There would be musk between their thighs. I said yes to Jenny. My voice said yes. My hands were at my sides.

'Kneel before me, Beatrice.'

I did. My head was bowed, my hands clasped together. I prayed for goodness. Edward's mother used to undress with her door half open. We could see her as we went past. Her bottom was big. I told Edward that she should close the door. He smiled. His eyes were small and neat. Like his pine when it was not stiff.

'Kiss my thighs,' Jenny said. She raised her skirt, gathering up the folds. I was blind. A milkiness, a perfume. Her drawers were split both back and front. It was the fashion then. Women could attend to their natural functions without removing them. In my mother's early days women had never worn drawers.

The curls of her slit, her love slot, honey pot, were framed by the white linen. My palms sought the backs of her thighs. Her knees bent slightly. I could feel her smile. My tongue licked out, sweeping around the taut tight tops of her black/stockings. Her skin—white like my white. She tasted of musk and perfume and the scents of flowers. My lips splurged against her thighs.

'Ah, you lick! Like a little doggy you lick,' Jenny laughed. After a moment or two she pushed me away with her knees. 'It is too soon,' she said. I wanted to cry but she would not let me. I was brought to my feet even as the door opened and Jenny rearranged her dress. My aunt led Caroline in and frowned a little at Jenny, as I thought. The window of the linen room was set high up at the other end from us. The light was morning soft. Caroline wore, as I did, a woollen dress of fine skein.

'You will see to them, Jenny,' my aunt said. From our distance I heard Arabella enter the house. There was a tinkling of glasses, laughter. The door closed, leaving the three of us alone.

'Remove your dresses,' Jenny said. My hands went to the buttons of mine, but Caroline hesitated. Jenny smacked her and she squealed. 'Quickly!' Jenny snapped. We stood naked except for our stockings and boots.

Jenny drew us together, face to face, thighs to thighs. From a drawer she took cords and bound us tightly together—ankles, thighs, waists. We could not move. Our cheeks pressed close. Placing her hands beneath Caroline's bottom she urged us slowly into a corner. I stood with my back to the meeting of the walls. Caroline's breach flowed over my breath.

'Your bodies merge well together,' Jenny said, 'are your breasts touching fully? Move your breasts. Your nipples must touch.'

Yes, I said, yes Jenny. Our nipples were like bell-pushes together. Mine grew and tingled. Caroline's grew. Her toes curled over mine.

'Please, don't,' Caroline whispered. I knew that she wasn't speaking to me but in her mind speaking. I moved my lips against her ear. Jenny had gone.

'You like it,' I said. I wanted to make her happy. I coaxed her. She had had the cane. Was it nice? 'Do you like it?' I asked. I made my voice sound as if we were going on a holiday. If she liked it we would be happy.

'I don't know,' Caroline said. Her voice was smudged. Our bellies were silky together. I could feel her slit warm, pulsing. It was nice standing still. I moved my mouth very slowly from her ear to her cheek. I felt her quiver. Had she kissed Auntie's slit? I would not ask yet. I would ask later. The tip of my tongue traced the fullness of her lower lip, the Cupid curve. Caroline moved her face away. Her cheeks homed. Our nipples were thorns, entangled.

'Do not!' she choked.

'Jenny will come,' I said. Caroline moved her mouth back to mine. The bulbous fullness of her breasts against mine excited me. Our mouths were soft in their seeking. I sought her tongue with my tongue. It retreated, curling in its cave curling. Sipping at her lips I brought it to emerge. The thrill made us quiver. Our nipples moved, implored. My belly pressed in tighter to hers. The door swung open of a sudden. It was Jenny. She scolded us and said we had been kissing. Working her hand between us she felt our love mouths, secretive between our thighs. They were moist. Her hand retracted. Her fingers sought our bottoms.

'You must practise—you love one another. Caroline—put your tongue in her mouth.'

We swayed. Caroline's tongue was small, urgent, pointed in its bickering. Hidden by our lips our tongues licked. It was a secret. I wanted.

'Open your mouths—let me see your tongues,' Jenny commanded. We obeyed.

'Half an hour,' Jenny said. She moved to the door and we were alone again. Birds sprinkled their songs among the leaves outside. I was happy. The richness of our bodies flesh to flesh was sweet. Caroline's eyelashes fluttered and tickled against mine. I could feel her belly rippling.

Our tongues like warm snakes worked together. Our thighs trembled. The ridged tops of our stockings rubbed.

Perhaps the door would remain closed forever.

Our minds whispered together like people in caves.

* * *

We would go to meadows, my aunt said. She saw my look of incomprehension. We had been released exactly upon the half hour. Dressed again we sat in the garden and drank champagne and lemonade. It was a reward, Jenny said, because we had not cried or protested when she untied us and made us dress again.

'Meadows—it is a country house I have recently bought,' Aunt Maude explained.

'We may go indoors first?' I asked. I was referring to our own house. My aunt nodded as if surprised at the question.

'Do not tarry—we leave at noon,' she told us.

Jenny accompanied us into our house. She was pleased and curious, I believe, to see it again. When I began to assemble clothes she stopped me. 'Not that many, Beatrice. Simple dresses only. Be sure to include your riding attire.'

I took but one trunk, as did Caroline. A sense of curious excitement seized me. The years rolled back. We were children again preparing for a holiday. We would paddle in the sea or descend from bathing huts whose steps led down into the water and were drawn there by ponies. Ladies were not permitted to expose themselves on the beach, though men could bathe naked so long as they were a far distance from the females.

Unseen by Jenny I took a bottle of liqueur and secreted it. I whispered to Caroline to do the same. She shook her head. Munching a biscuit we waited upon Jenny to conclude her discreet inspection of the house. When she came down she was wearing an ornate hat that Mother had left behind.

'May I have this?' Jenny asked. I do not know why she asked. Perhaps it was to test me. I said no. Not put out, she handed it to the maid and asked her to return it upstairs. 'We shall have fun,' she said and led us out.

In the roadway stood a large six-seater carriage of a kind not too often seen outside of London or the larger market towns. We ensconced ourselves. The manservant who had accompanied Arabella placed our trunks on top, protected by a guard rail. Our aunt joined us, then Arabella. She had changed into a riding outfit with a three-cornered hat—a small one that perched attractively on her hair. She smiled at us with the distant smile of a stranger. The coach, led by four horses, started with a long cracking of a whip. The manservant whose name was Frederick sat up beside the coachman. It was a long and sultry run. I think he enjoyed it little. Arabella toyed with her crop frequently and once or twice teased it playfully about my aunt's thighs. It was a pleasant enough drive, the countryside rolling about us once we had passed through the town. Arabella and Aunt Maude conversed of plays we had not ourselves seen. There was talk of a private theatre at which the actress had evidently appeared.

'We must contrive one,' Arabella said, 'in the barn perhaps.'

'The attic would be splendid, surely,' my aunt replied. 'It is extremely large,' she explained to Arabella. Then she gazed at us as if we were about to speak. I busied myself with counting trees. Auntie had shown she knew what attics meant to me. Mother must have told her a long time ago. Or perhaps she had peered with a telescope from her own to ours. I must tell Mother. I would write coded messages, use French words, invisible ink. There would be spies.

Twice on our journey we stopped at inns and took refreshments. 'A yard of ale!' my aunt called jovially, as if herself a gentleman, on entering both, though she had no intention of drinking one. People regarded us curiously. We were strangers. At the second resting place we ate meat pies with thick forks that looked not too clean. Jenny sat with my sister and I ate at a separate table.

'Keep the children quiet, Jenny,' my aunt said. We drank ale from pewter mugs. I was constrained. I wanted to sit outside the inn and watch the farm workers pass, wearing their rough smocks. Through the thick panes of leaded glass that was ringed with circles I could see their small images. Mother on the water floating. My dress billowing. Fish nibbled at my garters while we embraced. It was said that Nero had boy slaves who swam under water while he was bathing and attended to his penis in the same way. I had read that in a book whose binding was broken. The leathered boards of the book had flopped as Edward's penis had flopped against my thigh.

Jenny took us out while Auntie settled the bill. A woman bearing a basket and leading a small child passed along the roadway. The child stared and pointed at us.

'Shush! They are from the town,' the woman said. She endeavoured to curtsey as she walked. The child wailed and was dragged on. Like the woman its feet were bare.

We journeyed on. The coachman and Frederick had eaten at a table outside. I could hear the coachman belching frequently above the rumbling of the wheels. The coach jolted exceedingly. I dozed. The talking of my aunt and Arabella was like a murmuring of bees. Jenny had not spoken to them nor been addressed except briefly at the inn.

At last I sat upright as the coach made a sudden turn, the coachman hollering at the horses. There were hedges, stone walls, a rougher road. The coach swayed, throwing us about, as it descended a long slope. Then the house appeared. There were outbuildings. The house was long and made of grey stone. We passed beneath an archway and were in the courtyard.

'Neither of you are to speak,' Jenny said. We waited while the others descended and then she bustled us out. A woman wearing a black dress and the cap of a housekeeper stood waiting on the steps. A youth ran past and began to assist the coachman and Frederick in removing the trunks.

'To your rooms,' Jenny told us when we entered the hall which was circular.

'May we not see the house—the gardens?' I asked. Jenny stared at me. There was a battle of eyes. 'Later,' she declared. I sought a softness in her tone and found but a wisp of it. The staircase was circular and broad. The stonework on the surrounding walls provided ledges for the windows. I wanted a white dove to sit in one. Its pink eyes would gaze at me as I passed.

I would throw crumbs. It would peck busily. I would wear a white dress with a pink sash.

The sails of Mother's ship billowed in the wind. With whom was she talking? Feet trod the boards upon the deck. Men peered at horizons. Beyond them the bronzed women waved and waited.

Our rooms lay together, side by side. We would undress to our stockings and rest, Jenny said. There were pitchers of cool water to drink. We waited while Caroline disrobed and lay down.

'Lie flat on your back and keep your legs apart,' Jenny told her. She obeyed. Her blue eyes blinked. Her arms lay at her sides. The soft fern around her pussy lips betrayed its gold, its gleaming pink. Closing the door upon her, Jenny turned and kissed me, mouth to mouth. I knew her desire. Our tongues touched. A melting.

'Do you love her?' Jenny asked. I had no need to answer. 'We shall have her together,' she said. 'Do not throw your clothes upon the floor. Be tidy.'

I blushed at her silly words. I yearned to be her accomplice, to write messages on trees. She would follow and read them. I would ride on a white horse with my hair flowing. An archer would run beside me.

The room was stark—the stonework not plastered within as I had expected. A large bed stood in the centre of the floor. The foot of it faced the door. The headboard was mirrored with three ovals of glass set in gilt frames. On either side of the bed a cabinet. There was a single wardrobe, heavy in aspect. Its doors were mirrored as was the headboard. A thick pile carpet was the only comfort:

I removed my bonnet and dress slowly, then my chemise and drawers. I was to keep my knee-length boots on, Jenny said, and to keep my stockings straight and taut at all times. My lips must always be slightly parted.

'Why are we here?' I asked. I lay down as Caroline had lain, arms straight at my sides. Jenny nudged my ankles to make my legs part wider. The moisture of the long journey was around and within my Gunny. Jenny moved to the end of the bed and gazed at me.

'Erect your nipples,' she said. I licked my lips and passed my palms lightly over my breasts, flicking the tips until they rose. The cones pointed from their surrounding circles of crinkled flesh.

'You are to be trained,' she told me. 'No harm will come to you if you obey.' She moved along the bed to the cabinet on my left. A long leaded-glass window with a deep stone sill was also on my left. A vase stood upon it with a single withered flower. Dipping the tips of her fingers into the pitcher of water she sprinkled it upon my breasts. The sudden cold made me start. My nipples quivered and stiffened harder.

What is the purpose of our training, I asked, but the question stayed in my head like a wasp in a jam jar. It buzzed and spun. Jenny turned and gazed down through the window at the meadows beyond.

'Did you want to kiss Arabella?' she asked. 'Answer quickly!'

I did not look at her. I knew I must not. I said yes. Questions poured over me. I said yes. I said yes I would like to see her breasts, to kiss her thighs, to tongue her slit. I hated Jenny. She knew it was true.

She had turned away again. She seemed no longer amused by my meanderings. 'There will be a reception this evening, Beatrice. I shall instruct you in what to wear. A servant will come for you in an hour. Obey her.'

She was gone. A key turned in the lock. I made to rise. Were there cracks in the stone? Watchers? Seekers? My aunt might come. I closed my eyes and walked down corridors of thought. Would Mother return?

Mother's footsteps had sounded down the drive when she left, certain, uncertain. A crack of a whip and the coach was gone. Dust rose in the roadway upon its departure. I thought to catch the dust in a jar and watch it swirl forever. It would not do that, Caroline said, when I told her. In the evening I chased a butterfly towards the sun.

I had dozed. A servant was shaking my shoulder. She was the house-keeper I had seen on the steps. I sought my dress, my chemise, my drawers, but they had gone. She tossed a grey cloak down around my feet.

'Come!' She did not call me M'am. I cast the cloak about me. We went up to the floor above and along narrow passageways to a second, smaller staircase. At the foot of it Caroline waited. She was garbed in a cloak as I was. Beneath she wore only her stockings and boots.

'Go!' the woman said. A side door with an iron latch was opened for us by a young servant girl who curtsied. We passed outside onto the stone flags through which grass and weeds sprouted. There were smells of chickens, pigs and hay 'Go forward to the stable,' the woman said and pointed. My shoulders nudged Caroline's. The knuckles of our hands touched beneath our cloaks. Our feet stumbled over rough grass. The doors of the stable loomed. large, yawned open. We were within.

Open shutters allowed rays of sunlight to enter the stable. We passed through the bars of the light to the further wall. There were iron rings, chains. We were made to stand side by side while the woman removed our cloaks. Our arms were raised, spread apart, our wrists secured to rings. The tip of my nose almost touched the timbered wall, as did Caroline's.

Our legs were parted roughly a full three feet so that our stockinged and booted legs were strained. Metallic clicks. Our ankles were secured. Our breathing was tremulous. We dared not to look at one another. The bales of hay about us dreamed of past summers.

There were voices beyond. I felt the woman's return. My head was drawn back. A leather gag was inserted between my lips and tied behind in the nesting of my hair. Caroline's lips would not open to the gag. She received a loud smack. Her yelp gurgled away behind the leather.

'Wash them down,' a voice said. Pieces of rough cloth were bound tightly around the tops of our thighs to prevent water trickling down our stockings. There came water, wetness, cold. I jerked. My spine curved. The sponging was insistent. It passed beneath my bottom, cooled my slit. Fingers quested at my love lips as they urged the sponge. I was forced to strain up on tip-toes. The sponge passed beneath my armpits, in the curls there. It roamed over the hillocks of my breasts. Water tickled me, trickling down my belly. There was laughter as I squirmed. I did not know the voices.

Caroline was attended to next. The sponge trailed longer beneath her quim, I thought. Was I jealous? Her love mouth pouted no more tightly than my own. A rough towel dried us. Our nipples perked against the wall. The iron rings, the manacles, the bonds about our ankles, clinked.

'Six,' a voice said. I sensed a movement new—a soft, insinuating sound as of leather passing across a palm.

Cra-aaaack! Broad width of leather seared across my bottom. Ah! I jerked. My belly to the wall I jerked. Cheeks wobbling, tightening, I received another. The sting was sweet, laid full across my buttocks.

A humming whine behind the gag. My own or Caroline's? Mother—no! Mother would not permit this. Surely her ship would turn, its tall sails straining. Commands. Feet urgent on the deck. My eyes screwed up. The heat flared in my bottom at the next.

'Harder!' I had heard my mother say when Jenny stayed that night.

'Neeynnnng!' Cries strangled in my throat. Flame-searing, the strap took me again. Again. Again. The trees could not see me. The grass did not care. Tears pearled down my cheeks. In my rudeness I squeezed my scorched cheeks tighter.

'Ah, the fullness of her—the thighs, the cheeks. What delicious plumpness,' a voice said. Was it Arabella? I heard the cries, unheard, of Caroline. The strap attended to her next. 'Let me feel the heat,' a voice said. It was the same cultured woman's voice. Palms palmed my wriggling bottom with womanly tenderness. They felt its fullness, the throbbing. Caroline's hip bumped against mine in her squirming. The loud slap-crack of the leather sounded. Fingertips sank insistent in my burning bulge. Cupped, held, I sank my weight upon the palms. My big plum, my pumpkin.

The last crack of the leather.

'Let me feel her,' a voice said. Another came whose perfume was as Arabella's. Behind us they stood side by side, controlled our squirmings with their seeking hands. I heard kisses. I could feel tongues. An urgent jerk from Caroline nudged me hard. A small laugh, husky, intimate.

'Not now—not yet,' the woman behind me said. Her fingers unclasped as if reluctantly from beneath my bottom. 'Is she wet? Tell me,' she said, 'Ah, give me your tongue!' She had spoken of Caroline. She was wicked. I could not restrain the working of my hips. Long tongues of flame licked through my buttocks still. Baby fingers of warmth moved in my groove. My love-slot pulsed gently. My nipples stiff.

'Leave them—they have been well attended to. What sweet young mares. They can be watered now.'

The voice was her voice. I knew her as Arabella now. Our gags were loos-ened. A tin mug passed between the wall and my mouth and tilted just suffi-ciently to let water trickle between my lips. I did not want it. I wanted wine. Had the servant unpacked my trunk? She would find my flask of liqueur.

The water had slopped down over Caroline's chin in her blubbering. I could feel it. Globules of water fell and decorated her nipples. Then the doors closed, the big doors in their closing. We were left alone.

I wanted to speak but I knew not what to say. Caroline hung her head. Her forehead rested against the wall.

'I love you,' I said. The fleshiness of our hips touched. She would not answer me. She made silly, babyish sounds. With my legs wide apart I closed my eyes again and dreamed of the stemming of phalluses, held by women, behind me—the nubbing thrust between my open lips. When my bottom was thrust over the end of the rocking horse, the taut cotton had outlined the lips of my honey pot beneath. I had rubbed against the haunches—felt their pleasure.

'It hurts,' Caroline whined. I shushed her. We must not be heard. 'Squeeze your cheeks,' I said. I wanted to touch her bottom, its polished roundness. There were footsteps—a slurring of feet upon the ground, the wisps of hay.

'What have you been doing?' Jenny asked. 'Have you been wicked?' She released us. Caroline covered her face. She was ignored. 'Put your clothes on—you cannot be seen like that. There are workmen about—rough men,' Jenny said.

We donned our cloaks. The tops of my stockings were damp. It was a feeling I liked. The stinging moved in my bottom still, but it was sweeter now. It made me walk differently. My hips swayed more.

'That is good,' Jenny said. She could see. She walked behind us. The doors were open again, huge in their hugeness. Two men with pitchforks stood beyond. They touched their caps at our passing. We did not look at them. Their voices were country voices. They breathed of warm milk in stone jars, left overlong on windowsills. Stale cheese—dried scraps of bread. They were rough men. My bottom moved—a silky bulb of heat beneath my cloak.

Beatrice

* * *

There were crumbs around my mouth. I wiped my lips delicately with my napkin and yawned. After the meal which the servant had brought to my room, I had sipped my liqueur. It had not been taken. The servant who brought the tray was the young girl who had curtsied to us when we had been taken to the stable that morning. Her name was Mary. She was unlearned but pretty. It pleased her to wait upon me. The flush of pleasure lay on her cheeks.

She appeared not surprised to find me naked except for my stockings and boots. On her coming back for the plates, the wine bottle and the glasses, I took her wrist and sat up. I swung my legs over the bed.

'M'am?' she asked. The housekeeper had not called me M'am. I sensed ranks, classes within classes, initiations. I drew Mary down beside me. 'I dare not stay,' she said, 'they will punish me.'

'With the strap?' I asked.

She gazed at the floor. Her feet were shod in neat black boots. Small feet. I would lick her toes perhaps. No. Crumbs of dirt between them. My nose wrinkled with distaste. My hand slid from her wrist and covered her hand. She trembled visibly. Her rosebud mouth was sweet. Such gestures are fatal. They have meaning—like commas, dashes, question marks. I have walked between words. I know the dangers of the spaces between them.

I passed my hand up the nape of her neck and felt her hair. It had not the silkiness of mine, but it was clean. I turned her face, moving my lips over hers. She started like a fawn. I held her. There was a taste of fresh bread in her mouth.

'Tell me,' I said.

'There are no answers,' a voice said. It was Jenny. She had entered qui-

280

etly. I neither moved nor sprang up as perhaps she wanted me to. Instead I pressed my mouth again upon the girl's. She trembled in her freshness, a salty dew between her thighs. I felt intimations of boldness. Jenny's hand fell upon my shoulder.

She drew Mary up from my embrace. The girl turned and went, leaving the plates. I made to rise when Jenny fell upon me, spreading my legs by forcing hers between them. The hairs of her pubis were springy to mine through her thin cotton dress. It was a new dress. Small mauve flowers on a blue background. I wanted it.

'There is a wildness in you,' Jenny said. Her tongue licked suddenly into my mouth and then withdrew.

'Let me kiss your thighs,' I begged. She laughed and rose, pushing herself up on her forearms slowly so that her breasts bobbed their juicy gourds over mine.

Bereft I lay. Would she seek my tears—kiss the salty droplets? At Christmas Eve I had been carried upstairs with my drawers down. The sea-cry, the wind-cry. Jenny turned to the window and looked down. The darkness now beyond—the mouth of night.

'The stations are all closed—the people have gone. The ships have sailed,' she said. I began to cry. She turned and shook me roughly. 'The reception will begin soon, Beatrice—get dressed. Stand up!'

Words stuttered in my mouth but knew no seeking beyond. I wanted my nipples to be burnished by her lips. Instead I obeyed quietly as she told me to remove my boots and stockings. In place of the stockings I was to wear tights such as dancers do on the stage. They were flesh-coloured. The burr of my pubic curls showed through. They bulged. A top of the same material was passed over my shoulders. It hugged my waist and hips, fitting so tightly that my nipples protruded into the fine net.

'Longer boots,' Jenny said. She pointed to the wardrobe. I padded to it. They had been made ready for me, polished. Sleek-fitting, I drew them on. The heels were narrow and spiked. 'Brush your hair—make yourself presentable,' Jenny said, 'I shall return for you in a minute.'

I had not then seen the house except for the back stairs and the entrance hall. There was buzzing of voices as I was made to descend with Carolina—she dressed as I. The grooves between our buttock cheeks showed through the mesh. A piano played. It stopped when we entered. People in formal evening dressed gazed at us and then turned away. Gilt mirrors ranged the walls with paintings between them—one by one around the room. Mary and another girl moved among the visitors with champagne. On sideboards there were canapés in numerous colours. They looked as pretty as flowers on their silver trays.

The piano played again. Mozart, I thought. Men looked at my breasts and buttocks. Their eyes fanned Caroline's curves. The high heels made us walked awkwardly, stiffly. The cheeks of our bottoms rolled.

To the one blank wall farthest from the doors Jenny led us, a hand on each of our elbows. There were clamps, chains, bands of leather.

Caroline first. Her legs were splayed, her ankles fastened. Her arms above her head.

'Hang your head back—let your bottom protrude!' Jenny snapped at her. I wanted to be blindfolded. I knew it was good to be so. Black velvet bands swathed our eyes. In darkness we stood, our shoulders touching warm. The manacles were tight.

I had seen my aunt. She watched upon our obedience. I heard her voice. There was silence in the room. The last chords of the piano tinkled and were gone. A wink of fishes' tails and gone.

Caroline first. I heard the intake of her breath as Auntie passed her hands up the backs of her thighs and squeezed her bottom cheeks. 'My doves,' she breathed. She placed a broad, warm palm on each of our bottoms. People clapped. The room stirred again, came alive.

We were left. Knuckles slyly nudged our bottoms from time to time. Were we forbidden? Female fingers touched more delicately than the men's. With the protrusion of our bottoms and the splaying of our legs, our slits were at pillage. Mine wound into the mesh of the tights as slender fingers quested and sought the lips. And found. I tried not to wriggle my hips.

Champagne was passed between our lips from goblets unseen. I absorbed mine greedily. I could hear Caroline's tongue lapping. There was dancing. I heard the feet. The plaintive cry of an oboe accompanying the piano. If it were a girl playing I would know her by her slimness, her tight small mouth that only an oboe reed would enter. Her face would be oval and pale, her breasts light and springy. She would speak little. Her words would be dried corn, her days spent in quiet rooms. At the high notes I envisaged her on a bed in a white cell. She would not struggle. Her stockings would be white, her thighs slender.

Laid on her back, she would breathe slowly, quietly, fitfully through her nose. Her dress would be raised. Knees would kneel on the bed between her legs. Her knees would falter, stir and bend. Her bottom would be small and tight. Hands would cup and lift. She would wear white gloves of kid. I had almost forgotten the gloves. They would be decorated with small pearl buttons spaced half an inch apart.

No words. Her mouth would be dry. A small dry mouth. Her Gunny would be dry. A small dry Gunny. A tongue would moisten it—her fingers would clench. She would close her eyes. Her eyelashes would have the colour of straw.

Her knees would be held. The knob-glow of an ivory phallus three times the girth of her oboe would probe her slit. A small cry. A quavering. In her dryness. Entering, deep-entering it would enter. Lodged. Held full within. The tightness there. In rhythmic movement it would move, the lips expanding around the stem.

Silently she would work the white shaft. Her buttocks would twitch and tighten. A crow would alight at the window. Pecking at stone it would be gone.

There were no words to speak for her. In the white cell of her room a rag doll would smile and loll against the wall. Through her nostrils now her breath would hiss. Music scores would dance through her mind. The oboe of flesh would play in her.

'Pmniff!' Her breath explodes, mouth opens. She ravages her mouth, she struggles, squirms. Faint velvet squelch between their loins. Her cunt lips grip the dildo like a clam. Her tormentor clamps her bottom, draws the cheeks apart. Mutinous still, her tongue retreats, unseeking to her seeking.

Her face is pallid. She is finally spent. Her dress is straightened. A vague fussing of hair. Quiet as a wraith she descends.

'You will have tea now, dear? You have had your lesson?' she is asked. She nods. Her knees tremble, a warm trickling between her thighs. The oboe, yes, the tall ship sailing.

I emerged from my dreams. We were loosed and turned about, our bonds replaced. My bottom to the wall, I waited.

* * *

There was quiet again. The music ceased again. I had not liked it. Its feebleness irritated.

The Lady Catherine was announced. I turned my head, though I could not see.

'Let her enter and be brought here,' I heard my aunt say. There was a sound as if of a heavy table moving. Jenny's hands moved about my face. I knew the scent and taste of them. Her fingertip bobbled over my lower lip. The blindfold slipped down an inch beneath my eyes.

'Look,' Jenny said. I saw the woman enter. Her coiffure was exquisite. A diamond choker, a swan neck. Her curves were elegant beneath a swathing white gown of satin flecked with red. The collar of her gown was raised slightly at the back, as one sees it in portraits of the Elizabethans. She wore a look of coldness and distance. Her lips were full, her nose long and straight. Her eyelids were shadowed in imitation of the early Egyptians.

She made to step back as my aunt reached her. Her fingers were a glitter bed of jewels. Behind her entered a man of military look, impeccable in a black jacket and white trousers, as was the evening fashion then. I judged the years between them. She was the younger.

'Not here. It is unseemly,' she said.

Jenny covered my eyes. Did she then uncover Caroline's? I heard not a sound beside me.

'No,' the woman said in answer to some muttered remark. There was movement past me. I felt it. As the air moves I felt. Hands touched my thighs, caressed. A finger traced the lips of my quim which pressed its outlines through the fine mesh of the tights. It was removed quickly, as if by another. I heard the jangling of bracelets.

'Not here,' the woman said again. I felt her as if surrounded, jostled. They would not dare to jostle, but they had touched me. Was I an exhibit?

'B-Beatrice…' A croaking whisper from my sister. I ignored her. I heard her squeal. She always squeals. She was being fingered. Her bonds jangled. The girl with the oboe would be tight. The sperm would squirt in her thinly. Would she feel it?

Jenny favoured me. Once more my blindfold slipped. The chandeliers danced their crystal diamonds. The Lady Catherine was moving forward. As if through water she moved. An older woman moved beside her, a hand cupping her elbow. The older woman wore a purple dress. Her vulgarity was obvious.

'Catherine, my sweet, you will come to dinner tomorrow night? The Sandhursts are coming.' Her voice cooed.

'I do not know. Perhaps, yes. I must look in my diary, of course.'

Catherine's look was constrained, her lips set. Behind her, as I felt, the woman who had escorted her in was feeling her bottom. It was of an ample size, though not too large by comparison with her stately curves. Her face turned to her escort as if pleading. She shook her head. I saw the table then. It had indeed been pushed forward. Upon its nearest edge was a large velvet cushion. Her long legs appeared to stiffen as she approached it. Her footsteps dragged. Her shoes were silver as I saw from the occasional peeping of her toes beneath the hem of her gown.

Jenny covered my eyes again. I had not looked at Caroline. Her veins throbbed in mine. Her lips were my lips. We had been bound together naked. I had sipped her saliva.

There were murmurings, whispers, protestations, retreats. The doors to the morning room opened and closed, re-opened and closed again.

'It is private,' I heard my aunt say to others. The room was stiller. I heard a cry as from Catherine.

'Lift her gown fully,' a voice said, 'hold her arms.'

'Not here…' She seemed unable to say anything else. Not here, not here, not here, not here. A rustling sound. Slight creak of wood. A gasp. Plaintive.

'Remove her drawers-.'

'She was unseemly?' It was my aunt's voice. To whom she spoke I knew not. I guessed it to be the escort. Her voice was dry and thin.

'Improper,' she replied. The word fell like the closing of a book. 'Take them right off. Do not let her kick,' she said.

'No! Not the birch!' A wail from Catherine. Would she have her bound, my aunt asked. It was not necessary, she said, but her wrists should be held.

I envisaged her bent over the table, the globe of her bottom gleaming. Her garters would be of white satin, flecked with red. The deep of her groove—the inrolling. Her breathing came to me, filtering its small waiting sobs. The dry rustling sound of a birch. I had never yet tasted the twigs. It was said that they should be softened first.

'Not bound,' my aunt said. Her voice sounded almost regretful. 'Hilda—you will hold her wrists tight. Stretch her arms out.'

'Noooooo!'

The long, sweet aristocratic cry came as the first swishing came. It sounded not as violently as I thought. I wanted to see. My mind groped, grappled for Jenny. Perhaps she had been sent with others to the morning room. Beside me Caroline uttered a small whimper. Did she fear the birch? She would not receive it. I would protect her. I ran through tunnels calling Mother's name. Edward had used his stepmother's first name. She had permitted it. He had lain upon her.

'Na! Naaaaah!' A further cry. Her sobbing rose like violins. A creaking of table. Beneath her raised gown, her underskirt, her chemise, the velvet cushion would press beneath her belly. There was comfort. I comforted myself with the comfort.

The sounds went on. The birch swished gently but firmly as it seemed to me. First across one cheek then the other, no doubt. The bouncy hemispheres would redden and squirm. Streaks of heat. Was it like the strap? I did not like the stable. Did I like it?

'Ask her now,' her escort's voice came. There was whispering—a quavering cry. A negation. Refusal. 'Three more,' she said, 'her drawers were down when I caught them together.'

My aunt tutted. The small dots of her tutting impinged across the sobs, the swishings. They flew like small birds across the room.

'Whaaah! No-ooooh! Wha-aaaaah!' Catherine sobbed. I felt her sobs in my throat, globules of anguish swelling. They contracted, slithered down. There was quiet. Her tears would shine upon the polished wood of the table.

'Ask her again.' The same voice, impassive, quiet. The sobs were unending.

'Have you before?' my aunt asked. It was her garden voice, clear and enquiring. The lilt of a question mark that could not fail to invite.

'Twice—but she resists. What does she say?' She asked as if to another.

'I cannot hear. Catherine, you must speak, my dear, or take the birch again.' It was undoubtedly the voice of the woman holding her wrists. Who held the birch?

'I c... c... do it to me!'

I saw nods. Through my blindfold I saw nods. I envisaged. There was a shuffling. Wrists tighter held. A jerk of hips. The arrogant bottom outthrust, burning.

'No! Not there! Ah! It is too big! Not there!'

The floor drummed in my dreams. The dildo extended, flesh like but harder, cooler, entering. The chandeliers glittering with their hundred candles. I could see no more who was holding the dildo than who had been holding the birch. Was it the same tormentor or yet another?

Her sobs died, died with their heaving groans. 'N... n... n... ' she stuttered from moment to moment. At every inward thrust the table creaked. Was she still being held? I needed voices, descriptions.

'Work your bottom, Catherine! Thrust to it!'

My aunt spoke. Their breathings flooded the room. I cannot. No—yes— oh do not. Do not gulping gasp. A last sob. Silence. 'Have her dress,' my aunt said at last. 'Hilda—see to her hair, bathe her face, she has been good. Have you not been good, Catherine?' A mumbling. Kissing. 'So good,' my aunt said. Bodies moved, moved past us and were gone. Was the dildo gone as well, or did it remain?

The doors to the morning room were re-opened. A flooding of people, a flurry, voices. Enquiries. My aunt would not answer.

My limbs ached, yet I was proud in my aching that I had not struggled. I was free in my pride. We could speak but we had not spoken. Our minds whispered. We were wicked.

A chink of light. Our blindfolds were removed. Caroline blinked more than I. She had not seen before. People stared at us more strangely now. They were of all ages. Eyes glowed at the bobbing of our breasts.

'You must go to bed. A servant will bring you supper,' Jenny said.

I moved carefully, cautiously—wanting to be touched, not wanting to be touched. My hips swayed. I thought of Catherine.

As we reached the bottom of the stairs she began to descend. We waited. I wanted to be masked. Accompanying her was the older woman in purple. I knew then that it was she who had held her wrists. Their eyes passed across us unseeing.

'And there will be a garden party—for the church, you know,' the woman in purple said.

Catherine's eyes were clear, her voice soft and beautifully modulated.

'Of course—I should love to come,' she replied. They entered the drawing room together as we went up.

'Did you see?' Caroline asked me the next morning.

'There was nothing to see. People were making noises,' I replied. I wanted her to sense that I was more innocent than she.

'Auntie felt my breasts,' she said.

She looked pleased.

* * *

I like the mornings, the bright mornings, the sun-hazed mornings.

It was so when we sat in the breakfast room that morning, Caroline and I. The chairs had been taken away save for hers and mine.

'You will breakfast alone in future,' our aunt said. 'Eat slowly, chew slowly. Have you bathed?' We nodded. Jenny passed the door and looked in at us. Her face held the expression of a sheet of paper. There was a riding crop in her hand. It smacked a small smacking sound against her thigh.

The drawing room had looked immaculate as we passed—its doors wide open, announcing innocence. The walls against which we had been bound were covered with mirrors, paintings. Perhaps we had dreamed the night.

There would be riding, Aunt Maude said. We were not to change. Our summer dresses would suffice. Arabella passed the window, walking on the flagstones at the edge of the lawn. She wore a long white dress that trailed on the ground. The neck was low and frilled. The melons of her breasts showed. Her straw hat was broad-brimmed. There were tiny flowers painted around the band. She carried a white parasol. Her servant walked behind her in a grey uniform.

When we had eaten Jenny came again to the door and beckoned us. We followed her through the grounds and beyond the fence into the meadow.

Frederick stood waiting, holding the reins of two fine chestnut horses. They were gifts to us, Jenny said. The leather of the new saddles was covered in blue velvet.

We were told to mount. The servant looked away. He studied the elms on the high rise of the ground in the distance.

'Swing your legs over the saddles. You will ride as men ride. No side-saddle,' Jenny told us. The breeze lifted my skirt, showing my bottom. We wore no drawers. I exposed my bush. Frederick had turned to hold the reins of both horses. The stallions stood like statues. The velvet was soft and warm between my thighs. The lips of my pussy spread upon it.

Jericho.

Jenny said we were to ride around her in a tight circle, I clockwise, Caroline counter-clockwise. The servant turned my horse. I faced the house. It looked small and distant. A doll's house. When we returned and entered it we would become tiny.

Jenny clapped her hands and we began. The movement of the velvet beneath me made my lips part with pleasure. Caroline's face was flushed as she passed me, the flanks of our steeds almost brushing. Our hair rose and flowed outwards in the breeze. We kept our backs straight as we had been taught. Mother could not have reached up so high to smack me.

'Straighten your legs—lift your bottoms—high!' Jenny called. She stood in the middle of the circle we made. The breeze lifted our skirts, exposing us. The hems of our skirts curled and flowed about our waists. The sky spun about me.

'Higher!' Jenny commanded. Our knees straightened. Frederick had gone. I was pleased. In profile the pale moon of Caroline's bottom flashed past me. I heard her squeal, a long thin squeal as the crop caught her, light and stinging across her out-thrust cheeks. And then mine! The breath whistled from my throat. I kept my head back. In the far distance near the house two figures were watching. My aunt was watching. Arabella's head lay on her shoulder, her parasol twirling.

Again the crop. It skimmed my naked bottom cheeks, not cutting but skimming as if it were skittering across the face of a balloon. Who had taught her that? It stung, lifting me up on to my toes in the stirrups. I leaned forward, clutching at the horse's mane, breathing my whistling cries to the far-deep empty sky.

At the twelfth stroke of the crop upon each of us, Jenny raised her hand. We slowed, we cantered, we reined in. Panting we fell forward, exposing our burning bottoms to the air. The breeze was cool across our pumpkins hot.

'Dismount!' Jenny called. Frederick the servant was returning. He carried things. 'Stable them!' Jenny ordered him. She referred I thought to the horses, but he ignored them. My bottom tightened as he approached. The ground would receive me—surely it would receive me. I would bury myself in the longer grass and hide until I was called in to tea. I would be eighteen again.

The leather collar bands that I now saw in the servant's hands were broad and thick, studded with steel points on the outer surfaces. My eyes said no but he did not look. I wrote a question silently on my lips as I used to do with mother in the attic. The servant could not read. He fastened the first collar around my neck. A chain ran down my back. The tip of it settled in the outcurving of my buttocks. From behind me then where Caroline stood I heard a small cry.

'No, Caroline, be still!' Jenny hissed. 'Walk forward to the barn now!'

Behind us the servant held the chains, one in each hand like reins. We stumbled over the grass, the rough hillocks.

'Why?' Caroline asked. It was only to herself that she spoke, but Jenny answered her. She walked beside us, ushering our steps.

'Love is firmness, Caroline. You are the privileged ones. Halt!'

We had neared the stable doors. They were open. The darkness within yawned upon the meadow, eating the air that came near it. Arabella was there. She closed her parasol and leaned it against one of the doors.

'Leave this—I will see to them,' she told Jenny.

'Yes, Madame,' Jenny answered. Was she not queen? Who was queen? The chains snaked against our backs, urging us forward. And within. In the flushing of Caroline's cheeks I could feel my flushing.

'Over there,' Arabella said and pointed. There were two stalls—too narrow for horses. The dividing wall between them was but a foot high. I saw the chains again, the wall rings. Caroline wilted and would have stepped back. She was prodded forward. The manacles, ankle rings and chains all were secured. We stood side by side, the low wall between us. I wanted the back of my hand to touch Caroline's hand, but it could not.

'Their dresses, you fool—raise their skirts,' Arabella said. I felt Frederick's hands. They were strong but delicate. Not touching my legs or bottom he bared me to my waist. Caroline quivered and bit her lip as he repeated the action with her.

'Wash their flanks,' Arabella said.

I heard a clink of bucket. The sponge attended to us both. Water trickled over our buttocks and thighs. It ran down into the tops of my stockings and lay in rills around the tight rims. Patted roughly, we were dried.

'They are fair mounts. What do you think, Frederick?'

'Yes, Madame.'

His voice was stiff, expressionless. I relaxed my bottom, feeling its glow—the aftermath of the cropping. The outcurving cheeks above my damp thighs were roseate. I could see them in my mind. I wished I could see Arabella now in her white dress, but my back was held to her. She is very beautiful. Her dark hair flows down over her shoulders.

'Display, Frederick!'

Her voice was curt. She waited. I could hear her waiting, the sound of her waiting, like a bell that has stopped tolling and waits for the rope to be pulled again.

'Madame?'

His voice was a croak. Was he afraid? I felt not afraid. The day lay upon me, soft of the morning. My flesh bloomed. The damp upon my flesh was warm with my flesh. The tops of my stockings chilled. Caroline breathed through her nose. There were noises, shufflings, small metal noises; cloth noises.

Cloth makes noises like fog.

Display? What was display?

'Turn them!' I heard Arabella say. Ah, it was strange. He held his loins back as he obeyed so that the wavering crest of his pintle-pestle would not touch us. It was long and thick. I like long and thick now. The chains rattled. We were turned. I saw through the barn doors as through a huge eye. The world outside disenchanted me. There was an emptiness. Arabella sat on a bale, her legs crossed. Her skirts were drawn up to show her knees. She smiled at me a light smile, a wisp of a smile. Caroline's face was scarlet. The servant was naked. His balls were big. His penis was a horn of plenty.

We stood side by side still—children waiting to be called to the front of the class, for punishment or to be given prizes? Frederick's body was slender, muscular.

'Come!' Arabella said to him. He turned and moved to her. His back was to us, but he did not look at her. I could feel he did not. His glance was high. Above her head, in homage high. There was a trestle close—two pairs of legs shaped in a narrow V with a bar across. He moved to the front of it and stopped. His back touched the bar. Then he bent—a backward bend—so that his spine arched over the bar, his palms flat on the floor beyond. His penis stuck straight up.

Arabella moved her long wide skirt with an elegant gesture and slipped down off the bale. She came to us. We had kept our legs apart. She was pleased.

'Caroline will lie with her face between my thighs tonight, Beatrice. I shall wear black stockings—pearls around my neck. My thighs will clench her ears. Will you see? Do you wish to see?'

My eyes pleaded. She laughed. She squeezed my chin until my lips parted. 'You can see his cock,' she breathed. Her tongue snaked within my mouth. I tasted the breath of her, warm and sweet as Benedictine. She twirled her tongue, then moved to Caroline.

'Put your tongue in my mouth—Caroline!'

Oh, the fool—she should have obeyed immediately. Arabella slapped her face. The tip of Frederick's prick quivered.

'I shall commence exercising you soon, Caroline. Do you understand?'

'No.' My sister's voice was small as if she were hiding behind a pew in church.

'You say, `No, Madame."

'No, Madame.'

Caroline can be dutiful. I like her body. It curves so sweetly. Her breasts and bottom are plentiful.

'You will learn,' Arabella said. Then Jenny entered. It was a play—a private play, I felt. She stood in the doorway, hands on hips, observing us. Was she jealous? When Arabella turned, Jenny's hands dropped immediately to her sides. There were no words yet. It was a mime.

'Let him rise,' Arabella commanded. Jenny smiled. She walked forward and flicked her crop against his straining tool. He groaned in his rising. His eyes were haggard.

Beatrice

'You may choose,' Arabella told her. Jenny tossed her head. She looked from one to the other of us. She strode—strode to Caroline and pulled her forward.

'Please no,' Caroline said. Her feet skittered, dragged. Her free hand pleaded to the air. The chauffeur had turned to face her. He had tucked our dresses up sufficiently tightly for them to remain so. I wanted to kiss Caroline's bottom. The cheeks are firm and plump. Her pubis pouts.

'Bend her over the trestle,' Arabella said.

Caroline shrieked. Jenny had hold of the chain from her neckband and pulled it tight, forcing her over. Caroline's shriek dropped like a fallen handkerchief and lay there, crumpled and used. Her back was bent until she was forced to place her palms on the floor. Her bottom mounded. The sweet fig of her slit showed.

The servant waited. His erection remained as stiff as ever. There was excitement.

'Dip!' Arabella said.

There were new words. I was learning them. Display—dip. His eyes burned. Caroline's hips were high. He took them, gripped them. Rebelliously she endeavoured to twist them but he held her. His lips moved. I wanted words to come—a revelation—but no words came. His loins arched. The crest of his penis touched, probed.

'Caroline! Do not move or speak or you will be whipped!' Arabella said.

She stood observing, as one observes. It was so in the drawing room the night before when my aunt watched the waiting penis enter between the cheeks of Catherine's bottom. I could see now only the servant's haunches, his balls hanging below. Caroline bubbled a moan. Was it speech? His shaft entered—slow, but slow—the petal lips parting to receive it. The straining veins, the purplish head, the foreskin stretched.

Caroline's head jerked up and then was pulled back down by the tensioning of the chain in Jenny's grip.

'No, Caroline!' Jenny said softly.

Four inches, five. Caroline's mouth opened. Perhaps she had not, as I thought, sucked upon the penis. Her love mouth gripped. The ring of truth. Cries gurgled from her lips. Six inches, seven. The fit was tight. I saw her buttocks squeeze, relax. His hands moved to the fronts of her thighs, suavely gripping them. A burr of stocking tops to his palms.

'No-ooooh!'

A soft, faint whimper. In! Ensconced. Buried to the hilt, his balls hung beneath her bottom.

A second ticked. Two. Three.

'Out!' Arabella snapped.

Gleaming, his shaft emerged. I saw his face in profile, the lines etched as by Durer. She jerked her head. He moved towards his clothes. Caroline blubbered softly, her hips wriggled as if she still contained him. Jenny drew her up by the chain. Caroline's eyes floated with tears. Her face suffused.

In the house—not until in the house—were our neck halters removed. We stood in the morning room. We waited. Arabella moved to Caroline and stroked her cheek.

'Are you learning?' she asked. There was summer in her voice.

'Madame?'

Caroline's voice was blank, soft as the sponge that had laved us. Arabella shook her head. 'It does not matter,' she said. We shared secrets, but I knew not what they were. The secret between Caroline's thighs tingled. I could feel its tingling like a buzzing on my lips. Caroline was wicked. I felt certain that she was. Her containment had been too great. She should have cried. Would I have cried? Kathy turned away.

Beatrice

'You know I will whip you if you do not tell me, Caroline.'

Caroline's lips moved, burbled, hummed. 'Mm…' Her thighs trembled. Kathy turned back to her.

'That is better,' she smiled, 'you are naughty, Caroline, you know you are. I have to train you. Edward is trained. Do you not think he is well trained?'

Caroline bent her head. She was alone. Each of us alone except when we are kissing, touching. Sometimes when I am being touched I am alone. There was a small cloud around her lips, pretty lips. It said yes. Arabella was pleased again. Aunt Maude entered. There was movement. Unspeaking she took my arm and led me out.

Upstairs in my room she removed my dress. I saw the bed and it was not my bed, not the bed I had slept in. The headboard was different. Wrist clamps hung from the headboard. She made me lie down. She straightened my stockings and drew my legs apart. I waited for my ankles to be secured. I was passive. She drew my arms above my head and fastened the wrist straps. Her face bent over mine.

'It is for your good, Caroline. Are you happy?'

I said yes. I wanted to please her. Proud in my bonds I lay. My belly made a slight curve.

'Perhaps,' she answered. It was a strange word. 'You will grow happy. Edward was weak for you, was he not?'

I nodded. The morning light grew and bloomed over my body. I had fine breasts, good haunches, a slender waist, Aunt Maude said. Was Jenny nice to me, she asked. I thought yes, no. I wanted to be kissed. I parted my lips as Jenny had told me to. I was not sure, Aunt Maude said. I would be sure soon. She bent over and kissed me and laid her fingers on the innerness of my nearest thigh. Her mouth was warm and full.

'Flick your tongue a little, Beatrice. Quick little flicks with half your tongue.'

She was teaching me. Our mouths fused together. Her forefinger brushed my button—too lightly. My hips bucked. My aunt stopped kissing me and smiled. She sat up. Regarding me, she unbuttoned her dress and laid it back from her shoulders. Her breasts were heavy gourds, the nipples dark brown and thick. Brown in their darkness brown. The gourds loomed over my face, brushed my chin, my nose. My aunt purred a purring sound. Her breasts swung like bells across my mouth. The nipples grew and teased between my lips. I wanted to bite.

Arabella entered. She waited and my aunt rose.

'He has not whipped her yet?' Arabella asked. Aunt Maude shook her head.

'Soon, perhaps.'

'Yes,' Arabella said. She removed her dress, the filmy folds. Her stockings were silver, banded by black garters of silk. Her drawers were of black satin, small, such as a ballet dancer wears. Her breasts jiggled free. She sat at the dressing table beside my bed. Aunt Maude stripped off her own dress and stood at Arabella's back, brushing her hair. They smiled at one another in the mirror. The smile would stay there for a moment like the impress of my lips when I used to kiss myself after mother had spanked me.

Arabella rose. My aunt looked superb in her stockings, bootees, a corset, frilled knickers. They exchanged sentences with their eyes as if they were posting small, personal notes. My aunt nodded. Arabella mounted the bed over me at my shoulders, facing my feet. The moon of her bottom loomed over my face.

'Her legs,' she said.

The board of the bed to which my ankles were now tethered and spread moved forward, making my knees bend. It was an ingenious device, as I later discovered. The upright board was fixed to the legs which rested on heavy castors. Being slightly wider than the bed itself, the legs and the board were able to be moved at will. My knees were bent up, splayed. The globe of Arabella's knickered bottom brushed the tip of my nose. It descended. In a darkness of bliss it squashed upon my mouth, my eyes, my face.

I tasted her.

'Do not move your lips, Beatrice—it is forbidden!'

I could not breathe. The flesh weight of her hemispheres was upon me. The impress of the lips of her slit in their silken net were upon my mouth. Her bottom bloomed its bigness over me. I panted.

Her bottom moved, ground over my face. It lifted but an inch. I gulped in air. Smothered again, I grunted, gasped. Aunt Maude had a feather. The tip of it, the tickling tip of it, passed upwards in my cunny. I gurgled, choked. The feather twirled, inserted and withdrew. Air whistled through my nostrils and was squashed again. My loins shifted, jerked.

The agony of ecstasy was intense at the feather's touching. A wisping of wickedness, it passed around my clit, tickling and burning. My bottom thumped. The bed creaked. The sides of my face were gripped tight between Arabella's silken thighs. Long tendrils of desire urged their desire within my cunny. My bottom lifted, pleading, in my smothering. Musk, perfume, acrid sweetness—I knew them all.

Let me be loved, in my desiring.

No—Arabella swung off me. Her panties were wet. Sweat glistened on my brow, my cheeks. My loins itched, stung. My mouth was wet with her. I closed my eyes and whispered with Caroline behind a pew. We wore candy-striped blouses, pretty bonnets. We chewed bonbons. I wanted one.

They turned me quickly, unloosing the shackles swiftly. Once on my belly the bonds were refastened. The board at the foot of the bed pressed farther up, forcing my knees up almost to my breasts. The cleft of my pumpkin was exposed.

Something nosed between my cheeks. A velvet touch, a thin dildo of leather swathed in a velvet sheath. The oiled nose of it probed my rose, the tight puckering of my secret mouth, the O of my anus.

'N... n... n...' I choked. It penetrated sleekly, entered. My mouth mouthed in my pillow. In the heat of it, the ice of it, I felt it, slender, long, like Edward's penis. Edward had never attempted my bottom. He did not know it had been smacked.

'Oooooh!'

One should not cry out. Should one cry out? I am quieter now. I accept. I am given, loved, I submit. In my moods. It was different then. My bottom mouth gripped it in a grip of treachery—the sleek black velvet of my velvet love. The pointed nose oozed in and twirled. My bottom was riven. In the wild twisting of my face and hips I saw Arabella's legs. Thighs of ivory splendour. Rotating, it withdrew. I was opened. I bit my pillow. The stinging sweetness trembled in my loins. The oil which had been smoothed upon it made it slippery. I grimaced, cried. Arabella laughed.

'Enough—it is enough. How sweetly she sobs—how her bottom bulges to it.'

'It was so when she was spanked. She should be whipped now,' my aunt said. A faint succulent plop and it deserted me. I was hollow, empty. I needed. My O was a bigger O. I dived beneath sandcastles of shame. My toes wriggled.

Was Mother's ship sailing back? It would beach at Eastbourne. People on the beach would run screaming, the pebbles sliding beneath their feet. My mother would descend to save me.

They released me. The board moved back. My legs straightened. My wrists and ankles were freed. I sank down, curling up. I would become a hedgehog. Gypsies would catch me.

'Shall we go out now, Beatrice?'

It was Arabella's voice. I turned. She was putting on her dress. My aunt was putting on her own dress. She buttoned it with the air of someone who had had it accidentally removed, or by a doctor perhaps. I hid my eyes.

'Yes,' I said. I felt shy. Arabella clapped her hands with pleasure. She reached down and pulled me up.

'Come—get dressed you silly girl. How old are you?'

'Twenty-five,' I said. I had said that to mother. They all knew. Why did they ask? Aunt Maude scolded me to brush my hair.

'Don't be a naughty girl, Beatrice,' she said.

Facing the open gates the coachman sat holding the reins of the horses. The cab was the same that we had arrived in.

Caroline and I wore straw boaters, plain high-necked white blouses and long black skirts. Our hair was drawn back with ribbons. My aunt and Arabella entered with us.

'Keep your hands still,' my aunt said. There was a jerk and the carriage started up the slope. It bumped exceedingly again. At the top we turned right—in the opposite direction to which we had come—and proceeded along the lanes. A few yokels moved aside at our coming, but otherwise no other carriage passed us.

Aunt Maude and Arabella toyed with their gloves and spoke of balls, receptions, dances. I envied their pleasures.

My face was demure. I wanted to ask where we were going but I knew it was forbidden. After some six miles we reached a place that was too small for a town and yet too large to be a village.

Over the cobbles of the streets we rattled until we came to a house facing a pond and a green. Two children ran playing with hoops over the grass. The house was of stone, the windows small. It was set amid a walled garden.

'Shall they come in?' Arabella asked. My aunt nodded. They descended first. The coachman helped us down.

Aunt Maude led us forward towards the gate to the drive of the house as if we were approaching for a family portrait to be taken. The door was black, inset with frosted glass. The knocker was of brass in the semblance of a lion's head. There was a bell which Auntie pulled. It tinkled with broken notes somewhere within. Almost immediately a servant maid answered. She curtsied at the sight of my aunt.

My aunt presented her card as we entered the hall. The maid took it upon a small silver tray and vanished. In but a moment she returned and ushered us within a drawing room where a middle-aged couple sat in high-backed chairs. They rose as one. Not having the advantage of facing the sun, the room had a certain gloom.

I waited to be introduced. Instead, Arabella pointed to a small love-seat in one corner. 'Sit there,' she said. We threaded our way through the furniture and sat like doves, side by side, our hands in our laps.

Port was dispensed. We each received a glass. To my astonishment and amid the blushes of Caroline my aunt spoke of us to the lady she addressed as Ruby. She gave our ages and certain details of our training. We sat mute. Only our Christian names were given.

'They are most certainly quiet and well-behaved,' the lady said. She turned her gaze upon us and appraised us. We kept our eyes lowered—

Beatrice

Caroline out of shyness and confusion, I out of discernment. I felt it would please her. It did. One particular lady displayed a greater interest in us. Leaning forward in her chair she spoke in a low voice to my aunt. Twice she nodded then the mysterious lady rose. She approached us. We stirred not.

'Do not move,' Arabella said quietly to us, 'Look up!'

We raised our eyes. She was a stocky woman in her prime. Caroline gave a little jump as she bent down and placed his hands upon her blouse, cupping her breasts. I could feel their warmth and weight as on my own hands. She attended next to my own, running the balls of his thumbs about my nipples. They stirred and pointed into the cotton of my blouse. Her hands trembled exceedingly.

She returned to his seat, her Sapphic breathing sounded laboured. Arabella's eyes remarked his condition, I know. Her glance came to us again.

'May we take them upstairs?' she asked.

My aunt inclined her head. 'I regret…' she said. Her voice was formal as if she were writing the words on parchment. 'We should see Amanda, perhaps.'

There was a nodding. The servant was summoned. Miss Amanda would be asked to come down, she was told. We waited. The clock upon the mantelpiece threw tiny arrows of sound into the carpet. My nipples grew turgid again and softened. Footsteps. The door opened. A young lady of about twenty-three years appeared. She was dressed in simple attire: a blue dress that clothed her form admirably.

A tasselled cord of blue velvet drew the material in at her waist. She was slender. Her legs were long. Her high breasts made themselves appealingly visible through the material. Her dark hair was swept back behind her ear. A pearl necklace and matching earrings adorned her. Her eyes were large and faintly wondering. Her mouth had a petulant look.

There were introductions from which my sister and I were again excluded. Amanda looked towards us. We avoided her glance as if by inverted politeness. Amid the chairs she stood like a hunted fawn.

'I do not want to go,' she said. Her voice was shrunken, distant. Arabella's eyes absorbed the delicate outcurving of her bottom.

'It will take but a month, perhaps less,' my aunt said. She spoke as if Amanda were not present. The séance it seemed was then at end. There was a rising as if of marionettes.

'Take your cloak,' the lady said to Amanda who had laid small white teeth into her lower lip.

'But if I promise...' Amanda began.

'It is a nonsense—she will not even be spanked,' the lady said, addressing my aunt. In the same moment Arabella took Amanda's wrist. 'Come!' she said sharply. We knew that the word was addressed to ourselves as well. A bustling, a rustling, an opening and closing of doors and we were gone. The carriage kicked up a fine dust with its departure. The children with the hoops stared after us. Amanda sat pale and quiet between Caroline and I.

'Amanda—you must not be dismayed, we shall treat you well,' my aunt said, 'There will be strawberries and cream for tea.' Caroline and I smiled because we were meant to smile. The passing countryside had the remote look of scenery painted on canvas. I wanted to return to my room and lie still. To my surprise Caroline and I were sent upstairs freely on our own upon our return.

No one followed us. The doors to our rooms lay open. We lingered uncertainly between them.

'Was it too big?' I asked. She knew my mind and that I was speaking of the stable. Transparent shutters came down over her eyes.

'It was naughty,' Caroline said. Teeth like pips of a pomegranate showed between her lips. 'Why did she?' she asked. There was a childish breathlessness in her voice that I sensed she considered appealing.

I brushed tendrils of golden hair from her forehead. I removed her boater and my own and guided her into my room. A boldness seized me. I closed the door.

'You have to be trained,' I said. I knew the words. I felt older. The scent of beyond was in my nostrils. The air was clean in my eyes.

I was truthful. 'I do not know, Caroline.' We stared at one another. 'When Aunt Maude was caning you began. I wanted to know.'

Caroline said, 'It was tight and it stung.' The wonder around her mouth was like traces of cream. I kissed her lower lip and sucked it in. A bee's kiss. The tips of our tongues touched and played. My hands held her hips lightly. We both thought of Amanda. I knew that.

'In the linen room…' I said.

Her eyes were hot. 'I know…' Her form was limp as I began to raise her skirt. My hands sought her stocking tops, the sweet warm flesh above. Caroline placed her hands on my shoulders. 'It was nice,' she said thickly. A small unravelling of lust was within me. I moved my hands up to the tie of her drawers and loosed it: They sagged, fell to her knees. I knew my wickedness. The curls about her cunny tickled my palm. I felt her moisture.

'You were long in the summerhouse,' I said. I had not forgotten. The rolled lips of her slit were oily on my palm. 'Was it good?'

Caroline's arms clasped my neck. She seemed about to faint. Her thighs parted so that her knees held her drawers taut. 'Yes,' she said. I felt dizzy with a sweet sickness. The, sea waves lapped us.

'It is good,' a voice said. We jerked and clutched one another. I did not want to look. It was Arabella's voice. 'But you were told not to—were you not told?' she asked. My hands dropped. Caroline's skirt half fell but remained coiled about her knees. The legs of her fallen knickers showed.

Arabella beckoned me. 'I know your devilment,' she said and smacked me hard about the bottom. I jumped and squealed as Caroline often squealed. Her hand was as sharp as Mother's. There were old photographs in my mind, tinted with dust. The wing of a dead bee on my sleeve.

Caroline sat at command, forlorn. My wrist was gripped. The door to the bedroom left wide open, I was taken upstairs. 'The second door,' Arabella said. She unlocked it and pushed me roughly within. The room was long and bare. There were cages, the bars of slender ironwork. Three cages in a triangle stood, each the size of a small closet. There were benches, leather-covered. A wooden bar hung across trestles stood in the centre of the floor. Two skylights misted with dust allowed the day to enter.

Arabella stripped me quickly of my dress and drawers and placed me, booted and stockinged, in the nearest cage. I wailed a small wail as the door clanged and closed. A bowl of strawberries and cream, a plate of brown bread and butter and a bottle of white wine lay in the small space at my feet.

Arabella walked to the door. Opening it she glanced back at me and said, 'You are lucky, Beatrice. You are the chosen.' There was silence and she was gone.

I crouched to eat and drink. There was no spoon with which to eat the strawberries. The cream dripped from my fingers. I licked it. A small drop lay upon the springing of my pussy curls. The wine had been uncorked. I sucked upon the neck of the bottle. The cool gurgling. I did not want the bread.

The door looked at me beyond. It was padded with thick black leather, rimmed all around with metal studs. I liked it. The door would be my friend.

Beatrice

Half an hour passed. I leaned back against the bars and felt one of the cool round rods between the cheeks of my bottom. The sensation was pleasant. I pressed against it but the contact was not as I wished. I could not bend forward.

The door opened. My aunt Maude led Amanda in: Unbound, her dark hair was as long as my own. At her pubis the triangle of curls was crisp and neat. Her stockings were banded at the tops by metal rings. Her long legs teetered in the same mode of high-heeled boots that Caroline and I were made to wear. Her breasts were pale mounds of jellied glory. She held her head high in her nakedness, her pride stung by shame.

'I did not want to come,' she blurted. My aunt ignored her. The door of the cage next to mine swung open. On the floor the same meal awaited her that I had received.

'You would not obey—you know you would not obey,' my aunt said. The lock clicked. 'Beatrice, be still and finish your wine. It is good for you.' Her heels sounded loud upon the floor. The studded door closed. All was still. I drank my wine. If there were two bottles I would have poured some over my breasts. I would have raised my nipples to the bars so that Amanda could lick them. Her bottom was quite delicious. Tight and small. Like half a peach it jutted. Had she been tried, trodden, mounted? I was naive then. I should have known that she had not been.

Amanda tried to look at me. She could not. Her hand gripped the bars. Her other arm fell lax. In sagging she showed the sweet curve of her hip.

'It is hateful,' she said. She did not ask me who I was. I had wanted her to ask.

'You have not been spanked,' I said.

Her eyes were lidded. She had a small, delicate voice. 'Have you?' she asked.

'Often.' I poured a little wine over my finger and sucked it. I did not want the cage between us. We could have kissed with the cage between us. Her face was oval, cold. There were no mirrors in her eyes. I nibbled a piece of bread. I forgot that I did not want it.

'What will they do?' Amanda asked. Her mouth was small. Under pressure it could be made to kiss with succulence. I like succulence. It is like *foutre*.

'They will train you,' I said. She stared at me with her mouth open. The metal bands around her thighs fascinated me. They fitted by being slid up her legs where, at the greater swelling, they stopped and gripped as a finger ring does. They had been made for her, she said. She had kicked exceedingly when they were first fitted a month ago. She had been held and had been made to wear them ever since.

'Who fits them?' I asked. She blushed and would not answer. I felt a small impatience with her. 'Drink your wine,' I said. She needed to be unlocked, eased, made supple.

The thought stirred me. It was my first revelation.

* * *

Jenny appeared and passed my drawers to me through the bars.

'Put them on—your aunt is coming,' she said. I scrambled into them just in time. My hands were pious over my breasts.

Auntie did not look at me. Jenny opened Amanda's cage and brought her out. She cowed under her gaze and tried to hide her pubis. Jenny smacked her wrists. There was a strap in my aunt's hand, broad and thick—the same perhaps that our bottoms had tasted in the stable.

Amanda's ankles twisted, causing her to stumble. Jenny took her to the bar which was at waist height. The wood was round and polished. In the centre where her belly would rest was a slight dip.

'Bend and keep your heels together. Grip the lower bar tightly,' my aunt told her.

Was her voice more authoritative than the one Amanda had known? Her eyes were dull. For a moment she stared at the wall and then obeyed.

'Please not too hard. May I go then?'

Her voice was a Sunday School voice. Jenny bent and fastened a broad strap round her ankles. Stepping back she glanced at me over her shoulder. I looked at the door, my friendly door. It would grow warm if I leaned against it.

My aunt approached Amanda whose display was quite delicious. Of a purpose, as I realised, her hands were not tied to the lower bar. The orb of her bottom was flawless—the cleft tinted with sepia in its innerness. The strap lifted and uncoiled.

Cra-aaaaack! Ah, the splat of it—the deep-kissing leather kiss across her girlishness! Amanda winced in anguish, her mouth sagged. A low wail came. The strokes were slow and lazy—insistent. The weight of the leather appeared to need only an indolent movement of arm and wrist. Sometimes it fell across, sometimes under—under the offered apple where the long thighs met and the skin made small creases as if puckering itself in readiness for the out bulge.

Each splat brought a higher gasp from her. Her bottom became a haze of pink and white. Her knuckles whitened where they gripped the lower bar.

'Noo-Noo-Noo-Noooooo!' she pleaded. Her hips began to make more violent motions of rejection. At each stroke the tight cheeks tightened. A big man's hands would have encompassed both cheeks together. A split melon. I wanted my tongue to pass around it in its warmth, its heat out—giving, receiving. I counted ten, twelve, fourteen. Amanda gritted her teeth. Was she crying far within herself? The glow of her bottom was luminous, yet no marks showed. I have since learned the art of it, have heard it called indeed, 'French polishing.' The leather must never be thin. Thin would be cruel.

The metal bands that held the tops of Amanda's stockings rubbed together. Her knees sagged, making her bottom orb out more. A low whooooo-hooooooing sound hummed from her lips. It is the sound one waits for.

My aunt ceased. I could hear Amanda sobbing, but it was not a sobbing of pain. It was the sobbing of a child who has lost her toys. The sobbing of a child who has ceased to cry when nobody listens.

'Be quiet, Amanda—Quiet!'

Jenny's voice was a voice of love. She unfastened the strap around the girl's ankles, drew her legs wide apart and fastened each to the sides of the stand. The salmon-pink of her love lips showed. Amanda cried out and made to rise, but Jenny took the nape of her neck and forced her down again. My aunt turned away. I wanted her to look at me, to acknowledge my existence, the modesty of my posture with my palms cupped over my breasts.

But she was otherwise occupied. She reached into a bag she had brought with her and pulled out a phial of warm, sweet oil and a long thin dildo.

I watched, I listened. An oiled finger moved about Amanda's restlessly rolling globe. It sought her rose, her bottom mouth. Jenny's hand was laid now on her down-bent head. All was silence save for her rushing gasps. The dildo when it entered her did so fraction by fraction, upwards between the cheeks, parting their parting.

'Nnnnnnnnn!' Amanda hummed. Her neck and shoulders strained against the pressure of Jenny's hand in vain. Her hips twisted wildly. The dildo rotated slowly in my aunt's fingers, half embedded. Twirling it, she began to glide it back and forth.

'Sweet mare—you will take the piston yet,' she murmured. Her voice was without malice. It spoke of hushed rooms, drawn curtains, a muted sun.

'No-oh-OH!'

Amanda's voice rose on a long singsong note, but there was no reply. The dildo entered another inch and then withdrew. Jenny unstrapped her and led her back to the cage. Amanda slumped down sobbing, her face covered. Her elbow tilted the bottle of wine. The neck fell trapped between the bars.

'Why does she cry? We are a benediction,' my aunt said.

'They are tears of wrath,' Jenny answered. She looked uncertain as if she had collected the wrong words together. She looked to Aunt Maude for refuge. My aunt frowned.

'The spirit of NO is being driven from her,' she said. She motioned to my cage. The door was unlocked. I was led without as if I were going to communion. The bar received me. 'Caress her first—she is the worthy one,' my aunt said.

With my thighs together I was bent as slowly as a mechanism under test. I grasped the bar. My fingers lay upon the ghosts of Amanda's. Jenny's fingers felt for the pouting of my nest, the love lips pursed. With her free hand she palmed the warm cheeks of my bottom. The upper crease of my slit into which her fingertip wormed, parted just sufficiently to allow her to love-tease my button. I murmured softly in my mind. Pleasure-travellers voyaged through my nerves. The cheeks of my bottom quivered to the urging in-thrust of Jenny's other forefinger.

From the other side of the bar my aunt bent and fondled my breasts very gently as if she. were handling hothouse fruit. Her thumbs spoke to my nipples, whispered over them, erected them. Rigid cones on hillocks of snow.

'It is enough—she holds the pose well,' Aunt Maude said.

I knew the strap then—knew its bite. Jenny who wielded it permitted me to sway my hips, catching the left cheek as I swayed left—the right as I swayed right. I knew the humming sound in my head—the burgeoning of images, pictures, wickedness's. The heat was tempest to my flesh. I moaned in my undoing.

Twelve? Did I count twelve? My knees sagged. I needed a mouth beneath my open mouth. Amanda was a wax statue in a cage. I parted my knees. The gesture was not unseen.

'Come,' Jenny said. There was comprehension in her voice. My moist hand in her cool hand. Wriggling like a schoolgirl I was taken to a divan so narrow that when I lay upon it my legs slipped down on either side.

'Heels firm on the floor—head back,' my aunt said. The heavy heat of my bottom weighed upon the black leather beneath.

Jenny moved behind, took my arms and drew them far back above my head. She held me lightly, fearing no rebellion perhaps.

From her sleeve my aunt drew a long white feather with a curving tip. It passed across my vision. My hips jerked.

'No, Beatrice,' my aunt intoned. Her words were chiding, soft. The stinging in my bottom from the strap deepened and splurged. 'Look at me, Beatrice. Peep your tongue between your lips. Just the tip.'

My eyes were Aunt Maude's eyes. They knew countries of the past I had not visited. My tongue peeped. Amanda would lie on her bed at home. The veils of her undoing would be raised. The strap would rise and fall. The metal bands would become gold bands. The roseate hue of her bottom would dwell in her mornings, illuminate her evenings.

'Good... so... remain... do not stir,' my aunt admonished me. The feather tickled and moved between my thighs. I bit my lip. My tongue retreated.

My aunt was kind. She waited. A bubble of saliva floated from the re-emerging tip of my tongue. It dwelt on my lower lip. I sang in my throat and felt the twirling of the tip—the white heat of it around my button.

Aunt Maude's eyes dared me to turn from hers. I held. Up, down, the feather teased. It entered me. My buttocks rose, fell, rose again. My eyes were saucers on and on. I writhed——the ceiling in my vision swimming in its blankness. On and on.

I broke the rules.

'Na! Na Aaaaaah!' I choked.

Starbursts in my belly. My bottom heaved, my heels chattered on the floor. I bucked, absorbing each long inflow of sensations. Starwheels of white heat spun around my clitoris. Out-shooting tendrils of fire swept my body. My tongue protruded. A quivering cry and I slumped, stilled, vacant in frustration. The empty skylights stared at me. A swallow passed across one. Here, now, gone.

In a moment I crouched in my cage again. Amanda and I stared at one another like strangers who have too many questions to ask.

* * *

Were they good today?' my aunt asked that evening, though she knew the answer well enough.

We were dressed once more in clinging dresses of the finest wool, our curves displayed. Our boots were thigh boots. Stockings. Otherwise we were naked beneath.

'They played in the garden. It was sweet to see them playing in the garden,' Jenny replied, as if reporting on goings on that had eluded Auntie.

Arabella was dressed in black—a high-necked dress. A pearl choker adorned her neck. Jenny was dressed identically. My aunt was less formal in an ordinary day gown. Amanda was absent. We sat formally.

'You may talk,' Jenny told us.

Caroline and I looked at one another. We had nothing to say. It was all in the looking. Her nipples peaked through the wool of her dress as did mine. Our globes were outlined. Arabella rose and played softly at the piano. We waited for dinner.

Arabella smiled at us. 'They do not talk very much,' she said.

My aunt inclined her head. 'No—they are lost in their dreams,' she replied. She clapped her hands. There was a tinkling, footsteps. It was Amanda. She bore a tray sparkling with glasses. A tiny white lace cap perched on the side of her glossed hair. The pale-pink of her breasts showed through a thin white blouse. The black maid's skirt that she wore had been shortened to show her thighs. With the swaying of its hem the metal rings showed, ringing her black stocking tops.

Walking to my aunt first she bent and offered her a dry sherry. The skirt rose at her bending. Her naked bottom shone pale. No one spoke. When she came to Caroline and me a flush showed on her cheeks. I posted a small smile between her lips. My look was motherly.

Jiggling her bottom cheeks self-consciously, she left. Our eyes were pasted on the half-moons of her bottom like mementoes of a journey.

'She will train better here than at home,' Aunt Maude said. There was a nodding.

'She will give you jewels,' Jenny said and pouted. There was laughter. I contained my own. Caroline's laugh was a small apology of nervousness. There was the sound of carriage wheels beyond, a crunching of gravel. The housekeeper flurried to the door. It was Catherine. Her cloak removed in the hallway, she entered in a dull-red dress of silk with elaborate overlays of white lace about the neck. Her diamonds sent messages of light. Without a word she stepped daintily past our chairs like one who is uncertain where to sit. A glass of sherry waited at her elbow.

'The days are good,' my aunt said and smiled at her, raising her glass. Caroline and I were as invisible. 'You have passed the days well?'

'There was hunting,' Catherine said. She looked faintly bored, as aristocrats often affect to do. Leaning back in her chair she crossed her legs with an audible swishing of silk. 'Three girls—pretty and sprightly. They ran not far. We used the walls of the enclosures and the rose garden beyond. They squealed louder than rabbits upon being caught. We pinioned them and carried them within. There were pleasantries. The gentlemen mounted them in turn. They were common girls—field-girls given to such lusts, I believe. Of no account.'

Rising, she opened her purse and took out a cigarette from a paper packet. It was not too new a habit then, but few women indulged in it in public. Her hands trembled slightly as she lit it from a candle. The aroma was Turkish.

'You have not behaved. Have you behaved?' Aunt Maude asked her. 'The reports have not been good.'

The Lady Catherine's face was blurred through smoke. Did Caroline recognise her voice?

'I did not want,' Catherine began. Then the gong for dinner sounded. We entered the dining room. Frederick and Amanda served us. Our glasses were refilled constantly. They were the finest wines. My aunt conversed with Aunt Maude and Arabella about the house, the grounds, the farm. There would be a new summerhouse, she said. I squeezed Caroline's thigh. She had the grace to blush.

'I did not come for this. Will there not be an entertainment?' I heard Auntie ask Catherine.

'You know why you were sent again. Disobedience ill becomes you,' my aunt told her. Catherine glanced at us for the first time to see if we were listening. Our heads were bowed. We absorbed ourselves in lobster and *Chateauneuf du Pape*.

'They were blindfolded before,' Catherine muttered.

My aunt waved her hand. 'It is of no account,' she said, 'come, you must permit at least a little display.' Rising, she moved behind Catherine, bent over her and unbuttoned her dress at the front. I saw the purpose of its buttoning there. As the sides slid away her breasts were lifted out in all their splendour. Her nipples were rouged. Arabella slid her chair back and did the same to Caroline and I. Aunt Maude smiled, took her seat once more and brought a goblet of wine to Catherine's lips. Her throat worked as she drank.

'So you must sit in future when you return—it is more seemly,' my aunt told her.

Amanda entered. Frederick followed and cleared away our plates. He went out. In Amanda's hand was a silver jug.

'You have brought the cream?' Arabella asked her. 'It is warm?'

Amanda nodded. There was bemusement in her face. A cloud of unknowing lay upon her features. Her lips were rouged, her eyes shadowed. She looked beautiful, I thought. At the flaring of her skirt as she passed I saw faint pink marks upon her bottom cheeks. The hem fell like a broken promise and then lifted again. She approached Arabella's side.

'Not here—to the Lady Catherine,' Arabella said impatiently. My aunt's hands disappeared beneath the table at Catherine's side. Catherine's face suffused. Her body seemed to lift a little. There was a loud rustling of silk.

Her skirt had been drawn up. Amanda's footsteps were quick, small and elegant as she moved around the long table to Catherine.

She appeared to be learning quickly—in hope, no doubt, that she would be released. Would she run to the woods and hide? There would be a hunting. She would be trussed and taken home, her skirt wound upwards amid the tight cords.

'Pour,' my aunt said. She appeared to grip Catherine's hand nearest to her own beneath the tablecloth.

Catherine gave a start, her chair creaked. Amanda had bent and poured the warm, rich cream between the valley of her breasts, the deep divide. I wanted to rise and see its trickling—the white lava. I dared not.

'Be still—it will flow down—let it flow,' my aunt told Catherine.

We were virginal in our sitting, Caroline and I. We looked and did not look.

'Down, girl!' my aunt said to Amanda. Their eyes clashed like rapiers. The jug was empty. Its creaming oozed its last over the lip. Falteringly Amanda placed it on the table. Her knees bent. She disappeared. Beneath the polished table of oak I felt her. Her bottom nudged my toe. Catherine's eyes rolled, she leaned back. A soft gasp. I could feel her legs open, guided no doubt by my aunt's busy hands. The warm cream made a white trail down between her luscious breasts and disappeared beneath the looseness of her dress where Aunt Maude had slipped the tie at her waist.

'You liked the horses?'

'Yes.'

Voices spoke.

'Let us be quiet for a moment,' my aunt admonished as if we had been chattering constantly.

I wanted my boot to slide off to feel with my stockinged toes the bulge of Amanda's bottom as she knelt, her face most obviously now between Catherine's thighs. Tasting cream. Cream on her bush, her pouting, her sticky.

Catherine gave a little jump. Her eyes half closed. 'Drink your wine,' my aunt told her. The goblet was raised to her lips anew. Her lips slurped. Beneath my feet there came another slurping. Catherine bubbled and spluttered into her goblet.

'Mounted but twice indeed since you visited,' my aunt said to her scoldingly. 'Are you not bad, my love?'

Catherine's eyes closed. She moved her lips away pettishly from the goblet. Wine spilled its fall on to her breasts. 'P... p... p... p....' Little explosions of sound from her mouth. Her hips worked, breasts jiggling. The slurping noise beneath the table increased.

'Such ripeness—it is always pretty to see,' Arabella murmured. My aunt glared at her. Arabella smiled. For a moment I thought she would embrace me but instead she got up and passed around behind me to Caroline. Bending over her and drawing her face round, she covered Caroline's mouth with her own and passed her fingertips suavely about the snowy hillocks which stood revealed. I could feel the tingling in my mouth of my sister's nipples. Arabella's tongue delved. I could feel it delve.

The feet of Catherine's chair were scraping. The chair rocked.

'You are difficult, too, Caroline, are you not?' Arabella purred. Her mouth was a rose. Would I ever kiss her fully? She desired to make me jealous, I know. The sound of Amanda's lapping tongue was in my ears. Small noises of hysterical sound wisped from Catherine's lips. My aunt held her.

'Look at me, Caroline—haven't you been difficult?' Arabella coaxed.

'Yessssss,' Caroline gritted. 'Oh, but it was so big and...'

'What nonsense she speaks,' my aunt laughed, 'you have sucked it—I know you have. Amanda, rise, leave her!'

A scuffling, Amanda appeared, face hot, lips wet. My aunt beckoned her. Her skirt, caught up, betrayed the wantonness of her bare bottom.

'Your report was no better. Worse, indeed,' Aunt Maude told her. 'Is it not true?'

'Ma'am?' Amanda asked thickly. Her eyes were bleared, her expression slightly vacant. I expected Auntie to draw her forward and fondle her bottom. To my surprise she did not. I thought of Mother. She lay on the beach, perhaps. Pebbles stirred as people approached and stared down at her. She rested in her waiting.

A murmuring beside me, a soft moist sound of lips. I hated Caroline. I would whip her.

Catherine lay back against the high back of her chair. Her mouth was open, a look of languishing upon her face. I judged her about twenty-seven. Her hand wore no wedding ring. Her fingernails glistened, perfectly manicured. My aunt's hand worked gently beneath the table, between her thighs. Catherine's eyelashes fluttered.

'Take her upstairs,' Aunt Maude said abruptly to Arabella. Led out in docile tread, Caroline did not look back. Footsteps on the stairs. Arabella returned.

'As to Amanda....' Arabella said. Everyone waited for her to speak except perhaps Catherine who was floating still in a luxury of sensations. 'Amanda, stand in the corner there facing us. How wicked you have been!'

My aunt rang a bell. Frederick entered. He carried a small silver bucket wherein stood a wine bottle packed around with ice. Placing it on the table, he removed the bottle, wiped it with a napkin and left it there. The door closed again behind him. The cork of the bottle was round, black and polished.

'Lift your skirts—part your legs,' Arabella ordered. My aunt did not turn to look. Amanda's eyes were lanterns. The black flaring of her bush. The curls looked thicker now. The creamy tint of her flat belly.

'Wicked!' Arabella intoned. She took the bottle and moved to Amanda whose eyes hunted the ceiling. The neck of the bottle lowered and hovered beneath her pubic mound. It hung in a straight line down between her stockinged thighs. 'Draw your legs together, Amanda—grip it!'

A long hush-rushing sound like a sudden movement of water surged from Amanda's throat. Her eyes screwed up. Her long eyelashes trembled. Ice-cold, the bottle was gripped between her trembling thighs. Expressionless, Arabella placed her fingers delicately beneath the base of the bottle and urged it gently up.

'Noooo—Aaaaah!' Amanda moaned. The black, round shiny cork parted her love lips and was gripped within it.

Arabella drew down the tiny skirt.

'Whooooo!' Amanda jittered. Her skirt hid all but the base of the bottle. Her teeth chattered. Small pearls of white. I want to run my teeth around them.

'Finish the wine,' my aunt said. She rose—an avuncular host—and filled our glasses. Catherine's head had sunk. Her spirit moved through forests afar. The cream had long been lapped from her slit, her tight-purse, her nutcracker, her penis-pouter. Her bottom cheeks relaxed in their fullness, naked upon her seat.

I dipped the tip of my tongue in my glass. It swam like a goldfish. I wanted to French-drink again. Was it forbidden? Catherine had opened her eyes and sat up. She seemed more composed. Her head inclined towards Aunt Maude's. Sitting beside me again, Arabella slid her hand on to my thigh and caressed it. I would not look at her. I cast my eyes down upon the tablecloth, the white, the serene.

'Are we loved?' she asked me. My mind had already begun to catch at the corners of reason. Amanda stood in her aloneness. I did not reply. I wanted to catch the words my aunt was speaking. Of them all, the Lady Catherine intrigued me most. Her coming was totally voluntary, I felt. Her body held an arrogance of desire, unfulfilled until it was drawn forth by persuasion. Were we all the same? To what dark altars were we led? Darkness was strawberries—the sunlight cream.

'It excites me—I fear it,' Catherine said,

'The root of desire is fearing. When you were caught with your drawers down, did you not intend to be caught?'

'I was dragged to my room,' Catherine muttered. Her voice contained a sulkiness of satisfaction.

'And mounted admirably,' my aunt said dryly, 'as you were here, after your birching. You prefer to be birched?'

'Not always, but the strap…'

'It subdues you, yes, but you must not grow reliant upon it. Marriage will be no cure for you. It will dilute the very qualities that give you such attraction, my dear. I shall recommend that you are blindfolded in future. It will enclose such modesty as you have.'

My aunt twirled the stem of her wine glass. Even as I, she stared at the tablecloth and appeared to muse. She said nothing, though, and the dinner ended with me still wondering what had been held back on her tongue.

* * *

The laurel leaves of the garden hedge were dry. I moved my cheek against them. The breeze fluttered my skirt. For two hours on the following morning we had been caged, Caroline, Amanda and I. Then

Jenny had taken us out one by one and accorded us twelve strokes of the strap across our naked bottoms.

'Your morning exercise—you may be given more pleasant ones shortly,' she said. Amanda blubbered quietly. Each of us sank down in our cage again, our bottoms seared. We were not to talk, we were told.

Released first and dressed, this time in a white wool dress with a gold chain at my waist, I was sent into the garden. I loitered palely. My hands toyed with twigs. The maidservant Mary brought out lemonade. It cooled my body with a sheet of cold within. My eyes were quiet against her own. I felt intimations of newness within me.

Mother on the high seas sailing. I would write to her. By fast packet-ship my letter would arrive shortly after her landing. I returned within the house, not knowing whether I was permitted to return, and asked my aunt. The space where the two leather seat-supports had been the night before was now filled again by a small table. Bric-a-brac and vases stood upon it. I looked for the impress of the feet of the chairs in the carpet but saw none.

Aunt Maude sat embroidering. I asked if I might write. Her expression issued surprise. I would find paper, pen and ink already placed in my room, she said. As I made to go she beckoned me. I stood close. Her hand passed up beneath the clinging of my dress—perhaps to satisfy her that I was wearing no drawers.

'How firm and fleshy you are,' she said, and sighed. The heat of the strap was still in my bottom. It communicated itself to her fingertips. Her hand slipped down, caressing the backs of my thighs as it went. 'Write well and clearly,' she told me.

I ascended to my room. All was put ready for me as if it had been anticipated. A small escritoire stood against one wall. I seated myself and drew the paper toward me. The ink was black. I swirled it gently with the decorated steel nib of the pen. 'Dearest Mother…' A bird's wings rustled against the window. I rose, but it was gone. No message lay upon the sill. I leaned my forehead against the glass. 'Dearest Mother…'

I started and turned at the sudden entrance of Arabella.

'There is nothing to say,' she said, 'it is all in the doing.'

'It is not true,' I said. I wanted to cry. Her arms enfolded me lightly as one embraces a child who must leave soon upon a feared journey.

'It is good that you know. If you had not known you would be writing swiftly. Is that not so?'

Her voice coaxed. I nodded against her shoulder. A simple movement of her supple form sufficed to bring her curves tightly against mine. Half swooning I moved my belly in a sinuous sleeking against her own. She released me too quickly with a smile that I could feel passing over my own mouth in its passing.

'There is to be a reception. Brush your hair, wear a boater—it suits you,' Arabella said. She waited while I obeyed. Descending, she took hat and gloves from Mary who stood waiting. Two horses pawed the dust outside. This time the carriage was a hansom.

'May Caroline not come?' I asked. My question was ignored. I entered first, followed by Arabella who sat close beside me.

'We are going to see a friend,' she said.

The journey took an hour. We passed the house where Amanda lived. The children with the hoops had gone. They sat in some small schoolhouse, perhaps, learning the directions of rivers and the trade winds. Arabella had not conversed with me except to ask if I was thirsty. When I nodded we reined in at an inn. A potboy brought us out mugs of ale. The coachman quaffed his own loudly. With a belching from above and a cracking of the whip we were off again.

The house at which we arrived lay like my aunt's in rural isolation. Stone columns adorned with Cupids ranged at the entrance. The drive was long and straight. Immediately the hansom braked, a butler appeared and ushered us in with the grave mien of one who has important people to announce. We entered a drawing room where, to my astonishment, Catherine sat picking at crochet work. From a chair facing her own, the man with the military moustache who I had seen with her before rose and greeted us. Catherine nodded politely and smiled at Arabella. Her long fingers worked elegantly.

The gentleman, whose name was Rupert, drew Arabella aside to the end of the long room. I caught but a few words of their whisperings. 'It will progress her,' I heard him say. I glanced at Catherine. Her lips had pursed tightly. I perceived a slight tremor of her fingers.

Arabella turned back to me. 'We shall go upstairs,' she said. I wondered in my wonderings. The room was one of great charm. An Adams fireplace stood resplendent. Two small lions carved in stone rested on either side of the big brass fender. Blue velvet drapes were abundant. The furniture smelled of newness.

Arabella's voice seemed to encompass Catherine also. Her hands flirted with the piece of crochet work and fell. The gentleman spoke her name. She got up, her eyes uncertain. The lacework fluttered to the floor. Preceding us she advanced into the hallway and up the wide, curving staircase. There, at the first landing, several doors faced us as did also three young girls in servant attire who appeared to be in-waiting. They stood side by side against a wall. Their hands were bound behind them, their mouths gagged. Their black dresses, white aprons and morning caps were of the utmost neatness.

'This one,' Arabella said. She selected the smallest girl who looked about eighteen, her fulsomeness evident in the sheathing of her dress about her curves.

Rupert jerked his head and the girl detached herself and followed us, her gait made slightly awkward by her bound wrists.

We ascended again to the second floor where a lady of singular beauty, in her middle years, appeared as if to descend. She halted and appraised us. 'A progression, yes,' she echoed as the gentleman spoke to her, 'it will be good for her. Catherine, you will obey, my dear.' Kissing her on the cheek she passed on and down. To untie the other two maids, I thought. I knew their posture, the inward-seeking of their thoughts, the tightness of their bottom cheeks. Their thighs would tremble in the mystery of their beings.

A door opened. We entered a room that was longer than the drawing room beneath. Four windows ranged along the farther wall, the drapes drawn back. The double doors closed heavily. Catherine, the maid and I were ushered to the centre of the room.

I saw then the paintings which hung along the wall facing the windows. There were men and girls in bonds. The men exhibited penises that were either bound in leather or protruded boldly in their nakedness. Each vein was so cunningly painted that one could have touched and felt the slight swellings. Women lay bound, naked or in curious attire, one upon the other. Men with their wrists bound and their eyes blindfolded knelt in their penis-seeking between the splayed thighs of naked ladies.

My eyes passed through them as if through mirrors. Except for one. It was of a girl who wore thigh boots and black tights. The tights had been lowered to her knees. Each hair of her pubic curls had been painted separately with the finest of brushes. She was bound to a post that stood alone in the centre of a planked floor. She wore no gag. Her head was upright and her eyes proud. Her long golden hair was as mine. The cherry nipples of her breasts peaked proudly.

Arabella moved beside me. 'It is better to be bound than to see others bound, is it not?' she asked me. I sought Catherine's eyes but she would not look. Her white dress was as simple as my own. I divined her nudity beneath.

'I do not know,' I murmured.

'Come—we shall know the answer,' Arabella replied. Close to the far end of the room a stout post stood, even as in the painting. To the back of it was fastened four lengths of wood in the shape of a square that protruded on either side. Led forward, I was turned so that my back came against the post.

'Raise your arms,' Arabella instructed. I did so. My wrists came against the lengths of wood. Taking cords she bound them so that I was held as on a cross. 'He will not have seen you before,' Arabella said and threw a smile over her shoulder at Rupert who had moved closely behind Catherine. I watched her head jerk nervously as he palmed her bottom.

Arabella bent and raised my dress, coiling the wool up until it wreathed tightly about my hips. My pubis bared, I blinked and endeavoured to stare past the pair facing me, but the increasing wriggling of Catherine's hips was lure to my eyes.

Drawn wide apart, my ankles were next secured. The lips of my slit parted stickily, warmed and moistened as they had been by our journey. Catherine murmured and choked a small cry. Her dress was being slowly lifted at the back by Rupert. The maid stood like a small tree waiting.

Arabella beckoned her. In her awkwardness she came. Arabella pushed her to her knees before me and removed her gag.

'Have you taught her to lick?' she asked Rupert, whose hands were now busy beneath the back of Catherine's dress. The young woman blushed deeply but seemed frozen to the spot. At the back her bottom was now bared, lush and full in all its proud paleness. At the front the material of her dress looped with some modesty still to hide her pussy.

Rupert shook his head. With such treasures of firm flesh as bulged into his hands, he was equally entranced by the vision I presented.

'Dearest Mother...'

The paper lay forlorn where I had left it. No signals flew. At the first touch of the maid's nose to my belly I quivered in my longings. Arabella nudged her and she sank lower as one who makes to drink from a tap.

She kissed my knees. Her mouth absorbed itself above and circled in an O about my thighs. Her lips teased the tight banding of my stocking tops. Her tongue sought the soft-firm flesh of my inner thighs. I bent my knees slightly. I offered, sought. As through crazed glass I watched Rupert's hands desert Catherine's bottom and glide beneath her armpits to unfasten the front of her dress.

I wanted her. Her mouth, her tongue. I sought to reach her with my eyes, but hers were dazed. As her breasts were bared she whimpered and struggled. Pink of face she held her. Her nipples extended through his fingers. The jellied mounds stirred beneath his seeking.

I felt the out flicking of the maid's tongue ere it reached me, touched my lovelies. I wanted not to moan. I must not moan. Thumbs parted my lips and sought my clitoris, my button, my ariser. The tongue tip swirled. I knew its cunning. Ah! she was good. Starshells burst in my belly. I whimpered, ground my hips. Her tongue would not reach into me. I wanted it.

Did I cry out? On the brink of my salty spray, my spilling, I trembled in a cloud of delight.

'There is nothing to say. It is all in the doing,' Arabella had said..
Catherine was as one swooning. The arms of Rupert upheld her. Her dress
was raised in front—her thighs, her longing. Her bush was plump—a perfect mound of Venus. Had it been creamed, or only her bottom yet? I knew
the answer soon.

'Enough!' Arabella said. She stirred the maid with her foot. The girl fell
back and twisted sideways. Her shoulder bumped the floor. Her small pink
tongue licked around her lips.

Catherine's struggles renewed at Arabella's turning. Her eyes were wild
as hunted fawns. Traitorous, her nipples shone erect. Her thighs clenched
together. Her stockings of light grey silk rubbed. The noise made an electric hissing. Did she not know it as an invitation?

I held upon my cross. The maid beneath me did not stir save to glance
slyly up between my legs. I used the coldness of my eyes upon her. She
blushed and hid her eyes. They were eyes that would move and rustle in
the grass at night. In her truckle bed she would lie at evening beneath a
coarse blanket. Upon heavy footsteps waiting. A cottage smallness. The
cramped places of lust. A heaving of loins. Lettings of desire. Globules of
sperm upon her pussy hairs. Small legs, perfectly shaped, stirred beneath
her skirt-.

I would buy her, perhaps.

'No!'

Catherine screamed foolishly as she was borne to a couch of purple velvet, her dress raised high to bare her belly.

'Wha-aaaaah!' Her screams became hysteria as Arabella assisted in
thrusting her down, mounting upon her shoulders as she had mounted
upon my face. Wildly as Catherine kicked she could not escape the scooping back of her knees by Arabella. Her slit showed pulpy in its fullness.

For the battle now Rupert prepared, casting off his jacket and lowering his breeches. His cock pronged a full nine inches long. The head was purplish, swollen. His hands assisted Arabella's in parting Catherine's long milky thighs. Catherine's shoulders bucked. She was held. Her anguished cries half-extinguished beneath Arabella's skirt bubbled away.

'You have had her bottom only?' Arabella asked.

'Thrice—including her penance over the table when she was birched. How magnificent she looks!'

For long moments while Catherine blindly squirmed her hips, he gazed upon the fount of his desiring. I wanted the maid again—her tongue. In my pride I did not ask. Only the silent pulsing of my quim beseeched.

Yet just then he was called by a voice I did not recognize but one he felt compelled to obey. Delayed and with great pain, he wedged himself back into this trousers and only consoled himself with the thought of future delights.

'Tonight, then,' he said. He patted her bottom. Her eyes would not look at my eyes. Turning away she patted haplessly at her hair and then covered herself. I knew her wetness.

'In your silences shall you be saved, Beatrice,' Arabella murmured to me. There was approval in her look. Releasing me, she fussed about my tidiness like a nurse.

The maid, ignored, was left to her own devices. Sedately we descended, walking quietly as people entering a theatre after the curtain has risen. In the drawing room the lady we had encountered above sat drinking wine. A maid entered and filled the glasses that awaited us on a sideboard.

'Catherine—you dropped your crochet on the floor,' the lady said. Her tone was reproachful.

'I am sorry,' Catherine replied in a muted voice. She picked it up from where it lay and took it upon her lap again. There was a flush on her cheeks but otherwise she appeared composed again.

We sat drinking our wine and spoke of mundane things.

* * *

'Ah! How she will be fucked tonight!' Arabella said as we entered the hansom again.

I had never heard such coarseness. I stared at her. Her eyes had a light in them I had not seen before.

'Should not he have fucked her—spilled his semen within her richness? When he buggered her, over the table—ah, how we had to hold her—his cock disappearing within her cleft. Come, kiss me, Beatrice!'

Her arm enfolded my shoulders. Our lips met in a haze of sweetness. Deep her long tongue delved within my mouth. The jolting of the carriage added to the excitement of our embrace. I felt her hand pass up beneath my skirt. I parted my thighs to her seeking. Her thumb brushed the lips of my slit. I choked my little gasps within her mouth.

'Seven years—seven years it has taken him to bring her to that—yet she obeys us now. He will fuck her tonight. How timid she will be at first, how flushed! His tongue will lick at her nipples, stir her being. Her thighs will move awkwardly, seeking to be opened and yet not. Their tongues will meet. Falteringly her hand will find his cock. She adores bottom fucking now, though he has had her that way but thrice, each time held down. She will come to the strap and birch more easily now, knowing her reward—the slug of flesh within her bottom gripped. Do you hear me, Beatrice?'

I could not hear. I knew not her wording. My slit creamed, bubbled, spurting. Sliding from the carriage seat, I all but fell on the floor. My dignity, my being, lay scattered about me like dying petals. I clasped her, in my falling clasped.

'I love you,' I said.

Arabella laughed and pushed me roughly into the corner. Her fingers glistened. Would she lick them?

'Did you not like my litany?' she asked.

I nodded. The words had been thrown at me out of a box. I had caught them yet I needs must arrange them. A sullenness crossed my features. I wanted to cry. I sought greater fulfilment. Cock. He had lain upon her and given her his cock. I hated the crudities. I shuttered them off in my mind. They tapped at the shutters. I ignored them.

Arabella's eyes were mocking. 'You did not like it?' she asked.

Was I under test? I shook my head. 'I do not know,' I said.

Arabella laughed. 'You fool. There are clues. You have not found them yet, Beatrice. Be silent now. Await the teaching.'

Dinner that evening was formal. Caroline sat quiet, attentive. She had been a good girl, my aunt said. Amanda, it seemed, was caged upstairs, her meal taken to her. I wore black, the wool clinging as tightly as ever. There was a new serving maid, a woman of about thirty, comely and plump. The dull black dress and white apron suited her. During the whole meal she was not required to say a word. I wondered if she had eaten and drunk before us. Such things engage my mind sometimes. It is a kindness. Mother told me once that it was my old-fashioned way.

We took coffee in the lounge, then turned to liqueurs. There was a festive air. I could feel it. We lounged at our ease. The shackles were cast. Caroline laughed occasionally with Auntie. We were tamed.

When the maid brought in the *Cointreau*, Arabella took her wrist.

'Drink with us,' she said.

'M'am?' The maid's cheeks coloured.

'Drink with us—sit with us—here at my feet—take a glass.' Arabella's words were pellets. They stung against my skin. The woman skimmed a nervous look around where we sat in a circle.

'Look, I will hold your glass while you sit,' Aunt Maude told her.

The maid obeyed at last, discomforted in her sitting on the floor. Her legs coiled under her. I liked the shape of her calves. Her ankles were slender. Slender ankles and plump thighs often betoken sensuousness to some degree.

'Lean back and be comfortable,' Aunt Maude said. She dropped a cushion onto the carpet for the maid to lean upon. She looked like an odalisque. Auntie was whispering to Caroline. What were they saying?

'Attractive women often sit on the floor,' Arabella remarked. The maid looked at her and did not know whether to smile or not. Arabella's smile was a cat's smile. With a flip of her toes she kicked off one of the gold Turkish slippers she was wearing and, to the woman's startlement, laid her toes on her thigh. Her toes curled.

'It is nice,' Arabella said. Her foot moved upwards along the maid's hip and felt its curving. 'Drink your drink,' she said sharply. The woman obeyed. My aunt eased a shoe off in turn. Sitting obliquely behind the maid she lifted her leg, eased her stockinged foot beneath the woman's chin and lifted it.

'Lie down—down!' my aunt said.

The maid's arm made a querulous seeking gesture, but she obeyed. The cushion squeezed itself from under her. Arabella circled her leg and moved the sole of her foot lightly over the woman's prominent breasts. She started and would have sat up if Aunt Maude's foot had not then moved with a twist of ankle to the front of her neck.

The maid's eyes bulged.

'M'am—I don't want to,' she whined.

'Oh, be quiet!' Arabella said impatiently. Her foot slid back down. Her toes hooked in the hem of the maid's skirt and drew it up above her stocking tops. Plump thighs gleamed. The simple garters she wore bit tightly into her flesh.

'No, please, M'am.'

Neither listened. Aunt Maude's toes were caressing her neck and up behind her ear. Arabella's toes delved upwards beneath the hang of the up flipped skirt. The woman's hands scrabbled on the carpet. My aunt's toes soothed over her mouth. A choking little cry and the maid's back arched. The delicate searching movements of Arabella's toes up between her thighs made the black material ripple. The maid's cheeks were pink. Her lips parted beneath the sole of my aunt's foot which rubbed suavely, skimming her mouth. Arabella's toes projected up into the skirt. Her heel was rubbing now.

The maid moaned and closed her eyes. Beside me, Caroline puffed out her breath. The maid's eyes closed. Her bottom worked slightly. She drew up one knee. Aunt Maude slipped down on to her knees beside the maid and began unbuttoning the front of her dress. The ripe gourds of her breasts came into view. Her nipples were stark and thick in their conical rising.

Arabella slid down onto her knees in turn. Her hands swept the skirt of the maid's dress up to her waist. A bulge of pubic hairs sprouted thickly. The maid covered her face and made little cries.

'Open your legs properly!' Arabella told her sharply. Still with her eyes covered the maid began to edge her ankles apart. It would be her first such pleasuring, perhaps, though female servants who shared bedrooms frequently fingered one another.

Auntie loomed up before me. She smiled, drew my hand towards her.

'We shall go upstairs,' she said. I was bereft. Caroline would see. I would not see. We entered the hall and ascended. I did not want to go in the cage. But the room was empty and the cages were empty. 'Go to the bar—raise your dress,' my aunt said.

I wanted to see what would happen to the maid, but I obeyed my aunt. Would she be ripe in her desiring? I did not want Arabella to kiss her. But I obeyed. A bulbous symphony in black and white. I gripped the lower bar, my bottom bared to her. She knew me in her seeing now. The door reopened but I did not look. Footsteps quiet. Tapering fingers, coated with warm oil, massaged the groove of my pumpkin. At my rose, my O, the finger lingered, soothing. High heels clicked again and our visitor was gone.

Strained in my posture I kept my thighs, my heels together. The purse of my love-longing peeped its fig like shape beneath my cheeks. I waited.

At the first crack of the leather I cried out my small cry, my head hung. The stinging of the strap assailed me three, four, five, six times. I clenched my nether cheeks, their plumpness hot. Tears oozed.

The quiver-cry that burst next from me was at the first biting of three dozen thongs. My whip had come—it lived—it sang. I hated, loved it.

'Auntie, don't!'

My little wail, the dying cry. I choked in my choking sobs. The tips of the thongs sought me, burnished the blossoming of my cheeks and sought the crevices. Rain of fire, down-showering of sparks. My hips squirmed, my heels squeaked on the floor. Mistress of my arching beauty now, Auntie stung me deeper till my sobs came louder. My shoulders lifted, fell. My hands slipped on the bar and gripped anew.

At the dropping of the whip at last—betraying clatter on the floor—I made to rise. My hand reached back and sought my dress.

'No, Beatrice, stay!'

'No more!'

My bottom scorched, my wail beseeched. Hands at my hips. They gripped like steel.

'Down, Beatrice, down!'

The cheeks of my bottom held, parted, spread. My rose exposed. 'No-ooooh!' The last cry of my frailty fluttered, fell. I felt the flare of my own heat released when the dildo pierced me behind. I made to rise. 'Down, Beatrice—down, girl, down!'

I blubbered, squirmed. I wanted, did not want. The rubbery ring of my anus yielded to invasion—the swollen leather phallus. Quarter inch by quarter inch the shaft entered. My mouth gaped. The thick peg urging urged within. Then with a groan Auntie sheathed it to the full, my brazen cheeks a butterball of heat.

Within me now it stirred, pulsing and throbbing with the rhythms of my own insides. Then it withdrew—the slow unsheathing I both feared and sought. A faint uncorking sound. I felt the tip of the dildo touching my cheeks.

'Go to your room,' my aunt said.

I did not look. I feared to look. I had received. I rose, legs shaking, scuffling down my dress. My bottom sucked in air and closed. Finding the door I ran down to my room.

No one came.

In my sobbing I fell asleep clothed, squeezing my bottom cheeks until oblivion came.

* * *

The days of strangeness closed in upon us further. We were stripped and taken to the cages 'to meditate,' my aunt said. In my aloneness she asked me my dreams. I knelt while I told her, my face bowed. During my speaking she would allow me to raise her skirt and kiss her thighs. In such moments I was truly her slave. I buried my lips against the smooth skin above her stocking tops and licked.

'You are naturally wicked by, nature,' she said to me once when I had recounted a particularly vivid dream.

Maria—the maid with whom she and Arabella had toyed—stayed on. On the morning after her pleasuring she became more acquiescent and submissive to commands. Her skirts were hemmed excessively short. Whenever my aunt looked at her thighs she blushed.

One afternoon we had what my aunt called 'an amusement.' At lunch Maria had been complimented upon her serving of the wine and food. She looked foolishly pleased. On our retirement to the drawing room I was intrigued to see a large camera of mahogany and brass standing upon a stout tripod. Its lens faced inwards from the windows, no doubt to gather light. Before it was placed a simple wooden chair. Other furniture had been pressed back against the walls.

Upon Maria's bringing-in of the liqueurs, my aunt said to her, 'Maria, we shall take your portrait today—your likeness. Will that not please you?'

Maria smiled and curtsied. 'As it please you, M'am,' she replied. As I learned afterwards, my aunt had rooted her with her dildo, over the dining room table. She had not struggled unduly, it seemed. Arabella enlivened us by playing on the piano. It was an old melody, sad and wistful. Jenny—who had not lunched with us, having been attending to Amanda upstairs—-came and joined us.

'Bring the manservant,' Arabella told her.

Jenny disappeared and reappeared. There was a clattering from the distant kitchen while Maria tidied up. Once again Frederick was naked, led by his collar and chain. A blue bow was tied about the root of his penis which hung limp. Jenny led him to the chair and turned him to stand beside it, facing the camera.

Aunt Maude wiped her lips with a lace hanky and went out. A sound of scuffling came—a slap—then a silence. In a minute or two my aunt entered with Maria who wore now open-net stockings, knee boots, a tiny black corset which left her breasts and navel uncovered, and a large feathered hat such as one might see at Ascot. Her face was well adorned with powder and rouge. Her eyes were heavy-lidded.

At the sight of Frederick she started back. A loud smack on her naked bottom quickly corrected her.

'Go and sit in the chair—act as a lady—this is a formal portrait,' my aunt told her. Marie's large bottom cheeks wobbled as she obeyed Auntie. Her bush was dark—thick and luxuriant. Hot-cheeked she sat and faced us.

'Cross your legs, Maria—how dare you show yourself!' my aunt snapped at her.

Arabella lit a cigarette. The smoke coiled about us like incense.

Aunt Maude moved to the camera and bent behind it, casting a large black velvet cloth over her head and shoulders, as over the back of the camera itself. Her hand sought forward and focussed the big brass lens. Marie's eyes had a sullen look. Aunt Maude took one slide of the pair, cautioning them to be still for a full minute. Then my aunt rose and assisted her in changing the glass plates.

'Raise your right hand, Maria, and let his prick lie on your palm!' Arabella said.

There was hesitation. Imperceptibly Frederick's prick stirred and thickened as it lay on Marie's warm, moist hand. Maria would have bitten her lip in dismay if my aunt had not told her sharply to keep her expression fixed in a smile.

With small variations Aunt Maude continued photographing. The light was excellent, she observed. By the fourth attempt Frederick's prick stemmed fully upright, the flesh swelling around and above the neat blue bow. Maria was forced to hold it now. Her face had a dull, vapid took.

'It is done,' Aunt Maude said at last. She collected the heavy glass plates together. They would be framed in gilt, she said.

'I will take them now,' Arabella said. Walking across to Frederick whose penis had not lost its fine erection, she took hold of his chain. 'Get up,' she said quietly to Maria. She smiled across at me. Did she know I wanted her?

'Where shall you take them?' Aunt Maude asked.

'To the stable. It is time they were coupled.' A short squeal came from Maria as Arabella moved behind her and inserted a finger upwards between the globing cheeks of her bottom. 'So tight and plump—she will milk him deeply,' she smiled. Her smile had a taste of olives.

Maria jerked forward and went to kneel at my aunt's feet.

'M'am, I beg you!' she pleaded.

Arabella clicked her fingers and Jenny came forward with a leather neck-band and chain which she secured quickly around Maria's neck.

My aunt's eyes were kindly. She gazed down at the top of Maria's bent head.

'Beg me you should, Maria. What a foolish woman you are.' Her hands raised her skirt. The dark V of her pubis was apparent to all our eyes through her white, split drawers. Her bared thighs came warm and sleek to Maria's face. Maria lifted her head slowly. Her tongue emerged, mouth hovering about the plump mound whose curls sprouted so thickly. The lips moved against her lips. My aunt's legs spread a little. Maria's tongue made a broad wet smudge around her pouting.

'Rise now!' my aunt said to her. The chain clinked. Jenny pulled on it and drew the woman to her feet.

'M'am...' Maria's lips quivered. She looked like an overgrown girl who did not know what to do. Her nipples protruded thickly on her large, milky breasts. The surrounding circles were broad, crinkly. The flesh was firm.

'You will obey, Maria. Mare and stallion in the stable—it is fitting. Go now!' Aunt Maude ordained.

Arabella led them out. Through the windows I could see the trio crossing lawn towards the paddock.

Aunt Maude funned to us. 'Go upstairs,' she said, 'you should not have watched.'

In my room I made to remove my dress. We were never permitted in our bedrooms to remain clothed. Frequently now we were inspected. The hairs of my mount were occasionally trimmed to form a neat line below my navel. It would make the rest of my curls cluster more thickly, Arabella had said. She entered as I drew my dress up to my waist in preparation for removing it. Without halting her pace she stepped quickly forward and cupped the naked cheeks I exposed. I wriggled immediately to her fondling touch.

'Do you want to go to the water closet?' she asked. I nodded. I had drunk much wine. 'And I—come with me.'

The water closet had been newly installed. There were not then many in use. The annex in which it stood was large. A mirror was fastened to the door which faced the white and blue-flowered basin. Leading within and bidding me to lock the door, Arabella immediately raised her dress and squatted.

'Hold me—hold me while I do it,' she murmured.

I held back. I hesitated, but she seized my wrist and drew my hand between her thighs. The hairs of her sex around the pouting lips tickled my fingers. A murmur escaped her mouth that I recognised as one of deep pleasure. I felt her moistness, tire oily slit. Her arm came up and drew my face down. Our mouths merged in a misty sweetness. My senses swam. Impulsively I cupped her furred treasure which of a sudden gushed out a fine golden rain over my palm as her tongue intruded into my mouth. Its long wet coiling around my own tongue together with the warm flooding over my hand hypnotised me. She gripped my wrists until the last trickle.

'You now—you do it,' she said.

I protested weakly. Rising, she moved me around and raised my dress. My bottom was presented to the bowl. My knees trembled. I loosed my waiting flow in turn, drenching her palm and fingers while we kissed. She held me until the last seepings. Then we dipped our hands into a bowl of water and dried them on a thin towel that hung on a nail.

Emerging, Arabella laid a hand on my shoulder. 'Your aunt wishes now to see you,' she said. 'She waits in the study.'

I had not visited the sanctum before. My footsteps along the passageway slowed. Arabella's hand pressed lightly against the small of my back. 'Do not be wilful,' she urged. The kaleidoscope of my thoughts spun. The moment we entered, my aunt's arms engaged me. I pulsed in her arms like a small bird taken in the hand. She was so much stronger than I had ever felt a woman be.

'Has she been good?' she asked of Arabella over my shoulder. A laugh came from her. A sprinkling of falling silver leaves.

'She wet my hand in the closet,' Arabella said, 'her thighs are wet still. Feel her.'

Moving swiftly up behind me she raised my dress clear to my hips, then caught my arms and drew them tightly behind me.

'Open your legs and show her. See—the damp is still on her thighs,' she said. My face was scarlet. I writhed helplessly in her grasp while my aunt surveyed me at her leisure, the slimness of my calves, upswelling of thighs, the trimness of curls where my treasure was entrapped. White of belly.

Of a sudden then I was flung against her. In falling she drew me with a simple motion over his lap, my jellied breasts exposed in turn by the up wreathing of my dress.

'No, Auntie, no!'

My gasp came in the upsweeping of her hand which blasted down on to my naked bottom.

I yelped, I cried. The burning was immense.

'No, no, no, NO!' I sobbed again. My training had left me. Fire blazed in my cheeks. My legs kicked. I clawed at the carpet. The splatting of her palm came down again and again. I was woman and child. My bottom reared and flamed. Pearls of tears cascaded down my cheeks.

'Ya-aaaah!' I screeched again and again until she stopped and I lay limp, helpless to her caressing. The palm glossed my globe, her fingers delved. I burbled out my sorrows. Her free hand sought my dangling gourds.

'Get up, Beatrice!' Arabella intoned.

Blear-eyed and wriggling like a fish I came upright. Her arms clasped my waist tightly, allowing the insensate wriggling of my bottom to continue. Her mouth sought mine. I choked. Salt tears were at my lips. Her voice coaxed me, murmuring upon my mouth, breath to breath. A haze of wine and perfume. She had raised her dress. Our stocking tops rubbed together. The cream of my bubbling bubbled to her lips. Cunningly she parted her legs, rubbing her slit against mine, her hold not lessening about me.

'How oily your quiet—how stiff your nipples, sweet.'

I gulped her words within my mouth. Wildly they swam, my head invading. Gulping to pulping of lips and tongues. Hot tongues in my bottom licked my groove. Long she held me, coaxing, kissing. My torso shimmered. A stickiness between our bellies grew—a mist of perspiration. In silence my aunt sat behind me watching.

The stinging in my bottom eased, became a throbbing. Lost in time and space I stood, Her mouth was my haven. A strange torpor seized me. I felt my legs parted until I stood straddled. Arabella's fingertips quested my globe, parted its cheeks.

'Let her see—let her see, Beatrice. She has stilled you, has she not—after your whipping?'

'St...st...st...' I stuttered. Her fingers clawed the opening of my cheeks. She held me but loosely. An insolence of power.

'Stilled, yes, Beatrice. Her dildo in your bottom. A single plunge within. We call it that. Move backwards now. Move slowly, inch by inch.'

In the cobwebs in the corners were there words? Released, my hands caught empty air, fastened upon the wraiths of yesterdays. With a small shriek I fell back where my aunt had expertly positioned the phallus to penetrate my rearward rose. My bottom churned, uplifted, fell—the velvety leather piercing my cheeks.

I bounced, I burbled, twisted and was held. Then Arabella bent over me. My chin upraised. Her working fingers on the dildo worked. Her knuckles grazed my slit. Her eyes were laughter. Her hand moved faster. His hands beneath my armpits weighed my breasts. The bud of my slit swelled, my rosy clitty. A finger sought my nest and rubbed.

Finally, Auntie's hand on my breasts, I melted, died. I moistened her the dildo in my spending. My breasts swelled. I swayed back to feel it deep, legs apart.

'Go,' Arabella said. She pulled me up, my dress high-wreathed. The door mouth opened, swallowed me. There was quiet in the house as always, as if everyone had left. From the landing window I looked out upon the lawn and saw Caroline lying on the grass. Jenny was kissing her.

I lay down on my bed. The ceiling darkened and lowered until it enfolded me.

I ran through caverns and saw magic lights.

* * *

Aunt Maude wakened me in my early morning warmth. She brought me tea. I sat up and drank from a translucent cup.

'You were bad yesterday—do you know you were bad?' she asked. She fondled my hair while I drank. I did not know what to answer. Often in those days I did not know.

My aunt drew down the sheet and tutted. 'Your stockings are laddered.' she said. I had not bothered to take them off. She rose and took new ones from a drawer. The sheet was laid down to the end of the bed. Caressing my legs she drew off my stockings and replaced them. The new, black ones were of openwork style that came to the very tops of my thighs. 'It is better so,' she said and waited until I had finished the tea.

'You will be a good girl now, Beatrice, will you?'

I said yes with my eyes. My eyes were soft with the morning. My aunt removed my nightdress and attended to my face with powder and rouge.

'Maria was bad—do you remember?' she asked.

I said yes. My voice was soft with the morning. It was yesterday or the day before. I had forgotten the day.

'Amanda improves a little. Catherine is properly settled now of course,' Aunt Maude continued. She glossed my long hair with a brush. Its bristles tickled my back. 'They are not as you are, Beatrice. Turn over now—your bottom up, well up.'

I obeyed. I drew my knees up. I was to be punished for my wickedness in the water closet and the study. My wrists were strapped to the sides of the beds where the iron supports ran beneath the mattress. Then my ankles.

'Dip your back properly—present yourself, Beatrice!' Her tone was sharp. When I did, she moved back behind me. I laid my cheek on the pillow and waited. 'Such a perfect bottom—you surpass us all,' she breathed.

The whip was in her hand, taken from beneath my pillow. The thongs flicked out, making me arch and rear like a filly. I turned my face inwards and bit into my pillow. The tips stung and searched me—messengers of seeking. They sought my crevices. Their small mouths nipped and made me writhe. Heat expanded. Tendrils of fire—hot in their seeking. The hissing hissed to my bold cheeks, my pumpkin, skirting my offered fig, my honey pot. Much as I squirmed and gasped the sensation had its bitter sweetness. The straps held me.

A sound beyond. The whip fell. My face rustled in its hiding in the pillow. I struggled at my straps. My hips weaved. My eyes closed, opened, closed. The bed sagged between my legs—my legs splayed wide.

'No, Auntie, No!'

'Be quiet, Beatrice!' Her hand stroked my hair.

I gargled, gurgled, squealed. Thong-kissed, my cheeks were parted. The wicked dildo again brandished and nosed against my O, the puckered rim. Hands clasped my hips and stilled their wayward motions. The rim yielded. I received an inch of the oiled leather. I endeavoured to tighten. Too late. The piston pistoned. It was sheathed.

'How tight she grips!' Auntie complained, my obedience wanting. Subtle and smooth she urged it more within. 'What a bottom of glory—hot, hot, how clinging!'

I heard their lips, the licking. Her hand slipped beneath my belly, fondled the lips of my quim and parted them, seeking my clit. I bucked. The movement allowed my aunt's fingers to bury itself farther in my slit.

My aunt moved back, forcing her way beneath me where I knelt. My head swam. My moistening anus held its velvet grip. Half-emerging, the dildo sheathed itself to the full again, emerged, and then repeated the gesture. Sparks sprinkled in my belly. My hot cheeks churned against her form.

Aunt Maude drew my mouth down upon her own.

'Move your bottom, Beatrice—move it on my dildo.'

I blubbered in her mouth. Her tongue lapped my seepings. A sharp tingling sweetness in my slit increased.

'Move your bottom—you are on the rocking horse—pretend.'

Coarse in her excitement, my aunt clasped my cheeks. Our mouths were sucking sponges together. I lapped as greedily as she. I moved my hips. Lewdly I churned my bottom.

'Yes!'

In my aunt's mouth I moaned.

'Fuck the dildo with your bottom, Beatrice.'

'Yes!'

'Do you not know your power, my love? Ram the dildo!'

The words… were they the words… the power? I moved, I choked, my senses swirled. My tongue in my aunt's mouth, I drew the cheeks of my bottom forward until I could almost feel the tapered end at my rim.

'Hold now!' Aunt Maude instructed. She had slid from beneath me and watched closely the ins and outs of her treasured leather phallus.

Head hung, my lips pursed tight beyond her seeing. A final test of my total obedience? The leaves of old albums turned their pages slowly in my mind. My teeth chattered briefly. The lure was now exquisite. I urged back. A certain oiliness between us had eased the passage. My bottom expanded comfortably but tightly round the leather tool. Auntie's tongue touched my anus, travelling along the leather in its travels.

small husky sob escaped me. I began to jerk my bottom in little frenetic stabs. Each one allowed me to feel the full length of dildo provided me. The rubbery rim of my anus mouthed it more tightly. I could accommodate my pressure, as it seemed.

'At your own pace, Beatrice. Are you coming?'

I could scarce breathe for the excitement of sensations. The feeling was unique. The heat in my bottom added to the wicked, itchy-burning of my submission.

I had come twice in far-faint thrilling spillings. Lifting my head slightly, I rotated my bottom with the phallus half lodged within me.

'Y… y… yes,' I stammered. My voice was a small girl voice. Sunlight in the attic, hazed with dust. The stone cooler where the wine had waited in our aftermaths. The wrigglings of my bottom as I descended the ladder, my mouth clouded with summer.

A deep quivering seized me deep inside my belly. The mouth of my O gripped it as in a velvet vice. As of an instinct I held my plump cheeks now tight and squirmed.

Swimming in sensations, I collapsed. The phallus, unsupported by Auntie's forceful hand, plopped out, its wet nose upon my thighs. My bonds were loosed.

Drowsy in my sweet fulfilments I was turned. I lay upon my back. Her mouth touched mine. Fingers felt my wetness both at my mound and my bottom.

'It is good,' Aunt Maude murmured. My body fluttered and trembled still. My thighs lay open, wanton. Our tongues touched. My lips were petals to her stamen—seeking. My aunt turned the pages in my mind and read from them silently, slowly.

'What do you want?' she asked.

I sought a word. 'Everything,' I said. The word was a butterfly caught in a net. Its wings were unbroken. Her eyes released it again. It flew about us and melted within me. Her finger traced my lower lip, causing me to pout. Without meaning to I giggled.

'Jenny is in a cage,' my aunt said.

I did not believe her. For a moment I did not believe her. I tightened my thighs together but she tickled me and made them lie wide again, my legs straight in their net stockings.

'Dress now. Wear drawers. Be firm with her. Tell her what you would have her do.'

In my rising I stared at her. The room yawned about me. I fussed with my dress.

'It is true?' I asked.

Aunt Maude laughed and lifted my chin. 'Why else were you sent? Do you not know yet your beginnings and your endings? Have you not been nurtured, led to this? Would you be as Caroline, Amanda, or Jenny?'

My head would not move. I was rigid in my knowing.

'Even so, there may be lewdnesses—at your permitting. Your freedom is entire now, Beatrice. I shall mark your progress. Instil, train, command. Do you understand?' She loosed my chin. I nodded. The air about my eyes had lost its mist. The sperm had bubbled from Caroline's bottom, perhaps, long ere this. I made appraisals, promises—within myself I delved and sought. The cheeks of my bottom were heavy, warm, fulfilled.

'How firm and fleshy you are,' my aunt had said. I sensed my perversities. The air of the house hung now about me like an old cloak.

Jenny was naked in a cage. Amanda lay upon the couch on her back, tightly bound from head to feet. I unlocked the cage. Jenny's arms were strapped to her sides. She wore black stockings and a long string of pearls which hung between her melon breasts. She was sitting. She stared at me dully. I motioned my head and she rose with an effort, rolling for a moment against the bars. Then she recovered herself and stepped out.

I led her to the bar. I intended to strap her. Her small, tight bottom had a fascination for me. It was like Amanda's except that Jenny was shorter than she. Her hair had been trimmed in an urchin cut.

'Do not speak until I speak,' I said. I bent her over the bar and gave her bottom a sharp smack. With her arms bound, it was needful for me only to touch the back of her down-bent head lightly. The sound of the smack coupled with the resilience of the cheeks and the wild little gasp that she uttered thrilled me tremendously. Slowly I left her and walked over to the wall where the straps hung. I selected the shortest and thickest. Amanda's eyes beseeched me briefly. I gave her a small tight smile that betokened nothing.

'When we were younger, did Mother have you with whip or phallus? Did she kiss you where no one else had?' I asked Jenny. In uttering my words I brought the leather across her bottom with a loud Cra-aaaaack! Her hips swayed and jerked inwards so far as the bar would allow them to. A dull flush spread across her hemispheres.

'You intend not to answer, Jenny?'

Her face was suffused. A second, sharper stroke of the leather made her yelp more.

'Yes, Beatrice.'

'When you came to sleep in the guest-room?' The double doors of the past opened more clearly to me now. They yawned upon our yesterdays.

'Yessssss!' she hissed as the loud-smacking strap again seared her bottom.

'You will tell me later in precise detail. Rise!'

Her face contorted as she did so. She swivelled round on her heels and stood before me. Her head hung. I smiled and tweaked her nipples.

'How delicious you must have been for her,' I said coldly. I felt no emotion. It was an observation. I led her downstairs by her string of pearls which I knew she would fear to, have broken. Her small feet padded silently on the carpet. Leading her into my room which was empty again, I gave her a further smack, making her jump. She skittered nervously forward and then stood still.

'Kneel!' I told her. A sense of severity entered into me, but I was as yet not entirely tutored. A few months hence and I would have handled her even better. Kneeling and with her head and shoulders bowed dutifully, she looked as one seeking protection. It was part of her attraction. I wanted her tongue—her small darting tongue—but it was too soon as yet.

I walked round her, inspecting her slowly. She had grown little through the years, I thought. Her body was small, curves tight and sweet.

'You were strapped that night?' I asked.

'Yes.'

The little word upon the carpet lay. I stood before her once more and raised my foot, bringing the sole of my boot down gently on the back of her head. Her lips touched the toe of my other boot and kissed it.

'Begin, Jenny.'

Her mouth mumbled against my boot. Her lips smudged its glossy surface. I edited her text in my mind as she spoke, sensing her slyness. Her conversion that night had been swift, as she would have had me believe. In the double bed to which she had been carried while supposedly half asleep, her nightgown had been stripped; her bottom poised. Fearful to cry out lest she woke me, the strap had scorched her. Confessions had been drawn from her that she said were false. After a score of strokes she had been stilled, even as my aunt had stilled me long ago.

On being carried back at last to the guest room, she had felt isolated, lonely. The silence of the house at night had hung about her like bat's wings. Her bottom knew heat and emptiness and longing. In her tinglings she had lain.

'Go on,' I said when, at this part of her narrative, she halted.

'There was no more,' she mumbled. Her mouth moved over my boot even more fervently.

'Do you believe her?' It was my aunt. She had entered unseen, unheard. Her look ignored Jenny. She came across, lifted my chin and kissed me. The kiss endured. My aunt's hand reached down and sought Jenny's hair while our mouths were locked. She drew Jenny's face upwards, beneath my skirt, between my thighs. Open, warm and seeking, Jenny's lips nuzzled into the V of my drawers. I felt the pleading lapping of her tongue. I did not move. My hips were unresponsive as if by instinct. By placing her free hand beneath my bottom, Aunt Maude could tell it was so. Her lips moved with pleasure upon mine. Our salivas mingled.

'Do you believe her?' she asked again.

I would not answer. I wanted what I knew within myself. My bottom squeezed in my remembering. My aunt's mouth swam back from mine. 'Tell her,' she said quietly.

I looked down. The front of my skirt was looped over Jenny's head. Her tongue worked industriously, tracing the lips of my quim through my drawers. Despite a faint trembling of my knees I moved not.

'Down!' I commanded. The surge of power was within me. I knew the power. Jenny's response was instant. She sank down again. Her mouth deserted me. 'Go! go to your cage!' I said. With the closing of the door my aunt took my hand and guided me to sit upon the bed. Going to my closet she poured a liqueur for each of us. Returning, she sat beside me.

'You will continue your meditations,' she said, 'plan your plottings, manoeuvre them to your will.'

The freshness of cool water was within me after my handling of Jenny.

'All?' I asked.

Aunt Maude did not answer me directly. 'You dealt well with Jenny. It shall be so with Caroline and—upon your need—with Arabella. Observe the males. How proudly their cocks rise. Hidden sometimes beneath their breeches—at others lewdly exposed. Frig them, toy with them, play with them. The bubbling jets expel. Their faces soften, their cocks soften. They are as putty. Their training is no more arduous than that of the girls. They shall service you only at your bidding.'

'Service?' I sensed the meaning, yet I asked.

'In your lewdnesses, Beatrice your slit, your bottom. Never your mouth. Mouths are for others.'

'Such as Caroline?'

'Sly in her sweetness, she has sucked upon their bubblings, yes. Had you not known this? She is shy, acquiescent. Her mouth lends itself like a rose to the sperm, imbibing deeply. In her demureness she wipes her lips secretively and blushes. Did you not know.'

I hid my face. It was my last shyness. 'Perhaps,' I said. Spiders' webs glistened in my mind, broke, fell apart. I envied her for a moment—the big knob purplish at her lips, her tongue gliding beneath the veins. The urgent gliding, sliding. The silence save for the sucking of her lips. Sweet throbbing of the tool—its jets out spurting. Mouth salty, creamed, her limp form raised. Her bottom fondled.

I came to myself again. 'Shall we return soon?' I asked.

'At your wish, Beatrice.' A last flourish of her glass and she was gone. I leaned back. The wall was cool to my back. In the summer I would have cages on the lawn—between the shrubbery and the summerhouse. I would have my whip. My eyes would be as fire, my breasts uplifted.

* * *

The letter I had begun to Mother lay as I had left it. I imagined her gazing at it. The Chinese, I have heard, never destroy a piece of paper once it has been written upon. Characters once imparted to it acquire a being, a magic, a presence. They rest upon the surface like the silhouettes of birds who have no wish to move again.

I took up the pen again. Dearest Mother, I await your return. Beatrice. It was enough. Now in my subtle shifting it sufficed. She would move among the words at night as a poacher moves among the larches and the elms. Taking an envelope, I addressed it to her at the tea plantation in Malabar which her father had bequeathed her. She would return from thence with dust on her dresses—the musk of strange men in her nostrils, the dream of a rocking horse.

I would place the horse on the lawn, perhaps, in a larger cage for Caroline. When the rain came it would stand forlorn and waiting. Raindrops in their crystal glittering on its stirrups.

I bathed and listened to a twittering of voices from the garden— Caroline's and Jenny's among them. Upon my descent for lunch I employed subtleties rather than assertions. At the serving of the soup I asked Maria what wine we were to have with the fish.

Beatrice

'With the fish, Riesling...' Maria began and looked as if towards Arabella, my aunt being seemingly deeply engaged with the unfolding of her napkin.

'Not the Riesling—we will have Piesporter, Maria, and you will address me as M'am. You understand?'

The poor woman almost curtsied in her confusion whereat Arabella swept a look along the table to Aunt Maude whose placid quietness gave full reply. I had additionally had Amanda brought down. She sat as one who is at a party without friends. Arabella's look passed to me. I received it briefly with a slight affectation of boredom.

'Caroline, you will gather flowers from the garden after lunch. The rooms have a slightly drab air. Place some in my bedroom first. Amanda will assist you,' I said, and turned immediately to engage my aunt in conversation. Arabella was thus neatly isolated.

I rose first from the table. Normally, in the conventions, Aunt Maude would have done so and I would have waited upon her to do so. By this small sign, however, a silent Arabella received my further tokens. When I moved of a purpose into the conservatory she followed me—a slightly wounded falcon, I felt, though I bore her no malice. To the contrary, she attracted me both physically and mentally.

'There is change, then,' she asked quietly.

'As to all things,' I replied. I placed my arm about her waist and then slid my hand down very slowly to feel and fondle the quite perfect globe of her bottom. Beneath the light material of her dress the twin hemispheres had the smoothness of peach skin.

Arabella compressed her lips slightly and endeavoured to hide a smile of pleasure at the lightly-floating questing of my fingers. That she wore no drawers was evident by the way I could gently urge a single fold of her dress into the tight groove of her bottom.

'You have not yet given us a performance, Arabella.'

'No?' Her voice was light but shaky. She endeavoured to recover her usual poise and move away but a warning inward pressure of my fingers stayed her. 'The subject was forgotten,' she said. The faintest of blushes had appeared on her cheeks. It pleased me.

I drew her to a small bench where we sat side by side. The scent of fuchsias was rich in my nostrils. Earth smell, loam smell—a nostalgia of flower-pots, some straight, some tilted.

'Your performances have been few? I mean for your private theatricals, Arabella.'

'*Le Theatre Erotique*? There have been some amusements in the past. I engaged Lady Ridge's three daughters upon a delicious masquerade last summer. It made excellent preliminary training for them. It is extraordinary what licences the erstwhile modest permit themselves when they believe themselves inhabiting a world of fantasy.'

'Wherein they also believe themselves full hid by their costumes?' I asked.

Arabella's look of appraisal would have been flattering in any other circumstances.

'Exactly. They had not so much as raised their skirts before nor shown their ankles. I had them attired at first in glittering tights with knee-boots and transparent bodices. Music entranced them to display themselves. A small orchestra was discreetly screened from the proceedings. We acted out at first an innocent game of circuses. The estate ponies were perfect for that. We used a large marquee. The audience was naturally small and the champagne flowed. I allowed the girls to imbibe freely between their frolics. In their giggling and foolish ridings around on the ponies I gave them several twitches of the crop to enervate them.'

I laid my hand upon Arabella's thigh and fingered up the material of her dress slowly until her nearest leg was bared to me almost to her hip. My fingertips ran sensuously around her stocking top. She leaned back. Her lips remained slightly parted for a moment as if seeking breath. The transition from stocking top to silk-smooth skin was delicious.

'And the entertainment?' I asked. I guessed it was called that from my aunt's photographic interlude with Maria and Frederick.

'There was to be trick riding, I told them,' Arabella continued. She moved her knees wider apart to allow my hand to glide up more easily and fondle the warm inner surfaces of her thighs. 'The ponies were exchanged for three fine Arabian horses from Lord Eridge's stables. The door to the marquee was then tightly closed. The musicians, being in a separate marquee that abutted our own, could see nothing.

'I blindfolded each of the girls and had them mount the steeds, whereat their arms were secured about the horses' necks. There was a little fretting on their part about this, for fear they would fall. I comforted them,' Arabella went on with a smile and a half-closing of her eyes as I delicately touched the lips of her quim. Her bottom shifted forward slightly on the seat.

'You strapped their ankles to the stirrups—yes, go on,' I said confidently.

'First I had them ride in a circle. Unknown to them three of the men folk guided the stallions by their reins. The sisters thought themselves most adept and laughed shrilly, if sometimes nervously. Occasionally I gave them a harder twitching with a schooling whip than they had before received. By then they were quite flushed with all the excitement. I judged them ready. The horses were stilled and to multiple shrieks from the three lovely heroines of the piece their tights were swiftly drawn down. Then with a single bound a male leapt up behind each of them, raised their bare bottoms from off the saddles and…

I leaned to her. Our lips, tongues met. My forefinger circled the increasing sticky lips of her slit.

'Each was fucked more than once?' I asked. I had not intended to use a word of such coarseness. It spilled unbidden from my lips. Arabella's tongue swam around my own.

'In succession from the males—who had long waited upon such an occasion—each girl received a triple dose. They had quieted considerably by the time a second foaming lance entered their pussies. The gentle jogging of the horses as they continued to move round slowly in a circle added to their pleasures, no doubt.'

'Their bottoms were feted, too?' I asked. Arabella's parted legs had straightened. I sought right beneath the sweet orb of her bottom and found her puckered rose.

'No… n… no…. not then,' she stammered. 'That pleasure had been reserved. Half fainting with untold pleasures, the girls—were finally dismounted and taken blindfolded into the house, their wrists secured, their tights removed as well as their boots. Their naked bottoms were quite rosy after their ridings, of course. In the main bedroom of the manor all had been prepared beforehand. Taken within, the three were strapped side by side upon the bed with pillows piled tightly beneath their bellies to elevate their bottoms.

'The squire—entering then ready for the fray with his penis bobbing—exerted his efforts valiantly in each of their bottoms in turn, stilling each while they moaned and squirmed fretfully. Then, taking the elder—whom I placed in the middle—he pumped her bottom fully, fondling the other two meanwhile. Such was his pleasure that the rose hole—from which he finally withdrew—frothed most fully, I can tell you. Oh, Beatrice—your tongue, dearest, I implore you!'

Her beseeching for my mouth between her elegant thighs was to my satisfaction since I intended then to ignore it. She had asked and been refused. It suited me perfectly. Taking her chin I pushed her face back and ceased the toying of my fingers.

'Later, perhaps,' I purred, 'upon your continued good behaviour. You have not finished your recital. What then occurred?'

'His prick considerably limper, of course, he left the squirming and blindfolded beauties to their wonderings as to the possessor of the doughty staff which had cleft their bottoms—not entirely to their dissatisfaction, as it later transpired. They were then released, bathed and cosseted—by myself and Jenny, as it happened. We said nothing of the lewdnesses to which they had succumbed and indeed brought wine and cakes and made merry as if the afternoon had been nought but gaiety.'

'Their training began thereafter, Arabella?' My hand held her chin still in a commanding pose.

'Yes. They were clothed henceforth as you have been—in close-fitting wool dresses with nothing beneath save their stockings and boots or shoes. Frequent but light applications of the birch did wonders. With sisters—they were eighteen, twenty and twenty-two respectively—it is best to keep them herded close at all times. The breakfast room, being large, was transformed into a recreation room for them. To a large circular table I had a short centre post fixed. Each girl was spread across the table with her wrists secured to the post. Their ankles were tied by a rope which circled the table and looped around their outstretched legs.

'For the first week they continued to be blindfolded when brought down, their dresses secured up around their waists. Into the breakfast room I patted them, one by one. They had adorable bottoms and were quite quiet and obedient when secured in a circle around the table. A dozen swishes of the birch came first, bringing a pink glow to their offered bottoms. The twelfth stroke was always the sternest, bringing loud shrill squeals—for they quickly learned that it was followed by the stiff insertion of the throbbing staff into each of their bottoms.

'At the end of the first week, immediately after each had been birched, I released Samantha, the eldest, while leaving the other two bound. Cautioning her to be silent, I bound her wrists and removed her blindfold. Though not so Sapphic as the rest of us, the sight made her blush violently, she made to turn away from the upright majesty of the cock that awaited her, but I twisted her about to face it.'

'You made her ask for it,' I murmured.

'Of course.'

Arabella's voice was husky, her eyes wild with pleading for the attentions of my tongue.

'How crude,' I said softly and rose, looking down at her. 'Arabella, draw your skirt up fully—well beneath your bottom. Good. Spread your legs more. Excellent! A delicious thatch, my sweet. Has it been watered of late?'

Before she could reply I strode to the door and gazed back at her. She looked indeed a picture of wantonness, her breasts heaving. The tint of her thighs above her stockings was as of pale ivory. The bush of her quim was thick and luxuriant.

'Wait!' I said coldly, quickly removing the key from the door and turning it on the other side as I went out. Unmoving she sat, the beseeching of her eyes following me. 'I shall show you the delights of the dildo that I have become so accustomed to.'

I hastened to Aunt Maude and told her of my immediate intentions. Her eyes glowed. 'I will get it ready,' she said, 'it will take but a moment to clean and oil it after you made such use of it.'

When she returned with it, Arabella gazed with horror.

'B… Beatrice! You cannot!' Arabella implored. Imprisoned and shafted upon him thus, she looked adorable. Her nipples already sprouted thickly, I noticed.

'A merriment—did you not think?' I asked Aunt Maude.

My aunt nodded. 'It will do her no harm. She has long inhibited herself, I am sure.'

It was an unnecessary question, as her eyes told me. There were permutations into which I had not yet entered nor thought to enter.

'I shall make her Mistress of the Robes,' I said, and laughed. We placed our ears to the door briefly and caught their muffled moanings. 'She will speak not a word to her out of pride,' I said, 'and neither will she dare address her despite the fact that we will have her plugged. An almost perfect conjunction, I think.'

Leaving her penetrated thus, holding it in with her own thighs, not knowing the moment of our return and when she can remove it, Auntie and I left happily.

'You have grown in your knowing,' Aunt Maude replied.

'Of course,' I said pertly. The exercise had given me a heady feeling of conquering without cruelty—the path I was thereafter to follow in all my knowing. Eight persons out of ten have a willingness to submit in the right circumstances and guided by the right hands. Therein is a safety for them. They are led—permitted. In their enforcement are they permitted. I had moved beneath the sea and raised my skirts. The water had lapped me. A tongue had lapped me. Fishes had nibbled at my garters.

I would have a dozen pairs of gloves of the finest kid, reaching to my elbows, I told my aunt. The idea of the very sensuousness of their touch communicated itself to her immediately. She would have her glove-maker bring them she said. They would be extremely close-fitting. 'Their come will bubble over your fingers,' she smiled. 'When I wish it,' I said. 'Come—I want you on the rocking horse.'

Aunt Maude stepped back. 'I?' She jerked, but my hand already had her elbow. 'Do you mean it, Beatrice?' I had no need to answer. Her docility came as from one who had half expected it. Stockinged and booted, but otherwise naked, she looked superb. Her figure had a rubbery firmness in all its outcurving aspects. Mounted on the horse, she stretched her bottom back brazenly, her slit gleaming juicily.

I accorded her no pleasure other than three dozen biting flicks of the whip. The enforced bending of her knees—together with the orbing of her bottom—as she fought to keep her heels dug into the stirrups, provided the very aspect of eroticism I had long envisaged of myself.

I had entered my domain.

* * *

It was a full forty minutes before I released Arabella and drew her up. Her nipples were rigid, her breasts swollen. Following me in with a distinctly awkward gait after the whipping I had accorded her.

An exceedingly pretty half laugh broke from her lips, accompanied by a small, emerging 'Oh!' that had all the colour and perfume of a budding rose. I drew her dress down as a mother might with a child and soothed her hips.

'You will not make me again?' she asked. The invitation was so blatant that I all but laughed.

'Obedience is necessary at all times, Arabella,' I replied softly and kissed her brow. It was damp still with her exertions as were her peach like bottom cheeks which held a faint mist of moisture between them. It would have pleasured me distinctly then to have guided another leather man root into her bottom while holding her down beneath my arm. Perhaps she read the wish in my eyes for she simpered and pressed into me.

'I should never...' she began. I knew her intention. It was to apologise to me for what had gone before. Perhaps she thought I had come in disguise to test her.

'You may have Jenny as a handmaid—for today, Arabella.'

* * *

Caroline lay waiting for me upon my bed with a look of such tremulousness that I slid down upon her. The petals of her lips grew softer under mine.

'Do you remember French-drinking?' I asked her. She blushed, nodded and murmured softly, drawing me more protectively upon her. I toyed with her thighs gently and with my other hand ran my forefinger along the succulent curve of her lower lip. 'You liked it?' I asked. She hesitated, then lisped a sibilant yes. Her breath flooded warm over my cheek.

'When we return I will dress you as a little girl,' I said.

She giggled and clutched me tighter. 'Will you?' she asked shyly. Her heart palpitated, our breasts bulging together.

'There shall be sweetness, punishments and pleasures, Caroline. I shall bring you to them all. Fetch wine now—an uncorked bottle—go!'

So astonished was she at my sudden command that she leapt up immediately as I rolled away from her. 'And a napkin,' I added. Clattering with unseemly haste she was gone and had returned within several minutes. In the meantime I had stripped to my boots and stockings and told her to do the same. Then, before her wide-eyed look, I lay back with the napkin beneath my bottom and my legs spread and dangling over the edge of the bed.

'This is the way we shall French-drink in future,' I told her and motioned for the wine, at the same time making her kneel between my legs. The bottle came cool, between my breasts. I inverted it so that the neck pointed downwards towards my belly, laid flat. The ball of my thumb held tightly over the neck.

Raising my feet I laid them against her back, impelling her mouth inwards where the lips of my quim awaited her first salute. Ali! the sweet brushing of her mouth, half shy, half bold. Slowly I eased my thumb from the bottle neck until it but covered half. The wine trickled down. Down in its trickling down it meandered. Over my belly coursing, into the bush of curls seeking.

'Lick—drink,' I whispered. The cool flowing of the wine which I released in bubbling streams was sweet to my skin, yet no sweeter than the more eager lapping now of Caroline's tongue. The tip curled and filtered between the lips of my love pot, seeking upwards to my sprouting bud as the wine rolled gaily upon it and was received into her mouth. I longed to buck, but I dared not or the wine would have shivered in sprinkling sparklings everywhere. My legs quivered and straightened, sliding down from her back. Brazenly I parted them wider, arching my toes as a myriad of delicious sensations overtook me. The gurgling of Caroline's throat as she received the increasing flood of wine was itself music, yet I must not forget my place, my purpose, nor my disciplines.

'You shall French-drink so, Caroline—the prick in your bottom,' I husked. 'Wriggle your bottom as if now you were receiving it—lick faster!' I desired to cry out that I was coming, yet some instinct told me not to divulge even to Caroline the degrees of my pleasure. Muted whimpers broke from my pursed lips as a thousand tiny rockets seemed to soar and explode in my belly. The saltiness of my spillings in their spurtings no doubt communicated itself to her in a fine spray over her tongue.

I sighed, relaxed, and knew at long last my pleasure. My thumb covered the mouth of the bottle anew. I permitted no more to flow. With a tender but firm motion I pressed her mouth away. I was truly soaked.

'Bathe me,' I murmured. I rose and preceded her into the bathroom. 'Do not speak—you may speak later,' I told her. The sponge laved me. I arose and was dried again. I took her then to the basin, bending her over it with my hand gripping the nape of her neck and washed her face.

We returned to the bedroom where I lay back full length. A scent of saffron came from the drawer of my dressing table where Mary or Maria had evidently sprinkled it with herbs. Waiting with owl-like eyes of blue, Caroline sat tentatively beside me and gazed down upon me. My fingers played with the backs of hers.

'Do you understand?' I asked.

Her lips moved as if to seek words that had long flown.

My arm reached upwards, looping about her neck and drawing her down of a sudden so that the corner of her mouth came to mine.

'You will know your purities, Caroline. The O is a purity. It circles within and without itself, knowing no otherness. Your mouth is an O—your bottom presents an equal roundness. Between your thighs the O has surrendered itself to an oval, an ellipse. Within its knowing is the O—between your bottom cheeks another. The O of your roseness. The male stamen will enter it and impel the long jets of its succulence within. You will receive, absorb—even as your mouth absorbed. Did it not?'

I seized her golden hair, making her squeal. Her face lifted in startlement. Then, by a loosing of my clutch, she slithered down and buried her nose between my breasts. Her arms encircled my waist.

'Do not punish me for it,' she murmured.

I played with her locks, running my fingers through the silky curls.

'Punishments and pleasures, Caroline. Have I not told you? You will suck it in my presence, bent upon your task. The while that it throbs in your mouth your bottom will receive the whip.'

'Oh, please no! Beatrice, no!'

'There shall be stables, too, Caroline. I have engaged Maria to keep them clean—to monitor my captives. Shall you be one?'

Caroline dared not to raise her eyes. Her mouth nuzzled between the orbing of my breasts. I waited long on her reply. The whisperings of shyness, shyness in her mind breathed their illicit thoughts upon me.

'Shall... shall it be as with Frederick?' her whisper came to me aloud.

'Penis-bearers?' I mocked her lightly. 'I shall have you blindfolded sometimes, my sweet. You will not know who your stallion is.'

'Will you not love me, Beatrice?'

I drew her up slowly until her face came over mine. Broadening my stockinged thighs, I allowed her legs to slip between mine and pecked at her lips.

'In obedience there is love—in love there is obedience,' I said. I slid my hand upwards beneath the long fall of her hair at the back and took her neck between thumb and fingers. It pleased me to do so even as I sensed that it pleased her to be held in this way. I felt her trembling. The moist lips of her pussy nestled into my own.

'Have you not been stilled, Caroline?'

'Please kiss me, please, I want your tongue,' she husked. I smiled. Her moods were as the light passing of summer clouds. I could reach up and touch them.

'Suck upon it,' I breathed. Possessed as I am of a long tongue I inserted stiffly into her mouth. The suction of her lips was delicious. She moved them back and forth over the sleek, velvety wetness and murmured incoherently while I squirmed my hand down between our bellies and cupped her plump little mount. The curls frizzed to my fingers. Caroline squirmed, endeavouring to bring her button to my caresses, but I laughed within her mouth and smacked her bottom suddenly with my free hand making her yelp.

'D... don't!' she bubbled. Her face hid itself against my neck. 'What is stilled, Beatrice?'

'The male stem in your bottom, my love—urging, gliding, deep in. There it stays for a long moment and is withdrawn.'

'Oh!' I could feel the heat of her blushing against my skin, 'it... it would be too big!' she stammered.

I laughed. The ceiling received the pleasure in my eyes. A warmness flowed over me. Caroline had, after all, been reserved for the cock I would present to her.

'Your bottom cheeks are deliciously elastic, Caroline. The first time you will experience considerable tightness, but you will yield. You will feel the veins, the knob, the inward pushing—the breath will explode from your lungs. But on the second,' I went on, ignoring her wrigglings that were meant together with her silly, tumbling words to express refusal, 'on the second bout, my sweet, your rose hole will receive the repeated pistoning of the cock until you have drawn forth his spurting juice.'

'No! I don't want to!' she whined.

'Then you will be whipped first—or strapped perhaps.'

With each word then I smacked her bottom loudly, ringing my free arm tightly about her slender waist while she jolted and struggled madly. Finally I let her roll free. Her pert bottom was a perfect picture of pinkness, splurged with the paler marks my fingers had imprinted. Drawing up her knees she sobbed and lay with her face against the wall.

I waited. After a moment when she had not moved I rose and put on my dress. Immediately she spun over and lay upon her back.

'What... what are you doing?' she asked. Her eyes were blurred with tears, her hair mussed. In such disarray she looked at her prettiest.

'Maria will learn to use the strap on you now,' I said severely. Without looking at her I brushed my hair in the mirror.

Caroline rolled immediately off the bed and, kneeling, hugged my legs.

'If I say that I will—please!' she begged.

I glanced down at her and then resumed my brushing. 'It is not for you to say, Caroline,' I answered briefly. I moved away from her by force so that she slumped upon the floor, looking as forlorn as she could contrive. It was a game that she was learning, I could sense, yet her knowing must not be too great. Not as yet. In a year or two perhaps. The fine balance of yes and no was truly here.

I looked down upon her once more. The violin troves of her hips were indeed sweet, the upsweep of her bottom infinitely appealing. With a slightly greater plumpness than Amanda there possessed, Caroline would surrender eventually to her pleasures more than she knew.

Head hanging and eyes clouded, she rose slowly to her feet and endeavoured to hug me. I stood unmoving.

'Do not let Maria strap me hard,' she murmured. Her fingertips fluttered about my back like petals falling. When I did not answer she snuggled into me closer, manoeuvring one thigh and trying to press it between my own. 'Do you not love me?' she whispered.

I raised her face at last.

'In all my being,' I replied softly and kissed her mouth. 'Now go upstairs. I shall strap you myself. You will learn.'

'Yes,' Caroline whispered. It was a plea rather than acceptance. Another moment and I might have relented.

'Go,' I said again, 'wait for me—over the bar. Leave your dress here.'

Her footsteps slouched. Her look was lost—sweet and well contrived. It passed across my mirror and was ignored.

Five minutes later the strap swathed heat across her cheeks.

In her sobbing cries as she gripped the bar beneath was her surrender.

In the week that followed I made ready for our departure. Arabella made her future appointments with me. Maria's husband, Ned, was interviewed formally. He would come into service with me, I told him carefully. His uniform would be that of a valet. He would be put to many different tasks. Maria—I was pleased to think—had evidently scolded him into agreement beforehand since his continued nodding during my conversation became almost tiresome. His physique, however, was entirely suitable—his thighs good, his loins muscular.

There would be Frederick also, as I apprised Arabella. He had been permitted no further licence with her. To ensure that, I had kept him to the house while she was elsewhere. The day before leaving I called her to my room.

'You will devise a play—not too simple a one, Arabella. I will have it performed a few weeks after we have settled in again.'

She curtsied playfully. I had not asked her to sit. 'Shall there be many players? Six or eight, perhaps?' she asked.

I merely nodded as if my thoughts were already elsewhere. It is a simple enough trick. It keeps those I need, desire—or would work to my will—in a state of slight imbalance.

'You will engage Amanda in it,' I said. 'We shall then best see her progress—and her silver stocking bands, no doubt. And the maid at

Catherine's house—the young one who attended upon us. I want her. You will obtain and bring her.'

The play itself would be of no great importance. The words, the acts, could be peeled away at my discretion and replaced by others. Catherine possessed a controllable wantonness, as I had witnessed. She would present a voluptuous example to occasional novices. As to the young maid who had lain at my feet after tonguing me—the sly-eyed, sloe-eyed one—there was a hint of impudence in her eyes that I could quell at will or use according to my whims.

On the morning of our departure I made Caroline ready in the prettiest of blue dresses with matching bonnet and patterned stockings of the same shade. For myself I wore a modish back dress, severely buttoned to the neck, with a pearl choker. My bonnet was a three-cornered one. It gave me a slightly swashbuckling air without looking flirtatious. As to the kid gloves I had desired, I had now a dozen pairs in different shades.

The house waited for us, bereft of servants. My aunt had dismissed them. It was wise. Only the older gardener, Perkins, was left. He was too withered for my purposes. Appearing at the approach of our carriages, he doffed his hat and acted as footman in opening the door. I gave him the most gracious of my smiles.

The rooms at least had been aired. From the kitchen came smells of butter, cheese and herbs. Mingled withal was the scent of bread which had been left that morning. Milk waited in stone jars, covered with fine net. In the stonewalled larder, lettuces shone their fine diamonds of cool water. All was well. My letter to Mother floated upon the oceans. Maria and Jenny removed their cloaks and moved about us. Curiously nervous as they appeared of the windows and the gardener's eyes, I had them don dresses. The proprieties had to be observed. With the drawing of the curtains at night, our world would be enclosed.

'Shall there be visitors?' Caroline asked. Maria made tea. We took it in the drawing room.

'Many. There will be masquerades, amusements, entertainments, Caroline—garden parties. You will enjoy those.'

I would chain the girls to trees at night, I thought. Chinese lanterns would float and sway among the leaves. I would move among them with a feather, their dresses raised. One by one they would be carried in for pleasuring. The stables would be candlelit.

Did Caroline read my thoughts? Laying down her cup she rose and looked beyond the French windows to the lawn where the silver larches swayed in their slender beings.

'You will not love me as the others—I know it,' she said sullenly. 'Will all the girls be young?'

'No.' I rose in turn and moved to her. My hand rested upon her shoulder. Her head lay back. Her fine hair tickled my nose. 'Some will be matrons—firm of body. The summerhouse is large within, is it not?'

Caroline nodded. I could not see her eyes. 'Yes—why?'

'We shall furnish it to our tastes. What is within?'

'A divan—no more.' Her bottom in its roundness moved its globe against my belly. 'Mother said stopped her.

'I shall ordain. There shall be ottomans, rugs, silken cushions, shaded lamps, a small scattering of whips and birches to tease your bottom. We shall have our privacies there—our secrets, our voluptuousness. Do you understand?'

'Yes,' she husked. She turned and nestled in my arms. 'Will you... will you make me do it there? No one will see, will they?'

'No one—no one but me. You will offer your bottom as you gave your mouth.'

So saying, I raised her dress at the back and fondled the satiny orb. Feeling between the cheeks I circled the ball of my thumb about her rose hole, making her clutch my neck and quiver.

'It will b... b... be too big!' she quavered.

'Be still!' I said sternly, 'hold your legs straight, reach up on your toes. Hold so, Caroline!'

'Blub!' she choked. Easing my thumb within I felt her warm tightness to the knuckle, her gripping. Her gripping was as a baby's mouth. With a smooth movement of my free arm I scooped her dress up at the front and cupped her nest. It pulsed in its pulsing. My thumb purred between the lips and parted them.

'Still!' I commanded her. 'Hold your dress up—waist high, Caroline!' She obeyed, swaying on her toes as she was. Her eyes glazed as I moved my thumb up deeper into her most secret recess, toying with the small perky button of her clitoris at the same time. 'I...' she began. Unable to keep her balance, her heels chattered on the floor.

'Whoooooo!' she whimpered.

I allowed her the sounds, the small outburstings of breath. The warmth emanating from between her silky thighs was delicious. Had I not intended now to keep her separated from the others I would have had Maria or Jenny enter and tongue her.

'Be quiet now—be quiet now, darling,' I coaxed. I had moved to her side in the moving of my hands. Her fingers sought to release her uplifted skirt and clutch at air, but by some silent command they stayed. The folds drooped but a little. The pallor of her thighs gleamed above the blue darkness of her stocking.

The natural elasticity of her bottom eased a little until I was able to insert my thumb fully, my fingers flirting with the nether cheeks. The oiliness of her slit increased—its pulsing fluttered.

Beatrice

'B… B… Beatrice!' she stammered. Her head hung back until I almost feared she might collapse. An intense quivering ran through her. The curving of her straightened legs was exquisite. Of a sudden then her head snapped back, her shoulders slumping as I withdrew my thumb.

'Oh!' she choked and would have slid to the floor had I not caught her. 'Oh, Beatrice!'

'So, it shall be,' I smiled and kissed her mouth. She would make much of it in the beginning. In time she would kneel for it with glowing pride—an altar of love. After two years, as I had promised myself, she would return to her everydayness, free to leave or to stay.

You ask why—and I know not. Who shall be free and who not? I had chosen to ordain. There were those who would follow and those who would not. Through the dark glass of unknowing they would seek my image. At night they would huddle in the woods, the shrubs, among the wet leaves—crying for my presence. I would untie their childhoods. The last drums of their youth would beat for them. In their submission would be their comforting. Wailing and crying they would succumb to that which they had longed for. The whip would burnish their bottoms in their weepings. The velvet curtains would be drawn—receive their tears. The dry leaves of the aspidistras would accept their lamentations. In the mornings they would be as choir girls, clothed in white. Calmed from the storm they would talk softly, twittering. I would absolve their sins. I would teach. In time they would learn the inferiority of men—the penis-bearers, the money bringers.

For as such only would men be used. I would teach.

Now we composed ourselves again. Caroline sat fidgeting a little while Maria removed the tray. She would prepare a meal for Frederick and her husband on their arrival later; I told her. Together with herself and Jenny they would eat in the kitchen.

Maria bobbed and nodded in her going. She saw herself perhaps as the head of a small conclave of servants, but I would know how to split and divide.

'Caroline, you will have a maid shortly,' I said when the door had closed. She looked at me in astonishment. We had lived in comparative modesty before. 'I?' she asked.

I smiled and seated myself beside her, rolling her warm and slender fingers in my hand.

'A young servant who at present serves Catherine and her family,' I explained. The idea had come sudden upon me. It would serve to elevate Caroline above the others.

'She shall be unto you as a handmaid. You will train her,' I said. 'She will attend upon no one else other than at my bidding.'

'Train her?' Caroline's face was a picture. 'Oh! Shall I be as you, then?' she asked naively but I forbore to laugh. Her sweetness was apparent. She would lend herself with the seeming innocence of an angel to all that I intended.

'In time perhaps, Caroline. You have been stabled, at least. Was that not splendid? Did you not enjoy it?'

She nodded, her cheeks suffused. 'No one will ever tie us together again,' she said.

'But I may tie you together with your maid,' I laughed. The shyness in her eyes darted with the delicacy of moths. 'She is pretty—a perfect body. Pleasures and punishments—did I not tell you?'

'May I… may I strap her? Just sometimes?'

The question was unexpected. Deep pleasures were in my being at such questions. I had the power to answer or not—to assuage, persuade, refuse, mollify or conquer.

'You wish to? Who else did you wish to strap?'

A knowingly attractive pouting of Caroline's mouth offered itself to me.

'Amanda. She wanted silver stocking bands—did you know?'

'Yes, I knew. What else did she say?'

Caroline's eyes retreated. They appeared to take an immense interest in my corsage. 'She… she said if they were silver, solid silver, she would let him.'

I breathed lightly, betraying no surprise. Ah, Amanda! The depths of you! But no doubt she had seen no other escape and so sought to make her excuses. Caroline had obviously probed and asked. We know not those we know when they are away from us. Mother would lie with women in their bronzeness. She would swish their bottoms with a fly-switch. Languorous they would lie, the sweat between their nether cheeks, up-bulging, offering—the delicate twitching of flesh as the switch descended. Servants would come and go, bearing tea, blind in their unseeing.

'You may strap her, yes, but only playfully,' I said, recalling Caroline's question. I would draw her into my plans a little, yet leave her always on a fringe of wondering—the last lines left undrawn, a mid-air hesitation. Workmen would come shortly to commence the building of the stables, I told her. I had promises that the work would be completed in two weeks. The main bedroom which Mother normally inhabited would become now my own. Caroline would take the room next to it. The stables would have an annex that would form a caging room.

My plans expanded with every breath—her face a mirror to my thoughts. Withal a question poised itself on her lips as a bird alights and rests upon a sill.

'But when Mother returns?' she asked.

My face was blank. 'And naturally we shall furnish the summerhouse last,' I said as if there had been no pause in my words. Clearly she was about to speak again when the doorbell sounded. Jenny hurried to answer. In a moment she returned bearing a *carte de visite* on a tray. I took it and read. The name meant nothing to me:

'He seeks but a moment and is accompanied,' Jenny said. I did not ask by whom. Such questions tend to indicate some unsettlement of the mind. I waved my hand languidly for her to admit them. Caroline adjusted herself, fanning out her skirt. Her composure at such times pleases me.

In a moment the door opened to admit a gentleman of not unpleasing aspect in his middle years. He was alone. He sought my indulgence, he said. His dark suit and clerical collar gave him a slightly hawkish air. They had travelled from Kent, he explained, to inspect a neighbouring house he intended to purchase in the parish. Alas, the hub of one of the wheels of their carriage had collapsed and the house agent had not arrived with the keys, as promised. They had waited an hour in the gardens. Now with the lateness of the day he sought to find momentary shelter for his daughters. 'They are waiting beyond?' I asked.

'In the hall, Madame. I thought not to disturb you overmuch...'

'Oh, but you must bring them in!' I interrupted swiftly. 'My sister will see to it. Will you not have a sherry? Of course we shall afford you all that you need. What a hopelessness you must have felt in your waiting.'

Overwhelmed by my reception as he appeared to be, he took the preferred glass and sat as the door reopened to admit two young ladies of apparent exceeding shyness. Both were prettily dressed and bonneted, but their boots had a sad and dusty air of those who have travelled far.

In seconds they were introduced. The taller, Clarissa, was it seemed eighteen. Jane was her junior by three years, but already with sufficient nubility to attract my eyes. Both were brunettes with pert noses and pleasing mouths. Their ankles were slender, though mainly hid.

'How were you to return and when?' I asked. I affected a great bubbling, flooding him with words while Caroline attended to the girls with refreshing drinks. By some fortune, Frederick and Ned made their appearance during my discourse. I summoned the latter immediately to the wheelwright who I knew sometimes put carriages out on hire. Within the hour the fellow returned bearing the solemn news that only a small phaeton was available with scarce room for three for a longish journey.

In the meantime, however, I had gathered much. The Reverend Ames was to replace the present incumbent vicar. Yet, it seemed, he had business that very night in Gravesend, where he must return.

'Then the girls must stay,' I proclaimed immediately while both sat darting the most timid yet enquiring glances at me. No doubt like he they wondered at my Mistress-ship of the house in my relative youth.

'Nay—it would be a terrible imposition, Madame. In particular since I shall be unable to return for a week. Is there no hotel or hostelry close?'

'Where they would stay unchaperoned?' I asked. The thought soon mended such objections as he had tendered with obvious civility, hopeful as he had obviously been that I would take them in. They were after all of our own class. The conventions were being observed. The additional presence of Caroline placed a perfect seal upon the matter.

At five-thirty, having partaken with us of a cold collation which Maria had prepared, he was ready to depart. His daughters sat demure as ever, the dutiful kiss imprinted on their cheeks with his parting. Crowned as I was with his gratitude, I saw him to the driveway where the phaeton waited.

Clarissa and Jane would be well seen to, I assured him. His hand received my own and held it rather warmly. He was a widower, I had learned.

'They will be in the best of care—of that I am now certain,' he proclaimed and kissed my hand gravely before ensconcing himself on a rather hard seat.

'The very best,' I assured him, 'they will be seen to in all respects.'

'A week, then,' he said and waved his hand. He seemed rather enamoured of my gaze, I thought, as his carriage trundled forward. I watched it to the gates. The door lay wide still—invitingly open for me. Its panes of coloured glass fragmented glittering streaks of light along the wall of the hall where the sun struck. The light brushed my cheek as if in benediction as I walked through and entered the drawing room.

Caroline had engaged herself more animatedly, it seemed, in conversation with the girls. Perhaps in her knowing, she thought as I. I clapped my hands and smiled, expressing my pleasure at their presence.

'First we will bathe you and refresh you,' I said. They had removed their bonnets. Their hair flowed long and prettily about their shoulders. I reached down and took the hand of Jane. 'Come—I will see to you first. Then Caroline may attend upon Clarissa,' I said.

A light flush entered Clarissa's cheeks. 'Oh, but… she began. I stopped her with a further smile.

'I know,' I said softly. I induced infinite understanding in my voice. 'Normally you bathe alone, but in a strange house—and the taps are really so difficult…'

I allowed my voice to trail off vaguely in leading Jane out. She had the perfect air of a Cupid, I thought—an impression that increased as I first ran the water and then undressed her. Her form was exquisite, her breasts the firmest of pomegranates on which the buds of her nipples perked as if beseeching kisses. Her bottom had a chubbiness that my hands sought slyly to fondle in removing her drawers. In stepping out of them she betrayed with many a blush the pouting of her cunny lips which nestled in a sweet little bush of curls.

Tempted as I was to finger them I urged her into the water where she sat with the warm scented water lapping just beneath her breasts. 'I shall soap you—may I?' I asked. Seemingly not wishful to escape the admiration in my eyes she sat mute, pink cheeked, as I passed my soaped hands first over her deliciously firm breasts. Plump and silk smooth as they were, her nipples erected quickly, her lips parting to show pearly teeth as I playfully nipped the nearest between two fingers.

'How pretty you look,' I breathed, 'may I kiss you?'

In speaking I passed my free hand up the sleekness of her back, cradling my palm beneath her hair. Hot-flushed as she was, her lips came peach like to mine with sufficient parting for me to intrude my tongue. For a long moment her own coiled back, but then came timidly to meet mine. My hand passed over the succulent weight of her other breast. Its nipple burned like a thorn to my palm. Her lips moved farther apart in her wondering, but I intended not to spoil her yet. I assumed an air of loving fun and joviality that would disperse itself as a balm to her conscience.

'It will be fun, Jane, will it not?' I asked and received a shy, lisped yes. For the rest I soaped her carefully, fondling every crevice and hillock I could reach without making my further gestures too obvious. The drying took longer—particularly in the gentle, urging motions of my towelled hand between her thighs. Her flush rose considerably then, her knees bending as she clung to me.

I said no more, donating but a light kiss to her mouth before putting her into a robe. In a week I would work wonders with her. And night had yet to fall.

Hearing the opening of the bathroom door from below, Caroline brought Clarissa up. The water lay warm still. It was the custom then for two people to use the same bath, the water supplies being often uncertain.

Clarissa's eyes grazed mine in their coming. I knew her eyes. I would neither fondle nor kiss her in the bath. While Caroline escorted Jane to her room, I led Clarissa within and waited as one waits while she disrobed. In chemise and stockings her figure was similar to Amanda's save that her bottom was larger. Nervously fingering the straps of her chemise, she waited evidently for me to leave. Instead of doing so I gathered up the clothes she had discarded. I did so as by reproof. Then with a pettish gesture she removed her last garment and stood in her stockings. Her mount was plump, her thighs elegant, feet small. Her breasts, though not large, were of perfect roundness.

'Call me when you have bathed and I will bring you a robe—or the servant shall,' I told her.

The relief in her eyes was evident. A smile of assent meandered to her lips. Removing her stockings and stepping daintily into the clouded water, she sat down.

I went out, leaving the door ajar and placing her clothes where she would not find them. Jane would be easy. I knew her kind. Loving, warm and submissive, she would absorb the cock with wriggling wonder. A week was almost too much. With Clarissa it would be different. I had allowed her but one small victory, and her last. The surprise of the strap would come all the more clearly and stingingly to her that night. Maria would hold her.

I moved in my musings beyond, into the lumber room from whence the ladder led to the attic. A sadness of dust was upon the rungs. Beneath me, the water in the bathroom splashed as it would splash upon the prow on the tall ship in its sailing.

And it's returning… it's returning… it's returning.

GRACE AND ANNA

I. GRACE TO ANNA

Lago di Garda, 5 June p.m.

My dear Anna,

At the moment that there happened to be a randy young bitch arriving at the Villa Lola, I was in my room dressing for dinner. Hearing sounds of her in the next bedroom, I could not resist making use of the convenient peep-hole which a previous master had installed. It was not mere voyeurism on my part, Anna. I had already watched Miss Jones display herself to her admirers in a manner which had clearly given her a secret satisfaction, however much she appeared to scorn their attention. Now I longed to see what the true effect of it would be upon the little wriggler herself.

Making not a sound, I sat on a chair, removed the little round shutter, and applied my eye to the aperture.

Miss Jones was standing before the long mirror, admiring herself. The dark slanting eyes with their tight heavy lids were motionless, the tall brow, sharp nose and fine-boned features made a study in immobility and composure.

Without drawing her gaze from the contemplation of her own mirrored beauty, she adjusted the three glasses of the dressing-table this way and that. I did not at first understand the purpose of what she was doing. However, Miss Jones undid her working-pants and pushed them down, stepping out of the tangle of cloth which lay about her ankles. She also unbuttoned her blouse and shrugged it off so that it fell to the dark richness of the Persian carpet. At last she was naked, like a randy little gold-skinned odalisque or a lewd almond-eyed temple dancer.

Then she turned and walked across the room with that tight lascivious little swagger of her trim hips which is her most characteristic movement, I began to understand why she had altered the angles of the triple mirrors on the dressing-table. As she walked, the randy little piece could watch herself reflected from front and rear, thanks to the triple mirror in one corner and a finely framed costume mirror that stood against the opposite wall.

She made her way to the long Regency sofa with its thickly padded crimson velvet and its ornamental scroll at one end. It was on this that all the mirrors had been trained. As she lay there, on whichever side, she could see her light gold beauty reflected from the front and the back simultaneously.

She stretched out naked on the soft crimson velvet, the upper half of her body turned over a little on her front and one knee drawn up slightly, which gave a delightfully saucy distortion to the perfect shape of her bottom-cheeks. Posing like this, she was the boudoir beauty—lascivious and per-verse—of which Romantic Europe has dreamt this past century!

There is, to be sure, a perversity in the manner in which Cara Jones uses her body, the lewd postures which she so instinctively adopts. Yet her true perversity is in her cunning young mind. By the aid of the mirrors, she was now using the sight of her own body to excite herself! As she saw the slim upward branching of her Levantine-coloured thighs, her straight slender back and narrow waist, the smooth tan of her trim bottom-cheeks, she began to caress herself gently. At first it was no more than a gentle self-stroking of those parts which are agreeable to stroke—the flanks and belly, a little firming of her nipples between finger and thumb. But the sight of her doing this to herself was as if she had been spying on a pair of lesbian lovers. Unable to resist, Miss Jones slid a hand down and intruded her fingers between her thighs.

She manualised with the slow expertise of one who has had ample prac-tice—and expert tuition!—in the art. I have always thought it of the utmost importance that a slave-girl of whatever age should be obliged to self-love regularly and should be taught to do so with skill. It relieves those trouble-some feminine tensions and leads to more ready obedience of one's own commands. So, like a lewd little harem wanton, Miss Jones performed upon herself now.

Yet I cannot too strongly insist that her pleasure was ten times the greater for being able to see herself do it. She is entirely self-sufficient for she loves no one as intensely as herself. I watched her enjoy the most ecstatic bliss of honeymoon romance with no other person near her. She brought herself off twice, shuddering and groaning, before the time when the maid knocked at her door to announce that dinner was to be served in half an hour.

The nimble fingers seemed to heed no warning. They parted the trim gold buttocks, stroked and tickled her between them. They plagued the slippery pussy again and again, tickling the little clitoris until Miss Jones shuddered and groaned with the delicious torment of it. They milked her sly cunt until she threshed and squirmed her thighs on the fine sofa.

Once she tried, without success, to spank herself. How eagerly I would have done that to her, for the little bitch made me late for dinner!

Your loving cousin, Grace

II. GRACE TO ANNA

Lago di Garda, 11 June
Anna, dear!

I really think, my love, that Dr. Raspail has proved a disaster in the matter of your neurasthenia. Will you not reconsider, Anna my dear? Will you not, after all, leave England and come to us here in Italy for the season? The light and air would do you good. The Italian way of dealing with such problems of the heart as yours would at once put many matters into perspective for you.

I promise you there is entertainment enough! Since I last wrote, matters have developed most amusingly here. Not only do we have Carissima Jones at our disposal but the nymph Marit, a Scandinavian student of eighteen who has been put under Mr. Bowler's tutelage for a month or two while she learns the language and customs of Italy. I assure you, dear cousin, that Marit will offer you all the charms of Julie with the added thrill of a young girl whose body and mind have not yet reached the full growth of womanhood, so that you may train her in the way you would have her develop so that she adequately appreciates the pleasures of her own sex.

You do not believe me? Very well. Imagine yourself in this resort, somewhere near the pink paving of the promenade and the palm trees stirring in the breeze. The youth of the town and the young students gather there in noisy groups. Among them you would find Marit and some other girl who takes language lessons at the summer academy. One sight of Marit would make you forget the little tart by whom you have been ensnared!

To be sure you shall have her dressed in the same blouse and tight denim of your idol. What would you see? A pretty little creature, charmingly indifferent to the authority of her elders and betters, Marit has those firm and pert little features which match the lightly sun-browned silkiness of her fair skin. The tilt of her nose and the tight little chin are as charming as her blue eyes and the light brown waves of lustrous hair which are worn loose and trimmed just where they lie upon her shoulders. You might see her in some cheeky little summer cap, sitting at a cafe table with the others, smoking a forbidden cigarette, and you would long only for her.

Marit's figure is just of the sort you prefer. Indeed she likes to show it in the tightest jeans-denim of beachwear. Her legs and thighs are still narrow and straight, quite as slender as those which you admire through the bookshop window! Her hips are lean as those of any fourth-form schoolgirl and Marit's bottom-cheeks are still slim and tightly rounded.

You have only to join us here, dear Anna, and this nymph of Norway shall be yours with all her adolescent promise.

You hesitate! Perhaps you worry that Marit is not ready for such things as you envisage? You would be quite wrong in that, my dear, and I will prove you so with the evidence of my own eyes. Marit has the certain knowing hardness about her which betrays her plentiful knowledge of some men and many more women.

How do I know all this? Last night there occurred the most amusing incident of all. The Signora with her bold eyes paid us a call after dinner to share coffee and liqueurs and to inquire most charmingly after our well-being during Mr. Bowler's short absence in Venice. At a late hour, she took his leave and was shown from the room by Miss Jones.

Marit had long since been dispatched to her room so that we might talk of things freely in her absence. The Signora is most intrigued by the Scandinavian surname Aas, which she feels sure must be derived from a vulgarity of some sort!

Ten minutes after she had left my company, I went upstairs to my own room and was soon aware of a murmuring which came from beyond the wall. Our randy young Miss Jones was not alone in her bedroom! You may be sure that I lost no time in drawing up a chair and applying my eye to the spy-hole in the wall. One does not hear very much, for the walls are conveniently thick and I do not suppose that Miss Jones or the Signora who was with her now thought that anything of their activities could be overheard.

To my astonishment, Miss Jones was dressed as if for her work the other afternoon, in tight pants and blouse. Indeed she was now performing the very chores which had attracted the attention of several gentlemen to the shop window. The Signora sat in a chair behind her, one hand playing between her own legs while she watched her.

The Signora was for all the world like the young woman whose trouser bottom had been deluged while she watched Miss Jones at work on all fours!

With the small round brush she was now stirring up the pile of the bedroom carpet, the crop of her brushed curls lowered and her almond eyes flashing their occasional challenge at the woman who sat behind her. As she worked her way back towards the Signora, Miss Jones's slim and upward branching thighs offered a lewd and enticing prospect to her mistress. Her rear cheeks so round and trim, so suggestively separated, swelled and writhed. The route between the rear of her legs lay tantalisingly open. By hollowing her waist downwards, the randy little piece was trying to offer herself still more brazenly for the Signora's attention.

As soon as she was close to her chair, the Signora put her hand down and began to fondle the cheeks of Miss Jones's backside in the tight denim. She stopped at once, waiting on hands and knees with her head still bowed a little, as if to discover what her pleasure might be.

It will not surprise you to learn that the Signora began to undo her at the waist and to work the denim, with Miss Jones's panties inside, well down over her taut young hips and trim thighs. A moment more and her pants were round her knees as she knelt at his disposal. The great lady slipped her fingers between her warm gold thighs from the rear. With gentle stroking and squeezing she roused her, for all the world as if she were milking some compliant female creature in her stable!

If Miss Jones felt the indignity of such a situation, she showed no sign of this. She braced herself on hands and knees, her head lowered as if she were trying to look back between her legs at what she was doing to her. Her slim Levantine thighs writhed together in the most exquisite of Cupid's torments and the cheeks of her backside seemed to tense and relax in a furtive telltale rhythm. From time to time the Signora drew her hand away, causing her a gasp of deprivation, and administered a ringing smack on the coppery smoothness of Miss Jones's bottom, that forced a squeal of alarm from her. Then she moaned and quivered gratefully as the hand resumed its former labours between her thighs.

You may be sure that the Signora was not going to bring her to a conclusion so easily, Anna. Anyone who had possession of this lascivious little piece would want to make it a long session with her. She was merely working her up to a point at which she would never regain her equanimity without first having a climax.

She told her to remain on all fours and I guessed at once that there was to be some kind of bedroom sport. Getting up from her chair, the Signora went over to the table and took a fine mauve candle from its silver-gilt holder. In a moment more, she stooped over the girl as she knelt on hands and knees. To be sure, she was more than ready for something of the kind. With a little careful insertion of the candle-base between the rear of her legs, she found a most convenient holder for it—a holder which received the round mauve wax with grateful tremors and sudden gasps of pent-up excitement! The ornamental wick protruded back between the rear of the slim gold thighs in a most provoking manner.

Somewhat to my alarm, the Signora struck a match and applied it to the wick. It burnt with a small and perfect flame. I hoped she did not intend it to burn down until it scorched randy young Miss Jones *ou vous savez*, as the saying is! You may be sure, though, she is too much of a gentlewoman for that. The proletarian zeal whose torches found their way between the thighs of certain aristocratic beauties in '92 is foreign to her.

Who can tell what preliminaries a pair of lovers may adopt to excite them to greater prodigies in their coupling? Miss Jones waited on all fours while the Signora with her eyes staring, went down on all fours behind her. A spot of hot wax fell on her bare thigh and she gave a sudden start, for which the Signora chided her. The rules of the game must be observed.

Presently the Signora clapped her hands sharply to make the sound of a starting-pistol. In her own bedroom, this *cavaliera* would have fired off a pistol in earnest but she was more prudent as a guest at the Villa Lola.

When the signal was given, Miss Jones scampered forward on hands and knees, the little flame of the candle fluttering like a flag. Grinning madly, the Signora set off in pursuit. She did not, it is true, use her utmost energy for she wished to prolong the fun a little. The object of the sport was to blow out, snuff out, or snap out the life of the little flame whose candle was sunk so firmly in the girl's love-nest.

At first the Signora tried to blow in sharp gusts of breath but the randy young minx merely twisted her arse this way and that to frustrate him. Foiled in this, the Signora took from her pocket a pair of snuffers and tried to smother the flame by pinching it out. She was not successful, though she once pinched the flesh high up on the rear of the girl's thigh, which caused an amazing shriek. The Signora told her, somewhat ungratefully, to shut her noise.

As the sublime noblewoman scampered after her beauty, lured on by squirming thighs and writhing hips, there was nearly a catastrophe to put paid to the Villa Lola and all its occupants. Our randy young odalisque was greatly excited by the sport and by the promise of what was going to be done to her at its conclusion. This, combined with the agreeable presence of the candle base in her pussy had made her lubricate copiously. Her energetic movements made her feel the candle more exquisitely than ever and her natural feminine slipperiness had spread even down the inner surfaces of her trim thighs.

I swear it was this state of her excitement which now caused the candle to shoot backwards from between young Miss Jones's legs as she scampered forwards. Like a splendid *jeu d'artifice* it sped out from beneath her thighs and described a surprising arc across the bedroom, the flame still fluttering at the wick. It fell quite six feet away and was at once in danger of setting on fire the silk cover of the bed. The Signora, *galantuoma* that she is, ignored this mere threat to life when there were more important matters to be decided. It was Miss Jones with a charming little scream who sprang across to the bed and began to beat out the infant flames with the back of a hairbrush.

At no point had it been agreed that the rules of the game were suspended. The Signora snatched a silk cord from the curtain and, as the object of her lust knelt over the scene of the little conflagration, she ran the cord round her wrists and tied her by it to the bedpost. There she knelt, or rather knelt over, the edge of the bed, her hands tied and able only to look round with a sudden fright in the slant of her enigmatic almond eyes.

How busy the Signora was with her now! She knelt down behind the lewd young shop girl, just like a dog who sniffs a bitch. Se kissed the coppery smoothness of her bottom-cheeks, her trim young thighs, and even between her legs, much to the cost of his immaculately waxed whiskers. She gave her a hearty smack on the bottom and then another. This excited him so much that the Signora continued until Miss Jones wailed plaintively to know if she was to be spanked or ravished.

'A little spanking, Car',' she murmured, 'A smack or two to make you lively! Do you want to go home, Car? Have you had enough, Carissima Jones?'

She smacked her bottom a little, and rode her again.

'Untie my hands, then,' she murmured in her charming Celtic lilt.

The Signora merely chortled at the suggestion and gave another sharp smack on her coppery-toned bottom-cheeks as if to reprimand such sauciness. Miss Jones gave a little squeal, whether of discomfort or excitement, who can say? Perhaps it was a little of both.

There is, alas, no scale of enthusiasm in these matters by whose Fahrenheit or Centigrade one may measure the thrill of desire. Yet our almond-eyed beauty writhed and whimpered in a manner which made such exact measurement unnecessary. The Signora feasted her lips on the delicate whorls of her ears and the fine moulding of her neck. She bit her lightly on the shoulders and his fingernails raked the smooth gold flanks of her trim thighs. Car, in turn, twisted her face round and the tight-lidded slant of her dark eyes begged kisses for her greedy lips.

A series of sharp rising cries announced the approach of her climax while the Signorina licked at her sopping cunnie. They lay entwined on the dark blue-and-crimson of the Persian carpet, writhing and panting together a little in the moment of their supreme satisfaction. Presently there was another sharp smack on her bottom to prepare the randy little piece for an encore.

Just then I heard a sound in the corridor. Opening my door as softly as I might, I peeped through the crack and took young Marit entirely by surprise. What do you suppose? She had stripped to her white blouse and her denim drawers—which was not unusual at that hour of night. She was also kneeling at Miss Jones's keyhole, which was charmingly lewd!

You may guess the sequel. Her features were hidden somewhat by the light brown tresses which lapped about her collar. Yet as she sat upon her heels and viewed the scene in the bedroom, Marit's slim young hand was thrust within the waist of her pants at the front. Her fingers were moving with a most lascivious knowingness between her slender thighs.

Though I could not quite see her face for the silken waves of hair falling about her features, I was certain of her mood all the same, if only from the manner in which her glossy young hair trembled and the gasps which issued from her!

Do not condemn her too easily, Anna. Desire is strong at her age and yet the proper conduct of society requires that its yearnings must be repressed by its elders. How else, then, is Marit to relieve her feelings?

So the little minx worked herself harder and harder, until at last the spasm came upon her. She shuddered as if with horror and yet surely the pleasure was exquisite. Indeed, she was so overcome that she sank down and lay upon the tiles, hugging her knees to her breasts and her fingers busy in her panties all over again!

What momentous events are passing in the Villa Lola, dear cousin! What stories I may have to tell you by the time that I dispatch my next letter to England!

Your own loving Grace

III. ANNA TO GRACE

Wight, 14 June, afternoon
My dearest Grace,

I received your letter with its charming and most amusing anecdote of Miss Jones. Yet I fear, my dear cousin, that I am hardly a good audience for such tales just now. To tell you the truth, I do not know whether to rejoice or despair.

Before you cry alarm at my obsession and write to Dr. Raspail about my condition, let me inform you that all my suspicions have proved well founded, as I saw for myself last night. Would you credit it?

Thinking this room of mine unoccupied, the two girls did not so much as draw a curtain over any window. I saw all that passed as clearly as if then in the best box at the theatre and they performing on the stage a dozen feet from me!

But first you may be sure I had not missed the opportunity of taking many a view of Julie during the day, while she sat on her stool behind the shop counter in her plain black dress and coquettish little red shoes. I watched her as, having changed into the working pants of tight denim, she lifted the books and filled the shelves again. At a discreet distance, I followed her through the streets on her route to the rooms where Sian waited. How I adored the spread of her fine golden-blond hair on her shoulders as it rose and fell a little with the rhythm of her agile steps! How my eyes caressed her slender thighs in the skin-tightness of smooth faded denim which creased across their backs and behind her knees at each movement. Though she is, I hear, nineteen years old, Julie's thighs have the endearingly fragile look of a little girl's. My desires grew harder as I watched in the tight denim seat the lewd little movements, while she walked, of the saucy little cheeks of Julie's bottom!

When we came to the narrow street, I hurried up to my window and sat there discreetly behind the curtain. Every room opposite was open to my view—bedroom and kitchen, even toilet and bathroom—so little did they imagine themselves to be observed and so little, perhaps, did they care.

Sian was watching for her girlfriend's arrival. I saw the image of her face and the short tresses of red hair shaped about her head and lying here and there on her forehead. In anticipation of the passion and seduction to come, she had darkened the lashes of her blue eyes with the mascara brush and painted red the sensuous little bud of her lips. With her pert young nose and the slight weakness of her chin, she appears the most blatant sensualist.

They met at the door of the sitting-room and at once slid their arms about each other in a writhing and smoothing embrace. Each of them seemed to be trying to stifle the other with the pressure of mouth upon mouth. Sian, the tendrils of dark red hair lying over her brow, was quite shamelessly unbuttoning Julie's blouse with all the moist eagerness of frustrated passion. In a moment more her hands had firmed up those pert little breasts which I vow ought only to be accessible to my own adoring hands. I was so vexed, Grace, so very vexed that I cannot describe my state of mind with any lucidity. It pains me even to recall my feelings then.

They led one another off, with arms twined lewdly round waists and heads resting together, pausing to kiss and nuzzle at every few steps. The door from the bathroom to the toilet opened and Julie went in, undoing her pants in preparation. At least, I thought, the door would be shut and she would be separated from Sian for a few minutes. Perhaps I would contrive some scheme for getting the slut with the mop of red hair into my power by then.

I was so enraged, my dearest, that I trembled afterwards at the images which had occurred to me. Yet I cannot say I regretted what I would have done to Sian if fate had delivered her to me in some harem from which no scandal ever emerges. How I hated her painted little mouth and her round chin, the slant of her cheekbones and the way she mascara thickened the lashes of her wide blue eyes. I raged at the mop of red hair trimmed short where it just lapped over her collar, its stray plumes falling on her brow. I would have handed the leather strangling-strap to my major-domo and ordered him to do his worst to Sian.

Vain dreams, indeed, and yet most agreeable to me in my jealous fury—and surely justified by what I saw. The door of the toilet did not close. Sian and Julie both entered. Julie sat on the pedestal with her knickers round her ankles and released her flood on the porcelain. All the time, Sian hung over her and browsed with lips on lips. Julie sat a little longer while her friend busied round her. Then I saw that my treasure was winding her golden blond hair into a strand, holding it forward from the crown. With Sian's aid she once more pinned it into that delightful little top-knot which gives her the look of such a saucy little madam of a child!

Even before Julie rose from the pedestal, Sian knelt before her and removed the panties and denim which were round her ankles. To my fury she seemed to be telling Julie, in a sly and sluttish manner, that she would need to wear nothing of that kind again this evening and that indeed she might not be permitted to. I wonder, Grace. Do you suppose it could be contrived for the sharp bodkin point to enter Sian's belly button at such a snail's pace that she might live a whole day and night upon it? I cannot wish for less that that!

I watched them return kisses again. Now it was Sian who undid her pants and sat upon the pedestal. I tell you, Grace, I nearly swooned with horror when I saw how she had led my girl astray. For now it was Julie who hovered over Sian, lips to lips, while the redhead pressed the pale softness of her hips and bottom on the seat and then let loose such a flood upon the porcelain.

Is the world mad? Has decency deserted the entire female sex? Do you recall the way we had to hide our Sapphism, living underground and not entering toilets together like common sluts? Like a pair of dirty little schoolgirls, Sian and Julie fondled and played in this inauspicious bridal suite.

That was but the start. Sian stood up and removed her own pants from the tangle round her ankles. Naked from the waist down, arms about one another, they slunk from there into the bedroom. You may well believe that the boudoir of such a pair was a place of extreme disorder and that the cover of the bed itself was littered with the brushes and patch-boxes, the rouge and mascara, by which beauty is applied to certain female features. Among this debris, down they lay. Each pulled the other's blouse up to bring their breasts into play, nipples teasing nipples into hardness while I watched them. Then it seemed that Sian coaxed Julie to mount astride her thigh by cocking a leg over and to have a ride. My view was of Julie's saucy little bottom-cheeks and the rear of her thighs as she did this. How she squirmed! How her seductive little bum-cheeks clenched and writhed, her thighs squeezing upon Sian's in order to excite the sensitive folds of her vaginal flesh.

I saw that Julie's passion rose easily and this made me lament all the more that she was not spending it upon me. Her hands were clenched into fists and she ground her teeth with frenzy. She clenched her thighs upon Sian's with such vicious energy that you might have thought she was trying to crush to death her ticklish little clitoris.

What was I to do? Alas, I was doomed to be merely the spectator of a pleasure enjoyed at my expense.

Julie had been easily seduced. She now turned about so that she knelt astride Sian's face, indeed almost squatted on Sian's lips, while she bowed her own face so that she could employ it between the other girl's open legs. In this manner they made love for the next half hour. First it was with fingers, diddling one another quickly up and down the pleasure slit, working a finger in and then quickly in-and-out. Next it was kissing and tongue-flicking of the other girl's love-button. During this, Sian moaned with happiness all the time and twice screamed out at the intensity of her arousal. Presently to my horror, I saw Julie move a little and kiss Sian upon the cheeks of her bottom.

What was to be the end of this? I had not expected to see Julie climax first for though she may appear a sullen little thing, her moodiness did not seem to be of that kind which sometimes cloaks the sensual nature of a woman. And yet it was Julie who orgasmed first. She jigged her hips and her thighs—so slim and fragile— shuddered with the overmastering thrill of the release. She cried out the names of Sian, of her loutish boyfriend, and of several other partners with whom she has enjoyed a rub and a squeeze in the past.

Sian, unable to wait longer for her own release, slipped a hand down and completed her own pleasure without any assistance from Julie. With her eyes closed and the tendrils of her red hair lying over her forehead, she began to gasp and tense herself until this randy trim-thighed little shop girl came off with shudders and murmurs of passionate gratitude to her own fingers.

Those who tell you, Grace, that jealousy is like the torture of the rack do not at all exaggerate. The cruelty of it is in the way it pulls a man in opposite directions so that he is no longer master of his feelings. At one moment I saw Julie in the arms of another and could have wept for the loss I felt. Then, with no effort on my part, I felt only a savage anger towards the girl for whom I longed. It was as if, since I could not have her, I wished to see her tortured and abused. Then this feeling too would pass and I was once again desolate in the hopeless state of my exile from her joys.

To see Sian and Julie toiling at one another was the keenest punishment of desire which I could ever have imagined.

They lay head to tail on the bed, closely inspecting and fondling the spread of each other's thighs and buttocks. The most intense spasms of their mutual desire seemed to be past. Now they were content to stroke and fondle more gently. Despite the wedding-ring on her finger, Sian has trim young thighs and firmly agile bottom-cheeks. Julie licked her fingers and began to draw wet patterns on the white skin of Sian's trim young buttocks and down her thighs. Now the redhead returned the service to the slim young blonde. They wetted and drooled over each other in the lewdest possible manner until their unwholesome conduct excited stronger passions and they began to pry and insert their fingers, each watching what she was doing to the other at a few inches distance in order to inflame her own lewdness.

I cannot envisage what means may be used to drive these two girls apart and to speed Julie into my arms. I do assure you, Grace, they now began to play upon the bed like the most lascivious little kittens. There was not one nook or cranny of either girl's body which was not lingeringly probed and caressed by the tongue of the other little slut! You see where despair born of jealousy had brought me? I now began to think of Julie as a slut!

I will leave you to imagine what I wished for Sian when I knew how deeply she had undermined the purity of my passion! Were it in my power, I would order a display behind the plate glass of the shop which should have the crowds a-gape! Sian with her mop of red hair, her white-skinned lasciviousness and blue eyes, a rope round her neck and her feet dancing on air a full hour! A steel bodkin-tip tickling her bare belly-button and beginning to demand entrance!

Have no fear, Grace. It is not yet within my power— but it shall one day be! I shall not be called to account for it. Our friend, the Lord Chief Justice, will be my security! Dr. Raspail shall plead my neurasthenia. Have I not been provoked beyond the endurance of a woman in perfect health, let alone one in my questionable condition?

Despair overcame my curiosity and I turned from the window. Presently I knew that it would be impressible for me to endure another moment in the rooms I had hired to keep my observation upon the pair. Taking up my hat, I went down the stairs and shut the door. Above the little street, I now saw the light shining from the uncurtained window of the room in which the two girls lay, naked and writhing in each other's arms.

I departed, my regret at the disappearing sight of them only equalled by my knowledge that I had done what I must to preserve my fragile health.

IV. GRACE TO ANNA

Lago di Garda, 25 June
My dearest Cousin,

Only the postscript to your letter lightened somewhat the apprehension which I have long felt on your behalf. Lord Rupert will furnish you with all the necessary introductions you require and will esteem it a pleasure to do so. There are public disciplines attended by the justices which you might witness. Yet when the door is locked upon certain scenes, it is only the chastiser who is present with the girls. I am sure you will understand why!

Your failing perhaps is one of moral resolve. Cannot you see what may be done in the name of moral discipline? We have had a charming example here in the past few days and, indeed, it is I who have helped to bring it about. Were you to join us here, you would find that I am now spoken of as the strictest duenna who ever watched over the girls of the Villa Lola. And yet, I assure you, I have never enjoyed myself half so much in my life as I do now with Miss Jones and Marit Aas.

By your outrage at the lewd little romps of Julie and Sian it is evident that you have much to learn about the amusements in which the female sex may indulge today that we never could in our day. Truthfully, though, I have long wanted to see young Marit's panties as her only covering, solely for the pleasure of stripping them from her.

Were I a fool, which I trust is not the case, I had by now attempted a romantic seduction of our Scandinavian nymph. And what would have been the result? Outrage and scandal; the end of a pleasant summer by this warm Italian lake.

What then was I to do? It was evident that I must become a moralist of the kind only found among the higher orders of English female society. Marit herself gave enough pre-text for that. She is not quite an *immoraliste* and yet her conduct is a little questionable. In her singlet, saucy little cap, and tight denim pants on her slender thighs and tightly rounded rear cheeks, she parades each day in the town. With her soft young face and the waves of her brown tresses lapping silkily over her collar, she is to be seen sitting at cafe tables with other girls and boys, smoking a cigarette with the studied manners of a little coquette.

It is also evident that Marit plays with herself between the legs, furtively enough in the privacy of her own bed. Put all these things together and does she not call for the strictest moral supervision? I summoned her to my presence, with all Mr. Bowler's authority to support me. Marit will be a real beauty with her firmly rounded chin, wide and charming smile, her short pert nose and light blue eyes. How she blushed now when I spoke to her of her delinquencies, ending with the worst.

'Stand up, Marit, and turn about so that I may see you. Such pretty legs for a girl of your age, in those tight denim pants! I'm sure your bridegroom will find them to be graceful and elegant when he undresses you on your honeymoon night! Narrow hips and tight young bottom-cheeks, Marit! Not quite a proper grown woman yet, perhaps! All the same, your backside begins to show a woman's shape! Even in your wedding-dress, I'm sure those rear cheeks will still be taut and agile!'

The velvety smoothness of Marit's lightly suntanned face coloured up a little at these compliments but she blushed far more deeply at my next words.

'I think you like to make love to yourself, don't you, Marit? When did you last do it?'

Imagine the blushings, the stutterings of protest now!

'Don't pretend to misunderstand, Marit. When did you last play with yourself?'

Believe me, Anna, I was the master inquisitor of our Nordic nymph. There was such shame-faced hesitation, a few gulps and whimpers. But I would tolerate no prevarication. To my delight Marit confessed to doing it *twice* the day before, once in the bathroom during the afternoon and then in bed at night! I shook my head, as if my heart were heavy with sorrow at the news.

'I am more distressed, more disappointed in you, than I can say, Marit! So, if I did my duty as I should, it would be to send you home at once to your unhappy parents with a full explanation of your conduct. A girl so predisposed to these things is a moral danger to herself and to those with whom she associates. You know, I imagine, to what I refer.'

Grace and Anna

There is something so exquisite, Anna, about true repentance. Marit's knees pressed the carpet before my chair as she begged for anything—anything!—rather than the disgrace which now threatened her. I was not easily moved, you may be sure. We had tears from her before I was softened a little. A fool would have gone too far. Not I. With great seriousness I explained that her moral welfare was my sole consideration. Against my better judgment, she might stay at the Villa Lola. There was, however, to be a condition.

Anything, Marit assured me. Anything!

Very well, I explained. In order to maintain moral vigilance over this frail adolescent conscience, Marit was to be inspected twice a day for evidence of immoral conduct. In order to spare her blushes it would be done anonymously. There was a convenient hatchway between two rooms in the cellar. She would bend through it and the hatch would be lowered until it was locked in place, just touching the small of her back. Marit would not be able to straighten up or free herself until the hatch was unlocked. We should be able to strip off her denim skirt or pants, pull Marit's knickers right down and fiddle with her all morning or all night if we wished to. Best of all, this was to be done in the name of the strictest moral supervision.

A duenna of less imagination than I, would have fallen upon the girl at the first opportunity. I was struck by a more poetic notion. Miss Jones should carry out the examinations of Marit each morning and evening. I had no doubt that a randy and depraved young bitch of Miss Jones's sort would have an effect upon Marit. I should soon have two girls in a lewd and lascivious state rather than one.

So it was that yesterday morning, Marit went slowly down the steps to the lower rooms. She hesitated long before the hatchway but then bent forward through it, the washed blue denim tight on her slender thighs and the tight little rounds of her bottom-cheeks. The hatch was lowered into place and locked. You may be sure I spied from a corner where I could see both sides, the silken waves of Marit's collar-length hair falling about her face in the most charming disorder.

Miss Jones appeared cautiously, walking with the usual tight little swagger of her hips, the warm gold of her face with its almond eyes and sharp nose appearing like a Turkomean mask. She studied the slim little figure presented to her from the waist down and then very slowly undid Marit's denim. Even this caused the victim to squirm a little with apprehension. The young mistress pulled the drawers down until they were a puddle of denim round the girl's ankles. Marit's thin graceful thighs looked almost frail and yet one had not the least regret at what she was about to undergo. Marit's panties were no more than a pair of tight briefs in white cotton. For the moment she was made to wear them.

Miss Jones began her inspection. Her slim nimble fingers entered between the rear of Marit's bare thighs and closed upon the little pouch of secret flesh moulded by the tight cotton gusset of her panties. How the younger nymph flinched and squirmed at the delicious forbidden touch of Miss Jones's fingers. But Miss Jones makes love to herself regularly and so has the skill of a devil when she takes other girls in hand. A demure young debutante like Tracey was heard to scream with the sharpness of the pleasure when the pale ovals of her bottom cheeks and her pussy flesh came under the handling of our randy little temple dancer!

Marit gasped and whimpered, tossed and twisted her head, squirmed her slim bare thighs as if trying to press the excitement back into her womb. The thick and pearly dew of her passion began to gather and, in no time at all, Marit's knickers clung between her legs. Miss Jones, randy little minx that she is, was aware that the feel of the cotton pants in this state would make Marit even more exquisitely aware of her own arousal.

Only when the pupil had been fully roused did Miss Jones pull the panties right down. How narrow were the trim young hips she now revealed, while Marit's slim bottom-cheeks seemed hardly on the threshold of womanhood. Now the agile fingers of the older girl moved in the most remorseless rhythm, rubbing and squeezing, stroking and tickling. You may imagine how Marit squirmed and gasped, for all the world as if in true distress, whose sounds are often hard to distinguish from the cries of pleasure. She knew not whose fingers were working the magic spell upon her, which added to the charm of the situation. Yet, as one watched, it was evident after ten more minutes that the pattern of her movements changed. She ceased to tighten herself or resist. Opening her slim young thighs wider, she accepted Miss Jones's caresses, even showing how she yearned for them. Marit's lips parted, she breathed deeply, and her eyes closed gently and flutteringly in a dream of love. Presently Miss Jones knelt behind her and applied her open mouth between Marit's slender thighs, whose inner surfaces shone wet with the youngster's slippery dew. There are as many secret lusts as there are human beings. Miss Jones has a perverse relish in tasting other girls during their excitement. She brought Marit off with sly dartings of her tongue and constant kissing of the roused and moistened folds of puss-flesh. Marit cried out softly, her legs trembling visibly and her tight young arse-cheeks squirming.

Holding her firmly after the climax, Miss Jones parted Marit's trim little buttocks and began to caress or tickle her between them. My own future plans for Miss Aas involve a degree of unusual pleasures and I was pleased to see that Miss Jones had begun to sensitise her in the forbidden valley already!

Our Scandinavian nymph squirmed and whined in protest for the next half hour. But the little beauty had her buttocks tickled and her bottom-crack caressed pitilessly. In a few weeks more we shall have awakened all her erotic responses in that sensitive area. By the time that Miss Jones finished with her, it was an hour before lunch. The hatch was unlocked and raised. Marit rather forlornly pulled up her knickers and denim. Presently she retired with eyes downcast. Do not lament for her, my dear. I was able to observe her through the spy-hole between our rooms. Marit dropped her pants again, lay down on her bed, and played with herself between her legs until it was necessary to knock on the door and remind her that lunch was ready.

She will be a changed girl by the time she leaves here. And yet, Anna, who will dare to deny that I have acted in the most moral fashion? Do you now begin to understand? I do hope that, having received these most encouraging reports of the goings on here, you have decided to come join us. I assure you that given the encouraging state of Sapphism in Italy, you will not regret it.

Your own adoring Grace

SUSAN ANN

S usan Ann in boots and tights—The thighs and bottom of a college-girl waitress—A lewd wager and a challenge—Miss Jolly, an almond-eyed devil—Her wicked tricks upon naked Sue! —Susan Ann in love at last—Her delicious forfeit

I had taken my dear friend Laura to my club and we had just been seated when there was a tap at the fine white door with its gold inlay. When it opened, my dining companion and I stared in astonishment and absolute delight, for we had only just been discussing Susan Ann and her repudiation of sex following a bad ending with a recent gentleman. It had been our suspicion that she wanted for the sort of awakening only another woman could offer.

Let me describe Miss Susan Ann to you. There was indeed a hardness in her potentially pretty face. The fair-skinned features were well cut but her mouth was set tight, her light blue eyes rather narrow, and her chin a little shallow. There was a hint of pretty freckling round her nose. I could imagine her laughing easily and behaving quite skittishly among her girlfriends, but towards men she showed a chill of bitterness. Her tresses of medium brown hair just overlay her collar, a style that suited her, and were shaped quite close to her head with a short, parted fringe.

What caused my quiet gasp of delight was the sight of Sue's figure tantalisingly displayed. She was an averagely tall girl with firm, well-kept curves, which by the age of twenty-five had nonetheless a proud young maturity. Perhaps it was to smuggle herself past the porters that she now wore a short blue jacket with brown leather boots to her knees, and skin-tight denim riding trousers!

I doubt if it was simply a disguise. In her bitterness to the male sex I suspect that Sue derived satisfaction from showing men the delights which they would never be permitted to enjoy. Even the most aged Albany porter would scarcely have mistaken her figure for that of a stable boy from the cavalry!

As she served the meal, my attention was drawn to the superbly delineated shape of her body from the waist down. So much so that I cannot remember a single one of the succulent dishes we devoured or even one of the fine old clarets which accompanied them. The blue denim of the riding trousers fitted her like tights, creasing across the backs of her knees and upper thighs with the tension. She had long firm thighs whose upward and outward branching was perfectly outlined by the tight denim.

As she approached with platter or decanter my eyes followed the bow of her trim legs, then dwelt upon the taut triangle of cloth leading down to Susan Ann's love-nest, which had caused so many problems. As she turned, at my elbow, and reached across the table, I could scarcely keep my hands off her. The denim was drawn splittingly tight across the proud cheeks of Sue's bottom. Like many girls at that time, she wore the protection of tight silken briefs under riding trousers to give extra insurance against saddle soreness. So taut was the denim that I clearly saw the elastic hem of the briefs outlined, arching up high and tight over each cheek of Susan Ann's backside.

The meal was done at last. Coffee and brandy were brought, our cigars were lit.

'Now then, Sue,' said Laura softly, 'are you ready to put your renunciation to the test?'

'If you like,' she said indifferently. It was the prim, cool voice of the college girl.

'Then take off your trousers and boots, Sue,' Laura said, 'and your jacket. Wear just your briefs and your breast halter. Then lie on your back on the dinner table. You have my word that no man will touch you against your will.'

Susan Ann obeyed. I would like to have taken her knickers down there and then fingered her among the crockery, turned her over, smacked her arrogant young bottom long and hard, and done all manner of things to her. But a gentlewoman keeps her word. Soon, in tight glossy briefs and silk breast halter, she was lying on her back among the debris of our banquet.

'Your hands through the cuffs, Sue,' Laura reminded her.

Since we had given our word, it was agreed that Sue must allow her wrists to be strapped to the table frame on either side of her. She made no protest, as if she no longer cared what happened to her. When she was secured there, Laura got up and went to the door of his study. She opened it. This time I very nearly shouted with laughter, though I had half expected what would happen. Can you guess?

The answer, in two words, was Miss Jolly, or Cara Jolly, or Car' as she was more familiarly known. You haven't met her before, of course. May I introduce you?

Miss Jolly was a tight little wriggler of twenty-two or twenty-three summers. She had a neat figure, golden skin, and an almost Egyptian or Mediterranean beauty. The sharp nose, dark lynx-eyes, and tall forehead held a promise of passion and perversity. Her hair was cut short of her collar and brushed upwards in short dark curls. She had the neatest young breasts, a slim straight back, and narrow waist. She was, by the way, wearing tight silk knickers and blouse. The knickers encased her from waist to knees, showing slim thighs and hips without a pinch of excess fat. Yet the pale coppery cheers of Miss Jolly's bottom were perfectly and exquisitely rounded. Indeed, she emphasised their appeal by walking with a tight lascivious little swagger for the benefit of those behind her.

This, then, was the hot, almond-eyed little beauty who was to restore the warmth of love to our frozen Susan Ann! Laura had kept his word. No man would lay a ringer upon Sue.

Miss Jolly needed no instruction. She walked across to the table where her golden figure made a piquant contrast with Sue's fair-skinned body, now almost bare. There was a devilish gleam in Miss Jolly's slanting eyes as she lowered her head and fastened her mouth on Sue's in a vigorous kiss, trying to force the taste of her tongue into Sue's mouth. Sue resisted with tight lips and immobility. Then she tried to break away, twisting her body among the dinner debris. A coffee cup rattled and the slops splashed the back of her thigh, trickling down to gather behind her knee. Inadvertently she sat against a saucer, where her seat was not covered by the briefs. A large grey smudge of cigar ash blemished one proud young cheek of Sue's bottom!

Miss Jolly stood back and pulled up the halter, clear of Sue's soft white breasts. She worried the tight pink nipples between finger and thumb. Despite herself, Sue's eyes closed and her lips parted slightly. Miss Jolly opened a little tin containing pale brown powder which smelt of hot spice. She took some on her tongue and watered it in her mouth. Then, still with her tongue, she washed over the first of Sue's nipples, adding a little more powder and settling down to a lick-flick, lick-flick mouthing of Susan Ann's tit-cherries.

Sue gave a soft cry, mingling protest and longing. The tightness of her mouth was gone, her nipples were hard and erect, she was arching her torso up as if to offer them to Miss Jolly's urgent attention. Still she would not confess the wager lost.

Very gently, the golden-skinned tormentress drew Susan Ann's knees up to her chin and secured them there by a strap round the lower thighs connecting with another round Sue's waist. Sue was still on her back but now in a squatting position. Miss Jolly went down to the other end of the table for an under view of her subject, the spread of thighs, cunt, and arse which a squatting girl presents to the ground. Laura and I moved our chairs slightly so that we too could concentrate upon this sight from a range of a mere few inches! The tight translucent silk of Sue's briefs showed the lightly mossed lips of her womb and the deeper cleft of her backside with its dark narrow entrance revealed by her spread posture.

'Oh, no! No!' Sue implored as Miss Jolly's nimble fingers began gently and tantalisingly to stroke the furry vaginal lips through the thin tight silk. But the dark almond eyes were pitiless. Against the silk we heard the light whisper, whisper, whisper, as Miss Jolly stroked remorselessly, ending each caress with a gentle pressure on the clitoris. The remorseless rub-and-squeeze soon produced visible and audible results. Sue's protests grew quieter and gave way to gentle, wistful sighs. The wet of her pearly love-juice began to darken the silk of her pants.

'You wicked girl, Susan Ann!' said Laura, playfully stern. 'You can't resist temptation, can you?'

She made no reply, only lifting her hips readily so that her briefs could be drawn well down her legs. She was warm with excitement, the love-juice and perspiration gathering. The musty girl-scent of passion reached us from between her thighs and bottom-cheeks.

Miss Jolly opened the little tin of spice again, and despite herself, Sue cried out in alarm. But on her elbows with head lowered, Miss Jolly licked the hot stinging excitement into the wet cleft of Sue's nether lips.

The last cold disdain had gone from Susan Ann by now. She was itching lewdly. Miss Jolly had only to put her slim agile hand there and Sue rode it like a saddle, rubbing herself from the tip of her clitoris all the way back to her bum! The wicked Eastern spice was so constituted that she was desperate to assuage its virulent titillation, and yet the more she rubbed the worse it teased her.

There was no harm in the cunning spice, of course. Once washed off, its effects died away. Indeed, Sue had only to retire to the bathroom afterwards and water herself in order to be free of it. Its permanent and beneficial effect was upon her mind.

Miss Jolly had not done with her yet. She took three small balls, the size of blackbirds' eggs, moistened them, and took them one by one into her mouth. Then, bowing her head, she slid them on her tongue high up into Sue's cunt. Gently she turned Sue on to her side. Even this movement produced a sudden gasp from the patient at the deep and thrilling arousal of the smooth little globes moving in such a sensitive place.

Next Miss Jolly took the thin, empty tube of a corona-corona cigar, thick as a thumb and about eight inches long. With great care she lubricated Susan Ann's rear and slid the rounded end of the tube into the girl's behind. Sue gave a cry of alarm as she felt what was happening, but pleasure rather than harm was all that resulted. For a moment she lay there. The tight mouth was relaxed, the blue eyes wider and more appealing. Inside her lay the three magic eggs. The end of the cigar tube peeped out saucily between Susan Ann's bum-cheeks.

Now Miss Jolly began in earnest. With one hand she manipulated Sue's sensitive cunt lips and clitoris. With the other she moved the cigar tube in a gentle in-and-out movement in Sue's bottom. The three little eggs were thus manipulated from both sides at once, jiggled by the masturbation between Sue's thighs and stirred by the tube in Sue's behind beyond a thin diaphragm of skin.

Sue responded with wild, rising cries of joy. In a delirium she screamed the names of her lovers, as if calling them to witness her triumph. She cried out to have this one's prick in her mouth, a tool between her legs, and a third up her bottom. Miss Jolly pressed another kiss upon her, while continuing to masturbate Sue at the same time. Sue's mouth opened greedily, drawing in the almond-eyed girl's tongue, sharing the tastes of Miss Jolly's mouth in her own saliva.

At last Sue reached the zenith of her ecstasy and the bubble of passion burst. Without a pause, Miss Jolly continued the masturbation and Sue was riding again towards love's reward for the second time. After three orgasms, Miss Jolly stopped, and Sue lay panting on her back. The wicked lynx-eyed bitch now gently blindfolded Susan Ann. When this was done, she took a velvet soft rubber penis which had been warmed to blood heat in water.

Caressing Sue's cunt lightly, she presented the knob of the rubber dildo to the parted lips of the blindfolded girl.

Deceived by this, Susan Ann gave a sigh of relief, as if for something of which she had long deprived herself, and sucked as contentedly as a baby on a dummy. She groaned with the pleasure as a second diddler entered between her legs. Without a word of command she turned on her side, her proud pale bottom arched out, inviting a third intruder. The rubber prick up Sue's backside must have stretched her to the limit. Yet she had no wish to be spared even this ordeal.

When the three rubber phalluses were presently withdrawn, we heard only Sue's imploring whimper for their return. Yet the time had come for comfort and reassurance. After so much care, we had to be certain that her return to the delights of love was not spoilt by later remorse or self-disgust.

When she was released, Laura said gently, 'Pull your pants up, Sue, and go into the bedroom.'

She dressed quickly without looking at either of us or at Miss Jolly. Yet I sensed that Susan Ann was not ashamed. Rather, she was proud of herself for being a woman again.

HENRIETTE, BERTHE, ROSINE, THÉRESE, MARTHE, JANVIER & BLANCHE

Henriette de Barras

16 Avenue Matignon

'Everybody for me, and myself for everybody.' Such is the incredible and audacious motto that this miniature beauty puts on her letter paper, emblazoned in a multitude of colours. We must not forget that she is one of the few high-class demireps who enjoys the advantage of a good education. She is a little lady, born in 1861, and she left her comfortable home at the age of seventeen with a young officer who deserted her after a few months. One of the

Henriette, Berthe, Rosine, Thérese, Marthe, Janvier & Blanche

daintiest little creatures in Paris, with a wasp-like waist that she contrives to make smaller still with tight lacing; a plump figure; small, regular features and a most candid, innocent manner of speaking. She is very friendly with her female companions and likes to be petted and cuddled by any possessed of Sapphic tastes. She pretends to be descended from her namesake, the general famous in French history, but what does that matter to our reader, on carnal thoughts intent? Who cares whether she be of blue blood or humble birth, so long as she be good-natured, healthy and lascivious? She is rather dear, being greatly in the fashion.

Berthe Béranger
14 Rue Sainte Anne

Yet another actress of the little bandbox theatre, the *Palais Royal*. She has played all over the provinces, notably at Bordeaux and at Nantes. A fair slight woman, of medium height, much addicted to the use of cosmetics. The bistre shade under her bright eyes, sign of too earnest devotion to the sports of Venus, is always brought into great prominence, as if her mistress were proud of the two lascivious languishing circles. Berthe, called by her friends, Bébé, which sounds like the initials of her name, pronounced the French way, is inordinately fond of lesbian love, and is always pleased to give herself up to the clinging kisses of her female friends. Like most of her kind, she is very greedy after money, and we may excuse her , as she has a little swarthy girl to bring up. She is pleased to accept the homage of one or other of the actors of her theatre, regardless of their sex. Should this siren tempt any visitor to Paris, let him (or her) be chary of his cheques. Her photograph is to be found all over town, as, indeed, are those of most of the ladies who are dubbed actresses. We need scarcely say that the stage is merely the ante-chamber of their luxuriously furnished bedrooms.

Rosine Bloch
21 Boulevard Haussmann

In 1865, this handsome Jewish girl left the National Academy of Music (the Conservatoire) with flying colours, having gained every prize. She had no artistic ambition, but only tried to make her fortune. Being very beautiful, she quickly succeeded. She is tall, above the average height of women, very largely built, with beautiful almond eyes, rich crimson lips and queenly carriage. Although now about thirty-six years of age, she is still a marvellous morsel. Her pet vice is passive tribadism, and a very pretty little Israeli maiden, Lilia Herman, is often to be found beneath her tent or on her knees, drinking the sweet consolation that is distilled from the alter of female friendship.

Thérèse Bréval
60 Boulevard Malesherbes

One of our prettiest harlots, but what would be called in London 'a hot member'. Her splendid bust, large black eyes and pretty face have been in circulation since the age of fifteen, when her mother sold her in the Alsatian town where the family lived. Her maiden-head was paid for several times, until it was impossible to deceive the purchasers any longer. Her father suffered imprisonment for robbery, and since then she has lived with her mother, who makes her work very hard. She is twenty-six now, and has never perfected her early education, not knowing how to read or write. She was a ballet-girl for a time, but soon grew tired of kicking up her legs for such small wages. So she gave herself entirely to prostitution, and, thanks to mamma, prospered greatly. She has had as many mistresses as lovers, and a favourite after-supper diversion is the spectacle of Thérèse making love to one of her own sex. She cannot possibly sleep alone, and if by accident she should come home by herself, invites her maid to jump into bed with her.

Marthe Cerny
21 Rue Berlioz

In the year 1858, Marthe came into the world at Rouen, where her mother and father worked hard at making copper saucepans. Trade grew bad, and papa emigrated with wife and daughter to Paris, where madam treated herself to a sturdy lover, who not only satisfied the old lady, but also debauched the head of the family by taking him out to suppers and giving him tastes for high-priced whores, champagne suppers and other expensive luxuries which are generally unknown in the iron mongering trade. But the false friend was soon found out, and the door shut in his face, while the adulterous wife died of galloping consumption, brought on by her insatiable desires. Marthe was then packed off to boarding school, so as not to be in her father's way. The provincial beauty was soon taught the pleasures of tribadism in the silence of the dormitory, her school chum being none other than Thérese Bréval, who not only taught her the mysteries of Minette, but also how to 'frisk' the fraternal till. Since then, she has been up and down on the ladder of lust, and spends all her money on women, being passionately fond of the pleasures that she learnt in school. Marthe is a fine, tall woman, with long black tresses, large eyes, good teeth and a beautifully shaped bosom, albeit small withal.

Janvier
Opéra

All the women at the National Academy of Music are venal whores, and to trace their biographies would necessitate a volume devoted to that building alone, which is nothing more than a gigantic bawdy-house. From the apprentice ballet girl, just out of her teens, down to the high salaried principal songstress, all are to be had for the asking—the payment varying from a supper and a new pair of boots, to hundreds of pounds. We mention this lady because she is an insatiable devotee of lesbian love, and pursues her prey in the corridors of the Opéra like a man. She is short and dark, with a splendid pair of legs and thighs that cause her to be chosen to play pages. She is a very good-looking woman, with a large mouth, the lips of which are of a bright crimson colour , borrowing their feverish warmth from the youthful, unfledged tails she is so fond of chewing.

Blanche Delaunay
Athenée Théatre

All that we can learn about this brilliant beauty, fat and fair, is that she was formerly a servant in a bawdy-house. Her beauty soon found her many lovers, and , after a variety of changes in life, we find her at the theatre above-mentioned, where she plays small parts, such as silly servant girls, when her enormous bubbies are freely shown to the astonished spectators. Since her appearance on the stage she has got up in the world, and her tariff, from silver, as it used to be, now reaches to the golden standard. She became the heroine of innumerable orgies, and grew to be a ferocious lesbian. But some woman with whom she was madly in love, having behaved badly to her, she returned to the muscular arms of the male sex. At this present moment she fondly adores her dog, Azor, and makes no secret of her attachment to the faithful and patient animal.

DENISE

his story is a reminiscence; a fond recollection of my colourful days as a youth. I can safely say (with the clarity of hindsight) that my youth was extraordinary. My upbringing was unlike any other young woman knew at the time, and to this day, many years later, I have yet to meet a soul whose story can compare with mine in its bizarre nature. For while sexual inversion has become more tolerated in modern times, it was still rejected quite harshly when I was young. Seeing my obvious inversion from an early age, my family had a pressing interest in keeping it from general knowledge. My story, then, is one of daily theatrics and secret erotic releases that made it possible for me to negotiate the society of the day.

My erotic rearing gave me a great sense of alienation, yet also a feeling of being absolutely rare and precious. Of course, later in life I learned that I was not alone in my sexual proclivities; proclivities that flourished and were fostered from the time I was very young on through my early adulthood. I have since had the pleasure of finding others who share the same delicious tastes that I have enjoyed. I was cared for by my strange and beautiful stepsister, Helen, with the delicate attentions that one gives a fragile, unique flower. It was my lovely stepsister who helped me to find the 'true' self that was hiding inside me.

Ever since I could remember, I had a great fondness for the female sex. Indeed, I felt about my gender the way other girls felt about the opposite one. It was Helen who really prodded me to discover my true nature and created an environment in which I relished the world of women. Thus, the following words are the tale of what I shall call my 'becoming.'

The episode that I am about to relate is a description of my sexual awakening, and the pivotal event that shaped the rest of my life.

As you can imagine, I had been wallowing in a state of some confusion as to the nature of my sexual orientation since the onset of my adolescence. I had been reluctant to leave my home, which had been fairly bleak since my father had become a widower.

When I was first sent away to an English boarding school, I took great pains to hide my feelings from the other girls, but it was still a disaster. Apart from the pleasure I derived from stealing long glances at my schoolmates— I was fascinated by their soft curves and small forms; their feminine ways held a great exoticism to me, as well as exciting me greatly—I had little pleasure. In fact, I was ashamed and stood up to much ridicule during my time at boarding school. I was miserable and terribly out of place. I found that my one solace was daydreaming, and I took to staring out of my window, and the windows of the classrooms, remembering the peace and solitude that I had once enjoyed at Beaumanoir.

Many was the night that I lay alone in my bed, creating images of delight, picture fancies of the lovely gowns that Helen wore and all the accoutrements of her station and sex. I would worry, on such sleepless nights, about my future when I was to take over as mistress of the household. I felt that I should look forward to that day with much hunger, but in truth, I was not anticipating the day with gladness. In fact, I knew deep within my soul that I had no taste for marriage and the station I was expected to inhabit, but I did not know how to escape my destiny. If I had only known at that time that my fate was already decided, I would have worried considerably fewer hours away.

But those hours during which I lay awake were not without their pleasurable moments. It was during the secret quiet of the night that I began to discover the pleasures my own body had to offer. Because I was not obliged to share a room with anyone else, I could spend hours lightly stroking my body and bringing myself to pleasure over and over as I massaged my breasts and downy quim. During these wonderful moments, I would always imagine a lady dressed in the finest of women's clothing. I fantasized that my hands ran over her body encased in kid gloves, and that her breasts were softly caressed by the fine lingerie or the harsh lacing of a corset. These thoughts aroused my fancy almost more than the actual touch of my hand did. The potency that these fineries held for me is impossible to describe in detail. I can safely say that the deep hours of the night were among the only happy ones that I spent at that boarding school.

I devised elaborate passion plays in which Miss Priscilla dominated me, while Helen enjoyed toying with my breasts, or even better still, I liked to imagine Helen's lovely full lips on my cunt while Miss Priscilla lightly abused my nipples with her fingers or her mouth. Of course, during these imaginary scenes, the two women would be dressed in the most exquisite of gowns. Oh, the hours of pleasure I afforded myself thinking these wickedly delicious thoughts.

I had yet to see another woman naked, so it was hard for me to imagine. But there was an instance that I liked to draw upon during my hours of fantasizing. One time, a few years previous to being sent to school, Helen and I were sent to the shore. I will never forget the moment when Helen bent over and gingerly removed her shoes and then her stockings, revealing the most beautiful pair of feet that I had ever seen. I watched with jealous hunger as she ran to and from the sneaking tide. Oh, how I wished that I were the sea, that it was I caressing her perfect white feet with my tongue, with my hands and fingers.

But I digress! I was to relate the story of the fateful evening in which a turn of events happened that shaped the entire course of my life.

It was a night like any other previous to it. I lay alone in my bed, lightly stroking my slit with one hand, my lovely little breast with the other. I was recalling an elegant evening dress of satin and tulle that Helen had worn at a spring party the season before. I was enjoying my solitary pleasure so greatly that I never heard the door of my bedroom creak open. As I was quietly moaning into my pillow, I felt a pair of cool hands stroke the soft flesh of my buttocks. I sat up instantly, quietly yelping in surprise when I was met with Heather Repton's hungry eyes. Heather Repton! Here was the girl who had taken such pleasure in tormenting me, and now she had caught me in nightly pleasures.

'Heather! What are you...'

'Shh!' she hissed, and covered my mouth with one hand, while the other began roving around my body freely.

I began to struggle, and she pushed me roughly against the pillows. My heart raced, half in fear and half in a new lust aroused.

'Heather, what do you think you're doing?' I whispered desperately as I felt the lovely weight of her small body pinning me to the bed.

'I know what you've been doing in here, you nasty little thing,' she said. She reached between my legs, and grabbing my quim in her hand. 'I came to join in your fun.'

I felt my face flush painfully, especially because her hand was wet from my leaking slit. Not only that, but I was painfully aware of my breasts and tried to cover them with my arms.

'Oh, Denise, don't cover those lovely things. I came to see them too!' Heather laughed, pulling my arm away from my chest with her free hand. 'I want to put my lips on your titties.'

Without waiting for an answer from me, Heather plunged her head down upon my chest and hungrily began to suckle at my soft pink nipple.

Oh, if I could describe to you the exquisite joy and heated pleasure that I felt course through every inch of my flesh! No one's hands but my own had ever stroked or paid lusty attentions to my secret boobies. And now, in a moment's time, Heather Repton had fallen upon me, and with her lips she kissed and bit and sucked my tit. With her hand, she reached between my soft thighs and took cunt in her hand and began to stroke and fondle the lips of it. I had know her to be bold in her torments, but I had never imagined she would be bold in such ways. It was exhilarating. I arched my back involuntarily to meet the kisses that she continued to lavish upon one nipple and then the other.

'Oh! Oh! Heather!' I moaned, my pleasure very nearly exploding.

Just as I was about to spend from Heather's deft fingers, the door of my dormitory room burst open. There in the frame of the door, her face lit underneath from a kerosene lamp, was the dormitory mistress.

I shrieked and recoiled from the light that the headmistress brought in with her, while Heather shouted and tumbled off of me and the bed. She tried to madly scramble underneath the bed, but of course it was a futile attempt at escape. I was horrified and utterly shattered that I did not get to finish my passions. And I knew, as did Heather, that we would both be expelled for our 'disgraceful' behaviour.

The events that immediately followed at the school were dreary, and I was very glad to get away from the dreadful place as soon as I had been booted. Had I known that the episode was the greatest thing that could have happened to me at the time, I would not have been so ashamed. As it was, I feared Helen's wrath, and thought about it the whole ride home. Well, almost all of the ride—if the truth be told, I did offer a moment here or there to the delicious memory of Heather Repton's hand on my cunt and his pretty mouth clamped upon my nipple.

Accordingly I returned home, and nobody knew what to do with me. I could not go to another school. I was too young for the University. I stayed at home for six months. My father was already sickening with his last illness. There was no one to control me; and no doubt I bullied the servants, was tyrannical and threatening to the tenants, rude to Helen, and contemptuous of Miss Priscilla. Miss Priscilla had precise old-maidish neatness which it was a pleasure to me to offend. I would stamp about the drawing room in noisy muddy boots and fling myself on delicately upholstered sofas in dirty football clothes. These things I delighted to do because I saw how much they shocked her and offended Helen. Finally Helen made a suggestion to my father that I should attend a sort of school of her choosing, a school in Paris, in fact, one she was sure would work for my kind. My father was delighted with the idea. He was very ambitious for me. He was unwilling to face the disturbing realities of my unusual inversion.

* * *

Once the household became acclimated to my new habits, we became quite happy while we awaited my departure for school. It was like a new world that I awoke to, finding the sun streaming in the open window. Phoebe brought a cup of tea to my bedside. How delightfully different everything was from the rigid severity of my life in the girls' school. My marble-tiled bathroom seemed a paradise on this summer morning. I was allowed to choose my own frock, and Phoebe dressed me according to my choice. I wore a short walking skirt and coat of plain white silk with a white lace blouse that had a low baby collar that left my throat free. With this cool dress, I wore pale grey silk stockings and grey suede shoes with high Cuban heels. A belt of pink satin, a big straw hat, and elbow-length grey suede gloves completed the costume. I went downstairs and had a walk in the garden until Helen's friends came down. Then we went into a delicious breakfast with fruit and hot rolls.

Everyone from Helen to Doris was as kind to me as it was possible for anyone to be. Helen of course was pursuing her policy: She wanted me to enjoy my life as an invert. She wanted me to love it.

After breakfast Doris was driven off in one of the motorcars to her school in the neighbouring town of Mark's Cross. I was free from tiresome lessons and long hours in the schoolroom. I took up the *Daily Mail* and settled down on a cushioned chair on the veranda with a cigarette. Violet, who was a few months younger than I, joined me. Helen came upon us with a smile upon her face.

'What do you girls want to do this morning?' she asked. 'You won't want to stay in and I should be very glad, since I am busy, if you would drive down in the governess cart together to the village and take some messages for me.'

'That will be jolly,' cried Violet and she looked at me with a smiling face. 'I shall love going out with pretty Denise.'

'Then I will order the cart for eleven,' said Helen. 'You won't want a groom with you. You can always find someone to hold the pony in the village.'

What a change for me! For two years, I had never gone out except with a governess who made us walk two and two and forbade us to talk. Now Violet and I were to drive alone! Thus began a delightful day of freedom for me. The freedom was certainly tempered by some dainty tyranny exercised by Violet. But she was so sweet and loving that I adored being tyrannized by her. For instance, just before the time we were to start off she came to me and said:

'I like your coat and skirt, dear, immensely. But you have prettier hats than the one you are wearing, I am sure, and although those little grey suede shoes and gloves are no doubt very comfortable, I don't think they are smart enough for you to wear when you go out with me.'

'All right, Violet,' I said laughing, and I ran upstairs to my room. I chose a very big leghorn hat adorned with a broad ribbon of white velvet on the crown and tied with an enormous bow and a row of pink roses to match my belt. And I changed into white transparent silk stockings with little, new white shoes, with sparkling buckles and high Louis Quinze heels. Instead of the grey suede gloves, I put on very long delicate gloves of white that disappeared under the elbow-length sleeves of my white silk coat. I took a pink parasol and ran downstairs to Violet.

'Shall I do now, Violet?' I asked.

She looked me over.

I extended a kid shoe and Violet smiled in approval.

'Yes, buckles and high heels suit you Denise. You look delicious now,' and she flung her arms round my neck and kissed me rapturously. 'Oh how silly you are, Denise, to want to not want a husband when you are such a lovely girl,' she cried.

A groom was holding the pony at the door. We got into the trap. Violet took the reins. I put up my parasol and we drove through the beautiful grounds to the park gates. How I enjoyed the sunlight and the fresh air and the country after being cooped up for so long!

Oh, the contentment and joy I felt in being alone with Violet that lovely morning. The warm spring sun and the wonderful pleasure of Violet's company was a luxury of freedom that I had not experienced ever. Yet Violet's disposition; her wish to be my tiny tyrant brought to mind and heart a sweet nostalgia for my lovely friend Nellie.

Nellie was my closest companion and dear love during the time I attended the French girls' school. When I first arrived at the school, I was filled with apprehension and anger at my predicament. I was feeling a great and terrible excitement, which I now understand as a forceful erotic awakening. I was sensually overwhelmed by the future that entailed masquerading. I had been shamed into going to the school, and so upon my arrival, was rather complacent as Helen and Miss Priscilla arranged everything with the headmistress. It began quite unpleasantly. I was still quite exhausted from my channel crossing and the long carriage ride to Paris, and Helen had great fun explaining to the headmistress, in lurid detail, about my indiscretion with Heather Repton and the consequent expulsion from my former school.

Denise

'She is really quite a monster, and so as her guardian and executor of finances, I have decided that a few years among the refined company of young ladies will only do her good,' Helen explained to the stern head-mistress. 'As you can see, she is capable of acting quite normal already, and we have arranged for two personal maids to attend to her needs and make certain that her true nature is not revealed.'

The headmistress looked me over disparagingly as Helen explained everything to her, and after Helen concluded she paused for a long moment before she answered.

'Well, Miss Deverel,' she said, 'I am certain that we shall be able to remodel your charge into a refined young lady of society. I must only ask if she is willing to undergo these changes, for if she is here entirely against her wishes, our task will be next to impossible.'

Helen turned to me and said, 'Denise, answer the headmistress.'

I lowered my eyes in shame and said quietly, 'I wish to be here, Madam. Please accept me.'

'Very well,' said the headmistress. 'You shall stay. You really do look more a normal girl than an invert. You know that, don't you?'

I kept my eyes lowered and nodded yes. I was hiding a smile, for I was inwardly exploding with joy. Indeed, I saw the potential of having the best of both worlds. I would lose the stigma of an invert while gaining in the attention and affection of the sex I longed for. In truth, the events that had started as a consequence of the episode with Heather Repton, the impend-ing punishments, and imprisonment among the lovely young ladies of the school were the greatest and happiest events of my life. But I did not com-pletely understand that at the time.

'She shall have her own room so that the maids can help him dress, and attend to the special regimen that I have constructed for her,' said Miss

Priscilla. 'She will be needing massages and special care in order to keep her appearances as feminine as possible.'

'Yes, and we have had sent a wardrobe befitting a girl of her rank. I do hope this arrangement will be to your satisfaction, Madam,' said Helen to the headmistress.

The headmistress nodded, and then instructed us to say our farewells, for I had a lot of adjusting to do as a new pupil in her school.

My eyes met Helen's as we said good-bye, and within our gaze a mutual agreement was passed. I would acquiesce to her power. She understood me more than I understood myself at that moment. Power became her, and her lovely dark eyes gleamed with an unnatural glow.

'Good-bye dear Denise. We shan't be seeing each other for quite a while. Be a good girl, Denise, and mind what the mistress says.' She kissed me lightly on the lips, and left the room, Miss Priscilla following her out.

Soon the headmistress returned to the parlour, and her stern presence frightened and excited me. This was supposed to be a punishment, and I did not want to betray the exquisite sensation of happiness that was beginning to flood my being. I was afraid that if the women who were controlling me knew what a great coup this was for me, they would retract and redesign their plan for me. I kept my face as expressionless as possible and my shining eyes cast to the floor.

'Now,' said the headmistress sternly, 'we shall design some rules for you. You are to obey them stringently or you shall be severely punished. As much as you look and behave like a young lady, the truth of your nature remains. You are not to reveal to *anyone*, with the exception of the maids and myself. If you do, you shall be unconditionally expelled. You are to behave in a modest fashion at all times, and I expect nothing more than perfect submission to all the ordinances that apply to all the other girls here. Is that understood, Denise?'

Denise

I shuddered with excellent joy. 'Yes, Ma'am,' I stammered, not venturing to look at her.

The headmistress rang a pretty little bell, and a lovely young maid entered the room. Her golden red hair was tied up in an elaborate braid, and she had striking green eyes and the fairest skin I had ever seen. It was unbelievable to me that this magical creature was a maid. She was beautiful, and I could not help but staring at her enviously.

She curtsied in front of Miss Priscilla, and said, 'How can I help you, Ma'am?'

'Nellie, take Miss Denise to the suite upstairs. Her maids will be arriving shortly with her trunks. While you are waiting for their arrival, draw a bath for Miss Denise, and see that she is well groomed for supper.' And with that, the headmistress dismissed both myself and my lovely Nellie.

As we walked up the stairs, I could not take my eyes off the perfect form of her buttocks, which rubbed against the black fabric of her skirt as she walked.

'Where are all the other girls?' I asked.

'They are all on a picnic for the afternoon, Miss,' Nellie replied.

I couldn't wrest my eyes from her perfect complexion, or the unusual fullness of her pert breasts, which strained at the fabric of her apron. She had dainty, small feet that were enclosed in a simple pair of black boots with many grommets for the high lacings. She had tiny hands, uncharacteristic of a maid. Her general beauty and manner seemed much more refined than any maid that I had ever known. I was falling hopelessly in love with her.

'You are such a pretty thing,' said Nellie as she went about preparing my lovely new room. 'I do hope you like it here at the school. Most of the young ladies are such nice girls. I think you will be very pleased here, Miss.' Nellie approached me as she paused, and took a lock of my hair and twirled it on her finger. 'You are a pretty thing,' she repeated.

So I passed for a normal girl. I was shocked and pleased. I was equally surprised by Nellie's forward behaviour as a servant, but then I realized that I was unfamiliar with the ways and manners at this type of school. In a sudden rush of impulsive affection, I reached out and drew Nellie to my breast.

'Thank you for saying so, Nellie. I think you are lovely too. I am so happy to be here!' I gushed. I felt the warmth of her large breasts against my own, and felt her arms encircle my waist. My heart sang. Her hair smelled sweet and clean, and her skin was as soft as butter.

'You are so lucky that you will be in a room of your own, Miss,' said Nellie as she pulled away from my embrace. Her face was suddenly flushed and probably as red as my own.

'Nellie, don't be ashamed of being kind to me. I think you are a wonderful creature, and I do hope we will be friends,' I said, stroking her hot cheek.

'Oh yes, Miss Denise. I would like that ever so much,' she cried as she smiled.

I could scarcely believe my fate! I was the happiest youth in the world. The possibilities of the next two years unravel as a delicious fantasy within my mind's eye. My dreaming was interrupted by the thrilling, shocking sensation of Nellie's delicate fingers pinching my nipples.

'Nellie!' I cried, but did not move away. She meant to draw her hand away from my bosom, but I grabbed her wrist and guided it back to my breast.

'You like that, Miss? I overheard the headmistress say that you will be getting special massages, and I just wanted to please you, Miss' Nellie's face

Denise

was still quite red, but there was a mischievous gleam in her eye.

'What else did you *overhear* the headmistress and my cousin Helen discuss?' I asked, continuing to keep her hand pressed to my tittie.

'Nothing, Miss,' Nellie insisted.

'Are you certain that you didn't mistakenly hear something you shouldn't have?' I pressed. I felt certain that she knew my true identity and that she was simply toying with me.

'Yes, Miss Denise. I didn't hear anything. Nothing that I shouldn't have heard, that is,' she retorted with growing confidence.

Ah, so she was going to blackmail me. How absurd the thought is in retrospect, but at the time, I was terrified of being discovered and expelled from the school; a place I desperately wanted to stay.

'You would like to see my titties, wouldn't you?' I said suddenly.

'Oh, Miss! I—I,' she could not finish her sentence.

I laughed and let her remove her hand from my tit. Without hesitation, I undid the buttons of my simple travelling blouse, and shimmied out of the straps of my chemise, thus revealing my full breasts and pink nipples to the randy maid.

'Oh, Miss Denise, you have lovely titties,' she stammered and stared at my heaving chest; I was excited by the sudden turn of events.

'I have shown you mine, don't you think it fair for you to show me yours now, Nellie? It looks as though you are carrying a lovely set of globes. I want to see them,' I coaxed her.

'You are right Miss I will show you my bubbies.' She undid the ties of her apron, and then the small buttons of her blouse. Once she was released of her cotton chemise, she revealed a deliciously large pair of milky white breasts with large pink nipples.

'Oh, Nellie,' I cried. 'You have lovely titties. Let me feel them!' And without waiting for an answer, I reached out and took her flesh between my fingers. She returned the loving caress immediately.

The thrilling sensation of her light fingers, gently at first, and then more forcefully, teasing and tickling my nipples, was making me delirious. It seemed inevitable that I would deluge the hair of my nest. Would she sense this?

'Let me kiss them,' Nellie whispered. 'I've seen the other young ladies of the school doing this with each other at night. They thought I wasn't watching, but I was. Oh how I longed to join in their fun. They are always giggling and embracing each other when they tickle each other's bubbies and quims.' Nellie paused suddenly and arched her eyebrow. 'Let me see your quim,' she said.

I pushed her away in terror. Thoughts that she might blackmail me returned. Was that what she did to the young ladies here? While I was thinking, Nellie had come forward and put her delicate red lips to the most nervous part of my breast. She began sucking and licking me, and the feeling was exhilarating. I did not want her to stop, but I was still afraid. I continued to fondle and pinch her breasts, enjoying my task immensely. And then suddenly, as I was lost to the pleasures of Nellie's lips on my breasts, she reached between my legs and felt the sopping wet fabric there.

'It is true, then. I did hear. You are a true Sapphist, aren't you? Oh, Miss Denise, how exciting. Oh please, please, let me see you. Please.'

I was utterly shocked on two counts. Firstly, I was astounded that Nellie had the nerve to reach between the folds of my skirt and grab my quim, and secondly that she was not frightened or repulsed by finding out my true nature.

'Please, my pretty pet,' she pleaded. 'We could have such a lovely time together.'

Denise

I slowly began undoing the buttons of my skirt, never taking my eyes from her luscious breasts. Suddenly, I had a brilliant thought.

'Why don't we both get undressed? In fact, why don't you draw a bath for me, and then if you would, you might join me in the warm soapy water.'

'Oh yes, Miss Denise. That is a lovely idea. I do so love baths.' She turned and went into the bathroom, where I heard the water running and her pretty voice humming.

I was beside myself with expectation. I had never seen another woman completely nude. I had never had the opportunity to be touched by another girl except Heather, nor had the fun of freely exploring one's body with my hands. My cunt ached with built-up tension and desire. Carefully, I stepped out of my skirt and went into the bathroom.

I found Nellie bending over the bathtub, her clothes neatly folded in a stack on a shelf high up so that they would not get soaked. I had the pleasure of admiring her full buttocks for a long moment as she bent, completely exposed, over the porcelain tub. I could see a fringe of hair peeking out just below her little rosette anus.

'Nellie, you are lovely,' I whispered.

'Oh, Denise, you frightened me,' she jumped. And then without hesitation, she came toward me. I took in her creamy flesh, her voluptuous tit, her white belly, and the cleft between her soft white thighs, the crack of her pussy surrounded by light blond hair.

'Come now, Miss Denise, take off your underthings. It is time you had your bath,' she said mischievously. She reached out and undid the drawstring of my drawers.

'Why, you have such a luscious one, don't you? How wonderful!' she cried gaily, and without hesitation fell on her knees and kissed my throbbing clitoris.

She looked up at me, and asked me if I liked the way that felt. I could only nod vehemently. It felt absolutely divine. She put her full lips over my clitoris and tickled the end of it with her tongue, and then after doing that for a few moments, she thrust her mouth over nest itself and thrust her tongue as far as it would reach inside. As she did this, with one hand she caressed my anus and with the other, she lightly touched her own nipple. I felt involuntary moans escape my lips, and I thought with horror that I was going to spend at any given moment.

'Oh! Nellie, that feels so marvellous. Oh! Oh!' I cooed and groaned.

Gently, I pulled her up so that she was standing. We embraced, and I kissed her lips which were swollen and bruised from sucking my quim. I let my tongue play at the soft vulnerable flesh of her mouth and tongue, while she did the same to me. Our nipples grazed and touched one another as we held each other in a tight embrace. One of her delicate little hands was wrapped around me gently working the cheeks of my backside, while her left hand seemed to have disappeared inside the folds of her own flesh. I groped between the soft flesh of her thighs, and found her hand there lightly stroking her own pussy.

'Let me,' I whispered. I knew instinctively what to do. Nellie guided my hand at first, leading my fingers deep into her warm, wet quim. I felt a thrill of the mysterious nature of women overwhelm my sensibilities, and for a moment I was slightly jealous of Nellie's pretty folds of pink wet flesh surrounded by the soft curls of her blond hair. Her hands guided my finger to a point inside her nether lips where it seemed to be harder, a little pearl of pulsing flesh. I was fascinated, and began to delicately massage her. As I did this, she moaned and thrust her hips against me and pressed her mouth against my own more forcefully.

Soon I felt that I could hold back no longer. Nellie had one hand on my nipple, which she pinched harder and harder, as her strokes on my clitoris became more fierce and rapid. My hips moved back and forward to meet her fingers, as my fingers drew out a natural rhythm from her beautiful body. Suddenly, I thought I was going to swoon from lack of oxygen, and I gave myself over to my orgasm. As soon as I did this, I felt Nellie stifle a moan, putting her mouth to my neck and I felt her warm sex juice flow all over my fingers.

Afterward, we both began laughing rather sheepishly at our rather bad behaviour, Nellie dressed herself while I climbed into the bathtub. I told her my whole story. I told her everything about Miss Priscilla and Helen and my father. I told her of my real desire for women how coming to the school was, in a sense, the best possible solution.

Nellie listened with a wide smile as she gently soaped and rubbed me in the bathtub. I realized that by telling her my whole secret, I was trusting someone I hardly knew with my deepest, darkest truths. I remember that I felt instinctively that she would never hurt me. And I turned out to be correct. During my two years at the school, Nellie was an unfailing friend, a patient confidante, and an exquisite lover. She was the most lovely companion a girl could ever want.

I wept piteously when we said good-bye, for I knew I would never return to the school after I left it. We had shared so much together, and I feared that I would never find her equal. But when I met Violet, I realized that she had the potential to fill the space that leaving Nellie had created. Violet was much more the tyrant than Nellie, and this is what I had grown to need. I loved Violet almost as fiercely when I first saw her as I had loved Nellie.

* * *

One afternoon, my French friend Violet was teaching me the finer points of acting the role of a French lady. She was instructing me as we were riding in her carriage.

'You won't want your parasol up, Denise,' she said, 'so put your hands behind your back and place your beautiful feet together, the smart shoe buckles level. That's right.'

After luncheon Violet instructed me to change my dress because we were going shopping and then having tea. I went upstairs relieved by her words. I wanted nothing more than to shop with Violet. We were to have the big motor-car to ourselves, tea at the flower show. The prospect was delightful. I put on a lovely trailing dress of rose voile, tied well in below the knees with a scarf of tulle and a blue hat with a crown of pink roses. Violet was in dark grey with a grey satin hat. We drove off in the luxurious big motorcar to the neighbouring town.

'Show me your feet,' said Violet, as we rode along. I raised my skirt obediently.

'As I thought,' she said. 'You don't pay enough attention to your feet, dear.'

I protested. I was wearing a very smart pair of patent leather shoes, laced with black silk ribbons tied in big bows on the insteps, and black silk stockings.

'These are lovely shoes,' I cried indignantly.

'For morning wear, perhaps. How high are the heels? I don't believe they are three inches.'

'But, Violet, heels that are too high look improper.'

'Nonsense,' said Violet. 'For the afternoon nothing looks so fascinating as a neat, tightly fitting pair of dainty very high-heeled boots with black leather legs that button over the ankles without a wrinkle. Look at mine!' She extended an exquisitely booted foot before my eyes. 'Luckily we are going to fetch some new ones that have been made for you. I will have you buttoned into a pair before I take you to the flower show, though really I don't know that we ought to go now.'

Denise

'Oh, Violet!' I pleaded.

'I don't see how I am going to find time to punish you for your carelessness about your feet, Denise,' she said. 'Take care that after luncheon I never see you again without exquisite boots on your feet.'

Violet bought some hats for herself and for me and then we drove on to Binot, Violet's boot maker.

'You have been making some lovely black leather boots for this young lady, Miss Denise Beryl,' said Violet to the girl who came forward.

'Oh yes, Madam, some very pretty boots with high heels. This way please.'

She led us into the ladies' showroom upstairs and produced some beautiful flashing boots with legs of black glacé kid that would reach up to the beginning of my calves. The boots had dreadfully high and slender Louis Quinze heels, with escalloped edges around the buttonholes. The shopkeeper buttoned them onto my feet. They were exquisitely cut, fitting me very tightly but not pinching me.

'But the heels are much too high,' I said as I teetered on them.

'I like them,' said Violet. 'They are becoming to your feet and ankles.'

'They are only a little more than six inches high,' said the shopkeeper calmly. 'Stand up, Miss, if you please,' and I stood up. 'But they suit you beautifully.'

'I can't wear them, really, Violet,' I cried.

The shop girl looked at me sternly, 'I think that young ladies who want to be slovenly and object to the high heels of their dainty boots ought to be punished.'

'She will be,' said Violet sternly.

'Stand up on your chair, Denise.'

'Violet!'

'At once! And hold up your dress to your ankles.'

I obeyed.

'I will leave her under your charge in this position,' said Violet to the shop girl. 'I shall come back in half an hour for her. Will you see that she doesn't move? If she does, you may rap her on her pretty buttocks.'

'Certainly,' said the shop girl, arranging my feet with the ankles together and the toes turned out. I had to stand on the chair for half an hour in the showroom, while ladies came in and tried on their boots. Each one naturally asked what I was doing perched upon the chair, and the shop girl explained my fault.

Violet came back after what seemed to be an eternity and took me to the flower show. We had tea together at a little table on the grounds.

'Show your smart boots dear,' said Violet. 'Cross your feet in front of you and let everyone see them. You must be grateful now that I took you to the boot shop.'

I blushed and said, 'Yes, Violet.'

I couldn't help but appreciate the admiration of the men and the envious glances and disparaging remarks of the women. I was having a lovely time.

We drove back to Beaumanoir, bringing with us other girls who came in and played tennis until half past six. Then Helen sent for me to come to her boudoir.

'You have had a pleasant day, Denise?' she asked affectionately.

'Oh, Helen, it has been lovely,' I exclaimed kissing her.

'I am glad, darling,' she said. 'Now run away, have your bath and get dressed for dinner. Phoebe is waiting for you. I am going out to dinner myself, but I want to see you looking your very prettiest before I go. Phoebe will bring you to my room.'

Denise

As Phoebe began to bathe me, I suggested to her that she perhaps give my titties a nice little massage.

'Oh, Miss Denise, you are as impudent as they say you are,' she laughed contemptuously and reached down and took both my nipples between her fingers and gave me an excruciating pinch.

'Phoebe! You're hurting me!' I cried.

'Silence, or I'll hurt you more,' she said fiercely.

I bit my lip and tried to keep the cries of mingled joy and pain muffled within. Just when I thought that I could stand it no longer, she released her iron grip.

'Now, stand up, Miss High Heels,' my maid commanded me.

I did as she requested reluctantly, fearing some further torment. I lifted my body out of the soapy water and it was revealed to Phoebe that I had the fingers of my right hand quite far up my quim.

'Well, well, Miss Denise, it seems you like that kind of torment.'

I was too ashamed to answer. I hung my head, looking greedily at my poor bruised nipples.

'Come here!' barked Phoebe, holding out a bath sheet for me.

I stepped out of the tub, and as soon as I did, Phoebe took my hand off my cunt and put her own inside instead. I was shocked because she had never done this sort of thing before but of course I did not object. I moaned despite the self-control I was trying to exert over my emotions. But it was impossible: I was nearly climaxing under the pretty tortures my maid was suffering unto me.

'You like this don't you, Miss Denise? Don't you? Tell me you like it. Say you love what I am doing to you,' she whispered hoarsely. I could see that she had her own hand stuck up her skirt and was rubbing herself fiercely between her legs.

'Oh yes, Phoebe, I do! I do love it. Kiss my titties, they are so sore from your tortures. Put your pretty mouth on my poor nipples,' I begged my maid pathetically, enjoying the desperate sound in my own voice.

Phoebe obliged me, stealing vicious kisses and little bites of my flesh. She sucked and licked my nipples, all the while circling her fingers over my clitoris.

'Oh, Phoebe! I am coming. Oh, yes, yes!' I cried exuberantly.

Quite suddenly, she stopped.

My eyes flew open in wild disappointment. 'Phoebe,' I cried, 'don't stop. Please!' I begged.

'There,' she said heartlessly, as she walked away from me. 'This little punishment serves you well for being such a spoiled little tart. Mine is far worse torture than being caned, is it not?' She laughed at me heartlessly.

I sobbed and pleaded and begged for her to finish me off, but of course, she refused.

She led me back into my bedroom. There she dressed me in a lovely pair of new tight white kid gloves. They reached all the way to my shoulders and were buttoned with hundreds of little brilliants, while the seams on the back were embroidered in silver. She put me into the most wonderfully fine underclothing, all threaded with blue satin ribbons. I wore a filmy petticoat, a tight corset of pale blue satin, and a lovely frock of white satin covered with embroidery of silver and diamonds. Over this frock I wore a tunic of blue chiffon through which the silver-embroidered satin rippled like water. The corsage was extremely décolleté, the sleeves being mere shoulder straps of paillettes and diamonds, and on the left side of the corsage a bunch of big pink tea roses was fastened.

The tunic reached below my knees, where it was caught with a bouquet of the same roses and finished with a band of blue satin, which held the dress in with a great buckle in front, and was fastened behind with a large bow. The skirt was so tight and clung so closely to my figure that my legs felt as though they were tied in it. From the bottom of the tunic, the white satin skirt, with its shining embroideries, fell to my feet, but cleared the ground all the way round. I wore exquisite transparent white silk stockings through which my flesh showed pink. My slippers were of plain white satin, pointed and deliciously cut without bows but with oval diamond buckles, and heels over six inches high. A blue ribbon of satin filleted my hair. I wore earrings of diamonds and pearls, a rope of pearls around my shoulders, a string of diamonds with a diamond pendant around my throat, and diamond bracelets over my kid-gloved wrists. Phoebe gave me a little fan of ivory and lace.

'Now you are ready,' she said, 'and I am very proud of you, Miss Denise, I can tell you. Stand still.' She placed one strong arm around my waist, and the other under my knees and lifted me up in the air as though I were a baby.

'What are you doing, Phoebe?' I cried indignantly, while I wriggled in her arms. 'I am not a child. Put me down on the ground at once.'

Phoebe held me still tighter.

'Keep still, Miss Denise, and hold your silly tongue or I'll punish you,' she said sternly. 'I am obeying my orders. Your hands behind your back at once.'

I was waving my luxuriously gloved hands in protest, but at the sound of her peremptory voice, I obeyed her.

'That's better,' she said. 'Now press your ankles and feet together! Arch your insteps. Make the most of your beautiful buckled slippers.'

Blushing with shame, I obeyed her again. I could see myself in a mirror held in her arms, a grown-up young lady in a lovely evening frock! I could see my lovely feet in their high-heeled satin slippers obediently placed together with the insteps arched, and my legs dangling over her arm.

Phoebe carried me along the corridor to Helen's bedroom and kicked at the door. Helen's French maid, Leonce, opened it. Helen was dressed in an exquisite long gown of pale green chiffon over white satin. She turned with a smile and pointed to a spot between her two large mirrors.

'Place Miss Denise on her feet there.'

Phoebe set me down. Yes, I had never looked so well. My blue tunic with the silver embroidered white satin underdress set off my fair hair and skin to perfection. I was so happy. There was a colour in my cheeks, and my eyes sparkled. I had enjoyed a lovely day of fresh air, exercise and freedom, and now in my delicate underlinen and dainty frock, I was dressed for dinner. I was conscious of a voluptuous feeling of well-being and delight. My dress was short enough to give a glimpse of my pink insteps in shimmering cobwebs of white silk stockings. I could see my feet, which looked more slender and elegant than ever in their slim little pointed slippers, ornamented with the big oval diamond buckles.

'You look sweet, dear,' said Helen. 'Let me see how prettily you can walk in that those high heels!'

A strip of white kid was unrolled on the floor by Leonce.

'Keep on the strip,' said Helen; and I walked, turned, and came back, pointing my toes and flashing my slipper buckles. The dress rustled deliciously about my ankles as I walked. I could take only the tiniest steps, which exaggerated my submission.

'My skirt is so tight that my legs are actually tied together,' I said smiling at Helen, 'and I have an extra half an inch on my Louis Quinze heels.'

'I know,' replied Helen. 'They look lovely. In fact, darling, I think I am going to tie you still tighter.'

She was smiling radiantly. She held in her hand a black leather strap with cruel steel buckles.

'Sit down on this chair, and give me your beautiful feet.'

I had learned enough to know that obedience must be prompt. I extended my feet to Helen, who kneeled on one knee and took them onto the other knee.

'But Helen, what have I done?' I asked.

'This isn't punishment dear,' she replied as she delicately crossed my slim ankles. 'But it is very, very important that there should not be the slightest mark even on the white soles of these exquisite new high-heeled slippers when you have your conversation with Aunt Priscilla.'

Why, I wondered? She adjusted the gleaming strap round my crossed ankles and bound them tightly together. Oh how delightful the sensation was! The blood rushed into my face, and into the more intimate parts of my body.

'Now, to keep your gloves clean,' she said as she tied my hand in the same way with a smaller strap.

'There, darling, now we are certain that you won't walk and soil the shoes,' she said. 'Be very obedient to Aunt Priscilla.' She kissed me, and Phoebe once more lifted me in her arms. The voluptuous thrills which had been coursing through my veins redoubled. I saw myself in the glass. With my white shoulders and bosom rising from my delicious décolletage, I looked like some wonderful doll in Phoebe's arms—except that my bosom heaved rather spasmodically. Phoebe, in order not to ruffle or tear my dress, had raised the skirt, so that not merely were my buckled feet and crossed tied ankles visible, but my silk-stockinged legs as well, to halfway up the calves.

'Oh, Helen!' I murmured, my eyes swimming with languorous yet heated longings. I was pricked by desires I knew I could not act on. A world of these fantasies were expressed in my sigh. Helen smiled. It was her policy and wish to keep me, tonight of all nights, stimulated by passionate yearnings. She even provoked and increased my desire as she caressed my legs, sliding her hands up over the smooth shining stockings under my dress, feeling all the way up to my knees and garters.

'Are your garters of white satin dear, with big bows and buckles?' she asked.

'Yes, Helen,' I answered blushing.

'You are very happy tonight, Denise, aren't you?'

'Oh yes, Helen.'

Phoebe carried me downstairs to the drawing room and placed me on a sofa, propping up my back with cushions and drawing down my dress so as to cover my ankles.

'Now lie like that! Don't put your feet to the ground, Miss Denise,' she said.

'I won't, Phoebe.'

I was left alone, and in a few minutes Violet came in looking very pretty in a white gown of *ninon de soie*. She leaned over the sofa and looked down at me. A hungry smile and a blush came upon her face. She teased me by running her gloved hand over my satin slippers.

'Do you know, Denise, that I am falling love with you? Not because you are a lesbian of course, but because you are a girl. I am in love with you only as girls can love one another.' After this strange utterance, which excited and flattered me, she cried, 'Oh, you have got your hands and feet tied! How delicious! I must look.' She turned back my frock, and asked me why. I explained.

'I wonder what Miss Priscilla is going to do to you tonight,' she said slowly. 'I am jealous of her.'

She bent her head down and kissed my lips long and ardently, letting her tongue play over my hungry lips and even coaxing my tongue to lace with hers. Then she drew a breath of pleasure and smiled.

'Violet, that was lovely,' I said breathlessly.

Denise

She bent down again passionately, lifted my bound feet and I felt her warm lips pressed upon my insteps. Oh! A delicious spasm of emotion shook me. How my passions were ignited! Suddenly, Miss Priscilla, dressed in a high-necked black silk robe and flat square-toed shoes, joined us. Netta announced dinner. Phoebe carried me in and placed me in a chair and freed my hands. A clean white satin footstool was placed under my bound feet and we dined. How I enjoyed that dinner. Violet was on one side of me, and her kiss seemed to still burn and tingle on my lips and insteps. At times she dropped her napkin, and as she stooped down to pick it up, she would give an affectionate squeeze to my slippers or a sly caress to my legs. Even Miss Priscilla's face looked pleasant. I was carried back to the drawing room where Violet and I were allowed a cigarette over our coffee. Miss Priscilla rose.

'I shall send Phoebe to bring you to my boudoir in five minutes, Denise,' she said. 'I am just going to see that all is ready. Meanwhile put on your gloves and button them carefully. Perhaps Violet will help you.'

'Of course I will,' cried Violet. She kneeled by the sofa and, with caressing fingers, drew on my long delicate gloves and buttoned them up to my shoulders, smoothing them over my arms, so that not a wrinkle should show. Then she pressed my hands passionately.

'I should love to tie them together, just as your feet are tied, only ever so much tighter.'

I blushed, and realized that I loved her and wanted to possess her.

'You may if you like,' I said after staring at her hungrily for a long while.

'There's no time now. Someday when we are alone I will.'

'But, Violet, you said you loved me,' I remarked with a smile. She frowned in perplexity.

'I do Denise. Yet, do you know what I would *really* love? I would love to see you dressed just as you are now in that beautiful evening frock tied to a chair in Mrs. Pettigrew's dark room with those buckled satin slippers and slender ankles in the fetters, while the laundry girls feed you on bread and water.'

My face grew scarlet.

'Oh, Violet, that would be dreadful,' I cried, and yet the picture her words evoked fascinated me strangely! Oh, how I wanted Violet to torture me with her fetters. Oh, how I wanted her to torture me with her tongue.

Unfortunately, Phoebe came in for me then. Violet and I kissed one another good-night, and then Phoebe carried me up the stairs. Miss Priscilla's boudoir was furnished in the Empire style with an elegance out of keeping with her puritanical appearance. A small fire was burning cheerfully, but to keep the room from growing too hot, the window was open, letting in the summer night.

'Untie Miss Denise's ankles,' said Miss Priscilla at once.

I was placed standing in a blaze of light on a square of white kid between two great mirrors, so that I could see myself back and front. Miss Priscilla drew up a chair and sat facing me, but a little to one side so as not to obscure from me my reflection in the mirrors. Phoebe went out of the room.

I was excited and a little frightened too. I looked at Miss Priscilla timidly. She crossed one leg over the other, showing me her ugly flat shoes and lisle-thread stockings.

'Lift your dress, Denise! A hand on each side of your skirt! Lift it prettily above the ankles. That's right. Press your high heels tightly together and turn out your toes! That will do. Now watch your pretty reflection in the mirror, while I talk to you and, above all, never lose sight of the truth in the glass in front of you.'

449

I blushed rosily and smiled, 'Very well, Miss Priscilla.' I trained my eyes on my mysterious image.

'Now listen to me, Denise,' she went on, 'some day you will be allowed to lay aside your dainty frocks, but I think it's a great pity. Helen and I are determined, however, that we will not have a repetition of your outrageous conceited conduct. We will not tolerate your untidy ways or your disrespect.'

'I am cured of that Miss Priscilla,' I said humbly, watching my feminine lips answer.

'Perhaps,' she replied calmly, 'but we mean to make certain of the cure. We want you to willingly submit to the rule and authority of women.'

'Forever?' I asked in dismay, but my dismay was coloured with a passionate warming in my heart. I wanted to be under their authority forever.

'Always.'

I hesitated.

'Miss Priscilla!'

'Yes.'

'It seems natural to me that I should be kept in subjection,' I said timidly, 'so long as I am wearing girls' corsets and long gloves, earrings, and pearl necklaces, while I am wearing décolleté dresses, girls' frilled lingerie and pretty petticoats, girls' silk stockings, and satin slippers with high heels. I don't resent discipline at a lady's hands while I am dressed this way.'

'That's better. You *are* improving. And yet, Denise, even in your satin slippers, you are not as obedient as you profess your willingness to be. You are looking straight at me instead of at your own reflection in the looking glass.'

My eyes sought my image in the mirror.

'I am very sorry. I forgot,.' I said humbly.

'That is no excuse, Denise,' said Miss Priscilla placidly. 'Gather in your pretty frock, until it is stretched quite tight over your behind, and bend double.'

She rose. Red with shame, I obeyed her.

'I can't whip you with a cane, Denise, for a cane would tear your fragile dress. But this will be quite as effective.'

She took up a very thick short stick of rubber covered with white satin. It was like a policeman's truncheon, except that it was flexible.

'Bend well down. Your skirt tighter. Gather it in with your kid-gloved hands, dear.'

Oh, how ashamed I was to be punished in this humiliating childish way in my lovely clothes, yet I felt that familiar thrill of sensuous pleasure.

Miss Priscilla ran her hand languorously over my stretched bottom as I stood bent at the waist.

'We will punish the right globe first,' she said. 'One, two, three, four,' and at each word the elastic stick danced upon my bottom stinging me dreadfully.

'Oh, Oh! Miss Priscilla. It hurts worse than the cane. Oh!'

'Keep still! Five, six.'

She held her dress aside with her left hand. I saw her common flat shoes and cheap stockings. How extraordinary and bizarre it seemed that an elderly skinny woman dressed so humbly should be whipping the posterior of a beautiful, luxuriously dressed girl who was holding up her pretty frock with to receive the punishment. She flogged me methodically. I think I could hear her moaning almost imperceptibly. The pain was intense. My eyes filled with tears; the tears rolled down my cheeks.

'You are moving your satin slippers, Denise,' she said. She stooped and yanked my heels and ankles together with her hands. 'Watch your diamond buckles! Each time they flash, I shall add three more strokes.'

'Oh, Miss Priscilla,' I wailed. 'Please tie my ankles together then. I can't help moving, the pain is so dreadful.'

'I shall not tie your ankles, Denise. You would love that, wouldn't you?' she said. 'You must stand quite still of your own free will while you are being punished. Now for the left globe. One, two.' I screamed.

'Three, four—yes, this is the weapon, Denise, to bring fashionable young ladies in dainty frocks to their senses.' Smack, smack, my bottom danced and writhed. 'This will teach you obedience, pretty Miss Satin Slippers.'

Smack, smack. She fairly cooked my flesh, up and down and now across, smack, smack fell the heavy elastic stick on the thin delicate skirt. 'High-heeled young ladies,' bang, bang, 'are improved by a good whipping on their haughty impudent flesh.' Her voice had become hoarse and deep.

'Now perhaps you will watch your shoe buckles, will you?'

'Oh, Miss Priscilla, I will, I will,' I cried.

'Good!' She laid the truncheon aside. 'Now stand up, Denise.'

She contemplated my tear-stained face and my quivering bosom with pleasure.

'Now loosen your frock, but take care that it doesn't fall over your ankles.'

'Yes, Miss Priscilla,' I jerked out between my sobs.

'And mind that you don't move your pretty buckled satin slippers.'

She dried my eyes with her handkerchief and resumed her seat.

'We will go on where we left off. If you wish, you are to be made a will-ing slave under woman's authority. The one method certain to make you that is to make you love your subjection. It is obvious that you already have the disposition of a slave. It is quite clear that you love to be punished in your pretty frocks even though the punishment costs you pain and tears. But to make that love the overwhelming influence of your life, it is necessary that you should be made to associate supreme pleasure with a picture of yourself. You must love the image of yourself dressed in women's gloves, girls' corsets and frocks, silk stockings, girls' high-heeled dainty slippers, and then, of course, the delightful sensation of exquisite lace-frilled lingerie. Therefore, answer me this question: Have you ever loved a woman?'

I was scarlet with confusion. I felt that to answer the truth would somehow give her a hold on me that would be dangerous. Yet of course she knew the truth. She was simply forcing me to admit it.

'You must not ask me such questions,' I said.

Miss Priscilla rose, never losing her temper.

'Bend down again, Denise! This time you will raise the dainty skirt altogether and I am going to whip you over your thin pantalets.'

'Oh, Miss Priscilla, I will answer.'

'After I have whipped you, Denise.'

Miss Priscilla was implacable. My tears were hardly dry, my skin still burned terribly, yet I was made to bend down and suffer the punishment again, even more acutely this time. I bent down. She lifted my skirt and turned it back over my shoulders, leaving my girlish bottom exposed in my batiste drawers.

'Now lift up the dress in front until the frills at your knees are exposed.'

I obeyed her. She took up the elastic truncheon and stood behind me.

'Keep quite still, dear! Can you see your high heels reflected in the mirror behind you?'

'Yes, Miss Priscilla.'

'Fix your eyes on your glistening slender satin slippers and I'll tan you thoroughly and well.'

Smack, smack, smack, the thick rubber stick danced and jumped upon my batiste drawers. I screamed as it bruised my tender flesh. The pain she was giving me was intolerable and deliciously cruel.

'The feet still, Denise, or I will punish them too. There's nothing half so good for the dainty derrieres of satin-slippered young ladies as the stick. Oh these girlish globes can dance, my dear, as much as you like, so long as the girl's buckled shoes are quiet.' She breathed as she brought the truncheon down again and again.

She flogged me until I yelled with pain, and the tears streamed down my face in floods. My white bosom strained and heaved. At last she stopped and carefully readjusted my dress. 'Stand up now, Denise! Hold your skirt as before. That's right,' she said as she dried my eyes. 'Answer me now, Denise. Have you ever enjoyed a woman?'

I answered through my sobs, 'Never!' I lied for I thought she would reject me if she knew the depth of my inversion.

Miss Priscilla's thin lips smiled with contemptuous satisfaction.

'I thought that anyone as feminine as you would hardly be acceptable. But I wanted to be sure. Had you known a woman dear, you would have been more difficult for Helen and me to deal with. We should not have been able to mould you, or to indelibly write your subjection upon your character as upon a blank page.'

Miss Priscilla settled herself in her chair with a look of satisfaction. I felt singularly helpless. I understood that every answer I made handed me over more and more as a slave. Yet if I did not answer I would be cruelly punished until I did.

'I pass to another subject, Denise. When you have admired women, what is it in them that you have admired? When you think of women, what about them do you think? What about women attracts you so?'

I was startled; I would not answer her.

'If you don't answer immediately, Denise, I shall lock a bright pair of steel handcuffs over your delicate white gloves.'

My heart gave a jump. I blushed rosily—with pleasure. I saw the little white-gloved hands, which so daintily held up my lovely frock. To have them handcuffed by Miss Priscilla! A divine longing filled me. I looked at my little buckled slippers of satin. Oh, to be handcuffed while wearing those fairylike ballroom shoes. The strangest sensations overcame me.

'If you handcuffed me,' I said timidly and not replying to her question, 'I should not be able to keep on holding up my dress.'

'I will prove to you that you are wrong, Denise.' She took up a shining pair of handcuffs; thin broad bands of steel linked close together. She was actually going to handcuff me. Oh, the expectation was delicious!

'Let your skirt fall. Now your hands together, palm to palm in front of you.'

My hands met at once in position. I could not help but admire the tight unwrinkled gloves of spotless leather.

Miss Priscilla took my hands and roughly fitted me with the handcuffs. What a stimulating picture met my feverish eyes in the mirror! An elderly sharp-faced woman, in a black robe, looking just as I should imagine a prison Mistress would, chaining the exquisitely gloved hands of her pretty young prisoner. Click, click, the handcuffs snapped to. I was helpless. She then took a long chain with a spring hook at each end. She snapped one end onto a ring on my left handcuff. Then lifting my skirt all around so that my ankles were visible, she drew the chain tightly around behind me, under the up-swell of my thighs, and fixed the other spring hook to the right handcuff. The chain thus did three things: It held down my handcuffed hands, bound my thighs, and kept my dress up. I smiled at my reflection in the glass. I felt and looked so deliciously helpless. Miss Priscilla sat down again, calmly watching me.

'Now, Denise, perhaps you will tell me what you admire in women.'

'Their feet and ankles,' I replied shamefacedly.

A gleam of triumph shone in Miss Priscilla's eyes.

'In what way, Denise?'

I hung my head. I had told so much; however, I went on, 'I like the smart patent leather boots with leather legs and high Louis Quinze heels. And elegant patent leather shoes laced with satin ribbons tied in big bows on the insteps. And little buckled high-heeled satin slippers.'

Miss Priscilla nodded with satisfaction. 'Shod then, just as we keep you shod.'

'Yes, Miss Priscilla.'

'I thought so, I have watched you Denise. You are a *fétichiste du pied*.'

So that is what the phrase meant! How well she knew me! I was dreadfully ashamed.

'But that is not enough, Denise. Don't twitch your pretty fingers. Let your chained hands rest quietly against your lovely frock. I have not finished with you yet. The mere sight of a lady's pretty feet in her dainty boots attracts your eyes, fascinates you, but it does not trouble your passions, as they were troubled last night when you stood in the corner.'

'Yes,' I said in a whisper. 'But, oh Miss Priscilla, don't ask me any more questions; I am so horribly ashamed.'

'I must ask them,' she returned implacably. 'You must remember that you are an invert of enormous wealth, enormous power, and responsibilities for which you are quite unfitted, and that Helen and I are responsible for you. If you ever obtained your liberty, you would abuse your power. We are bound therefore to keep you in bondage and for that purpose I must know every detail of your character. Since ladies' boots on ladies' feet by themselves do not arouse and delight you, what does? Tell me at once.'

'Miss Priscilla, I can't,' I cried in despair.

She rose calmly. 'Lift up your head!'

I obeyed. Her hands were clothed in the long black kid gloves that seemed to be the uniform of the house. She took the point of my chin in the fingers of her left hand and held it firmly. With her right palm, she deliberately smacked my cheek with all her strength.

'So, you won't answer, won't you? You disobedient, impertinent girl!'

'Oh, oh, oh! Your leather stings my face dreadfully, Miss Priscilla.'

I struggled in vain to wrench my chin free from her fingers.

'It is meant to sting your pretty silly face.'

Slap, slap, slap, slap. 'Now we will make the other as red as this one is.'

She began to slap my left cheek in the same way. My hands were chained down to my legs. I could not resist. I burst into tears from the pain which I was suffering.

'Oh, Miss Priscilla, you are too cruel!'

'Why don't you answer the questions then? What a pity that I have to smack this pretty face and spoil its delicate complexion! Your satin slippers are moving, dear. I shall have to turn my attention to your dainty white feet in a moment.' She slapped me a few more times and then said, 'There that will do! You are as red as a dairymaid, you silly girl.'

She resumed her seat, while I stood and sobbed helplessly.

'What is it that chiefly enthrals and delights you, Denise?'

The question was asked again. Oh, through my tears, I had to answer it! I had to reveal that entrancing, shameful dream-world in which I liked to wander.

'I love being punished by normal girls, by girls in dresses and frills.'

457

'You are delighted now?'

'Oh, Miss Priscilla!'

'Answer!'

'Yes.'

'Did the idea, the thought of being punished excite you before it was actually done to you?'

'Yes.'

'Since when?'

'Since I was a girl and I realized I wasn't like other girls.'

'What was the first occasion?'

The horrible catechism, making me reveal all my hidden fancies, was getting on my nerves.

'Of course, I knew that you longed for women to punish you,' Miss Priscilla continued calmly.

'You knew that?' I gasped. I was astounded.

'I guessed it from your ways. It is not unusual in lesbians. But it's important that I should know how the idea first came into your head.'

'Oh, Miss Priscilla, I can't answer you. It isn't a fair question. I won't answer,' I cried out passionately.

'In that case,' she said looking at me with a malicious smile as she rose from her chair, 'in that case Miss Satin Slippers must have her pretty face slapped again.'

'Oh, no, Miss Priscilla! I can't endure it. I won't have my face slapped again,' I cried, and before she even raised a hand to touch me, I burst into a flood of tears and turned away.

'Stand still, Miss Satin Slippers,' she said fiercely, coming towards me.

'No, no, I won't,' I sobbed passionately. I stamped my feet in a rage as much as the chain around my thighs allowed me to do, and then I tried to run away. She seized me at once. My hands were handcuffed, I could do nothing to defend myself.

'How dare you move?' she hissed, her voice frightening me. 'Do you think that we dress you up in the finest silk stockings specially woven for you at ten guineas the pair and have your shoes cut and finished and buckled in the most exquisite style with the daintiest heels for you to stamp at us in them?'

At her quiet tones my anger vanished. A fresh flood of tears burst from me remorsefully. 'Oh, Miss Priscilla, I didn't mean to be impertinent to you.' I sobbed, and in a fit of penitence, I, the fashionably dressed Miss Satin Slippers, as she termed me, buried my face in her bosom.

She took me in her arms and patted my white bare shoulders soothingly. 'There, there, Denise!' she said gently. 'Don't pull at your handcuffs, dear, like that; you can't get them off and you will only spoil your nice gloves. Come dry your eyes.'

She dried them with her handkerchief, holding me affectionately in her arms.

'You forgive me, then?' I said imploringly.

She shook her head.

'You must be cured for your own sake, Denise, of these foolish fits of passion. You must recognize the necessity of having your pretty feet punished before your face is slapped.'

'Punish my feet?' I exclaimed, a queer thrill of pleasure shooting through me even at that moment, as I looked down at them. 'In these shoes and stockings?'

'Yes.'

In the corner by the fire, with its back to the wall, stood a chair upholstered in white satin and gold, a solid chair with arms. To it was attached a pair of stocks for the legs. She placed me in the chair, turned back my skirt, and opened the stocks.

'Put your legs in the stocks.'

The stocks were made of polished mahogany, the holes lined and padded with satin so that they could hold the legs in a vice and yet not tear the most delicate of silk stockings. I put my legs in the grooves. Miss Priscilla shut down and locked the upper plank of the stocks and wheeled a big three-sided mirror in front of me. I could see my ankles and feet sticking out from the stocks in their dazzling finery of high heels and diamond buckles and lace. There was not a mark on the new white soles. They were the slippers of a wealthy debutante and I was going to be punished in them. My blood frothed and boiled with erotic anticipation.

Miss Priscilla kneeled and took my right foot in her hand and, in an instant, piercing shrieks from my lips rang through the room. She bent down my instep until I was sure that the bones must snap. Then she twisted it to the right until I was certain my ankle must break, then again to the left.

'Oh, please, Miss Priscilla, this is dreadful. It's torture! Oh, oh, my foot! You have lamed me for life.'

But she was a doctor. She knew exactly how far she could punish me without breaking bones or spraining sinews. Then she clasped my leg just above the ankle in both hands and sawed her hands different ways, pinching my tender flesh and provoking screams from me. Then she took the slippers delicately off my foot and whipped the bottoms of my feet with a little whale-bone rod until I yelled again through a blinding storm of tears. She replaced the slipper and treated the left foot in the same way. She released my legs and said, 'Your feet won't forget that lesson very quickly, Denise. Stand up!'

'Oh, my feet are too tender.'

She forced me to stand. To touch the ground tortured me.

'Go back to your place. Will you stand quietly while I slap your face?'

'Yes, Miss Priscilla.' I wept but kept my eyes lowered humbly.

She smacked me cruelly again until my cheeks were fiery red, and I thought my sobs would choke me.

'Now we will get back to business, Denise.'

She sat down calmly in her chair, and looked at me hard. 'When did you first feel that you wanted ladies to punish you?'

'When my governess took me over her knee to punish me, I was seven years old. While she slapped me, I was looking down and I saw just below me her feet which were shaped very prettily and shod in elegant buttoned patent leather boots with high heels.'

Miss Priscilla nodded and said, 'I thought it would be something like that. You understand now, Denise, why we are subjecting you to discipline. If you loved the mere idea of it, how much more would the real thing appeal to you! How much more easily you could be subdued and held in subjection!'

Yes, the whole terrible plot these two women had concocted to turn me into their willing prisoner was now revealed to me, yet I seemed incapable to resist it. Miss Priscilla rose, clasped my waist, and caressed my bosom.

'You are not going to give us much trouble, Miss Satin Slippers.'

She took the handcuffs and chain from me.

'Stand in the corner until I am ready for you. Put your face to the wall, your dainty heels together, your hands behind you.'

I obeyed. I heard Miss Priscilla moving the furniture. She led me out of the corner and stood me between two long mirrors. I saw a high stool of solid mahogany. It had a padded seat of black leather, and at the edge of the seat, there were white satin straps to tie down the legs above the knees. In the front of the solid stool, a little bar of steel with a ring at the end of it jutted out for an inch or two just at the place where the ankles would be if anyone were sitting on the stool. It had a flat back padded with white satin, and arms stretching out in the form of a cross rose behind the chair. At the extremities of the arms of the stool, little handcuffs were fixed to hold the arms extended.

'I think your stockings can be drawn tighter up your legs, Denise.'

Miss Priscilla raised my skirt and carefully strained the fragile stockings up over my knees, shortening the suspenders.

'Now mount the stool,' she commanded me.

She placed a little gold footstool in front of me, and I climbed onto the stool by means of it. I sat on the stool with my legs dangling. She took away the gilt footstool. She strapped my waist with a leather strap tightly to the back of the stool, and extending my gloved arms one on each side, fixed them with the handcuffs to the cross. I allowed it all timidly.

'You need not be frightened, Denise. I am not going to hurt you.'

She fondled my bosom with her gloved hands and kissed me for a long time. I was terribly excited. I waited in an extraordinary suspense. Then she tucked up my skirt in front and underneath me until my white satin garters with the big bows and buckles and the lace frills of my drawers were exposed. She strapped my thighs down together to the edge of the seat just above the garters, so that my knees, showing delicately pink through the filmy sheen of the tightly strained stockings, projected a little beyond the seat, and my feet hung down clear of the little steel bar and ring.

'Can you move them? Try!' Miss Priscilla mocked me.

In the bright light reflected from the mirror, I saw my round legs tapering down in their shimmering meshes of silk to my neat little ivory ankles and my exquisitely slippered slender feet. I tried to move them.

'I can only move my insteps, Miss Priscilla,' I said smiling. 'I can make my shoe buckles flash, that's all.'

'I don't mind you doing that, dear. Watch your beautiful legs and feet!' And then without warning, she took my satin-slippered feet in her hands and began to caress and fondle them as she had fondled my breasts. The feel and the sight of her hands in their white kid gloves, playing delicately with my shining satin slippers, sent me into ecstasy. She played with my heels, and it sent thrills of voluptuous pleasure through me, causing my nipples and prick to respond to the feeling.

'Isn't it ridiculous, Denise,' she said in a gentle insinuating voice, 'to want to go back to heavy boots when with the flash of your diamond buckles, you can attract everybody's admiration to the beautiful shape of your feet and ankles and the loveliness of your shoes and stockings.'

I smiled and blushed. 'Perhaps, Miss Priscilla,' I whispered shyly.

'I am sure, dear,' she replied.

Her hands crept up to my insteps, where she patted and tickled them. She then pinched my calves affectionately, and reached up to my knees. I was trembling from head to foot. I watched my legs and feet with a delicious expectancy. A mirror was tilted underneath me in such a way that the new white soles and satin-covered heels were reflected in the big glass and were made visible to me. Oh, my round soft legs in the shimmering gossamer of the tightly stretched silk stockings, and the leather strap binding them deliciously together at the delicate ankles; oh my little feet in their feminine finery! My slim slippers of glistening satin looked sensuously perfect, and the added sensation of Miss Priscilla's touch was the living end. Oh, my arched insteps, my high curving narrow heels! How exciting that these ladies had perched me up in them as a punishment. Oh the blazing diamond buckles! Ladies had had them set for me, had sewn them on the exquisite slippers as a badge of subjection, and to attract all eyes to the loveliness of my feet.

Miss Priscilla seemed to read my thoughts. As she fondled my knees, she said: 'Weren't we right to dress you as the lovely girl you are? Why should ladies put up with a clumsy youth in ugly trousers, when they can have a prettily corseted, long-haired girl tripping about the drawing room in rustling satin frocks and light little high-heeled slippers that are a positive joy to their eyes?'

She continued to fondle my feet with slow, sensuous attention.

'Oh, yes, Miss Priscilla,' I murmured languorously. 'You were right.'

'And when we had dressed you and gloved you and corseted you, weren't we right to take your silk-stockinged legs and cross the dainty slippers, binding your ankles with satin straps and your gloved hands with handcuffs?'

I stared at the reflection in the mirror, and saw a beautiful girl with a flushed face and a wanton smile upon her red lips. I saw the white high-heeled slippers fitting with such perfection over the exposed glistening white silk stockings. I admired them, bound with leather straps and hand-cuffs. I was thrilled to be at the mercy of this thin shrivelled old woman in her black plain dress.

'Oh, you were right,' I murmured wildly, almost losing control of myself. Her caressing hands extorted my admission.

'Reflect,' she said 'that no lady would punish you with this treatment were you dressed in the boyish way you used to dress. It is only because you are corseted and curled and white-bosomed and are wearing satin slippers with high heels that you are subjected to this exquisite degradation. Don't you love your subjection?'

'Oh I do! I do!' I cried, nearly swooning with erotic pleasure.

It was I, Denise Beryl, the young woman with the great fortune and the lofty ambitions who was speaking. But her kid-gloved hands caressed me. I could give no other answer. It was in that moment that I gave up my will, my life, to her and to Helen. I leaned toward Miss Priscilla as far as my handcuffs and my bonds would allow. I writhed in an ecstasy. To live satin-slippered and corseted with handcuffed gloved hands and strapped ankles in beautiful décolleté frocks—yes, I learnt that night from Miss Priscilla's hands that this was the supreme joy life held out to me.

'Keep me tied and daintily frocked! Oh, Miss Priscilla, thank you!' I gasped and sank back with a dropping head as I found my body racked with joy.

Miss Priscilla sprang up with a cry of triumph. She freed me from my bonds, led me over to a sofa, and stretched me out upon it on my back.

'I am going to cover your face,' she said and she took up a black silk handkerchief. She gazed down with the utmost contempt at my outstretched form.

'It is all over with you now. Do you remember how you used to annoy me with your dirty shooting clothes and your heavy noisy boots? No more noisy boots Denise—ever! Only the daintiest little things of patent leather with slender tapering heels for the future.'

I was floating back now into the ordinary world of men and women. I was ashamed. I moved restlessly.

'Lie still.'

She covered my face and left me. She snatched the handkerchief from my face.

'Stand up, Denise!'

I stood up. Miss Priscilla rapidly unlaced the back of my dress, took my arms out of the shoulder straps, and let the dress fall in billowy daintiness about my feet. My singular delicate petticoat followed.

'That will do,' she said, contemplating my jerking helpless figure with undisguised contempt. 'Your education is complete.'

She gave me a glass of champagne, and then, with a disdainful smack on my bottom, she said: 'Now take your pretty feet back to the drawing room.'

Ashamed, I curtsied low to her and went out of the room. But the venom was in my veins. As I walked down the stairs, the rustle of my frock, the feel of it clinging delicately about my ankles, the lightness of my slippers, and the sensation of high slender heels all ravished me. Yes, I wanted to be kept in subjection as a beautifully dressed girl. Forever.

I entered the drawing room where I found Violet alone, reading a novel in an armchair. How pretty she looked in her frock of *ninon de soie*, and her little slippers! Oh, the venom was in my veins. For the moment, I saw her as young and pretty and dainty, yet I longed to be punished by her. Miss Priscilla had accomplished her aim.

'You have been a long time,' Violet said peevishly. 'I have been here alone and it has been very dull.'

She was annoyed. I smiled and blushed.

'What has Miss Priscilla been saying to you?' Here was my chance and I took it.

I flung myself into a chair, crossed my knees and swung a satin-slippered foot indolently to and fro.

'You must find out, my pretty one,' I said.

Her eyes flashed dangerously.

'Don't be impertinent, Denise. And uncross your legs at once! Put your heels together and turn your toes out and answer me.'

I swung my foot more violently.

'I warn you, Denise,' she said violently.

I began to unbutton a glove with an impertinent smile.

'Very well. It is your fault, Denise. Go and fetch me a cane.'

She sat up sternly.

'A cane?'

I was horrified. I had not meant to provoke her to inflicting so severe a punishment. I wanted no more whipping.

'You will find one in the punishment room. Bring it here and be quick!'

My face clouded over.

'Oh, Violet!' I begged, falling at her feet.

'It's too late to plead for mercy. Be quick,' she said.

Reluctantly I rose and fetched a cane. Oh, I had been a fool to provoke her.

'Hold out your hands straight from the shoulder, one on each side. Your feet prettily in position.' And then without hesitation, Violet brought down the cane on each of my outstretched hand.

'I'll teach you to be impertinent, Denise,' Violet was furious, her pretty face convulsed with rage.

'Oh that's enough, Violet,' I wept.

'Not nearly,' Violet laughed triumphantly. 'This will teach you to obey me in the future.' She brought the cane down again and again. My breasts heaved with passion for the little tyrant. I loved my little torturess.

'Oh, Violet, I will, I will,' I sobbed.

'Oh you will,' she cried. 'Don't rub your knees together, you naughty thing. Stand quite still, Miss High Heels.'

She flung the cane down, after she had pleased herself with the torments. 'Your hands behind you,' she commanded me.

She fetched two thin white cords of silk. And while I stood with my bare shoulders shaking with sobs, my pretty love bound my hands together with savage cruelty.

Denise

'Now kneel on the sofa.'

She raised my skirts to help me, then she brutally pushed me down.

'Perhaps you will put your pretty feet and ankles together now. '

She tied my ankles, my high heels and my insteps tightly together. Then she said, 'Lean over the back of the sofa.'

'Oh you are not going to cane me again.'

'No, I am not going to cane you, Denise,' she said sternly, as she turned back my pretty frock and took my drawers down to my knees. 'I am going to birch you—do you understand, pretty fool? I am going to birch your tender white flesh,' and she pinched my bottom with her fingers. 'I am going to cover it with red stripes and wheals.'

'Oh, Violet.'

'Silence.'

She ran quickly into the punishment room and came out again with a terrible birch.

'Oh, Violet, you couldn't be so cruel!' Of course, I was hoping beyond hope that she was.

She ran lightly over to me in her satin slippers. Oh, a girl so pretty and so young couldn't mean to punish me so severely for so trivial a fault. It was too good to be true.

'Bend well over,' she said, flourishing the birch. She made it whistle in the air. I was helpless.

'Oh, Violet, if you must birch me, please lock the door first and gag my mouth. I know I shall scream, and it would be so disgraceful to be seen tied hand and foot in my dinner dress being birched by a girl younger than myself,' I said piteously.

'You don't deserve it, Denise,' she said. 'But I love you, darling, so I will spare you unnecessary humiliation.'

She went and locked the door. Then she carefully gagged my mouth. She stole a delightful moment in which she fondled my breasts freely. She pinched my nipples and lightly slapped my bosom. I felt my quim stir from the pleasure.

'I am sorry, Denise, but you must be soundly birched,' she said and took her place. How cold the air was on my naked flesh, how shameful my position!

The twigs whistled through the air and slashed my tender flesh. I would have shrieked at the first stroke, had my mouth not been gagged. My bottom was already so tender.

'Is this your first birching, Denise?'

I nodded my head.

'A virgin bottom! That makes it more delicious to punish.' She was like a young fury. 'Fancy violating your bottom, darling. A regular rape isn't it?' she cried gleefully, and again the twigs fell. I twisted and writhed, my bottom danced and flinched, the tears streamed down my face. 'The fat pretty soft thing is already striped with red, dearest, but you shall have a purple bottom before I am done with you.' Her strength seemed to increase with each stroke. 'A purple moon of a bottom to show to your friends!' she laughed. 'There's still a little white place here, and another here.' She flogged me daintily, carefully, never breaking the skin, but making it swell, covering it with bruises and wheals. And then once more my sobs began to diminish. Suddenly, I ceased to feel the pain. As I leaned over the sofa, I surreptitiously rubbed my aching clitoris against the bolster. Violet was giving me such pleasure, such pain, that I simply had to rub myself against the couch. The friction on my genitals stimulated me even more!

Violet finished.

'Now to wind up properly, I will give you six strokes with the cane across the thin soles of your pretty slippers.' I could not protest, but I jerked and writhed in my sweet bondage. Violet took up the cane.

'I won't tear the slippers. I'll keep to the soles, you pretty vain creature! I know your vanity was troubled lest I should spoil your dainty shoes!'

At last she untied my feet and took the gag from my mouth. She led me to a mirror, and holding up my dress, for my wrists were still tied behind my back, she showed me my posterior. What a dreadful condition I was in. A few minutes before it had been white and pretty; now it was a discoloured ugly thing with black patches of congealed blood and purple stripes. It felt dreadfully heavy too, and the pain tortured me.

'Oh, Violet,' I exclaimed piteously. 'How could you spoil it!'

'It was good for you to have it spoiled,' she said. She rubbed it gently, the sight obviously pleasing her. Clearly, she liked to dominate me, too! Oh, how had I become so lucky?

After admiring her handy work, she fixed my drawers, readjusted my dress, and put her arms round my waist. Her anger was all gone. She looked at my piteous face with gentle eyes. She dried my eyes affectionately.

'Kiss me, Denise darling.' Our lips clung passionately for a long time. She put her sharp little tongue inside my lips, and bit my lips with endearing little love-bites.

'Stand there!' she said, suddenly pulling away from me.

She replaced the birch and the cane and picked up the fragments of twigs from the floor. She burnt them in the fire. Then she unlocked the door.

'Phoebe will know, of course, when she puts you to bed,' she said. 'But no one else need know of our little secret. Come here!'

She was folding a big white handkerchief. I crossed the room to her timidly.

'You are not going to punish me anymore.'

'I am going to see, darling, whether you will now put your high heels together and turn your dainty toes out when I tell you to. I am going to blindfold your eyes, stand you up on a chair with your face to the wall, just by the armchair in which I am sitting.'

I blushed with great pleasure. My eyes danced and my mouth smiled. She fixed the scarf over my eyes and tied it at the back of my hair. Then she turned me round, clapped her hands delightedly, and kissed me ardently on the lips. She led me to the chair and guided my little satin slippers up onto it. She placed me in position. Then she sat down in her armchair at my side and resumed her book. I stood there for an hour blindfolded with my hands tied. Every now and then I felt her dainty little hand steal under my dress and touch my feet to make sure they had not moved. She would caress my ankles, and play with my slipper buckles and high heels. Miss Priscilla had done her work well that night. The hour was an hour of bliss.

LESLEY

When the summer was over, memories of Paris dwelt in the minds of the lovers like phrases of a song.

During the long months of the winter city, remembrance of Paris in its season possessed their imaginations like a ghost. It waylaid them at the rainy corners of the fashionable shop lit boulevards, as the glass treasure-houses were closing and the December crowds pressed homewards.

Other men and women in the winter city evoked the summer images and voices at their leisure. They conjured them from the warm resonant air of the theatre or the recital-room, white their companions sat still as prisoners of an enchanted castle before the rich keyboard dramas of Beethoven or Schumann.

To all the lovers, the Paris I knew was a dream of villas and gardens. Its air was the scent of mimosa in the silence of long, deserted corridors. A golden twilight of blinds drawn against strong afternoon sun dimmed the deep colours of Persian hangings and tall vases. At the stairway curve, a florid window-arch framed a distant flash of blue water.

The days of summer were unvarying and unalterable in such a place. Morning was a time of hot pearl-grey sky beyond white-painted rails. The calls of children rose among a dull salvo of breakers at the sea's limit Blue and immaculate at midday, the afternoon tide glared silver in the sun's decline.

Every evening the disc of dark fire sank in the haze beyond the cypress trees, engulfed at last in a violet sea which lay calm as an Italian lake.

In the formal evenings of the winter city, while the salon music played, the lovers sat primly in long dresses dwelt privately with the images and voices of the girls whom they had possessed in the secret places of the summer. For the lovers at Paris, were ladies, their prey, girls. Paris was an island like Sappho's own, where the fairer sex was devoted almost solely to itself.

In the Villa Rif at Paris, within its deep gardens and behind its protective walls, such possession was complete. The lovers were the guardians of that place, the supreme arbiters of its laws. By removing the privilege of refusal, they bestowed on the girls another gift. It was the pretext of surrendering under compulsion to the most extreme fantasies of the lovers which removed from the girls all remorse and self-reproach. Once past this threshold, the girls relished their freedom and often graduated to become lovers themselves.

At the centre of the Villa Rif lay a courtyard garden, built upon the site of ancient cloisters. Above its arches an inscription had been carved long before, the words drawing a charmed circle about the girls and the men who possessed them.

The sun was the servant which laid bare their beauty.

The grilles were the eyes which watched them.

The walls were the ears which heard them.

The carpets were the hands which caressed their nakedness.

The air was the gentle touch which ravished them.

To those who had known it, Paris became a state of mind rather than a town with population figures and mean temperatures. Women in the winter city assured themselves that they need only travel there the next day to find the same azure sea and warm winds which they had known in June or August.

At Paris, under the tutelage of the lovers, a girl would permit suggestions and acts of passion which she would reject elsewhere. She would submit to entreaties condemned as perverse in any place not wholly dedicated to pleasure.

The pleasures of the Villa Rif were not to be judged by the standards of the winter city. For the young women who possessed them, much was possible at Paris that would have been unthinkable in another place, at a different season, or with the male sex.

* * *

Afternoon light, cool and neutral as a gleam of water, filled the elegant modern bedroom where the young woman stood. Filtered by the pate scooped lace of the window curtains, the aqueous cloud-light broke in sudden jewels of radiant colour on the crystal pendants of the lamps. Shimmering lozenges of red and blue, green and violet, dappled the wall hangings of warm pearl.

From every wall the plain angled glass reflected the young woman's proud image, like mirrors held by the discreet hands of admiring servants. Above her, the tiny panes of the domed skylight seemed shaped to be the spy holes of her lovers. The wide bed awaited her with a cover of apricot silk.

Lesley stood before the mirrors for a moment longer, a thoughtful connoisseur of her own beauty. The plain glass held the image of a quite tall and trim young woman, twenty-eight years old, whose firm pale features and blue eyes were composed in an expression of self-possessed arrogance. She had the classic, fair-skinned beauty of an English middle-class girl, from the aloofness in her clear blue eyes to the slight sulkiness of her mouth and chin.

Her straight fair hair was cut in an urchin-crop, shaped close to her head from the high crown to the jaw-line, and worn in a long, centrally parted fringe. This boyishly unfeminine hairstyle was her boast of being an educated young woman, one who was modern enough in her outlook to be emancipated from any sense of belonging exclusively to her marriage and children.

It was perhaps the impatient flick of her fringe, the wilful self-indulgent line of her mouth, which suggested a certain resentment against the world—or at least the male sex. Conventional morality dismissed Lesley as a promiscuous young wife because she had given herself to other men during seven or eight years of marriage—and because she had now walked out on her husband and infants in order to live with a succession of lovers. Yet, in the true sense, she was not unfaithful with other men, Lesley was as contemptuously dismissive of them as any prude. She was not a demure and courteous girl of eighteen with the world before her. At twenty-eight, resenting the years of submission to marriage and child-bearing, she gave herself almost exclusively to women and always on her own terms. To the admiration of the rest, Lesley returned the cool and disdainful stare of her blue eyes.

Turning from the bedroom mirrors, this modem young woman closed the door beyond which lay the peach-blossom marble and gold taps of a sumptuous bathroom. As she moved, the glass on every side reflected her figure in the chic Mack cotton of a coolie trouser-suit.

Lesley had the firm erotic maturity of a Spartan soldier-girl. As she drew off the short black jacket, a white singlet underneath moulded her breasts. Though softly developed in the years of marriage, they retained all their youthful poise and pride. The tight fit of the black cotton trousers showed that her long thighs were still trim and lightly muscled. Two well-controlled pregnancies had done no worse than impart a marginal broadening to her hips, a slight firming out of the cheeks of Lesley's bottom.

To the placid gaze of the mirrors, the young wife revealed herself more fully as she undid the Mack trousers, taut across her hips, and eased them down. Even in so simple an action there was, in Lesley, a curious mixture. She undressed with self-assurance, pushing down her pants to her knees, drawing first one slim foot out and then the other. Yet, as she turned to lay the trouser-suit on a chair, she walked in stockinged feet her head bowed, the urchin-crop parting under her own weight upon the nape of her neck, for all the world like a scolded child. Behind the challenge of her firm chin and parted fringe, she was both an arrogant young woman and, it seemed, an imploringly defenceless schoolgirl.

Like a pupil presenting herself for a ballet-class, Lesley was now dressed in nothing but the snug white singlet and a pair of sheer and translucent tights, whose deep honey-tone gave a warmth to the pale beauty they could not conceal.

The clinging white cotton of the singlet showed that her nipples were

Lesley

already erect as she faced the mirrors again. Standing before the glass in a moment of self-criticism, she combed the long fringe of her short fair hair briefly with her fingers. From the front, the sheer honeyed gloss of the tights showed the trim length of her thighs, the slight proud curve of her belly, the pubic hair pressed in the triangle of her loins as prettily as sea-fern seen through water.

Still inspecting herself, Lesley turned, her face twisted over her shoulder as she examined the seams which ran up her calves. She watched herself draw a hand over the seat of her tights as if to ensure that everything was as it should be. The angular mirrors framed this view, the lightly muscled rear of her thighs, the firm proud cheeks of Lesley's backside under the stretched film of the tights. The moonlike pallor of Lesley's buttocks was seen through this final veil, the cheeks pressing dosed the dark forbidden valley which divided them.

Bowing her head again, Lesley watched her stockinged feet as she walked with the precise and practiced steps of a dancer to the silk-covered bed. Without bothering to turn back the apricot-coloured sheen of the covering, she knelt upon it, then slid down until she was lying on her back with her head supported by the pillow.

For several minutes she gazed up at the white ceiling with its mouldings of Viennese stucco. In the stillness of the room she listened to the sounds of the spring afternoon. The traffic in the street, below the balconies of the fashionable apartment buildings, was light and infrequent. It was the stirring of the linden trees just beneath the window which came more dearly to her. In the house itself there was no sound of the others, neither Connie nor Judith, Christine nor Fatima.

Pulling up the hem to her ribs, Lesley slid her hands under tight white cotton and tentatively circled the nipples of her breasts with the tips of her fingers. She played with herself in this way for a while, her wilful young mouth relaxing, her lips parting, and her blue eyes staring into some unfathomable distance of her own mind.

Her long, well-exercised thighs began to stir at last. Without taking off her tights, Lesley drew her knees up to her breasts so that she lay on her back in a squatting position. Mirrors at the foot of the bed, reflected her from underneath, her hips and thighs stretched to their broadest by the squat, the mesh of the tights shaping the lips of her sex like a second skin.

Shaking her fringe into place, the young wife allowed her hand to move up her legs from the knee, as though it were that of a lover approaching her. With the back of her nails, within the whispering film of the tights, she began to stroke the parted vaginal lips.

There was no hint of shame or excitement in her action. She shifted a little, opening herself more fully to her own caresses, and stared at the ceiling above her without the least self-consciousness. Lesley made love to herself often, and however strange it might seem, she had done so more often during her marriage than at any other time.

It was not the failure of a lover which had prompted this. Like many modern young women of her class, Lesley held the view that her body belonged to her and that she would use it as she pleased. To explore her own sexuality and learn the routes of pleasure was the privilege of any intelligent and sexually liberated young woman. How else was she to determine those things which she would ask a lover to do to her—and those things which she would forbid her? Moreover, there were things, she had discovered, that only a woman could do to her. She was loathe to deprive herself any of it.

She had usually chosen the afternoon, when the children were still at school and her husband at work. Then she would leave her task in the garden or the house and go upstairs to the bedroom. There she would lie naked under the silent gaze of the mirrors and play with herself intermittently for two or three hours. It was both self-indulgence and experiment. For part of the time Lesley masturbated, slowly and intricately. For the rest she curled naked on the bed, lost in thought.

Now, in the spring afternoon of another main house, Lesley emitted a long shuddering breath and the wetness of her love began to form a sheen in the crotch of her tights. Her fingers opened as she rubbed and squeezed more vigorously, her thighs tightening in a slight and convulsive rhythm. There had been times when Lesley had brought herself to such a pitch that each of her knees had caused bruising by its pressure on the inner surface of the opposite thigh.

Lesley caught her breath, as if from exertion, and turned on to her side. Her knees were still drawn up and her fingers moved with irregular vigour over her clitoris and vaginal lips in the wet gusset of her tights.

Dreams of her lovers rose in her thoughts and faded again. As she abandoned herself to pleasure, she lost the power to control those ghosts which lurked in the recesses of her mind. There were men whom she had loved and deserted. There were men whom she had dismissed with contempt And there were men who had taken a vindictive delight in humiliating her.

It was not by her own choice that her thoughts turned to one of the last group as her knees pressed together impatiently and the wetness of her tights spread down her legs.

The incident had been trivial enough and yet it haunted her, its memory woken by the sight of the black trouser-suit lying on the chair. As she played with herself, breathlessly and with fevered energy, Lesley saw again the sunlit garden in the last year of her marriage. She had been wearing the black suit then.

She had been picking flowers, the older child close by her. At first she had not even noticed the woman, who was a well-dressed stranger, rather old and matronly, reminding her of the type who was the only female in a group of men. Even when she saw her, she had not observed the camera in her hands. The wall and the trees had shielded it from her. She was also indifferent to any woman in whom her interest was not aroused. It was the child's fidgeting and turning of the head which made her realize at last that the faint clicking was the sound of the camera's shutter and that the woman had been surreptitiously photographing her for half an hour.

The woman had not touched her or spoken to her. Yet any doubt was dispelled when she held the child against her and turned to the voyeur. She covered the camera lens and met her startled blue eyes with a wide smile of amusement at her shock and indignation over the use she had made of her. Before Lesley could even recover breath to protest, the woman had turned and walked away. She was bold like a man, the sort who took the philosophy course at university or became the first female member of the medical faculty. Lesley felt herself bettered and the feeling was unwelcome.

The incident might have been trivial enough, though an emancipated and self-possessed young woman like Lesley was angered and humiliated. Yet a certain fear and curiosity coloured her thoughts when she wondered what enjoyments and ordeals the woman inflicted on her in the person of her photographic image.

The true fright had come several days later, when the post brought her a package of finished full-plate photographs. There were portrait studies of her face, in every mood from a sulky turn of the mouth to a thoughtful softness in her blue eyes under the fair parted fringe of her hair. Other pictures showed her standing, sitting, holding the child against her, her breasts perfectly outlined by the white singlet. Some poses were erotically suggestive or comically vindictive. One had been taken from just behind her as Lesley stooped to pick a flower. Her firm thighs were braced apart a little and her knees bent forward. The thin black cloth of her trouser-seat was drawn skintight over the fully rounded and widely parted cheeks of Lesley's bottom. The woman had scrawled some words below, fantasies of whips and impalement, leaving Lesley in no doubt as to the desires which she had stimulated in Frau Doktor, as she had taken to calling her.

What caused her heart to jump with a strange fear and excitement was the knowledge that the woman who wished to do these things to her had gone to the trouble of tracing her name and where she lived. Was it only in order that she might send these mementoes of her lust to her? Or did the good Doktor's private moments of enjoyment seem more exquisite because the photographs bore the identity of a real woman?

The incident was some months in the past, half-remembered like a lesson from her schooldays. Yet the thought of it still affected her profoundly. As she dwelt upon the details, Lesley had without realising it stopped playing with herself. Her hand lay motionless on her stockinged thigh and the blue eyes under the boyish fringe of fair hair stared at the onyx boxes on the glass tables without seeing them.

Slowly she began to caress herself again, the wilful young mouth tightening as she determined to bring herself to a climax. Sudden contrary surges of longing and its appeasement throbbed in her loins, her lips parted softly and her breathing became audible. The blue eyes closed, fluttered open briefly, and then closed again, as if to capture and hold the pate dream of pleasure.

She had mistimed it. As her fingers moved again, now gentle and wet with the slippery dew, there was a light sound beyond the double dove-grey doors which led to the landing. The square onyx dock on the peach mirror table with its chromium banding stood with its gold hands at four o'clock. She knew that it was Connie.

Though Lesley stopped what she was doing to herself, it was not with any sense of shame or alarm. Connie, the young oriental servant, had seen such things before. Lesley lay with her hand on the soft inner swell of her thigh again and waited for the doors to open. She heard the metallic movement of the coffee pot in the dish, the diminutive rattle of china, as Connie balanced the tray and turned the glass handle.

Entering, closing the door behind her, Connie was a vision of the demure oriental maiden at twenty-two years old. The sheen of black hair falling to her shoulder-blades was held back from her face by a silver clip on either side.

Like a Thai temple-dancer in her movements, Connie's almond eyes and flat features were set in a pretty heart-shaped face. The moods of Asian beauty changed easily upon her lips and in her eyes, from beautiful impassivity to a devil-mask of laughter, and then to a quick glancing apprehension. Narrow-waisted, slim at shoulders and thighs, Connie's saffron yellow smoothness had the more neatly developed breasts and the less fully-rounded buttocks which made such Asian girls resemble children.

That afternoon Connie came to her mistress at the usual time of four o'clock. The almond-eyed girl seemed as if she had intended to come naked to the room but had been timid lest one of the men should see her as she went up the stairs. She wore a black silk cord, doubled, so that it ran round her waist, down her loins and under her legs, drawn up to the back of the waist between the demure pale yellow cheeks of Connie's bottom.

Without a word she set the tray down on the glass table and poured the coffee for her young mistress. As Lesley drew herself up against the pillow, Connie knelt at the side of the bed, like a handmaid of this fair-skinned Venus, offering her the petal-fine Meissen cup.

Lesley

In the silence, Lesley took it and drank slowly, handing it back to Connie when she had finished. The fine-boned Chinese girl kept her eyes lowered as if not daring to gaze at the hips and thighs of the pale beauty. Presently she raised her face, looking at the dark line which the coffee had left on the fair skin above Lesley's upper lip. Connie leant forward slowly, as if about to kiss her. Instead, the tip of her tongue protruded and, with eyes closed, she licked the coffee smear from Lesley's mouth and took it into her own.

Then it was Connie who, like a well-trained servant, assumed the management of their relationship. She stood up and stooped over the bed, Lesley raising her hips a little from the silk cover so that her stocking-tights might be peeled well down her thighs. Then Connie, lay gently on the bed, her head towards Lesley's knees, her slim feet on the pillow, and her knees drawn up a little. Their two bodies formed halves of a complementary curve. Lesley's head was pillowed on Connie's legs just above the knees as they lay in their inverted embrace. Connie's face was level with the opening of the English girl's thighs. Lesley's view was of the slim saffron smoothness of Connie's bottom and the rear of her thighs.

Connie undid the black silk cord which had covered her most intimate body-furrows, and dropped it on the floor.

'You like to see me,' she said with gentle firmness. There was no suggestion that Lesley was required to reciprocate in making love, only that it would be more exciting for her if she could see the Asian girl's vaginal lips and anus while Connie's fingers and lips performed their humble service.

Connie had been taught the arts of female masturbation by a domineering mistress when she was twelve years old. Her fingers stroked the wetness which matted the fair hair on Lesley's flushed vaginal lips.

'You have made love to yourself!' Connie said, in a quiet voice which mingled reproach and admiration. Then she began to exercise her own skill with gentle fingers upon Lesley's clitoris and labia, rubbing and squeezing, rubbing and squeezing, rubbing, rubbing, rubbing, until it was Lesley's turn to utter the first muted, questioning cry.

The vaginal lubricant was wet on the inner surfaces of Lesley's upper thighs. Not disdaining the moisture, Connie began to lick it away with an agile tongue. Tantalising, she allowed these lingual caresses to come closer until she touched the pink sliver of the clitoris and brought a sharper cry from her proud young mistress. Holding Lesley firmly by the open thighs, the pretty Asian witch lunged her tongue between the widened and imploring lips, thrusting in and out, in and out, in and out...

Despite her years of marriage and her lovers, Lesley had never been able to bring herself to perform such a service for any partner—man or woman. Sometimes she would explore Connie with her fingers while the other girl's tongue made love to her. The slim Chinese beauty accepted gratefully the inexpert fingers between her legs. Once Lesley had brought her fingertip to Connie's anus. The saffron-skinned girl had tightened instinctively with apprehension and refusal, only to relax her seat-cheeks and offer herself at once, as if for fear of offending.

At present, Lesley was self-absorbed in her own erotic torment. Her head rolled from side to side on its pillow of smooth Asian skin. She pulled restlessly at her lower lip with her teeth, her breath was like the victim of a fever and her cries grew higher and more plaintive.

The mingled saliva and vaginal lubricant was in danger of running down over the curve of Lesley's bare thigh and blemishing the apricot silk of the bed-cover. Connie wiped the wetness with her own hand and then wiped her hand on her flank. She lay quiet and impassive as her mouth served the English girl's pleasure. There was a mute innocence about the yellow tan of Connie's bottom-cheeks and the vaginal entry peeping back between her thighs as she patiently presented herself to Lesley's view.

Lesley saw a timeless tranquillity and submission in this pose. Connie lay quiet and timid as the daughter of a defeated city who knows that she must be ploughed and rent by the brutal soldiery of the conqueror, among the fires of destruction and the cries of butchery. She lay as if awaiting, one after another, the pitiless javelins of flesh which the drunken victors would plant between her legs and in her backside. She lay as if for a drama whose end must be the impaling pike-handle up Connie's behind and the keen blade drawn across her throat.

Lesley began a crescendo of sharp, hard cries, like a young animal in pain. Connie teased her further and further along the narrowing path of ecstasy, swelling the balloon of pleasure fuller in her loins before it should burst. In her delirium, Lesley's tongue ran aimlessly on her own parted lips. Her thighs began to tense spasmodically as if striving to beat together. In the erotic frenzy of her orgasm, anything was possible to her—betrayal, murder, torment—either to be inflicted or undergone.

With a final violent sob she had reached the crest of her ecstasy and was falling into the abyss, deeper and for ever.

In a few moments she lay calm again. Connie slipped from the bed, took a linen towel, raised Lesley's hips and spread it under her, in order to spare the apricot silk. Then the Chinese girl went to the bathroom and turned on a gush of warm water from the gold taps. In a moment more she returned with a bowlful, now lightly scented by orange blossom. Taking as much care as if she were making love to Lesley again, Connie began to sponge and dry the vaginal tract, the buttocks and their cleavage, the thighs, legs, belly, breasts, back, and neck of the young woman whom she served with such obedience.

By the time all this was done, Lesley's composure had returned, the self-possession filled her fine blue eyes again and the line of her mouth was firm and wilful. The singlet and the soiled tights were left in a crumpled tangle on the floor for Connie to dispose of. Lesley dressed herself in a pair of black briefs of stretched cotton web, whose elasticised fit encased her hips, loins and buttocks tightly and revealingly as to their shape. She chose a matching breast-halter. Honey-toned translucent stockings were drawn sheer and smooth up her legs by the elastic straps of her black suspenders.

Standing before the mirror, she added to this ensemble a cream silk blouse with a tied neck, and a long brown skirt which came tight round her legs like a peasant girl's. When she had drawn on the smooth brown boots which encased her legs tightly from the foot to the top of the calf, she was almost ready.

Lesley, like the confident young woman she was, showed her emancipation by disdaining to wear make-up. This omission made her arrogant pale beauty all the more seductive to men and women who dreamt of subduing and punishing her. It was one of love's paradoxes, of which she was unaware and which, perhaps, she would never understand.

There were sounds outside of the servants carrying cases and portmanteaus so that all should be ready for the night train. Lesley watched Connie pick up the singlet and tights from the floor, beginning the last chores before the house was closed for the summer.

Only then did Lesley walk across to the Chinese girl, who stood naked and demure before her. She kissed Connie on the lips and felt the quick, brief pouting response.

'You shall go to Paris with us,' Lesley said quietly, 'Christine has arranged it because it pleases me.'

She walked slowly away and onto the narrow landing of the circular stairway under the grey glass dome at the centre of the house. The pale marble stairs with their smooth brass rail and openwork design of the banisters, wound down to a hallway paved with what might have been cabbalistic signs. With one hand on the wide brass rail, Lesley went down the stairs, past the closed bedroom doors at each of the three levels.

Christine was standing at the bottom, still in white riding breeches and tunic. The stern cast of her features softened in a smile as she took Lesley's hand and kissed her lightly on the cheek. Her voice murmured in her ear, little more than a breath.

'There is a ceremony to be performed before we leave. Had you forgotten?'

* * *

Lesley brushed her parted fringe impatiently and turned her blue eyes to Christine with a glance of doubt and resentment.

'Ceremony?' she said with distaste, 'What ceremony?'

'Frau Muller and Judith,' Christine held her with a smile, affectionate yet mocking, 'The solemn farewell of the teacher to the pupil.'

'No!' said Lesley sullenly, 'Muller is a brute! She has no right to do such things to her. You must tell her so! Please!'

They walked across the marble design of the oval hallway together to the ante-room with its gilt cornices and its long Egyptian settees of emerald velvet and carved scrolls. Christine took Lesley's hand again.

'Don't be foolish,' she said, the harder edge to her voice proclaimed her the mistress of the situation, 'It is my parting gift to Frau Muller for teaching her so assiduously in the past few months.'

Between the sofas the ante-room was carpeted by the blue and tawny patterns of Persian runners. The deep walnut gloss of a Steinway piano with its lid raised reflected the cloudy afternoon outside. On the music-stand of the keyboard someone had left a copy of Schumann's *Etudes Symphoniques*, the familiar cover of an Augener edition, white with an inset border of blue and the composer's name in bold black script.

Lesley, her hand still held by Christine, pulled back.

'No!' she said in the same peevish voice, 'I won't go in there! I shall go back upstairs.'

Christine kissed her gently on the cheek again and murmured in her ear.

'If we may not go into the other room with them, at least stay with me here. Who will there be to intercede for Judith if you go upstairs?'

It amused Christine that Lesley's indignation on behalf of Judith faded so easily at the prospect of being caressed and aroused. She led Lesley to the partition which divided the ante-room from the drawing-room beyond. One section of the mirrored doors separating the two rooms had been folded back by about six inches. It gave a full view of the long salon which lay on the far side.

They stood there, Christine holding Lesley back to front, looking over her shoulder, so that both shared the view of the other room through the gap. Immediately in front of Lesley, between her and the screen, was a round leather-topped table. Christine kissed the crown of the Lesley's fair boyish crop and felt her relax a little.

In the drawing-room the first preparations were being made. The maid-servant, Maggie, came in. She was a sturdy young blonde of twenty-one, dressed in black, the lank golden hair worn loose to her shoulders and parted, like Lesley's, in a fringe. Maggie turned the flower-patterned sofa so that the light from the long terrace-windows fell upon it. She cleared the loose cushions from its surface.

While she was busy with this, Frau Muller came in from the terrace. She was a woman of fifty, her hair silver yet her shoulders were strong and straight. She looked round the room and then nodded at Maggie.

'Very well,' she said abruptly, 'You may tell her to come in now.'

There was a pause as she waited for Judith. During this moment, Christine's lips brushed Lesley's ear.

'Lean forward, Lesley. Support yourself with your hands on the table.'

'Why?' She half turned her head without looking back at Christine. 'What have you brought with you?'

'Do as you are told, Lesley.'

She hesitated a moment more, as if to indicate that she obeyed as a matter of her own choice and not under her compulsion. Then she curved forward from the waist, her palms well spaced out on the leather inlay of the table.

There was the sound of a door opening in the far room and then a girl of eighteen came into sight. Dressed in her school uniform, Judith had none the less the tall elegant figure of beauty. Her light brown hair swept like a veil from her high crown to her shoulder-blades, framing the pale oval of her face with its wide-set hazel eyes and its demure regular features. Judith was a beautiful woman of eighteen dressed in a uniform of childish simplicity. Her white school blouse and tie were covered by a navy-blue cardigan which was thin and tight. The little grey skirt was absurdly skimpy and brief for a girl of her height and age, coming down only to mid-thigh and leaving bare the slim pale grace of Judith's legs. Below that she boasted only a pair of tight black knee-socks which shaped her legs from her feet up to the elastic tops gripping tightly just below her knees.

She stood before Frau Muller, her teacher, with her hands clasped behind her neck and her head bowed a little in a gesture of good manners. She had learnt early in life to be demure, quiet, and submissive.

'You know what must happen now, Judith?' Frau Muller raised her girl-ish chin with her finger and almost seemed to smile as she looked into those beautiful young eyes. 'I have kept a careful inventory of all your misde-meanours in the past six months so that there should be a reckoning before we parted. You are a young woman now, Judith, and cannot be forgiven like a mere child. You know what I mean, I think?'

She dared not meet her gaze. What an unusual tutor she had been, so strong and proud a woman yet so cruel and unsympathetic to the girl in her charge.

While Judith was forced to listen to her recited the catalogue of offences, Christine occupied herself with Lesley, who still leant forward with her hands on the table at their vantage point. She worked the hem of the skirt up over her calves and thighs until the material was gathered in an untidy tangle about her waist. Glancing down, she surveyed the gold-en sheen of her stockinged legs, the bare pallor of her upper thighs, and her hips, which were tightly shaped by Lesley's black stretch-briefs. Christine's hand slipped between Lesley's thighs from the back and her fingertips began to tickle the soft warmth of her vaginal lips through the warm web of elasticised cotton. Christine was amused to find that she was a little wet from her self-love on the bed and her fulfilment with Connie. Christine's lips kissed her ear and she breathed to her as her fingers stroked between her legs.

'You've been a secret little girl, haven't you, Lesley? At Paris we shall insist that you do such things more publicly.'

Christine felt Lesley tighten at this. Was it the outrageous suggestion, or did her thighs tense involuntarily on the hand which gave her such satisfac-tion? Lesley spread her feet a little and lay further forward over the table, resting on her elbows, each breath becoming longer and audible as

Lesley

Christine played with her. She wondered if Christine had brought it and can satisfy her as Connie hadn't been able to.

Just then Christine revealed her secret: a rubber penis that she had been hiding. Lesley greeted the feeling of it between her thighs with joy. She made short, thrusting movements to impale herself on it. Her woman-sounds were in part gasps of exertion and in part muted whimpers of frustration. In her greed for satisfaction, she cared nothing more about Judith's fate.

As they made love, Christine and Lesley watched the scene in the next room. Christine had planned this and even Lesley, who had so indignantly denounced the barbarism of what Frau Muller would do to Judith, now seemed to derive some excitement from it in her present situation.

'Your skirt, Judith?' said Frau Muller peremptorily, 'Slip it off and leave it on the chair!'

Muller and the two voyeurs watched as Judith undid the skirt, slid it down her long fair thighs and drew her feet from it one by one. She laid it on the chair and turned to her teacher again. Apart from her smart black knee-socks, Judith's only garment below the waist was a pair of white stretch-briefs, the traditional underpants of a sixth-form schoolgirl. Her long elegant legs with their slim grace would have been the envy of a ballerina. Where her tight briefs made a narrow triangle at her loins, a single tendril of Judith's fine light-brown pubic hair had escaped them to curl against her thigh. She turned, and now the seat of the tight briefs outlined a pair of elegant oval bottom-cheeks which the prettiest nymph in mythology might have coveted.

'Kneel on the sofa, Judith!' said Frau Muller quietly, 'Kneel facing the padded back. Good. Now, lift your hips from your heels and go right forward. Kneel over the sofa-back so that it supports your belly. Like that.'

Muller studied her in this posture. There was a charming innocence in the sight of Judith's slim bare legs, so fair-skinned and womanly. The seat of her knickers showed a taut resilience in the shape of her tightly rounded and gently parted bottom-cheeks.

'We must have your panties down, Judith, so that we can whip you properly.'

'No! Oh, no!' In this imploring protest there was, for the first time, a catch of tears.

'Don't be foolish, Judith! You've never been chastised before, I understand. It will make very little difference to the amount of pain whether you wear your knickers or not. You may just as well have it properly, without them, so that you know what a real whipping is like!'

Without further delay, Frau Muller took the waistband of the white stretch-briefs and pulled them down, working them over her hips and thighs. The warmth of the day and her own slight perspiration, caused the thin white cotton to gather a little under her legs and in Judith's bottom-crack. Even before the agony of the whipping she had to undergo an ordeal from the fingers of her middle-aged teacher, who could not resist exploring between the thighs and buttocks of a tall and beautiful eighteen-year-old girl. At last Judith's stretch-briefs were twisted round her ankles. Frau Muller was prepared to begin.

Muller's choice was not the cane or the birch of the schoolroom but a length of sash-cord which she held at its two ends so that it dangled as a loop about eighteen inches long. Judith's sweep of light brown hair brushed across her back as she craned round fearfully to watch her tutor turned tormentor. Muller had eyes only for the long pale thighs above her black knee socks and the bare moonlike ovals of Judith's bottom-cheeks.

With lips drawn back from her clenched teeth like a vengeful wraith, Muller raised the whipcord and lashed it down across Judith's bare buttocks. She let out a wild scream and her hands clutched and tore at the sofa covering. Writhing desperately, she prevented the next two strokes from finding their mark—but only at the cost of taking the first lash of whipcord across the backs of her thighs and the next across the backs of her knees.

'Right forward over the back of the sofa, Judith!' said Frau Muller sharply, 'At once. Don't twist on your hip like that! Quite still!'

Yet as soon as she raised the whipcord again, Judith could not control her fright.

'Take your hand away from bottom, Judith! At once! Very well, I see that I must tie your wrists out of the way!'

Judith wept and sobbed, imploring with all the tearful beauty of her pale oval face and its brimming hazel eyes. But Frau Muller was unmoved and the girl knew better than to dare physical resistance. She allowed her wrists to be tied tightly together with another length of stout cord. Then she knelt forward, bending right over the sofa-back so that her hands might be tied, with her arms at full stretch, to the iron frame which supported the sofa at its base.

A tall and beautiful schoolgirl in this posture was made to appear at the same time absurd and yet extremely provoking. The tears in her wide-set hazel eyes and the downward curve of her mouth as she pleaded with her teacher, made the pale oval of her face in its frame of fine nut-brown hair no less appealing. As she knelt tightly forward over the back of the sofa, there was a rear view of her slim fair-skinned thighs rising to the tautly rounded nymph-cheeks of Judith's backside. Demurely rounded, yet wantonly parted, their womanly charm completed the paradox of her appearance.

High up between the rear of her thighs it was just possible to glimpse the rear view of the lightly haired adolescent pudenda which the pupil had exposed much more fully as she tried to evade the first three strokes of the whip. Between the parted ovals of her buttocks was the tight dark bud, its surround like a lightly veined leaf—Judith's anus which the punishment posture obliged this innocent girl to offer in so lewd a manner.

Frau Muller sat down on the sofa, holding a strap which she had taken from the side-table. With this she pinioned the girl's legs together tightly, just above her knees, also drawing the strap through a metal strut under the cushioning to hold her in place. Muller continued to sit a moment longer, her eyes dwelling on the rear pout of her vaginal lips and the dark closed bud between her buttocks. Like the modest maiden she was, she had washed these areas before reporting for the punishment she knew had been decreed. Yet the day was warm. Already the clean scent of soap was mingled with the mineral and musty girl-scent from between her thighs and from between the cheeks of Judith's bottom. Muller breathed it in.

The cruel tutor stood up and turned the hem of her white blouse back, well above her waist, so that Judith's hips and buttocks were properly bare. The girl twisted her face round further, more anxiously than ever, the veil of fine silken brown hair spilling forward over her shoulders.

Tight-lipped again, Muller raised the loop of whipcord and lashed it down with a vicious energy across the pale oval cheeks of Judith's eighteen-year-old bottom. For a moment the long-legged beauty seemed frozen by the paralysing anguish of the impact. Then she gave a frantic cry and contorted her buttocks in a wild surging.

The teacher tamed her by a second and a third whip-stroke, raising sinuous weals across the twin curves of Judith's behind. In angry crimson the looped tracery of the cord began to pattern her buttocks, sometimes curling round to catch the flank of her hip or the inner edge of her seat-cheeks where they curved in to meet. Judith screamed for forgiveness, for pity, even for a moment's respite.

The prints of the whipcord began to merge into two crimson patches, centred on the crowns of her buttocks. Frau Muller deliberately aimed the next twelve strokes at those very areas of her behind where she had already hurt her so badly. In desperation, Judith tried to twist her backside away but the whip followed her pitilessly. A wickedly aimed stroke of the lash drew an irregular row of ruby dots from her thrashed seat-cheeks. As though she could not see it for himself, Judith screamed at Muller that the lash had made her bottom bleed.

'Control yourself, Judith! When a beautiful girl like you is whipped, a bead or two of blood should be drawn from her bottom! Round your backside out properly. You must learn to offer it prettily for your punishments!' It could be assumed that Frau Muller spoke with authority.

With these last words, she slashed her with the cord across the softer undercurve of her bottom-cheeks, just along the faint crease where Judith's buttocks and thighs met. Judith had exhausted the first energy of her cries and she now responded to the strokes with an abrupt shriek after each impact of the whip. It seemed, after more than twenty strokes, that she had lost the breath to do more.

The teacher met the eyes of the weeping beauty with a mischievous smile, her tongue touching her lip as if in promise of some devilment. With all her strength Frau Muller lashed her eight times across the tender and softer lower curve of her bottom.

Her head went forward over the sofa. The tall schoolgirl was clenching the woollen ribbing of the sofa in her teeth to brace herself. Lower down, the cloth cover of the furniture was torn where her fingernails had ripped at it in her frenzy.

Muller lashed her twice across the backs of her knees. For the next few days, Judith would not walk a step without being reminded of it by the discomfort which the movement caused.

Again the cruel tutor cut her across the bottom but her rescue was in sight. Under the final strokes, Judith screamed for her parents, her boyfriend—all those who could or could not hear her—to come and save her. Yet the teacher was indifferent to the last, finishing and without another word to her getting up and walked from the room. It was Maggie, the blonde maid, who came in almost at once, to untie Judith's hands.

Christine still held Lesley over the table, impaled on the rubber replica of the male member. Christine moved it gently inside her as they watched Judith. The girl sobbed uncontrollably as a broken-hearted child. Yet even as she wept, Judith began to move slowly and painfully from her position. She stood up, brushing away tears with her hand and gulping down some of the sobs which rose in her throat. Then, like a well-trained young woman, she turned the sofa round and moved the table a little to its usual place in the room. These pieces of furniture had been moved for use in her punishment. It was her duty to put them back.

Cautiously and with many a wince, she managed to put on her short grey skirt. Her school knickers remained crumpled and concealed in her hand. Judith's buttocks were so swollen and bruised from the whipping that it was unthinkable for her to endure the tightness of her panties until she had sponged herself with cool soothing water.

Even so, she could not resist going to the drawing-room mirror and turning her back to it. She lifted her brief school skirt and looked round over her shoulder in a long and thoughtful inspection of her whipped backside. The agony of the ordeal did not quite conquer all her natural feminine fascination with what had been done to her. She picked up the sash-cord with which she had been flogged and ran it through her fingers. Her long brown hair fell forward about her face as she looked at the whip with the same unmistakable curiosity. Then she put down the lash, turned, and walked slowly from the room.

Christine held Lesley's pale flanks with either hand as she bent in front of her in imitation of the way a man might fuck a woman from behind. How excited she was! Christine could feel the amount and rapidity of her lubrication. It was certainly a consequence of her misbehaviour in the bedroom, Christine thought. Yet, for all Lesley's protests at the severity of the punishment, she had lubricated copiously while watching Judith being thrashed.

She came with short spasmodic cries. Christine kept the phallus in position until the last trace of Lesley's pleasure subsided. Then she removed it and they turned towards each other. With eyes closed she gave Lesley her tongue in her open mouth. Then Christine smiled and held her away from her body, addressing her as if she were a little girl rather than a promiscuous young woman.

'Go upstairs and put on clean panties, Lesley. The car will be here in half an hour.'

She walked away with her short fair hair slightly bowed as if her young pride had been in some way humbled by the manner of her dismissal. Christine withdrew to the drawing-room, the scene of Judith's chastisement.

In the idle minutes that followed, talk of Paris and its season occupied every room of the house, even among the servants who were closing shutters across windows which would not be opened again until October. There was a sound of hat-boxes and portmanteaus being assembled, the baggage which would accompany the travellers, although by a different train.

When the car came, all six women, some young, some old, some girls, some lovers, were ready. Christine and Fatima rode in front. Behind them were Judith, Lesley, the governess, Maggie and Connie, the two maids. Judith was now dressed in a manner more fitting to her beauty. The green velveteen dress with its narrow waist suited the pale oval dignity of her young face, the wide hazel eyes, and the veil of fine light brown hair.

Judith had wept a good deal after her punishment and the traces of that weeping were still evident in her face. She had cried with the pain of her buttocks wealed and swollen by the whipcord. Yet her tears flowed even more for the thought of what had been done to her. She walked slowly and uncertainly. The chauffeur came to help her into the buttoned leather interior of the car but Christine waved him away.

'There is no need of that! She was whipped by her teacher this afternoon and feels a little sorry for herself. She can manage well enough on her own.'

Throughout the drive to the Zoo station, the driver kept glancing at Judith in his mirror. When he caught her eyes he gave her a smile of quiet amusement. At length, to avoid this, the girl laid her head on Lesley's lap, allowing the young woman to stroke her hair and comfort her.

Rain in the winter city caused the wet black streets to soak up moisture-clouded lights along its shop-lit boulevards. The opulent window displays seemed to shine more splendidly against this curious black radiance. The long glass cases of the stores offered their treasures like the burnished and silken booty of an imperial campaign. These riches of conquest were tendered by a frieze of slim wax mannequins, like slave-girls in the victor's triumphal procession.

The round green poster pillars on the broad pavements offered Salome at the Opera, *Wallenstein* at the Schauspielhaus. A vintner's window displayed dark bottles on deep bloodstone velvet. One blue-black Madeira label bore *Gran Cama de Lobos* in thickly stamped gold. A small inset window by a fashion boutique appeared like a votive niche with a glass front. It held a pine statuette, oiled and polished, the symbolic sweep of a young female nude with sloping shoulders and turning thighs, half pirouetting among objects of tribute. To one side a pure silk scarf swept with casual elegance down the length of its wire stand, the crimson sheen patterned by a key motif in silver and bronze. On the other flank of the nude figure, the coffee brown gloss of a child's riding-switch curved slightly against the hessian-covered wall of the niche.

To Christine, the sight of such shops brought back a first recollection of Maggie, when she and Fatima had made her acquaintance several months before. Maggie, with her coltish figure and the golden blonde hair worn loose and lank to her collar with a parted fringe, just like a little girl. Maggie at work in the window, the faded blue jean-trousers and close-fitting black singlet. Maggie with her fair-skinned face and blue eyes, features a little crude like a *jolie laide*. Maggie with her slut's brazenness and child's innocence so alluringly mingled. Maggie with her tongue pressed against her upper lip in a thoughtful moment. Maggie fooling energetically with the young men at work. Maggie on all fours brushing energetically. Maggie's bottom, full-cheeked under the tight jeans-seat as she bends, drawing the attention of passers-by. Maggie pretending to lose a pin and looking for it. Kneeling with back to the window and head touching the carpet as she scans about. Maggie's bottom-cheeks tightly rounded and lewdly parted under her tight jeans in this posture, even the soft purse of pubic flesh outlined. Smiles and cameras among the onlookers. A boy playing with himself furtively under his coat, adoring Maggie's sluttish young rump through the glass.

And Maggie, finally, confessing to Christine and Fatima that while she did it with men she dreamt of doing it with women. It was at that moment that Christine and Fatima knew they would take her with them to Paris.

Christine smiled at the memory. Presently the black car drew up by the echoing glass temple of the departure hall. Judith, who had been holding Lesley's hand to her cheek as she lay with her head on the young woman's lap, now took the hand and kissed it, tasting her own tears upon it as she did so.

All stations, it seemed, had their individual association and odours. The travellers to Paris were embowered by the perfume of flowers and scents of fresh fruit borne in from the stalls near the Kantstrasse. Departure boards carried the names of distant cities and resorts like the verses of a poem. Close to the damp parks and lit shop-fronts of the city, the long nave of the terminus was adorned with frescoes which showed men and women beside a lavender sea, under pink pergolas hung with purple grape. However distant Paris might be, the flowery coasts of its perpetual summer, even the minarets and the arches of Moorish palaces beyond, were first perceived under this great glass roof in the winter city.

* * *

Evening, under the echoing glass nave of the departure bay, the night express to the summer coasts stood waiting. From the tawny shades of its cabin-lamps a warm amber flush was diffused through the windows of the softly carpeted wagon-lit and restaurant car. Here and there a darker rectangle of glass reflected the dim blue glow of a sleeping-light. At the diminutive dinner-tables as the white-coated stewards brought ice and glasses, the talk was already of villas and tennis courts, polo grounds and casinos, hotels where the ranked flags signalled the opening of the summer season.

In the long lamp lit restaurant car, women were dressed for their journey as if for the formality of the opera. Young ladies in plain backless gowns like the maiden slaves of an Egyptian queen. Young lovers in white satin, smooth and tight on their thighs and hips, with the short curled hair of page-boys. Women in cotton trouser-suits and a pair of amorous girls dressed alike in blue matador pants, coats and cloche hats.

The table at which the two men sat with Lesley and Judith attracted the glances of other men and women alike. There was a piquant contrast between Christine's blonde self-confidence and the darker sophistication of Fatima's. Lesley, the self-confident young Venus of twenty-eight, made a suggestive partner for the pale beauty of Judith, the sweep of her light brown hair from her high crown to her shoulders catching the warm slanting light of the lamps.

Pine forests and the gleam of early moonlight on flat grey lakes moved in a panorama beyond the windows of the restaurant car. The sudden movement of small animals in the light of the express and the isolated glow of a hunter's lamp animated the still and sombre scenes.

By ten o'clock, only a single couple remained in the dining coach, smoking and delaying the moment of their intimacy. For the other men and women, the long hours of the journey in their sleeping cabins had begun.

Christine, as usual, had reserved the three compartments which made a self-contained area at one end of the royal blue wagon-lit. These little rooms had an air of antique luxury, for the coach had travelled between Paris and the inland cities for many years. Its imperial dignity appeared in the dark polished wood, the rich and slightly faded upholstery of the deep banquettes. Flame-patterned mahogany in the wooden panelling had been waxed to a liquid gloss. On each side of the cabin, a bed was made up with crisp white linen and the air was freshened by a perfume of California poppy.

On Christine's orders, one cabin had been allocated to Connie and Judith, another to Maggie and Fatima, the third for Lesley and herself. As the air raced past the steel flanks of the express with the sound of a stream in torrent, Christine watched Lesley close the blinds of the sleeping-car and begin to undress. She shook her fair parted fringe clear of her face and stepped out of her skirt. The skin and her blouse were neatly hung in the narrow mahogany cupboard.

The white breast-halter showed the soft but resilient rounds of Lesley's breasts, which despite her experience of child-rearing had retained an alluring tautness of outline. For all the moodiness of her fair-skinned features, Christine noticed with amusement that the tight white cotton showed her two nipples erect with expectation.

'Keep your breast-halter on for the moment, Lesley,' Christine said quietly. The young woman hesitated but obeyed. Christine noticed that after her fucking by the dildo that afternoon, Leslie had taken off her stockings, possibly because the wetness on her thighs had marked them at the top. She had put on another pair of translucent stocking-tights without panties. This pleased Christine who liked her in such misty, mysterious veiling and often ordered her to dress in that way.

Christine kissed her on the lips.

'Lie on the bed, Lesley,' she said softly, 'this one. Over here.'

She sat down, drew her legs onto the cover and arranged herself, lying on her side with knees drawn a little upwards as she looked at her older lover, the one who had been her first after her marriage, her first woman after men, and still her favourite. Christine took her hand.

'I should like to strap your wrists together, Lesley. Will you object to that?'

Lesley gave an impatient flick of her fringe, as if bothered by a stray hair on her face.

'No,' she said uncertainly, 'I won't object.'

Lesley

Christine took a one-inch strap, drew it firmly round the young woman's wrists and used it to tether her hands to the frame of the bed. When Christine turned towards the door, Lesley said quickly, 'Must I stay like this?'

Christine smiled.

'It is better that you should. It pleases me that you should.'

With that she went out, leaving her in the half-lit cabin until Lesley turned on to her side, lay down, and began to doze. The cabin-door opened an hour later and the two figures who came in were just discernible to her by the glow of the sleeping-light which had been left on all the time. They were Fatima and Maggie. There was no reason why they should have come to this cabin of the sleeping car to make love, except that they wished to perform certain acts in front of Lesley while she was obliged to lie with her wrists strapped down, unable to intervene in any way.

Fatima had made Maggie dress in her working costume because that was the way in which she pleased her best. Fatima, being of a people who so often served others, liked to make use of her while she was dressed as a common shop girl, reminding her of the first time she had seen her. So now, Maggie wore her snug blue singlet and the faded tightness of her blue working-jeans. Neither of the women paid the least attention to Lesley by word or glance, though she lay on her side watching them, her eyes open. They behaved as if she might have been asleep or, indeed, not there at all.

The light caught the bell of Maggie's golden-blonde hair, spilling loose on her shoulders like a child's, its fringe parted on her forehead. The fair-skinned face with its firm crudity of features had a look of insolence. She pressed her tongue to her upper lip in a manner of sluttish anticipation. Maggie was not a tall girl, her thighs and legs being short for the rest of her figure. Above the waist of her jeans, where the singlet-hem pulled free, there was a pale sheen of plumpness. Her breasts appeared soft but not over-weight in the tight singlet. Maggie was not a big-bottomed girl, yet as she walked the tight jeans showed a certain plump swagger of her lower but-tocks. When she had been working on all fours, in public view, many of her male admirers had chosen to watch her from the rear. Her buttocks were not large but they were quite broad and sturdy in keeping with Mag's coltish appearance.

'Kneel down, Maggie,' said Fatima softly, 'here, in front of me.'

Fatima pressed her to her knees beside the bed, until Maggie's face was level with Lesley's own, no more than eighteen inches away. Turning to one side, Fatima switched on the bed-table lamp so that its tawny light illumi-nated Maggie's face. Then Fatima produced the coup de grace, the very dildo that had been inside Lesley that very afternoon. Lesley's gasp went unnoticed by the couple, so intent were they on their progress. Christine must have given it to Fatima for precisely the purpose of this show.

'In your mouth, Maggie!' Fatima said gently, 'Remember you are to be my captive slave-girl tonight. This is the first tribute paid on all such occa-sions as that!'

Maggie hesitated only a moment. Her hand circled the rubber at its base, as if to prevent too great a length entering her mouth and choking her. She held the dildo like this and turned to Lesley. Teasingly, she showed it to the promiscuous girl in her helplessness. Little could Maggie know what Lesley knew about the flavour that Maggie was then tasting. Maggie's golden-blonde hair spilled forward slightly as she bowed her head and wet her lips. There was no false modesty about her. Mag sat on her heels and licked up and down the rubber shaft with her young and agile tongue. Maggie was a tart by birth and breeding, a girl of the lower orders who had known of such practices since she was ten years old.

Lesley

Opening her lips wider she circled the knob as if it were a real penis and began to suck with a rhythmic movement of her head. Fatima looked down at her, a smile of satisfaction illuminating her features as she watched Maggie performing this service of humility with her mouth, a service she had provided so often for men, now offered up to her female lovers.

'Suck more slowly, Mag!' she said gently, as if she herself were being kissed, not a shaft of rubber. 'Make more use of your tongue! Play with the tip! You are such an expert. What a loss for mankind that you do it now to rubber! What a bold and randy young slut you are, Maggie!'

Once or twice the rubber knob, tasting of Lesley, went too close to the back of her throat and drew from Maggie a slight choking protest. Involuntary tears smudged the mascara with which she had darkened the lashes of her blue eyes.

When Fatima decided she had finished with the rubber shaft, she turned towards neglected Lesley.

'Show her love with your tongue, Mag!'

Turning her face to Lesley, the blonde girl extended her tongue until it quivered a little with the effort. Fatima was aware that Lesley had been tensing her thighs rhythmically together as she watched and now there was a wetness of self-lubrication between them. With the hardened look of a slut, Maggie brought her tongue closer still to the lips of the promiscuous yet coolly arrogant young woman. Lesley hesitated. Then in a sudden access of frustrated desire, she closed her eyes and opened her mouth to receive Maggie's tongue and swallow all that the other girl had to give.

Fatima watched with amusement, the true mistress of the situation. She mercilessly ignored Lesley's sighs as Maggie left her.

'Kneel down, Mag. On all fours with your seat towards me!'

Once again it was arranged so that Lesley had a view of the lovers from about eighteen inches away. The shop girl now presented that view which so many of her passing admirers had stopped to smile at. In the tight jeans, firm but sturdily rounded, the cheeks of Maggie's bottom were suggestively presented. The outline of the stretch-briefs which she wore underneath was clearly visible.

Fatima undid and lowered Maggie's jeans with the panties inside them. Kneeling behind her Fatima gently milked the fleshy lips of her vagina from the rear with her strong fingers. Taking up the dildo, still wet from Maggie's mouth, Fatima pushed it into the blonde girl's sex from the same rear angle, causing Maggie to sob with relief. Lesley watched with aloof blue eyes. Yet the murmur of the bedsprings betrayed her squirming of her own thighs.

Maggie had one hand between her legs and was playing with herself quite shamelessly as Fatima made love to her with the rubber. Fatima paused, smiling. She opened a small jar and vaselined the dark inward dimple of Maggie's anus. The dildo, having already pierced two of her three holes, knocked for admission at this last hole, the tightest of the three. Maggie gave a child's cry of fearing hurt, perhaps to excite her. Then she uttered a short hollow gasp as her rear muscle yielded and her arsehole was stretched wide round the shaft. At no time did she ask Fatima to spare her.

Fatima sodomised Maggie vigorously with every inch of rubber. All this while the twenty-one-year-old servant girl never ceased to play with herself.

'Were your other lovers too timid to insist on this, Mag?' asked Fatima, 'I'm sure some of the men who watched you working in the shop must have imagined such things! Is this the sort of thing only a woman is brazen enough to demand of you? Keep your face turned to the mirror so that I can watch you! Squeeze the dildo with your backside, Maggie, you young slut! Ah, what ecstasy it is to watch you thus!'

Lesley

Fatima rammed the dildo in and out like a piston.

'Your head right down, Maggie, and your seat spread hard! I want you to feel this to the depths of your entrails! Now, my young slut! And now! Ah, you feel it pumping I think!'

When she had finally deemed the reaming of her bottom to be adequate, Fatima sat on the bed by Lesley. The wetness between Lesley's thighs was visible now, the dew collecting on her tights.

'Lick Maggie's fingers, Lesley!' Fatima murmured, as she masturbated Lesley gently. But Lesley bridled at the fingers held to her lips. Fatima stopped the masturbation of her and Lesley gave a forlorn little cry.

'Lick Mag's fingers, then!' Fatima said with gentle insistence, offering to continue with her fingers on the condition that Lesley tasted Maggie's fingers. Fatima began to mould the wet lips of Lesley's vagina through the thin tights. And this time, as Maggie held the fingers out, Lesley's tongue slid between lightly opened lips and licked, and licked, and licked. Fatima laughed and stood up. She led Maggie out and left Lesley to her thoughts.

It was almost another hour before Christine came back. When she did so, she was not alone. Beside her stood the demure fine-boned figure of Connie. The Asian girl was once again naked except for the black silk cord round her waist, running down between her thighs, under her legs, and up between the cheeks of her bottom.

Christine made Connie lie beside Lesley on the bed, but this time with her head towards Lesley's feet. Christine herself lay down so that she and Lesley looked into one another's eyes over the naked body of Connie, whose hips lay between them. She commanded Connie to suck her slit.

As Connie obeyed, Christine looked down at the Asian girl's beauty. Her sheen of black hair falling to her shoulderblades, was held back by silver clips from the warm-toned heart-shaped face with its impassive almond eyes. Connie had had her admirers too when she had worked as a shop girl. Men would pause to study her figure in tight denim as she arranged the season's fashions for display. Some of this casual admiration did not even attract her attention. There were other men whose smiles and questioning glances brought a wicked laughter to Connie's own slanting eyes.

Other men, with crueller passions, surveyed her in a different way. Unsmiling and sardonic, they watched her kneel, the tight denim showing the trimly rounded cheeks of Connie's bottom separated and giving an extra width to her behind in this posture. When she met the eyes of these men, the girl caught her breath with dismay. She read their thoughts of gags and restraining bonds, of their cruel pleasures indulged without pity. They would go on their way. Yet, later on, Connie would look round and see them standing there once again, contemplating her. Then her almond eyes would fill with fright, she would drop her dress-pins with a start and seek refuge somewhere beyond their gaze.

Now, where she belonged, spared the shop windows and in the company of women, a clitoris pressed against her tongue, her slim young breasts touched Christine's belly. Her eyes admired the slim-bladed shoulders of the girl, the delicate bone-pattern of her pale yellow back. She was glad they had found these two shop girls, Maggie and Connie. The young girls were so integral to the experience at Paris.

Connie's hips, level with Fatima's own face, were demurely trim and yet silken smooth. She parted the slim thighs and smiled at the sight of the thin veil of dark hair which scarcely concealed her little clitoris.

Lesley murmured to Fatima, with the slight peevishness of a little girl as she pulled at the bonds which held her wrists. Christine smiled and shook her head. She believed it good for Lesley to endure such frustration from time to time, to witness the enjoyment of others, to plead for a share of it, and yet to be refused. Hunger would sharpen her appetite.

Connie lacked the prudishness of an English girl in her acceptance of a admiration. She received gratefully the tributes paid to any part of her body and was not repelled by the manner of a woman's worship of her. Now she lay with her head motionless for a while, her tongue lapping the slit of her lover.

Christine stroked the slim satiny yellow thighs of the girl. She kissed her hips and belly. She allowed her lips to browse on the demure saffron cheeks of her trim Chinese bottom. Her fingers teased her clitoris, stroking lightly, tickling and withdrawing, until Connie whimpered with longing for a more systematic masturbation.

Christine began this gently with one hand, rubbing and squeezing the eager clitoris, rubbing and squeezing, rubbing and squeezing, without remorse. With her other hand Christine parted the saffron-toned buttocks and kissed those cool seat-cheeks. The hand between her legs moved towards the path leading to her womb. Christine began to kiss the warmer smoothness of skin where her buttocks curved in together. Settling down to rouse her, Christine moulded a long succession of light kisses to Connie's anus, feeling the delicate pattern of the flesh-bud under her lips.

There was no doubt that this prolonged loving by her lips in so sensitive an area excited her profoundly. Christine felt on her fingers the warm slipperiness of natural lubrication between her thighs. Connie still held her lips to her mistress's clitoris and tongue-washed it with sighs and moans of gratitude. Her nimble Asian fingers gently manipulated Christine's womb, as if to stimulate a stronger flow of passion.

Presently, Christine took from her dressing-gown pocket the same rubber penis. How intimate Lesley was coming to know it! While Christine and Lesley watched, the Asian girl raised her upper leg, showing them the widened lips of her sex in this posture. Slowly but with a firm pressure, she pressed the tip of the artificial penis into her body.

Holding the base of it in her demure young fist, Connie began to make love to herself vigorously with the dildo, working it in and out with a fevered energy. As her cries began to grow more shrill and uneven. Her naked body squirmed and writhed as she impaled herself with the shaft.

The long mirror at the foot of the bed showed Connie's bare back and her buttocks as she made love to herself in this posture. Now she took the rubber dildo in one hand, held it behind her, and touched it to her anus as she used her fingers to continue with her own clitoris. The thought was stronger than her resolve, for her eyes showed a mingled excitement and apprehension. Christine held her close, putting her own hand over Connie's.

More resolute than the girl herself, Fatima forced the way with the head of the phallus until Connie's almond eyes widened with alarm as her anus yielded. She gave a sudden cry and then subsided with the length of the rubber penis sheathed in her backside.

At the same time Fatima worked the dildo, she manipulated things so that Connie's lips and hands were free to play with Lesley.

With her hands inside the English girl's tights, Connie masturbated Lesley until the pale beauty came with cries of longing. This excitement precipitated the Asian girl's own crisis. Christine felt the quick tremor of her thighs and heard her first short, rhythmic gasps.

The cocooning luxury of the sleeping car was invaded by grey Parisian light. In a canyon, between tall stone houses with peeling shutters and mansard roofs, the express passed under the open ironwork of bridges bearing the shabby streets of La Villette or La Chapelle above the broad expanse of the iron rails.

Yet the destination of the lovers lay far beyond this. In another hour, the journey would resume, the slipstream of the express washing incessantly over the plate glass window and the polished royal blue flanks of the wagon-lit with a sound like lashing rain. Tunnels which pierced the centres of great cities or the spurs of remote hills threw the streaming air against the coaches with a sudden impact, the brick wall of the excavation flashing away at blinding speed.

There was to be darkness and night again before the journey's end. In these hours, the travellers crossed a dream landscape of flat moonlit pasture. Here and there an old manor house or hunting lodge showed briefly among its plantation of dark trees. From time to time the train halted at the station of some anonymous city. There was a view of a town-bridge crossing a broad commercial river on which the starlight glimmered faintly. The dark eminence of a hilltop fortress, sinister even by day, testified to ancient war and slaughter on the flat land below, where the vaporous wisps of cloud redoubled the radiance of the full moon.

At last Christine, Fatima and the other four women came to the place where the car was waiting for the last stage of their journey to Paris. There were no more cities or railway junctions, only remote and suspicious countryside, a place of little towns and scattered villages. Here was the land's end and the world's end, a realm of violent animal lecheries and strange cruelty practiced in the name of law.

A long road swooped straight, mile after mile, over wooded hills with apple orchards. Lonely and grey the gothic churches stood aloof, steps leading down to the sunken floors of their dim, candle-lit interiors.

At night the travellers came to commercial hotels in little market-towns, their courtyards hidden beyond archways from the street. Along the uneven corridors above were bedrooms hung with prints of old barbarities, thin carpets on pine boarding. They ate in old dark-panelled dining-rooms with deep window recesses, the deep copper tone of cooking pans hung on the walls and the slow beat of a tall clock made by a country craftsman.

By day they passed the fields of maize and the open land where old women in dresses and aprons the colour of terra-cotta, and dark conical hats, were digging potatoes.

At last the countryside began to change. There were yellow fields of mustard and the first rows of early vines. A warm wind blew from the sea and, for the first time, the travellers sensed the presence of Paris.

* * *

The journey south brought them to a land of vines, a landscape of rivers and flat fields, quiet canals and little inland ports from which the steeples of remote villages were seen at a distance. The purple Judas trees were now in flower and blue wisteria overhung the stone boundary walls of old manor houses.

In the silence of the car, Lesley would raise her eyes slowly to dwell on Judith's beauty. The girl sat demurely with her hands folded in her lap. In the pale oval of her face, her lips were lightly parted, the gaze of her hazel eyes unwavering as she looked ahead of her. When she turned, the sweep of light brown hair from her high crown to her shoulder-blades moved with the allure of a dancer's veil. Then, before Lesley could look away, Judith's eyes would meet hers, calm and yet question-ing, as if the girl who was within a week of her nineteenth birthday feared and longed for the future.

On the following day, in a white and blinding afternoon sun, they came to a high hill-town, a bastion, unknown to the world behind them. It was a place of wide spaces, brooding in heat and silence. Barracks and prison buildings with their shutters closed stood in a pale ensemble on a vast gravelled square. A narrow and deserted street of little shops with their awnings pulled out represented the commercial life of the town. There was another square, a gravelled space once more, with stunted plane trees. Beyond that lay the arid limestone hills and the descent to Paris.

That night was passed at a little town which was no more than a clearing among a tall forest of pines and spruce trees growing in the flat alluvial soil of the coastal plain. The whine of saw-mills and thick scent of pine resin hung in the warm air of the spring evening. Before dinner, Christine came to the room which Lesley was to share with Judith for the night. Se explained with a smile that she wished to supervise Judith's dressing for dinner now that she was to appear as a young lady.

The girl had just stepped naked from her bath with her light brown hair braided in a pair of plaits down her neck. While she was still drying herself in the bathroom, Christine dismissed Lesley and began to choose those garments which she had decided that Judith should wear. There were only two that she would permit for the moment and she summoned a maid to take them to Judith in the bathroom. Then she sat at ease in a chair, lit a cigarette, and waited for her to appear.

She did so reluctantly and with good reason for her timidity. Judith was dressed in the sheer silk of lilac-coloured stockings and a short plum-coloured corset which encased her young breasts, leaving her shoulders bare, came down to a narrow waist and ended with a frill of lace round the top of her hips. Between this and the stocking-tops at mid-thigh, the girl was bare but for the elastic suspender-straps of the corset which drew the stockings high and tight on her legs.

She stood before Christine uncertainly, her light brown hair now released from its braiding and once more falling in its veil about her pale oval beauty. Christine beckoned her until she stood at the arm of her chair.

At the front the corset came down in a short V-shape between her thighs, not quite covering all the fine moss of pubic hair.

Christine drew the girl's head down and kissed her on the lips, with such passion that Judith struggled breathlessly against her. Christine let her go and returned to her cigarette.

'Fold your hands behind your back, Judith,' she said quietly. When she had obeyed, Christine intruded a finger between her legs and touched her vaginal lips lightly. With a tightening movement of her long graceful legs, the girl began to back away.

'Stand still, Judith!' Christine's voice was sharp and impatient. Judith obeyed, looking down as if unable to take her eyes away from what the finger was doing.

'Look at me!' Christine said and a smile almost broke on her lips as she raised her hazel eyes to meet her gaze. 'Tell me, Judith, when did you last make love to yourself?'

In her eyes, the shock of the question seemed to register with the force of a blow she might have struck her. Judith waited before her, immobilized by it. The maid who had been emptying and cleaning the bath now stood in the doorway, astonished but also visibly amused at Christine's questioning. Judith bowed her head again and said nothing. Christine sighed.

'Very well, that is a matter we shall investigate properly when there is more time. Now, turn round, if you please.'

With her head still bowed to avoid the maid's smile, Judith obeyed. At the rear the plum-coloured corset had been cut high and seatless. It was rare for a girl of eighteen to have a figure which could do justice to such lingerie. Yet it suited this tall and willowy beauty to perfection. Christine surveyed the long elegant legs and the narrow waist. The frill of the corset arched high enough at the rear so that it merely touched the very tops of the pale oval cheeks of Judith's bottom.

Christine's fingers moved lightly on the cheeks of Judith's backside. She smiled to herself as she inspected the few fading bruises and weals of whip-cord left by the thrashing which her teacher had given her.

'I'm sure the learned Frau Muller enjoyed herself when she whipped you, Judith,' said Christine lightly, 'You are innocent in such matters as yet. Later on you will understand that for her to hurt you so badly was a true labour of love. Even you, my innocent Judith, must have guessed that there are women who enjoy doing such things to you.'

The maid giggled at these words and went from the room with a final conspiratorial smile in Christine's direction. Judith's pale resilient young seat-cheeks tensed together in her self-consciousness.

'Bend forward,' said Christine gently, 'Support yourself with your hands on the little table.'

Reluctantly she did as commanded. Her demure young buttocks spread broader and parted until Christine had a view of her rear cleavage and the backward pout of her vagina at her thighs. Christine's finger touched Judith's anus and the dark little inward dimple tightened with instinctive apprehension.

'Don't be foolish, Judith! You have overheard enough to know that we will use Vaseline whenever we violate you there. If you are well behaved, we will select only the narrow dildos!'

Christine kept her in this position for some while, fondling and caress-ing her, even kissing between her legs briefly, giving Judith a taste of the benefits of Paris before she drew her hand away.

'Choose a pair of knickers from your trousseau, Judith. Show me which they are before you put them on.'

She was not easily pleased. Judith chose one pair of panties after another without gaining approval. At last Christine consented to a pair of pale blue briefs, tight-fitting and translucent. Only then was she permitted to put on her petticoat and the simple but striking dress of green silk with its narrow waist. She sat at dinner with the others, beautiful as a young woman and yet submissive as a well-trained little girl.

The next afternoon brought them to Paris, the white villas in the Spanish style with their red-tiled roofs bordering a sheltered bay and overhung by wooded hills. Yacht sails hung like dragonflies on the glittering water beyond the pillars and stucco of the casino. Heat and tranquillity enveloped the pale sands, the gardens with their clipped hedges and tennis courts, the quiet streets with their fashionable boutiques and florists, the squares of whitewashed houses with Spanish balconies in black wrought-iron.

The way to the Villa Rif lay down a broad boulevard, a long vista of rhododendron trees on the pink paving, tall white buildings and the awnings of cafes with their interiors of dark buttoned leather and polished wood.

The Villa Rif was one of those residences in broad quiet roads which are seen only distantly through the wrought-iron railings that guard them from the world. As the day's heat waned and darkness came, the white lamplight of the street fell far short of its walls, the moon's glimmer lost in black foliage. In the stillness of night, there was no sound but the electric chatter of cicadas, no movement but the sudden looping of bats against the pale sky, no scent but the warm odours of the pines.

Within this villa and its grounds, the women might pass the entire season and want for very little. Neither Christine nor Fatima insisted upon such isolation. A demure girl like Judith and even a self-possessed young woman like Lesley might be more effectively imprisoned by means which required no locks and bars. Christine and Fatima, experienced lovers that they were, had long known the simpler truth.

Let all her ways be unconfined. But clap your padlock on her mind. Their pleasures which began at morning would occupy them until night. Connie and Maggie, though treated as servants, were not exempt from these lecheries. The older lovers, their authority and debauchery hand in hand, exacted their tribute in nobly furnished rooms of the summer villa, among dark wood and flame-patterned Spanish rugs. The cries of the girls in their surrender wavered in the sunlight of white bedrooms among lace and angled mirrors, the tiny shrillness of pleasure fading before it reached the locked gate leading to the world outside. There were long evenings spent by lamplight in the cloistered garden courtyard at the centre of the villa. In the stillness of the night, sounds would have carried further. Yet if extreme forms of enjoyment were contemplated, it was only necessary to employ restraining straps and a padded leather gag in order to reduce the highest scream to a plaintive mewing.

Christine took possession of Lesley on the first night. During their journey she had refused her any relief for her longings in order that she might be the better prepared when they reached their destination.

When she went with her after dinner to the wide bedroom above the garden, Christine realised that her own preparation had been even more intense than hers. Now she wanted Lesley with a sudden obsessive longing.

She stood before the mirror, having taken off her shoes, skirt and blouse. The glass reflected an image of the sulky fair-skinned beauty as she combed the fringe of her urchin crop in a habitual impatient gesture. Her white breast-halter and matching suspender-belt were accompanied by the tan of sheer stockings and brief tight panties of slinky and translucent apple green.

Christine turned her at once and took her in Lesley arms. Though she was quite a tall and trim young woman, Lesley in her stockinged feet seemed like a juvenile waif beside Christine's powerful build. Her hand smoothed over her bare belly with its slight proud curve.

They undid her breast-halter. Christine firmed Lesley's breasts with her hands, the white globes still taut and resilient. She tongue-flicked her nipples to erection and heard her first sighs of contentment. Her hand slid between her legs and Christine smiled as she felt that, in her excitement, Lesley's panties were already wet there with the vaginal lubrication which the thrill drew from her.

It amused Christine to think that under her disdainful manner and arrogant attitude, Lesley was so easily roused. Small wonder that she had walked out on husband and children in order to gratify the tormenting itch for her sisters which tickled her between her thighs.

'What a depraved young wanton you are, Lesley!' she said gently as she gave herself to her fingers, 'There are places for such as you, houses where the mistress will spare you nothing!'

Squirming under her caresses, Lesley kissed her face with a brief and breathless rhythm of her lips. Then, unable to wait longer, she lifted her hips a little and tried to tug the panties down her thighs. Christine drew her hands firmly away and obliged her to wait, after all, until she was ready. Lesley murmured in her lover's ear, wheedling her with every form of endearment and promise.

'A little longer,' Christine said softly, still denying her, 'You must reach such a pitch of desire that you would sell yourself to slavery for a release from it... Now, undress yourself.'

She obeyed with an eagerness which might have been more proper in a girl of ten or twelve greedy for a treat.

Lesley

Christine decided then to reward her and finally lowered herself before Lesley and began kissing Lesley's aroused slit. Lesley moved with a sudden spasmodic energy so that Christine had to restrain her at first in order to begin their mutual rhythm of tongue to clitoris. At last she adjusted herself to this and gave herself to the pleasuring without reserve.

Christine brought her easily to her first crisis. As she made love to the petals of her wet nest, Christine's fingers stroked her between her rear-cheeks and she felt an increased thrill in her movements. They continued thus through Lesley's second and third crisis, until she begged for Christine to let her rest before she spent herself into oblivion. Christine, in a merciful mood, let her be.

*　*　*

The events of that night, as of every other night, were a reminder to Lesley that she, as surely as Connie, had become Christine's possession. Did she ever consider returning to her marriage and children? If she did, the idea was not entertained for long. The constant seductive prying of women's voices and hands, the nights of loving which left her exhausted and calm at last, held her willingly in thrall. More important still, to return to her former life would have been an unbearable humiliation. By such a step she must announce to the world a surrender of her sexual freedom, of her emancipation, of her right to be the proud woman she wished to be. To an aloof and self-possessed young wife of her kind, it hardly seemed that there could be any indignity or punishment worse than that.

Lesley consoled herself by believing that her submission to Christine was of her own free will. At any moment, she thought, it would be possible to reclaim her freedom. The life of the Villa Rif was one which she could enjoy for as long as it pleased her, and which she would renounce when it pleased her no longer.

In all these beliefs except she was mistaken, but as yet she did not realize it. Indeed she would never return to any man, but this did not render her any more free than marriage, for Christine was more her mistress than she could know. The hot days were passed in the naked pleasures of elegant rooms, among brooding lamps and silent carpets. Her pale aloof beauty was the complement to ornaments of jade and ivory in cool recesses, alabaster and porcelain on painted shelves.

Afternoon drives in a shaded carriage took the lovers along the long elegant boulevards of white stucco, the imperial Parisian grandeur of hotels and the little boutiques with coloured sun blinds. The brilliance of the summer tide glinted on the fresh paintwork of the cornice, where pink tamarisk moved with feather-lightness in the warm breeze and yellow broom flamed in the gardens. The smell of tide-washed sand hung in the afternoon air as the emerald sea darkened in the heat to a black horizon line.

When evening light began to thicken, the carriage brought them again to the Villa Rif, the tall camellia tree and pampas grass, Italian cypress trees and white flowers in the depth of hot shade. As the pleasures of the evening turned to the passions of the night, blue tinted light shone on the white stucco of the grand hotels. In the gardens of Paris, the glass moons of the lamps on their wrought-iron mounts glimmered among dark evergreens.

Not every day was passed in this manner. After two weeks, Christine took Lesley alone on a journey which occupied them from dawn until dusk.

'Antonia wishes to photograph you,' Christine had said to her on the preceding evening, 'You can have no objection to that.'

And she smiled at her in a manner which assured her that the truth was yet to be learnt.

They drove from the little town past the lime-green stucco of Spanish arches round country villas, through a flat terrain of canals and fields. Here and there an estate and its chateau were surrounded by tall iron palings and dense trees. Nothing but the curve of a gravel drive and the conical roof of a baronial tower could be seen beyond the gates. Christine turned into one of these driveways and they came at last to the wide shuttered front of a manor house with a flight of curved steps before the door. A fountain played in the centre of the gravel space and the red tulips rose like tongues of fire from the trim lawns and flower-beds.

They were expected but not met by their host. Christine led her into the house without announcing herself. In a small room near the door she ordered Lesley to undress. When she had done so and while she was still naked, she brought Antonia to her.

The encounter filled Christine with a quiet amusement, all the more enjoyable because Lesley was too overcome to hide her desire. Of all the women she had met, Antonia would be the most beautiful, the most perfect. It was common for Antonia, so tall and fair at twenty-five, to have that effect on men and women alike. Yet Antonia cared little for women and none at all for men. She had only to kiss a woman's hand and the thrill of it made her spine tingle. She had only to look steadily into her eyes and her legs grew weak beneath her. Why it should be so, Christine did not know. Was it a trick of nature, of infallible animal attraction?

Antonia looked and saw in Lesley the familiar symptoms, her self-conscious attempts to keep her eyes lowered or turned away and the compelling fascination which drew them, despite this, to the young woman's face. Lesley cared nothing for her nakedness, nothing for the wantonness of her behaviour. To ignore Antonia, for a lascivious young woman like Lesley, was like a desert wanderer whose tongue is blackened by thirst turning back from a pure and sweet oasis pool.

Antonia smiled at her from time to time with courteous and studied indifference. The comedy was played with eyes and lips at a distance, a performance which Christine had witnessed many times before. Lesley offered no objection as they prepared her for the photographs which were to be taken.

They brought her into the stone-flagged hall of the baronial house and there dressed her in her costume. It was no more than a series of broad leather straps drawn tight on the trim pale body of the naked Lesley.

One strap was tightened as a collar round her neck with its loose end lying down her back between her shoulder-blades. The next formed a broad leather belt round her waist, drawn tight enough for the soft pale flesh to swell a little where the edge of the leather sank into it. There was a strap round each ankle and two more drawn tight round the middle of each long firm thigh. A leather cuff adorned each wrist.

Lesley, naked in black strapping, was drawn down onto the Persian rug in the stone-flagged hall of the manor house. Antonia, murmuring her instructions, viewed her through the camera's eye.

'Lie on your back, Lesley, head turned aside… legs open a little… again… again… now on your belly… hands behind you, holding the cheeks of your arse apart… again… Hold them wide apart and look back over your shoulder, into the camera… the collectors who buy the photographs need to see your face as you do it… a timid look now, frightened at what you've done… now shake that fringe and look disdainful… play the wanton slut, Lesley… now do a sulky little girl… sulky at being made to show herself, and a bit frightened, too… '

It began well, Lesley obeying Antonia as she had never obeyed anyone in her life. Next she led her to the wide stone stairs and made her climb a little. Antonia asked her to climb very slowly—and repeatedly. From the side she took the proud tilt of her young chin and the uplift of her pale breasts. Then she moved round behind her.

From the rear she photographed the slight submissive bow of Lesley's head as she saw the short fair hair parting under its own weight on her nape. The light caught the pale sheen of her back, the long firm maturity of her legs kept in trim by careful exercise and bicycling. As she climbed, the pale cheeks of Lesley's bottom seemed to swell out from under the constraining waist-strap. Her buttocks swayed and contorted with the movement, touching and parting in a soft erotic enticement.

Antonia photographed her methodically in these shifting postures. Presently she stopped her and approached. It was necessary to guide her movements a little. Christine smiled as she saw the smooth flank of Lesley's hip goose-pimpled with instinctive excitement when Antonia laid her hand there, touching her for the first time. She made her arch the back of her waist inward, increasing the swell of Lesley's pale backside somewhat and also causing her thighs to open a little more with a glimpse of the fair hair growing fine and soft on her vaginal pouch. Between her buttocks the forbidden cleft of Lesley's anal valley was wantonly and provocatively exposed.

Christine drew her down again, on her knees, facing the camera. With her palms on her strapped thighs she made her incline forward towards the camera and hold a slim leather riding-switch in her teeth. She was like an animal sent to retrieve some object for her mistress, except that in this case she offered to the viewer an instrument of torture to be used upon her.

It amused Christine—not only in Lesley's case—to see the effect of the camera on such a young woman. Even the most disdainful and arrogant beauty, once she was naked before the lens, seemed timid and obedient as a little girl in a dancing class. Before Antonia, Lesley had lost all her self-assurance and had become the forlorn child begging only attention and affection from an adult.

Antonia had not yet finished with her. In Christine's company she took Lesley out into the sunshine, naked still but for her straps and a pair of high-heeled sandals. They walked across the gravel space, blinding in noon sunlight, and through the cool shade of the trees. At a little distance, on a grassy mound in the park, there was a round mausoleum, its grey stone now lichen-covered with the passage of two centuries. From the rounded entrance arch, one stepped down onto the paved floor of uneven flagstones. Light came through narrow slits in the tall vaulted structure, above the railed niches round the wall where burials had taken place. So it seemed, though the mausoleum had the air of being built as no more than a garden folly.

Antonia took from a stone shelf the garment placed there for Lesley's visit. It was a black cloche hat and a mourning veil, the emblems of young widowhood. When she put these on, the line of her long fringe was just seen through the fine mesh of the veil, whose folds came down almost to the nipples of her breasts and to her shoulder-blades. Antonia then made her kneel with her forehead touching the ground and her hips rose. In this posture she attached one last strap. It was a black chastity-strap which ran from the front of her waist-belt down under her legs and tightly up between her seat-cheeks to fasten at the back of the waist-belt.

Keeping her kneeling with forehead touching the floor, Antonia motioned to Christine. It was Christine's task to stand astride Lesley and ensure, by holding her round the waist, that she remained in position. From the rear Antonia saw the firm proud cheeks of Lesley's behind stretched wide apart, tightly rounded and broadened. She took the long slim riding-switch of bamboo cased in smooth leather. She raised it and brought it down with a savage impact across the pale curve of Lesley's backside. A split-second of stillness passed in the warm noon and then the urchin-cropped young wife screamed with all the power of her lungs at the atrocious pain of the leather switch.

Antonia stepped back a pace and then forward. She raised the switch behind her shoulder once more and lashed the pale squirming cheeks of Lesley's bottom a second time. Her mouth opened in a wild shriek. As it died away she burst into a violent storm of tears.

'Hold her,' said Antonia to Christine, for Lesley was now desperately trying to wriggle free. 'She must bear one more.'

Lesley shrieked at her, pleading not to have it as Antonia touched the switch lightly across her buttocks to aim the stroke. Indeed, she had reason. Two merciless welts now glowed across her behind and a bead of blood drawn from one of them had trickled down her seat-cheeks to her thigh. But Christine held her firmly and Antonia brought the switch down across Lesley's arse with a viciousness that caused the hairs on her nape to rise.

They moved her gently so that Lesley in her widow's veil lay curled and weeping on the floor before one of the tomb entablatures. With her face hidden, pillowed in her folded arms, she lay on her side with her knees drawn up, her hips turned to present the three blazing weals across her buttocks to the camera's eye. Antonia placed on the tomb a laurel wreath and the switch, as if the latter had been the favourite implement of a dead husband for whom the young widow wept. Antonia took a dozen photographs, camera studies of this affecting scene. Then the veil was raised and the studies were repeated with Lesley obliged to show her tears as well as her stripes. She was required to lie there while Christine stood over her, the toe of her shoe between her rear-cheeks as if about to complete her subjection by rousing her with it. Only then was the photographic session complete.

Antonia put the veil back on the ledge and took Lesley with her to the garden lake. Christine walked back to the house alone. There was no camera now, only Lesley and Antonia together. In her gentle arms she checked her tears and allowed Antonia to guide her to the wooden landing-stage where a skiff had been moored.

She lay in the boat while Antonia took the oars and rowed it to the opposite side of the lake, sheltered from the burning-mirror of the pale noon sky by the overhanging willows. She undressed and plunged into the lake, swimming easily and strongly. When she returned, she stood on the bank, drying in the sun, like a figure of Venus

The pain which Antonia had caused her and which still burnt across her hind-cheeks was nothing to Lesley compared with her need. Antonia was well accustomed to situations of this kind and knew that in the aftermath of punishment even the most resentful and contentious young woman may become soft and wheedling, like a smacked child seeking to be forgiven.

Antonia lay naked in the boat beside her, stretched out at her ease and then began to sleep. Lesley had not dared to touch or embrace her statuesque form, only to lie there quite unable to speak or to take her eyes off her. Antonia, dozing in the warm afternoon on the summer lake heard the drone of insects, the light murmur of grass and guessed at Lesley's feelings. She was moistening despite herself, she thought, for Antonia was almost able to detect the humid mineral odour of feminine arousal. Lesley's eyes had moved down from her face and she was staring at the curves of her inviting hips and thighs.

Antonia heard and felt the movement as she slipped down in the boat. Lesley's hand brushed aside the long fringe of her fair hair. Her arrogant fair-skinned features were level with the photographer's loins. Lightly at first, Lesley's fingers touched her there and began to play in her tight curly hair in slow repeated patterns of caressing. Antonia, hands folded behind her head, watched Lesley through half-closed eyes. In a moment more Antonia was wet and hungry, and yet she made no movement.

Lesley turned her long-lashed blue eyes upon Antonia's with expectant curiosity. Antonia ignored her. It amused her to see Lesley hover on the verge of an act which rumour had it she had never before performed with any woman. Her decision was suddenly made. Lesley bowed the short cut of her fair hair and touched her lips to the lips of Antonia's lush flower in a brief, uncertain kiss. She repeated the kiss slowly, and then with more ease. Accustomed to the sense of her mouth touching the sex of another woman, her last resistance was overcome. She ran her tongue between Antonia's legs and began to lick with her eyes closed.

Antonia looked down at her, stroking her neck gently as Lesley made her submission in this manner.

'What a hypocrite you have been, Lesley! Did you truly reject your marriage in order to enjoy your own freedom and rights over your body? I think not! At the first pangs of desire between your legs, there is nothing you would not perform to win a lover's attention to you there! All your freedom and self-possession comes to no more than that.'

Even the words by which Antonia mocked her appeared only to add to the young woman's excitement. Lesley had grown so eager that the moisture of her thighs was just visible when her legs parted a little. Antonia continued to watch her, making no attempt to embrace her yet.

'Shall we have you watched in such an act by those who know you best, Lesley? It would be the simplest thing in the world. Would it please you for your own children to see you now, the marks of the whip across your buttocks as you give yourself like this? A camera lens would accomplish that.

Ah, I believe the thought of such humiliation excites you still further… It shall be arranged at a later time.'

They had removed her chastity-strap in the mausoleum. Now, as she worked her own wet lips over Antonia's, the stimulus of her words made the excitement shine more abundantly on her inner thighs. Presently, Lesley knelt upright and straddled her. She was no longer self-conscious or demanding. Her face showed only the breathlessness of exertion and desire. She began grinding her pubis against Antonia's, like a needy girl or a deprived widow. She put her leg between Antonia's legs and began to rub her thigh where her saliva had wet Antonia between her legs. She panted hungrily, urgent to do anything that would send them higher. Her lips were parted, her eyes closed, and the perspiration began to gather on her face, her neck, and in the hollows of her shoulders.

Antonia permitted this for a while longer before shifting and letting Lesley grind wantonly on the thigh Antonia offered between her legs. Lesley now was astride Antonia's thigh, rubbing in spasmodic movements, pressing hard. Antonia's fingers stroked her back, the white cheeks of Lesley's seat with their sheen of perspiration. She touched the tight inward bud between them. Then she reached out to the bank of the lake and snapped off a frond of nettles.

It was a pain no greater than that which children inflict on one another in a game. Lesley cried out as much with excitement as discomfort when the leaves of the nettles brushed her bare bottom-cheeks, the spike edges leaving a scarlet rash of white sting-blisters. By now she was in her first ecstasy, the short fair hair lowered as her hips pumped harder along Antonia's thigh. Antonia smiled and applied the nettle leaves more intimately between Lesley's buttocks. Yet her cries were drawn out in the compulsive spasmodic obbligato of joy. After Lesley' hard-earned crisis, she lowered herself and lay next to Antonia in the boat. In the long warmth of the afternoon the two lovers fell into a doze at the edge of the calm glittering lake.

The sun had left the sky's main vault and begun its last descent to the lakeside trees when Antonia led Lesley back again to the house. After dinner that evening, since she and Christine were to return to Paris in the morning, she made her confession in the presence of the two women.

'I love Antonia,' she said simply. 'I am in love with Antonia.'

They looked at her as if not understanding the purpose of the statement.

'How can that be of the least significance?' said Christine, smiling at her indulgently, 'It matters only to you.'

They were not obliged to explain further, though they did. Antonia produced a set of photographs. Lesley recognised them at once, with a sense of shock, as those which the unknown woman took surreptitiously of her in the garden with her child during the last months of her marriage. She was too dismayed even to ask how they had come into Antonia's possession.

'The woman who took these,' said Antonia quietly. 'She loved you in ways that you would have found repellent. Yet she loved you with all sincerity. It did not matter because you lived in a world where you were the arbiter. Love was yours to allow or deny. Here things are different. The decision of love is ours, not yours. You are permitted to love—who can stop you? Yet now you may only do so as a supplicant—as the woman who took those photographs loved you. It cannot matter to us.'

Yet Antonia made love to her that night until she wept with joy. The next morning, Lesley returned with Christine to the Villa Rif.

* * *

The days which followed the visit to Antonia were different from those which preceded it, just as the summer at Paris that year differed from the season of the year before. It was only in little things that the change could be shown clearly. Yet in these it was evident that the distinction between Lesley as the mistress of the Villa Rif and Connie or Maggie as the servants had altered. Now it was Christine and Fatima who were the mistresses, as they had always been. Lesley and Judith, no less than Maggie and Connie, were cast in a role where submission or obedience was required without hesitation.

Lesley was left to console herself with dreams of the summer day by the lake, where she had been allowed to love Antonia so briefly. Now, when she met the love for her in the calm hazel eyes of Judith, it was as if the ideal image was blurred and distant, distorted by her feelings for the young Venus. Yet she was haunted as well by the quiet demure presence of Judith, the pale contemplative beauty and the veil of light brown hair which suggested a life of devotion to some adored object of desire.

If the events of the previous summer at Paris were now recalled in the long dusty days of August, it was because of an announcement that Claire was to be a guest at the Villa Rif in a few more days. The visit would be a short one, but it marked in every way the median point at which the high season of pleasure began to darken. The house and its tenants were marked for a more sombre and dramatic fate.

The truth about Claire was known only to Christine and Fatima. She was a tall slim young woman who, like Lesley, wore her red hair in a short cut. Her face was marked by green eyes with a hint of cruelty and vicious-ness in their slant. Who was she?

Christine and Fatima knew the whole truth. To the young women at the Villa Rif, Claire was the mistress of 'the other house,' which lay beyond frontiers and a mountain range. It was a place which they had never seen and whose darker reputation was known only by hints. During every season at

Paris there were girls whose eventual destination was that other house. Whether they went willingly or as captives remained an unanswered question. They did not return to Paris, nor were they ever seen again in the winter city.

* * *

Several girls had made the journey to that other house in the previous summer. Nothing was known of them after that, except perhaps to Christine and Fatima. Among them was Laura, a pretty girl of nineteen, of medium height and slim figure. With Diane, Ruth and Jacqui, she had passed into Claire's keeping. There was a mingled appeal of innocence and coquetry in her softly rounded, high-boned face and blue eyes, the page-boy style of light, golden brown hair brushing her collar. In tight riding-jeans her belly and loins showed flat and firm, her thighs having the slimness of adolescence. The tight seat of the jeans shaped Laura's bottom, its apple-firm cheeks seductively lithe.

Such girls as Laura went to their fate apprehensively but without resistance. This was not the case with others. Lesley recalled Noreen, a nineteen-year-old girl, tall and strongly built. The firm pale features, the insolent brown eyes, even the lank dark hair cut at her shoulders and fringed on her forehead, promised a struggle. So it was. Noreen had twisted and wrestled in the grip of the two men who dragged her to the closed car. In the tightly strained jeans, her strong young thighs had braced against her escorts. As her hips twisted, the firm full cheeks of Noreen's bottom received many a smack through the thin denim. After they had secured her in the car, one of the women went back to the house and fetched a pony-whip—a necessity for the journey.

Now, a year later, Claire returned to the Villa Rif. She was accompanied as always by one of her girls who had been trained to the most perfect obedience. On this occasion it was Laura.

After dinner on the first evening, in the lamp lit salon of the Villa Rif, Lesley and Judith were present as the partners of Christine and Fatima. When Claire came in she as accompanied by Laura, dressed in the sleeveless silk blouse and figure-fitting jeans, in which she might have swung through the streets of Paris with the agile young strides of a nineteen-year-old nymph. Laura walked a few steps behind her mistress, like a well-trained young animal, and stood by obediently while Claire sat down.

From beside her, Claire took a leather collar to which had been attached a four-foot leash.

'Stoop down and have your collar fastened, Laura,' said Claire.

The girl lowered the long page-boy waves of her golden brown hair until her mistress had clipped the collar round her neck. Then Laura sat on the carpet with her legs drawn under her, close by Claire's foot. The pretty high-boned face was lowered a little to hide her blue eyes from the inquiring scrutiny of the others. The fine gold hair, brushed across to either side of her forehead from its central parting, was all that could be clearly seen.

Claire and the Mistresses talked about Laura while the girl was obliged to listen.

'It was a great advantage,' said Claire, 'that Laura had been so strictly brought up by her parents. Such girls are always the easiest to train in obedience, even the obedience of a concubine. Laura's self-discipline and subservience are quite admirable.'

The young mistress went on to explain that Laura had been abducted almost on the eve of her marriage to a gross and common youth who would never have done justice to her charms. In answer to Christine, Claire explained that the girl's virginity had been taken by a leather phallus in the mistress's presence. Some weeks later, a favoured friend had been the only woman so far to insert said phallus in Laura's bottom. The way had been so strait that Claire and an assistant had been obliged to hold her narrow waist and trim hips still while the phallus was oiled repeatedly and finally forced in to its hilt.

'Laura's training must continue, however,' said Claire with a smile at her pretty slave, 'Such a lively little creature is apt to grow conceited if the lash is laid aside altogether.'

This caused a good deal of amusement among the guests and very little surprise. None of the other working-girls, Diane nor Wendy, Ruth nor Jacqui, had been so polite and eager to serve their customers as Laura. Yet that would not excuse her from such training as Claire had planned.

It was Christine who asked to have charge of the lead and drew Laura to her first. She raised the girl's chin and swore she looked sullen and resentful—though her expression was one of startled prettiness. She laid her facedown over her knee and ran her hands over the jeans-denim stretched so taut and smooth upon the firm young cheeks of Laura's behind.

'I cannot forget,' Christine said, 'that Laura was perverse enough to give herself in betrothal to a common young boor, when there were such women as the ones in this room who would have employed her far more fully. I believe she should be corrected for that!'

Laura knew the meaning at once, for her slim young buttocks tightened visibly with apprehension in the tight jeans-seat. Christine returned the girl to Claire.

'Laura,' said the young mistress quietly, 'slip off your jeans and underpants.'

With head lowered apprehensively, Laura's slender bare arms moved to obey. The lamplight caught the sleek waves of her golden brown hair. Laura pushed down her jeans with her panties inside them and stepped clear of the tangle. Claire jerked the lead a little and drew the girl towards a sturdy table. The four onlookers admired the easy movement of Laura's slim legs, the puff of fair hair at her loins and the high tight shape of her young buttocks. Claire bent her over the table and attached the heavy collar to the far side to hold her.

Claire used the dog-leash to inflict discipline on Laura. She doubled the thin leather and lashed it across the backs of the slim thighs. By the singing crack of leather and the redness of the weal it was evident that Lesley or Judith would have screamed out at once. Yet this stroke and a second one across her legs drew from Laura only a sudden intake of breath, released in a half-controlled sob.

There was a sense of excitement among the spectators in the room. During her first year at the other house, Laura had not only been trained to obedience, she had also been trained to take punishment. How many such whippings had it taken to teach her that pleading and screaming were not only useless but would actually be punished in themselves? Christine and Fatima exchanged their first smiles.

Claire brought the leash down hard across Laura's bottom-cheeks, half a dozen times. The eighteen-year-old girl tensed her buttocks desperately and cried out softly. Yet she neither squirmed her buttocks aside nor gave vent to screams. Once or twice the loop of thin leather curled round and caught her flank. On a few occasions it fell short and curled between her rear-cheeks.

Then they heard Laura scream, her face twisted round, the golden brown page-boy tresses tumbling aside as she looked in terror at the witnesses.

Yet her hands had not been tied, though the collar kept her bending over the table tightly. Once, in the extreme anguish of another stroke catching her between the cheeks, Laura swung her arms behind her. Yet the hands with which she might have tried to cover her bottom remained stretched out at either side of it. So well had Claire trained her pretty slave-maid that even in such an extremity Laura knew better than to commit the offence of impeding the whip.

There came a moment when even the best training was of no avail. Laura was whipped in this manner for a considerable time. Before the session was over they saw her slim young buttocks contort and twist wildly, they heard her scream without respite. Once or twice the thin leather wrought havoc in a line of pinprick dots across the trim cheeks of Laura's backside.

At midnight the others left Laura alone with Christine. Brushing away her tears on the edge of her hand, the girl knelt before her chair and lowered her lips to the demanding quim at her eye level.

Claire had chosen to enjoy Connie's Asian beauty in her room. What passed between them remained a mystery. Yet next day, when Claire and Laura were to leave the Villa Rif for the other house, the result of that lesbian passion was revealed. Lesley came face to face with Connie, led by two women down one of the long corridors of the villa in the cool sunless light of early day.

Connie was naked. Her wrists were strapped behind her back and the men held her arms on either side, as they held Noreen when she was led away a year before. Unlike Noreen, Connie offered no resistance. Indeed, there was a leather collar round her neck, though without a leash. A gag-strap was drawn between her lips, and her beautiful almond eyes regarded Lesley with a mute appeal.

Claire appeared and smiled at the sight of Lesley's dismay.

'Connie must go with me,' she said simply in reply to Lesley's questioning indignation, 'It is time she was taken to the other house. Christine has agreed to it. Since Connie belongs to her, she may dispose of her as she chooses.'

In this, Claire was quite right. Yet while Connie was led away, Lesley ran to Christine, begging her to deny all that had been said. She sat in the leather smoking-chair and drew Lesley onto her knee, as if she were a child. She smiled at her, as if she were truly indulging a sulky little girl by offering her an explanation.

'Connie will go to the other house with Claire and Laura. She goes of her own free will, having declared her love for Claire in their bed last night. The use of the straps and the gag is entirely logical. It is the first rule here that a wish expressed in the height of passion cannot be withdrawn in the calmer moments which may follow. To allow such a thing would be to deny the supreme authority of love. Have no fear, Claire will train Connie to accept her fate as she has already trained Laura.'

To Lesley's protests, Christine responded by revealing something further, news which in itself brought a deeper shock to Lesley's aloof blue eyes.

'I shall go with them,' said Christine gently, 'It must be so.'

'And what is to become of me?'

There was no mistaking the peevish arrogance in Lesley's voice, like a little girl denied a treat.

'You will wait here,' said Christine gently, stroking her silky hair, 'You will be kept here with Fatima, Judith, and Maggie.'

She moved quickly, turning her face to her at the words 'kept here.'

'Come now,' said Christine smiling at her, 'I do not think there is anywhere else for you to go. It may console you to know that my place here will be taken by Antonia. You cannot object to that, Lesley! How plaintively you confessed that you loved her!'

Lesley

Under the parted fringe, Lesley's face was a study in uncertainty. To be close to Antonia seemed to make her pulse beat faster at the very thought of it. Yet the news that she had no choice but to remain seemed to intimidate her.

'Connie is mine and I give her to Claire,' said Christine softly. 'Maggie is mine and is given to Antonia!'

A frown of displeasure crossed Lesley's sulky face at the news that she was to have a rival in the shape of the blonde shop girl.

'Judith is mine,' said Christine slowly, 'She is eighteen now and therefore I give her to Fatima.'

'Fatima!'

Lesley's cry was one of despair and defeat, the sound of it bringing a smile of satisfaction to Christine's lips. The thought of Judith's demure pale beauty at the mercy of Fatima's pleasures was terrifying.

'Please!' Lesley took Christine's hand and kissed it as she knelt before her chair, 'Fatima will be cruel to her! She will use her in ways which we both know. Judith is too young for that, too beautiful!'

'Fatima will enjoy her all the more for her youth and beauty.'

'No!' Lesley gave a tearless sob of protest, 'I love Judith! Not as I love Antonia, but as a woman loves a woman! Give her to me if she must be disposed of in such a way!'

Christine laughed at the absurdity of it.

'She is already Fatima's, Lesley! It is all arranged.'

At this, Lesley relapsed into a sullen silence.

'And to whom have you given me?' she asked bitterly after a few more minutes.

'To those who want you. You have always been so disdainful and dismissive in granting your favours, Lesley. Now in a house of love, it is you who must be a beggar for love! You may beg from Fatima.'

'No!' It was the same wailing of a spoilt little girl.

'Then you may beg from Antonia.'

She did not reply and so Christine added a warning.

'Remember, Lesley, that neither Judith nor Maggie is your property. If you attempt to seduce either, it will be a crime against the mistress who possesses her. By the rules of the house, she may flog you for it, or have the penalty inflicted by another. Consider carefully, if you are tempted by another girl's beauty, whether the pleasure will be worth the pain.'

Christine bowed her head, kissed the crown of Lesley's head very gently, and then stood up. Before she could recover her wits and go after her now former mistress, the door was locked. From the window, Lesley watched as the car containing Christine, Claire, Laura and Connie set out on the first stage of the long journey to the other house.

* * *

With the departure of the travellers, the long summer, even at Paris, passed its meridian and began to wane. The pastel-coloured blossoms of the earlier months and the rich perfumes of the evening gardens gave way to the first rattle of dry leaves in the light wind, scorched by months of hot sun. The bougainvillea climbed in a last purple blaze on the villa walls and the oleanders grew gaudy in the carnival of the dying Saturn.

Antonia arrived at the Villa Rif on the evening of Christine's departure. She remained courteous but distant in her treatment of Lesley, never allowing her to forget her duty of submission. Antonia took Maggie to her bed, seduced by the hard sluttishness of her pale face and the childlike golden blonde hair which lay lank and fringed upon her.

Fatima had not yet possessed herself of Judith. When she did so,

Lesley

Lesley would be sure to know. The sleeping arrangements in the Villa Rif required that Judith should occupy a bedroom which could only be approached through Lesley's. Indeed, the door between the pupil and the governess was often left open at night. Yet the days passed and Fatima did not appear.

In the warm nights of August, Lesley lay upon her bed in the black breast-halter and stretch-briefs which were all the covering she needed. The scents of the garden and the distant salvoes of breakers on the sand came through the window which, though barred for safety, stood open above the lawns and shrubberies.

Beyond the open door, she sometimes heard the light rhythm of Judith's breathing in her sleep. For Lesley herself, this was the first time of sexual denial. Yet her liberation from emotional servitude of the conventional kind gave her the right to explore her own body, to masturbate as often and as much as it pleased her.

Lying on her back with her eyes closed in the starlit room, there was a quality of innocence in the firm fair-skinned face. Lifting her hips a little, Lesley would ease the black stretch-briefs down her thighs until they gathered untidily just above her knees. With her eyes still closed, perhaps in a dream of Antonia, she slid a moistened finger between her legs and began to play with her clitoris.

Presently her breath would be released in long, uneven gasps. Her body would stir restlessly with a sudden convulsion of her long trim legs, like a patient in a fever. Turning her head aside she would muffle her sudden cries with a pillow pressed to her mouth. When that other hand could be spared, it would fondle her breasts and erect their nipples as if it belonged to an imagined lover. Later she would turn on her side as the tension rose, her knees pressed hard together, her thighs tight on her own hand almost in fear that it might escape. By then Lesley was wet with excitement, her finger deep in her vagina and her thumb still massaging the impatient young clitoris. Then her other hand would sometimes go behind her. She would fondle her own buttocks as a lover might while preparing her for a dildo or the whip. Men and women who had watched her and lusted for her in vain, would have stared in delight to see Lesley's finger-tips playing between her buttocks as she lay there, the spasm of joy coming in her loins at last, and Lesley fingering her own arsehole at the same time to increase her sense of wantonness.

Her thighs wet with vaginal lubricant, Lesley scaled the peak of her orgasm, her face pressed into the pillow to muffle her cries. At last she lay there relaxed and fulfilled, not daring to move again for fear of waking Judith in the next room. Did Judith ever hear the muffled cries and think that Lesley was trapped in the toils of nightmare? Slowly pulling her panties up, Lesley would lie there thoughtfully, her fingers still stroking her moist pubic sheath through the gusset of black elastic cotton.

A young, once-married woman like Lesley had lost a good deal of her modesty by her middle twenties. Regular exercise by her husband's penis and two experiences of the nozzles and squirts of the maternity ward had banished the bloom of bridal innocence. Sometimes she would fall asleep with her panties still round the base of her lithe firm thighs. It was so frequent for her to stir during the night and play with herself again that she could pull them up then.

Bereft of Christine and Connie, dismissed by Antonia, Lesley was imprisoned in the Villa Rif by her love for Judith and her yearning for Antonia despite her indifference. Yet she seemed almost like a figure of bereavement among the others, a young widow who knew no consolation but that of her own fingers during the warm summer nights. The others

Lesley

ignored her, Maggie looked upon her with casual curiosity. Maggie would have consoled her and felt not a tremor of affection. But now even Maggie, the sluttish blonde shop girl, belonged to Antonia. It was only Judith, with her pale oval beauty and steady hazel eyes, who looked upon Lesley with pity and adoration.

Despite her former promiscuity with men, Lesley could not bring herself to seduce a tall and graceful nymph of eighteen. Judith knew so little of such matters that she would feel soiled and humiliated by the grosser acts of lesbian passion. It was impossible. Lesley stroked the girl's fine brown veil of hair, kissed her lightly on the cheek and allowed her to indulge the innocent romance of a schoolgirl's passion for the governess. To the hazel eyes so full of innocent pity, Lesley returned a calm gentleness which she pretended with difficulty.

It was past midnight on a night when Lesley lay uncovered on her bed, the breast-halter fallen to one side and her briefs completely discarded on the cover. She slept fitfully and had no notion that Judith with the oval beauty of her face framed by the sweep of light brown hair stood, as she had so often done, and looked down in adoration and pity upon Lesley's sleeping body. Nor had Lesley any notion that Judith stood white and naked in all the splendour of her lithe young figure. It was then that Lesley stirred so far in her sleep that to Judith's eyes she seemed to wake—though in truth she had only half woken. This time Judith did not withdraw hastily on tiptoe to her own room. She eased herself gently on to the bed, which woke Lesley at last. Then Judith stretched out her own body so that it lightly covered Lesley's and assaulted her with an inexperienced passion which under other circumstances would have been comic.

She began kissing Lesley hard and repeatedly on the lips until Lesley responded as if to calm the girl. At the same time Judith's inexpert hand thrust between Lesley's thighs and began to rub her with a vigour which expressed her own love rather than rousing it in the other. Breaking away from Lesley's mouth, Judith gasped as if she might almost be weeping.

'I love you! I love you! Oh, how I love you!'

Despite the wild confusion of her thoughts, Lesley gently drew away the hand which still rummaged between her thighs. She kissed Judith's face, mouth and eyes, tasting indeed the saltiness of tears upon her. The cruelty of sending the girl back to bed with a rebuke or a scolding was impossible. However arrogant Lesley had been towards men, she found that she softened more easily towards her own sex, as if in the face of a common enemy. Indeed, though she would not permit Judith's stroking between her legs, Lesley could not bear to part with the girl just then. After being deprived of Christine and Connie, after being rejected by Antonia, she so desperately needed a warm naked body to hold against her, if nothing more.

So the young girl and the young divorcée lay naked on the bed hugging and kissing like a pair of children. At last Judith took one of Lesley's hands to her lips and kissed its knuckles. She led it to her own breasts.

'Touch me there,' she pleaded, 'Oh, please do!'

Lesley massaged the cool softness of Judith's firm young breasts until the girl sighed softly in her arms. Then Judith led the hand to stroke her smooth pale back with the fine indentations of its vertebrae marked in adolescent clarity. Soon Lesley was persuaded to stroke the cool oval nymph-cheeks of Judith's bottom and then the hand was drawn into the rear opening of the thighs where it stopped at once. Judith cried softly in her need.

'Please, my love! Please!' There were tears in the intercession.

Lesley complied at last, stroking the soft-haired mound of Judith's vagina as if to calm a fretful child into sleep. Judith sighed in long-awaited con-

Lesley

tentment and allowed her lips to browse on Lesley's face, neck, shoulders and breasts. Despite herself, Lesley could not draw back now. Even if she could curb her own longing, Judith sobbed with dismay every time the beloved hand seemed about to withdraw from between her legs. There was dismay even when it was drawn back so that Lesley could run her fingers between the cheeks of Judith's elegant young backside.

Learning from what Lesley was doing to her, Judith's hand returned between the thighs of the first love in her young life. This time the thighs relaxed and opened, accepting the tribute. Judith's orgasm came with quiet cries of joy in Lesley's arms and Lesley herself had to bite back her sobs of happiness as she reached a shuddering spasm. There was a point where shame and decorum were cast aside. Love became pitiless in its intensity. As the first dawn light cast a wan glimmer upon the bed, Judith lay with her head towards Lesley's feet and kiss-teased the warm vaginal lips. Lesley gazed on the upward-turned cheeks of Judith's behind, kissing the tight anus-bud between them before darting and lingering her tongue upon the girl's clitoris.

When morning came, there was no remorse, no fear or dismay at the joys shared during the night. In the gardens of the Villa and on the cornice, Lesley and Judith walked hand in hand or arm in arm like lovers. Their happiness defied the world.

Fatima, who might have sought revenge for this now that Judith was put at her disposal, maintained an ironic detachment. Fatima saw that Lesley had lost none of her self-possessed coldness in other respects, which suggested that love was without an improving effect on her. She was soon a witness to the truth of this.

At one side, the villa gardens were divided by a tall fence of wire mesh from a neighbouring boys' institution. The area was strictly forbidden to the boys who were savagely whipped across their bare buttocks by the warden for such trespass. Lesley knew this and chose the opportunity to avenge the female on the male sex.

In the trouser-suit of thin black cotton she would go down to the land by the fence and pretend to weed it. Seeing a young woman in the distance several of the lusty young boys would risk a sadistic whipping to reach the wire fence.

Lesley would simultaneously taunt them and pretend to ignore them from a few yards beyond the fence through which they watched her. Though they were only half her age, the boys allowed their eyes to wander over her in wistful admiration. They began with the straight fair hair cut short as if to boast her liberation from feminine subservience. They were undeterred by the dismissive contempt in Lesley's clear blue eyes or by the sulky weight in her mouth and fair-skinned features. They loved the shape of Lesley's spruce young breasts in the cotton singlet. They adored her trim thighs in the tight black trousers. Her vagina was something they yearned in vain to see.

Yet as she shook her parted fringe clear and bent to weed the land, turning her back on the boys in contempt, they enjoyed some reward. With her Spartan soldier-girl thighs braced apart and knees bent a little forward, Lesley bent tight to her task. The thin black cloth of the trouser-seat was drawn drum skin tight. The boys stared open-mouthed with delight at her in this posture. Their eyes settled like summer flies on the erotically firmed-out cheeks of Lesley's bottom!

With a vindictive feminine perversity, Lesley bent like this at her weeding a few feet beyond the wire fence. Furtively at first, one of the lads drew out his young tool and began to exercise it with his hand. Soon the others followed his example, half hidden from one another, their eyes

Lesley

staring at Lesley's tight black trouser-seat and hips as she stooped to her labours.

What dreams and ambitions did this view inspire in them? Did they envisage worshipping Lesley's backside on the bridal bed, the nuptial veil lifted, lips saluting her between her rear thighs?

Was Lesley to be their cabin-girl on a long oriental voyage? With her waitress-pants pulled down, did these landlocked sailors ride the rear way to her vagina, in their dreams, or sodomise Lesley vigorously as she lay over the bunk of her youthful captain?

In fantasy no image is too outlandish or bizarre. Which of the lads imagined a miniature garden-carriage with two bars across the shafts? Lesley, pale and naked but for her harness straps, stood in the shafts with her back to the driver. She had been bent forward over the rear bar, her leather collar and wrist-cuffs secured to the front one. She must run at the young driver's command, her firm hips swaying, her proud fair-skinned buttocks arching and rounding in a constant temptation to the carriage whip. Did the lad imagine a day's outing to such garden beauties as schoolboy humour might devise? Horsewhip Hill? Canewell Woods? Long Birching? In the intervals of spurring with the whip, how easily his hand might enter between the thighs of this pale young mare and tame her by soft caresses. Perhaps the more adventurous among them saw a pair of beauties between the shafts, the young mare and her own filly.

Yet even as these boys dreamed their dreams, Lesley would walk to the nearby summer-house and alert the warden to their trespass.

Then she would return and pose before them again, taunting them expressionlessly as she plucked the weeds. In their desperate state, the lads had lost all hope of escape from the most sadistic thrashing. In their plight they did not scruple to show their excitement to the treacherous young woman. With active hands, tongues running on their lips and eyes glazed, they brought on their crises. The tribute of several young loins fell only a little short of Lesley as she stooped before them.

Then, still ignored and despised by the arrogant young woman, the boys woke to the agony of the whipping which awaited them in an hour or two. They crept fearfully away. Indeed, Fatima had seen occasions when, having made her complaint to the warden, Lesley would merely stand and survey the young masturbators with cold indifference. How the lads begged her to return to the weeding, to offer them some view on which they could fix their hearts in the final moment of orgasm. To reply to this was, in her view, contemptible, and Lesley watched their sperm fly vainly and wildly. Disgust and triumph shone in her blue eyes.

Fatima held no strong views on this and yet she could not grudge the lads a chance of retribution when it came. Lesley was a demanding and faithless young woman, randy and greedy, the seducer of Judith who was hers by rights. She had little cause to be so snooty over the young boys admiring her breasts, bottom and thighs. So it seemed to Fatima.

Lesley and Judith did not share a bed throughout the night but visited one another as they felt moved to. On the nights when there were no such visits, Lesley was left alone on her bed to dream at first of Antonia, who was unattainable, and then of Maggie, who lay bereft in her own bed as Lesley did.

What images of Maggie possessed Lesley's mind in that hour? They were perhaps only the unremarkable sights of Maggie as her admirers first saw her in the attitude of a working-girl. The young shop girl had been sitting on her heels regarding the world with a certain slack-jawed vacancy, the lank pale gold hair parted aside on her forehead and a hard wantonness in her fair-skinned features. The incidental details of Maggie on all fours, pol-

Lesley

ishing hard with a damp cloth. As the hem of the singlet pulled away from the jeans-waist, a lightly dented softness of pale flesh was revealed. The soft taut weight of Maggie's breasts shaped by the singlet. A slight stockiness of Mag's thighs in tight jeans, reducing her height. The firm full cheeks of Maggie's bottom as she laboured on all fours in the tight denim pants. Her little-girl-liveliness with her companions. Maggie's look of sluttish indifference to the world.

Perhaps even Lesley herself could not have told the truth about her motives as she got up from her bed and walked softly into the passageway outside the room. In a furious confusion of fear and longing, desire and revulsion, pride and submission, she opened the door of Maggie's room and then closed it behind her.

Maggie lay naked on the cover of her bed in the warm night. She was alone. In the lighted room the eyes of the two young women met and neither, for the moment, showed terror at the predicament they were in—for they must inevitably be found together in the morning. Instead, Lesley went straight to the bed and took the blonde girl in her arms.

It was surprising that though Lesley was the beginner of their pleasure, Maggie soon took the initiative. Underneath her slut's appearance, she had a warmth and responsiveness. It was certain that the two young women would be vindictively punished for their night together. There was no way to lull their terror but by pleasure. Yet Maggie did not reproach Lesley for what she had done. Instead, she took her in her arms, lulling and soothing her in a soft voice. They lay together for some while with no more sexual passion than a pair of affectionate schoolgirls. In the moonlit gardens of the villa the black spears of cypress trees rose against the pale night sky. Far off, a storm flickered and rumbled beyond the sharp ridge of the mountains.

'I love you, Mag,' said Lesley at last, 'I want you so much!'

These were no more than the words of a cold young woman intent on her own pleasure, yet Maggie responded to them. A bold look on her firm, crude features, she sought Lesley's mouth and at the same time slid her hand between the taut erotic maturity of the bare thighs.

The two young women squirmed together naked, moaning and yielding in their passion. Maggie was not the sort of girl to win a husband easily, yet she had learnt the arts of love from her boy-friends in the dusty rooms of city slums. She bit lightly on Lesley's back, shoulders and breasts, exciting the young wife with the gentle sharpness of love-bites which left a red mark of wantonness.

Fondling each other as they did so, the two beauties turned head to tail and admired each other's upward squat of hips, thighs and rump. A drawer of the bedside table rattled as Maggie opened it. She took out a box of glass beads, each perfectly round, smooth and the size of a large grape. Lubricating the first one in her mouth, she brought her lips close to Lesley's vagina, kissed the warm opening and then with her tongue inserted the glass bead gently inside. The sullenness of Lesley's face was softened into a yearning languor by the pleasure of this. She cried out softly as Maggie repeated the process with two more glass beads. But Maggie had not finished yet.

She took a larger pendant, oval in shape and the size of a small egg. Oiling it, she pressed it between the parted curves of Lesley's pale buttocks until her anus yielded and then closed over the intruder.

Since proclaiming her sexual freedom some months earlier, Lesley had allowed several other women to masturbate her. Yet none had used such devices as this. When Maggie's fingers manipulated her vaginal pouch, the movement of the three glass beads inside her gave Lesley an

Lesley

excruciating degree of pleasure. In her frenzy she was incapable of words. The soft 'Ahs!' of ecstasy rose to cries and then almost to screams of uncontrollable desire.

The short cut of Lesley's fair hair twisted from side to side in the fury of her first orgasm. The lubrication of her vagina was so copious that it was clearly audible when she moved. No sooner was one climax achieved than Maggie's fingers began once more to mould the inflamed vaginal lips.

At first Lesley's middle-class reserve had been too strong to obey Maggie's other whispered request, which was to expel the larger glass oval by contractions of her behind. Yet soon there was no depravity she would not perform in her passion. Her lips sought Maggie's pudenda and her tongue ravaged the moist warm depths. Between the smooth pale moons of her buttocks, Lesley's anus seemed to tense and swell, the round end of the glass oval peeped out. Lesley's arsehole widened to expel the rest and the oval rolled at last into Maggie's hand. It was replaced by a larger one, and then a larger one still. Throughout their pleasure, Lesley's bottom received and expelled these devices several times in each minute. At last the multiple orgasms and the labours of her behind left her panting and exhausted in Maggie's arms.

Maggie's charm was in the combination of a slut's hardness and a child's innocence. There was an undeniable boldness in her blue eyes, firm features, the slovenly chewing of candy and her way of standing slack-hipped like a whore. Yet the ripe yellow hair which lay fringed and straight to her shoulder blades was still cut in the style of a little girl. Now she was frank as a little girl and brazen as a whore. Kneeling on all fours so that Lesley might enjoy watching her, Maggie played between her own legs with one hand. Then, pausing, she took the glass oval and inserted it in her own backside. Maggie played with herself, front and rear, until Lesley began to yearn for her in the colder hours before dawn.

'Come to me, Mag!' she whispered to the blonde shop girl, 'Ah, come to me, my love!'

The rest of the night they lay in one another's arms, exhausted and sleeping soundly as children.

* * *

As summer turned to autumn, the stars glittered more coldly above the tide-washed sand and the white terrace of the casino. By late afternoon the sun was low in the sky and the wide boulevards of Paris were empty of all movement but the dry scuffling of fallen leaves.

The Villa Rif stood untenanted and desolate in its deep gardens. Those whose voices and passions animated it in summer had gone, some to the winter city and a few to that other house beyond frontiers and a mountain range. The very furniture had been removed from the spacious rooms, leaving only the bare floors and the walls and ceiling from which footsteps rang back harshly.

One boy, a solitary youth with private dreams and passions, noticed the open and untended gates on a fine autumn afternoon. Unchallenged, he walked along the driveway to the house, the grass and weeds already luxuriant after several weeks of neglect.

The windows of the house were shuttered and its doors still locked. Yet the first of the equinoctial storms had blown down a small tree and broken a catch on one of the window shutters. The boy heard the irregular clatter of the hinged wood, swinging back against the stucco of the wall.

No one would come there again until the winter was past and the early spring brought a time for refurbishing and painting the villa in readiness for the new season. The boy followed the sound and found the open shutter. It could only be secured from the inside. The boy knew that it would be an easy matter to open the window, close the shutter and the catch from within, then let himself out by one of the doors which would lock again by means of its fastening.

As he swung himself through the space of the open window and into the first room, the boy paused and gazed at the ghostly grandeur of the bare walls, dimly lit by the rays which filtered through the slats of the closed shutters. He walked slowly through the echoing apartments until he came at last to a room which was brightly lit by contrast with the others, for its windows were covered by iron bars and it needed no shuttering.

The floor of the room was paved with marble and the walls with their white tiles seemed like those of a prison or institution. It was strangely furnished. A hand-basin and a toilet-pedestal gave it the appearance of a wash-room. Yet there was a padded leather sofa with no back but having a heavy scroll at one end. This was almost the only piece of furniture left in the villa and stood at the centre of the paved floor. At intervals on its mahogany frame, restraining straps had been strongly riveted to the wood.

The boy was intrigued by the disorder of this room, as if it had been left forgotten by the occupants of the villa. No attempt to tidy it had been made in the days before their departure.

On the sofa lay a young woman's panties, a brief film of apple green translucence. The boy's interest quickened as he picked them up. A bamboo cane and an open jar of Vaseline were on the floor beside the divan. As he lifted up these curious items, he noticed that where the restraining straps were low down beneath the padded scroll, the varnished wood bore tiny scratches, as if from the frenzied nail of strapped hands. The wiping-rag from the hook by the toilet-pedestal and the box of tissues from its holder both lay on the sofa. A pulse of excitement and curiosity beat harder in the boy's throat as he tried to conjecture what had been done in this room. On the padded leather of the sofa lay a soft pliable gag-strap, upon which it was just possible to see the impress of a woman's teeth clenched in desperation. A pencil-shaped glass squirt and the liquid-soap dispenser from the hand-basin had been left on a nearby stool.

Entranced by these objects, the boy examined the brief silk panties eagerly. They were not the knickers of a schoolgirl or a teenage nymph but belonged, he thought, to a mature young Venus.

The rest of the villa was empty, devoid of furniture or even discarded clothing. It was only as the boy walked through the rooms for a last time that he noticed the white leaves of paper in a grate.

There was no doubt that the bundle had been placed on the fire in order to be burnt. Some charring of the paper suggested that a match had been set to it and that it had been left to blaze. Whether it was carelessness in arranging it or some quirk of down-draught in the chimney would never be known. Yet the boy picked the papers out and found them unharmed. There was also a small package, which contained a recording.

The boy's heart jumped as he saw that most of the papers were full-plate photographic prints, ten inches by twelve. At the top of the pile was a sur-reptitiously taken picture of a young woman standing in a garden with a child often or eleven. The boy looked at the firmly mature young figure, the fair urchin-crop and the regular fair-skinned features. He turned the print over and saw the name 'Lesley' pencilled on the back.

There was no time to examine the rest in detail. A glance at them proved that most had been taken in the tiled toilet room of the villa at night. They showed Lesley stripped and at the mercy of two sadistic prison guards. Anticipation rather than unease made the boy collect these discarded treasures quickly and make his way from the Villa Rif.

Returning home, he locked the door of his room to guard against intrusion and began to investigate the photographs and the recording. But first he read with great eagerness a short dossier describing Lesley. He learnt her full name, where she was born and the fact that she was now twenty-eight years old. Her education was described and the seven or eight years of her marriage during which she had borne two children before turning to her current Sapphic ways. Then there was an account of how the young wife had walked out on her marriage and children in order to sleep with woman. Now it seemed, she had committed some grave moral offence. The dossier ended with the condemnation of Lesley to a judicial whipping on her bare buttocks with no mercy to be shown!

At the promise of this, the boy's heart beat faster. He took the pile of photographs and examined them in sequence. At the same time he played through the recording, for it was an accompaniment to these images. The recording was amateurish and indistinct in places, yet it was undoubtedly an authentic record of what had passed in the tiled punishment-room.

The photographs had been taken at night by the magnesium brilliance of flash. Though they were less subtle than camera studies made by daylight, there was no doubt that they were the work of a true artist.

The boy began to examine the photographs carefully, at the same time playing the few moments of the recording which belonged to each picture.

1. The young woman's bedroom at night. Lesley in white singlet, tight translucent panties, suspender-belt and stockings, lay on the divan. Her back was to the camera. The boy admired this view of her, the high-crowned urchin-crop, the long trim legs, the firm young hips and the erotic maturi-

ty of Lesley's bottom-cheeks seen palely through tight slinky panties. The two other women who were going to thrash her had come to fetch the young woman. To the boy's delight, the two women and their photographer had caught Lesley masturbating. There was no doubt of this. Her hand was seen between her legs, massaging her vaginal lips thought the tight gusset of her briefs.

'You like to play with yourself, Lesley, don't you?' said the voice on the recording, 'Let's see if a prison whipping will cool your randiness!'

2. The two women had seized her. Lesley was on her back on the divan. One woman had drawn her knees up to her breasts so that the full spread of her hips and thighs was offered to the camera. This same woman had stripped Lesley's panties down, revealing the flushed and roused love-lips between her thighs. She fingered Lesley there. The other woman held her head between her hands to make her face the camera. Her arrogant blue eyes and spoilt young face under the parted fringe were now a study in dismay.

'Look into the camera lens, Lesley!' said the voice on the recording, 'You'll have a complete portfolio of photographs taken of you during punishment. The men who buy sets of the pictures aren't just paying to see women do these things to each other. They want to see your face at the same time, to see how you take it… ' The second woman smiled. 'Look at the young minx! She can't help bedewing her thighs even when she's waiting for the whip!

3. In the next photograph the first woman sat on the edge of the bed, holding Lesley facedown over her knee as if she were a child to be spanked. Her left arm circled Lesley's waist tightly to steady her. The fingers of her right hand were snug between her thighs at the rear. Her legs squirmed in unavailing protest as her tormentor squeezed her vaginal lips gently, and skilfully excited her clitoris. As she masturbated Lesley to her unwilling cli-

max, the recording caught her gently mocking words.

'I must finish you off with my fingers before your punishment, Lesley! It would never do to allow you secret pleasure by squeezing your thighs during discipline! Nothing must be allowed to distract you from the whip!'

She gasped and struggled but the hand moved with firm assurance.

'Relax and enjoy it, Lesley. I'm going to make you come. Once you've got it out of your system, you'll be more in the mood for a whipping. Ah, you can't help moving your hips in time to the rubbing can you, Lesley?'

'Don't turn your face from the camera, Lesley!' said the other woman, 'Look into the lens properly or must I hold you? Collectors pay well for pictures like these. They'll expect to see your face as you climax.'

Presently the young lesbian's capitulation to pleasure began. A series of short rising whimpers ended with a long shuddering cry of release.

4. This was the first of the photographs to have been taken in the white-tiled punishment-room which the boy had entered inadvertently at the Villa Rif. The clock on the wall showed that it had been almost 11:30 at night by then.

Lesley was facedown on the black buttoned leather of the heavy sofa, her head now pillowed on her folded arms. Black rubber cushions under her loins raised and broadened the pale swell of her bare seat. No one could question the aptness of the costume she wore, for the area to be thrashed was admirably framed by the white elastic arch of the suspender-belt across the back of her waist, the elastic straps drawn down either flank and the honey-eyed gloss of stocking-tops at mid-thigh.

As one would expect, the young woman was looking sidelong over her shoulder at the two other women who made the preparation for her punishment. Leisurely the boy who held the photograph admired the high crown of Lesley's coiffure, the way her straight fair hair had been cut at the jaw line and shaped so closely to her head. A last chill of self-possessed arrogance still lingered in her fine long-lashed blue eyes. Indeed, the fear of what lay in store for her had not yet dispelled all the slight sullen hardness of her mouth and chin.

So far, the women had used only the restraint of their own hands to position her on the sofa, though her left ankle had been strapped to the heavy frame of the furniture at one end. Their hands were running expertly on her long trim legs, especially on the bare pallor of her thighs above the tops of her glossy stockings. One woman's finger touched a wisp of fair pubic hair which peeped between the rear opening of her legs. The other woman had her hand on the firm pale maturity of Lesley's bottom-cheeks, her fingers touching the secret humid warmth between them.

It was the recording which gave life to this cameo, for the sharp indignation of Lesley's voice did not quite conceal a tremor of fear.

'You have no right to bring me here like this! Let me go! Please! I've done nothing to deserve it! Please!'

One of the women laughed.

'Don't be foolish, Lesley! You're going to get a beating—that's why you've been brought here. Just like the delinquent lads in the next building.'

'No... No!' There was a sound of struggling and gasping. Then, it seemed, they were holding her still.

'Why make such a fuss about such a little thing, Lesley? You won't be the first young woman to get a good whipping—nor the last. You've got a firm proud bottom to take it on.'

The sound of struggling began again.

'Don't hurt me! Please! I couldn't bear to be whipped!'

The other woman answered her.

'No need for such panic, Lesley. There are other things which must happen before your punishment.'

Lesley

There was a further sequence of breathless protests and the shifting of sofa springs. Then the first woman spoke again.

'Open your legs wider, Lesley. Wider still. Lie forward more tightly over the cushions. Now let me feel you. I shall expect to find you well prepared for this after what you were doing to yourself in the other room!'

The boy listened to what followed, hardly daring to move for fear of missing some detail. There was a pause in the recording after the first woman had finished and, when it resumed, the voice was that of her companion.

'Maggie parted her buttocks the first time, several weeks ago. I imagine she must be well used to such things by now. Lie still, Lesley! I can't believe that the touch of a finger and Vaseline in such a place is a novelty to you...'

The first woman fondled the cool smooth cheeks of Lesley's firmly mature young bottom. She parted them and admired the tight inward dimple of Lesley's anus. Where the cheeks curved in together, the satiny whiteness of the skin assumed a tint of yellowed ivory.

Then the first woman stepped back and the second prepared Lesley by taking a glass marble and dipping it in the jar of Vaseline. Coating it well with the grease, she pressed the little glass ball firmly into Lesley's anus until the tight rear muscle yielded and then closed over the intruder. The boy thought he could hear Lesley's gasp. For a few moments, they allowed her to lie there while they kissed and fondled her between the legs, stroking the warm pubic sheath through the back of her thighs. Then the first woman told Lesley to return the marble to her hand.

Shocked by such a demand, she could not—or would not—at first. The second woman took the thin leather belt and dispassionately lashed her twice across the buttocks with it. She cried out, twisting away on the bed. Then, lowering her fringe to the pillow to hide her face, she lay on her belly and yielded the marble into the woman's hand, waiting, cupped under her rear cheeks. Several more times she coated it with Vaseline and inserted it until Lesley was well lubricated. Each time, the boy heard her gasp as she strained to comply and return the marble to her tormentor. Then the second woman explained gently to her that, for all her other experience in the marriage bed and with other women, what came next would be an agonising ordeal unless the way was well prepared.

The first woman showed Lesley what awaited her. She took from her pocket a dildo which was much thicker than her thumb. She began to struggle a little but the second woman held her firmly round the waist with one arm, looking down at the moon-pale cheeks of Lesley's bottom until she lay still again. Then she pressed the rounded tip of the dildo firmly between her buttocks until Lesley yielded under the increasing pressure with a muted cry of alarm. She exercised her with this device for five or ten minutes. At the same time her other hand manipulated her between her legs until she shuddered with a first spasm which the boy could clearly hear on the recording.

5. The preliminaries were over now and Lesley was sprawling on her belly over the cushions, still strapped by one ankle. Her face was turned in dismay towards her ravishers, one of whom had now picked up a long slim cane. The light caught a trace of wetness at the rear parting of her thighs and a slight oily smear at the meeting of Lesley's buttocks.

'Take your hands away from your bottom, Lesley,' said the voice of the woman on the recording, 'You won't like the cane across your knuckles.'

'Wait,' said the second woman, 'She needs more cushioning under her belly, so that her arse is properly lifted. Lift your hips a little, Lesley. At once! Or must we add a refusal to your punishment?'

There was a sound of the cushions being arranged and the bamboo being touched lightly across the young lesbian's buttocks. Then the cane lashed down in a vicious stroke across the bare pale cheeks of Lesley's bottom. There was a split-second's pause of total silence. And then Lesley screamed.

Again the bamboo rang out across the firm pallor of Lesley's bottom-cheeks—and again she screamed at the swelling agony of the impact. Eagerly the boy counted the strokes to himself to see if it would be six—but it was more—or twelve—but that passed too.

6. The clock in this photograph showed that it was half an hour after midnight and that a dozen strokes or so of the caning had been given. The bamboo had left deeply coloured weals across the firm erotic maturity of Lesley's bare bottom, as well as two marks across the backs of her thighs. Frantic with the burgeoning smart, the young woman had twisted round on her hip and was clinging hard to the arm of her chastiser to prevent her raising the cane. Under the parted fringe, Lesley's blue eyes were imploring her as if her life depended on the answer. Her mouth had the woebegone, down turned shape of a penitent little girl who pleads with her teacher.

7. The next camera study was made only a few moments later. Yet there was a significant and predictable change in the scene. To avoid such an interruption as had taken place, Lesley's wrists were strapped together to the far end of the sofa frame and the caning had continued. Her finger nails had clawed at the polished wood until they broke, in the agony of the thrashing. Her hands had clenched into fists until the nails drew blood from her palms.

Her head was still turned, her mouth and eyes wide under the fringe of her short-cut fair hair as she screamed for a respite. But the two women replied to the desperate appeals of the promiscuous young minx with smiles which promised a long ordeal. The woman with the cane had thrashed the crowns of Lesley's twenty-eight-year-old bottom-cheeks to deep crimson. Now she was measuring the bamboo across the softer, sensitive undercurve of her backside, just above the crease dividing her buttocks and thighs.

On the recording, the boy heard Lesley scream at the first of these savage lashes of the cane. Yet even so he was able to hear how the women had taught her to accept the inevitability of her punishment. Half an hour before, under the first stroke, he had heard the young woman cry out not to be caned. It amused him now to hear Lesley screaming instead only to have her strokes delayed. The boy hoped this would be denied—and it was.

8. It was almost one o'clock and the boy felt a stiffening excitement in his loins at the knowledge that the two women had made Lesley's punishment last so long. Indeed, it was by no means over, though the scene had once more altered. From the voices on the recording the boy had heard that Lesley was crossing her legs desperately, jamming one knee into the back of the other to contain the appalling smart of the bamboo. The women had already denied her this relief by strapping her ankles a few inches apart to the sofa frame.

To take the cane upon the flank of her hip was painful enough. Yet the boy had counted at least fifty strokes of the bamboo across Lesley's bottom and knew how frantic she must be to shield it from further punishment. So she had begun to twist on her side, away from the woman with the cane. It was the second woman who came to her colleague's assistance. Smiling at the folly of Lesley's attempted evasion, she perched on the edge of the sofa, tightened her arm over Lesley's waist, and turned her seat back to face the punishment. She remained like this, holding her, so that only Lesley's bottom and legs were visible in the photograph. It was on the recording that the chastiser's voice explained the consequences of her disobedience.

'Your punishment will continue in a moment, Lesley. First of all you

Lesley

must receive properly the stroke which you tried to avoid. Then there will be six extra strokes for your failure to keep still.'

The boy listened with his pulse racing to the sounds which followed these words. He heard the extra strokes given with vicious skill. Lesley screamed for her lovers, her children, anybody, as if one or all of them could hear her and would come to her rescue.

It was also in this photograph that Lesley, in her writhing, had thrust her bottom out to its fullest extent and thus offered her most complete rear view. The boy took a magnifying glass and scanned the picture with prurient curiosity. He saw, between the rear of her thighs, the light pubic hair matted by the moisture of previous sexual excitement. Between her buttocks, the few stray hairs near Lesley's anus were plastered flat on the smooth skin by the sheen of Vaseline.

9. At this point, for the prison thrashing was still continuing after one o'clock, the boy could not resist glancing at the piquant contrast offered by Lesley in the days before her enslavement. There was a photograph of her gardening in the black trouser-suit, not long before she had renounced her married life and children. Her present ordeal was all the more exciting for this portrait. The picture showed Lesley standing to face the camera, holding a child with its back to her. The arrogant blue eyes looked a little away from the lens, and the fair-skinned facial beauty under the parted fringe was marred by her customary sulkiness, seen most clearly in her mouth and chin. How much more the boy preferred to see her contrite and weeping under the bamboo.

10. From this portrait of an emancipated young woman, the boy turned to a full-plate study of Lesley's face during the present caning. He held the two pictures side by side and saw how the arrogant self-possession had crumbled at the first strokes of the cane. The picture of Lesley's face while she was chastised was one which any true disciplinarian would have hung

among the treasures of his collection. Under the long fair-haired fringe, the aloof blue eyes were now wide with pain, the mouth forming a howling oval of torment.

11. Lesley's bottom was once again the centre of the composition. Now, however, tight strapping round her waist held her down without the need of a woman's firm arm. The hands of the clock showed that the picture had been taken just before half-past one in the morning.

There was no longer any part of Lesley's behind which was not deeply coloured by the cane, except for a strip of whiteness where her buttocks curved in together. The cane was unable to touch her there and, for that reason, a whip was kept in readiness.

The chastiser was now caning her hard and sharply across the earlier weals of the bamboo. Lesley's voice was shrill with panic.

'Don't cane me any more! Not yet! Please! Oh, please!'

'Lie forward properly over the cushions, Lesley,' said the woman impatiently, 'Don't clench your buttocks like that!'

'I'm being tortured!' Her cry made the stone walls ring.

The other woman laughed.

'You shall learn the true meaning of that word, Lesley, in the place to which you are being sent.'

12. With astonishment and delight, the boy saw that the caning had still not finished. The supple bamboo rod smacked and lashed across the woven crimson which marked Lesley's buttocks.

For the first time the boy paused to consider his own reactions as he followed the events of the photographs and the recording. In truth, he had first heard Lesley's cries and outbursts with a profound shock. By now, however, he was intrigued enough to consider them more rationally. He noticed, from the intensity of her screams, that the initial impact of the cane across

Lesley

Lesley's bottom seemed to swell for several seconds to an unbearable torment, sharpening her cry to a wild shriek.

It was also evident that her screams were now more abrupt than they had been at first, perhaps from so much crying out and pleading. It could scarcely be that she noticed the pain less. Between the strokes and the screams, Lesley gave vent to a storm of sobbing, rising in shrillness or falling in despair, like the arpeggios of punishment.

The boy wondered if the drama was merely acted for the camera and recording. Perhaps it was. Yet he knew by instinct that no actress, of however consummate ability, could mimic such a performance as Lesley's. In the photographs, there was a sense of authenticity which the onlooker saw immediately.

In the present photograph, Lesley's high-crowned head was turned, so that she faced her chastisers in pain and panic.

'You've cut me!' she cried out, 'I can feel it!'

The boy looked quickly at the photograph. Where the bamboo had landed aslant Lesley's right-hand bottom-cheek it had raised a well-marked weal. It was plain to see that several ruby dots had welled up along this line and that the largest of them was trickling down the lower curve of Lesley's backside to gather in the crease which divided her thigh and her behind. The cruel women dismissed her frantic cry. How they treated her. The boy couldn't help but be shocked at the way the fairer sex could treat its own members.

'You have much to learn about prison thrashings, Lesley. You are not a little girl being smacked by a teacher. A young woman of your age and type must expect a prolonged judicial punishment. A well-used bamboo will cut your backside a number of times before the thrashing is over. Lie forward properly over the cushions. There is much worse to come yet!'

There was much following this which had not been photographed, yet was to be heard in fragments on the recording. At one moment it seemed that Lesley was undergoing a softer ordeal in the hands of the two women, for she sounded like a spanked little girl now pleading affectionately to be loved and forgiven.

Soon after this she cried out in panic and seemed to wrestle vainly with the women who positioned her. A woman's voice said, 'Don't be foolish, Lesley. You're here to be punished. We want you strapped bottom-upwards over the sofa-scroll, bending very tightly forward.'

13. It was shortly before two in the morning. Lesley was indeed strapped down kneeling very tightly forward over the heavy padded scroll at the end of the sofa, her arms strapped at full stretch to the base of its frame. In this posture her firm pale buttocks were pulled hard apart, showing the yellowed-ivory smoothness of Lesley's bottom-crack where the skin curved in towards her anus.

They were punishing the young victim for her arrogance, using a pony-lash with a stout handle and a short tail of braided leather. It was the second woman who whipped her now, either because it was her forte or because the first had become too tired. She cracked the snakeskin lash across the bare pale moons of Lesley's bottom in a sinuous weal. The whip curved and clung agonisingly to her first seat-cheek, curled down into Lesley's bottom-crack, and then curved up over the further cheek of her behind.

Lesley's face was twisted round towards her tormentor. Her blue eyes under her parted fringe matched the expressive frenzy of the shriek on the recording. Every muscle in her thighs and hips seemed contracted by the anguish, her knees were jammed urgently together and her toes curled with the sheer intensity of the impact.

Lesley

Unmoved by this, the woman who held the lash took aim across Lesley's backside, even including the rear of her thighs, and whipped, and whipped, and whipped.

There was a pause in the discipline, allowing Lesley to check her sobs a little. It seemed that the women wished her to understand exactly what was going to happen.

'Now you must undergo the last part of your thrashing, Lesley. It will be the hardest for you to bear. The full rigour can only be exercised when you are already supremely sensitive from the previous strokes. Let us have no hypocrisy about punishment. I want to take you far, far beyond the limits of punishment, into a twilight world where nothing exists for you but the anguish of the whip across your bare buttocks. Don't twist your mouth from the cotton wad, Lesley! It is prudent that you should be gagged for this last adventure!'

Even before the first stroke was given, the recording caught the small sounds of Lesley's frenzy. Her shrill pleading and protests were reduced by the gag to an urgent mewing. The sofa springs echoed the strapped writhing of her thighs and hips. He heard the young woman's bare belly slithering vainly on buttoned leather in the sweltering southern night. Unable to contain her panic, there was no restraint of feminine rudeness from Lesley's behind.

14. Was it all a charade or did it truly happen as promised? The boy heard a wild mewing as the smack-cuts of leather across Lesley's bottom made the stones ring. As for the next photograph, it had been taken just after half-past two.

In this full-plate study, the whipping was over, the last stroke just given. Lesley was unfastened and her gag removed. Indeed, the two women had raised to her feet this urchin-cropped young Sapphic, her firm erotic maturity laid pale and bare. As they assisted her upright it seemed that Lesley's bottom patterned the floor with red petals from the final tapestry of the pony-lash.

There was one more detail, deeply exciting to the boy as proof of how far she had been taken. Lesley's head drooped on the woman's shoulder as she held her, her arms limp at either side. The second woman stared in wide-eyed admiration and open-mouthed delight. Like a ravished virgin-bride, Lesley had swooned in her chastiser's arms!

15. The last photograph of the sequence had been taken at dawn. Lesley again facedown on the sofa. She now slept, showing the softer feminine gentleness of her face in repose. It was as if the drama of the whip had been necessary to the deep and tranquil exhaustion of this slumber. Lesley slept at last, all anguish and passion spent.

The boy roused himself from reverie and saw a last scrap of paper, written by Lesley—a smuggled appeal for rescue slipped into these camera studies. The place of her captivity was written on the other side. The boy hesitated, not turning the paper over. He knew how often and with what fascination he would play the recording and brood on the sequence of photographs. Yet he feared that in a moment of weakness he might take pity on Lesley's continuing slavery and respond to this final appeal for help. Once the paper was turned over, he would know the place of her servitude and the knowledge must remain with him.

He glanced at the final photographs of Lesley whipped. The smooth prints reflected the mute images of her mouthed frenzy, the beads and trickles of the lash-marks on her bottom, her swooning, the smelling salts and the punishment resumed. Then he made his decision.

Without turning the message, he went to the fireplace, dropped the paper on the glowing coals, and watched it darken and flake to ashes.

* * *

From time to time in the hot weeks of autumn an unrelenting African wind blew sand-coloured dust about the house on the rocky plateau

Lesley

where young Madame Claire was absolute mistress.

At times the dust-storm veiled the sun itself, hiding the broad stony valley and the distant limestone escarpments. Then the dust would clear and the wind would drop as unexpectedly as it had risen. From its eyrie, the house with the barred windows looked down on a landscape of lizard and lynx, three-hundred feet below. Among the olive trees and umbrella pines on the slopes, the sun's heat shimmered from the time-eaten Roman arch and the last ruins of a great arena. During the white heat of the day no man was to be seen on the dry and rocky terrain. Even at night it was only crossed by those visitors whom the mistress of the house invited.

Those who had known Lesley as a self-possessed and indifferent young wife watched her with interest. Many of them hoped that her natural resentment and arrogance at the thought of slavery would break into rebellion—for the pleasure of seeing her punished.

Yet her new guardians were accustomed to young women of this type and knew by what trivial means obedience and humiliation might be enforced. Constant beatings would make her useless for other pleasures. She would be whipped and caned, of course, but when it happened it would be for the pleasure of a woman of particular stature. Lesley's educated and emancipated poise, her insistence on the rights of her womanhood were easily undermined by treating her as a little girl whose most menial bodily needs can be denied or compelled by those who possess her.

Like the other girls, Lesley was at the service of those guests who visited Claire's Sapphic treasure house from far and near. This was never more evident than in the evenings when the young women were made to act as waitresses at the dinner table before being put to other uses. The perverse appeal of Lesley's fair-haired crop and the firm, pale maturity of her body made her a frequent choice for such duties. Claire would stipulate the costume to be worn. As a rule this consisted of a white breast-halter and suspender-belt with sheer stockings, a pair of panties—brief and tight in thin apple-green silk—being the sole concession to modesty.

It was easy to detain the young woman as she stood before a guest or bent across the table to reach for a plate or glass. By the time the meal was over, Lesley had been well fondled between the legs in consequence of this. Through the tight thin silk of the panties, the glow of a smack-print was often visible on Lesley's bottom. This was how she was treated by some of the most prominent and hungry of the Paris's lesbians.

Claire would also assert her authority over Lesley by making the young woman stand by while the mistress recited her history to the dinner guests in sardonic terms. Claire would begin by describing Lesley the spoilt middle-class schoolgirl, then the promiscuous college student. She spoke of Lesley the greedy and pregnant bride, the brief period of child-rearing and then the series of lovers.

All this had changed now that the promiscuous young wife was the slave of those who had abducted her. Before proceeding to their pleasures with her, the mistress and guests amused themselves by passing around the dinner-table those photographs which showed Lesley being enjoyed as only a slave-woman can be.

In one set of pictures, not only was Lesley herself punished for some misdemeanour. At the same time she was made to 'horse' a charming adolescent pupil to be thrashed at the same time. The photographs showed Lesley naked, bending forward tightly along a vaulting-horse, upon which she was firmly strapped down. A schoolgirl nymph with fair shoulder-length tresses, solemn blue eyes and a firm pale beauty was the second culprit. She was made to sit naked astride Lesley's waist, then to bend forward tightly until her breasts and belly pressed hard on Lesley's bare back. In this charming posture, 'horsed' astride Lesley's waist, she too was strapped down.

The sequel was enacted by the appointed executioner, carrying a slim rod with a short tail of whipcord. She was confronted by two faces twisted round to her in double trepidation. Fearfully her movements were followed by Lesley's eyes under her long parted fringe and by the solemn blue eyes of the younger nymph with the fair tresses. The chastiser's excitement would have been great even on seeing the full pale moons of Lesley's bare backside as she bent tightly with legs strapped together. To see such a prospect crowned by the resilient youthfulness of Rachel's bottom-cheeks as she lay horsed astride the older culprit's waist was irresistible.

With a smile at Lesley, Claire conceded that the whipping far exceeded the limits of any permissible prison discipline. Indeed, the executioner's superiors were obliged by the rules to reprimand her for its severity. Yet they did so with smiles of reassurance. To have two such beauties presented in such a manner made restraint unreasonable. The executioner was assured that her advancement would not be impeded and that when the two young women received their next month's whipping it should be in the same manner and by her hand.

Such experiences curbed Lesley's arrogance. Indeed, she was made to humble herself in countless ways. Sometimes, they sat her in the stone stoup of a pedestal in the courtyard where the guests gathered. There she was fastened, clad only in breast-halter and the film of honey-toned tights.

They detained her until a liquid pressure forced from her a self-conscious request. Claire would deny it at once. The guests watched with curiosity the urgent compression of Lesley's thighs, the slither of the tights in her restless stirring. At last the flood broke. With head bowed, Lesley yielded in a long liquid whispering, until she sat in the torrent which filled the hollow.

These libertines would keep her sitting in her pool until her filmy honey-toned tights were well soaked, the backs of the thighs and the flanks of her hips, as well as the seat and crotch. Then they would make her turn on her belly over the stoup for their inspection. The wet seat of the translucent tights clung to her rear contours like a second skin. Its thin filmy mesh shone wet and was a little darkened by moisture. Soaked and clinging smoothly, the tights made her upper thighs and the proud cheeks of Lesley's mature young bottom seem fuller and fatter in this posture.

Her female admirer, seeing this and knowing that Lesley was well fastened, bending over the pedestal, was seduced by the sight. She remarked that a punishment strap was the lot of little girls who misbehaved in this way. For half an hour she used a broad leather thong to spank Lesley's behind in wet tights. With eyes gleaming and lips pressed vindictively hard, she strapped her backside with explosive smacks of leather. Lesley's cries, her storms of sobs, her desperate pleas to be spared brought only a smile to her tormentor's lips. Lesley's blue eyes under her little-boy fringe were in floods of tears after only a few minutes. By the end of the vigorous and smarting bottom-smacking, the crimson soreness of Lesley's firm buttocks was a visible glow through the seat of her tights. Sometimes the woman would then peel the wet tights down and employ whipcord across the wet trembling cheeks of Lesley's seat.

So far as Lesley's backside was concerned, its most natural function was easily controlled by master or mistress. If she was to attend the guests, it was necessary that she must be able to perform any act demanded of her. Therefore, when she woke in the morning, two attendants fastened a broad leather belt firmly round her bare waist. From the front of this, a broad strap ran down her belly, tightly under her legs, and was then strained upwards, deep between Lesley's buttocks, to lock at the back of her waist. A thumb-sized projection fitted into Lesley's anus. Besides muzzling her natural needs, the wearing of this device, two or three times a week, was gradually curing the natural and extreme tightness of Lesley's arsehole. Her wrists were strapped in front of her to prevent interference. She could thus walk, lie or sit in her usual clothes until summoned for the pleasure of her admirers that night.

Even the muzzle was a reminder of her slavery rather than a necessity for the pleasure of the guests. To this educated and promiscuous suburban ex-wife it was an abject humiliation to be denied the use of the white-tiled closet on the grounds that she must be in a state to perform such acts before the guests if so required.

The guests had no taste for such things, but their amusement as Lesley was made to listen to an account of her predicament, was none the less for that. There was, it is true, one woman whose passion was to have Lesley adorned with straps holding her wrists together in front of her and a choke collar round her neck with a long leather leash. She would allow Lesley to wear a white breast-halter and a white suspender belt whose straps pulled the sheer gloss of filmy gold stockings well up her long pale thighs. Lesley's panties were not, of course, permitted.

It amused this particular guest to take her into the moonlit olive grove, as 'a young bitch who had been mated a couple of times.' There she brusquely commanded her to do what she had to, like a young bitch taken for a walk by her impatient owner. On hands and knees, even with one leg raised a little to avoid splashing herself, Lesley released her water in true canine fashion. Often the mistress would jerk the choke-collar, forcing her to follow before she was done. A few times she had ordered Lesley on all fours with knees together, a small bowl set on the backs of her calves, its rim pressing the rear of her lower thighs. On the first occasion her peremptory command, as she stood behind her looking down, had shocked Lesley into immobility. She drew the pouch of Lesley's vagina well back between her thighs so that even there she would not escape her impatience. Then, with a dog-whip, she thrashed Lesley's buttocks until she obeyed, continuing the discipline even while her body performed its menial task.

In all these things, Lesley underwent the lessons of submission, humility and obedience—so necessary to this arrogant woman with her illusions about her own right to sexual freedom, and emancipation from the duties of marriage and child-rearing.

There were other forms of obedience imposed, which would have been impossible in the world outside. Lesley would be told to lie on the carpet of a nobly furnished room in front of the guests. Her black stretch-briefs were pulled down and her singlet drawn up, baring her from breasts to knees. One of those sitting round her would give the commands.

'Make love to yourself, Lesley! Show us how you like to do it!'

Disobedience to such orders had long ago been subdued by punishment. Now she closed her eyes, in modesty or pleasure. Then her self-possession melted as she surrendered to this natural enjoyment which she had practised so often in private that public reticence was absurd. The spectators' murmurs accompanied her.

'Pull your singlet higher and show us how you fondle your breasts at the same time, Lesley... Lift one leg a little, my dear, so we may see you diddle your clitoris... Your left hand, Lesley! Use it behind you! Play with yourself between those cheeks at the same time... That's better! See the little madam! How it excites her! You play between your buttocks when you make love to yourself in bed, Lesley. Our keyhole spies have watched you do it, never fear!'

Voices alone would enforce Lesley's sense of slavery, for she was compelled to answer all questions, listen to all remarks and perform all acts, upon pain of severest retribution as she lay naked.

Lesley

'Describe your first time with a woman, Lesley. Leave out no detail… Tell us which of your lovers' dildos and tongues gave you most pleasure… Repeat the lewdest things your lovers said while she courted you… Now your great lover, Lesley!. Your first partner in adultery! The lewdest thing she ever did to you in bed! The randiest thing you ever said to her!

Repeat them to us at once! Did you truly take the rubber dildo and show us exactly how you did it!'

The voices entered her mind and echoed there until even in sleep they seemed to possess her still and she would wake with the phrases on her lips.

By the rule of the house, Lesley saw only those other girls who were brought to her bed or who were summoned for the pleasure of the guests on the same occasion. The weeks passed without a glimpse of Judith, Connie, or Maggie. Her questions about them, as those about Christine, Antonia, and Fatima, were chided and unanswered.

Claire had not yet taken Lesley to her own bed but she had decreed a number of love-matches between Lesley and other girls. At first Lesley had protested the impossibility of such passion. Claire had stroked her fair crop, kissed her forehead lightly and chided her a little.

'Be sensible, Lesley! You cannot deny that you enjoy making love to yourself. Do you not respond to the first caress of a hand between your legs? If you find pleasure in being roused by another young woman, it is absurd to make such bother over which young woman she is!'

'But I care!' A note of defeat sounded in her plaintive wail.

Claire stroked Lesley's fringe and kissed her again.

'Ah, you still cry for Judith! Is that it, Lesley? You must make up your mind that such things cannot be. Yet when you take Kim or Mandy, even young women like Maggie, Jennifer or Pat, in your arms, you need only close your eyes and imagine it is Judith. You may cry her name in your ecstasy, if you wish.'

In the weeks which followed, Lesley was made to accept a series of bed companions. First they chose Kim for her, a gently shaped and wide-eyed nineteen-year-old with blonde hair cut even closer than Lesley's. Yet in tight smooth trousers, the soft young cheeks of Kim's bottom and her flat loins soon won her a male admirer. Her new possessor employed her vigorously in bed, though not disdaining to use the bamboo often across the soft pale cheeks of Kim's bottom.

The next partner chosen for Lesley was Mandy, a tall and strongly made girl of eighteen. Mandy's lightly curled brown hair was worn in a cluster on her forehead and cut short at her nape—ah admirable setting for firm pale features and brown eyes. Yet the guests admired this young Amazon in her tight blue jeans and singlet. The strong young legs and hips, as well as the strapping young cheeks of Mandy's bottom won her the same lover as Kim. The fortunate woman took them both to her bed simultaneously. When displeasure had to be avenged, the two girls lay naked, side by side, on their bellies over the bolster. The whipping was all the more severe in the excitement offered by a double target, the softly rounded pallor of Kim's bottom-cheeks and the more sturdy spread of Mandy's buttocks.

There was only one girl whom Lesley was required to make love with over a long period of time. Her name was Tania and she was nineteen years old. Unlike the other girls in Claire's protection, Tania belonged to a man who had lodged her in the harem of the young mistress, so that he might visit the girl when it suited him.

Tania, like many of the others, was a softly shaped young beauty with a neat straight nose, a demurely tucked in chin, her pretty olive-skinned face showing a tendency to dimples when she smiled. The short crop of brown curls clustering over her forehead and cut clear of her collar gave her a rather cherubic appearance. Perhaps it was only her eyes which betrayed. Their pale blue loveliness seemed strangely shadowed, in pan by her high cheekbones. Yet the shadowing also gave her the air of a masturbatrix.

To see Tania in the tight wool of her white vest and the still tighter fit of her working-jeans was to appreciate at once her lover's interest in her. The same softness which gave her face its charm also characterised her figure.

Where did her admirer see her first? Perhaps it was as she leant forward, elbows on the counter, chin cupped in her hands as she read the newspaper and smoked a cigarette. In this pose, the softness of Tania's breasts weighed in the tight wool of her vest. With her waist hollowed downward and her hips thrust out in this posture, the soft cheeks of Tania's bottom were broad and full in the tightened seat of pale blue jeans. It was visible that in a few years more, she would have reason to be self-conscious at a certain fatness which she showed in this position.

Tania was a polite and well-spoken girl, eager to please her customers. She smiled quickly, the whites of her blue eyes all the more radiant by contrast with the olive tone of her face. Yet her lover had never entertained any intention other than that she should be her slave-girl, held safely by Claire for her visits.

In consequence, Tania was left to her own devices for long periods of time. Rather than permit her to be corrupted by private debauchery with Gillian, Fiona or her other companions, it was judged best that she should be commanded to spend her love upon Lesley under the supervision of their mistress.

So it was that the girl of nineteen and the young wife of twenty-eight were first brought together. At Claire's insistence, they lay naked upon the bed, each facing the other with doubt and hesitation. Claire's patience soon failed her. She gave orders that they should be fastened together by a strap round their waists and that the most stimulating mixture of spices should be applied between their thighs and buttocks as well as to their nipples. No sooner was this done than the two young women began to stir and gasp under the teasing heat. Claire leant over them and used one hand on each. She fondled each between the thighs until both Tania's lips and Lesley's were wet with their mutual kisses.

Soon their hands were more than eager to finish the work which Claire had begun. Looking steadily into one another's eyes—for love now overcame all sense of shame—Lesley and Tania masturbated one another as skilfully and intricately as they knew how.

Neither of them was, in truth, averse to such exercise. Once the first veil of shame had been torn aside, no demand was too extreme. What the world scorned as lesbian depravity became for them the expression of the truest and most tender affection. Many nights were passed with Tania and Lesley lying head to tail, each presenting her spread hips, thighs and buttocks to the other in an upward squat. The love which began with fingers now proceeded to the velvet caresses of lips and tongue in the most secret places of the female anatomy. Shivering with pleasure and cooing with the softness of a pair of doves, each rendered to the other the tribute of her orgasm.

Lesley longed for Tania every night, as if her life depended on such satisfaction. Yet she was not in love with the girl. The pleasure which she derived from their caresses was merely for her own gratification. When Tania's rare male admirer paid his visits and took the girl for his own enjoyment, Lesley felt the pang of physical bereavement. Yet for Tania's fate she experienced no pity, only a curiosity as to what Tania suffered at the hands of her possessor.

Lesley

On many occasions there was little to learn beyond the expected truth that the man had stripped Tania's young body with its slightly muddy pallor of bare skin, laid her on her back with legs spread and performed upon her the common act of copulation.

Sometimes there were variations to this. He would sit in his chair with Tania kneeling before him. Obliging her to bow her brown curls, he would lead Tania to suck his erection either until he laid her on her back or else until he paid his tribute into the mouth of this nineteen-year-old beauty.

The sight of Tania bending with her chin cupped in her hands on the counter was not without its effect upon him. By the way her waist was hollowed downward, Tania's broad full buttocks had been suggestively parted under the tight blue denim. Indeed the ridged outline of her stretch-briefs, arching up over each cheek of Tania's bottom, showed clearly.

Making her assume this position, the man would undress her and use a Vaseline-coated finger between Tania's buttocks. She made this ultimate sexual surrender of her body only under compulsion and with teeth clenched in the ferocity of the violation. He determined that she must yield him the tight enjoyment of her behind more readily, sought Claire's advice. It was decided that though it would be unthinkable for another man to employ her thus in the lover's absence, a dildo would provide the answer. Every afternoon Lesley lay in the next room and heard Tania cry out at first as the rubber phallus was employed. Yet the cries grew rarer and less shrill as the weeks passed. By the time of her lover's next visit, Tania yielded him this pleasure with no more than her sighs and whispers of satisfaction.

* * *

Winter in that hot limestone country did not come as it had done in the northern city. The heat scarcely diminished during the days of white sunlight over the broad valley and olive slopes which led the eye to distant mountain escarpments. Even at the feast of Saturn and the return of the year the sun still set in a slow disc of fire, its resting place not far distant along the ridged horizon from where it had been when Lesley and her companions first came to the house.

Yet the nights were colder, the starlight more luminous and the moon more brilliant. The cry of jackal and lynx grew sharper and more menacing in the darkness. Yet the house and the little whitewashed town on the plateau seemed as much a state of mind as Paris had once been and the winter city soon became.

Lesley was parted from Tania, since Claire now chose to take the young wife into her own bed. They gave Tania to a lewd and soft-figured young blonde of twenty-five, named Jackie. With her bell shape of blonde hair, her pale and sulky features, Jackie had something of Lesley's aloof manner and appearance.

Lesley saw no more of Judith or of Maggie. She asked if Connie was still in Claire's possession. The young mistress would only say that the Asian girl now belonged to a man, to whom Claire had given her.

Lying naked with Claire in the cold moonlight which lit the bedroom, Lesley did not dare at first to ask about Judith or Maggie for fear of what she might team. Yet she found courage at length to inquire in an indirect way about Tania's fate.

Claire took the young woman in her arms.

'You have much to learn, Lesley, much to learn about such houses as this. Caress me while I tell you.'

Lesley's fingers moved slowly between the thighs of the slim cropped redhead.

'In houses like this,' said Claire, 'the logic of a woman's existence is her attraction for those who enjoy her. You are now, perhaps, more appealing to some men than when you were a bride of twenty. Tania's soft charms at nineteen will become gross in a few years. There is one answer to this. All houses of this kind have a certain room. When a girl is taken there, she does not return.'

She paused, feeling the abrupt cessation of Lesley's movements in the moment of shock. Then Claire stroked the young wife's cropped fair hair as if to calm her while the explanation was continued.

'There are a few men—very few—who have the taste and the money to inflict such final severities, when the time comes. In Tania's case, the arrangements are already made. There is a man who will take her into that room, where the walls are hung with whips and strange implements, blades and batons. After a few days—or a few hours—he will come out alone. The same fate is decreed for Noreen, a young trollop of nineteen, though she does not know it. No warnings are given. You have seen the photographs of Vanessa, the snub-nosed tomboy with her lank fair hair and insolent manner? Vanessa Cox was taken to that room while she was still eighteen, for her impudent charms were almost over and she would have grown into a drab. There was never such an array of whips or tiny implements in the brazier coals as was provided for the man who accompanied her. Two days and a night passed before her body was tumbled through the oubliette onto the rocks below, to be snuffled as natural prey by the predators of night.'

Later that night, Claire kissed Lesley and asked gently, 'Tell me truly, my sweet. Have you ever loved anyone but yourself?'

'I have loved Judith as a woman can.'

'Will you prove it?' Claire stroked the moist vagina skilfully.

'Yes!' The word came as a whimper of longing, imploring forgiveness for the past, 'Oh yes, if you will let me!'

'Will you share her life for ever, as her lover?'

Lesley nodded, blinking away her tears. Claire got up and left her for a while. When she returned as if by a feat of magic, she was leading Judith, who stood naked in the moonlit room, taller and more graceful than ever at the close of her sixteenth year. Lesley stared at the vision as though it might be the ghost of beauty which would vanish at a touch. Claire led Judith to the bed and let her lie in Lesley's arms. She left them together.

For the First time, Lesley wept for some cause rather than her own, weeping for love of Judith. They lay in each other's arms, crying and kissing away each other's tears, brushing back one another's hair and feasting with their lips on every feature of the partner's face.

When the first storm of tears was over, they touched each other softly between the legs and began a long and gentle act of mutual masturbation. Then they kissed each other's bodies, scorning no crack or crevice. It was dawn when they fell at last into sleep with their arms entwined about one other.

Claire returned a few hours later and woke them. She spoke to Lesley.

'Will you share Judith's life as her lover from now on?'

'Yes!' Lesley looked into Judith's lovely eyes as she spoke.

'Will you share every pleasure with her?'

'Yes!'

'Will you share every punishment or torture?'

'Yes!' The reply came without hesitation. 'Even if you must accompany her to that room from which there is no return?'

'Yes!' The reply was quick but Lesley's voice trembled a little.

'One moment!' Claire smiled, 'Judith will be sold, like many girls in this house, sold as a slave to a master or mistress. Do you swear that the man or woman who owns Judith shall own you too? Own you as a slave? Will you submit with Judith to be cherished or chastised, to suffer those final severities of the leather noose or the blade, if your master or mistress decides?'

As she asked these questions, smiling, Claire's hand was between Lesley's thighs, bringing the promiscuous young wife to orgasm. Claire felt a tremor run through the pale limbs at the mention of the belly-skewer and the leather collar. But Lesley was now on the delirious edge of her orgasm and the answer was demanded.

'Yes!' she cried softly in her passion, 'Oh, yes!'

Claire smiled again, satisfied that Lesley had at last learnt to know a type of love which was not mere selfish indulgence.

Not a night passed after this without Lesley and Judith being required to make naked love under Claire's gaze. Irretrievably lost in their infatuation, no persuasion was necessary. Lesley and Judith would have loved nakedly and wantonly even if all the world was watching them because they could no longer help themselves. Often they would come to Claire in the heat of the day and ask if they might also spend the afternoon on the bed. The request was granted.

When there were guests in the evening, Lesley and Judith would be chosen together or separately by those who wished to enjoy them. On these occasions the nobly furnished rooms with their Moorish colonnades and verandas displayed twenty or thirty of Claire's young women as they gave pleasure to those who had chosen them. It was on one of these occasions that Lesley had her only other sight of a girl who had been at Paris in the summer. After dinner, Judith was in the arms of a young Arab woman, the mistress of a pasha who allowed her this alternative diversion occasionally. Lesley, on the far side of the room, was naked but for her black strapping while the pasha himself fondled her at full length on a sofa. There was a disturbance of some kind and then two attendants brought in the padded birching-horse, whose presence suggested judicial punishment.

The news was whispered that one of the guests had chosen Maggie and Noreen for his diversions. Their admirer had made them lie head to tail, each presenting an upward squat to the other's lips. He then demanded the performance of acts so extreme that Noreen, a strongly built young woman at nineteen, had refused and resisted with violence.

Maggie was brought in first, naked from the singlet hem at her waist down to her heels. The guests admired her pale coltishness of figure, the slight stockiness, the lank golden blonde hair cut short at her shoulders and fringed. Though she had not offended, the rather hard sluttish features of her fair-skinned face made sure that not a voice was raised on her behalf. Being rather short in the leg, Mag was drawn up on tiptoe to bend tightly over the padded horse, secured at full stretch by the strapping of her wrists to the base on the far side.

Nineteen-year-old Noreen came next. She was still dressed in her snug white singlet and the pale blue jeans worn tight on her lower limbs. Her taut strong thighs were clearly shaped, as were her firm sturdy hips and seat-cheeks, which, though broad, were not marred by surplus fat. The dark brown hair, lank and fringed, just covered her collar, framing the determined lines of her fair-skinned face and the insolence of her brown eyes.

She began to struggle at the sight of the horse, with anger as well as fright. Yet soon she had been bent over it and secured, a yard or so along from Maggie. A canvas screen on two wooden supports was next arranged, having the appearance of a banner. It was placed so that it ran along above the birching-horse, the base of the canvas framing the backs of the girls' waists. However hard they twisted their heads round, neither Maggie nor Noreen would be able to see what was happening behind them or the identity of the chastiser. Noreen, in particular, was a strong girl who would certainly bear a violent grudge. This method was therefore judged prudent.

Lesley

Those on one side of the birching-horse could see only the heads and upper halves of the two girls as the gag-straps were fitted to protect their teeth in the frenzy of the ordeal. To the other side of the room, where the guests now gathered, the upper half of the two girls was concealed by the screen. The onlookers saw only two pairs of buttocks, hips and legs as Maggie and Noreen bent over tightly.

For many of their admirers this seemed sufficient. They clustered round, certain that the two girls would never identify them. For almost an hour, the fondling continued. Maggie's pale thighs, so firm and stocky, were eased astride. The young thighs themselves were lingeringly kissed and handled, the vaginal pouch flushed from the embrace of expert fingers. Young slut that she was, Maggie scarcely showed any evidence of this to those who saw only her face. The rather crude pale features were brazen as her blue eyes, only the straight cut of her lank golden hair giving a little-girl innocence to this young woman of twenty. Other men fondled her seat-cheeks, more than one finger exercising her between them.

Noreen's determined and defiant look never faltered, whatever her feelings, as she shook the lank dark brown hair into place repeatedly. Through the thin tight covering of pale blue denim, her admirers handled her firm working-girl's thighs and the broadened sturdy cheeks of Noreen's bottom. Over her robust young buttocks the jeans-seat was taut and smooth. In her vain resentment she tried to twist away from the hands which roved over her two rear hemispheres. The seat of her jeans was divided by a stout central seam, drawn deep and taut into Noreen's bottom-crack. Strained under her legs by her bending posture, the stout seam even parted her vaginal lips whose soft shape was clearly seen in the tight denim between her thighs.

The tensing and squirming of her hips and legs redoubled as they undid her waist-belt and drew down her pants. In the tight denim the outline of Noreen's knickers, a pair of snug stretch-briefs, had been clearly visible. These too had to come down, baring her from waist to heels. Two hands at once made for her vaginal pouch. Others wandered over Noreen's bottom-cheeks and soon their insistent fingers vanished deep between the two pale mounds. A few men were so indifferent to public censure that they knew no shame whatever. When the chastiser arrived, the tributes which these libertines had paid were visible upon her thighs and buttocks.

The man who now entered carried the familiar pony-whip with its short tail of woven snakeskin. He pinioned each girl's ankles and her legs just above the knees. Noticing the blemishes which the lust of their admirers had left, he went into the adjoining room which the girls used and came back with a convenient rag in his hand. The clout was naturally dampened and, as he clutched it, he frowned in disapproval at the libidinous state of the rear views which both Maggie and Noreen presented. Neither of the culprits could see him or had any idea of what was about to happen. Yet as the spectators watched, he wiped over each pair of rear cheeks, first Noreen's and then Maggie's. The application of a communal cloth in so public a place and manner caused much attempted squirming but to no avail. Yet it was not the chastiser but the pasha's pretty little Arab mistress who tore the rag in half and used it to muffle the culprits' protests.

Noreen was punished first. She had no idea of her precise fate until the man trailed the cold leather of the pony-whip across her pale statuesque buttocks. Noreen's rear cheeks tightened with instinctive fright. Indeed, that cruel promise of the leather whip on her bare backside caused a visible thrill of terror. For the first time the man who carried the lash smiled. Reversing the whip in his hand, he pressed the rounded butt between the strong pale cheeks of Noreen's bottom in a promise of the most sardonic violation. It was impossible to say whether the high, wadded mewing which penetrated the folded cloth was a cry of fear or fury at such an affront.

Yet she was made to undergo it without further delay. For a young trollop of nineteen so sturdily built, Claire regarded this as a mere indignity rather than a torment.

The man withdrew the butt at last. He raised the slim whip above his shoulder and brought it down with a sharp crack in a wickedly sinuous weal across the firm pale cheeks of Noreen's bottom. The nineteen-year-old girl rose up on her toes with the intensity of the anguish, yet her cry was still one of rage rather than hurt alone. But the next ten or twelve strokes soon altered that. Noreen screamed into her gag, and screamed and screamed again. The flashing leather whip performed a dance of torment across her lash-marked buttocks, often catching her between them. To those who watched on that side of the room, divided from the other half by the canvas screen, Noreen was a bottom and little more! Yet Noreen's bottom was the most interesting thing about her to such men and they did not complain. The tail of the lash caught the flanks of her hips and the backs of her thighs occasionally, yet repeatedly it drew a ruby beadlet from the whipped seat-cheeks or, more wickedly, near the closed anus-bud between Noreen's buttocks.

The girl's mistress could not witness this for it seemed that she held Noreen's head on the other side of the screen, caressing and encouraging her gently.

'A little more punishment yet, Noreen! Come, let me lift your head a little. Soon you will understand why I would not let you wear your tight cotton briefs for the whipping, Noreen. You would never have known the undiminished agony of the leather whip on your bare buttocks. You might have wondered all your life what it would have been like without your panties on! It was my wish that you should experience such a thing at least once. Come, Noreen, breathe a little more from the bottle to fortify you. Ah, I think he cut your bottom with his lash just then! Did he not, Noreen? That is common in such punishments!'

When the drama had ended, it was Maggie's turn, though she was dealt with more leniently. The cane thrashed a score of times across the pale broadened cheeks of Maggie's backside and then she was reprieved.

It was Lesley who, without premeditation, provided the last act of the drama. She lay with a man on the sofa, her tongue caressing the head of his penis gently. She had been profoundly moved by Noreen's ordeal but not in the expected manner. Her tongue still circling the knob of the pasha's penis, she looked up at him, a cold desire in the arrogant blue eyes under her urchin fringe.

'Let Noreen be punished again but with the switch,' she said softly, 'Let her be made to wear a persuader for it as I was once!'

Such requests were never to be denied when the guests made them. The pasha, in gratitude for Lesley's devotion with her tongue, soon asked for what she wanted. The others knew it was Lesley's own suggestion. While the two culprits still bent, fastened side by side, over the padded punishment-horse, the persuader-strap with its row of needle-points down either edge was brought and attached to the front and rear of Noreen's waist-strap. The onlookers could not see it as it ran down the girl's belly, only where it was strained back under her legs to run deep and tight between Noreen's bottom-cheeks. Gasping with the intensity of the needle tips, the strongly built nine-teen-year-old girl could find relief only by bending very tightly with backside thrust right out, and by keeping absolutely still. Even then, it was possible to see how the needle points dented the smooth skin of Noreen's bottom-cleavage with piercing imperiousness. Indeed the strap had been drawn vindictively tight to ensure that one or two of them pressed home.

Lesley

The necessity of absolute stillness under a whipping with the slim wand of the pony-switch was evident. Yet the anguish of the switch made it impossible. Intrigued as never before, the onlookers witnessed the frantic drama of Noreen caught in this appalling dilemma.

To some, Lesley was the true object of interest. Claire thought so. She had truly come into her own. After this summer at Paris, Lesley would never be the same.

* * *

The end came unexpectedly. Lesley opened her eyes, coming to the plateau of consciousness like a swimmer regaining the surface of a lake after a long shallow plunge. The square onyx clock on the peach-mirror table was striking four. It was surely this which had roused her from the long afternoon dream of Paris, the Villa Rif and that other house over which Madame Claire presided.

It was a shock to recall the cruel and humiliating fantasies which her mind permitted in sleep. Had the dream truly been so brief? The entire sequence had passed in her unconscious thoughts between the moment when she saw the hands of the onyx clock approach the hour and the moment when the dainty metallic strokes of its mechanism roused her.

She was lying on the apricot silk of the bed cover, her hand still between the thighs of her panty-tights feeling the wetness of her own arousal. In the severe modernism of that bedroom in the winter city, the cloud-light still broke with the cool neutrality of water on the angular mirror and the crystal lamp-pendants which dappled the wall with prismatic lozenges of red and blue, green and violet.

'It's time to go!'

The woman's voice spoke again. It came from beyond the double dove-grey doors which opened on to the landing of the fine circular staircase at the centre of the house. Lesley listened and knew that the words were not directed toner.

She waited for a knock, for Connie to enter with the tray and the coffee things. Then she looked and saw that the tray was already there on one of the glass-topped tables. Had it been left there while she slept? Had Connie come to her in reality or was their love-making no more than a dream?

Judith! Antonia! She realised with a shock that Judith was real enough but Antonia had been the creation of a brief afternoon dream. Lesley got up from the bed and began to dress quickly. Someone was playing the Steinway in the drawing-room below. She heard the sublime leaping chords of the last of Schumann's *Etudes Symphoniques* and knew that it was the music whose score had been folded on the piano in her dream.

Whose voice had said, 'It's time to go?' Not Christine's or Fatima's. Had she truly woken from her dream? Lesley opened the dove-grey doors and went down the graceful circle of the stairway under the glass dome above the vestibule. Her heart beat a little faster and yet she was drawn with longing as well as dread to the riddle's answer. One might dream of reality or unreality, the past or the future. Yet surely what she saw now was just a dream.

Frau Muller had stopped playing the *Etudes Symphoniques*. Judith was walking, with head bowed in modesty or submission, across the marble circle of the hall and into the drawing-room to which she had been summoned.

Christine was standing at the foot of the stairs in her riding breeches and jacket, looking up at Lesley as she descended the shallow curving steps. In a little while she would change and then be ready for the car which would take them to the Zoo station for the Paris express. Just at the moment she was flexing in her hands a supple bamboo which was no part of her riding costume.

Lesley stopped, one hand on the smooth rail of the elegant metal banister.

Lesley

Her heart beat in her throat with fear and longing.

Christine smiled up at her, vindictive in her amusement.

'There is a ceremony to be performed before we leave,' she said, pointing the cane towards the room where Judith attended her teacher's summons. 'Had you forgotten?'

Then she stepped forward and took the arm of the young woman who seemed about to swoon on the last step of the staircase.

Magic Carpet Books

m C

Catalog 2005-2006

The Collector's Edition of Victorian Erotic Discipline
Edited by Brooke Stern

Fiction/Erotica · ISBN 0-9766510-9-2
Trade Paperback · 5 3/16 x 8 • 608 Pages
$17.95 ($24.95 Canada)

Victorian erotica is replete with all manner of discipline. Indeed, it would be hard to find an erotic act as connected with a historical era as discipline is with the reign of Queen Victoria. The language of erotic discipline, with its sir's and madam's, its stilted syntax and its ritualized roles, sounds Victorian even when it's used in contemporary pop culture. The essence of Victorian discipline is the shock of the naughty, the righteous indignation of the punisher and the shame of the punished. Today's literature of erotic discipline can only play at Victorian dynamics, and all subsequent writings will only be pretenders to a crown of the era whose reign will never end.

The Collector's Edition of Victorian Lesbian Erotica
Edited By Major LaCaritilie

Fiction/Erotica · ISBN 0-9755331-9-3
Trade Paperback · 5 3/16 x 8 • 608 Pages
$17.95 ($24.95 Canada)

The Victorian era offers an untapped wellspring of lesbian erotica. Indeed, Victorian erotica writers treated lesbians and bisexual women with voracious curiosity and tender affection. As far as written treasuries of vice and perversion go, the Victorian era has no equal. These stories delve into the world of the aristocrat and the streetwalker, the seasoned seductress and the innocent naïf.

Represented in this anthology are a variety of genres, from romantic fiction to faux journalism and travelogue, as well as styles and tones resembling everything from steamy page-turners to scholarly exposition. What all these works share, however, is the sense of fun, mischief and sexiness that characterized Victorian lesbian erotica.

The lesbian erotica of the Victorian era defies stereotype and offers rich portraits of a sexuality driven underground by repressive mores. As Oscar Wilde claimed, the only way to get rid of temptation is to yield to it.

The Collector's Edition of Victorian Erotica
Edited by Major LaCaritilie

Fiction/Erotica · ISBN 0-9755331-0-X
Trade Paperback · 5-3/16"x 8"· 608 Pages
$15.95 ($18.95 Canada)

No lone soul can possibly read the thousands of erotic books, pamphlets and broadsides the English reading public were offered in the 19th century. It can only be hoped that this Anthology may stimulate the reader into further adventures in erotica and its manifest reading pleasure. In this unique anthology, 'erotica' is a comprehensive term for bawdy, obscene, salacious, pornographic and ribald works including, indeed featuring, humour and satire that employ sexual elements. Flagellation and sadomasochism are recurring themes. They are activities whose effect can be shocking, but whose occurrence pervades our selections, most often in the context of love and affection. This anthology includes selections from such Anonymous classics as *A Weekend Visit*, *The Modern Eveline*, *Misfortunes of Mary*, *My Secret Life*, *The Man With A Maid*, *The Life of Fanny Hill*, *The Mournings of a Courtesan*, *The Romance of Lust*, *Pauline*, *Forbidden Fruit* and *Venus School-Mistress*.

The Collector's Edition of the Lost Erotic Novels
Edited by Major LaCaritilie

Fiction/Erotica • ISBN 0-97553317-7 ·
Trade Paperback 5-3/16"x 8"· 608 Pages
$16.95 ($22.95 Canada)

MISFORTUNES OF MARY —
Anonymous, 1860's:
An innocent young woman who still believes in the kindness of strangers unwittingly signs her life away to a gentleman who makes demands upon her she never would have dreamed possible.

WHITE STAINS —
Anaïs Nin & Friends, 1940's:
Sensual stories penned by Anaïs and some of her friends that were commissioned bya wealthy buyer for $1.00 a page. These classics of pornography are not included in her two famous collections, *Delta of Venus* and *Little Birds*.

INNOCENCE —
Harriet Daimler, 1950's:
A lovely young bed-ridden woman would appear to be helpless and

at the mercy of all around her, and indeed, they all take advantage of her in shocking ways, but who's to say she isn't the one secretly dominating them?

THE INSTRUMENTS OF THE PASSION —
Anonymous, 1960's:
A beautiful young woman discovers that there is much more to life in a monastery than anyone imagines as she endures increasingly intense rituals of flagellation devotedly visited upon her by the sadistic brothers.

The Story of M — A Memoir
by Maria Isabel Pita

Non-Fiction/Erotica • ISBN 0-9726339-5-2
Trade Paperback · 5 3/16 x 8 · 239 Pages
$14.95 ($18.95 Canada)

The true, vividly detailed and profoundly erotic account of a beautiful, intelligent woman's first year of training as a slave to the man of her dreams.

Maria Isabel Pita refuses to fall into any politically correct category. She is not a feminist, and yet she is fiercely independent. She is everything but a mindless sex object, yet she is willingly, and happily, a masterful man's love slave. M is erotically submissive and yet also profoundly secure in herself, and she wrote this account of her ascent into submission for all the women out there who might be confused and frightened by their own contradictory desires just as she was.

M is the true highly erotic account of the author's first profoundly instructive year with the man of her dreams. Her vividly detailed story makes it clear we should never feel guilty about daring to make our deepest, darkest longings come true, and serves as living proof that they do.

Cat's Collar - Three Erotic Romances
By Maria Isabel Pita
Fiction/Erotica • ISBN 0-9766510-0-9
Trade Paperback · 5 3/16 x 8 · 608 Pages
$16.95 ($ 20.95 Canada)

Dreams of Anubis

A legal secretary from Boston visiting Egypt explores much more than just tombs and temples in the stimulating arms of Egyptologist Simon Taylor. But at the same time a powerfully erotic priest of Anubis enters her dreams, and then her life one night in the dark heart of Cairo's timeless bazaar. Sir Richard Ashley believes he has lived before and that for centuries he and Mary have longed to find each other again. Mary is torn between two men who both desire to discover the legendary tomb of Imhotep and win the treasure of her heart.

Rituals of Surrender

All her life Maia Wilson has lived near a group of standing stones in the English countryside, but it isn't until an old oak tree hit by lightning collapses across her car one night that she suddenly finds herself the heart of an erotic web spun by three sexy, enigmatic men - modern Druids intent on using Maia for a dark and ancient rite...

Cat's Collar

Interior designer Mira Rosemond finds herself in one attractive successful man's bedroom after the other, but then one beautiful morning a stranger dressed in black leather takes a short cut through her garden and changes the course of her life forever. Mira has never met anyone quite like Phillip, and the more she learns about his mysterious profession - secretly linked to some of Washington's most powerful women - the more frightened and yet excited she becomes as she finds herself falling helplessly, submissively in love.

Praise for Maria Isabel Pita...

Dreams of Anubis is a compellingly erotic tale unveiled in one of the world's most romantic and mystical lands... Ms. Pita brings together both a sensually historic plot and a contemporary Egypt... her elegant style of writing pulls at your senses and allows you to live the moment through her characters. The language flows beautifully, the characters are well drawn, the plot is exciting and always fresh and riveting, and the setting is romantic. I highly recommend Dreams of Anubis for anyone with a love of erotic romance with a touch of magic and mysticism.   Just Erotic Romance Reviews

Maria Isabel Pita is already one of the brightest stars in the erotic romance genre. If you're unfamiliar with her work, she specializes in transporting her readers effortlessly between the past and present, while indestructible true love weaves its eternal spell on her characters' minds and souls.   Marilyn Jaye Lewis

Beauty & Submission
by Maria Isabel Pita

Non-Fiction/Erotica • ISBN 0-9755331-1-8
Trade Paperback · 5-3/16" x 8" · 256 Pages
$14.95 ($18.95 Canada)

In a desire to tell the truth and dispel negative stereotypes about the life

of a sex slave, Maria Isabel Pita wrote *The Story of M... A Memoir.* Her intensely erotic life with the man of her dreams continues now in *Beauty & Submission*, a vividly detailed sexual and philosophical account of her second year of training as a slave to her Master and soul mate.

"A sex slave is very often a woman who dares to admit to herself exactly what she wants. Absolute submission to love requires a mysterious strength of character that is a far cry from the stereotype of sex slaves as mindless doormats with no self-respect. Before I entered the BDSM lifestyle with the man I now call "my Master" as casually as other women say "my husband" I did not believe a sex slave could lead a normal, healthy life. I thought my dreams of true love and my desire for a demanding Master were like matter and antimatter canceling each other out. I have since learned otherwise, and Beauty & Submission continues the detailed account of my ascent into submission as an intelligent woman with an independent spirit who is now also willingly and happily a masterful man's love slave." From Beauty & Submission

Guilty Pleasures
by Maria Isabel Pita

Fiction/Erotica ISBN 0-9755331-5-0
Trade Paperback · 5 3/16 x 8 · 304 Pages • $16.95 ($21.95 Canada)

Guilty Pleasures explores the passionate willingness of women throughout the ages to offer themselves up to the forces of love. Historical facts are seamlessly woven into intensely graphic sexual encounters beginning with ancient Egypt and journeying down through the centuries to the present and beyond. Beneath the covers of Guilty Pleasures you will find eighteen erotic love stories with a profound feel for the times and places where they occur. An ancient Egyptian princess… a courtesan rising to fame in Athen's Golden Age… a widow in 15th century Florence initiated into a Secret Society… a Transylvanian Count's wicked bride… an innocent nun tempted to sin in 17th century Lisbon… a lovely young woman finding love in the Sultan's harem… and many more are all one eternal woman in *Guilty Pleasures*.

Select Reviews:

'Guilty Pleasures' is a collection of eighteen erotic short stories. These stories take you on an erotic journey through time, each one taking you further back in time than the story before it, until there is no time at all. Maria Isabel Pita is an imaginative writer with a skill for writing beautiful prose. She has taken her love for history to create a collection of stories that makes you want to keep reading. Her heroines are strong and the tales told from their point of view pull you in and make you want to know more about their individual stories. The author's attention to detail and historical accuracy makes it easier for the reader to fall into the stories as they read. This collection has something for everyone. I would highly recommend this collection of short stories. There is nothing guilty about the pleasure received from reading it. Romance Divas

Pita does indeed take us through the ages, from the near-future time of 2015 A.D., back through the 20th century, then the 19th, 18th, 17th, 16th, 15th, 12th centuries, back to 1000 B.C., 3000 B.C., through to another solar system, and on to a parallel universe. What will amaze you, if not even alarm you, is Pita's eye for detail and her uncanny feel for the everyday lives of her distant characters. When you read her stories of ancient lovers, for example, you will believe that Pita herself has visited those times and is merely recounting to you first-hand what she observed, endured, and felt while she was there. The storytelling is seamless and flowing. The erotic encounters between her characters are sexually explicit and arousing, sometimes emotionally raw, and often thought-provoking for the reader. Pita's unique imagination is unleashed and she spares no punches. Guilty Pleasures *is an absolute must for any fan of literary erotica.* Marilyn Jaye Lewis – Erotic Author's Association Review

My Secret Fantasies – Sixty Erotic Love Stories

ISBN: 0-9755331-2-6 • $11.95 U.S. / 16.95 Canada

In *My Secret Fantasies*, sixty different women share the secret of how they made their wildest erotic desires come true. Next time you feel like getting your heart rate up and your blood really flowing, curl up with a cup of tea and *My Secret Fantasies*…

The Ties That Bind
By Vanessa Duriés

Non-Fiction/Erotica · ISBN 0-9766510-1-7
Trade Paperback · 5 3/16 x 8 · 160 Pages
$14.95 ($18.95 Canada)

RE-PRINT OF THE FRENCH BEST-SELLER: The incredible confessions of a thrillingly unconventional woman. From the first page, this chronicle of dominance and submission will keep you gasping with its vivid depicitons of sensual abandon. At the hand of Masters Georges, Patrick, Pierre and others, this submissive seductress experiences pleasures she never knew existed…

"I am not sentimental, yet I love my Master and do not hide the fact. He is everything that is intelligent, charming and strict. Of course, like every self-respecting master, he sometimes appears very demanding, which pains and irritates me when he pushes me to the limits of my moral and physical resistance. My Master is impassioned, and he lives only for his passion: sadomasochism. This philosophy, for it is one, represents in his eyes an ideal way of life, but I am resolutely opposed to that view. One cannot, one must not be a sadomasochist the whole time. The grandeurs and constraints of everyday life do not live happily with fantasies. One must know how to protect one from the other by separating them openly. When the master and the slave live together, they must have the wisdom to alternate the sufferings and the languors, the delights and the torments...."

A Brush With Love
Maria Isabel Pita

Non-Fiction/Erotica · ISBN 0-9774311-1-8
Trade Paperback · 5 3/16 x 8 · 254 Pages · $12.95

The cobbled streets of Boston wind back into a past full of revolutionary fervor and stretch passionately into the future inside the thoughts and desires of Miranda Covington, a young and beautiful professional artist's model.

Michael Keneen knows exactly what he wants to do in life, even if it means disappointing his parents by not continuing a tradition of three generations in law enforcement. For Michael, artist models are only aesthetic challenges on the path to his Master in Fine Arts, until one freezing December afternoon Miranda Covington takes the stand, then suddenly getting her beauty down on paper isn't all he wants to do.

Lost in hot daydreams that often become reality when she poses for handsome clients in private, Miranda doesn't notice the sea of faces around her while she poses, until Patrick's penetrating blue eyes meet hers. He might not be a cop like his father, but his arresting personality is irresistible, especially when he discovers hidden longings in Miranda that challenge all her conventional ideas about love in ways that excite her like nothing ever has...

Secret Desires: Two Erotic Romances

ISBN: 0-9766510-7-6 • $12.95

DIGGING UP DESTINY by Frances LaGatta:

Atop Machu Picchu - lost Inca City in the Clouds - archeology professor Blake Sevenson unearths a sealed cave marked by a golden sun god. Behind that stone wall resides a priceless ransom of gold and silver. Hope Burnsmyrehas has a brand new PhD, no field experience, and high hopes. She and Blake clash at every turn, but the chemistry between them makes the jungle feel even hotter.

DREAMS & DESIRES by Laura Muir:

Poet Isabel Taylor buys a stack of magazines for inspiration, and discovers the man of her dreams staring back at her from a glossy full-page electric guitar ad. That night she has a vivid encounter with Alex Goodman in her dreams, and when his band comes to town she joins a crowd of groupies backstage. When he whispers, 'Don't I know you?' the first thrilling note is struck in a romantic tour-de-force in which their desire challenges all rational limits...

MAGIC CARPET BOOKS

Order Form

Name: _____

Address: _____

City: _____

State:_____ Zip:_____

Title	ISBN	Quantity
_____	_____	_____
_____	_____	_____
_____	_____	_____
_____	_____	_____

Send check or money order to:

Magic Carpet Books
PO Box 473
New Milford, CT 06776

Postage free in the United States add $2.50 for
packages outside the United States

magiccarpetbooks@earthlink.net

Visit our website at:
www.magic-carpet-books.com